THE EDGE

OF

THE NEST

THE EDGE

OF

THE NEST

THE SOLITUDE OF
IVAN TURGENEV

CHRISTOPHER CRUISE

Matador
9 Priory Business Park,
Wistow Road
Kibworth Beauchamp
Leicester LE8 0RX, UK
Tel: (+44) 116 279 2299
Fax: (+44) 116 279 2277
Email: books@troubador.co.uk
Web: www.troubador.co.uk/matador

ISBN 978 1784620 899

British Library Cataloguing in Publication Data.
A catalogue record for this book is available from the British Library.

Printed and bound in the UK by TJ International, Padstow, Cornwall
Typeset by Troubador Publishing Ltd, Leicester, UK

Matador is an imprint of Troubador Publishing Ltd

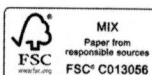

To Pat, Jo Jo, Amanda, Lawrence and Oliver
and in memoriam I.B., without whom…

From the Dead, for him who is immortal.
Inscription on a wreath at Turgenev's funeral, for which political prisoners from all over Russia had subscribed.

PREFACE

Fictionalized biography is a dangerous genre: history purists chafe at anything that cannot be one hundred percent verified, while novel addicts perhaps lose patience with information that doesn't immediately carry the story forward or reveal new aspects of the characters. In an effort, if not to please, at least to mollify both parties, I can claim not to have tampered with the essential facts of Turgenev's life (e.g. where and with whom he was at any given time) but my interpretation of these facts has been coloured according to the dictates of my imagination.

I have tried always to bear in mind some lines Umberto Eco wrote on the subject of fictionalized biography: 'In order to give us a vivid image of a character, the author reconstructs dialogue that may not have taken place exactly as he described; we may accept this but we demand that the writer's reconstruction be based on documents which, if they do not confirm those conversations, at least do not render them implausible.'

The small, austere living room of a dilapidated apartment on the Fontanka Embankment in St Petersburg, some time in the winter of 1843, is filled with a dozen or so young men in their mid-twenties. There is barely room for them all: some perch on high-backed wooden chairs; others sit on the edge of tables, swinging their legs; one, the tallest and youngest, is sprawled out on a sagging sofa; the latecomers huddle on the floor, knees hunched up to their chins.

It is well after midnight and a tallow candle provides the only light. In a corner a samovar bubbles; tea, the only beverage available, is sipped out of tall glasses accompanied by dry, stale biscuits. Cigarette and pipe smoke makes the air thicker than the fog outside, stealing up from the Neva to add its murky contribution to the ill-lit streets of the city.

The host, from the vantage-point of his thirty-two years, guides, leads, dominates the conversation. Vissarion Grigorevich Belinsky, the brilliant, controversial, what would now be called *engagé* critic, has for some years been the guiding spirit of a group of idealistic young men, all, in their different ways, seeking to break free of the stifling stranglehold of Czar Nicholas I's Russia. A few are of noble birth, the rest the sons of doctors, lawyers and government officials. Among them are Ivan Sergeyevich Turgenev, Pavel Vasilovich Annenkov and Mikhail Aleksandrovich Bakunin. Turgenev – the one on the sofa – has just returned from three years at the University of Berlin and unenthusiastically taken a job as a minor functionary at the Ministry of the Interior. In his spare time, of which he takes care to ensure there is plenty, he has begun to write poetry, mostly on the twin themes of love and nature. A few literary journals have started to publish him, and it was as a young poet that he was first welcomed into Belinsky's circle.

Annenkov, who is to remain a lifelong friend, comes from an affluent landowning family and, apart from a brief period as a civil servant, will spend his life as an inspired dilettante; his unrufflably affable nature enables him to remain on friendly terms with many of his contemporaries who will later become bitterly divided by political differences.

Bakunin no longer forms part of the circle, having quarrelled with Belinsky five years earlier. The eldest son of minor nobility from the province of Tver, northwest of Moscow, he and Turgenev had met in Berlin, where for several months they had shared rooms and plunged enthusiastically into the alluring whirlpool of German idealism. During a holiday at the family estate of Premukhino, Turgenev had formed a romantic attachment with one of Bakunin's four sisters, Tatyana. But by the end of the summer he realized that, whereas he had been intrigued by a close intellectual affinity, she had fallen passionately in love with him. His attempt to extricate himself by means of a rather clumsy letter left the girl distraught; but her brother, who happened to be heavily in debt to him, showed no signs of resentment and for a while their friendship continued as before.

This was not the case with Belinsky who, on a previous visit to Premukhino, had fallen in love with another of the sisters. But Bakunin had resented his plebeian guest's wooing of the beautiful Aleksandra and, accustomed to being the dominant figure in any gathering, was jealous of Belinsky's superior intellect. Their unlikely friendship had ended in a violent quarrel.

This night, as always at these nocturnal gatherings, the arguments have ranged around the same three or four topics: social injustice, Russia's relationship with Western Europe, literature, the future of humanity... At this moment there has just been a lively exchange of opinions about a review Belinsky has written for the monthly *Otechestvennye Zapiski (Annals of the Fatherland)* of a recently published romantic novel. Someone, the gentle Annenkov perhaps, has expostulated that it was too scathing, too cruel: "After all Vissarion Grigorevich, to write such things is not a crime."

"You are wrong." Belinsky leaps up and paces from one corner of the room to another, waving his arms, the helter-skelter flow of his words flowing uninterruptibly and frequently ungrammatically from his thin, slightly twisted mouth which rarely smiles – though when it does, as his closest friends know, it reveals the inherently sweet nature that belies his nickname of 'the furious Vissarion'. "You are quite wrong. A crime is exactly what it is. A crime against thought, a crime against feeling, a crime against humanity."

"Against humanity?!"

"Yes, against humanity. What are all these noble sentiments, these fervent declarations of undying love, these pious pronouncements, these trials you know will be overcome, these reconciliations you know are pre-ordained, these treacly happy endings with church bells tolling and gently falling snow? They are an insult to intelligence, and as intelligence is all we have, that's an unforgivable sin. They are soft viscous pap to smother over the harsh outlines of reality, to lull the reading public into a sense of mindless apathetic somnolence, to prevent them from ever questioning, even in the privacy of their own minds, the fiat that all is eventually well, that our dear rulers are looking after us like wise and kindly grandfathers, chiding us gently from time to time, punishing us ever so slightly once in a while, but always for our own good…everything for our own good…"

A violent burst of asthmatic coughing brings a temporary respite. Katkov, who was a contemporary of Turgenev's at Berlin University, takes the opportunity to goad Belinsky and embarrass the young poet, of whom he is secretly jealous.

2

"And yet you were one of the very few to praise our dear Ivan Sergeyevich's poetic effort, *Parasha*. Hardly a beacon of modernity! A pure young girl suffering the pangs of adolescent love, a hero – if you can call him that – afraid to commit himself to any decision more binding than choosing between beef and pork, a *mariage de convenance* which leaves everyone vaguely dissatisfied but – ah, you know how it is – life must go on… You remember what your colleague Panaev called it: 'A weak dilution of Pushkin with a couple of spoonfuls of tepid Lermontov'. But you lavished superlatives on it. You, the prophet of the new, the plain, the unadorned, wrote of the poem's 'piercing sense of observation, its profound thought, its delicate, gracious irony'."

Belinsky's brilliant blue eyes, usually half-hidden behind heavy lids, widen and flash from his pale, bony face, now mottled from the exertion of trying to control his coughing. "I would have thought that you, Mikhail Nikiforovich, would have been able to read beyond the words. What I was praising in that review was not the poem but the potential. The writer of the drivel we have just been discussing is fifty-four and – we may hope – nearing the end at least of his creative life. But Ivan Sergeyevich was only twenty-five when he wrote *Parasha,* and it was his first narrative work. Before that, just a handful of poems, no better and no worse than so many others. But here, for all the conventionality of form and expression, was an acuity and a sensibility which could go on to finer things. Here was a tender young talent to be nurtured, not uprooted. If, along with all the others, I had destroyed the poem, I might have destroyed the poet. And that, I think we can now all agree, would have been a pity."

Turgenev, who up to now has tried to maintain the languid, indifferent manner he affected in those days in the face of criticism or praise, cannot resist a grateful smile in the direction of his champion. But it is soon replaced by a sardonic grin as he turns towards Katkov. "Of course what even one of your omniscience couldn't know was what Belinsky wrote to me in a private letter immediately after his review was published. After ripping my poor little poem to pieces in a much more devastating way than the other critics, because I knew that what he said was true, he ended: "I would be happy to read your next efforts, but please before you send them to me, have them copied to run on without being divided into lines, otherwise I keep being plagued by the idea that they are supposed to be in verse."

Belinsky doesn't join in the general laughter, but drives home his point. "And the result, my friends, was his tale, *Andrey Kolosov*. Only eight months separate *Parasha* from *Andrey Kolosov*, but what a difference! Sinewy prose, not flabby verse. A recognizable picture of student life today, not the predictable twitchings of marionettes in a never-never-land at a never-never-time. And above all, real behaviour, real feelings, real *life*. Let me tell you what my favourite moment in the forty pages of that tale is. Not the quick sketches of the minor characters in the student community, acute though they are. Not even the creation of the gruff,

3

boorish retired lieutenant Sidorenko, nailed down with such economy and precision. No, it's the moment when the eighteen-year-old storyteller, who thinks he's deliriously in love, goes to ask Sidorenko for his daughter's hand. He's already won her reluctant consent, even though he knows she's in love with his friend Kolosov; all night long he's been in raptures of joy, but as he makes his way to the house, his ecstasy is punctured by tiny darts of doubt. And when he arrives and sees Varya sitting there between her father and her aunt, he surprises himself by looking at her in the objective way a man with a full stomach contemplates dishes of food laid out on a table for his benefit. And what is his first reflection? 'I found she had rather red hands'. *There* is talent, gentlemen. Those red hands are worth all the slender necks and dainty ankles in our literature."

Flushed with pleasure, leavened with a touch of embarrassment, Turgenev stands up and announces that he will have to leave. "Tomorrow I have to be at the Ministry by ten," he announces ruefully. Nobody else shows any signs of movement, so Belinsky accompanies him to the door and leads him down the dark rickety staircase. Helping him into his greatcoat, he asks him if he is contemplating a career in public service.

"For the love of God, no," is Turgenev's immediate reply. "I have been at the Ministry for eight months and am already bored beyond belief."

"Then why do you stay? You have money of your own, and the salary cannot be very high."

"The salary wouldn't pay the rent of my lodgings. No, I depend entirely on my mother, who sends me a regular allowance. Without that, I wouldn't be able to live in St Petersburg."

"Unless you scratched a living like the rest of us and burnished your talent for putting words on paper."

"That would be even less likely to pay my rent. And besides, if I left the Ministry my mother would surely reduce my allowance, if not cut it off altogether."

"She sounds like a formidable lady, this mother of yours." Belinsky opens the door to let his visitor out on to the street. "And you seem to be very much under her influence. You must tell me about her."

"There is much to tell. And a great deal more that I don't even know about."

"Meaning?"

"How she came to be the way she is."

"Is there no one you can ask?"

Turgenev thinks for a moment before venturing out into the icy blackness of the night. "Perhaps my uncle Nikolai. One of these days I must find an opportunity to put some questions to him…"

It took him ten years. Nikolai Turgenev, his father's brother, had been in his childhood the person for whom Turgenev had the greatest affection. He felt much closer to him than to his unapproachable father. 'If I had wings,' he wrote to him from Moscow, aged thirteen, 'I would fly to you. I would press you to my breast strongly, strongly, and kiss you again and again.' After Turgenev's father's death in 1834, his mother appointed Nikolai to be her estate manager. It was a stormy relationship. Varvara Turgeneva was perfectly capable of running Spasskoye herself, and most of the time did so; all she wanted was a compliant figure to whom she could, from time to time, give orders that would unhesitatingly be obeyed. Nikolai, inherently lazy in any case, soon settled back to enjoy the fruits of his position without bothering overmuch about the responsibilities. But he never knew where he was with her. Insistent on keeping up the fiction that her marriage had been one of untroubled happiness, she would one day tell her brother-in-law that every time she looked at him she saw her Sergey, which made her 'love you like my soul'; the next, after noticing some discrepancy in the accounts, she would accuse him of being her 'enemy', of stealing and trying to ruin her. Eventually she learnt from a steward that he had married a woman half his age and hadn't dared tell her. She accused him of 'disloyalty' and told him to pack his bags and be out of Spasskoye within a week. After her death Turgenev, knowing that the old rogue, with his young wife, Masha, and two small daughters, was up to his ears in debt, took pity on him and reinstated him. He was later to pay dearly for his kindness.

It was in the winter of 1855, while he was working on his first novel, *Rudin*, that Turgenev was finally able to draw his uncle out on the subject of his mother. At first even bluff, insensitive Nikolai avoided the subject of his sister-in-law unless he was recounting some anecdote in which the omission of her name would draw more attention to itself than its inclusion. Then, one day Turgenev suggested he read his *Mumu*, a tale which Carlyle, no less, was to call the most touching story he had ever read. It tells how a deaf and dumb giant of a serf was forced by the whim of an egocentric and capricious mistress to kill the dog he loved above all things in the world. This was based on fact, and there can be no doubt that the lady was a portrait of Turgenev's mother. Even Nikolai was moved by it, and the effect it had on him, along with the brandy with which Turgenev kept him liberally replenished, unblocked whatever reluctance he might have felt about talking to his nephew about Varvara. Once his tongue was unloosed, nothing could stop it; over a period of several long winter evenings, he would send his wife off to bed early so that his reminiscences would not have to be diluted by any need to spare her blushes.

"Of course," he began, "all I know about her early life was from hearsay. I was seven or eight years younger than her. And although our families didn't live all that far from each other, it wasn't as though they mixed in those days. The Lutovinovs were upstarts. Petty county nobility. Until a hundred or so years ago they were nobodies. Your father used to say his wife's ancestors were ugly as goats and stank like monkeys. But they certainly knew how to make money – and that's something that we Turgenevs, who can claim descent from the Tartar Khan, Turga, and have served the Muscovite princes since the fifteenth century, have never been much good at. And it doesn't look as if you, my dear boy, are going to be any different from the rest of us in that respect. At any rate, they bought the property of Kholodovo, together with half the land around here and, in doing so, acquired a reputation for being a rough, violent, dangerous lot. It didn't all start with your mother, you know. There's a story told about *her* mother – I don't know how true it is, but everyone around here believes it. It seems that a young serf boy, a ten-year-old lad, forgot to carry out some task she'd given him to do. At the time, the old woman was half paralyzed and confined to a chair. But she somehow managed to find the strength to knock him out with her stick and then smother him with a pillow."

"You mean she killed him?", Turgenev asked, horrified, remembering the reverence with which his mother had always referred to his grandmother.

"That's what they say. Of course it all got hushed up. You won't find a word about it in the police records. As for Varvara, God knows she was a difficult woman! Many's the time I'd have gladly speeded her way to a better place. She lashed me with her tongue almost as often as she lashed you and your brother on your bottoms. But I have to admit she didn't have it easy herself as a young girl…"

Knowing the broad outlines of his mother's youth but few of the details, Turgenev was happy to let his uncle ramble on.

"…Her father died before she was born and her mother married again almost immediately. Somov, the fellow's name was, a widower himself, with two daughters who were as pretty as Varvara was plain. It wasn't long before they were being treated like princesses whilst Varvara was looked on as little better than a servant. Her stepfather might have been a Lutovinov himself: coarse, brutal, an ugly customer when drunk, which was practically every evening. She told my brother that once, when the whole family was gathered together after dinner, he brought a servant in who played the violin and his two daughters performed the latest dance steps they'd been taught. When they'd finished, Somov told Varvara to dance. She'd never been allowed any lessons, so she refused. Somov tried to insist, but she was as proud as Lucifer even then, and she wasn't going to make a fool of herself to please anybody. Somov was so enraged at her disobedience that he put her over his knee and thrashed her in front of everybody, including the servants. Knowing her, I'm surprised she didn't kill him there and then."

"Is it true that she left the house the night after her mother's death and came to Spasskoye?"

"So she said. But there was something fishy about that story. At least the way

6

she told it. Never could quite believe it myself. I mean, it was the middle of winter. And Spasskoye was nearly forty miles from Kholodovo. We all know how stubborn your mother could be, but after all, she could have left the next day…"

from VARVARA'S JOURNAL

5 December, 1805. *I have now been in my uncle, Ivan Ivanovich Lutovinov's house for two days, and I must try to set down on paper the events which led to my coming here. If I leave it but a day or two longer, I shall begin to believe I was subject to some kind of hallucination brought on by grief at my mother's demise, or the victim of a peculiarly hideous form of nightmare. But if I am to find a way out of this dark, impenetrable forest in which, for the time being, I seem to have lost all sense of direction, it can only be by looking closely and clearly at the obstacles that lie in my path and the terrible dangers which, by the grace of God and, if it be not presumptuous to say so, a certain firmness of will on my part, I have hitherto managed to avoid. So, painful and repugnant though it will be, I must compel myself to recall and record what, in other circumstances, I should gladly consign to the farthest reaches of oblivion.*

It must have been about four in the afternoon when my dear mother – the Kingdom of Heaven be hers! – took leave of this harsh world. For a brief moment, a spark of the strength that had sustained her all her life flared up, only to be finally extinguished. As the priest was reading the prayer for the dying, he sensed that she might slip away before he had finished, so he handed her the cross to hold. My mother asked him sharply what all the hurry was about and assured him he had plenty of time to finish. But barely had she lain back and begun fumbling for something under the pillow, when the Good Lord called her to Him. When we reached for her hand, we found it was clutching a rouble. Knowing her husband's miserable avarice, she had wanted to be sure the priest would be paid for reading the prayer for her own death.

After closing her eyes and bidding farewell to the priest, I fell to my knees again in prayer, paying no heed to my stepfather and stepsisters who were grouped around the bed, and trying to banish the perhaps unworthy thought that their presence there was due more to the dictates of convention than the expression of any deeply-felt sorrow. But I was barely surprised when, after only a very few minutes, Vasily Osipovich rose to his feet and announced gruffly that he was going to his study; to be followed, a moment or two later, by his two daughters, behind whom the door had hardly closed before I could swear I detected the sound of suppressed giggling.

How much longer I remained kneeling at my mother's bedside I cannot truthfully say. I remember discovering to my surprise that I was giving voice to my thoughts and begging her departed spirit to continue to watch over me and guide me. She had not perhaps been the most affectionate of mothers – as, dear Lord, I had certainly not been the most dutiful of daughters – but she was the only living creature I had been close to, and I felt her loss, recent as it was, as an irreversible loneliness, an emptiness of spirit which the last two days have done nothing to mitigate.

I was summoned back to the world of the living – I suppose it must have been three or four hours later – by a discreet cough from the door which announced the presence of the old manservant, Tikhon. He gently asked me if I would not care to join the rest of the family in the dining-room to partake of some refreshment that he had had prepared. I shook my head but smiled my thanks and asked him if, instead, he would bring some tea up to my room before I went to bed. As I made my way upstairs, I tried to shut my ears to the sound of convivial conversation mingled with laughter coming from the dining-room.

When Tikhon came to my room, he brought me not only a tray of tea with cracknel biscuits and honey, but also a message from my stepfather which occasioned me no little surprise. Vasily Osipovich had asked if I would be good enough to pay him a visit in his quarters later in the evening, at my convenience, as there was a matter he wished to discuss with me. My immediate instinct was to refuse, but after a moment's reflection I decided, in view of my stepfather's exasperation at the least thwarting of his will, that it would be wiser to comply with his wishes. I told Tikhon to say I would go; but as soon as the door closed behind the old man, I fell to speculating on the cause of this unexpected summons. If it were some question regarding details of domestic engagements, or even a delicate problem to do with inheritance, surely it could wait until tomorrow. Could it be that he was feeling some remorse at his insensitivity in regard to my grief and wished to make his peace with me at this propitious moment? I decided it behoved me to try and see things in the most charitable light: perhaps it had been my mother's last wish that her departure should at least serve to narrow the hitherto unbridgeable gap that had stretched between myself and Vasily Osipovich?

And so, an hour or so later, when the house was dark and silent, everyone else having gone to bed, I knocked on the heavy oak door which led from the entrance hall to the wing occupied by my stepfather's apartment. It was soon flung open and he appeared, holding a candle, at the threshold, wearing a dressing-gown knotted loosely over an open shirt and trousers, and a pair of leather slippers. Although he attempted to greet me with an ingratiating smile, I saw at once from the flushed complexion with which I was so sickeningly familiar, that he had been drinking. I was hard put to it not to turn on my heel and flee back to my room. But I mustered up my courage and walked past him into the corridor which led to his rooms. Would that, at least this once, cowardice had prevailed over temerity!

When we reached his study he motioned me to a divan, sat down beside me, thanked me for coming and mumbled a few words to the effect that only he, who shared in it, could comprehend the depth of my grief. I detected little genuine sympathy in his

8

words: only a desire to have done with the proprieties in order to proceed to what was really on his mind. I felt we might have been burying my mother while her body still lay in the room upstairs. I asked him – I daresay rather coldly – if that was all he wished to say to me. His reply was to swallow a glass of brandy and say, no, he wanted to talk about the future. Changes would need to be made and he would like me to share in decisions that would have to be taken. With a smile I had never seen on his, or any man's, face before, he reached over and took my hand. It was as much as I could do to refrain from snatching it away. He went on to say that from now on I would have to take my mother's place. All that passed through my mind, other than my longing to be rid of him, was that this must be some stratagem to deprive me of whatever settlement my mother might have seen fit to make on me. But I replied, meekly enough, that I would be glad to do whatever lay in my power, in spite of my youth and inexperience... At this, he interrupted me to declare that he did not consider these liabilities: my youth would bring fresh ideas to the running of the household and – here his smile twisted into a horrible leer – it was the natural task of men of mature age like himself to help young girls to overcome their inexperience. There were more ways than one, he muttered thickly, in which I could take my mother's place. And thus saying, he pulled me roughly towards him and tried to kiss me on the lips.

I do not think that, however long God may grant me life, the stench of his foul, alcohol-saturated breath will ever quite leave my nostrils. But now I must pause for a moment before I can summon up the courage to relate what was to happen next. The very recollection of it causes my hand to tremble so violently that it is as much as I can do to keep the pen from slipping from my fingers...

6 December. *Last night I was unable to proceed further. Indeed, I could barely prevent myself from ripping out the pages I had already written and throwing them into the fire. But the cold light of morning has brought me strength and renewed my determination to continue to the end – though God forbid that this journal should ever come into anybody else's possession. I shall keep it hidden as secretly as its contents are hidden inside my breast.*

I pushed him away from me with all the violence I could muster and, calling him by what names I do not care to remember, tried to make my way to the door. But he followed me, seized me by the wrist, swung me round and pushed me back against his desk. His whole manner was changed now: his bloodshot eyes and heavy, panting breath demonstrated that he was much drunker than I had realized. He blurted out some vile, unforgivable words about how his wife had been ugly, crippled and no use to him for years, and it was time her daughter made up for her inadequacies. He pinned me back against the edge of the desk, thrusting his face against mine as I twisted my head to avoid his insistent, slobbering lips. I tried to cry out for help, but he put a hand over my mouth and, with the other, took one of my hands and held it pressed

9

against the lower part of his stomach. All that prevented me from fainting was the thought that I should then be unable to offer any further resistance. By pure chance my free hand, groping along the surface of the desk in an attempt to keep my balance, came in contact with some large round object which I now know to have been a glass paperweight. I seized it and brought it down with all my force on the crown of his head. He gave a short, sickening groan, sank to his knees and fell with a heavy thud to the floor, where he lay quite motionless.

I was convinced I had killed him. God help me, I felt no remorse at all; only the clear-eyed conviction that I must leave the house without a moment's delay. But where to go? The only place that came to my mind was this house, where I had been taken to visit my uncle two or three times. I knew it was a long way away – though little did I dream that it was actually sixty versts – but I could think of no other refuge. My uncle was a bachelor and had never shown the smallest interest in me. But he was my mother's brother and surely would be moved by the plight of someone so close of kin. I was terrified of going back into the main body of the house, but remembered there was a french window which gave onto the garden. As soon as I opened it and stepped outside, I realized I would die of cold if I did not put on some warmer clothing. I went back into the room, opened a cupboard at random and, as luck would have it, found an old greatcoat my stepfather used to put on when he walked his dog. It was absurdly too big for me, but when I went outside again I was grateful for every inch of it.

I started walking along the road that led to Spasskoye like one in a dream. The snow that had fallen during the day lay crisp and firm underfoot, and I made good headway. No thoughts came into my head except the determination to put as much distance as I could manage between myself and that hated house before dawn. By the time the household woke to discover that there was a dead man in the downstairs room, I hoped to be half way to my uncle's.

I had not been walking for very long – not more than an hour or so – when I heard from behind me the creaking of a vehicle and the muffled sound of horses' hoofs on the snow. My first instinct was to slip into the woods at the side of the road and hide. But I then bethought myself that it was far too soon for my stepfather's body to have been discovered. Whoever was travelling at this hour of night was not coming in pursuit of me. So I stood and waited for the conveyance to catch up with me. The moonlight was bright enough for me to be able to make out, when it was still nearly a hundred paces away, a dilapidated telega, its two horses being urged on with snatches of song, mingled with oaths, by its obviously quite drunk driver. He pulled up as soon as he saw me and gazed at me in disbelief. Given the picture I must have presented huddled in my stepfather's coat, he probably took me for some supernatural creature of the woods. This would account for his even greater surprise when I addressed him and asked him who he was and where he was going. When he said his name was Stepan, I recognized him for the odd-job man who used sometimes to bring to the kitchen door grouse and partridge he had surely poached from neighbouring estates. I told him who I was, and he nearly fell off his seat in astonishment. He asked me what I was doing on the road in the middle of the night, and I told him it was no business of his, but was he going anywhere near Spasskoye? He said he was going in that direction, but not that far. I climbed up behind him and told him to take me there, assuring him that I would make it worth his while. (Now I come to think of it, I must find some way to procure money from my uncle and have it conveyed to him, otherwise the wretch will start to blab.)

It was an excruciatingly uncomfortable ride. A network of interwoven rope, stretched from one side of the cart to the other, served as a seat; but it did little or nothing to cushion the violent jolting caused by the four wooden wheels, not one of which, I imagine, can have been of the same size. At first, the fellow turned his head and tried to engage me in conversation, but I soon discouraged that. He was not totally without respect, however; seeing that I was bareheaded, he offered me his fur cap. I was about to accept it, but when he took it off and I saw the lank, greasy locks that had been lying under it, I changed my mind. I pulled the high collar of my stepfather's coat up around my ears and fell into a sort of stupor. Every now and then my thoughts would revert to the scene in my stepfather's study, but I would force myself to blot it out and try instead to concoct some sort of story to explain my sudden and entirely unexpected arrival at my uncle's house.

Shaken and bumped about though I was, I must somehow have dozed off. I was woken by a particularly violent jolt which nearly threw me off the seat. When I had collected myself, I perceived that the horizon was streaked with light. I leaned forward and asked Stepan how much further it was to Spasskoye. He replied that we would be there in an hour or so. My short sleep must have cleared my brain, for I was now able to come to a rapid decision. I told him that when we were a little less than half an hour away, he was to drop me and I would walk the rest of the way myself. I said I was of course unable, then and there, to give him any money for his pains, but I would see to it that he received the handsome sum of fifteen roubles, on one condition: on no account was he to breathe a word to anyone about this night. If I heard the slightest rumour that anyone knew about it, I would see that he was flogged within an inch of his life. At the mention of the money, his oafish head started bobbing up and down like a pigeon's, but he seemed to take in what I had told him, and stammered a dozen times that red-hot pincers couldn't make him betray our secret. The words 'our secret' brought forcibly home to me the humiliation of entering into a state of complicity with riffraff like this, but under the circumstances I had no choice. Thirty minutes later I climbed down, stiff and aching, from his cart and walked the last few versts to Spasskoye.

I need not have worried about explanations to my uncle. His indifference to everything not directly related to his own pleasures and interests saw to it that he barely listened to the story I had prepared with such care during my invigorating walk in the early dawn. He made a sardonic joke about my appearance, expressed mild astonishment *that I had walked all that way during the night – 'But then you always were a tough little thing,' he added. 'Should have been a boy, really!' – said that he was sorry about his sister's death – 'But then it was about time she died' – and saw no objection to my staying with him for a while – 'As long as you make yourself useful and don't get in my way' …*

There. It is done. It has been a laborious task, but I think not an idle one. If I ever need reminding of the depths of depravity to which human nature can sink, I have but to refer to these pages. What will become of me now, I know not. I have received word that Vasily Osipovich did not die from my blow, and I thank Heaven for that. It seems that, to cover his shame, he has given out that it was hysterical grief at my mother's death that led me to flee. Well, let it rest there. All that I am certain of is that I will never return to that house. If it be God's will that I stay on here, I shall submit to it patiently enough. I cannot say that the prospect is very pleasing to me, but I have little other choice. Indeed, if my uncle should turn me out, perhaps all that would be left to me would be to seek to curtail a life that could only offer further humiliation and degradation. With all the guns I have seen in this house, the means would certainly not be wanting.

"Be that as it may," Nikolai Turgenev was anxious to get on with his story, "here she came and here she stayed. And to the best of my knowledge, she never went back to the house where she had been born and grew up. Except once."

"When was that?" Turgenev asked.

"Your little sister, Bibi, told me about it." Nikolai rubbed his hands together and emitted the throaty chuckle that always accompanied any reference to his favourite topic of illicit amours. "Of course, we didn't call her your sister in those days, did we? Your mother's 'ward', perhaps I should say. A sour, grasping young woman she's turned into, but she was quite sweet as a child. When she was still very young, your mother took her over – God knows why! – to see Kholodovo. Falling apart, it was. Hadn't been lived in for years. Somov had died not all that long after your mother left – of apoplexy, I think – and the two girls had married into the aristocracy and moved to Moscow. While your mother was talking to one of the peasants who acted as a sort of caretaker, little Bibi wandered off on her own. She came upon an old door which was still locked, even though it had already come off one of its hinges. She started to pull at the rusty padlock, to see if she could open it. Your mother came up behind her, seized her and dragged her away, almost wrenching her arm out of its socket. When Bibi asked her, in tears, what she'd done wrong, Varvara, with a look of deranged hatred on her face, the likes of which, Bibi told me, she had never seen before or since, screamed at her that she was not to go near the door again, that there was a curse on that room. Bibi remembered thinking it must have been haunted or something."

"My mother didn't believe in ghosts," Turgenev remarked thoughtfully.

"Well, we'll never know now. The house burned down shortly afterwards. At any rate, your mother spent the next ten years here at Spasskoye, under the…" he chuckled again and paused, as though searching for the right word – "the 'protection' of her uncle."

Turgenev humoured the old man by pretending to be ingenuous. "What are you hinting at now?" he asked.

His uncle's eyes sparkled with malignant glee. "Oh, there were stories that went around about that too. You know how it is in the provinces, a middle-aged bachelor living alone with his young niece. But I mustn't speak ill of your mother. And there was probably nothing to it anyway. I mean, a rich landowner like Ivan Lutovinov was never going to be short of female company. And, begging your pardon, my dear boy, but your mother wasn't the world's greatest beauty even then. Ivan Ivanovich's bastard son, the local people used to call her. And, by God, she was more than a match for most of the young men around here. She rode to hounds and shot and swam with the best of them. And what a competitor! She hated to be beaten at anything."

Turgenev laughed. "Yes, I remember her challenging my brother and me to billiard matches when we were home from university. She usually beat both of us. And the odd time she didn't, there was hell to pay. It was always the servants' fault. They'd been tampering with the balls, they hadn't prepared the cues properly… Kolya and I had a tacit agreement that it was better to let her win anyway."

"We all thought that was the chief reason she didn't marry earlier, that indomitable competitive spirit of hers. After all, there were many things in her favour. She was well educated. She went away to a good boarding school and she was a great reader. French novels, mostly. You probably got that from her. I don't remember your father reading much. Not to mention her prospects. Devilish tempting catch, she was. And she wasn't *that* bad-looking. Face was a bit off-putting: determined chin, tight-lipped mouth and that big nose of hers with the wide nostrils. But she had beautiful eyes and she could be a real charmer when she wanted to be. Fine figure of a woman too. She looked magnificent on a horse. Trouble is, courtships don't take place on horseback. Most of them, anyway. And the young men were afraid of her. They didn't want someone who was going to bring down more woodcock than they were. They wanted a wife who'd stay at home and see to their comfort and have babies popping out all the time. Like my little Masha. Can't say I blame them, really. She was a forbidding sort, even as a 25-year-old."

"You say she was a great catch," Turgenev observed, curiously. "But was it generally known that she would inherit her uncle's money?"

"By no means. Not all of it, at any rate. It could reasonably be expected that he would leave something to her. But no one knew Ivan Ivanovich's intentions in these matters. He was a tight-fisted old codger, apparently. Money was no object when he gave one of his hunting parties. Champagne flowed in the evening, orchestras were hired for dancing. But Varvara told me that every time she asked for housekeeping money, there were terrible scenes. Just like the ones she used to lay on for me, come to think of it. He used to beat her and punish her in all sorts of ways. He was always threatening to throw her out, and she was always threatening to leave. But she had the greater reason for sitting tight. I've heard it suggested that she knew he'd left her everything in his will, but just before he died they had an even more vicious fight than usual, and he shouted at her that he was going to disinherit her. He was a very sick man, and there are those who say that she substituted the medicine the doctors had prescribed with something a little stronger."

"Are you aware, Nikolai Nikolayevich," Turgenev asked wryly, "that in the course of the last hour or so, you have intimated that both my grandmother and my mother were murderesses?"

"Rumours, my dear boy, rumours. Probably not a word of truth in them. Just wanted to show you come from pretty wild stock – on your mother's side, that is. Not that there's any of that in you. Mild as a May morning, you are. Sometimes a bit too mild for your own good, I'd say."

"So she inherited everything?"

"She made damned sure she did! Every last rouble. A superhuman achievement. You know how cases involving rights of succession can drag on for years, decades even. And yet, in less than a month, Varvara got herself recognized as sole heir to an estate of thousands of acres, twenty villages and five thousand serfs. Her uncle's sisters were caught napping; by the time they heard of Ivan's death and wrote to the court putting forward some claims of their own, it was too late. Overnight, at 26, the little orphan, unloved and unwanted, became a totally independent, immensely rich woman. She once had all her silver stacked on a platform scale used for sacks of corn. It weighed two thousand pounds. I heard that myself from one of the bailiffs who was present. All she lacked now was a husband, and she set out to find one with the single-minded determination we both know about."

"Unless the local gentry were much less mercenary than they are now," Turgenev observed, "I wouldn't have thought she would have had much difficulty."

"Well, at first she wasn't short of suitors. But soon that little element we were talking of just now made its appearance."

"You mean she frightened them off?"

"Exactly. Your Russian gentleman, as we know, keeps his eye on the roubles all right. But his gaze might become a bit deflected if he fears he's not going to be master in his own house. And Varvara's way of wooing was, apparently, very direct."

"You mean she proposed to them?"

"In all but words, yes."

"How do you know all this? After all, my father hadn't yet put in an appearance. Where did you get all this information from?"

"If you like, you can hear an example from the mouth of one of the suitors himself."

"You mean one of them still lives in the neighbourhood?"

"Indeed he does. Pavel Petrovich Krupensky. And he has a story to tell about your mother that will singe your ears off."

During these days, Turgenev was essaying an early sketch, in Rudin's hostess, Darya Mikhaylovna Lasunsky, of a type that would obsess him for the rest of his life: the domineering woman who would overwhelm a man – at least for a while – by her charm, before either she lost interest in him or his eyes were opened to her ruthless egotism. He was intrigued by the prospect of being able to use his own mother as a part-model. The next evening Krupensky was invited to dinner, and this time, as Nikolai assured her there would be no references to anything improper, Masha was part of the company.

Nikolai had told his nephew that Krupensky had been extraordinarily handsome as a young man, and Turgenev had no difficulty in believing it. Pavel Petrovich must have been nearing seventy, but his bright blue eyes, mane of iron grey hair parted in the centre and falling to his shoulders and tall, erect frame bespoke a man who had made the business of charming women one of the main occupations of his life. He appeared delighted to meet Turgenev, complimented him on his stories and entertained his hosts to a succession of amusing anecdotes throughout dinner. When the men, with Masha's permission, lit their cigars, he turned to Turgenev and, with no prompting from Nikolai, asked him if he would like to hear about his brief rapport with his mother.

"It has never been my habit," he added with deliberate courtesy, "to speak ill of any lady that I have had the pleasure of knowing. But the story which, with your permission, I am about to tell you is so remarkable, and the principal character – your mother – such an extraordinary personage, that I think all ordinary conceptions of correct behaviour no longer apply. Determination such as hers transcends whatever society, in any epoch, lays down as *comme il faut*. It just is, it exists as a phenomenon in its own right, and all we weaker mortals can do is take note of it and marvel."

Turgenev begged him to tell the whole story and not, out of delicacy, to omit any details. This is what Krupensky had to relate.

"The first time I really became aware of Varvara Petrovna was one evening in Orel at the governor's ball. We had met previously at other people's houses, but I had never paid much attention to her nor, I believe, had she to me. Naturally I had heard of the extraordinary fortune she had inherited from her uncle but, although, like most young men, my means were as limited as my appetite was voracious, it didn't make any great impression on me. I don't think I am flattering myself when I say that a woman's wealth has never been of much interest to me. Their sex is

15

endowed with so many qualities of infinitely greater attraction.

"I mention this à propos of that evening in Orel, when I found myself increasingly drawn to her. She seemed to single me out for her attention with a boldness which was most unusual in young ladies of those days. We danced several times, and I was struck by her intelligence and the forthright way in which she expressed herself on a wide variety of subjects. In short, she was far from being the most beautiful girl in the room, but she seemed to me the most interesting.

"The evening came to an end, and a few days later I returned to Moscow. Life resumed its normal course, but I confess that the image of Varvara Petrovna often came to my mind. Certainly the fact that she had sought out my company played its part. A young man's vanity knows no bounds. Nor, for that matter, does an old man's; it's just that, alas, the chances of its being tickled are far more rare. But there was more to it than that: there was – how shall I put it? – a fire in her that made a challenging contrast with the bashful timidity of most of our young Russian maidens. I made up my mind that when I next went to the country I would find some way of renewing our acquaintance.

"But the initiative was taken out of my hands. A few days later I received a rather unusual invitation to a ball that Varvara Petrovna Lutovinova was to give at Spasskoye on the evening of the 17th of June. Now that happens to be the day of Saints Peter and Paul, and consequently doubly my name day, as it applies both to my given name and my patronymic. And there was something about the handwritten note that accompanied the invitation that implied, without any vulgar specification, that the ball was being held in my honour.

"This was clearly not an occasion to be missed. And in my carriage on the journey down I found myself surprised at how eagerly I was looking forward to the evening. Young as I was, I was already beginning to find most of those balls rather tedious affairs. Always the same people, the same conversation, the same music... But this time my curiosity was well and truly aroused. As we drew near to Spasskoye, I was surprised at the lack of other carriages on the roads. I had imagined somehow that this was going to be a big occasion, with invitations sent out to hundreds of guests. But my surprise turned to astonishment when we drew up in front of the house and there was not another carriage – or indeed another human soul – in sight. The journey from Moscow had been long, and I had even been a little afraid of arriving late. Of course my first thought was that I had come on the wrong day; but the fact of it being Saints Peter and Paul's day eliminated that explanation.

"I was completely at a loss as to what to do. But just as I decided that I had better drive to the nearest village and make some enquiries, the front door opened and the majordomo came out, walked up to my carriage door, opened it and said that his mistress was expecting me inside. I stepped down and followed him through the hall into an anteroom where Varvara Petrovna was sitting on a divan, her hands folded in her lap, an expression somewhere between mockery and exhilaration hovering around her eyes.

"She held her hand out to me, invited me to sit down and began, in a slightly bored tone of voice, asking me a series of the most conventional questions: was I tired after my long journey?… how long had it taken me?… would I care for some tea before being shown to my room?… I played her game for a while, until I was able to interject into a pause in the conversation: 'Varvara Petrovna, where are the other guests?'

"There was not a trace of embarrassment either in her expression or in her voice as she answered: 'There are no other guests.'

"I stammered out that I had understood there was to be a ball.

"'There is to be a ball,' she replied. 'But I have invited only you.'

"I don't think ever, before or since, have I been so utterly baffled. For a moment I harboured the idea that this must be some sort of elaborate joke. But there was no denying the absence of any sign of other guests. I could think of nothing appropriate to say. Nothing at all. I just sat there, looking across at her in vacuous disbelief.

"She returned my gaze for a few seconds and then asked, with nonchalant coolness: 'Have you any objection? If you have you must tell me. I rather thought you'd be pleased.'

"'Pleased!', I gasped. 'But, Varvara Petrovna, this is madness. Apart from the awkward situation in which you place me, have you given no thought to your reputation?'

"She snapped her fingers contemptuously. 'That's what I give for my reputation. But if it's your reputation you're concerned about, you have no cause for alarm. Throughout the entire evening, we will not be alone for a moment. The servants will be in attendance during dinner. And the orchestra will be playing until the early hours of the morning. After which,' she added with a touch of malice, 'I can, if you wish, provide a chaperone to escort you to your room.'

"Seeing that this did little to allay my unease, she concluded briskly: 'You seem to need time to reflect. I will have you shown to your room, where you can think it over at your leisure. If you decide to stay, dinner will be served at seven. If you choose to leave, no great harm will have been done. You will have wasted a couple of days. And I shall be left with the conviction that there is not a man of independent spirit left in this benighted Russia of ours.'

"She rang a little bell and a servant appeared immediately and accompanied me upstairs. Alone in my room, I looked around and saw that my luggage had already been unpacked and its contents neatly arranged in cupboards and shelves. This air of – how can I put it? – temporary permanence came to my aid in making my decision. And I cannot pretend that I reflected for very long. 'After all,' I argued to myself – and aren't we always our most understanding interlocutors? – 'this is an adventure that can do no harm to me. On the contrary, if word of it leaks out –

which it undoubtedly will – it will give me a certain cachet, lend me an aura of mystery which ladies of all ages have always found irresistible.' And as far as my conscience was concerned – and, believe it or not, I did have a conscience, albeit a not overly troublesome one – I absolved myself with the consideration that if she didn't care about her reputation, what business was it of mine to force the dictates of what is loosely known as 'good' society down her throat?"

Lupensky paused and looked around, as though to see if anyone would challenge this observation. Nobody did, so, with a little chuckle, he continued: "And having said all that, what really induced me to stay was, of course, that the idea of spending an entire evening in her company intrigued me. I could not have said the same of many, indeed perhaps of any of her contemporaries; but there was no doubting that there was something about Varvara Petrovna's boldness, her unconventionality, her sheer 'differentness' that I found both challenging and appealing.

"I won't abuse your patience by dwelling overlong on the details of that remarkable evening. I went downstairs shortly before seven, but had to wait a full half-hour before she joined me. She was wearing a ballgown she had brought back from Paris: a rather *osé* dress in cream-coloured tulle (*tulle illusion*, as they used to call it in those days), with bouffant sleeves which left her arms bare and a high waist setting off her already excellent figure. Altogether she made a handsome impression, and I remember thinking that if it hadn't been for the excessive broadness of her nose and the traces that smallpox had left on her complexion, she would have been a distinctly attractive woman. In any case, this was only a question of first impressions, because a few minutes later all thoughts of physical appearance had been driven from my head by the intelligence of her conversation and the vivacity of her company. As we dined – excellently – she talked little about the past but freely and enthusiastically about the future. She was ambitious and optimistic: I had the impression that the hardships and humiliations of her childhood had made her doubly determined to fill the rest of her life with experiences of every sort. She longed to visit other countries, her travels up to then having been limited to Germany and France. I told her of my love of Italy, and especially of the magic of Venice. She announced that she would go there that autumn, with a hint, I rather fancied, that I might accompany her. When we had finished dinner, an orchestra, which had been playing quietly in the background, struck up a lively series of polkas and mazurkas and we danced for what I seem to remember as hours on end – though no doubt my damnably failing memory is playing its usual time tricks on me. At first I found it rather a daunting experience, performing the familiar steps with no other couples to either side or onlookers laughing and chattering in groups around the walls. But the awkwardness soon wore off, and I found myself enjoying the freedom to make minor variations on the well-known steps without causing eyebrows to be raised at my temerity. She was a spirited, almost over-energetic dancer and, young as I was, I was ready enough for the moments when we would sit a dance out and refresh our – or at any rate my – flagging energies with a glass of champagne."

Lupensky's cigar had long since gone out, and he re-lit it with studied care. Turgenev, himself an expert raconteur, guessed that he was searching for the most effective way of bringing his tale to a close. Nikolai, who had heard the story many times, told his guest that this was no time to let his energies flag, poured some more brandy into his glass and, with a knowing wink to his wife, urged him to continue.

Lupensky, still taking his time, pursed his lips thoughtfully, blew a couple of smoke rings, took a sip of brandy and, with what seemed to Turgenev almost an air of reluctance – whether feigned or genuine, he was unable to decide – launched into the last part of his story.

"It must have been around two in the morning when Varvara Petrovna dismissed the orchestra. A servant or two were still discreetly present and my hostess asked me if I wanted another slice of veal or glass of wine. I declined and, with a joking reference to our moment of tension a few hours earlier, said that I thought it was about time my chaperone accompanied me to my room. She gave me a long look and then, with a light smile, said: 'I'm afraid I am going to go back on my word. I would like you to come with me for a minute or two into my office.'

"I was a little puzzled, but by then I felt so easy in her company that I followed her unhesitatingly. She led me to the room which I believe you still today use as an office" – Nikolai nodded in confirmation – "and after closing the door behind us, went over to a large desk and opened a drawer. 'Pavel Petrovich,' she said, 'I would like to give you a present in celebration of your name day. I'm an hour or two late, I know, but I wanted you to receive it when we were alone. And your punctilious sense of honour made that eventuality impossible until now.'"

"I was somewhat taken aback at this and, to hide my embarrassment, mumbled that in all conscience the evening up to now had been present enough. But she shrugged her shoulders and said that had been simply a *divertissement*. This seriously alarmed me. If the dinner, the wine, the orchestra had been a *divertissement*, what in heaven's name was she thinking of giving me as a present? I remember offering up a silent prayer that it wouldn't be anything I would be unable to accept. My prayer went unanswered. Without another word, she drew from the drawer a large roll of parchment and handed it to me. My heart, despite my best efforts to control it, was thumping hard as I untied the ribbon. I don't know what I was expecting, but nothing could have prepared me for the shock I received. For what Varvara Petrovna had handed me was a deed to one of her properties, with no less than five hundred serfs attached to it. My mind started to race. I had been led along like a little boy being enticed with his favourite chocolates to behave as his mother wishes. The ball had just been bait, and I had swallowed it whole like a famished carp. In plain words, she was bribing me to marry her. I had the devil of a temper in those days – another attribute that, mercifully in this case, attenuates over the years. Acting on impulse, I took the only course that seemed honourable to me. I tore the deed in two and threw it to the ground. I might as well have taken up a dog-whip and lashed her across the face. The blood drained from her cheeks and I could see from her clenched fists that she was digging her nails into the flesh of her palms. There was something superhuman about the effort she made to control herself. We stood there staring at each other for God knows how long, and then she forced her lips into a smile. 'I don't think that was wise,' she said. 'Perhaps you have drunk too much champagne. May I suggest that you have a good night's sleep and see if the morning doesn't bring you a little wisdom. You are turning down an opportunity that is unlikely to come your way again.' And she swept past me and left the room.

"The rest can be quickly told. When I reached my room, I was trembling all over. I splashed some cold water over my face and sat down on the bed, taking deep breaths and waiting for my heart to stop pounding and my brain to start functioning. I had to decide with a clear mind what action to take. To accept her gift was, of course, out of the question. But I asked myself if my impulsive gesture hadn't been an act of unpardonable discourtesy after the lavish welcome I had received? Should I make my apologies in the morning, thank her for her hospitality and take my leave, hoping that we could remain on friendly terms? I had almost decided that this was the course I should pursue when I saw again the expression on her face – condescension verging on contempt – and heard the tone of her voice when she'd said those last words to me: 'You are turning down an opportunity that is unlikely to come your way again.' She was counting on my making my calculations and regretting my rash behaviour. At that very moment, she was probably thinking: 'We'll see in the morning how much is left of our debt-ridden little *hobereau's* pride!' I didn't give the matter another second's thought. I packed my bags, went downstairs and woke my servant, who fortunately I knew had been installed in a room above the stables. Together we harnessed the carriage by torchlight and drove away before a glimmer of light appeared in the night sky. By the evening of the next day, I was back in Moscow."

Turgenev was the first to break the long silence. "What did she have to say to you when you next met?' " he asked.

"From that day, Ivan Sergeyevich," the old man replied, "I never again laid eyes on Varvara Petrovna."

"Amazing story, eh?" Nikolai exclaimed, as uncle and nephew took up the threads again the following evening. "You can lay many faults at Varvara's door, but inconsistency, never! You knew where you were with her." He gave a dry chuckle. "In trouble, usually!"

Turgenev smiled his agreement. "I haven't been able to get Lupensky's story out of my head. I couldn't write a word this afternoon. The idea that kept nagging at me was that perhaps, if things had gone differently with Mama and Lupensky, they would have made an excellent match. It was their intransigence that made it impossible. If she had expressed regret for her gauche behaviour, but explained that it was an attempt to show how highly she thought of him, or if he had tried to make her understand that, although it was impossible for him to accept her gift, he appreciated the generosity behind it, perhaps the mutual attraction that was clearly there might have broadened into something of lasting value to both of them. And then this very intransigence of theirs might have worked to their advantage."

"I don't follow you."

"Surely what my mother needed was a man with a character as strong as hers. I won't say stronger, because I can't imagine such a being. And Lupensky, by his rejection of her gift, showed that he was that man. Given time, this clash of wills might have resolved itself in a very stimulating synthesis."

"Or in a series of bloody battles ending only with the annihilation of one of the two parties!"

"Yes, of course. Very possibly. But even that might have been better than the cold, polite but immense distance I remember separating my mother and father."

"That came later. It wasn't like that at the beginning."

"Ah, that's what I wanted to ask you. I have in mind a story about a marriage in which, inside the shell of conventional appearance, there is a vacuum. Neither love nor hate. Just nothing. And the effect this has on the only son. But originally there must have been something inside that shell. For instance, how did Mama manage to snare my father? I doubt whether even she would try the Lupensky trick again."

"You know, that's always been a bit of a mystery to me. Sergey was never very communicative about it. Matter of fact, he was never very communicative about anything. But when I asked him about his courtship with your mother – and it was a lightning courtship – he would mumble 'Love at first sight' and there was nothing more to be got out of him."

"Perhaps it was love at first sight. That's the impression Mama always gave."

Nikolai allowed himself a sceptical grunt. "That's the impression she wanted to give. Otherwise, what meaning would her life have had? Apart from you, of course. But I've never been able to see my brother in the role of passionate lover. He was a great ladies' man, mind you. The women adored him. Handsome devil, too. But a bit of a cold fish, if you ask me. How well do you remember him? You were what when he died? Thirteen? Fourteen?"

"Sixteen. I have very clear memories of him, although I never felt particularly close to him."

"There you are, you see. I don't think he was ever really close to anyone. Certainly not to me. People were always remarking on how different we were. I was no Adonis and was forever tumbling in and out of some sort of scrape or other. But no one could say I didn't have an open heart. Always ready to lend a helping hand if a friend was in need…"

'And always ready to help yourself when you were in need,' Turgenev couldn't help reflecting.

"… But Sergey wasn't someone who found it easy to give anything of himself. And he, swept up in a whirlwind romance? Never! No, there was something there that I've never really understood. Her money played a part, of course. No getting away from that. His debts were all but strangling him. But that's not all there was to it. And why did they get married so quickly? Your brother was born a regular ten months after the wedding, so that takes care of the usual explanation."

"Tell me how they first met."

"Ah, now that I do remember. Sergey was a young lieutenant in the Cuirassiers. Twenty-two he was at the time. His regiment was short of mounts and they sent him out on a sort of scouring expedition with orders to buy as many first-rate horses as he could find in the neighbourhood at the cheapest possible price. One of the first places he visited was Spasskoye, because he'd heard of the eccentric rich landowner who kept a magnificent stable. She had a fine selection of animals paraded in front of him and allowed him to ride as many as he wanted. But when he'd made his selection and started to negotiate a price, she proved, for all her wealth, a very tough bargainer. This put him in a difficult spot, because although he knew the horses were worth what she was asking, he'd had strict orders not to pay more than so much per head. Seeing him dithering, she proposed a wager: the next day, with the pick of any horse he wanted, she challenged him to a cross-country race. If he won, he could have the horses at his price; if she won, she'd insist on hers."

"What was the result?" Turgenev asked eagerly, fascinated by this tale, which was quite new to him.

"Here their accounts differ," Nikolai answered with a laugh. "In later years, both claimed the victory. But I'm inclined to believe her. Sergey, till his dying day, swore she was the finest horsewoman he'd ever known. And that was a subject he was an expert on. When they were first married, in his tenderer moments he used to call her Penthesilea. At any rate, it was of no matter. Two days after his visit they announced their engagement and the date of their wedding."

Turgenev pondered for a moment and then suggested: "Could it be that she offered him the same enticement she had tried with Lupensky and he was less fastidious?"

Nikolai shook his head. "I don't think so. Sergey was a cautious character, even as a young man. He wasn't one to plunge in head first without having calculated the depth beforehand. Had she offered him the deed to one of her properties, if I know my brother he'd have taken time to think it over and then given his answer. And remember, she was six years older than he was. He was gaining a lot… but he was throwing away his youth at the same time. No, take my word for it: something happened that night which neither of them ever wanted to talk about. And it's no use our guessing now. We shall never know…"

INT. THE DINING-ROOM AT SPASSKOYE – EVENING

Varvara Petrovna Lutovinova, in a low-cut evening dress of emerald green satin, and Sergey Nikolayevich Turgenev, wearing full dress uniform, have just finished their dinner. Varvara Petrovna mutters some instructions to her butler and then dismisses him. Turgenev takes an appreciative sip at his glass of wine.

SERGEY

Your cellar seems to be as well stocked as your stables, Varvara Petrovna.

VARVARA

I hope you're not expected to buy wine for your colonel as well.

SERGEY

That was not part of my orders. But I'd be a very popular fellow if I came back with a couple of dozen bottles like this.

VARVARA

From what I have heard of officers' mess behaviour, the quantity consumed seems to take precedence over the quality.

SERGEY

(with a young man's pride)

Not in the 5th Cuirassiers, madame. Drunkenness is frowned

upon. We have splendid parties from time to time, of course. I hope you will pay us the honour of attending one soon.

(She smiles and nods her head in assent)

But we are expected at all times to behave like gentlemen.

VARVARA

Ah, like gentlemen! Well, that sets my mind at rest.

(ignoring his puzzled look)

No, Sergey Nikolayevich, my wine is not for sale. As I have all the red brought from France and the white from Germany, I only keep enough for my own needs. Whereas horses I am always picking up here and there. À *propos des chevaux*, it has occurred to me that perhaps our little wager tomorrow is not fair on you.

SERGEY

(piqued)

I assure you, Varvara Petrovna, as a cavalry officer…

VARVARA

(with a reassuring smile)

I am not in any way suggesting you would not be a worthy opponent. On the contrary, I'm amazed at my own boldness in daring to challenge you. But I have an unfair advantage. I have ridden this country for fifteen years. I know every hedge and brook so well I could draw them from memory. And my mare knows them as well as I do.

(overriding his attempted objection)

No, no, we will have our race, of course we will. But let us not make the price of the horses depend upon the result. Let's leave that to the cards.

SERGEY

The cards?

VARVARA

Yes. You play, I presume.

SERGEY

(ruefully)

Too often, I fear.

24

VARVARA

Ah! Have I hit upon your weakness?

(He doesn't answer, but the haunted look in his eyes reveals the extent of his debts. This is not lost on her.)

Well then, as one gambler to another, shall we let chance decide how much these animals are worth? If you win, you pay me your price. You don't have to tell your colonel I am practically giving these magnificent animals away. And with the difference you can perhaps relieve yourself of some tiresome obligations.

SERGEY

You are suggesting I cheat?

VARVARA

Oh, cheat! Such a big word! The 5th Cuirassiers acquire some horses that, if it hadn't been for you, they would never have even thrown a leg across. I'm not in the horse-trading business, you know.

(filling his empty glass)

But you have a very persuasive way about you, lieutenant. Any other emissary would have been sent packing. And you would be able to discharge a few debts, which all young officers occur from time to time. It seems to me a very satisfactory solution. If you win, of course.

(a pause)

Well, are you a real gambler or not?

SERGEY

(with at least a show of reluctance)

Very well.

VARVARA

Good. Let us adjourn to the card-room then.

She rises to her feet. He gulps down the rest of his wine, hurries over to pull her chair back and follows her out of the room.

INT. THE CARD-ROOM – A LITTLE LATER IN THE EVENING

Varvara Petrovna Lutovinova and Sergey Nikolayevich Turgenev are sitting opposite each other across a card-table. On a trolley nearby are a number of bottles and decanters. Sergey has a half-full glass beside him. Varvara is not drinking. They are playing vingt-et-un without chips or money, simply totting up the hands they have won. Sergey is dealer.

VARVARA

Carte!

Sergey deals a card face upwards. It is a seven. Varvara throws her two cards down on the table and we see that they are a ten and a five.

VARVARA

You win. Now let's see where we stand.
The best of how many hands did we say?

SERGEY

Fifteen.

Varvara flicks a pencil over some figures written down on a piece of paper beside her.

VARVARA

We've each won seven exactly. This is the deciding hand. Deal!

Sergey, who has been shuffling the pack, takes a sip of his drink and deals them each a card face down. When she picks it up, we see that Varvara's card is a six.
Sergey deals two more cards face up. Varvara's is a queen, his a ten.

VARVARA

Carte!

Sergey deals a five face upwards. Varvara has made twenty-one, but she immediately throws her cards face down on the table.

VARVARA

You win, lieutenant. Congratulations!

Sergey empties his glass and leans back in his chair with a satisfied smile.

SERGEY

But we're still going to ride that race, aren't we?

26

VARVARA

Yes. Tomorrow. But now I presume you won't refuse me another game?

SERGEY

You want to play some more?

VARVARA

Just one hand.

SERGEY

And what's to be the stake?

She looks at him fixedly, letting his question hang in the air.

SERGEY
(uneasily)

Well?

VARVARA
(in a level voice, without a trace of emotion)
The winner may claim anything he – or she – wants, that the loser is able to provide.

Sergey is stunned. For the first time we notice how young he is. Although he tries not to show his anxiety, his hands shake slightly as he pours himself another drink and two red spots appear in his otherwise sallow cheeks.

SERGEY
(stammering)
But...Varvara Petrovna...anything... could mean...

VARVARA
(inflexible)

Anything.

Sergey shakes his head helplessly from side to side, his lips framing words he cannot bring himself to pronounce. Varvara watches him for a while with barely concealed amusement. Then:

VARVARA

I thought we had established you were a gambler. Was I mistaken?

SERGEY
(his pride rubbed raw)

No. You were not.

(He takes a deep breath)

Very well, then. Let us play. Your deal.

Varvara takes up the cards and slowly and methodically shuffles them. Sergey hypnotically watches her hands as they deftly go about their business. He can hardly wrench his eyes away to reach for his glass, from which he takes a large gulp. Varvara finishes shuffling and raps the pack on the table to square it off. Then, still very deliberately, she deals them each a card face down.

Sergey picks his up and we see it is a jack. Varvara deals two more cards face up, an eight for Sergey and a king to herself. Sergey, with eighteen, has no choice.

SERGEY

I stand.

Varvara wordlessly lays down her cards: a king and a nine. Nineteen. She has won. Something – it could be remaining drops of tartar blood or it could be the imprint of military discipline – makes Sergey rise to the occasion. He is scarcely recognizable as the frightened youth of a minute ago. Nothing, except the involuntary twitching of a cheek muscle, betrays his apprehension. Quietly he asks:

SERGEY

Well, Varvara Petrovna, what is it to be?

And now it is Varvara's turn for a moment of indecision. She knows what she wants, but she doesn't know how to ask for it. She forces her features into a languorous, faintly flirtatious look which contrasts oddly with her normally determined, masculine expression. Finally she comes out with:

VARVARA

I think it would be indelicate, Sergey Nikolayevich, for a lady to put into words what she requires from an officer of the 5th Cuirassiers.

He understands immediately. With no show of surprise, or indeed of any emotion whatsoever, he gets up, walks round the table to her chair, puts his hands under her arms, raises her to her feet and kisses her. It is a long kiss. In detail, we see first her fingers digging passionately into his shoulders, then his fingers loosening her dark hair, which begins to tumble down her back...

CUT TO

EXT. COUNTRY AROUND SPASSKOYE – DAY

Varvara Petrovna and Sergey Nikolayevich are nearing the finish of their race. They jump a hedge almost neck and neck, but on landing Varvara's grey mare lengthens her stride and begins gradually to surge ahead. TIGHT ON the two riders: Sergey urging his horse on and flicking its flanks with his whip; Varvara imperceptibly reining her mare back and muttering 'Slow down!' noises under her breath.

EXT/INT. SPASSKOYE – DAY

Varvara and Sergey, in their riding clothes, run up the steps to the front porch of the house, laughing and chattering. She congratulates him on his victory, he modestly ascribes all the merit to his mount. Varvara calls for the butler and orders a bottle of champagne – 'Dom Pierre, Yakov!' She suggests, given the fine day, that they stay out on the porch. He agrees and they sit down on two wooden chairs around a wicker table. All sense of last night's strain has disappeared: they are now two young people quite at ease with each other. Varvara especially has softened almost beyond recognition; she is clearly in love with the handsome young officer.

SERGEY

Do you really mean to tell me, Varvara Petrovna, that all the land we have just ridden over is part of your estate?

VARVARA

Oh, just a very small part.

SERGEY

And those villages... we must have passed three or four.

VARVARA

I have over twenty.

Sergey purses his lips and gives a light laugh; but his eyes reveal that this information has reinforced an idea that has already been occupying his mind.
The butler comes out with the bottle and two glasses, which he fills.

29

VARVARA
(waving him away)
Off with you, Yakov! That will be all.

Sergey's eyes follow the butler thoughtfully as he goes back into the house.

VARVARA
(raising her glass)
To the victor! One of the finest horsemen I have ever seen.

SERGEY
(raising his)
To a gallant loser!
(he puts the glass to his lips and then adds, trying to conceal it's an afterthought)
And a beautiful one!

Afterthought or not, it has its effect on Varvara, who blushes slightly and lowers her eyes. Sergey pursues his line of thought in an anything but subtle way.

SERGEY
An estate that size must contain an immense number of serfs.

VARVARA
(simply)
Five thousand 'souls'.

This takes even the self-controlled Sergey's breath away. His jaw drops and he gazes at her in mock disbelief.
To fill the silence, Varvara adds:

VARVARA
Five thousand migraines.
(You feel she'd like to add 'for a woman alone', but doesn't quite dare. Instead she holds out her glass for him to refill and changes the subject)
You know, Sergey Nikolayevich, I think your victory today deserves a prize. I had my wish last night. Now what can I give you?

SERGEY

(with the sang-froid of one who feels he has nothing to lose)

Your hand in marriage, Varvara Petrovna.

VARVARA

(reaching out her hand to him across the table)

It is yours.

from VARVARA'S JOURNAL

<u>14 January, 1830.</u> *Today is the fourteenth anniversary of my marriage to Sergey Nikolayevich – not that he has remembered, of course, nor do I have the least intention of reminding him. And yet, upon reflection, it occurs to me now that it was he who chose the date. On the evening of that day when I so carelessly, so wantonly threw away any chance of happiness I might have had in this life, we were discussing when to celebrate the marriage. I tended to favour a lengthy engagement, believing, with how much justification I was all too soon to discover, that the period of betrothal was* un moment d'or *in the life of the bride-to-be; he, for reasons best known to himself and which he certainly never divulged to me, was all for the speediest possible resolution of the affair. With the giddy irresponsibility with which I conducted myself throughout that fatal day, aided no doubt by the quantities of champagne we had drunk, I suggested a final hand of* vingt-et-un *to resolve the matter for us. We played. He won and named the fourteenth of January, a mere couple of months away. He claimed that he was due for some leave after the New Year festivities and this would enable us to have a long honeymoon. I had no choice but to accept. Indeed, it seemed a matter of small moment, until I discovered that the date fell on a Friday. I have always harboured a superstition about Fridays –* ça m'a toujours fait peur, ce jour-là – *and I begged him to change it. A day sooner, a day later, what difference would it make? But he said that he was superstitious too and it would be unlucky to defy the decision of the cards. He was quite adamant about it and eventually I had to give way. For several years now I have never conversed with a young fiancée without warning her not to marry on a Friday. A curse hangs over weddings celebrated on that day.*

That said, I cannot lay all the blame for my arid marriage on the occult. The ways of this all-too-tangible world play their part too. I dared to step out of the role society had assigned to me. I wanted Sergey and I got him. And I have been punished for my presumption ever since. I should have waited until some toothless old man with breath like rotting straw paid me the compliment of asking me to marry him. But at that time I felt sure the world was mine. I had only to reach out and take whatever appealed to me. And oh how Sergey appealed to me! He was all I had dreamed of: wonderfully handsome, with all the ease of manner that comes from belonging to an old aristocratic family (the Turgenevs were provincial governors when the Lutovinovs were Lithuanian peasants) and the diffident, boyish charm which women could never resist. Women! There lay the problem, if only I had had eyes to see it. How could I ever have imagined that he, six years younger than I, would ever be content only with me? At the time, it never crossed my mind.

In recent years I have had occasion to think of little else. Not that I could not bring myself to overlook the occasional infidelity – that, no doubt, is part of our long-suffering sex's lot. But I cannot go into Orel without some brazen-faced young woman favouring me with a half-pitying, half-contemptuous stare. And even that could be tolerable. I could – and indeed do – avoid their society on all but the rarest occasions. But when it happens in my own house, with my own servants… ah, ça, c'est le comble! I would like to have them flogged on the merest suspicion, but that would bring out into the open what I suppose is best left buried under its layer of slime.

Perhaps what I find most intolerable is the sense of impotence. There is nothing I can do to alter the situation. I have tried to have it out with him, but he simply withdraws into an evasive, disdainful silence. I suppose I could defy l'usage du monde and turn him out of the house, but I cannot bring myself to do that: the ashes of our old affection flare up from time to time – though ever more rarely; and the children must be brought up with a proper respect for both their parents. No, this is my cross and I must continue to bear it. It is my punishment for having dared to choose my man instead of waiting to be chosen… like all the rest of the grateful, submissive little wives around here. Ah, mon Dieu!, I would sooner have died a barren old maid than have ended up like them.

My one consolation is my son Ivan. Nikolinka will never amount to much, but Ivan, even at the tender age of twelve, already shows exceptional promise. A bit too much of a dreamer at the moment, perhaps; a spell in the army later on will do him a world of good. But in some form or another, I feel sure that one day he will make his mark on the world. He also has a great affection for me, though being a boy he does his best to hide it. But my conviction that he and I will always share a closeness and an understanding is some compensation for his father's distance and indifference. Perhaps my relationship with my son will be my reward for all my suffering at the hands of my husband…

Having gleaned as much as he thought he could from his mother's social equals, Turgenev decided it would be interesting to take a look at the view from below. With this in mind, he paid a visit to a former serf who had once been a constant hunting companion and whom he had portrayed in several of his *Sportsman's Sketches*. Afanasy Timofeyevich Alifanov had not belonged to his mother but to a neighbouring landowner. Nevertheless, incorrigible vagabond that he was (he had rarely slept in the same place two nights running), he knew as much about Spasskoye and the way it was run under Varvara Turgeneva as anyone else. It had been ten years since they had last spent long days together with rod and gun, sharing an intimacy rare between master and servant in those times. And when Turgenev, who in the meantime had bought Alifanov his freedom, first caught sight of him, he noticed certain changes: domesticity (it turned out that he now spent most nights in the tumbledown hut he shared with his wife) had thickened his waist and fleshed out his scrawny neck. But he still wore the belted yellow nankeen coat and wide blue trousers from which he refused to be parted; and an astrakhan-bordered cap,

33

given to him many years before in a moment of drunken generosity by a penniless landowner, hung on a nail behind the door.

The only notable difference from the old days was the absence of Valetka, the mangy, cadaverously skinny setter that Alifanov never fed; when reproached by Turgenev, he replied that if the dog was clever enough it would find food for itself, if it wasn't it would never be anything but a liability. Nevertheless, Valetka rewarded his hard-hearted master with single-minded devotion and a skill in putting up and retrieving game that no pedigree hound in the area could begin to match. When Turgenev asked what had happened to him, Alifanov replied, as dispassionately as though they'd been discussing a broken saucepan, that he'd been shot a couple of years ago by a vindictive fellow-poacher. But when pressed as to why he hadn't acquired another dog, he just looked away into the distance and mumbled that he hadn't felt like it.

Turgenev noticed, when Alifanov greeted him with an almost effusive show of pleasure, that his breath reeked of stale alcohol. That, at least, had not changed. Remembering that, taciturn as the man was when sober, nothing could check the torrent of words once the liquor had started to flow, Turgenev suggested they take a familiar path through the woods which led to an inn where they could have lunch – "provided, of course, your wife has no objection." Alifanov, with a derisive laugh, called back into the hut: "I'm off with the *barin*. Don't forget to kill a chicken. And saw some more logs, I nearly died of cold last night." And, without waiting for any reply, he set off so fast down the path with his swaying, jerky stride that Turgenev had almost to break into a run to catch up with him.

They soon reached the inn and a couple of plum brandies were speedily despatched, Alifanov making a rapid sign of the cross before downing each glass. As Turgenev had hoped, it was not long before he started to chatter away like a blackbird. Knowing that the man would at first be reluctant to speak of his mother in any but the most respectful terms, Turgenev introduced the subject carefully, asking what changes he had noticed since Varvara Petrovna's death. "Oh, things aren't the way they used to be, you can take my word on that," Alifanov confided sagely. "No one knows what they're supposed to do and not do any more. Wasn't like that when the old lady was alive. Her people knew what to do all right. And… beggin' your pardon, Ivan Sergeyevich… God help them if they didn't do it!"

This was what Turgenev wanted to hear, and he threw out a little more bait. "You knew just about everybody who worked at Spasskoye in those days," he remarked. "Tell me, what did they think of her?" He was about to add, "You can speak absolutely freely", but seeing another glass going down, decided it wasn't necessary.

"Well she put the fear of God into 'em, I can tell you that. Oh, she could be a hard 'un, no doubt about it." His small grey eyes lit up with a reminiscent gleam.

"Real cruel she was at times. Remember poor Arina… no, how could you, you wouldn't've been more than five or six at the time."

"Tell me about her."

"Well, she was your mother's favourite maid, treated her almost like one of the gentry, she did, took her with her to Moscow, gave her her old dresses to wear and all that. Well one day this girl, lovely little thing she was too, comes and tells Varvara Petrovna she's fallen in love with one of the footmen and wants to get married. Whoo! What a fit your mother throws… 'You ungrateful girl, how can you do this to me after all I've done for you? I picked you up out of the mud and treated you like a daughter. Do you have any complaints about your situation here?' 'No, ma'am.' 'Well, what's this all about, then?' 'Nothing, ma'am, it's just that Petrushka asked me yesterday if I'd be his wife, and I said yes as long as it's all right with madam.' 'Well it isn't all right with madam. You know I don't allow any of my personal maids to get married. They're never the same again, their minds are always on something else, and before you know it they're having babies and any kind of decent service goes out of the window. Now I don't want to hear any more of this, you hear? Another word and I'll send you back to your village.' So Arina goes away, but a few months later what does she do but go and get pregnant, and reckoning that Varvara Petrovna's going to notice sooner rather than later, goes to her in tears and confesses everything and begs to be allowed to stay on in her employment. Flings herself on the floor, she does, and kisses her mistress's feet and sobs and beats her breast and all that. Well, you know what Varvara Petrovna did? She didn't even speak to her, she rang the bell and when the butler, Lobanov – you remember him – arrived, ordered that Arina should be stripped of her fine clothes and dressed in rags, have all her hair cut off and be packed off to the country before nightfall. And that's the way it was."

Alifanov shook his head in retrospective disbelief before lowering it to slurp up the soup which had just been brought to them. Turgenev asked if he knew what had happened to the girl.

"Arina? Oh yes. She married a miller over in Zheltukhina." He jerked his head back over his shoulder, as though the village lay just beyond the wall of the inn.

Turgenev was surprised. "You mean my mother allowed her to marry?"

"He had a bit of money – the miller, I mean. Arina had learnt how to read and write, and he thought she'd be useful to him. So he bought her off."

"Ah! And is she still living in Zheltukhina?"

"She's not living anywhere. She's dead. Popped her clogs young too. Can't have been much over thirty. Coughed up enough blood her last few months to fill a horse trough."

Turgenev couldn't resist a last question. "How is it, Afanasy Timofeyevich, that you know so much about her?"

35

Alifanov shrugged his shoulders and tossed down another brandy. "She used to talk to me," he said impassively.

Turgenev gave him an amused glance. "Over lunch with the miller?"

"You want to make fun of me, Ivan Sergeyevich! Well, you're a man of the world… and the miller was thirty years older than her. He used to send her over to me for a rabbit or two. And when I knew she was coming, I'd kick my old woman out of the house with some excuse or other and… well, you know how it is…"

"I hope you made the poor girl happy, Afanasy Timofeyevich."

"I did my best, Ivan Sergeyevich. That's all any of us can do, ain't it?"

There was a moment or two of silence as the innkeeper gathered up the empty soup bowls, replaced them with two plates of mutton stew and set down a large jug of kvass in the middle of the table. Turgenev saw Alifanov's eyes mechanically following the man's gestures (his thoughts no doubt still on his snatched moments of ecstasy with the unfortunate Arina) and decided that it was time for him to contribute something to the conversation. He told Alifanov of the first time he remembered being consciously aware of his mother's cruelty – though failing to add that it was also, and more significantly, the first time he was appalled by social injustice. When he was seven or eight, his best friend had been the son of one of the serfs, a boy of his own age called Grisha, whose mother was a housemaid. The two lads used to play for hours together in the garden, and sometimes inside the house as well, where in the evenings they would invent elaborate versions of hide-and-seek. One of these games ended up in Ivan's bedroom, where it developed into a fast and furious pillow fight. Varvara Petrovna, hearing the noise, came into the room just as Grisha was hurling a pillow at her son. He was immediately sent off to be whipped for daring to raise his hand against the young master of the house. And although little Ivan immediately burst into tears and begged his mother to spare his friend, she was not to be moved. Turgenev said he could still feel the agony in his stomach at the double sense of injustice: Grisha was flogged although he had done nothing wrong; and he was deprived of a friend – because Grisha took good care from then on to keep a large distance between himself and his former playmate.

The morsel provided by Turgenev elicited from the now garrulous Alifanov an unstoppable flow of anecdotes, some of which Turgenev knew, (though he didn't admit it, for fear of drying up the source) but many of which he was hearing for the first time. He was told how all the gardeners were flogged because someone had cut one of madame's favourite tulips, of which there were over a hundred varieties.

"And then there was the day poor old Semyon Mikhailovich got the chop." Alifanov's gurgle of relish at the thought led Turgenev to think that there can't have been much love lost between him and the victim. "You remember him, he was the butler before Lobanov?"

"Yes I do, just. But not why he was dismissed."

"Oh he was the real gentleman, Semyon was. Thought no end of himself. Looked down his nose at all the rest of us. Used to get the under-footman to polish the buttons on his brown tailcoat for hours, till they shone like gold. Thought he could do no wrong with the mistress, too. But he had another think coming. Seems that even Varvara Petrovna found that hoity-toity manner of his more than she could stand. So she started complaining every time he brought her a glass of water. (I got this from Matryona, her lady's-maid at the time, so every word of it's true, so help me God!) Sometimes it was too cold, sometimes it was tepid, sometimes it was cloudy, sometimes it smelt bad… and every time he had to go and get her a fresh glass. Well one day, when she was in one of her moods, she took a sip of water, practically spat it out in disgust, cried out, 'Can't I ever have a decent glass of water in this house?' and threw the water in his face. Matryona said you had to hand it to Semyon. He didn't say a word or move a muscle. He just wiped the water off his face with the back of his hand – or back of his glove, I should say, he always wore gloves – picked up the jug he had poured from and left the room. A minute or two and he was back again with the jug. He poured water into a clean glass and handed it to Varvara Petrovna, who took a sip and said: 'Ah, now that's what I call a glass of water!' So what does Semyon do but go over to one of the ikons, stand before it, make the sign of the cross and say: 'I swear before God that I didn't change the water in that jug!'"

"Brave fellow!" Turgenev exclaimed, admiringly.

"Drivelling idiot!" Alifanov retorted. "No more brown tailcoats and white gloves for him. The next morning all he had on was a rough old hemp shirt and a pair of trousers two sizes too big for him. And what was his job? Yardman. For four or five years all he did was sweep the courtyard, shovel up the horse shit and saw logs in the winter. Then he was replaced by Andrey, that deaf and dumb giant your mother had brought up from the country and liked so much… until he drove her mad with his dog. I seem to remember your uncle telling me you'd put him into one those stories you write."

Turgenev smiled and nodded his head. "One of these days, if you like, I'll read it to you."

"Yes, I'd like that. It's good to look back on the old days. You know, we can say what we like about Varvara Petrovna, and perhaps with a bit of drink inside me I've said too much," (Turgenev shook his head) "but you've got to hand it to her: she ran this place like a ruddy empress. It's all fallen apart since she died, what with you always being away and your uncle – beggin' your pardon again – not being made of the same stuff as she was."

"You ought to have seen your empress holding court in the morning," Turgenev said with a smile. "Every day at eleven o'clock, Monday to Saturday, she'd sit in her chair, which stood on a raised platform in her office – just like a throne, as a matter of fact – and receive the day's reports from her secretary, the bailiff, the intendant and goodness knows who else. Every now and then she'd make me attend the sessions – to learn something useful for a change, as she put it, instead of sitting around doing nothing all day. I used to spend most of the time watching her fingers; whenever she began to get dissatisfied with something someone was saying, they'd begin playing nervously with the beads of her rosary. Of course, everyone else knew this as well. So as soon as they heard the familiar clicking, they'd all fall over themselves to insist on how wonderfully everything was going, how there had never been a better harvest, how all the rents were coming in in double quick time, how profits from the sale of livestock were double those of last year…"

Alifanov broke in with a snort of disgust. "Crawling, slimy vermin! Cowards and bullies, that's what they were, the lot of 'em. Grovelling before the gentry, and cheating and bribing and squeezing the life out of the likes of us. They were the ones we really hated. I mean, the *barinya* – the Kingdom of Heaven be hers! – your mother, Ivan Sergeyevich…" – the effect of the alcohol consumed and the hard core of anger burning inside him made him start to slur his words – "for all that she scared the wits out of the best of us, did a lot of good around here too. There was that hostel she set up for all those old ladies down on their luck, and the school at Pokrovskoye… that was the first time any youngsters around here saw the inside of a classroom… more than I ever did, that's for sure. No, you can say what you like but, for all her faults, she was a grand lady… and I can't help thinking we were better off when she was alive than we are now. The lickspittles are still there – they breed like rabbits, no one'll ever keep them down. The difference is there's no one to keep an eye on them any more, they can get away with anything. Like a sheep dog without a master. If he's hungry enough he'll eat the sheep, if there's no one to crack a stick over him."

These words of Alifanov's occupied Turgenev's mind on the walk back. *Here am I, at home with all that is most progressive and liberal in Western Europe, and still bearing the stigmata of being an owner of men. Emancipation's in the air, but who knows how long it will take. And here's this fellow suggesting they were better off under the tyrannical rule of my mother than the easy laissez-faire attitude of Uncle Nikolai. How do you explain it? Ignorance, I suppose. They're so used to being treated little better than animals that any idea of independent activity is foreign to them. And yet my friend Herzen in London believes that the salvation of Russia lies in the 'sheepskin coat' of the muzhik! Not for a while, it doesn't. And in the meantime, it's very comfortable for the landowners – even the best of them – to go on having their dirty work done for them by stewards and bailiffs while they stay loftily above it all… and even win the respect of people like my poor friend here, who cannot hate more than one rank above his social station. To hate tyrants like my mother would be like hating God for the endless injustices of this world. Everybody's life needs some foundation, and perhaps theirs is provided by that very social hierarchy which liberals like myself find so demeaning...*

Alifanov, who had also been wrapped in his thoughts, now broke the silence. With his twisted grin he looked up at Turgenev and said: "You know, Ivan Sergeyevich, you should put me in one of your stories."

Turgenev smiled down at him. "Oh, I have, Afanasy Timofeyevich," he said. "I have."

Alifanov chuckled with delight and shook his head in disbelief, until a thought struck him and he looked up in alarm. "But that means everyone'll know all about me. And you and I know there are one or two things I did... well, it's better they stayed a secret."

"Don't worry," Turgenev reassured him. "You won't be that easily recognizable. We writers change things around, you know: a bit of someone here, a bit of someone else there... no one ends up exactly as he was in real life. And anyway, I changed your name."

"You did?" Alifanov wasn't sure he liked that. "What did you call me?"

"Yermolay."

"Yermolay... Yermolay..." He repeated the name several times, giving it different inflexions, as though weighing up its merit. A final 'Yermolay... hm!' appeared to indicate that he was reasonably satisfied.

from VARVARA'S JOURNAL

<u>18 February, 1839</u>. While inspecting the stables yesterday evening, I noticed that the guests' horses are being fed hay. This is ridiculously extravagant. Straw is perfectly adequate. I must tell Vasya to instruct all the stable-boys to that effect.

Told Fedosya to see if any of her under-cooks know one of their counterparts in the Krylovs' kitchen and could manage to worm out of her the recipe for their sausages. The ones we ate at Marya Krylova's luncheon yesterday were much better than mine.

What a bore! That idiot Borisov and his giggling fat sow of a wife are coming to dinner tonight. I cannot imagine what came into my head when I invited them. At any rate, I must tell Vasily not to serve the best champagne, as he did last week for the equally arrivistes Chernobays. Anything of quality is totally wasted on these people. A Rhineland sekt will be more than good enough...

And talking of the Rhine... five Fridays have now gone by without a word from Ivan. What have I done to deserve this neglect? It is a cross too heavy for me to bear. Jean is my sun. I see nothing but him, and when he goes into eclipse I cannot see clearly any more, I no longer know where I am. I knew I should not have let him go to study in Berlin; all that philosophy is simply going to unsettle him, make him forget his duties towards his family and render him unfit for a serious career in government service. I must suppress my pride and write to him again, though a one-sided correspondence is so hard to maintain; it is like casting a line into a lake where you know there are no fish. I must find a different tone from my other letters – not sound too anguished or reproachful, but equally not let him think that he can continue this unfilial behaviour with impunity for ever...

Perhaps I should channel a message through Porfiry. I had doubts about sending my husband's bastard to Berlin as Ivan's servant. But it appears to be working out very satisfactorily. He is an excellent young man and entirely devoted to Jean. My only lingering worry is that Ivan may end up on too familiar terms with him. After all, his mother was a dairymaid. And Ivan is so lax about remembering not to let the serfs rise above their station. But that is no doubt on account of his youth and will soon pass ...

Spasskoye,
21 February, 1839.

Mon cher Jean,

After five weeks' silence, I have today received a letter from Porfiry, so at least I know that – God be praised! – you are alive. Is it deliberate cruelty on your part, Vanichka, or just youthful selfishness that makes you cause your mother so much suffering? Either way, it is reprehensible. There was a time, not so long ago, that when we were separated you used to write to me almost every day. Is this change in your attitude the result of what you conceive as a rite of passage from adolescence to manhood? If so, I can only tell you that it is a poor sort of man who neglects his mother in this way. But enough of these lamentations. You know me to be a woman of mettle, not one liable to take this sort of treatment lying down. So this is what I propose.

I have today told Lobanov to send a letter to Porfiry with the following instructions, which I now repeat to you. If you do not wish to write to me, so be it. But then you must say to Porfiry: 'I shall not be writing to Mama by today's post.' At which Porfiry must take up pen and paper and dispatch me a note saying, 'Ivan Sergeyevich is in good health'. That will be enough for me for three postal deliveries, after which I imagine even my errant son will find a moment to write to his mother. You see how indulgent I am being! But now, read carefully. If both of you miss one post, I shall be forced to have your old playmate Kolya whipped. I shall be sorry to do this, because he is a good lad, I am taking him under my wing and he is coming along very nicely. One of these days he will make an excellent footman. But what can I do? You give me no choice. The poor boy will just have to bear it, voilà tout ...

Spasskoye,
28 February, 1839.

Mon cher Jean,

It is Friday, I have at last received a letter from you and perhaps now I shall finally be granted a night's sleep. For pity's sake, never do this to me again. Write, or I will not answer for my sanity... for my life, even. You do not know what your mother is capable of. Death could not be worse than what I have been through these past few weeks.

Let me try and explain something to you. I am very much alone in this world. All my life I have known nothing but hostility and envy. I have had to pay dearly for the blessings the Creator has seen fit to bestow on me. I have no mother, brothers, sisters, friends even... You two, you and Nikolinka, mean everything to me. I love you both passionately... but differently... and ssh, do not let anybody hear what I am saying – you are my favourite. I blush when I think of how much you mean to me. Perhaps it is a sin. But my life depends on you... like thread in a needle; where the needle goes, the thread must follow.

And now a word about your letter. (Ah, what a joy to be able to discuss things with you again! It is almost as though you were sitting opposite me in your favourite chair, gobbling up great spoonfuls of the blackcurrant jam you are so fond of and that I have had made especially for you.) You tell me you are writing poetry. Good! That is an excellent pastime for a talented young man like yourself... as long as it remains only a pastime. But a word of warning, Jean. Don't let your life assume too irregular a pattern. I fear you are becoming something of an eccentric. Remember that the world demands worldliness. All I am asking is for you to be like everybody else – everyone from your station in life, bien entendu. Go with the others. Limp with the lame.

So go on writing, by all means, and God be with you! If you are reasonably successful, you will continue; when you have had enough of it, you will stop. No one will notice, because you will not be famous. Your vocation is elsewhere: your country expects other services from you.

And now to something else you mention in your letter. You tell me I am always 'preaching sermons' about the way you spend money. If I am, mon cher Jean, it is because I have good reason. I received a letter the other day from Countess Benckendorff, who is visiting Berlin, saying she had seen you in one of the best restaurants, dressed according to le dernier cri, eating lobster and drinking Tokay in the company of a large group, all of whom appeared to be your guests. Is this student life nowadays? What happened to young men eking out a meagre existence in a garret, living on bread and cheese and sometimes being seen in the streets holding their caps out to passers-by in the hopes of acquiring an extra sou? You are fortunate; you can keep your hat on your head. But you do not have to play le grand seigneur. So let us come to an agreement on this. I will concede to your request that you may stop sending me an account of your expenses. Perhaps you are right in saying that the way you spend the money I send you is your business, not mine. But if this is to be the case, remember that when it has gone, it has gone. Do not bother to waste space in one of your all too rare and all too short letters asking for more...

Spasskoye,
6 March, 1840.

Mon très cher Jean,

Now I dare you to deny that your mother knows you as well if not better than you know yourself! Only a few weeks ago I recommended you to read Charles de Bernard's novel, Une Femme de 40

41

Ans. And today I receive your letter telling me about your little affaire with Mme Tyutcheva. You see? I read your heart before you did. Of course I am not at all sure, you naughty boy, that you should be writing to me about this sort of escapade. Perhaps your uncle or your brother would be more suitable confidants. But then again, perhaps not. After all, I am no ordinary sort of mother, am I?

As for Mme Tyutcheva... by now you know my mind on that subject. She is just the sort of woman I would wish for you. Women of her age are a godsend in these circumstances, and the advantage is mutual: they are flattered by attentions they no longer expected to receive, and young men can only benefit by their experience and savoir-faire. It is my fervent hope that you remain with her for quite some time. And now, not another word, you sinner! You have made your mother sin too. What a subject to be discussing in the first week of Lent!...

Spasskoye,
23 June, 1843.

Mon cher fils,

What pleasure your Parasha has given me! At first I started to leaf through it rather distractedly; you know that at Spasskoye, as in any self-respecting house, Russian poetry is not read; for the most part it is either imitative or incomprehensible. I assumed that your poem, although surely bearing the stamp of your intelligence and sensitivity, would be another of those pale little writings that appear and pass invisibly into oblivion, lacking the nerve and muscle to attract either praise or blame. But I was wrong. You certainly have talent. There are weak spots in Parasha, to be sure... but there are spots on the sun. No, all in all, it is an excellent piece of work... pleasing, delicate and discreet. And it made me very happy to see that you had signed it T.L.; I beg you to be a Lutovinov in your work, that would be a great comfort to me. In spite of what I have said to you before, you must not stop writing, you must not smother your talent. Lutovinov's Parasha is a good beginning. I am happy to adopt her.

Only one sour note in this Te Deum. I am, of course, pleased that your work was well received in the Annals of the Fatherland, but I trust you are not intending to become intimate with the group who contribute to that publication. I would particularly wish to warn you against Belinsky, whom I take to be their leading light... a very dim light, I hasten to add. He seems to be one of those young men who hold nothing sacred: neither their religion, nor their country nor even the most fundamental standards of decency and morality. If people like that are allowed to exert any influence, it will be the end of civilization as we know it. And it would be a sad business if a Turgenev-Lutovinov were known to be hobnobbing with a man who perverts the honoured craft of literature by using it as a platform from which to spew forth his ill-bred, spiteful, bitterly envious venom against a society he is, by any criterion of birth, talent or merit, totally unqualified to enter...

"**M**y mother would take to her bed with a migraine if she knew I were here. She thinks you're a bad influence on me."

Turgenev and Belinsky were walking through the pine forests surrounding Lake Pargolovo, to the north of St Petersburg. On the advice of his doctor, who hoped the country air might alleviate his asthma, Belinsky had rented a tiny dacha at Lesnoye, where he was installed for the summer with his wife and baby daughter. Turgenev went out there whenever his job at the Ministry of the Interior allowed – and often when it didn't. The two men, who were by now intimate friends, would talk for hour after hour, Turgenev trying to remember to shorten his giant countryman's stride to allow his thin, frail, stooping companion to keep up. But often he would forget, and Belinsky, who usually did by far the greater part of the talking, would be forced to come to a panting halt and collapse on the ground or lean against one of the great resinous trunks in order to catch his breath.

"I know she's a bad influence on you," Belinsky retorted. "Every time you come back from Spasskoye, you've regressed a little towards soft, pampered land-owning dandyism." Turgenev tried to expostulate, but Belinsky drove mercilessly on. "Oh, don't expect to hear pious platitudes about family ties from me. From everything you've said, it's quite clear that the woman is a monster – a model of everything Russia has to get rid of if it's ever going to have a chance of catching up with western Europe. It isn't going to be easy for you, *gamin*. I had a hard enough time freeing myself from a drunken doctor of a father and an ignorant, clinging provincial mother. But you have a battle royal on your hands. All I am saying is that the first step is to recognize your enemy. And you're fighting the devil."

"But what do you suggest I do?" At any kind of pressure, Turgenev's voice would rise to a petulant falsetto squeak, in surprising contrast to his huge frame. "If I anatagonize her too much, she's quite capable of cutting off my income. And what then? I can't live on my salary from the Ministry."

"I'm sure I live on far less," Belinsky commented drily. "And I have a wife and child."

"Yes, but you live for nothing but your work."

"And therefore I don't mind if I don't know where the next month's rent is coming from, is that it? Oh, the insufferable complacency of the aristocracy! 'We were suckled and reared in luxury, so how can you expect us to do without it?' You may find yourselves facing some ugly surprises one of these days. You, for instance, my dear *gamin*, might consider doing some worthwhile work yourself. When you finally rise from your desk after an exhausting three- or four-hour day at the Ministry, you could transfer your noble arse to another chair and settle down to write, instead of panting around every salon in St Petersburg after that opera singer of yours…" Turgenev again tried to protest, but was once more reduced to helpless silence by the unstaunchable flow of his friend's eloquence. "You have the talent, I'm sure of it. But without application, talent is useless. It's about time you made your choice: either you remain financially and emotionally shackled to your mother's entrails – in which case you will soon be leading the vacuous, useless life of your peers and I shall cease to have any interest in you whatsoever; or you leave lotus-land behind you and dirty your hands and make enemies and join those of us who think that the only salvation for this country lies with her writers. We have reluctantly to admit that for the moment there is nothing we can do about Russia, not while this Neanderthal Czar remains on the throne, with his bully boyars and hellfire-breathing bishops; but we can do something about Russian literature, and maybe some day – it may well be after our deaths – Russian literature will do something about Russia…"

He broke off, having run out, not of arguments, but of breath, and Turgenev was able gently to suggest that he could not imagine anything that he would ever write being of much help to Russia.

"That's because your head's still stuffed with all that German idealism you picked up in Berlin. *Parasha* was all very well for a beginner, but now you've got to grow. Write something about your own experiences, about friends, enemies, students, clerks at your Ministry, even your mother, for God's sake, but get down on your hands and knees and sniff the dirt, rub your nose in it if necessary, but above all rub your readers' noses in it. Don't try to be liked, Vanichka. That's the most dangerous temptation you face as an artist."

Turgenev gave a rueful laugh. "If I follow your advice, it won't be a question of whether I am liked or not; simply of my career in government service coming to a sudden end. I already feel the Minister can hardly wait to get rid of me."

"Best thing that could happen to you!"

"That's easy for you to say. But I would still have to find some way of supporting myself, and I won't earn enough by writing. The only other alternative is to beg from my mother, and you surely wouldn't approve of that."

"Oh, I'd have nothing against it," Belinsky said with a teasing grin. "What are the rich for? To what better use could they put their unearned wealth than subsidizing promising young artists? And besides, you hypocrite, you do it anyway! No, no, I say get all the money you can from her. Just don't let her use her roubles to bring you to heel like a well-trained setter. Tell you what!" He gave a yelp of laughter. "Persuade her to subsidize our journal and we'll give you a job as Assistant Editor at a thousand roubles a week."

Turgenev laughed too and took the opportunity of his friend's good humour to launch a mild counter-attack. "You were chiding me just now about my German idealism," he said. "But Annenkov tells me that only a year or so ago you were preaching it as violently as you are preaching the opposite now."

Belinsky's face wrinkled up in self-disgust. "It's true," he admitted. "And it was all the fault of your friend Bakunin. The moment he got back from Berlin, he started force-feeding me Hegel for months on end... and you know how persuasive the damn man is when he puts his mind to it. He even translated whole chunks of the *Encyclopaedia* for me, because I can't read German. And yes, I fell for it like a perch for a worm... gobbled it up whole and unfortunately spewed it up undigested for anyone who cared to read or listen to me. Oh, you know it all, of course. Imbibed it from the same source as Mikhail Aleksandrovich. *The real is the rational*! That's the great discovery, isn't it? Bakunin used to insist that the whole destiny of man was to understand and love – *love*, mind you! – reality. Whatever is, is for the best. Tyranny, bigotry, slavery are all in accordance with the immutable course of history and all we have to do is contemplate the perfect working of the world order and tune ourselves in harmony with the *zeitgeist*. What precious, pernicious nonsense! All I would ask of the immutable working of history would be to give me back those two lost years. It's unlikely I'll live very long anyhow, and to have thrown away so much time on that..." Words finally did fail him and he sank to the ground, his body convulsed by a racking fit of coughing.

Turgenev waited for him to recover and then spoke up in defence both of Bakunin and of the heady intellectual excitement of his Berlin years.

"As always, Vissarion Grigorevich," he said, "you leap from one extreme to the other. It wasn't all pernicious nonsense, what we discussed when we stayed up till dawn, night after night, talking, talking, talking... A lot of it was, of course. How could it be otherwise when a dozen young people are engaged in dialectic argument for the first time in their lives? What we were looking for was something to link all the disconnected ideas one or another of us would come up with – a common theme which would give some shape to our fragmentary perceptions of philosophy, art, literature, science, life itself. And this Michel, who was four or five years older than most of us, helped us to find. It didn't come originally from him, of course. And perhaps his eloquence led him to oversimplify; but we drank in his words as though they'd been delivered by the Delphic oracle."

"The problem with Bakunin," Belinsky said tersely, "is that his words will always remain words; they'll never become deeds."

"That may be. But at the time they gave us what we needed – some sense that nothing was completely accidental, that there was some purpose, some meaning, yes, even some rational necessity..." Belinsky was about to splutter into life again, but this time Turgenev held firm. "And it doesn't sound as if you and Michel have abandoned Hegel altogether. You've just reinterpreted him in a way that fits in better with your *Weltanschauung*."

"Oh, how you love your big German words! Well at least I know what that one means. But we haven't reinterpreted Hegel; we've just finally understood him correctly. The other interpretation was simply an excuse to provide a philosophic veneer of justification for absolutism on the part of the rulers and quietism on the part of the ruled."

"Whereas now?"

"Now we say, very well, if it is true that all that is real is reasonable, then opposition, protest, conflict, even revolution are reasonable too. It is up to each of us to give a hand to the working of history, which is anything but immutable. It's up to us, orphans of Russia, men without a fatherland, to mutate it. And do you know what opened my eyes to that? Studying the classics. What nobility there was in the ancient world compared to ours! There the foundation of life was personal pride; the dignity and sanctity of the individual. My God, how far we've regressed since then! Voltaire knew that. When he was attacking church and state intolerance, where did he get most of his examples from? Greece and Rome. Look what their poets and philosophers were able to write! Cicero on the concept of Hell: '*Non est anus tam excors quae credat*' – 'There is no old fool so stupid as to believe in it'. And Seneca, in one of his plays, I've forgotten which, had the chorus chanting up there on the public stage for all to hear: '*Post mortem nihil est, ipsaque mors nihil*' – 'After death there is nothing, and death itself is nothing'… which he later proceeded to exemplify by committing suicide with great dignity. And yet we never hear of them being even mildly reproved for these sort of pronouncements. And here we are, nearly two thousand years later, strangled by censorship, every word we write being scrutinized by the hired servants of state tyranny and religious obscurantism. 'Think the way we do, or don't think at all'. That's the message they want to drive into our skulls, and that's what we have to resist with every poem, play, story and article we write, otherwise Russia will sink for ever into the bog which Peter momentarily managed to heave her out of."

He relapsed into a gloomy silence, scooping up handfuls of pine needles, rubbing them between his thumb and his fingers and letting them slowly trickle back to the sandy earth. But Turgenev, so often the long-suffering butt of Belinsky's shafts of irony, wasn't going to let his friend off the hook. "But I've heard you, many times, condemn the use of art as a political weapon," he remarked.

Belinsky's head jerked up. "Don't misunderstand me," he said. "I'm not asking for social treatises – utilitarian tracts à la George Sand or the sort of rubbish the French socialists spew out. All an artist – if he is a real artist – can do is portray the truth as he sees it… and this is something, *gamin*, that you particularly should take to heart: never worry about trying to clothe ideas with flesh; if you have any worth as a writer, your work will contain these ideas whether you know it or not. Look at Gogol. When he started working on *Dead Souls* he thought he was writing a funny book. And so he was, by God. But he was also ripping open the viscous underbelly of Russia and setting down the most scathing denunciation of the regime ever penned."

"Which, it now seems," Turgenev observed, "he is bitterly ashamed of."

"That's because those voracious vultures of priests have got their claws into him. That was always the trouble with Nikolai Vasilievich. He's completely under the influence of the last person he's talked to. And now, from what I hear, this Father Konstantinovsky never lets him out of his sight; he's trying to get him to give up writing and enter a monastery. That would be another, and perhaps the most tragic, example of genius destroyed by ignorance and superstition."

"How they twist the message of Christ to justify all the things that Christ condemned!"

"I have an article in mind for our next issue along exactly those lines. No one can get near Gogol these days, but perhaps if he reads what all the people who encouraged and praised him think of the path he is taking, it might cause that wild mind of his to dart off in another direction." Belinsky looked keenly over at Turgenev, who was brushing some earth off his elegant velvet trousers. "Why don't you write it?" he asked.

Turgenev thought for a moment and then shook his head and said, with a deprecating smile: "It's not really the sort of thing I would do very well, is it? It wouldn't have any of the power that you would put into it. They don't call you 'fierce Vissarion' for nothing."

"A fine excuse," Belinsky snorted. "The truth is you don't want to stir up the mud. Isn't that it? What would your countesses in their salons be whispering behind their fans? 'What a pity poor Varvara Petrovna's boy has fallen into such bad company!' 'Fancy insinuating that our holy men could be anything but the faithful expounders of the word of Christ!' And this Spanish soprano you're so infatuated with... what's her name?"

"Pauline Viardot-Garcia."

"Yes, that's the one. She'd probably be shocked too. I can just hear her." He threw up his hands in a grotesque imitation of an operatic gesture and shrieked: '*Por l'amor de Dios, Juanito!*' Come to think of it, you probably still believe in God yourself. Do you?"

Turgenev, quite unperturbed, even by his friend's unflattering reference to the woman he adored, considered his question carefully and then said: "In a prime mover, some kind of supreme being, perhaps. Certainly not their avenging monster." And after a further pause for reflection he asked: "And you?"

Belinsky impatiently flicked away a handful of pine needles. "I find it impossible to penetrate even to the concept of a supreme being through our dense fog of parsons, bishops, patriarchs, metropolitans… It's as though they obscure even the possibility of any kind of benign deity. But then, the whole question seems almost irrelevant, there are so many more important things we have to think about, to commit our energies to…"

"Yes," Turgenev agreed, patting the bottom of his light brown waistcoat. "Like when we are going to have dinner."

Belinsky laughed uproariously, sprang up and held out his hands to help his lanky friend to his feet. "My dear *gamin*," he cried, "you are outrageous. Here we are, not having even begun to settle the vexed question of the existence of God, and all you can think about is your stomach!"

The conversation during the – for someone of Turgenev's voracious appetite – rather skimpy meal that Belinsky's wife served up lacked the morning's spontaneous animation. Marya Vasilyevna Belinskaya, who liked to be known as Marie, was a year older than her husband. She had been a schoolteacher in Moscow, but had been forced to relinquish her job because she too was plagued by chronic ill-health. The dacha they had rented was damp and draughty, the worst possible place, Turgenev couldn't help thinking, in the coldest, wettest St Petersburg summer for many years, for two people in their condition; but it was, of course, all they could afford. Fortunately Marie had lit a fire, and as he stood gratefully close to it, watching the neat, quick movements with which she placed plates and dishes on the table, he noticed what pains she took to appear lively and healthy, almost running backwards and forwards from the cupboard and the stove, and turning her back on the two of them whenever she was unable to suppress a cough. But it was only when they sat down to eat that he observed how desperately anxious she was to protect her husband from any over-excitement. Whenever some remark of Turgenev's would fuel Belinsky's scorn, anger or even just enthusiasm, her eyes, deep-set in her haggard, bony face, would flash imploring signals in his direction. The baby daughter, who seemed to have inherited her parents' sickly constitutions, bawled almost non-stop throughout the meal, and it was with a guilty feeling of relief that Turgenev found himself driving slowly back into the city in his droshky. He shared his meandering thoughts, as he often did when he was alone, with the old horse ambling along in front of him between the shafts. "Let that be a warning to me, Maksimka, old fellow! I could never live like Vissarion Grigorevich. I'm ashamed to say it, even to you, but domestic life of that kind would make me suicidal. All the more reason to follow his advice. I must take myself in hand, find some work that I enjoy doing and devote myself to that; not let myself degenerate into one of Pushkin's superfluous men. No time to lose! I'll find a way of earning enough money to make me independent of my mother. That way I can bury my guilty conscience and just let her rages blow over me. It will also extricate me from her periods of smothering love, which I find even harder to stomach. A new life, Ivan Sergeyevich, that's what you must fashion for yourself... and the sooner you start, the better. I'm afraid, like St Augustine, I'll have to say not quite yet... tonight, for example, I have promised Mme Viardot I will be at the opera to hear her *Lucia di Lammermoor*, and an army of Belinskys couldn't keep me away from that. But soon, Maksimka, very soon... " and feeling in the best of spirits and without a further thought for the future, he began to half-sing and half-whistle Lucia's first-act solo:

> '*Quando rapita in estasi,*
> *del più cocente ardoooore...*'

Spasskoye,
21 April, 1845

Mon cher Jean,

This is a black day for me. Your letter saying that you have decided to give up your job and leave government service plunged a dagger through my heart. Is it too late for a mother to plead that you reconsider this foolish decision? What is going to become of you, my son? Since returning from Berlin, you have idled your life away, giving yourself up to nothing but pleasure. I have heard from a reliable source that even when you were at the ministry, you spent most of your time reading novels and scribbling poetry. It seems that if it had not been for the distinguished name you bear (and which I fear you are going to drag into disrepute), you might well have been dismissed instead of so rashly dismissing yourself.

You must not think of me as someone who disapproves of a judicious enjoyment of the good things of this life. My young days were singularly lacking in any such gratification, but I do not think that has hardened my heart, making me bitter and envious. I think it quite natural for a young man of your age to sow a few wild oats before settling down to a life of domestic and professional responsibility. But there is a limit to all things, and it seems to me that, since ceasing to be a student, you have far surpassed that limit. What have you to show for these three years? Some verses of sound craftsmanship but no great distinction; an amorous involvement with that Bakunin girl whom, as far as I can tell, you first seduced and then abandoned; travels 'for your health', as you expressed it, though I must say your health seems sound enough to me; and now this panting around every salon in St Petersburg with your tongue hanging out like a mongrel cur in pursuit of a bitch on heat, after this damn gypsy of a singer.

I beg you, Jean, to listen to a loving mother's advice. You are now 26 years old – an age when it behoves you to put a stop to your puppyish frolics. I had – and still, malgré tout have – very high expectations of you. I had hoped that you would attain the sort of position in society I myself would have aimed at, had it not been for the damnable fact of my being a woman. All that is left to me now is to live vicariously through you, Vanichka. My happiness lies in your love for me, in your obedience and your respect. And I cannot feel you can have very much respect for me if you cover me with ridicule in the eyes of the world by quitting a post which could have led you to the highest reaches of the state.

I have to admit to a very small share of responsibility in this foolhardy decision of yours, insomuch as you justify it by your desire to gain time in which to write. (This is no doubt the nefarious result of the company you have been keeping, which I took some pains to warn you against.) It is true, hélas, that I have given you some encouragement by praising one or two of your literary products, but it was praise directed at an <u>amateur</u>, Jean, an agreeable way of spending your leisure hours. You cannot think that you have it in you to make a <u>living</u> as a writer! And even if you had, what a career for a Turgenev-Lutovinov!

I simply cannot understand your desire to become a professional writer. Is that a career for a gentleman? In my opinion, there is no difference between a writer and a scribe… both make daubs on paper for money. A gentleman should be at the service of the state and make a career and a name for himself in that service, not spend his time covering pages with black squiggles.

Allez, mon cher fils bien-aimé, make your mother the happiest woman in the world and apply to be reinstated at the ministry. If the head of your department should prove intractable, just tell me. I think I know the right ear into which to pour a little honey. You see, Jean, a mother, even when she's a tiresome old lady like me, can have her uses…

> '…col favellar del core
> mi giura eterna fè…'

The voice, caressingly smooth yet flawlessly agile, sent Lucia's first-act aria floating round the vast spaces of the Bolshoi Theatre and directly into the hearts of the nearly 3000 men and women present. But in the box of Avdotya Panaeva, the ambitious, attractive young wife of an influential writer and editor, the voice was all that could be appreciated. The view of the stage, where the intensity of the twenty-two-year-old Pauline Viardot would have held the audience spellbound even if she had never sung a note, was completely blocked by the huge frame of Ivan Turgenev; he stood at the very front of the box, gripping the ledge and leaning forward to put as little distance as possible between him and the object of his veneration. This had already occasioned glances of impatience and disapproval amongst the occupants of the box, which had not been lost on the aspiring hostess, whose other guests were far more important to her than the unknown – and uninvited – young writer. But when, after elegant embellishments on the theme, a perfectly executed high D, held for what seemed an eternity, finally floated down to close on the tonic G, and the same young writer bruised the tender ears of the ladies near him by bellowing '*Bravoooo!*' like a lookout boy who has sighted land, her small store of patience was rapidly exhausted.

At the end of the act she drew him aside and whispered with some acerbity: "Ivan Sergeyevich, that you come to my box uninvited I could overlook on the grounds of Panaev's and my warm feelings of friendship towards you. But when you then behave like an unmannered oaf and disturb my other guests, that is too much. I must ask you not to come back for the other acts.'

Turgenev spread his arms wide and protested in the high, squeaky voice with a slight lisp that he affected at the time: "But Avdotya Yakovlevna, don't you realize we are in the presence of genius? A goddess has done us the honour of visiting us. If we don't show our appreciation, she will never come back."

As the applause had only just died down, ten minutes after the curtain, his hostess was able to point out that appreciation had not been lacking. "But," she added, "your performance was more likely to attract attention to yourself than to her." Then, on seeing that this barb had really dismayed the besotted young man, she laid a conciliatory hand on his shoulder and favoured him with the practised smile she normally reserved for famous artists and eminent public figures. "Find somewhere else to watch the rest of the opera," she cooed, "and then come along to my reception afterwards. Lord and Lady Bloomfield have promised to come – he's the British Ambassador, you know, – and it might be useful for you to meet him."

"Useful? In what way?"

"Well, I imagine you're looking for some other work now that you've been… now that you've left the Ministry?"

"I left the Ministry in order to find time for my real work… which happens to be the same as your husband's. And I'm afraid I won't be able to accept your kind invitation, as I have a previous engagement."

One social quality the young Avdotya had not yet learned was that of suppressing her curiosity, so of course she asked him where he was going. Turgenev was only too happy to enlighten her.

"To Madame Viardot's dressing-room. A small group of her closest acquaintances, amongst which she does me the honour to include my unworthy self, meet there after almost all her performances. And now, my dear," countering her glare of envious fury with a low, ironic bow, "I must leave you to find a small space in which to park my frame for the rest of the performance."

Turgenev, as he often did, watched the next two acts of the opera from the gallery, where his enthusiastic clapping and roars for encores caused no embarrassment to his less sophisticated but more appreciative companions. In the intervals, however, he would come down and mingle with the cream of society. On one of these occasions he ran into a group of acquaintances including his friend Annenkov, who asked him why he chose to watch the opera from so far away.

"Ah, it's not a choice," he replied, airily. "It's a labour – even if a labour of love. I have organized a *claque* and I have to ensure that they are earning their wages."

The idea of a claque being necessary for the most popular artist ever to sing in a Russian opera house brought forth roars of disbelieving laughter. Annenkov drew his friend aside and asked him what the real reason was.

"The real reason, Pavel Vasilevich," Turgenev answered coolly, "is that a few days ago I received a letter from Spasskoye…

Spasskoye
3 October, 1845

Mon cher fils,

It is with some bitterness that I have to resign myself to the fact that the appeal I made to you in a letter of a few months ago has gone unheard. If my memory serves me correctly, I appealed then both to your good judgement and to your affection for me. It would seem that you are no longer in possession of either.

Hurtful though it be for a mother to discover such failings in the son she was once so proud of, I will not allow it to divert me from what I conceive to be a parent's duty. If your father were still alive, I would be only too happy to leave this for him to deal with, but in his absence I will not shirk from what I see to be my responsibility.

Your refusal to apply for reinstatement at the Ministry and your imprudent determination to try and make a living as a scribe presumably indicate a desire to display to others and, especially, to yourself, that you are now a man and therefore free to go your own way. This, of course, is the literal truth. But as there is always more than one side to the truth, I consider it my painful duty to now draw your attention to the harsher side of adult responsibility: namely, the obligation to pay your own way in the world.

When you were fulfilling a worthwhile task and paving the way for a splendid future, I was more than happy to implement your not very large salary with what I hope you will agree was a generous allowance. But now that you have defied my wishes and in all probability denied yourself the possibility of any future at all worth the name, I cannot believe that it would be any longer in your best interests to receive this allowance. So unless you can demonstrate to me that you are really in great need – and I shall require convincing proof of this – you may no longer expect to receive from me a monthly disbursement.

I need hardly add how unpleasant it has been for me to have had to take this step, but the blame for it must lie fairly and squarely on your shoulders. Of course, if you should see fit to change your mind even at this late hour and decide to re-enter public service – it doesn't necessarily have to be at your old Ministry – you would make me a very happy old lady who would be only too glad to revert to our former understanding.

May the Good Lord, mon cher Jean, see fit to tear the veil from your eyes…

The 'dressing-room', as he had described it to Avdotya Panaeva, to which Turgenev hurried after the performance, was in fact a much more elaborate affair than the poky, draughty holes in which even the greatest artists are often condemned to spend long off-stage hours. One of Pauline Viardot's first conquests on her arrival in St Petersburg had been Stepan Gedeonov, son of the boorish Director of the Imperial Theatres, who made up for his father's unconcealed dislike of actors and singers by doing everything in his power to please and humour them. It had been enough for Pauline to mention her fear of the effect the cold of a Russian winter might have on her voice for him to have a room especially built for her under the stage with its own independent heating system. It was there that she received her admirers after the opera. At first the room had resembled a busy railway station, with everybody who was anybody in the city – and many who were nobody but wanted to be thought somebody – crowding into the room in the hope of gaining the ear of the Franco-Spanish *diva*. But after the first flurry of enthusiasm had passed, Pauline performed her 'duty' receptions in her official dressing room, escaping, as soon as she could, down to her sanctuary, where she received her four principal admirers: apart from Turgenev and Gedeonov, these consisted of Count Matvei Wielhorski, an amateur cellist of great ability and charm, and General Pyotr Zinoviev, an immensely wealthy but dim-witted landowner, whose startling rise to so high a rank at the age of 34 was surely due more to his connections at court than his conversance with Clausewitz.

Some months before, the general had brought back the skin of an enormous white bear he had shot on one of his northern estates and presented it to Pauline for her room. The enterprising Gedeonov had had the idea of substituting the animal's claws with rather more substantial replicas made of gold. And after a while it became the custom for Pauline, usually dressed in a white peignoir, to recline in the middle of this exotic rug, while the four admirers each sat on the paw to which they were allotted. At that time, the hierarchy ran from Gedeonov on no.1, Wielhorski on no.2, Turgenev on no.3 and Zinoviev on no.4. Each in turn was supposed to entertain the *diva* with a story, either invented or true. Promotion or demotion from paw to paw depended, apart from the assiduousness of the courtship, on the quality or amusement value of the story.

When Turgenev had told Avdotya Panaeva that he had a rendez-vous after the performance, he had not been entirely accurate. In Donizetti's opera, the heroine dies in the third act, the fourth belonging almost entirely to the tenor. Genuine as Turgenev's love of music was, it was as nothing compared to his devotion to its mouthpiece. So as soon as the third act was over and the delirious applause in appreciation of the 'mad scene' had finally subsided, he hurried round to the sanctuary, hoping that the other three 'paws' wouldn't want to miss the old war-horse Rubini in one of his best-loved tours de force, *Fra poco a me ricovero*, Edgar's lament for his dead love. But within a matter of minutes all four, each trying to hide his disappointment at the others' presence, were gathered round a radiantly alive Lucia, who rebuked them for their musical insensitivity, but seemed in no hurry to send them back to their seats.

Without bothering to change out of the nightgown she was wearing, and in which she would soon have to take her final curtain calls, she settled herself on the rug and glanced round at the adoring young men. "Well, now that you're here, you might as well stay. But one of you will have to excel himself to make up for your discourtesy to my colleague. We have about twenty-five minutes before curtain – unless Giovanni Battista gives an encore, which he probably will, and that will make it half an hour. Now, which of you has some story that will make that half-hour go by in a flash? Ivan Sergeyevich," she turned to Turgenev, whose mouth was already opening, "you're our great wordsmith. Your companions are all doers; you're a dreamer. Tell us one of those true stories of yours which I never believe a word of."

"This time I won't tax your credulity, madame," Turgenev replied. "I have in mind a subject for a tale which has, as far as I know, no basis in fact. But I can't decide how to finish it. Why don't I give you an outline of the story, and then you can all tell me how you think it should end."

The idea meeting with general approval, Turgenev began: "Imagine a young lieutenant from the minor nobility, past his first youth, living a tedious existence in a dull provincial town. One morning his servant, a gruff but decent fellow, tells him that the bakery has run out of his favourite breakfast rolls. Unconvinced, he walks to the bakery and is given the last remaining roll by an attractive black-eyed young girl, the *boulangère's* niece, who had been keeping it for herself.

"Totally inexperienced in affairs of the heart, he falls hopelessly in love and invents excuses to go to the bakery at every possible opportunity. There he makes the acquaintance of the aunt, who senses a possible advantage from this nobleman's interest in her niece. He rents a room at the back of the bakery, where he consummates his love and now spends all his leisure hours, neglecting both his duties and his former acquaintances.

"But he soon realizes that his love for... let us call her Vasya... is not requited; what for him is an infatuation is no more to her than a mildly amusing game, which soon loses its appeal when his jealousy makes it difficult for her to see any other man. He starts to drink, and soon loses any appeal he might once have had for the girl, who delights in letting him believe that she is betraying him with a succession of lovers.

"When one night she fails to come home, he tries to make a complete break, telling the aunt he will no longer be needing the room. Unperturbed, she presents him with a bill for everything she considers he owes her, down to the sugar he has put in his tea. He goes back to his quarters and, to the despair of his servant, lies curled up in bed all day facing the wall. The servant invents a stratagem to lure Vasya into visiting his master, who, when she arrives, is very drunk. He apologizes for any trouble he may have caused her, takes all the blame for the failure of their relationship on himself and begs to be allowed just to stay around her, without making any further claims on her.

"Now the girl, who is not a bad sort, cannot bring herself, there and then, to give a flat refusal to this pitiful wreck of a man, although by now she no longer has any feeling for him at all.

"There, my friends." Turgenev looked around him with an expectant smile. "Now you tell me what you think should happen next."

Pauline was clearly diverted by the idea. She clapped her hands and issued orders. "*Très bien*, let's hear from all of you. In reverse paw order. You first, Pyotr Vasilevich."

The general wasted neither time nor words. "Perfectly obvious," he snapped. "The fellow wakes up the next morning, and when he's got over his hangover, if he has an ounce of spunk in him, he sends the girl packing and starts looking around for someone to take her place."

"Practical but unpoetic," Pauline remarked. "Matvei Yurevich?"

"I think," the Count said pensively, "that the girl would go home, think it over and, with her good peasant's common sense, realize that it would never work and, the next day, gently but firmly, tell him so."

"Ah, a Slavophil in our midst!" Pauline cried. She and her husband had become passionately interested in the intellectual battle raging in Russia between those who looked to Western Europe as a model and those who put their faith in the intrinsic sagacity of the Slav soul. "How do you like that, Ivan Sergeyevich? You, the epitome of the Westerner, with all the radical ideas you picked up in Berlin, having your story resolved by the untutored wisdom of a daughter of the soil?"

But neither 'paw' allowed himself to be drawn into an intellectual scrap, and Pauline turned to paw no.1. "What have you to say, Stepan Aleksandrovich?"

The Director's son had no doubts. "Oh, I'm a Romantic when it comes to stories. We all have far too much harsh truth to face in our everyday lives. I would like the girl to perceive the depth of his love, realize that she would never meet anything like that again and agree to marry him."

"And they would live happily together to the end of their days?" Pauline asked doubtingly.

"Surely we don't have to be as prescient as that," Gedeonov replied. "Ivan Sergeyevich would end his story there, would he not? If we had to guarantee the lifelong bliss of all young lovers, literature – not to mention opera – would be drastically impoverished."

Pauline nodded and turned back to Turgenev. "Well, there you are, Ivan Sergeyevich. You have heard three points of view: we might call them the cynical, the practical and the romantic. Now you must tell us which you are going to choose."

"Not yet, madame," Turgenev said. "I haven't heard from you. As the decision lies essentially in the girl's hands, your opinion is worth more to me than all the others. What do you think my little Vasya should do?"

Pauline's eyes lost their teasing sparkle and became almost grave. "I don't know what she *should* do," she said. "But I think I might guess what she *would* do."

"And what would that be?" Turgenev asked.

"Accept his offer… tell him that she would never send him away, but to expect nothing else from her."

"Ah, then you foresee a life of hell for both of them. After the cynical, the practical and the romantic, now we have the tragic."

"Why for both of them?" Pauline asked. "From the way you describe him, he doesn't sound as if he was going to have much of a life anyway. But if she played her cards cleverly, she could carve out a very pretty little existence for herself… Marry some young man of her own age and class and lead the sort of life she would have led if she'd never met him… except that there would always be this poor wretch around drinking himself into an early grave for love of her."

"And that would add to her happiness?" Gedeonov inquired drily.

"Why, of course it would!" Pauline said, with a ringing laugh. "You gentlemen should never forget that no woman can resist the attraction of being totally adored. Even if the adoration is hopeless. Perhaps especially if it is hopeless." She let the warmth of her Mediterranean smile melt each of her admirers' hearts in turn, before bringing it to rest on Turgenev. "Now, Ivan Sergeyevich, you can temporize no longer. What is your verdict?"

"You have completely convinced me, madame." The other three exchanged knowing glances of mock surprise. "I had in mind something of the kind myself, but now I have no doubts at all. That is the way my tale shall end."

"I am deeply flattered," Pauline said, and not a man there could say what proportions of mischief and sincerity lay behind her humble smile and lowered eyelids. What the other 'paws' would have agreed on, however, was that if Pauline Viardot had suggested that Turgenev should open a vein and dip his pen in blood instead of ink to write the story, he would have obeyed her without question.

n the spring of 1874, four French writers, Gustave Flaubert, Alphonse Daudet, Edmond de Goncourt and Émile Zola, plus one Russian one, Turgenev, took the habit of dining together in various restaurants more or less once a month. The group called themselves *La Société des Cinq* and referred to their meetings, in imitation of the Impressionists' *salon des refusés* as *les dîners des sifflés*, since each of them claimed to have written a play that had been greeted by whistles and catcalls in the theatre.

In the early days, the restaurant they resorted to most often was the Café Riche on the Boulevard des Italiens, with its elegant white and gold salon. It was there one spring evening, after each had gorged himself on a speciality of his native region (Normandy duck for Flaubert, bouillabaisse for the Provencal Daudet, caviare for Turgenev) that the conversation turned, as it usually did at this point in the evening, from literature to women. The Frenchmen loved to outvie each other in recounting priapic adventures, and also took a malicious pleasure in flaunting their cynicism, knowing that it ran counter to Turgenev's romantic sensibilities. That evening, for instance, Daudet, the most goatish of the four, boasted of the number of girls he had seduced within a few hours of first meeting them. "My only technique," he claimed, "was to pour into their ears a stream of the most indecent obscenities."

"How curious!" Turgenev murmured. Stretched full length on a divan in the private room they had taken that evening, he had listened to Daudet's bragging with a mixture of fascination, bewilderment and unease. "How very curious! The only way I have ever been able to approach a woman has been with respect, trepidation and a great surprise at my own good fortune. Have you never been touched by feelings of that sort? What memories, for example, do any of you have of your first meeting with a woman who was eventually to play an important part in your life?

Two of the company, Goncourt and Zola, immediately declared themselves out of the running, on the grounds that no woman had ever played an important part in their lives. Daudet tried to tell a scabrous anecdote about his courtship of his wife, the delightful and talented Julia Allard, but was soon shamed into silence by his friends, who had the highest regard for her, both as writer and woman. So it was left to Flaubert and Turgenev himself to divert their companions with accounts of their first meetings with Louise Colet and Pauline Viardot. Everyone knew, of course, the difference in the subsequent developments: Flaubert's stormy relationship had lasted, off and on, a mere nine years and had ended, almost twenty years ago, in the most brutal fashion: a note, hastily scribbled on the novelist's blue writing paper, saying: 'Madame: I was told that you took the trouble to come here to see me three times last evening. I was not in. And, fearing lest persistence expose you to humiliation, I am bound by the rules of politeness to warn you that *I shall never be in.*' Turgenev, on the other hand, had already adored Pauline for over thirty years and was rarely to leave her side for the next ten.

"Very well," Flaubert began. "If you want to know how I first met the woman it was to be my curse to love, I will tell you. It was a very unhappy time in my life. I was twenty-five and my father and sister had just died within two months of each other. One hot summer morning, I went to the studio of the sculptor, James Pradier, who was working on a bust of my father. I took with me the death mask of my sister Caroline, as I wanted him to do the same for her. Pradier had several times expressed the opinion that it was time I took a mistress, and had offered to present me with some suitable candidates from amongst his models. But I don't think for a minute he had in mind the model he was in fact using that day, who was Madame Colet. She was, after all, eleven years older than me, a married woman who wrote poetry of sorts and for some years had been carrying on a liaison with the Minister of Education, with whom she'd had a child. Hardly your run-of-the-mill *grisette*, you might say. Certainly not what I was looking for, if I had been looking for anything. But Pradier, who was one of those people who derive almost as much pleasure from pairing off their friends as from pairing themselves, had clearly let drop some insinuations about me which had aroused Madame Colet's curiosity. It would be dishonest of me, after all this time, if I were to deny the effect made on me by her almost naked body, which she made no effort, on my entering the studio, to cover. One consequence of my recent misery was that I had had nothing to do with a woman, not even a prostitute, for nearly three years. So, you see, I was as ready for plucking as a *Doux Amer* cider apple in October."

"And were you 'plucked' that very day?" Daudet asked.

"No, the circumstances didn't allow it. Pradier, while indulging himself in every sort of insinuation, never left us alone for a minute. But a day or two later I returned to the studio, and this time my fate was sealed."

"Which one of you took the initiative?" Zola asked.

"Difficult to say. Looking back on it, it almost seems as if the whole thing was predestined. After a while Pradier made some excuse of quite fatuous obviousness and went off on an errand, leaving me alone with Madame Colet, who was even less dressed than before. We exchanged a few platitudes, while I, with the awkwardness of youth, shambled round the studio. At a certain point my foot caught the edge of the stand holding the unfinished bust on which Pradier had been working. I reached out to prevent the armature from falling to the floor, caught it just in time and replaced the bust on the stand. As I did so, I became aware that my hands were cupping the breasts. I looked at Louise, who had also noticed and was smiling in a very suggestive way. With a certain embarrassment, I looked down at my hands, which were covered with wet clay. She threw me a towel and said, without a trace of emotion: 'Wipe them clean. Then you might like to try the real thing.'"

Daudet giggled happily. "And the gates of paradise were opened wide!"

Flaubert drained his glass of wine, wiped his moustache with a napkin and grunted gloomily: "Only to lead to the nether regions of hell."

Goncourt turned to Turgenev. "Now it's your turn, Ivan. Tell us about your first meeting with Madame Viardot. I fancy we will hear a rather different story."

Turgenev swung his legs to the floor and stretched lazily, his eyes full of unashamed tenderness. "Different, yes. And I fear rather less to you gentlemen's taste. But perhaps worth recounting nevertheless. The date was November the first and every year I remember it as if it had happened yesterday. But to tell the story properly, I must go back a few days…

"I was at a reception one evening – I don't even remember who my hosts were – when I became aware of a tubby little man at the far end of the room gesticulating in my direction and talking excitedly to a gentleman with a very long nose who was clearly not Russian. The little man's face was vaguely familiar, but for the life of me I couldn't put a name to it. After a while he came over and introduced himself. Although I had published very little at the time, and nothing of any merit, he claimed that he had read, and even admired, some of my work.

"'Aleksandr Aleksandrovich Komarov, sir, at your service. Major in His Majesty's Guards. A man of the sword, I fear, more than of the pen, but a follower none the less – dare I say, perhaps something of a connoisseur – of what it pleases me to call the spring tide of our great nation's literature: young men like yourself following in the glorious footsteps of the divine Pushkin… ah, what a tragic loss, what a pitiful waste! How long is it now? Six years already, and yet the wound that opened in my heart the day I first heard the fatal result of that insensate duel is far from healed, far from healed, sir… but why was I…? Ah, yes, you young men, I was saying, who have the honour to be his heirs, who bear the onerous responsibility of…'

"As he babbled uninterruptibly on, I stopped listening to what he was saying and found myself musing on the *roundness* of the man. Everything about him was round: round face, round eyes, round ears, a round little rosebud of a mouth, a round little dimple on his chin, a round stomach on which, from time to time, he complacently placed two pink, puffy, round little hands… When I returned my attention to his voice, – is it possible, I asked myself, that a voice can seem round? – he seemed to be about to get to the point – if indeed there was a point to get to.

"'You may be wondering, sir…' Indeed I was not, the only thing I was wondering was how to rid myself of him with as little offence as possible, 'you may be wondering why I have been so bold as to... not so much to make as to renew your acquaintance... ah, I have surprised you, have I not? Well, sir, we are not entirely strangers to each other. We are both practitioners of a noble sport, and some months ago we were fellow guests on the estate of Count Cherkassky, where I was not slow to note your prowess with the gun. We did not, it is true, converse with each other on that occasion, but on hearing that this excellent shot was the promising young Ivan Sergeyevich Turgenev, I reserved for myself the pleasure of exchanging a few words when the opportunity should next present itself. And what better opportunity than this, when here amongst us...'(at this point he clutched the sleeve of the foreign gentleman with the long nose and drew him forward) 'is another of Count Cherkassky's guests, who has already told me that he too has not had the honour of making your acquaintance. Allow me to present to you, sir, Monsieur Louis Viardot...' (the gentleman in question and I exchanged bows) 'man of letters, translator of that immortal masterpiece *Don Quixote*...' (which Viardot later told me Komarov had confessed to never having read) 'editor...' (and here he glanced round to make sure he was not being overheard and lowered his voice to a whisper) 'of a somewhat – how shall I put it? – subversive Parisian journal called *La Revue Indépendante* which propagates...' (with an embarrassed little giggle) 'every sort of horror: socialism, republicanism, anticlericalism and, oh dear me, I shudder to think what else... but nonetheless a keen sportsman and – dare I say it without offence? – above all the husband and, it might not be too much to say, the Pygmalion of La Viardot-Garcia, the divine Pauline, the toast of St Petersburg. Have you heard her, sir? Not yet? Oh, my dear young man, her Rosina, the passion, the purity of her *Una voce foco pa...*' (here Viardot and I both opened our mouths to correct him, looked at each other and shut them again) 'You know, gentlemen, it is a popular misconception that military men are incapable of appreciating art. Not so, not so. I have had the honour of risking my life for my country against the Turk and I can assure you that the sense of thrill and expectation on the dawn of battle is very similar to the excitement of waiting for the curtain to rise on a great performance. But, bless me, here I am, rambling on, instead of letting you two literary men start to grapple with each other, eh, eh?' And he stood there, his head darting from side to side with little birdlike movements, waiting for God knows what momentous debate to begin.

"Both Viardot and I later admitted that, in the silence that followed this avalanche of words – and believe me, my friends, I have been merciful and let you off with a mere summary – neither of us could think of a thing to say. I eventually mumbled something about how much I regretted not yet having heard Madame Viardot – the fact was that I couldn't afford the ticket – and Viardot immediately offered me a seat for her next performance in three days' time and invited me to a reception which he and his wife were giving the same morning. I asked him where they were staying and he told me they had taken an apartment in the Demidov house on the Nevsky Prospekt, opposite the Alexandrinsky Theatre. Before I could say a word, Komarov jumped in and offered to escort me there. Of course, I had passed the place hundreds of times, but I pretended gratefully to accept his offer in order not to offend him…"

Anyone hardy enough to linger, despite the bitter cold, on the Nevsky Prospekt on the afternoon of November 1st, 1843, could hardly have failed to notice a very tall man striding purposefully along, accompanied by a very short man trotting breathlessly at his side. The young Turgenev of those days cultivated a deliberately languid manner, and it was unusual for him to make any special exertion, even when he was out hunting. But today he had two good reasons for continually quickening his step: one was simply to keep warm; the other was the vain hope that tubby little Major Komarov would be forced, by lack of breath, to keep relatively silent. This was not to be. By the time they were five minutes away from the Demidov house, Turgenev was walking so fast that his companion literally had to break into a run. But not even this could staunch the flow: "I have had the honour, you know, Ivan Sergeyevich, of being received by Monsieur and Madame Viardot on two previous occasions and I can assure you, my dear young man, that rarely is one privileged to be part of so distinguished and cosmopolitan a gathering. Actors, musicians, writers, artists of every kind rubbing shoulders with the finest flower of the aristocracy; ministers, generals, ambassadors and goodness knows who else, all come to worship at the shrine of *la prima donna assoluta*, the uncrowned Queen of St Petersburg! And… you will see, you will see… she receives so graciously, so simply, you might think she was the wife of a provincial mayor, no airs and graces, a word with everyone. Imagine, the second time I went there she came up to me and greeted me by name, 'Dear Major Komarov, how delightful to see you again, I'm so glad you were able to come.' I can tell you I was overwhelmed… quite speechless…"

Turgenev spent the short time before they reached their destination trying to think of something to say which would have the same effect, but was forced to admit, even before he had met her, that in this, as in so much else, Madame Viardot had proved herself his superior…

Having assumed from what he had heard from Komarov that there would be a large crowd of guests, Turgenev was pleased, on entering the drawing room of the spacious apartment overlooking the theatre that the Viardots had rented for the season, to see that there were no more than forty or so. Several, he could tell from the way they were dressed, were members of the company: Rubini, generally considered the greatest tenor of his day, though now past his prime; the baritone, Tamburini; the conductor, Romberg; and a handful of lesser figures. General Gedeonov, Stepan's father, the Czar's Chamberlain and Grand Master of Ceremonies, stood haughtily erect in his full-dress uniform, glancing disdainfully around, probably in search of someone amongst this artistic rabble with whom it would not be beneath his dignity to exchange a couple of words. The others were a selection from the usual crowd who attended these functions, most of them known to Turgenev: a handful of society figures, hostesses on the lookout for an enviable 'catch', writers on the lookout for a generous patron. As soon as Turgenev and Komarov entered the room, Viardot came over and greeted them with the reserved courtesy which Turgenev was to learn to recognize so well. After ascertaining that Turgenev had received his ticket for the evening's performance, he led them over to the window, where Pauline was talking animatedly to a small group which included Rubini. Taking advantage of a momentary pause, he took his wife's arm: "My dear, I want you to meet Monsieur Turgenev, a young writer of whom great things are expected. Major Komarov, you already know…" Pauline favoured them with a professional smile of welcome, murmured how kind of them it was to come, and started to introduce them to the group she had been talking to. But the minute Rubini's name was mentioned, Komarov rushed up to him and started effusively to pump his hand. "Signor Rubini, this is indeed an *onore*, sir. You see in my humble self one of your warmest admirers in this city. How can I ever forget the series of recitals you gave here last spring! And your performance in *Il Barbiere* last week! I haven't been able to get it out of my head. Your…" And to Turgenev's intense embarrassment, the little major began, in execrable Italian, to sing to the world's leading tenor the baritone's famous aria: '*Figaro ki, Figaro ka, Figaro lì, Figaro là…*' Rubini, who was a tall man inclining to corpulence, looked at his leading lady as if asking permission to strangle the man. But Pauline, with an almost imperceptible flick of the eyes, charged her husband to deal with the situation, and Viardot linked arms with the major and drew him away, inquiring how the 'bag' had been last Saturday.

Without trying to banish the gleam of amusement in her eyes, Pauline said a few soothing words to Rubini and then turned to Turgenev. "My husband tells me you share his two great passions in life: slaughtering animals and literature. I have to confess that I care nothing for the first; indeed, to be honest with you, it fills me with horror. But I can never have enough of books. I am determined to learn as much of your wonderful language as I can while I am here, and there is no better way of doing that than reading. So I shall take the liberty of shamelessly exploiting my good fortune in having met you. You must come and see us some time… some time when we are not surrounded by people…" and here she looked around and lowered her voice, confiding in him as though he were a lifelong friend, "although I'm beginning to wonder if there will ever be such a time… and tell me what I should read. Simple things at first, of course, because with that fiendish alphabet of yours…" She raised her eyes to heaven and began to move away from him, but not before laying a hand on his arm and murmuring, with a smile of deep complicity: "I depend upon you. But now you must excuse me; if I don't melt a little of the ice around *mon général*, he will have our whole troupe transferred to Siberia! I'll leave you in the company of signorina Tadini, who I'm sure is dying to talk to you." And on the way over to Gedeonov she introduced Turgenev to a voluptuously handsome, raven-haired young woman whose self-confident Milanese beauty would have sent Stendhal into ecstasy.

Although Turgenev had not yet heard the Italian opera, he was well enough informed of the gossip to know that Pauline Viardot was Emilia Tadini's sworn enemy. The St Petersburg season had opened with *Il Pirata*, with Rubini singing the title role, which Bellini had written for him. But both Pauline and the other leading soprano, Assandri, had not yet reached the capital, delayed by the appalling travelling conditions of the time. So Tadini had been catapulted into a leading role for which she was by no means ready – and for which, according to the unkinder critics, she never would be ready. The result, apart from Rubini's predictable triumph, had been a rather half-hearted send-off for a season which had aroused such feverish expectation. So when, three weeks later, Pauline appeared in *The Barber of Seville* and almost every newspaper hailed the event as the real opening of the season, Tadini's already sensitive susceptibilities suffered a wound which was to remain raw for a long time to come.

Having watched every detail of Pauline's brief exchange with the handsome young giant, dressed in a careful imitation of Byronic slapdash elegance, complete with green velvet 'Don Juan' waistcoat, Tadini had come to the mistaken conclusion that her rival had been flirting with him. This made it imperative for her to attempt to seduce him, with no qualms about overplaying her hand. She was so tired, could they go and sit down for a moment, perhaps over there, in that quiet corner on the divan? Yes, it was thrilling to perform to such enthusiastic audiences in a new country, but one did get a little lonely now and then. After all, one only spent a few hours in the theatre, and how to while away all the rest of the time? *Sono italiana*, and you know, monsieur, we are not like you northerners, we shun solitude, we have a saying, 'There is plenty of time for that in the grave.' Perhaps you have visited Italy? *Ah sì, Roma, Pisa, Genova, ma Milano no, eh*? Well, next time you come, I will show you Milano, the lakes, Como, Garda… But in return (a suspicion of a pout here) wouldn't you spare me a moment or two and take me round your city? *È molto bella, Pietroburgo*, but so cold… *freddo, freddo, freddo*! (A melodramatic shiver, a chattering of teeth, a crossing of arms, a clasping of hands on beautifully rounded shoulders.) It is so sad to explore a new place by yourself. And my companions (an eloquent shrug of said shoulders) they are interested in so little: food and drink, *mangiare e bere*… I need to feel the pulse of a city (to make the point, a delicate hand round Turgenev's wrist) and I am sure you are the person to help me do this. After all, we are both artists, are we not? We *feel* things that others are not aware of… the eyes narrow in complicity, the superb bosom rises and falls and the normally hyper-susceptible Turgenev asks himself why he is not listening to a word she is saying. The answer, he soon realizes, is that his eyes refuse to linger on the perfectly formed features an inch or two away from him, but continually stray to where his hostess has now worked the miracle of eliciting a laugh from the constitutionally mirthless General Gedeonov. *What does this mean? The lovely creature beside me is throwing herself at me with an ostentation which, if she goes much further, will cause at least embarrassment, possibly a scandal. That woman over there, with her hair severely parted down the middle, her heavy-lidded, somewhat bulging eyes, thick fleshy lips and curved, slightly stooping shoulders is downright plain; she has paid no more attention to me than that required of a society hostess doing her duty towards an acquaintance of her husband; and yet she has completely monopolized my consciousness. I can't wait to break away from this chattering harpy, who is now resting a hand on my knee and squeezing my leg to emphasize some tediously trivial point, and find a pretext for engaging Madame Viardot in conversation again. How can I contrive this in not too obvious a fashion? Ah, she said she wanted to learn Russian. I could offer to give her lessons, to be her tutor. Better perhaps to suggest it to her husband. But that might make him suspicious. No, I could invite him to a shooting party next week and then bring up the subject in a casual way… But now to escape from this praying mantis…* "Of course, signorina, it will be my pleasure to show you St Petersburg, we must arrange it at the earliest possible opportunity, but now, if you will excuse me, I must go and have a word with Monsieur Viardot…"

"And so, *mes amis*, you see what sturdy edifices can sometimes be built on the flimsiest foundations." Turgenev looked at the four Frenchmen through the thick haze of tobacco smoke and added with a smile: "If it had not been for that ridiculous little Major Komarov, on whom I still look back today with the greatest affection, I might perhaps never have known the woman whom I consider to be one of the best, the noblest and the most gifted beings on this earth."

Flaubert, Goncourt, Zola and Daudet, all of whom shared some doubts about the ultimate benefit to Turgenev of his long association with Pauline Viardot, uttered appropriate little grunts of agreement, sighs at the gratuitous unpredictability of events and reluctant admissions that our destinies are so often beyond our control…

After which there was nothing more even for this garrulous group to say, and they all made their various ways home.

t was soon agreed that Turgenev would give Pauline Viardot Russian lessons at least twice a week, and more often if the time were available. But many of her days were taken up with rehearsals or attending obligatory social functions, and the two men often found themselves thrown together. They soon discovered that they shared many mutual interests: Turgenev showed Viardot round the art collections of St Petersburg, to gather information for a book he was writing on the great European galleries; and Viardot delighted his new young friend with endless anecdotes dating back to his days as director of the *Théâtre Italien* in Paris. But it was one passion above all that united them, and as often as they could they would drive into the country to indulge in their favourite sport. Viardot, wearing a *tulup*, the Russian peasant's leather jerkin, which blended incongruously with his plump, stocky frame and protruding nose, was grateful to his companion, who knew all the favourite haunts of grouse, partridge and snipe. And it needed only a carefully chosen question or two to release a flood of reminiscences about Pauline's early career, which kept Turgenev enthralled.

On one of these occasions Turgenev shot at a hare but only succeeded in wounding it. The poor creature tried to continue its flight, dragging its back legs and screaming horribly. A second later Viardot fired again. One last kick and the hare lay still.

"That," said Viardot thoughtfully, as he reloaded, "is the only thing that can spoil a day's shooting for me. There is no more dreadful sound than the scream of a hare. When I really wanted to insult one of my sopranos, I would tell her that's what she sounded like above the stave."

"It's lucky we can't hear the pain of wounded birds," Turgenev observed. "Otherwise we might both be looking for a different diversion."

Viardot grunted his reluctant agreement. "Whatever you do," he urged, "don't mention the hare to Pauline. She finds any kind of pain induced by violence unbearable. She's never yet come out for a day's shooting with me. She won't even join me for lunch."

"It's her artistic sensibility." Turgenev hastened to defend his idol, though no accusation had been made. "I noticed the other day, when she let me attend a rehearsal, how upset she became when two of the singers started a violent argument. It was *Don Giovanni*, and Tamburini was furious because his Leporello, who was very bad anyway, kept on forgetting his words during the recitatives, so the rhythm of the scene was always being broken. Eventually Tamburini completely lost patience and called the man an *imbecille,* or something like that, and Vesuvius erupted. You've never heard such a noise, both of them screaming at once. I was enjoying it enormously. My only regret was my Italian isn't good enough to understand half of what they were saying. But I could see Madame Pauline was in torment. She made a feeble effort to try and restore peace, and then she left the stage. White-faced and trembling. I would have thought that in an Italian company, this would have been an everyday scene, but instead…"

"It is," Viardot assured him. "But however often it happens, she suffers every time. Raised voices are anathema to her. The result, I'm afraid, of having witnessed so many of the scenes between her father and her sister when she was very young."

"Were they so violent?"

"Unimaginably so. I wouldn't have believed it myself if I hadn't happened once to walk in on one. Let's sit down for a minute and I'll tell you about it."

The two men settled themselves comfortably on the trunk of a fallen tree, and as Turgenev lit a cigarette, Viardot began evoking a day in Paris, twenty years previously…

He had gone round to pay a call on his old friends, Manuel and Joaquina Garcia. Garcia, one of the foremost tenors of his day, Rossini's original Almaviva, was now in his early fifties and was beginning to ease up on his singing to concentrate on coaching his eldest daughter, Maria, the future Malibran. The clash of temperaments was dramatic, because although Maria was only fifteen, she had inherited all her father's extrovert, flamboyant and stubborn character. At his best, Manuel was an inspiring teacher, but he lost patience very easily and absolutely forbade his daughter ever to say 'I can't'. She had simply to go on and on until she had mastered whatever arduous task he had set her.

When Viardot arrived he found Joaquina Garcia sitting in an armchair looking anxiously in the direction of the music-room next door. Her younger daughter, Pauline, aged three, was sitting on the floor in front of her, her head buried in her mother's lap, her body shaken with sobs. From the adjoining room came sounds more to be expected from a zoo than the home of one of the most musical families in Europe: a loud monotonous braying, over which a lark's repeated efforts to complete its song were frequently interrupted by heart-rending human wails.

In answer to Viardot's interrogatively raised eyebrows, Madame Garcia explained that father and daughter were practising a duet at the end of which Garcia had written a *point d'orgue*: while he held a bass note, Maria was supposed to execute an impossibly difficult cadenza. After a few unsuccessful attempts, Maria had cried out in desperation: "I can't do it, Papa", whereupon Garcia had given her a stinging slap on the cheek. "He hitting her, he hitting her," came the muffled voice of little Pauline, while her mother's eyes met Viardot's in a mute appeal. Determinedly, but with some trepidation, because Garcia's tyrannical behaviour in musical matters could extend to his friends as well as his offspring, Viardot opened the music-room door and went in.

Fortunately, this time Garcia's instinctively hostile glare at the intruder softened when he saw his friend. He decided to use the interruption. Turning to Maria, who was desperately trying to fight back her tears, he said, almost affectionately: "Now, *mi querida Maria*, you have an audience. A man of taste and culture. Sing for him as if he were a full house at La Scala. Show him what you can do. We'll go back… fifteen bars". The two of them began to sing again. When they reached the final bar, Garcia took a deep breath, held a long pedal dominant and looked expectantly at his daughter. And as though she were tripping up and down the easiest scale in the world, the young girl executed a dazzling series of roulades of satanic complexity with an ease, a purity, a hard-edged precision that Viardot who, though only in his early twenties, was already an experienced opera-goer, could not remember ever having heard equalled. Ending with a long trill of flute-like clarity, she and her father came triumphantly to rest on the tonic and for several seconds gazed at each other in silence. Viardot could sense the longing that was almost choking both of them: in Garcia to rush over and embrace his daughter, in Maria to luxuriate in her father's praise. But the habit of severe discipline won out over Mediterranean paternal pride, and with a curt gesture he dismissed her, saying: "You see? You can do it when you try. Don't ever tell me again that you can't. All right, run along now, I have matters to discuss with Monsieur Viardot." And with a bobbed curtsey in his direction and a smile in which Viardot thought he could detect a hint of triumphant mockery, Maria left the room, collected little Pauline and vanished upstairs.

When his wife and Viardot reproached Garcia a few minutes later for being too harsh on his daughter, he answered them with a smile: "I know, I know. Everyone thinks I'm a brute. But I tell you, this is a price Maria has to pay if she is to become the great artist she is capable of being. She has a rebellious nature, which can only be tamed by a rod of iron."

One of the earliest sessions with the 'four paws' took place after a performance of *The Barber of Seville*. Count Mikhail Wielhorski, amateur composer and paw no. 2, complimented Pauline on her discretion in the singing lesson scene, deploring the fact that most sopranos used it as a vehicle to show off their virtuosity. Pauline smiled her appreciation and told them a story she had heard from her sister, Maria, not long before her tragically early death. The curtain had just come down on one of Rossini's operas in which La Malibran had received an interminable ovation for an aria in which her dazzling *fioriture* had virtually submerged the original melody. The composer kissed her hand with his customary gallantry and said: "Magnificent, Marietta! Divine! The music wasn't bad, either. Who wrote it?"

"A lesson she never forgot," Pauline told them. "Although in works by lesser composers she still sometimes couldn't resist thrilling the audience with her extraordinary technique. But then Rossini would have forgiven her anything. He loved her… as did Bellini… and she loved them, different as they were. She used to say that Rossini expressed a sense of life, Bellini a sense of death…" As this set the 'paws' off on a heated discussion of the characteristics of the two composers, Pauline let her mind wander… *But the whole world loved her, as I found out to my cost… When I started, every role I sang had been* 'the Malibran role'… *how did I ever do it? The terror!… Everyone making comparisons – voice, acting, looks (no, not looks, there was no comparison there) – I could just imagine them thinking, 'Why is she so slow, Malibran took this passage much faster' or 'Malibran used to sink to her knees at the end of this aria, why does she just stand there?'… Perhaps that's why I adore St Petersburg, she never sang here…*

… But my 'paws' are getting restless, they sense I'm not giving them my undivided attention, especially that gangling young Turgenev; what am I going to do with him? He's so devoted and his Russian lessons are useful to me and he can often be very amusing, but he's so absurdly in love with me that he behaves like he's sixteen, not twenty-five… the other day, half way through our lesson, he complained of a headache, so I massaged his temples with eau-de-cologne, and what does he do but go around St Petersburg saying he has had a foretaste of paradise!… It's beginning to get embarrassing. Fortunately Louis doesn't mind because Ivan offers him such good shooting, but people are beginning to talk, I'd better be careful, perhaps a light rap over the knuckles is necessary…

A gracious smile to her four young admirers. "Well, gentlemen, I'm afraid I will have to ask you to leave. It's time for me to get dressed, or I shall be late for my appointment."

Turgenev was the first to spring to his feet. "My carriage will be waiting for you, madame, just opposite the artists' entrance."

A faint, perplexed frown. "But my appointment is not with you."

Turgenev was still young enough to blush. "Oh yes, madame. You were kind enough to say you would allow me to accompany you to the reception at General Gulevich's this evening."

Both hands flew to her temples. "Oh, my dear Turgenev, I am so sorry. I had completely forgotten. But I am afraid I will have to abandon you. Stepan…" (a charming smile flashed at paw no.1 cut to the heart of paw no.3) "is taking me to his father's, and that is a summons I must obey. He is, after all, my employer. And I must try to teach him to love his artists, instead of disliking and distrusting them. So good night, gentlemen. We shall see each other again the day after tomorrow… for *La Sonnambula*. I shall rely on your brilliant conversation to keep me awake!"

The 'paws' filed out: one ecstatic, two happy, and one dejected and crushed…

Poor Ivan, that wasn't a rap over the knuckles, it was a kick in the stomach… who knows if he'll ever speak to me again?…

She need not have worried. The slight rebuff only served to increase Turgenev's determination at their next reunion to outshine his fellow 'paws'. As he knew that the sleepwalking Amina had been one of Maria Malibran's greatest roles, he asked Pauline, from his paw, what had been her first memory of her sister on stage. "Oh, a very clear one," was the reply. "In fact, the first thing in my life that I remember as though it had happened yesterday. I must have been four or five at the time, and I was sitting with my mother in a box at the Park Theatre in New York watching Maria singing Desdemona for the first time. When it came to the moment for Otello, who was played by Papa, to kill Desdemona, he threw her down on the bed and raised his arm, about to strike her with his dagger – because in Rossini's opera, unlike Shakespeare's play, Desdemona isn't strangled but stabbed. Well, at that moment, Maria, instead of singing her part, suddenly cried out: *"Padre, padre, por Dios, no me mate!"* – "Father, for God's sake, don't kill me!". And I looked at her eyes and saw that she wasn't acting, she was really terrified. So I jumped to my feet, leant out over the edge of the box and started to scream: 'Stop him! Don't let him kill her!'" My mother had to pull me back into my seat and clamp her hand over my mouth until the scene was over and I saw that Maria hadn't come to any harm.

"What made her do that?" Turgenev asked.

"Maria explained it all to us afterwards. It seems that Papa had only decided at the last minute to put on *Otello* and had told Maria that she was to sing Desdemona five days before the first performance. *Five days* to learn and rehearse that role! So Maria, of course, said she couldn't and Papa was furious and told her that if she wasn't perfect he would really stab her at the end of the opera instead of pretending to. Naturally, neither of them took this seriously or ever gave it another thought. But after a performance of the *Barber of Seville* at the King's Theatre in London, where Papa had been singing Almaviva just before coming to America, an admirer had gone backstage and presented him with a dagger which Garrick had used when he played Othello. It was a beautiful weapon with a blade of Toledo steel and an ivory handle inlaid with rubies, and Papa had been proudly showing it to someone in the wings before going on for his final scene. Somehow or other, he forgot to change it for the harmless prop dagger; so when Maria saw him advancing on her with this weapon, which she had seen many times, she remembered his words, thought she must have given a very bad performance and was about to be stabbed to death."

Stepan Gedeonov, with his theatrical background, was more interested in the professional than the personal side of this story. "How did the audience react?" he asked.

"It seems that nobody was aware that anything out of the ordinary had happened. The fact that she slipped from Italian into Spanish would pass unnoticed in New York anyway. And it's proof of the intensity of Maria's performances, even that early in her career, that there was no visible difference when acted fright was replaced by real terror. I learned a lesson from that experience: if you make a mistake on stage and you act it through with sufficient conviction, the chances are that nobody in the theatre will notice."

On another of their shooting expeditions, Turgenev and Viardot, in the middle of a cold February day, were sitting in an *izba*, warming their bodies at the fire and their insides with steaming plates of *tstchi*, a pungent peasant cabbage soup, and frequent draughts of *kvass*. Turgenev, his storyteller's curiosity aroused by the anecdotes he had already heard, returned to the subject of Maria Malibran; during his student days in Berlin, electrifying reports had reached his ears of the meteoric career of the singer whose death, two years earlier at only 28, had plunged Europe into grief. And now he was able to hear first-hand accounts, both from her sister and from the man who had been her friend and confidant throughout her short life. Reminding Viardot of their previous conversation, he asked him if the relationship between Malibran and her father ever became less stormy.

"Not really. They were too alike. Proud as peacocks and stubborn as mules. Garcia could never see Maria as anything but 'his creation'. He was immensely proud of her, of course, but there was an element of jealousy too. The fact that she had become an international celebrity in his absence nagged at him. That was obvious when he and the rest of the family returned to Paris after their three and a half years on the American continent."

"By which time she was already famous?"

"In France and England she was being spoken of in the same breath with Giuditta Pasta, whom Rossini, who knew something about sopranos, called the most remarkable singer of his day. She hadn't conquered Italy yet. Her triumphs there came later."

"How did she manage to scale the heights so soon?"

Viardot thought for a moment. Then, weighing his words carefully, he replied: "I would say two-thirds talent, one-sixth determination and one-sixth charm. She enchanted everyone she met, men and women alike. She first burst upon the Parisian public when a countess, at whose house she had given a recital, forced the Conservatoire to grant her a public audition at a charity concert. The countess saw to it that *le tout Paris* was there. She sang Desdemona's 'Willow song', accompanying herself at the piano. She was a sensation. A critic wrote the next day that 'by the twentieth bar the audience was conquered, at the end of the first verse it was intoxicated, at the end of the aria it went mad.'"

"And so she was launched."

"Yes. A month or two later she was given a 'trial' at the Paris opera, singing *Semiramide*. The enthusiasm of the audience was so overwhelming that immediately after the performance, one of my predecessors as director of the Italian opera went round to her dressing-room and offered her a ten-week contract for the then unbelievable sum of fifteen thousand francs. Bear in mind that, at that period, I had a friend who was chief clerk at a ministry and his annual salary was fifteen hundred francs. And she was only just twenty!"

Turgenev returned to his initial line of enquiry. "But those perpetual quarrels between her and her father surely can't be explained by jealousy alone. There must have been some other, more concrete reason."

"Oh, there was, there was." Viardot indulged in the ruminative smile of one who can now look back on an embarrassing scene with amused detachment. "And I was unlucky enough to be present when it all came to a head. Not only present, but right in the middle. Even trying to mediate. And like all mediators, ending up by antagonizing both parties…"

Maria Malibran had renewed contact with the young journalist and art-critic, Louis Viardot, soon after returning to Paris from New York after her disastrous marriage. Having been a friend of her father's, he was always ready to lend a sympathetic ear and often a helping hand as the young girl struggled to rebuild her life. He had arranged for her to lodge with a certain Madame Naldi, an elderly widow whose husband had been a friend and colleague of Garcia's. He had also watched, with sympathetic understanding, as relations between the tempestuous young artist and the strait-laced old lady rapidly deteriorated under the strain of cohabitation. He had dissuaded her from setting up an establishment on her own, knowing the effect that would have on her already precarious social reputation; but had supported her decision to rent a house in the rue de Provence where, with Madame Naldi as her reluctant and disapproving duenna, she was able, when her professional commitments allowed, to preside over a *salon* which soon became a Mecca for all the leading young musicians, artists and writers of Paris.

Among the most assiduous frequenters of this salon were Viardot himself and a handsome young Belgian violinist, Charles de Bériot, who had already made a considerable name for himself. Viardot had noticed that de Bériot was very much in love with Maria. No surprise there; so were half the men in the room. What he could not be sure of was whether this feeling was returned. Certainly she seemed to single him out for attention, and was lavish in her praise after he had tossed off some dazzling feat of technical virtuosity. But was this professional appreciation of his talent or something more? Viardot was intrigued and puzzled.

One evening Maria asked him if he would accompany her the next day when she went to see her family, who had just returned to Paris after an unsuccessful attempt to establish a permanent opera company in Mexico City. She had parted with her father on bad terms, as he had vociferously disapproved of her marriage to Malibran. His motives for this may have been mixed, but prominent among them was undoubtedly his reluctance to lose his brilliant young *prima donna*. As for her, there can be little doubt that her chief reason for marrying Eugène Malibran, a French business man twenty-seven years older than herself, who had taken American citizenship, was a determination to get away from the stifling influence, both emotional and professional, of her father. The wedding, in front of the French consul in New York, was a sad affair. The rest of her family made a valiant effort to appear excited and happy for her, but Garcia was quite unable, as well as unwilling, to hide his detestation of his son-in-law, who was only six years younger than he was. He had, however, made generous provision for Maria, giving her a dowry of fifty thousand francs, which Malibran, who almost certainly knew at the time that he was on the verge of bankruptcy, managed to squander within two months of their marriage.

That had been three and a half years ago, and except for an occasional letter between mother and daughter, there had been no communication between Maria and her family since then. Garcia's Mexican fiasco had seriously depleted the family finances; at the start of their journey home a band of brigands on the road from Mexico City to Vera Cruz had completed the job, depriving them of everything they owned. In the meantime, the legend of Maria Malibran had taken wing: wealthy and beautiful, envied and admired, she was the most talked-about artist in the whole of Europe. The reunion of father and daughter was unlikely to be easy.

But just how difficult, Viardot hadn't realized until he found himself sitting beside Maria in the carriage which was taking them to their appointment. She was dressed in ostentatiously dramatic riding clothes: no sober dark blue habit, but an emerald green taffeta dress with a tight-fitting bodice, narrow sleeves and a voluminous skirt, under which, Viardot had noticed when she entered the carriage, she was wearing trousers. Under the wide sloping brim of a black felt 'Amazon' hat her curls cascaded down to her shoulders; pinned to her breast was a large gold brooch in the form of a tigress, with rubies for eyes. Viardot's thoughts about the inappropriateness of this costume for a confrontation with Garcia, who, in all but his own behaviour, tended towards the prudish, were interrupted by Maria's informing him that Madame Naldi had already been to see the Garcias. "And by the triumphant settling of her shoulders and the satisfied gleam in her eye as she saw me off, I have no doubt she has been speaking ill of me."

"What ill could she speak?" Viardot asked.

"Oh, any that comes into her head. She doesn't think I behave as a married woman should. As though my marriage had any meaning any more... in God's eyes or in men's. She says I'm 'too free with my kisses'! Perhaps when she was young, a kiss was a pledge for life. She doesn't understand that when I kiss someone after he's read a beautiful poem or played the violin like a demigod, it's just a more intimate way of applauding." She turned on him one of the languorous glances that sent young men at the back of the gallery into ecstasies for weeks on end and murmured: "Do you think I'm too free with my kisses, Louis?"

Viardot hastened to reassure her. "No, no, of course not. But you must remember that when Madame Naldi was a young girl, France was still under the *ancien régime*. Manners were very different then than they are for our generation. You mustn't be too hard on her."

Madame Naldi was dismissed with an expressive pout, and the main dish on the menu was brought out for Viardot's inspection.

"Anyway, it will be impossible for Papa to be angry with me. For once in his life he'll have to be grateful instead."

"Grateful for what?"

"Well, you know he's very short of money? So I'm going to give him whatever he needs until he's able to start earning again."

Viardot looked troubled. "And you intend to mention this to him today?" he asked.

"Yes, of course. That's why I'm going."

Viardot passed a hand wearily across his brow, fought off the temptation to keep silent and let events take their course, and finally ventured: "Maria, this is very generous of you, but have you forgotten how proud your father is? Don't you think it would be better to let a little time go by… give you and your family the chance to forget old feuds… and then, perhaps having consulted with your mother on the best way to bring it up, make your father this magnificent offer?"

The back stiffened, the nostrils flared, the eyes flashed with a regal imperiousness that, four years later, would make her Norma definitive for all who saw it. "Ah, I see! You want me to humble myself before him again! You want me to be careful not to hurt his feelings! Perhaps I should apologize for having made such a bad marriage, and say, 'Papa, Papa, you were right all along…'"

Viardot laid a restraining hand on her arm, but the flow was not to be dammed.

"Perhaps I should take singing lessons from him again, so that he can beat me when he doesn't like my *portamenti*! No, Louis, if that's how you feel, it's better that you get out of this carriage right now." She leant forward to give orders to the driver, but Viardot pulled her back.

"No, Maria, I'm coming with you. I think my presence might be useful… now more than ever."

This elicited a fiery sideways glance, after which she flung herself back into the corner, rested her chin on her cupped hand and gazed moodily out of the window.

In the few moments of silence that followed, Viardot had time to reflect that this time his usual acumen had deserted him. Of course that was why she had wanted him to come with her. Of course that was why she had dressed in this extravagant fashion. This was to be her revenge for all the humiliations of her childhood. This was to be a settling of accounts. He marvelled at the ingenuity of her scheme: the idea of the offer had certainly sprung from her generosity, which was genuine and inexhaustible; but at the same time it would make clear to her father that the Pygmalion/Galatea days were over; from now on, they met as equals. But would Garcia be able to accept this?

Of course, he too might have changed: perhaps the unfortunate Mexican experience had humbled him, toned down some of his rumbustious arrogance. Viardot's ruminations on the unlikelihood of this eventuality were interrupted by a gloved hand laid on his and the light brush of lips on his cheek.

She was gazing at him as her Amina gazed at Elvino. "I'm sorry, Louis" she breathed. "I'm a little nervous. But no one but you must know it. And thank you for coming. You know, if I wasn't already married, perhaps I would marry you. You understand me better than anyone in the world."

Viardot forebore to suggest that perhaps the guillotine would be a preferable fate, and contented himself with patting the hand that still rested on his.

"Did that mean that she had agreed to take your advice?" Turgenev asked.

"That was what I was wondering," Viardot replied. "And I was soon to have my answer."

The two men had finished their lunch and were about to set off for another couple of hours' sport before the light failed. But Turgenev wouldn't hear of leaving the table until he had heard the outcome, so Viardot contented him with a brief account of the momentous family reunion…

"The moment Garcia laid eyes on his daughter in that outfit I knew that the storm would break sooner or later. For a while, however, he responded to the appealing glances of his wife, and the opening exchanges were civil enough. Maria's elder brother, Manuel, and Pauline, who was only eight at the time, were overjoyed to see their sister again, and their excitement helped to lighten the already rather tense atmosphere. Maria had brought presents for everyone, and these were opened and compared and commented upon. Even Garcia seemed rather pleased with a score Maria had brought back from London, some lost work of Purcell's, if I remember rightly. But then there was a lull, and Joaquina said something about lunch being ready soon, and Maria said she wouldn't be staying for lunch. I saw Garcia stiffen, and he inquired icily if, after three and a half years, a couple of hours of her family's company was too much for madame to endure. Maria managed to laugh this off with a, 'No, Papa, it's not that. I have an engagement to go riding with some friends this morning in the Bois de Boulogne. I just came round to give you all a kiss and make you a proposal. You can talk about it, think it over, and in a day or two I'll come back and we'll have a long happy meal together and you can tell me how you feel about it.'

"Garcia's lips were pressed so tight together that I was surprised his voice was able to issue out from between them. But eventually he managed a, 'What is this proposal?'

"Maria took off her hat, tossed her head to shake out her hair and, with an air of assumed nonchalance that only I knew concealed her inner anxiety, said: 'Well, I heard that you lost all your money in Mexico, and as I've earned a lot recently and I'm about to leave for a very lucrative engagement in London, I would like you to accept 4000 francs a year from me until you are back on your feet again. I would also be very happy if Pauline would come and live with me. I would take care of all the expenses of her upkeep and education, and see that she had the best musical instruction that Paris can provide.' To fill in the gelid silence which followed her words, she added, hesitantly: 'Of course, if you would prefer to think of my offer as a loan, you could pay me back in your own good time. But I would much rather you would consider it a gift.'

"Garcia measured his words as though they were minims in a musical exercise. 'I wouldn't consider it either a loan or a gift,' he said. 'I would consider it charity.'

"This was too much for Maria. She went crimson in the face and exclaimed: 'Charity' How can you...'

"But her father silenced her as though she were still the little girl in the music-room. 'Yes, charity,' he continued. 'And that is something I have never in all my fifty-four years accepted from anyone. And I don't intend to accept it now from my daughter. As for your idea of taking Pauline away to live with you, it is out of the question. From what I have heard of this 'house' of yours, I wouldn't allow little Pauline to set foot in it.'

"Maria clenched her fists, and for a moment I wondered if she was going to strike him. But she took a deep breath and spat back: 'How dare you?'

"'How dare I?!' As Garcia's anger increased, his voice began to rise. 'You seem to have forgotten that I'm your father. And how dare you, I would like to ask, walk into your mother's house dressed in that outlandish fashion? Why are you wearing trousers under that skirt?'

"'Because I'm going riding,' Maria answered icily. 'And as we shall be jumping some obstacles, I shall ride astride.'

"'Ah!' Garcia's tone was now almost triumphant. 'So you can't even keep your legs closed during the day!'"

Turgenev couldn't believe his ears. "He really said that?" he asked incredulously.

Viardot nodded his head. "He did indeed. And the result was devastating. Joaquina put her hands over Pauline's ears and hurried her out of the room. I tried to intervene, but a butterfly might as well have sought to interpose itself between the antlers of two charging stags. Manuel, his eyes blazing with rage, said: 'Father, you should be ashamed of yourself,' and tried to take Maria's arm.

"And what did she do?" Turgenev asked.

"She smiled at her brother, gently removed his hand from her arm and, never taking her eyes off her father's face, began to put her hat back on. Garcia, realizing that he'd exceeded all limits, tried half-heartedly to make amends. 'I'll make *you* a proposal now, Maria,' he said, more quietly. 'And that is that you come back and live with your family. You could contribute to our expenses, if you wished, and...'

"This time it was Maria who interrupted him. She spat out a 'Never!', which might have been a rehearsal for those *Giammai!*s with which she was to electrify audiences all over Italy, whirled round on her heel and made the kind of exit that would bring them screaming and *brava*-ing to their feet."

Turgenev, who was already toying with the idea of writing for the theatre, was determined not to miss a detail. "And what did you do?" he asked eagerly. "Did you follow her?"

"No, no, I stayed behind to do my job. The job Maria had brought me along for. I'm sure she was expecting the reaction she received. I tried to make Garcia see reason, to convince him that he hadn't behaved very well. When the rest of the family gathered together again around a very glum luncheon table, Joaquina supported me as much as she dared, Manuel maintained a sullen silence, and even little Pauline, with tears in her eyes, said, 'Papa, why do you have to be so cruel?' But it was quite useless. In fact, counter-productive. Garcia might, perhaps, a few hours later, have been able to admit to himself that he had been too harsh. But never to us. Never to his family. When I told him I thought Maria's offer had been a very generous gesture, he dismissed it with one word: *cochonnerie*.

"Did they make it up soon afterwards?"

"Not for some years. Until just before Garcia's death, in fact. And never entirely. Because, you see, a few weeks after that meeting, something happened which made a bad situation worse."

"What?" Turgenev asked, impatiently. "What happened?"

Viardot took his time before answering, and then said slowly: "Maria wrote to her mother to tell her she was pregnant."

"With de Bériot?"

"Yes. She had two sons, Franz and Charles-Wilfred, before she was able to get her annulment and marry Charles."

"And how did Garcia react to this?"

Viardot gave a short laugh. "As a true Spaniard. He accepted that the baby would be brought up in his house – obviously Maria's career would have been seriously jeopardized if the news had got out – but he refused to see Maria and forbade his family to have anything to do with her."

"Did they obey him?"

"Only to his face. Manuel often went to see her, and when they knew Garcia would be out of the house for some time, Maria would pay quick, furtive visits to her mother and baby son."

Turgenev's curiosity was still not quite satisfied. "And how did you emerge from all this?" he asked. Did you still remain good friends with father and daughter?"

Viardot smiled. "Not quite such a good friend as before with either of them. I suffered the usual fate of people who try to see both sides of a violent quarrel. You often end up with the antagonists almost more hostile to you than to each other." As the two men rose and walked out through the door of the *izba* to collect their dogs and pick up their guns, he reached up to put a paternal arm around the young man's shoulders. "As one of these days, my good young Ivan, you will probably find out for yourself."

Turgenev was now so fascinated by the career and personality of la Malibran that he would badger Pauline with questions during breaks in their Russian lessons. When one day she expressed surprise at the extent of his interest, he immediately wondered if he was abusing her confidence. Hurriedly excusing himself, he asked if he had been indiscreet.

She thought for a moment, then shook her head. "No, I really am rather happy to talk about Maria. Perhaps it's good for me. It's seven years now since she died, and this is the first time I have allowed myself to confront certain issues."

Thus encouraged, Turgenev pressed on. "How often did you see her after the dramatic quarrel with your father? Do you have any clear memories of those days?

For a moment she closed her eyes and let a sad smile play around her lips. Then: "My memories of Maria, when we lived in the rue des Trois-Frères between our return from Mexico and Papa's death, are always a mass of contradictions: excitement and fear, happiness and pain. After the falling-out with Papa, her brief, occasional visits always fell into a similar conspiratorial pattern. The excitement of her arrival, as she swept me up in her arms and hugged and kissed me; then I would be left alone while my mother and Maria went to see baby Franz. I never spent much time with the baby; its very existence was kept as much a secret as possible, and they were afraid I would chatter about it to my friends. Then Maria and Maman would re-emerge and I would play or sing something for Maria. Those were my happiest moments; she would always compliment me and say how talented I was, a welcome change from the constant criticisms of Papa and my piano teacher and Reicha, with whom I was studying composition at the Conservatoire. Then, when I was ready to go on playing to her for hours, she would spring to her feet – she could never keep still for more than a few minutes at a time anyway – and say she must be off. Another enveloping embrace and away she would go, leaving me with the soft feel of satin on my cheek and the fragrance of her perfume in my nostrils. And I was left with my dreams until the next time…"

"And what memories do you have of her last years? Did you become closer as you got older?"

"Oh yes. I didn't really know the real Maria until after Papa's death. With that half-loved, half- hated figure out of the way, she was finally able to lavish her natural generosity on her family, as well as on all the lost and needy she was always helping throughout her life. As soon as Maman had observed a decent period of mourning, she and I were invited to stay with Maria and Charles in Naples, where Maria had been engaged for the season. They were living in a magnificent apartment in the Palazzo Badajo in via Toledo, and there I spent three or four months which, for sheer happiness, exceeded the wildest dreams of any twelve-year-old. Maria and I would often go off on our own, as Maman still didn't like to be seen very much in public. We would hire a carriage and go for long drives around that enchanting bay, visiting places with names that, at the time, sounded sweeter in my ear than any music: Portici, Posillipo, Castellammare, Solfatara di Pozzuoli… we used to fit them to arias and sing them as we drove along the coast on wonderfully warm autumn mornings. Ca—-a-a-a—astellama—-a-a-a-re to *Casta Diva*… that kind of thing. We'd stop somewhere and walk for hours along the beach, collecting brightly-coloured shells and pebbles, and I'd listen fascinated while Maria told me all the court and society gossip and the back-stage intrigues at the theatre."

"Was she popular with her fellow-artists?"

"With most of them, yes. A lot of her rivals were jealous, of course. But even the ones that loved her were sometimes driven to despair by her habit of changing her performance from night to night. They never knew what she was going to do next. But that was what made her so unique. Her audiences lived her characters' moods along with her."

"But you haven't followed her in this."

"Oh no. I'm much more down to earth. When I've discovered which moves and gestures work best for me, I stay with them. There are enough risks in our profession without deliberately running after more."

"And your mother? Did she fight with Maria as your father had done?"

"Never. But you don't know Maman. She's little short of a saint. She'd raise her eyes to heaven when Maria would do or say something extravagant, occasionally expostulate feebly, and there it would end. In the evenings after dinner, if Maria wasn't singing, the four of us would read or play cards or just chat amongst ourselves. There's one evening I remember particularly well. Maman and I were embroidering, Charles was playing patience and Maria was sitting on a low chair, surrounded by artificial flowers, ribbons of all colours, odd scraps of velvet and lace, plumes and goodness knows what else, making a hat. It was a passion of hers for a while, but like most of her passions, it didn't last long. And that evening it lasted all of ten minutes, after which she flung the embryonic hat down, rose from her chair and with a bored *Uffa!*, an exclamation which she'd learnt from her Neapolitan friends, suggested we all went for a drive along the coast road.

"'It's far too late,' Maman announced firmly. 'You have rehearsals all day tomorrow and a performance in the evening. You'll wear yourself out, child. Can't you ever keep still for a minute?'

"'You know what the Neapolitans say, Maman?' Maria replied. 'There's plenty of time for keeping still when you're in your grave. And it won't be long before I'm in mine.' (She was always convinced she was going to die young.)

"Maman put down her embroidery and said, with some exasperation: 'Don't talk such nonsense, Maria! You have no right to say such things. May the Good Lord forgive you! After all the blessings He has showered on you...'

"'And you know what the Greeks said! Those whom the gods love...'

"She stood there for a moment, biting her lip, and then, before the tears could well up into her eyes, she rushed over to me, pulled me out of my chair and practically dragged me out of the room.

"She hauled me up the stairs to her bedroom, closed the door behind us and flung her arms around me in an embrace which squeezed most of the breath from my body. Then she held me at arm's length, gazed with her tear-drenched eyes into mine and asked me (although she was really asking herself): 'Why do I say these things? I know they hurt Maman and Charles. And there's no sense to them. Look at me!' She gave a strangled laugh and glanced at herself in the mirror. 'I have the voice of Stentor, the body of Falstaff and the appetite of... of a cannibal! And yet...' She sank into a chair, gnawing her hand to try and control her sobs.

"I stood there, not knowing what to say. I was torn between embarrassment, wishing I could just disappear, and a desperate desire to say something which could help her. I went up behind her, put my hand on her shoulders, buried my face in her hair and babbled something about her being overtired, needing to rest, take a holiday...

"She patted my hand, looked up at my reflection in the mirror and, with a smile that was sadder than the most grief-stricken expression I have ever seen, said: 'You don't understand, my little Pauline. The reason that I never stop is because I don't want time to think. That frightens me more than anything. That's why I shut my eyes to everything except my career, my triumphs, my happiness. And you know what it is, this 'happiness' of mine? It's Juliet, dead, and I am Romeo weeping for her.'

"This really did leave me speechless. She must have noticed my discomfort, because she jumped from her chair with an energy designed to banish all morbid thoughts, went over to a cupboard and came back carrying an ornate jewel-case. 'I want you to have this', she said, opening it and showing me a superb diamond cluster. She interrupted my attempts at expostulation by telling me how she came to be given it. When she first came to Naples, she immediately conquered the public at the small popular Fondo theatre, but was warned that trouble was in store for her at the more aristocratic San Carlo. The King, Ferdinand II, usually attended performances there, and he was favourably disposed towards the reigning diva, a certain Giuseppina de Begnis, whose poverty of vocal splendour was made up for by the opulence of her physical charms. She was the current Desdemona and was determined to remain so. Maria's position was already precarious, as she had gone around the salons of Naples saying, '*Pour le roi je suis trop maigre*', and it would be a miracle if that had not reached the king's ears. A few days before her San Carlo debut in *Otello* she requested, with typical bravado, a royal audience and blatantly asked the king not to come to her first night. When the astonished Ferdinand asked why, she said she had heard that when the king was present in the audience, his subjects were discouraged from applauding unless the sovereign had set the example. She was afraid that he might be distracted and forget, and she was unable to give of her best unless she was encouraged by applause. Ferdinand was so impressed by her frankness and audacity that he went to the theatre and when Maria made her first entrance, stood up in his box and clapped before she had sung a note, thus guaranteeing her a triumphant reception. To de Begnis's fury, Desdemona was sung only by Maria throughout that season. A few days later, Maria was summoned to the palace to give a private recital, after which she was presented with the diamond cluster by Queen Cristina. When she opened the case in the privacy of her room to examine the royal gift, she found a tiny note in the queen's hand saying: *Jamais trop maigre pour la reine*.

"Maria's last words to me that memorable evening were these: 'When you're successful and famous, Pauline, as you surely will be, never be subservient to royalty. Curtsey to them when you're introduced, call them "Your Majesty", observe all the forms. But don't squirm before them. And never forget this: however much they might want to, they could never do what we do; whereas we, given the right circumstances, could do what they do just as well... and often a lot better.'"

It was with some trepidation that Turgenev finally asked Pauline about the events surrounding her sister's death. But even at the risk of being indelicate, such was his fascination with the woman he by now almost felt he had known, that once more his curiosity got the better of him. He reminded Pauline that she had mentioned her sister's conviction that she would die young. "There has always been a mystery about her death," he ventured. "I have heard so many conflicting rumours. Is it true that she was in some way responsible for it?"

"It would be more true to say that I was."

"You? How is that possible?"

She gave him a long, searching look before answering. "I have never really told all I know about those events to anybody. They left me with a feeling of guilt which I have never quite been able to shake off; so I suppose I made it easier for myself by consigning it all to the back of my mind. Perhaps the time has come for me to retrieve it. But not now. We'll keep it a secret from Louis, but instead of the next lesson, I'll give you an account of Maria's last days… however much effort it may cost me."

"When I look back," she told him, "on my relationship with Maria, I sometimes think of the last period of time I spent with her as though it were a recapitulation in a symphony. All the themes were there – joy, triumph, laughter, tears, anguish – and all played fortissimo. She and Charles, who were now married, had been invited to give a joint recital in Liège, and Maria asked me to accompany them at the piano and sing some duets with her. It was really my first professional engagement and I was beside myself with excitement. Imagine a girl of fifteen, fresh – or perhaps stale would be a better word – from three years of piano lessons consisting of <u>nothing</u> but finger exercises, being asked to appear on a concert platform with the world's most famous singer and a violinist whose name was mentioned in the same breath as Paganini's. But my exhilaration suffered a severe setback when I first laid eyes on Maria, who had just returned from a series of engagements in England. She looked like a walking corpse: her face was unhealthily pale and with bruises, which she'd tried, unsuccessfully, to cover and hide under make-up; her cheeks were hollow, and dark pouches sagged under her eyes, which lit up from time to time, not with their usual radiant vivacity but with a frighteningly feverish glitter. She had lost so much weight that her bones stuck out through her skin, and her natural grace of carriage had given way to a series of awkward, jerky, almost puppet-like movements. She joked about her appearance and said the bruises were due to tripping in her riding habit and falling down the stone steps of an English country house. Her poor health, she said, was the result of an impossibly punishing series of engagements at Drury Lane.

"Certainly this might have been true of any other singer: she had given 38 performances, including *La Sonnambula* and *Fidelio*, in 75 days, and goodness knows how many private recitals. But Maman and I, who knew our Maria, were sceptical of this explanation; in the past she had always thrived on gargantuan challenges like these. And I noticed something that perhaps escaped even Maman: as long as Charles was there, she managed to display her usual effervescent charm; but as soon as he left the room, it was as though the life drained out of her.

"I learned the reason for this the night after the recital. I had lived the first part of the evening like the heroine of the most romantic of fairy tales. Maria, somehow managing to look as beautiful as ever and singing with unparalleled mastery, reduced the distinguished, elegant audience to a stamping, cheering mob. Every time she returned to the stage to acknowledge the applause, she insisted on dragging me with her, however hard I tried to hold back and let her go out alone. And at the glittering reception afterwards, as the first families of Belgium competed in demonstrating to the newly-married Maria that 'de Bériot's concubine', whom they had snubbed for four years, was now their most precious personal possession, she never took her arm from around my shoulder, introducing me to prince after count after duke until my head whirled, and insisting that I partake in all the compliments and congratulations that were showered on her from every side.

"But it was when we finally extricated ourselves from the reception and got back to our hotel that I came face to face with the dark shadow which has to fall across every fairy tale. Maria was transformed as if by the touch of the demon's wand. During the drive back she had sat, still and silent, gazing ahead of her as though contemplating some fathomless enigma. On stepping out of the carriage, she staggered and would have fallen if Charles hadn't already had his arm round her waist. As we were collecting our keys, she told Charles she was going to spend the night in my room. 'It's so rarely that I'm able to have any time alone with Pauline,' she explained. 'And we have a lot to talk about, don't we, my angel?' Her eyes bored into mine, willing me to agree; quite superfluously, of course, as I was longing to unburden myself to her. Charles had no objection, as long as she promised not to stay up too late. She looked tired, he said, with male obtuseness, and needed to sleep. 'God only knows how much I need sleep', she whispered to me as we moved away. 'But it seems that sleep doesn't need me.'

"As soon as we reached my room we started helping each other out of our dresses. Still elated by the evening's triumph, and thrilled to be alone once more with the sister I worshipped, I promptly forgot how dreadfully ill she looked and proceeded, with all the egotism of youth, to gush out my own miseries. Just two weeks previously, on my sixteenth birthday, I had been sitting alone in the music-room of our house in Paris, playing the piano. For the past few months I had been taking lessons with Franz Liszt, with whom, of course, I was hopelessly in love. The week before, just as I was leaving, he had slipped me a couple of sheets of manuscript paper containing a composition he had written that very morning, asking me, as though it would be doing him a favour, if I would 'look it over' and play it to him the next time we met. Never had I put such ferocious energy into practising anything as I did into that short piece of Liszt's. And there I was, on my birthday, playing it with closed eyes – for I already knew it by heart – and imagining him telling me how beautifully it emerged from under my fingers. I must have been in some sort of a trance. At that moment, my mother came into the room, placed a Rossini aria on the music stand and told me to sing it. Since my father's death, she had been supervising my musical instruction, and though she was not as severe as Papa had been with Maria, she was not to be trifled with. So I sang it. When I had finished, she said to me, in a voice which brooked no argument: 'All right, I have now made up my mind. Shut the piano. From now on you will sing.'

"For me it was a calamity. I had always loved to sing, but had never doubted that my irresistible vocation was to be a pianist. There was already one female singer in the family, and she happened to be the greatest in the world. And then, no more lessons with Liszt?... Was it possible for so young a heart to break? But I was an obedient child. I had none of Maria's rebellion in me. So I bit my lip, nodded my head and submitted to my mother's will. The only concession that I made to the past was hiding the two manuscript pages of Liszt's composition in a drawer where I kept my most precious possessions. Perhaps I was hoping that one day he would come round to ask for it back. But he never did. And when I ran into him by chance a year later in Padua, he never mentioned it. He had probably forgotten he had ever written it.

"Maria listened to my pathetic little tale with conspicuous sympathy and understanding, but when I had finished she seized hold of my hand – we were now lying on the bed in our nightdresses – and said that she too had something to tell me, but I must swear swear swear not to tell anyone else, especially Charles. Of course I agreed – how I wish I hadn't! – and she proceeded to tell me about her terrible experience in England.

"As we all know now, the fall down the steps was pure invention. But to this day, very few people know the whole truth. She had taken part, against Charles's wishes, in a riding party organized by Lord Lennox at his estate just outside London. When the guests were choosing their rides, Maria, who took great pride in her horsemanship, had been shown a magnificent black thoroughbred stallion, but been told that it hadn't been properly broken in and was certainly no ride for a woman. 'I'm sure they said that to me on purpose,' she told me, 'daring me to defy their beastly smug English male condescension. And I'm afraid I fell for it. I couldn't resist the challenge. It was unforgivable of me... I had promised Charles not to do anything dangerous... and... no one knows it yet, Pauline, not even Maman... but I'm pregnant...' I couldn't resist an exclamation of 'Maria!', and she tightened her grip on my hand so that I almost cried out in pain. Then she went on, her eyes pleading with me for understanding and forgiveness. 'I mounted the horse – I could almost hear them saying to themselves, 'Now we're going to have a bit of fun!'' – and for ten minutes or so I was in complete control. He was a beautiful creature, and I was beginning to feel that wonderful sense of harmony between a human and an animal which is the intoxicating thrill of riding, when my luck ran out. One of Lennox's little sons had been trying to fly a big red kite in a nearby field, but the wind suddenly dropped and the kite fell like a stone right in front of the horse's nose. He reared up, but I managed, unfortunately, to stay on. And then he bolted, and there was absolutely nothing I could do. I knew I was never going to be able to stop him, so as we went under a tree, I seized on to a low bough, hoping to pull myself clear and jump down. But my foot caught in the stirrup and I fell to the ground. I must have been dragged along for quite some way until the horse stopped, but I don't know how far because I lost consciousness. When I came round, all the 'gentlemen' were kneeling round me, trying to force brandy down my throat and looking very sheepish. They patched me up as well as they could and Lennox drove me back to my hotel. But before I left, I made them all promise not to say a word about the accident to Charles. And they kept their word. He's never had any suspicion about what actually happened.'

"I told her that she absolutely must tell Charles, that he would arrange for her to be examined by the best doctors in Europe, but she simply shook her head and said she was past the care of doctors. 'I always knew I would not live long. I told you all, but no one believed me. I'm not afraid of death. Perhaps I was looking for it. Perhaps that stupid riding accident was an attempt to go half-way to meet it. But I know it will not be long now, and what I've just heard from you is like a confirmation. Maman told you you were to be a singer the same week that I fell from that horse. I'm sure she herself didn't really know why. It was Fate. The voice of Maria Malibran will not be extinguished. It will survive... stronger and more thrilling than ever. Because you will look after it better then I have. And so, my little Pauline, now you must make me another promise. As well as remembering not to tell anyone what we have talked about tonight, you must promise to obey Maman. I want you to take the torch from my dying hand and set beacons ablaze with it in every capital of Europe. We will defy the ephemeral nature of the singer's art. I shall die, but my voice will live on in you.'"

Pauline had become so engrossed in reliving these memories that she seemed to have forgotten her companion's presence. She now fell silent, and Turgenev saw that there were tears in her eyes. He had been listening with the concentration of one intent on storing up every word he is hearing. Now he encouraged her to go on.

"What, in heaven's name, did you find to say to that?" he asked.

"I stammered out a few conventional phrases, assuring her that she'd soon be well again and more beautiful and in more glorious voice than ever. But she shrugged these aside and, with something of her old imperiousness, insisted that I make the promise that she demanded. So I promised."

"Did you really think she was going to die?"

"It's difficult to say now. Of course, at the back of my mind there was always the memory of her melodramatic moments... 'My happiness is Juliet, dead, and I am Romeo, weeping for her'... but there was something about her that evening which transcended performance. Perhaps it was her calm. It was as though she were reading from a book she had written herself. I tried, as we always do, not to believe the worst, but I think deep down I knew she was telling the truth."

"Did you see her again before she died?"

"Yes, but never on the same level of intimacy. A few weeks after Liège she spent ten days at Roissy, the property she and Charles had bought just outside Paris, and invited all her closest friends to come and stay with her. I suppose her idea was to say a final goodbye, but it was hard to imagine it at the time. Seeing the enthusiasm with which she threw herself into entertaining her guests, you'd have thought she had another fifty years to live. Every evening there was music. She, Charles, I and many of the guests would sing and play late into the night. And Maria was the one who never wanted to stop. Later Charles was to tell me that was because she was still tormented by her inability to sleep. But I didn't know that, and as one happy day followed another, I became convinced that the scene at Liège had been just another of Maria's exaggerations. Only one aspect of her behaviour brought back my fears: that was her obsession with perfecting a song she was writing to words by the Italian poet, Antonio Benelli. It was called *Aprite alla Morte* – 'Open up to Death' – and she wanted it to be the final item in an album of her songs that she was preparing. She, who usually wrote with such facility, made draft after draft before she was finally satisfied. She dedicated it to Luigi Lablache, which in itself was ironic, as he was famous the world over for his *basso buffo* roles in Rossini, and is the most cheerful, life-loving man alive. But he's also a great artist; and when he sang it to us one evening, with Maria playing the staccato piano accompaniment representing Death knocking at the door as though she were hammering nails into her own coffin, I was not the only one to feel a sudden chill descending on the whole company."

"Do you remember the words?"

"All too well! The original was in Italian, of course, but the meaning was more or less this:

> *Knock! Knock! Who's there?*
> *Knock! Knock! It's Death.*
> *Quick, servant, open the doors,*
> *Open the doors to Death!*
> *For three months now,*
> *I've been trying to catch his eye,*
> *But he plays cat and mouse with me,*
> *Appears, then goes away.*
> *He's an ill-mannered reaper,*
> *Who keeps company with greybeards;*
> *He has a high old time with them,*
> *But he won't have pity on me.*

Knock! Knock! Who's there?
Knock! Knock! It's Death.
Quick, servant, open the doors,
Open the doors to Death.

Turgenev's natural sense of tact had a brief struggle with his unquenchable curiosity… and lost.

"Have you ever sung it?" he asked.

"Never!"

"Why not? You sing so much of your sister's repertory."

"Benelli died two months after writing the poem. One month after setting it to music, Maria was dead."

"So, after those few days at Roissy, you never saw her again?"

"No. Against everyone's advice, she insisted on going to Manchester, where she and Charles had been invited to take part in an important musical festival. At her first concert, she sang a duet which took so much out of her that she collapsed in the wings. The audience roared for an encore, and the stage manager went out to announce that Madame Malibran was ill and couldn't sing any more. Whereupon the 'civilized' English audience booed, hissed and started throwing their chairs at the wretched man, who was about to beat a retreat when Maria, who could never resist applause, came on and said she would give an encore. 'I will sing,' she whispered to him, 'but I am already dead.' When she had finished – and there were experienced onlookers there who said that she ended with the most perfectly executed trill the human voice could contrive – she swayed and would have fallen if Lablache, who was also taking part in the programme, hadn't rushed on and helped her off. This time, not even she could hide the gravity of her condition. She finally confessed to Charles about her fall from the horse, the finest doctor in London was rushed up to Manchester, but it was too late. She died a week later."

"And she was buried in Manchester?"

"Yes, at first. The city council, perhaps realizing that their townsmen had been in some way responsible, gave her a magnificent funeral and voted to build a monument in her honour. But Charles, when he recovered from his prostration, decided he wanted her to be buried in Belgium. With the blessing of the local curate, he chose a plot in the cemetery of Laeken, Brussels' most exclusive burial-place. And that's when the trouble started."

"What trouble?"

"An endless series of legal wrangles between the British and Belgian authorities. The Manchester councillors, having spared no expense for the funeral, were reluctant to relinquish the mortal remains of the distinguished foreigner whom, as a special mark of respect, they had buried under the south nave of the Collegiate church. This, of course, was a Protestant church, and the service had been conducted principally along Anglican lines, although two priests had been allowed to say the Catholic office of the dead at the foot of the deathbed before the procession moved off. The local religious authorities now became more jesuitical than the Jesuits: they contested the validity of Maria and Charles's marriage, claiming that the Paris tribunal had granted the annulment of Maria's marriage to Malibran, but not the full divorce… whatever that was supposed to mean. And if Charles was not legally Maria's husband, he had no right to claim her body. Charles sent a lawyer to Manchester, who found a way around this. He dug up some ancient law which said that parents could take possession of the bodies of their children, by violence if necessary, without rendering themselves liable to prosecution. So poor Maman, aged fifty-eight, crossed the Channel in midwinter during a storm, confronted bishops and city councillors brandishing a document containing her precious law, and eventually had the body exhumed at five o'clock in the morning. The coffin was driven through the city to the port, transferred to the ship and arrived in Antwerp the following morning."

"A happy ending, then."

"Oh, that was by no means the end! Now it was the Belgians' turn. The head of the Belgian church, the Archbishop of Malines, was wrongly informed that the service in Manchester had been conducted exclusively according to Protestant rites. So he reprimanded the curate of Laeken for having given permission for the body to be reburied in his cemetery and strictly forbade any Catholic priest to be present at the funeral ceremony."

"So it was a purely civil affair?"

"In the best sense of the word, yes. It was a homage to Maria on the part of people who had loved her and her art. Despite the short notice, they came from all over Europe: London, Paris, Milan, Naples, Venice… everywhere where she had captured the hearts of people who loved music. Looking back on it now, I can think of it as a glorious event."

"And at the time?"

"At the time, it was the most dreadful day of my life. Although three months had passed since her death, I still couldn't reconcile myself to the idea that she had really gone. The fact that I hadn't been able to kiss her goodbye, hadn't been able to mourn silently by her coffin, made it all seem unreal to me. And now, when she was finally back with her family, all gathered together in the villa at Ixelles, just outside Brussels, which she and Charles had bought four years before, she didn't belong to us any more. The place was overrun with visitors, mourners coming to pay their respects and crowds of inquisitive people just turning up to stare. I think Brussels must have emptied that day. The house and grounds were invaded. The drive, the front steps and all the ground floor rooms were one solid mass of humanity. I'm sure the panic that I sometimes feel in crowds stems from then. It was the first week in January, and one of the coldest winters in memory. Before the carriage bearing the coffin could pass, volunteers had to cut a path through the snow. Black drapes hung from the windows of all the houses along the route from Ixelles to Laeken. The clouds were so low and heavy with snow that the light seemed more that of early evening than mid-morning. I walked behind the carriage with Maman, Charles and Manuel, my feelings as numb, dark and chilled as the suburban streets of Brussels. The only thought that came to my mind was how Maria would have hated the repetitive drone of the funeral march and the monotonous rhythm, thumped out with military precision, by the drummers of a distinguished infantry regiment. And then the oppressive gloom was relieved, for a few minutes, by a moment of unsuspected beauty. When we reached the cemetery and as the pall-bearers were carrying the coffin towards the grave, boy choristers from the Cathedral choir, conducted by François Fétis, the director of the Conservatoire and a great friend of Maria's, started to sing a sublime four-part Miserere."

"I'm surprised the bishop allowed them to."

"He didn't. That was part of the beauty of it. Priests had gone round to the parents of all the boys with the best voices, threatening them with fire and brimstone if they allowed their children to sing. But Fétis retaliated by putting up notices in all the classrooms announcing that anyone who refused to take part in the Miserere for Madame Malibran would no longer be allowed to attend the Conservatoire. And not one boy failed to turn up."

"A triumph of Art over Bigotry. Achieved by a little painless twisting of arms. Voltaire would have approved!"

"I wish I'd had Voltaire to consult over the weeks that followed. Because Bigotry certainly got its revenge. And Art was powerless to offer any resistance."

"I don't understand."

"I had to stay on in that house for months with Maman and Charles, all three of us prostrated with grief. And devout and practising young Christian that I was, I tortured myself with the thought that if I had told Charles what really happened at Lord Lennox's, he wouldn't have let her go to Manchester, knowing she was so ill. After a few weeks of wrestling with this tormenting doubt, I decided to take it with me into the confessional.

"Was the priest able to help you?"

"Yes, I suppose so. But certainly not in the way he intended"…

INT. CONFESSIONAL – DAY

A confessional in a side-aisle of a large, gloomy gothic church in Brussels. Little of the grey winter light filtering through the high narrow windows manages to penetrate down to floor-level. The 16-year-old Pauline, shivering inside a thick black woolen coat, is making her confession. All she can make out through the screen is a cadaverous profile dominated by an immense beak of a nose. She speaks, especially at first, in a nervous whisper. The priest replies in a colourless drone, as though he were conducting a service or repeating a text he knew by heart.

Pauline has just explained the guilt she feels at not having told anyone about her sister's fall from a horse when pregnant, and her fear that she may be in part responsible for her death.

PRIEST

Your sister's life, my child, was in God's hands. Clearly He felt it had lasted long enough.

PAULINE

But father, she was only 28. And she had just remarried, only six months before. She had two small children and another one on the way…

PRIEST

The two children she had were born out of wedlock. And the validity of her second marriage was extremely questionable. Perhaps, if she had lived, she would have given birth to another unfortunate little creature who would have been illegitimate in the eyes of our Holy Mother Church.

PAULINE

If you only knew how overjoyed she was when her annulment was granted and she was able to marry the man she loved. She had waited six years for that moment.

PRIEST

She should have waited longer.

PAULINE

Father, none of us is perfect.

PRIEST

We are very far here from perfection. Your sister was a great sinner, and in my opinion the curate of Laeken was most ill-advised to allow her to be buried in his cemetery. I understand that her funeral service in England was conducted according to the Protestant rites. She should have been left there.

PAULINE

But her family wanted her to lie here. My mother, who is nearly 60, went all alone to Manchester to bring the coffin back. She never left its side throughout the long journey home.

PRIEST

Your mother's devotion is admirable, my child, but that is not our concern here…

PAULINE

Father, Our Lord taught us the virtues of mercy and charity…

PRIEST

It is not for you to interpret Our Lord's words. These are matters far above the head of one of your tender years. But take heed: you are, I believe, embarked on the same career as that of your unfortunate sister. Make sure you do not venture down the godless path that she chose to follow. Eminence in the artistic world sets many a trap for the unwary. And never forget that glory on this earth has the substance of a shadow; the torments of hell endure for eternity. For the moment you can set your mind at rest. Your refusal to break the promise you made to your sister was no sin. For all we know, it may have been part of God's inscrutable will. But beware of spiritual pride. Ask the Lord, in all humility, for courage to bear whatever burdens may lie in store for you. And say a prayer for the salvation of your departed sister's soul. Go in peace, my child. *Ego te absolvo…in nomine patris et filii et spiritui sancti…*

The priest's skinny claw of a hand makes the sign of the cross and he leaves the confessional. Pauline stays for a few more minutes on her knees, presumably following his instructions. But when she rises to her feet and walks out of the church, the set of her jaw seems more indicative of rebellious determination than pious submission.

❈

The spring of 1847 found Turgenev back in Berlin. Like many who revisit university towns where they have first tasted the heady wine of youthful freedom, he soon became conscious of a feeling of vague disappointment. He had been away six years and found the atmosphere much changed: 'Right' Hegelianism had had its day; the high-flown, dreamy, rhetorical theories which he had loved to discuss all through the night with Bakunin and like-minded friends, were out of fashion. 'Left' Hegelianism was now the rage, and its prophet, Feuerbach, who had sat at the feet of the master, enflamed the young with his denunciation of organized religion and despotic rule. This change coincided in part with a change in the new Belinsky-influenced Turgenev. Nevertheless, he missed some of the carefree camaraderie of his student days, and found the few friends that were still there disconcertingly serious.

But he had not come to Berlin for the sake of plunging back into the past. There was more than one reason why he was anxious to leave Russia for a while. He had begun to attract some notice as a writer: *Khor and Kalinych,* his story about two peasants, had attracted enough interest to encourage him to start writing others examining the rural world he had grown up in. These tales, many of which described, for the first time in Russian literature, the daily life and condition of the serfs, were published by the journal *Sovremennik*, 'The Contemporary', with a subtitle, 'from a Sportsman's Notebook'. But *Sovremennik*, originally founded by Pushkin and now revived by Turgenev's friends, Panaev and Nekrasov, was already viewed with suspicion by the authorities on account of its unconcealed liberal views, and he was told that his name was beginning to attract unwelcome attention in government circles; if he were going to write about Russia, perhaps it would be better for the time being to do so from abroad. Added to that, he found it impossible to spend more than a few days in his mother's company: visits to Spasskoye became ever more fraught with tension as he could no longer conceal his detestation of serfdom. Over the New Year festivities he had remarked that he found it inconceivable that human beings could be treated as chattels, to be moved around at their owners' arbitrary wishes, and that sooner rather than later they would have to be freed. The result was a fifteen-minute screaming fit, followed by the blank declaration that he must be mad.

But the overriding factor in his decision to go abroad was his inability to envisage any long-term separation from Pauline. Her third Russian tour, in the winter of 1845-46, had been less successful than the previous two: the craze for Italian opera was beginning to wear off and both Louis and their 6-year-old daughter Louise had been ill much of the winter. Turgenev had been in Paris the previous summer and had seen the Viardots, who had invited him to spend some time with them the following year at their château in the Brie country. So when he heard that Pauline would not be returning to St Petersburg for the next season, but would be appearing in a number of German operas in Berlin, he lost no time in applying for a passport. In January he was granted one 'to travel abroad for medical reasons'.

He soon learned, to his delight, that he was to be joined by Belinsky. Health was the reason for the critic's journey too, but in his case with all too real a justification. Belinsky hated the idea of leaving Russia. With no talent for languages, he felt as helpless as a child outside his native habitat. And cut off from all the sources which fuelled his violent energy, he dreaded the idea of long periods of time with nothing to do but brood over his illness. But his condition, aggravated by bitter grief over the death, after three suffering months, of his longed-for baby son, Vladimir, to whom Turgenev had stood godfather, was in fact deteriorating every day. His doctors felt, or at any rate said they felt, that only a period of cure at a spa could perhaps reverse the process. Money was the problem: although he worked himself unsparingly, driving his frail body to the limits of exhaustion, Belinsky and his family lived on the edge of poverty. Much of his work was done out of sheer conviction, without any hope of gain; and when an article was actually commissioned, he often had to wait months before receiving payment. But such was the love and admiration that his friends felt for him that, poor as most of them were too, they drummed up a subscription. This clearly wasn't going to cover the cost of taking his wife and child along, so the relatively wealthy Annenkov offered to accompany him. And the choice of spa fell on Salzbrunn, a Prussian watering-place in Silesia, since it was near enough to Berlin for Turgenev to join them.

Returning to his lodgings early one morning, Turgenev was astonished to find Belinsky slumped in an armchair. He had taken off his travelling clothes and was wearing a Tartar dressing-gown over his shirt and trousers. Turgenev's surprise and joy at seeing his friend again prevented him from noticing how tired and ill he looked.

"Vissarion Grigorevich!" he cried, embracing him with eager enthusiasm, "How wonderful to see you! *Willkommen in Berlin*! But what are you doing here, at this hour of night?"

Belinsky gave him a wry smile. "I waited a day for you in Stettin, but you didn't appear, so I came on alone."

Turgenev struck his forehead with the palm of his hand. Not even the keen-witted Belinsky could be sure if his puzzlement was genuine or assumed. "Stettin! Stettin!... Yes, of course, I was going to meet you there. But next week... surely next week..."

"Yesterday, *gamin*. But never mind. As you see, I am here."

"But I understood Annenkov was coming with you."

"Pavel Vasilevich was detained a few days in St Petersburg. He'll be joining me… us, I hope… in Salzbrunn."

"So you were travelling all alone. Oh, Vinya, I am so sorry. If I had known… When did you arrive?"

"About seven. I had thought we might sup together. But by nine my hunger became too much for me, so I asked for something to be sent up. They obliged with some goulash. It was not really what I wanted, but I couldn't think of the word for anything else."

"I'm sorry." Turgenev took his friend's hands in his, and now his penitence was surely genuine. "But when you hear where I've been, I know you'll forgive me."

"Let me guess. To an opera, perhaps?"

"Not just an opera. To one of the most extraordinary evenings in the history of the theatre."

"Madame Viardot was singing, I presume."

"Yes but…" Turgenev broke off and grinned. "You may tease me all you like, Vinya, but this time the world will bear me out. It will be in all the papers tomorrow. Do you want to hear about it now or in the morning, when you're less tired?"

"I have a feeling I'm going to hear about it now, whether I'm tired or not." Belinsky gave his friend a weary but encouraging smile. "Go on, *gamin*, tell me all about it."

"Well, they were giving Meyerbeer's opera *Robert le Diable*… I don't suppose you know it?"

"Never heard of it."

"You haven't missed much. The libretto's by Scribe – worse than usual – and there are just two women characters, Isabella, a Sicilian princess, and Alice, a sweet Norman girl who's a foster-sister to the hero, Robert, whose father is the Devil…"

Belinsky gently interrupted. "*Gamin*, I don't imagine it's the plot that made it one of the most extraordinary evenings in the history of the theatre."

"No, of course not. The important thing is that, in all the five acts, Alice and Isabella never meet. Now, when we arrived at the theatre this evening, there was an announcement that Mirella Steffanone, who was to sing Alice, was indisposed. So we were all about to go home, when another announcement was made that Madame Viardot would sing both parts. And so she did. And she was absolutely perfect in both: the haughty, aristocratic Isabella and the angelic, humble Alice. It was an incredible *tour de force*. I have never heard an audience so delirious. At the end, they simply wouldn't let her go. They must have called her back… oh, I don't know, fifteen, twenty times. And I heard several people saying, as they left the theatre, that if she did the same thing every night, there wouldn't be an empty seat in the opera house for the rest of the run."

"Do you think she will?"

"No, no, she wouldn't dream of it… for Steffanone's sake. She would never hurt a fellow artist. But it could be that Steffanone will not be better by the day after tomorrow, when there's the next performance, in which case I could take you to see the miracle for yourself."

Belinsky got to his feet, stretched and yawned. "Thank you, but I'm afraid I'll have to refuse. I'm rather tired after the journey, and the doctors made me promise to do nothing strenuous for the first week or so. And seeing the effect Madame Viardot's exploit has had on you, a similar experience could be enough to kill me." And he added, with a grim yet gentle little smile that made Turgenev's heart leap with remorse: "It wouldn't take much, you know."

Dresden,
Hotel Kaiserhof,
2 June, 1847
11.30 p.m.

Dearest Marie,

I have not kept my promise to write to you every couple of days, and I beg your forgiveness for this, even though I am sure you will soon understand why. You will be surprised to see that I am in Dresden, instead of Berlin or Salzbrunn. Let me start by explaining the reasons for this.

After I had been in Berlin less than twenty-four hours, I was already anxious to leave it. Of course it contains many treasures, but I had neither the strength nor the desire to see them; nor had I come all the way from St Petersburg to exchange one busy turbulent city for another. I was all ready to depart for the quiet of Salzbrunn, but Ivan Sergeyevich told me that it was too early, that the season did not start until the first week of June. This may well be true. It is also true that Pauline Viardot was to be singing in Dresden during the last week of May. So you see, here we are in Dresden!

You mustn't feel unkindly towards Turgenev. He has been a true friend, enveloping me in every sort of thoughtfulness several times a day. It is just that most of the time his mind is elsewhere. The poor fellow is completely besotted with his singer, whom I have now had the 'pleasure' of meeting… but I'll come to that later. The very evening we arrived here – it's not all that long a journey, but even a hundred miles is enough for someone like me, who has never sought to emulate Ulysses – what do you think we did? Settle ourselves in our rooms and go downstairs for a good dinner? Take a stroll around the streets of this wonderfully beautiful city? No, quickly into evening clothes and off, without time for a piece of cheese or a glass of wine, to the opera house, where they were giving an interminable work by Meyerbeer called Les Huguenots. *As you know, I am not a great lover of opera, but this might have been written to embody everything I detest about the genre: an absurdly melodramatic story, preposterously unbelievable situations, tragedies which could have been averted by saying the one word that anyone in his right mind – except for a character in an opera – would automatically say. All of this going on at unbearable length, propped up* (barely) by swathes of turgid, overblown music. Of course there were, every now and then – which means every hour and then – the odd tuneful aria and duet, and I have to say that La Viardot is really extraordinary, both as singer and as actress. But that's not enough to fill <u>five</u> <u>hours</u>. I shamelessly fell asleep through much of the fourth and fifth acts, and Ivan Sergeyevich was good enough to pretend not to notice. But when, at two in the morning, he said we must go and see Madame in her dressing-room, I drew the line, pleaded doctors' orders (they can come in very useful at times) and hired a carriage, which Turgenev was good enough to pay for, to take me back to the hotel.

A couple of days later we visited the picture gallery in the Zwinger museum, which has some fine paintings. Eventually we reached a small room where there is nothing but a Raphael Madonna. After duly admiring it, I was about to move on. But T. lingered… and lingered and lingered, until I asked him if he didn't want to see the other pictures in the collection. He blushed a little (it's a loveable thing about him that he still blushes) and admitted that he was expecting the Viardots here any minute and was anxious to hear Monsieur's opinion on the Raphael. (Monsieur is by way of being a great expert on art.) I started to leave, saying that, with all due respect, Monsieur's opinion was of little interest to me, but T. begged me to stay. The fact is that the poor man was as anxious for me to meet his diva as I was to avoid her. But there was nothing to be done, for a minute later, in they swept. T. made the introductions and there then followed a scene only Gogol could have done justice to. The problem was, there was no 'lingua franca'; I tried to stumble along with a few words of the sort of French that not even horses use, while she gallantly and courteously, realizing my incapacity, ventured a few remarks in Russian. Admirable as it is of her to have learnt any at all, this did not carry the conversation very far. She finally invited me to come with T. to a concert she was giving on Friday; this time she spoke in French and unfortunately I understood every word, so there was nothing I could do but accept. After they left – incidentally, Monsieur never pronounced on Raphael… or anything else, for that matter – T. was in the most ebullient spirits; I think he was convinced that the meeting had been a great success on all sides.

Marie, I must now let you into a secret, or rather make you an accomplice in my reprehensible behaviour. The concert was tonight, and I have returned to the hotel and am writing to you instead of joining in the subsequent celebrations. So I won't dwell long on the evening, as Ivan Sergeyevich may be back at any moment, and might look in on me to make sure I'm asleep, like all good invalids should be at this hour.

Inexpert as I am in these matters, there can be no doubt that musically the concert was very beautiful. For the first time I realized that all the hyperboles that are used about Pauline Viardot are simply the truth. She <u>is</u> a supreme artist – and so much more so in the songs and arias she sang this evening than in that ridiculous farrago of the other night. I have no shame in admitting that I was deeply moved by her artistry.

But I was nearly moved out of the concert hall by the audience that had gathered to hear her; whether by invitation or whether some had actually dug into their pockets to pay for their tickets I know not. But there they were – the local princelings and dukes and counts and barons with their overdressed, overbosomed wives – one exceeding the other in the fatuity and condescension of their remarks. T. seemed quite unworried by it – which would not have been the case if he had been facing our home-grown variety. But then, as I have already indicated, these days our dear Ivan Sergeyevich is only intermittently able to breathe the same air as us. This time he was quite upset when I said I was not going to accompany him to the reception *after the concert. I couldn't think of anything civil to say to those people in Russian, let alone any other language. To cut short his remonstrances, I had to trot out my doctors again.*

In haste, as I hear carriages pulling up in the street outside... The Viardots leave tomorrow for London. T. – probably in funeral garb – and I will go walking in the mountains for a couple of days to get some good Saxon air into my lungs and then we will move down to Salzbrunn, where we shall shortly be joined by Annenkov and I shall start drinking a lot of water.

My most loving thoughts go to you and our little Olyechka. Tell her that her Daddy will return, if not quite as Ulysses, at least as a fair imitation of Hercules. And try to believe a little of this yourself...

A few weeks after their arrival in Salzbrunn, Turgenev and Annenkov were sitting on the terrace of their hotel, sipping their breakfast coffee in the early summer sunshine. It was after ten o'clock, but Belinsky, who was usually the first to rise, still hadn't joined them. Fearing that their sick friend might have taken a turn for the worse during the night, they were about to go up to his room when he abruptly came out on the terrace and slumped into a chair beside them. His appearance seemed to confirm their anxiety: two angry, red-rimmed eyes glared out at them from under an unruly mop of uncombed hair; they found it hard to recognize the relaxed convivial friend they had said good night to only a few hours previously. But he reassured them, up to a point, when he told them that he had been up all night reading... "This!" And with a gesture beyond contempt, he threw a small book down on the table.

Annenkov picked it up and read out the title: *Selected Passages from my Correspondence with Friends*. "But this is Gogol's new book", he said excitedly.

"Yes. It arrived by yesterday's post. I didn't tell you, because I thought I'd read it first and spring a surprise on you both."

"And it isn't good?" Turgenev asked.

"It isn't just 'not good'. It's an abomination. I kept saying to myself during the night, he can't have written this. It's some forgery, put out by his enemies. But then I would come across some passage where the style was quite unmistakable, so I had to search for some other explanation".

"Did you find one?" Annenkov asked.

"It's too early to say yet. There could be several: he's been put under some intolerable pressure, or he's gone mad, or he's pathetically trying to curry favour with the authorities (I heard a rumour in St Petersburg that he's applying for the post of tutor to the Czarevich's son), or he's been told he's going to die and is grovelling around hoping to 'save his immortal soul'. But Gogol's immortality is enshrined in *Dead Souls* and *The Government Inspector*. This..." he picked up the book from the table with his thumb and forefinger, as though mere contact with it could transmit some repulsive disease... "is like a recantation of both. This can put everything we've been working for these past ten years back a century."

"Now, Vissarion Grigorevich," Annenkov protested, "you are surely exaggerating."

"Wait till you read it. If you didn't know, you'd think the author was some benighted Slavofart like Konstantin Aksakov… or even the Czar himself, if he knew how to write. It's an impassioned defence of autocracy, serfdom, censorship, priestly power… everything he held up to ridicule in *Dead Souls*. It's a flat denial of, almost an apology for, all the harsh, bitter truths he paraded for our inspection just five years ago." He started to cough and dropped the book into Turgenev's lap. "See for yourself. And tell me what you think is behind it all."

Annenkov, cautious and diplomatic as always, tried to extenuate. "Couldn't it be that this is a preparation for the second part of *Dead Souls*… mitigating some of the savagery? We knew it was going to be very different, that he was going to try and show us the redemption of some of the characters… even Chichikov himself. And we knew that he'd undergone some kind of religious conversion and was under the influence of this Father… whatever his name is. Perhaps this is just an attempt – an exaggerated one, from what you tell us – to show that the situation in Russia is not hopeless, that all is not lost, that things could improve…"

Belinsky almost choked in his attempt to control his coughing. "By leaving everything to the landowners and the bishops?" he gasped. Managing, somehow or other, to wrench his voice into a falsetto, he clasped his hands in front of his face. "Oh, flog us, little father, we know we deserve it, flog us to within an inch of our lives, and then we'll never touch a drop of vodka again and we'll till your fields sixteen hours a day for the greater glory of God and Holy Mother Russia…" He sprang to his feet, clamping a handkerchief to his mouth. "I'd better go and see if some healing Silesian water can cleanse some of the bile in my stomach." And he marched down the terrace steps and into the street, leaving his breakfast untouched on the table.

For a while the two friends watched the retreating figure hurtling away towards the baths. Annenkov, the classicist, remarked that he looked as though he were being pursued by the furies.

"He is," said Turgenev. "Or being devoured by them. It's strange, isn't it?" he added: "It's almost as though we'd got our old Belinsky back. He's been so meek and tranquil these weeks, I've sometimes had difficulty recognizing him."

Annenkov shook his head. "It would have been better if he'd stayed like that… both for his health and for his safety. I haven't told you, Vanya, but Belinsky's position back home is becoming more precarious by the minute. Every week there's some rumour that they're going to arrest him. These are bad times, and the longer he stays away from Russia, and above all keeps quiet, the better it will be. This book could be a dangerous catalyst. We have to try and take the sting out for him."

"If it's as bad as that, we must, of course," said Turgenev. "But God knows how! It's easier to tame a wild horse from the Caucasus than rein back Vissarion Grigorevich once his blood's up. However..." and he stretched lazily and started to get up, "let's go for a walk through these anodyne German woods and see if, like Schubert's miller lad, we can find a little brook to give us some advice."

If they had hoped that Salzbrunn's famous waters would have had some calming effect on Belinsky, they were to be much deceived. He didn't in fact return to the hotel until early evening, and when he joined Turgenev and Annenkov for a glass of beer before dinner, his mood of anger had changed to one of elation. The two friends had planned, without much hope of success, to try and deflect his thoughts, at least for a while, away from Gogol and his book; but they might as well have set out to deflect a whirlwind. Ignoring their feeble questions as to how his day had gone, he pulled from his pocket a notebook, opened it to show them several scribbled pages and started to read them some notes he had made for a piece he was preparing to send off to *Sovremennik* in the next day or two.

"Here, tell me how this sounds," he said, his hands trembling with excitement as he practically ripped out the pages in his hurry to find the passages he was looking for. '*I loved you as a man loves the pride and hope of his country, a leader along the path towards consciousness, development and progress... so how can I be silent when lies and immorality are preached – by you, of all people – as truth and virtue under the guise of religion and the protection of the knout. What you have failed to realize is that Russia has no need of preaching... she has heard all too many sermons and mumbled enough prayers... what she needs is the awakening in her people of a sense of their human dignity, lost for so many centuries amidst dirt and refuse... She needs rights and laws conforming not to those of the church, which grovel before despotism, but to common sense and common justice...*' then there's a bit more on the Church and its history of cruelty and intolerance... I bring in the Enlightenment and Voltaire... yes, here: '*Voltaire, who used ridicule to stamp out the fires of fanaticism and ignorance in Western Europe nearly a hundred years ago, is more a son of Christ, flesh of his flesh and bone of his bone, than all your priests, bishops, metropolitans and patriarchs...*'"

Annenkov couldn't help interrupting him. "Vissarion Grigorevich, you cannot say that!"

Belinsky gave a coarse, raucous laugh. "Oh, can I not?! And if they won't print it, I'll have it circulated round all the universities and student clubs of Russia. Here, listen, this is more or less how I want to finish. '*In spite of, and perhaps even because of, barbarous censorship, our writers are held in the highest honour, as no one knows better than yourself; the profession of letters has eclipsed even the glitter of gaudy uniforms. But poets who prostitute their gifts in the service of the powers that be soon lose their popularity. For the Russian people see in their writers their only leaders, defenders and saviours from the darkness of autocracy, orthodoxy and nationalism. Therefore, while always ready to forgive a writer a bad book, they will never forgive him a pernicious one.'*

He looked questioningly at Turgenev and Annenkov, neither of whom seemed anxious to commit himself. "Well, what do you think?" he asked impatiently.

Annenkov was the first to pluck up courage. "They're valuable ideas you've put together. When you've had time to think them over and… tone them down a bit, you'll have the basis for a good review of the book."

Belinsky laughed scornfully. "I have no intention of toning them down. Sharpening them up, if anything. And this isn't going to be a review, but an open letter to Gogol."

Annenkov turned, in a mute appeal for help, to Turgenev, who responded reluctantly. "I've only had time to glance through the book, Vinya, and I agree with you that it could have a harmful effect. But I don't think you should attack Gogol too personally, too directly. We know he's going through a crisis and perhaps this is just something he needed to write in order to come to terms with himself." He stifled Belinsky's gesture of impatience. "No, listen to me. Pavel Vasilevich and I have been talking about this all day, and I think I am beginning to understand what made Gogol write this book. We've all known for some time that he was having difficulty in writing the second part of *Dead Souls*. I think this shows that he's simply discovered he can't do it. He's realized that his genius was for pinpointing the *grotesquerie* of Russian provincial life and creating a gallery of unforgettable knaves and rogues. Now he wants to see them all redeemed and… God knows what… turned into saints, I suppose. And it's dawned on him, after four years of struggle, that he has no idea how to do it. And this must have come as a terrible shock to him. Hailed as Russia's greatest writer since Pushkin, announcing that his masterpiece was only a first imperfect part of a grand trilogy, keeping the world in suspense waiting for the sequel, and suddenly discovering that there isn't going to be any sequel. What can he do? Proclaim to the world that he's finished as a writer? Perhaps another man could do it, but not he. So what he does is write this… it's not really a book, is it?, it's a pamphlet… and under cover of ostensibly sharing some thoughts with friends, he tells everybody who can understand that this is the best he can do… this will have to take the place of the second part of *Dead Souls*."

Again Belinsky stirred restlessly in his chair, but Turgenev was not to be silenced. "What I am trying to say, Vinya, is this: I agree with Pavel Vasilevich that you shouldn't be too hard on Gogol, if perhaps for different reasons. I don't think he's suddenly turned overnight from being a reformist to a reactionary. I think he has simply found out that he can no longer write… not what he wants to say, at any rate. In other words, he's going through an artistic, not a moral, crisis."

Belinsky couldn't restrain himself any longer. "I don't care," he said, with icy deliberation, "if Gogol's crisis is artistic, moral or menopausal. And if I have to hurt someone I loved, so be it. This book doesn't deserve clemency. You two don't seem to see the vital issues that are at stake here." He stabbed a finger at Turgenev. "You showed me a draft of the story you're writing, which I think will be a fine one. And what does it portray? A landowner who has one of his servants flogged for forgetting to warm his wine and a bailiff who, with his master's connivance, gets the peasants into his debt, sends their able-bodied sons off to the army and then bleeds them dry till they pray for death. And this is the sort of thing that Gogol is now tacitly approving."

Turgenev tried to put in a word, but the old uninterruptible Belinsky was back with a vengeance. "Listen to this," he said, opening the offending book. His advice to landlords: "'*Gather your muzhiks, whom you should address as unwashed snouts, together and tell them you make them labour because this is what God intended them to do, not because you need money for your pleasures...*' God, God, everywhere God, he's dragged in to justify everything, and the priest isn't far behind him... here: '*Take the village priest with you wherever you go, make him your estate manager.*' ...and he recommends that education should be conducted solely by the landowners and the priests. Did you read that part? '*The peasant must not even know that there exist other books besides the Bible.*' So can you see now what the effect of all this will be? Can you see the parish priest patting his stomach and haranguing his flock: 'A fine example, my children, of how even the greatest sinners can see the light and repent. The smooth words of the Devil can seem temptingly attractive for a while, but sooner or later they will be revealed for what they are: falsity and wickedness.' And everyone we've been reaching out to, just asking them to think for themselves, will begin to say: 'Well, if Gogol himself says he was wrong, who are we to...?' It's as if Jesus Christ came back to earth and corrected a few beatitudes: 'Sorry, brethren, I got it wrong, it's not the meek who'll inherit the earth, it's the arrogant; not the poor who'll enter the kingdom of heaven but the rich! So you'll have to make a few adjustments; you can start by learning to love your Pharisees and your Roman overlords...'"

He looked at his two companions, saw that he had won them over, and continued in a gentler tone: "You know as well as I do, my friends, that I may not have much longer to live. We don't talk about it, but we know the threat is there. And if I die, who is going to denounce this sort of thing?" The emaciated face lit up with an irresistible smile. "A couple of comfortable, rational, bourgeois gentlemen like you? I think not. So you see, I have no choice."

Turgenev, unable to contradict this, stalled for time. "I'd like to see the final version of your letter."

"Of course. It won't take me more than two or three days. And soon after that my cure will be over and we can go on to Paris."

Turgenev shifted awkwardly in his chair. "Three days may be too long," he said. "I had a letter this morning which makes it imperative that, as soon as I've put the finishing touches to my story, I must leave for London."

"London! Why?" Annenkov asked.

"Oh, only a day or two," Turgenev replied evasively. "Business of a sort. I met a young Englishman in Berlin who works for a publisher, and he's written to say they might be interested in translating a few of my stories."

It was just as well he looked airily out of the window as he said this, otherwise he couldn't have missed the glances of mocking disbelief exchanged by Belinsky and Annenkov.

The 'day or two' turned into a week or two, and it was not until a hot afternoon in late July that Turgenev made his way to the shabby hotel off the Boulevard Saint-Germain where he had heard his friends were staying. Although he had written a note to announce his arrival, he found Annenkov alone. After greeting him with an affectionate bear-hug, he grew uncharacteristically solemn when Turgenev asked him where Belinsky was. "He's gone to see his doctor, but he should be back soon," he explained. When pressed, he admitted that he was far more worried about their friend's health than he had been in Salzbrunn. "They want him to go into a clinic, but he's convinced that once he does, he'll never leave. The trouble is, he hates Paris and despises the Parisians; the other day he told me he didn't want to die in the cuspidor of Europe. I think his only real desire now is to go home."

"Perhaps that's what he should do."

"What, with that letter he wrote to Gogol circulating around every ministry in St Petersburg? They'd arrest him at the frontier."

Turgenev couldn't bring himself to admit that not once during the time he had spent in London had he given the letter a moment's thought. Instead, he asked, ingenuously: "He didn't take our advice then and water it down a bit?"

"Water it down!?" Annenkov gave an incredulous snort and started rummaging in a drawer. "I begged him to, day after day. Who knows, if you'd been here, we might have succeeded. But I don't have even the little influence over him that you do. The result of all my efforts was this!" He pulled a tattered manuscript out of a drawer, found the page he was looking for and thrust it into Turgenev's hands. "Look at how he addresses Gogol! Can you imagine the effect this is going to have?"

Turgenev read a few lines out in an increasingly incredulous tone. "'Proponent of the knout, apostle of ignorance, champion of obscurantism and black reaction, panegyrist of Tartar morals – what are you doing? Look at the ground beneath your feet. You are standing on the brink of an abyss…'". He set the paper aside and gazed at Annenkov in horror. "You're right," he said. "We have to find some way of preventing him from going back, at least until the effect of this wears off… if it ever does. This is madness. It's playing into their hands. Even his warmest supporters will find it hard to defend him now. Nothing will keep him out of jail."

Annenkov gazed at him gloomily for a moment, and then said slowly: "Except one thing, perhaps."

"What's that?"

"If they were certain he was going to die soon, they might think they could reap more advantage by making a public display of their magnanimity. Christian charity, I suppose they'd call it. Leaving it to God to silence him for ever."

They considered this dark hypothesis for a moment in silence. Then Turgenev asked:

"So you think there's no hope, then? There were times in Salzbrunn when he seemed so much better."

Annenkov took some time to reply, and when he did he chose his words carefully. "I think hope is just about all there is. Of course the doctors say a period under their care in a clinic could work wonders. But it's in their interests to say that, isn't it? And who's going to pay their bills? And the clinic? He certainly can't." He shook his head. "No, Vanya, I'm afraid that, as usual, Vissarion Grigorevich knew exactly what he was doing." He reached out and tapped the manuscript on the table beside him. "This, I very much fear, is his last will and testament."

Another ruminative silence followed, broken this time by the arrival of Belinsky himself.

Turgenev's spirits lifted immediately at the sight of his friend who, the moment he saw his visitor, gave a cry of joy and flung his arms around his neck. "My dear Vanya," he exclaimed, "I am sorry I was not here to greet you. I told these Parisian quacks that nothing in the world could be better for me than the sight of my reprobate *gamin*, but of course you couldn't expect them to understand a thing like that. And now you'll have told all the news to Pavel Vasilevich. But there is one thing I want to hear before anything else. What did the publishers have to say?"

Turgenev looked at him in blank astonishment. "Publishers?" he stammered. "What publishers?"

A glance of mock bewilderment in Annenkov's direction. "Why, the ones who had taken an interest in your stories."

Turgenev coloured and looked around him vaguely. "Ah, yes... well, they've had some trouble in finding the right translator. And they said that anyway they'd need some more material... so they won't be making any decisions for a while."

Belinsky nodded gravely. "Yes, these things always take longer than you think. But you found other ways of occupying your time in London."

Belinsky's expression was so serious that Turgenev couldn't be sure whether he was being teased or not. Suspecting that he was, he mumbled a few platitudes about seeing a great deal of theatre and opera; but that only gave Belinsky the opportunity to pounce.

"You were able to hear Madame Viardot, I presume."

Now he was able to fall back more or less on the truth. "No, she was not singing. But we did meet by chance in the Haymarket. She and her husband had gone over to negotiate a season she will be giving next year at Covent Garden. It promises to be very lively. Grisi will be in the same company; they're forecasting an outbreak of Franco-Italian hostilities the likes of which have not been seen since Caesar conquered Gaul."

"So you saw each other a number of times?"

"Yes." Again a flush crept into Turgenev's cheeks. "As a matter of fact, we travelled over together yesterday, and they were kind enough to invite me to spend a few days at their château in the Brie country."

"So you'll be leaving us again soon?"

"Yes. Very soon, I'm afraid. In fact… tomorrow." On seeing the disappointment that Belinsky was unable to hide, he hastened to add: "But I'm sure they would be delighted to invite you both to Courtavenel for as long as you'd care to stay."

Belinsky quickly recovered himself. "That would be very kind of them. But there is so much to see in Paris… and I don't think I'll be here much longer. And then, I have to see these damned doctors every two or three days. They're trying to convince me to go into one of their clinics."

Remembering Annenkov's fears, Turgenev jumped at this chance of delaying his friend's return to Russia. "Yes, Pavel Vasilevich was telling me. We think you should go."

Belinsky gave them both a long look. "You do?" he said at last. "Well in that case, perhaps I should give it more serious consideration. But you would be able to come and visit me once in a while?"

"Of course," Turgenev assured him. "Courtavenel is only a couple of hours from Paris. I'll be coming and going all the time. And now I must be on my way. I have to settle into some rooms I've taken near the Palais-Royal, and I left most of my things behind in Salzbrunn, thinking I'd only be gone a day or two." A forced little laugh. "I don't suppose you were able to bring them with you?" Annenkov assured him they had, and said he would accompany him down to the *concierge*'s lodge. "But be prepared to put your hand deep in your pocket, or she'll deny she ever set eyes on them."

The château of Courtavenel, which the Viardots had acquired soon after the first St Petersburg season, was an impressive building, the oldest part of which dated from the time of François I. Pauline loved it unequivocally; it was the first house she had ever owned, and she and her mother had spent long, happy hours, whenever the exigencies of her career permitted, redecorating and furnishing it. It had taken them some time to introduce a touch of Spanish warmth into the stiff, formal north French atmosphere favoured by its previous owner, but by the time of Turgenev's visit it had an unpretentious charm which made it an ever-welcome goal for those of their friends who were anxious to put the busy social round of Paris behind them for a few days. Louis felt a little ambivalent about Courtavenel; he enjoyed the comfort and the calm it provided for his intellectual pursuits, and revelled in the superb sporting opportunities it offered; but when some of his radical political colleagues first set eyes on its stately grey stone walls, studded with elegant high windows, surmounted by pointed slate turrets and surrounded by a moat complete with drawbridge, he feared that the more rigorous amongst them might suspect that he had gone over to the other side.

Turgenev was as immediately enchanted by Courtavenel as he had been by its chatelaine. When he was first shown into the room he had been allotted, he was seized by a physical sense of having come home. Here was Spasskoye on a smaller scale, without the terrors of childhood, the frustrations of adolescence, the anger of youth. Pauline had accompanied him herself, and after looking round the simply but elegantly furnished room, with its willow-green wallpaper and the big window giving out on to the orangery at the back of the house, he felt like throwing himself at her feet and babbling words of gratitude. But there was nothing in her bearing, friendly but composed, to encourage this sort of demonstration. Instead she favoured him with one of her grave smiles, expressed the hope that he would be comfortable, and tapped her knuckles on a stout wooden table opposite the bed. "You'll be able to work here quite undisturbed. I'll tell the servants, once they have done the room, to leave you completely alone." She put out her hand and let a satin bell-pull slip through her fingers. "If you need anything, you can ring for them. You can even have your luncheon brought up here if you wish. But I hope you will always join us for dinner. We like to entertain our friends when we're here. We're away so much, it's almost the only chance we have of seeing them. I think you would find their company agreeable. And perhaps, in certain cases, even useful. Then there is music, reading, cards once in a while… But now I'll leave you. Your things will be brought up in a minute. Perhaps after you've unpacked you would like to join me for a walk. I can show you the garden and point out to you the way you and Louis will take when you go on your slaughtering missions." And with another friendly smile, she went out of the door; but before closing it, she looked back and asked him: "How long would you like to stay?" Seeing him completely at a loss, she continued: "Stay as long as you like… three days, three weeks, three months, three years, it's all the same to us."

It is unlikely that, at that moment, either Turgenev or she herself took these words very seriously. Both would certainly have ridiculed the idea that over the next three years Turgenev would spend more time at Courtavenel than anywhere else. And for none of that time would he return to Russia. His mother wrote vitriolic letter after letter, and when most of these went unanswered, she resorted to her well-worn method: after months of threats proved useless, she finally reduced his already meagre allowance to the merest pittance. Many of his friends warned him of the dangers of a young writer cutting himself off from the lifeblood of his native land. But none of this had the least effect on Turgenev. It was not that he ever made a definite decision to stay. He could just never bring himself to leave.

That first flash of illumination he had experienced on entering his room evolved into a persistent guiding light. Here, it told him, is where you belong. Here is where you can work – and for the first time in his life, he wrote for several hours every morning. Here is where you can discover what family life can be like – and he spent hours, especially when Pauline was away on tour, chatting with Madame Garcia, who asked for nothing better than a man who would sit happily listening as she related one rocambolesque detail after another from her adventurous life; or playing chess with Pauline's brother Manuel, who would become Europe's most famous and influential singing teacher; or giving piggybacks to the Viardots' little daughter, Louise, and laughing as she screamed, mostly from excitement and a little from fear, when he threw her up on his shoulders to a height which was, to her six-year-old imagination, close to the top of the world. And above all, here, it told him, is where you can broaden your experience – and over the next few months he found himself chatting with easy familiarity on literary matters with George Sand, Pauline's closest friend and confidante, who had played a prominent part in arranging her marriage with Louis Viardot; on art with Gustave Doré and Corot; and on music with practically every musician in France, who flocked to pay homage to Pauline's talent and charm, from the amiable, earnest Belgian, César Franck, to the witty, cynical, but always loveable Rossini.

After he had been at Courtavenel for three weeks without having given Paris a moment's thought, Turgenev received a letter from Annenkov. Belinsky was weaker than ever and his doctors had given him an ultimatum: either he was to go into their clinic and allow himself to be properly treated, or they would no longer consider him their patient. Belinsky, of course, had opted for the second alternative, but after hours of patient arguing, Annenkov had finally won him round. The day had been fixed for Tuesday of the following week and Annenkov was asking Turgenev if he would come to Paris on Monday so that the two of them could accompany their sick friend. He was sure that Turgenev's presence would be better for Belinsky than any tonic.

Turgenev immediately dashed off a letter promising that he would be there. Later that evening he mentioned to Pauline that he would be going to Paris for a few days the following week and was surprised to see her face cloud over in disappointment.

"Oh, why does it have to be Monday?" she asked. "Rossini's coming to dinner and I so much wanted you to meet him. He'll only be in France for a week or two: he's had to leave Bologna for some stupid political reason and he's taking up a new appointment in Florence next month. It may be years before we see him again."

Turgenev explained briefly why he had to go.

"But couldn't you visit him a few days later? After all, Annenkov will be there. The important thing is that there's someone to go with him. As a matter of fact, it would be better if you went later. It'll be a fresh face for him to see after he's been in the clinic for a day or two. Sick people are usually too weak to want more than one person around at a time."

Seeing him hesitate, she laid a beseeching hand on his sleeve. "Oh, please, Ivan. Gioacchino's like a guiding star for our family. Papa was his favourite tenor, Maria owed her entire career to him and I... well, you know what he means to me. I couldn't bear for you to miss him. It would spoil my evening."

Château de Courtavenel,
8 August, 1847

My dear Pavel Vasilevich,

I am afraid this letter is to countermand what I wrote to you yesterday. Something has transpired here which makes it impossible for me to leave for Paris on Monday. It would be an act of unpardonable ingratitude on my part towards people who have lavished on me the most unstinting hospitality.

I hope you will not have had occasion to mention to Vissarion Grigorevich that I would be there with you on Tuesday. If you have, please assure him that I will come to visit him in the clinic in a very few days' time. As a matter of fact, I think it is probably better this way. People who are as sick as he is usually prefer to have only one person around them at a time.

Please do not think badly of me for not being with you both on Tuesday. Remember to tell Belinsky that he is always in my thoughts and I count the hours until I will be once again in his inimitable company.

Your devoted friend,

Iv. Turgenev.

The Viardots were relieved to find on Monday evening that the notoriously moody Rossini was at his expansively mischievous best. Happy to be back in his beloved France after the professional spites, political imbroglios, domestic strain and recurrent illness that had been his almost daily lot since returning to Italy ten years previously, he blatantly basked in the beauty and warmth of his new wife, Olympe Pélissier, Vernet's model for 'Judith and Holofernes'. They had more or less lived together for fifteen years, but he had only recently been able to marry her after the death of his first wife, Isabella Colbran. Although the 55-year-old composer had written virtually nothing except the *Stabat Mater* since quitting the world of opera with *William Tell* in 1829, the sympathetic presence of Pauline, whom as a little girl he had made squeal with delight as he bounced her up and down on his knees while singing one of his *buffo* arias, brought back the days when he had been the lionized guest of every fashionable salon of Paris.

Chiefly for the benefit of Turgenev, who was the only person present he had never previously met, he began to reminisce about the Garcia family. "I often think the only opera I never wrote but wish I had was one about them. Of course, none of my incompetent librettists would have been up to doing them any sort of justice. That da Ponte fellow might have, but by the time I came on the scene he'd scuttled off to America. Incidentally, don't you think it's outrageous, the gifts the good Lord lavished on Mozart? Not only that unimaginable talent, but the luck to have at his disposal a librettist like that. How can the rest of us poor *musicisti* help being at least a little jealous? But to get back to our opera… " He looked at his host at the far end of the table. "What do you think of my idea, monsieur?"

"I have been wondering what your plot would be, maestro," Viardot replied.

"Oh plots, plots, you know I was never very interested in plots." He waved a gracious hand in the direction of Turgenev. "I'm sure our young friend here, whom I believe is a writer, could come up with something. Take, for instance, the premiere of my *Barbiere* in New York. Four members of the same family in the cast giving the first performance ever in America of an opera sung in Italian… announced, by the way, in one of the papers as 'H.Barbiora di Seviglia' by Rosina. There's enough there already to fill two good acts. But I tell you, it's not the plot that matters. It's the characters. And what characters! My dear friend Manuel *père*: fascinating, domineering, impetuous, unreliable." He turned to Pauline on his left. "You know, *cara*, if your father had had as much sense of measure as he had of music, he would have been the greatest musician of his age."

Pauline smiled away the compliment. "That honour, Gioacchino, would always have been yours."

"Oh very well then, let's say the second greatest. And then…" he leant over to kiss the hand of Madame Garcia, who was sitting on his right, "his complete opposite, the calm centre without whom the genius of the others would have been fatally dispersed. Manuel *fils*, a fine singer before he became a great teacher, was Figaro. And Marietta as Rosina, the unique, irreplaceable Malibran, object of the world's adoration, who never entirely ceased to be a little child. And you were there too, Pauline, more mature at the age of twelve than poor Maria would have been if she'd lived to be a hundred…"

"But I will never be unique and irreplaceable," Pauline put in provocatively.

But Rossini was too wily to get caught in this trap. "You will be unique in a different way," he said. "Maria was like a meteor blazing her way across the sky towards early oblivion. Théophile Gautier was right…" he laid an apologetic hand on Madame Garcia's sleeve, "from an artistic point of view, of course, when he said she had the genius to die young. But Pauline, if God wills, will go on singing for ever. Artists are like horses… and not only because you can lose a lot of money if you spend too much time in the company of either. There are sprinters and stayers. I ought to know something about this. I was the champion sprinter of all time. In my early days I wrote two, sometimes three, operas a year. Now look at this young Verdi fellow. One year's quite enough for him. But he'll probably still be composing when he's eighty."

"For the love of God, let us hope not!" Turgenev drawled. It was the kind of remark that had won him a reputation as an iconoclastic wit in certain St Petersburg circles, but it didn't seem to amuse Rossini.

"Why do you say that, young man?" he asked with an excessive civility in which Pauline immediately recognized lurking danger. But she had no time to intervene. Turgenev was only too ready to hold forth.

"It's peasant music, maestro… vigorous, yes… perhaps not without a certain grandeur now and then… but with such vulgar melodies, such straining after effect. Everything yelled fortissimo, especially those interminable unison choruses. I heard his *Lombardi*, rechristened *Jérusalem* for the Parisians, at the Grand Opéra the other night, and it was as much as I could do to stay in my seat. This is Saturday-night-in-the-piazza music, to be listened to with a glass of wine in one hand and a sausage in the other. This is not opera as you have taught us to hear it."

Rossini's eyes gleamed with sardonic amusement. "Then I have taught you badly," he said. "I am surprised that a young writer like yourself should be so ready to close his ears to the new. Surely it is not your dream to go on writing as everybody has written in Russia before you. Your Pushkin, for example… I, of course, am unable to read him, but some of your compatriots have assured me that he will have taken his place on Olympus. But you would not want merely to produce copies of what he has already achieved. Or would you?"

"If I could pen one line comparable to Pushkin, I would consider my life's work done, maestro."

"Ah! I am glad to hear the conception of modesty is not entirely unknown to the youth of today. It's a quality that has its importance. It must be used sparingly, of course. Like a sprinkle of tarragon over a roast. But we artists should never be completely without it. But to return to Verdi, may I have the presumption to suggest you keep an open mind, as well as ear. There is much of his music which is not entirely to my taste. But I heard his *Macbeth* in Florence earlier this year. Rough, earthy stuff, yes. But earthy as Shakespeare is earthy. Earthy with genius. Or is Shakespeare also perhaps too rough for your exquisite taste?"

This time the reply did not leap to Turgenev's lips. He had intended to flatter Rossini and had succeeded in antagonizing him. Besides, that anyone should question his admiration for Shakespeare! He left it to Pauline to apply her emollient touch.

"I think I'm closer to Ivan than to you, Gioacchino. I have heard nothing of this Verdi to make me think as highly of him as you do. And then, Shakespeare! Come now, you're pulling our legs as usual."

"No, *mia cara*, " Rossini smiled. "Just perhaps exaggerating a little. A weakness, as you know, I indulge in from time to time."

"Forgive me, maestro." Turgenev, emboldened by Pauline's support and the Italian's evident preference for charming his young hostess over insisting on his point, found his voice again. "I bow, of course, to your infinitely superior knowledge. But allow a humble lover of music and an ardent admirer of yours to say this: happy were our parents who were able to attend first performances of *Il Barbiere* and *Semiramide* while we are condemned to the likes of *Jérusalem*."

Rossini lifted his glass of Muscadet to the level of the candle flames and squinted thoughtfully at the delicate pale gold of the wine. "I would dearly like to agree with you. That quality of modesty whose praises I sang to you a moment ago has never, I have to confess, fitted me like a snug shoe. I think I have my place in the world of opera. My name will not perhaps be totally forgotten. But I cannot rid myself of the suspicion that, a hundred years from now, Giuseppe Verdi will be considered the composer of Italian opera *par excellence*, while my poor works are looked on as little more than light popular entertainment..."

Two days after the Rossini dinner, Belinsky wrote to his wife.

Clinique Sainte Thérèse,
Neuilly.
14 August, 1847

My dearest Mashenka,

As you see, they have persuaded me to enter a clinic. You must not be alarmed, my dear: it is not because they think I am a hopeless case, but because they are convinced that, with proper care, I can be as new again – or as near new as I have ever been.

Annenkov brought me here and made a great fuss about my being installed to his satisfaction. The dear fellow managed to get me changed from a ward of about 20 people to one of only 6, which was something of a relief to me – although my battle with the French language, which I can now declare well and truly lost, means that I am not obliged to converse much with those of my fellow-patients who make tentative moves in that direction. A 'Bonjour' on waking, a choice between 'C'est bon' or, preferably on their part, 'C'est mauvais' at mealtimes and a 'Bonne nuit' in the evenings fulfil the greater part of my conversational obligations.

Turgenev came to see me this afternoon, which touched me deeply, as I know he is terrified of hospitals. As I had nothing much to tell him, it was he who did most of the talking… and no prizes for guessing the subject! He regaled me with every detail of the life of the Viardots' château – the rooms, the grounds, the guests – except, strangely, any but the most passing reference to Madame herself – and then only as hostess (unparalleled) and musician (unique). Should this make us think there is something he wishes to hide? Or is he afraid that I shall start to tease him, as I have often done in the past? I really don't know. He speaks of Viardot with considerable warmth, and I think I know him well enough that if he were feeling uneasy on that score I would notice some embarrassment or reticence. Of course it is none of my business. Or at least, it shouldn't be. But I wish him so well and have such high hopes for his future that I should be sorry if he contented himself with simply becoming a French country gentleman. He could have done that in his own country if that was all he wanted. At any rate, he says he is writing regularly – continuing his stories based on his experiences around Spasskoye – so that is all to the good. I suspect that his talent is more suited to this type of sketch based on personal experience, rather than purely imaginative work.

The evening meal is being brought (I can already hear mutters of dégoutant from up the ward) so I must finish off. Be assured, my dearest, that I am already feeling better and, if the doctors are to be believed – a big 'if'! – I hope to be able to return home in a month or two. Incidentally, Iv. Serg. has said he will accompany me at least as far as Berlin, or even perhaps to Stettin. This would be very agreeable, but I am not counting on it too much. Tomorrow he's sneaking off back to La Viardot, and, as Mozart's Figaro says, if Madama calls…!

A big hug to Olyechka and tell her her papa will be back at the latest for the spring….

Your devoted husband,

V.B.

Some three weeks later, Turgenev heard from Annenkov that the doctors thought Belinsky was now sufficiently recovered to undertake the journey home. Knowing that he had mentioned the possibility of accompanying Belinsky some of the way, Annenkov wrote to warn his friend that the departure could be any day now.

Five days before he was due to leave, Belinsky received a letter from Turgenev.

Courtavenel,
10 September, 1847

Dear Vissarion Grigorevich,

It is with a heavy heart that I have to write and tell you that I shall not, after all, be able to journey with you back towards our homeland. Nor, alas, will I have the opportunity to see you before you leave.

Annenkov's letter telling me of your imminent departure took me by surprise – a happy surprise in that it means you must be much better, but a disappointing one in that it finds me at a moment when I am not able to make the journey from here to Paris – let alone to Germany. There are two reasons for this, one of which you will approve, the other which you will surely condemn. The second, to get it off my chest right away, is that M. and Mme. Viardot are throwing open their house next week for a large number of their friends and the high point of the proceedings is to be a theatrical entertainment in which they have persuaded me, against my better judgement, to play a leading part. You have never been a great enthusiast of the theatre, but you know enough to appreciate that woe betide anyone who misses rehearsals!

The second reason why I cannot afford to absent myself from Courtavenel is that I have set myself a rigorous writing programme – a minimum of four hours a day, which <u>nothing</u> is allowed to interrupt. I think that the stories I am doing are better than anything I have up to now achieved. Nekrasov is very keen to have as many as I can give him for Sovremennik, and I am very keen to receive the 250-300 roubles which he gives me for them. As my dear mother, who up to now has been sending me 6000 roubles a year, is now threatening to cut even that meagre allowance off if I do not immediately return, you can imagine how important this small but regular income is to me. I have set myself a target of producing 12 sketches this year; at the moment I have only completed seven, so I have my work cut out to write another five in the next three months.

All this, my dearest Vinya, to ask you to excuse me for once again seeming to fail you in your hour of need. I can but take courage from the fact that your health must be so much better if your doctors are allowing you to undertake that long journey. At any rate, I will surely be back in Peter by next spring, so we will not be parted for too long.

I do implore you to send me regular bulletins about your health – as well as an account of all that has been happening in our benighted land since our departure – my God, is it already eight months ago? Above all, try to restrain your anger... or at least your voicing of it! Your letter to Gogol is bound to have caused a stir, so give the dust some time to settle. The first and most important thing, even taking precedence over the state of our country, is the state of your health; and I don't need to assure you that any good news on that score will rejoice my heart. Even though I am only a gamin, and generally speaking an irresponsible sort of fellow, my attachment to you is imperishable.

Until the spring, then, my respected, admired and loved Vinya,

Your devoted friend,

Iv. Turg.

Belinsky didn't survive the spring. He died in May 1848, at the age of thirty-seven. Throughout his life Turgenev always referred to him as the closest friend he had ever had. On the rare occasions when he overcame his superstitious dread of death sufficiently to contemplate his own, he would say that he hoped to be buried near him. Thirty-five years later this wish was granted.

When he heard the news of Belinsky's death, Turgenev was alone... and for the first time in his life knew the full meaning of solitude. Pauline, accompanied by Louis, was on tour in Germany, and this time he was far too short of money to follow her. The few people he did see in Paris were no use to him: his familiarity with Mme Garcia didn't extend to outpourings of grief and shame; and with his Russian friends, particularly Annenkov and Herzen, he felt too guilty even to bring the subject up. He wrote regularly to Pauline, relating Parisian gossip, describing evenings at the opera and theatre, and lavishing advice about where to go and who to avoid in Hamburg, Berlin and Dresden. But he never even mentioned Belinsky's death. And it was to be many years before he did…

Twenty years, to be precise. It happened one evening in Baden-Baden, to which the Viardots and Turgenev, disgusted by the smotheringly bourgeois atmosphere of Second Empire Paris, had moved in 1863. At least that's why the Viardots had moved. Turgenev went to Baden-Baden because Pauline was in Baden-Baden.

Pauline was in semi-retirement and Turgenev, still trying to come to terms with the waves of vitriolic abuse from both right and left, which had crashed over him after the publication of his novel, *Smoke*, was engaged in no important work. The two of them, along with other diversions, began to write a series of operettas. On the evening in question, they had invited a number of friends to hear some of the songs from their current work-in-progress, *Trop de Femmes*, and make any criticisms or suggestions that might occur to them. Commenting on a not very original lyric Turgenev had written, wistfully recalling the insouciance of youth, a couple of the guests, having left that time of life some way behind them, had found the sentiments expressed a little cloying. Pauline now asked him whether they had corresponded with his experience as a young man.

"Far from it," Turgenev told her. "I can scarcely remember a day that was not somehow marked by guilt or fear – guilt over yesterday, fear for tomorrow. The carefree happiness of youth was as much a fiction to me as any of our old Russian legends. Our hero may remember his young days as filled with eternal sunlight, but after all that is the stuff of operetta. I am not being asked to, and would indeed refuse to, furnish a libretto for Herr Wagner."

"You certainly would not be asked to, as he writes them all himself."

"Yes, and I don't know which is more unbearable, the music or the text."

"Tourguel, you are becoming a crusty old conservative. I am a Wagnerite to my fingertips… in fact it is the only music which now interests me. And you'd better start learning to keep some of your opinions to yourself, because I've invited him to come and visit us soon… along with Cosima, who appears to be the current infatuation."

"Well, as long as he only talks, there can be no great harm… unless, of course, he talks at the same length as his operas. But never mind Herr Wagner. Let's get back to our little work. Doesn't my lyric ring at least a little true to you? Yours was surely a happy childhood."

"Happy, perhaps, but carefree, no. But then, I sometimes wonder whether I really had a childhood. With all the hours I spent studying piano and voice before making my debut at seventeen, there was very little room for frivolity. You know what they used to call me? The ant! Admirable though those creatures are, they don't give the impression of drifting around without a care in the world."

Turgenev considered this for a moment and then asked abruptly: "What would you most have liked to have done differently?"

"I have already told you," Pauline answered quietly. "I would have liked to be a pianist rather than a singer."

"You still would? After all your extraordinary successes?"

"How do you know I wouldn't have had my successes as a pianist?"

"I have no doubt you would. But there is less demand for pianists – especially lady ones – than for great singers."

"Clara hasn't found that to be the case... and don't let me hear you say that's because of her husband's music. Before they were married, she was much more famous than he."

"But surely, Clara Schumann is unique."

"I'll have you know, *mon cher Tourguel*, that when Clara and I played Robert's Andante and Variations for two pianos, Saint-Saens wrote that we played with *equal virtuosity*."

"But since Saint-Saens was always hopelessly in love with you, what would you expect him to say?"

She kicked him sharply enough on the shin to make him howl with pain. "You're a monstrous cynic. That's what comes of giving sincere answers to personal questions. But now I'll ask you one: what have you done in your life that you'd most like not to have done?"

Turgenev gazed into space. "Like many of the worst crimes, it's not what I did, it's what I didn't do. I can never forgive myself for not having gone to see Belinsky before he set off back to Russia. I had even promised to accompany him. But I never got even as far as Paris. And he died without my ever having said goodbye to him."

"Why didn't you go?"

"Oh, the excuse I gave was that we were rehearsing at Courtavenel. But of course none of you would have minded if I'd gone. It was just my cowardly way of avoiding seeing him looking so ill and having to face the fact that we would probably never see each other again. And finding the words to express that knowledge. It's so much easier always to say, I'll see you in the spring..."

Pauline looked at him sympathetically. "You poor man," she said. "How terrible to have carried this misery inside you all this time. Why did you never tell me before?"

"I have never told anyone. My shame was hard enough to bear without having to reveal it to someone else. The only other person who knew was Annenkov, and he, dear, kind fellow that he is, has never as much as alluded to it."

"Well I think you have suffered enough over a man who has been dead for twenty years. Besides, didn't someone tell me once that you made over a large sum of money to his wife and daughter?"

Turgenev's face broke into a sad smile. "A paltry sop to the conscience. No, the only thing that has helped to alleviate my remorse is that, for me, he has never really died. I talk to him sometimes as though he were in the room with me. And when I am working, I feel him there behind me. I hear him repeating the question he used to ask over and over again: the only question that really matters. Are you writing as though you were on oath to tell the truth? Still today, when I've finished a story, if I feel that he wouldn't have approved of it, I either tear it up or put it aside to rework. I would never submit it for publication."

Pauline laid her hand on his and smiled into his eyes. "I don't think I ever realized quite how much he meant to you. Tell me something: if he had lived, what do you think would have become of him?"

Turgenev smiled bitterly. "The Chief of Police in St Petersburg at the time was heard to say: 'We would have rotted him in a fortress'. And I fear they would. After all, remember the year he died: 1848. He was too close to death for us to know what he had to say about the February events in Paris. And by the time the spark of revolution had whipped round Europe as through a barn of last year's straw, he had already left us. The only thing we can be certain of is, had he not been such a sick man, he would have been unable to keep quiet…"

n March, 1848, a group of like-minded friends met in the Viardots' rented apartment in Paris to celebrate the present and plan for the future. February had seen the realization of their dreams: the senile King Louis-Philippe had abdicated, his hated minister, Guizot, had been forced to resign, the Second Republic had been proclaimed. The air of Paris fizzed with brotherly love and egalitarian fervour. Now, at last, everything was possible; now a new age could dawn.

None of those present had actually been in Paris during the February days. The Viardots had spent the winter in Berlin, where Pauline, as well as triumphing in a wide variety of roles, had persuaded Meyerbeer, at that time *Generalmusikdirector*, to let her create at the Paris Opéra the part of Fidès in his new opera *Le Prophète*; but they had kept closely in touch with events through Louis's colleagues on *La Revue Indépendante*, the left-wing paper he had launched in 1841, together with George Sand and Pierre Leroux. Turgenev had heard the news of Louis-Philippe's fall when a pageboy had burst into his hotel room in Brussels at six in the morning bawling, "FRANCE HAS BECOME A REPUBLIC!" In half an hour he was dressed and packed and managed, after an adventurous journey, to reach Paris by rail and road the same day. George Sand had also sped up from her country home at Nohant and had been appointed a sort of unofficial Minister of Propaganda by her influential political friends.

She tells them that Bakunin may be joining them. Since his university days with Turgenev in Berlin, the passionate, if muddle-headed, student of idealistic philosophy has become a revolutionary anarchist. In Russia his property has been confiscated and he himself sentenced *in absentia* to banishment to Siberia. In 1847 he had been expelled from France by Guizot for making an inflammatory speech on Polish independence on the anniversary of the 1830 rising. Since then he has been in constant correspondence with George Sand, but sent the letters to Pauline to avoid the prying eye of the censor. Now he has made a clandestine return to Paris, where he has been living in the barracks of the Workers' National Guard, the *Montagnards*. George tells them he promised her he would try to get away for an hour or two; but as Bakunin has never in his entire life been known to be punctual for any appointment, they agree to start without him.

George is a dynamo of enthusiasm; the revolution, comparatively bloodless and accepted by almost everyone, has rescued her from the dismal lethargy into which she had sunk after her break with Chopin. She asks them how they think they could each make the best use of their talents for furthering the cause of progress and reform. Viardot has no doubts; he is convinced that his lifelong devotion to the republican cause (had he not, only two years ago, broken off an engagement a week before the wedding when he discovered his fiancée supported a Bourbon restoration?) should automatically qualify him to take his seat in the new National Assembly. He asks George to put in a good word for him with her friend Ledru-Rollin, now Minister of the Interior.

George hesitates only for a second, but it is enough for Pauline and Turgenev to exchange a wary look; each knows that her husband, and his friend, enjoys the utmost respect for his forthright articles, pungent views and transparent sincerity; but would his dry, pedantic manner be what was needed in an assembly called to give voice to everything that was young and new in the country – an assembly whose spokesman was Lamartine, now nearly sixty, but still able to charm crowds with his eloquence, and remembered as the poet who had cried: *La France est une nation qui s'ennuie.* Louis, considered by some to be a bit of a bore himself, was hardly the man to reverse this trend.

George, quick-witted and tactful as ever, extricates herself with disarming ease. "You know, Louis," she says slowly, as though she has been giving the matter careful thought, "I think you'd be wasted there. You'd just be another voice amongst so many. What I think we should secure for you is the Directorship of the Opéra. You've already had the experience at the Théâtre Italien, and everyone knows what a success you were. Besides," smiling at Pauline, "when it comes to dealing with the whims of *divas* …"

Pauline throws up her hands in horror, part mock, part real. "Ah no, Mignounne, anything but that! I have just spent three months in Berlin trying to steer clear of the feuds between Meyerbeer and his fellow directors, and I have managed to survive with my contract intact. My debut at the Opéra. At last! And in a new role. And what are you suggesting? That my husband should become director of the Opéra so that all my enemies – just imagine Grisi and her pack! – can say: 'Well, you know why *she* got the part, don't you?"

George is in the middle of reassuring her that such voices could and should be simply ignored, when the door is flung violently open and a giant erupts into the room with a roar of welcome. It is Mikhail Aleksandrovich Bakunin. But a different Bakunin to the one they all remember. The leonine mane of fair hair is now trimmed and black. A walrus moustache droops over each corner of the wide mouth. The massive torso is encased in a blue French workman's blouse, and a pair of worn, dust-covered boots protrude from under the loose-fitting linen trousers. Turgenev is the first to voice his surprise. "Mikhail Aleksandrovich, what have you done to yourself?"

Bakunin seems astonished that anyone should ask such a stupid question. "I'm in disguise, of course. Didn't you know that all the gendarmes of Paris have orders to arrest me on sight?"

"But my dear friend, anyone who knew you would recognize you a mile away."

"They would?" He seems genuinely surprised. Then he throws back his head and roars with laughter. "Then that can only mean that the gendarmes have thrown in their lot with the workers."

Having embraced the men and kissed the ladies' hands with studied gallantry, he sinks on to a sofa, which sags ominously under his weight.

"What days, my friends! What times! All we have lived for… all we have dreamed of… and it's there… now…" he thrusts out a hairy paw, closes it with a snap and waves his clenched fist in the air, "there for the taking!"

Before he can continue, George, perhaps fearing that her self-appointed role as chairman is about to be taken over, breaks in: "Yes, yes, wonderful, wonderful! Before you came, Mikhail Aleksandrovich, we were talking about the composition of the new Constituent Assembly, the first to be elected by universal suffrage. Can you imagine? Instead of a quarter of a million voters deciding who shall rule France, now there will be nine million."

"And who knows what that will lead to," Louis Viardot puts in sourly. "I think the provisional government made a big mistake there. It's too soon, too soon. The peasant will vote for whomever his parish priest or his seigneur tells him to. What do you think, Ivan? You know more about the peasants than we do. What would your muzhik do in similar circumstances?"

"I fear you may well be right. Of course our peasants are serfs, ignorant as animals most of them, but with the animals' innate sense of survival. Yours are perhaps a little less primitive, but still it has been ingrained in them for centuries to do as they are told. Obedience is a habit it takes time to shake off."

Louis, pleased with the support, pursues his argument. "I fear that if the elections are held immediately, they'll return a government more reactionary than Guizot's. These friends of yours, George, don't see any further than Paris. They should postpone the elections for at least six months, get out of this city, breathe some country air and explain to their voters what is at stake and who can look after their interests."

Pauline takes up the argument. "Otherwise it seems to me there is a danger of democracy destroying itself. George is right, universal suffrage is a wonderful idea. The voice of the sovereign people. But what if the sovereign people should vote away their sovereignty… abdicate their power to control their own destinies? What if they should prefer to be slaves rather than free men and women? Can they be allowed to do that?"

No one hurries to answer this dangerous question. The truth is they are all waiting to hear a word from Bakunin, who has been staring out of the window, ostentatiously uninvolved in the discussion. George, uncharacteristically hesitant, ventures a timid "Mikhail Aleksandrovich?"

It is all that is needed – a feeble enough spark, but more than sufficient to set off the conflagration. The sofa groans with relief as the giant springs to his feet, strides over to the window, gazes out of it for a second as though drawing in strength from the air outside to counteract the stuffiness of the room, and then turns to face them.

"My dear friends, is it for this I have left my comrades whom I promised not to abandon for a minute? It is only because I love you, all of you, that I have been able to sit here listening to you twittering away like a flock of sparrows. Universal suffrage! What is universal suffrage? A step – a tiny step, an inch high – at the bottom of a ladder which is going to lead mankind to the empyrean. Haven't you understood that what has begun to gather strength here in Paris over the last few weeks is a tidal wave that will sweep away the whole of Christian Europe as we know it – carrying out to sea the helplessly kicking and struggling bodies of kings, bishops, generals, ministers, bankers, merchants, judges, yes, and many who have thought of themselves as leaders or representatives of the people; they will have to go too if they continue to think like you. Now is not the time, *chère madame*," this with a dazzling smile in the direction of Pauline, "to speculate about democracy destroying itself. The democratic principle, the pursuit of liberty and equality – absolute liberty, absolute equality – is going to destroy Europe. St Petersburg, Paris, London will be transformed into one gigantic rubbish heap. There will be no more arguments at banquets and in salons about what kind of state is best. There will be no more state. This is what I am telling my comrades in the barracks day after day. The revolution must be permanent and ubiquitous. We will not have finished when we have levelled the mountains and valleys of France; when there is equality of salary, equality of dignity, equality before the law. Then we must liberate our Slavonic brothers, annihilate the Austrian empire and create a Free Slav Federation where all the peoples of Russia, the Ukraine, Poland, Bohemia and the rest can climb out of their dungeons and reach up to the sun. For as long as there is one oppressive state left in Europe, all the others will be in danger. My comrades ask me – and you will ask me too – what will be left after this cataclysm? I answer them – and I answer you – in the words of Jacob Lenz: 'Clear a space! Destroy! Something will arise!'"

The beam from Bakunin's hypnotic eyes, switching from face to face, indicates that he has finished. Now it's your turn, it says. Challenge me. Confute me. But, as is frequently the case after one of the Russian spellbinder's perorations, no one can for the moment think of anything to say. His admirers claim that this is the result of the shattering power of his oratory. His detractors, that it simply reflects stunned disbelief at so much inflated, empty rodomontade. Sensing his friends' embarrassment, he cuts through it with a full-throated bellow of laughter.

"Of course, poor Lenz died mad. Young too – only forty-one. But I'm even younger. I have seven years to go still. And in seven years we can do great things. All of us." And switching effortlessly from revolutionary rabble-rouser to the young charmer who, first as officer in the Imperial Guard and later as idealistic student, had lightly conquered and as lightly discarded many a Polish, Muscovite and Berliner heart, he moves over to Pauline, takes her hand and kisses it.

"And you, madame Pauline, perhaps more than any of us. There never can and never will be enough great artists like you. I was wrong just now when I said that everything must be destroyed. Art is the exception. Everything will pass and the world will perish, but the Ninth Symphony will remain. And you…" and again he bends down and presses his lips to her hand for so long that Viardot's fingers begin to fidget, "you must be there to sing it. *Freude! Freude* for us all."

George Sand, happy to be back on the firm ground of art after the quicksands of destruction, pats her protégée's hand which Bakunin, to Louis's visible relief, has finally relinquished and proudly announces that she has written a cantata, to be called *La Jeune République*. Pauline will set it to music. "The musical world doesn't know it yet, but, mark my words, Pauline's gift as a composer will outshine even her genius as a singer."

Louis reveals that he has arranged for the cantata to be performed early in April for the opening of the Théâtre de la République. "There will be two soloists, my wife and Gustave Roger, who will create the tenor role opposite Pauline in Meyerbeer's *Le Prophète*; and a chorus of sixty girl students from the Conservatoire wearing long white muslin dresses with tricolour sashes."

A lewd yelp of delight from Bakunin. "Sounds like an invitation for a re-enactment of the Rape of the Sabines."

Pauline tries to look shocked, but isn't.

Louis tries not to, but is.

With another unpredictable key change, Bakunin turns to Turgenev. "And you, my old friend, traitorous *allumeur* of my poor sister, why are you so silent? Have you nothing to say? This is not like you." With malicious delight, he addresses the others. "Time was when his tongue was never still for a moment. He was always telling Tatyana stories or reading to her – the most ardent passages from the novels of Jean Paul or the poems of Novalis… not to mention his own. Which was the one you dedicated to her? How did it begin? 'Give me your hand and let us walk through the fields…'"

"That's enough, Michel!" Even Turgenev's patience is exhausted, and he silences his usually irrepressible countryman with a look that is as astringent as his words, at least to the others, are enigmatic. "I think, for both our sakes, it would be better if we left Tatyana out of this. As to your opinions which you expressed just now so forcibly, yes, I do have something to say, but it will certainly not be what you want to hear."

He stands to face Bakunin, and the three western Europeans stay seated like attentive, fascinated pigmies as the two immensely tall, handsome, eloquent sons of the Russian nobility – friends, rivals, wishing the same ends but differing violently over the means – confront each other.

"We are all," Turgenev begins, "as excited as you about what has happened up to now in Paris. You know that as well as we do. That is why we are here. But we also know that France is at a juncture from which many roads branch off, all of which she is at liberty to take. The question is which one is best – best not for the satisfaction of Mikhail Aleksandrovich Bakunin's latest theory (a theory he may well discard in a few months' time for an even more wilfully reckless one), but best for the men and women of France. What I fear is that the impetuousness of men like you will destroy what has already been achieved and leave the men and women of France worse off than they were before. I believe that the men behind the February days should adopt a gradual, step-by-step approach… yes, Michel, you can raise your eyes to heaven and beyond, but if catastrophe strikes France you will no longer be here, you will be in Italy or Germany or Poland, urging the people there to bring down the same catastrophe on themselves. I foresee that if events move too fast, one of two things will happen: either power will end up in the hands of men unqualified to govern, men who know how to burn but not to build…"

Bakunin can restrain himself no longer. "You see?" he appeals to the others. "Exactly what I was saying. You don't want a change, you want more of the same. Different faces, perhaps, but still plump, round, self-satisfied bourgeois faces. When will you realize that wisdom resides with the people, those men and women of France you were talking about?"

"Governing a country in the middle of the nineteenth century," Turgenev calmly replies, "requires greater skill and knowledge than steering a plough or hammering nails into the sole of a shoe. Guizot was not a foolish man, but he made mistakes."

"Guizot was a cold, inhuman monster."

"Perhaps, but a very able one. Have you read his *Histoire de la civilisation*…"

"I spit on his *civilisation* – and yours. Very well. You spoke of two possibilities you were frightened of. One is that everything will not go on exactly as before – *Guizotisme sans Guizot*. What is the other?"

"The other is that your rush to destroy will put muscle back into limbs long grown flabby. Monsieur Prud'homme, if, as a foreigner, I read him aright, is not politically a very sensitive fellow. If things begin to change a bit, if some of his privileges are extended to people he doesn't really think deserve them, he probably won't do much more than grumble into his soup. He may not even mind too much if some of the workers are actually given work to do – so long as part of the proceeds of their labours finds its way into his pockets. But if he so much as sniffs that someone might be trying to take something out of those pockets, let alone empty them altogether, then he will become a wild beast. And the resulting bloodshed could make the Terror of '93 seem like a Sunday pheasant shoot."

"And that," interjects Bakunin, jabbing a finger at his antagonist, eyes shining excitedly, "may be just what is needed to create the conditions for revolution."

Turgenev shakes his head sorrowfully. "I sometimes think you care more for the idea of revolution than the fact of human suffering."

George Sand, feeling control of the meeting has slipped out of her hands, decides to gather back the reins. She directs her broadest, but perhaps not her most sincere smile at the two Russians. "Now we mustn't let you two do all the talking. Of course, we can only be flattered that both of you, coming from so far away, take such an interest in our country, but..."

Bakunin doesn't let her finish. "That, madame, is because of the hopelessness of ever being able to do something for *our* country. Were it not for that, Ivan Sergeyevich and I would surely see more eye to eye."

Turgenev smiles his dissent. "I wouldn't be too sure of that. But," turning to the rest of the company, "allow me to waste a moment more of your time in telling you about a very strange encounter I had this winter. It may present our concern for the future of France in a new light. One morning, in late January, I was drinking coffee and reading the papers at the café de la Rotonde in the Palais-Royal when I heard a voice asking me in a harsh Provençal accent if he could share my table. I looked up to nod my assent and saw this tall, thin man, his dark hair flecked with grey, staring down at me through the smoked lenses of a pair of rusty iron glasses. His ill-fitting coat was creased and worn at the elbows, and when he started to speak to me I saw that half his teeth were missing and those that were left were stained brown and yellow. A man who has travelled a storm-tossed path, I thought to myself, one whose whole life has been a losing struggle against poverty and adversity. And yet there was a fire in his eye and an arrogance in his manner that didn't betoken humble birth or rudimentary education.

"After introducing himself – or rather telling me to call him Monsieur François, though I doubt that was his real name – he plunged straight into politics. His apparent familiarity with all the leading figures was only equalled by his contempt for them. He dismissed them with a lapidary phrase, one after the other. Guizot, Thiers, Barrot – he hadn't a good word to say for any of them.

"I asked him whether he believed that socialism – a cause with which I imagined he might identify – would triumph. He was scathing about this too. 'Socialism was born here in France, it is true,' he said. 'But take it from me, my dear sir, it is also here in France that it will die... if it is not dead already. The French are not cut out for socialism. Our political principles have two cornerstones: revolution and apathy. Nothing in between.'

"I confess that by this time I was so intrigued by the man that I asked him to venture a prediction as to what was going to happen. It was as if that was what he had been waiting for. He sprang to his feet, leaned his gnarled hands on the table and thrust his gaunt, wrinkled face close to mine. 'I will make two predictions, and I will meet you here from time to time so that you may either recognize my prescience or throw my words back in my face.'

"'The first?'

"'The first is that within a month France will be a republic.' I laughed my disbelief, but as we all know, that is now the case."

"'And the second?' I asked.

"The second was that before the end of the year, France would again be 'possessed' – strange word, but it was the one he used – by the Bonapartes."

This is met by a chorus of incredulity mixed with mockery. 'Madman', 'Drunkard', 'Fantasist' are just a few of the epithets levelled at the egregious Monsieur François. George sums up the feelings of all. "The only Bonaparte he could be referring to is that incompetent adventurer and charlatan, Louis-Napoleon. And the day that France is 'possessed' by him, I'll take the veil!"

Louis Viardot, as a fellow-writer, gives Turgenev a consolatory pat on the shoulder. "It's a pity your story has such a ridiculous end; otherwise you might have written it up."

But Bakunin, who has been listening attentively to Turgenev's account, now murmurs broodingly: "I wonder if it's so ridiculous. I would like to meet this gentleman; he may not be as crazed as you all think."

George Sand wags a finger at Turgenev. "You know what I think, Ivan? Your Monsieur François sounds to me more Russian than French – like a character out of that bizarre novel of Gogol's you translated bits of for me. I think you ran into some scoundrelly specimen of Parisian riffraff who was probably hoping to touch you for a few francs, and that fertile imagination of yours translated him into a character out of Gogol."

Turgenev smiles his denial. "No, no, he was exactly as I have described him "

"Have you ever seen him again?" Viardot asks.

"No, but I must confess I have been back to the café many times, rather hoping that he would appear to claim credit for his first prediction."

"He never will," is Louis's confident assumption. "He'll have been swallowed up into the insatiable maw of the great Parisian underworld."

But Turgenev shakes his head. "No, I feel sure that one of these days he will show up at the Rotonde, just as he said. These are troubled times, when men like him are in their element. He reminds me of one of those sea birds the English call stormy petrels. You only see them when a tempest is blowing. They fly low in the turbulent air, their wings skimming the rearing crests of the waves. And as soon as the weather turns fine again, they disappear…"

An hour later, Viardot and Turgenev are left alone in the room. Bakunin, after a lengthy and ceremonious farewell to Pauline ("Be sure to let me know the exact date of your concert – I wouldn't miss it for the revolution."), has gone back to his barracks, George has hurried off for a meeting of the Provisional Government, and Pauline has retired to the music room to vocalize.

Louis is finally able to unburden himself of his irritation.

"I hope your friend Bakunin isn't going to make a fool of himself."

Turgenev, although he knows perfectly well what his host is referring to, can't resist making light of it. "I think you can rest assured that, in one way or another, he will."

"No, no," Louis snorts, impatiently, "I mean as regards Pauline. Didn't you think he was rather overdoing his attentions to her?"

"Oh, on that score, you have nothing to worry about."

"On Pauline's part, you mean?"

"That surely goes without saying. No, I was meaning from Michel."

"You mean it's all bravado?"

"Unfortunately for him, I fear it is."

Louis smiles contentedly and rubs his hands. "All show and no substance, eh? Come to think of it, rather like his political convictions."

"Perhaps," says Turgenev, thoughtfully. "And perhaps sharing a common background. You see, I have it on very good authority that Mikhail Aleksandrovich is impotent."

Louis gives him a shrewd glance. "Good authority in that field can only mean a woman. Have you shared a mistress?"

"Not exactly."

Louis is intrigued. He ponders for a moment, then his eyes light up. "Ah, I have it. I noticed there was a certain tension between you two when he was talking of his sister. Perhaps a girl friend of hers discovered Bakunin's… inadequacy, confided in her and she confided in you."

Turgenev neither confirms nor denies.

"Oh, come now, you must tell me. Have I hit the mark?"

A slow shake of the head. "No, Louis, it is at once, simpler and more complicated than that. The woman that Michel and I 'shared', though not in the sense that you meant, was his sister, Tatyana. All through their childhood they had been very close. Too close, perhaps, for siblings. They and his other two elder sisters, Lyubov and Varvara, were in league against the rigid conservatism of their parents.

They formed what amounted to a German blood-brotherhood, with all the paraphernalia of codes, passwords, oaths and secret signs. And Michel, as the only male, was looked up to and adored by all of them. One summer I went to stay with them at their beautiful estate of Premukhino, and Tatyana transferred her adoration to me. For a while we were very much in love, but for me it was a passion of ideas that united us, a mutual, unquenchable appetite for literature. It was her mind I wanted endlessly to probe, not her body. As soon as I realized – and I have to confess that, young as I was, it took me far too long – that I had lit a fire that was threatening to consume me, I tried to explain my feelings to her. But she didn't want to listen. I went away and wrote her a long letter, telling her I had never loved a woman more than her, even though it was not an all-embracing, lifelong love; and that for me the bond between us was unforgettable and irreplaceable. She replied with a curt note saying she didn't understand the dry, contemptuous tone of my letter. And that was the end. We never saw or communicated with each other again."

"And she, as it were, 'went back' to her brother?"

Turgenev hesitates for a moment. "I've never talked about this with anyone before. Despite our differences, I am fond of Michel. And rumour and gossip are such ugly companions. All I have said up to now comes from my personal experience. What follows is hearsay and conjecture. But there is little doubt in my mind that, after my departure, she found from Michel the love that I had failed to give her. He had always been jealous of Tatyana and me. As oldest brother of a family of ten, he had, up to then, enjoyed unqualified adulation; I chipped off a splinter of his supremacy. It would be only natural for him to replace that splinter the moment I was out of the way. And, as you have seen for yourself today, he is not a man for half measures."

"And you think, because of that, he has never fully been able to love another woman."

"So I am led to believe. It's certainly not from lack of opportunity."

"And you also think that this may have something to do with his political extremism?"

"Ah, these are even deeper waters. But I have never forgotten a phrase he wrote to me from Berlin, soon after he embraced the revolutionary idea. 'The desire to destroy,' he said 'is also a creative desire.' Could it be that he is seeking compensation for an inability to find fulfilment in love in these grandiose dreams of ripping everything apart?"

"It could," Louis says thoughtfully. "It could indeed. A fascinating man. Who knows what will become of him!"

In May, the Viardots left France again, this time for London, where Pauline had a three-month engagement at Covent Garden. Louis hated the idea of being away from Paris, where he could follow – and possibly play some part in shaping – the events following the February revolution, but could not bring himself to renounce his duties as husband and manager. By the time they returned in early August, the euphoria that had followed the February revolution had been drowned in the bloodshed of the four 'June Days', and his dream of a reforming Republican government was seriously threatened. So it was politics, not art, that dominated the conversation at the dinner table on the evening of their arrival at Courtavenel.

All Turgenev, who had been in Paris those four days, wanted to hear about was Pauline's triumphs in *Les Huguenots* and her rivalry with Giulia Grisi, the beautiful, flamboyant Italian soprano who was in the same company. But Louis, tortured by the thought that his country was headed for another period of reaction, was in no mood for backstage gossip. He came straight to the point. "The situation is slipping out of our control," he said. "And it's our fault. We're incapable of uniting behind one common line of action. Everyone – Ledru-Rollin, Blanqui, Lamartine, Louis Blanc, Barrot – they all have the best of intentions, but each wants to ride his own hobby-horse. Each believes that he and only he has all the answers. There are more prima donnas in French republican politics than in all the opera houses of Europe! And while we spend our time arguing incessantly over details – limited or universal suffrage, arguments for and against the National Workshops – important issues, certainly, but to be decided in their own good time, what are our respectable, worthy friends on the Right doing? I don't imagine they can believe their own good fortune. That madness which happened in June – although I'm still far from clear what actually *did* happen – played straight into their hands. Now they can say to all the waverers, the *petit bourgeois*, the so-called moderates: 'There you are, you see! What else can you expect when you let the people take the law into their own hands. What a lesson for us it has been!' And now they are united, monolithically, behind one cause: to turn the clock back... to negate everything that was achieved last February."

"I doubt if they'll succeed in that," said Turgenev. "I don't see France becoming a monarchy again in a hurry."

"You don't?" Louis retorted. "Nothing would surprise me less. We're not in your country now, where nothing changes for centuries at a time. The French are fickle in their allegiance and deeply conservative in their temperament. I foresee a period of brutal reaction. But I want to hear from you, Ivan. You were here. What exactly happened during those four June days?"

The three of them moved from the dining room to a small salon where the men lit cigars and Pauline took up some embroidery. Turgenev stretched his legs out in front of his chair and gave a Louis a quizzical look. "I would be very surprised if there were one man in Paris who could tell you exactly what happened. All I can do is tell you what I saw."

"That will do to be going on with," Louis said with a smile.

Turgenev thought for a moment and then began: "I think the two things I shall always remember about those days were the heat and the confusion. It was the sort of heat that melts men's brains. Who knows? Perhaps in cooler weather the worst might have been avoided. But anyway, everyone had known since the beginning of the month that a confrontation was imminent. The tension hung in the air, like the smell of gunpowder. I heard, but cannot guarantee, that the spark which set the conflagration off was caused by the Minister of Public Works, Marie. He had summoned delegates from the National Workshops and told them the provisional government had decided to close the workshops down: all the unmarried workers were to join the army, on pain of losing their payments, and the others would be sent off to the provinces. From then on, the only thing people asked each other in the streets was: 'Has it started yet? Is it today?'

On the 23rd of June, I heard from the washerwoman who brought me my laundry. 'It's begun,' she said, and told me that a large barricade had been erected near the Porte Saint-Denis. I went immediately to look. At first, on my way, nothing seemed to have changed. Life went on as usual. But as I drew nearer to my destination, I began to notice there were no more omnibuses, and the shop and café owners were beginning to pull down their shutters. On the other hand, all the upstairs windows were wide open and heads, mostly the bonneted heads of women, were sticking out of them and cheerfully calling to their neighbours as though waiting for the curtain to go up at a theatre.

"When I came to the barricade, this festive spirit was still apparent. The men in their *blouses* were handing round bottles and inviting onlookers to share their wine. At one point one of them, who had probably drunk too much, raised his rifle in the air and cried out: 'Long Live the National Workshops! Long Live the Republic!', drawing an answering cheer from the crowd. It hardly seemed credible that anything calamitous could erupt out of this cheerful, friendly atmosphere. I stationed myself alongside the wall of one of the houses close to the barricade. The windows above me were open, but no heads poked out as the Venetian blinds were all lowered. Soon we heard an approaching roll of drums, and before long a column of the National Guard appeared about two hundred metres down the boulevard. They halted, and for two strange, unearthly minutes nothing happened at all. The laughter and the chatter died down. The men at the barricade stared at the column and the guards in the column stared at the barricade. Nothing moved except for one or two eddies of yellowish dust swirling in the intervening no-man's land and a small black-and-white spotted dog scampering about on thin little legs, turning his head inquisitively from side to side. Then, out of nowhere, came a dull thud that sounded, to my inexperienced ears, more like a massive iron bar falling onto the cobbles than a burst of cannon fire. For a moment there was silence of an intensity I had never known before. In the heavy noonday heat, the air itself seemed to stop and listen. Then from right above my head, with a suddenness that made my heart miss several beats, came a terrifying fortissimo crackling, like a huge piece of cloth being brutally ripped to shreds. It was the rebels firing through the Venetian blinds of the upper floors of the house.

"The tragedy had begun, although there was no way of suspecting at that moment the dimension it was to assume. I, at any rate, along with several other onlookers, decided it was time to be off. We edged our way along the walls of the houses and, just before turning into a side street, I saw my first two casualties of what are now called the 'June Days': a man trying to crawl on all fours out of the range of the gunfire, a képi with a red pompon having fallen from his head on to the cobbles; and the little black-and-white dog rolling on its back, legs kicking, a purple stain beginning to ooze from its scrawny ribs into the dust.

"On my way home, I saw something else which disturbed me to a degree I'd never have suspected. I was passed by another detachment of the National Guard who, no doubt attracted by the noise of gunfire, were hurrying towards the street I had just left. And who should I see in the vanguard, his rifle pointing forward with the bayonet unsheathed, his face distorted into a thin-lipped mask of cruelty, as though he couldn't wait to sink the steel into some poor devil's belly, but… you remember my story… the man who had introduced himself to me as Monsieur François."

Pauline's eyes lit up with interest. "Your prophet friend at the Palais-Royal café! Of course I remember. Had you seen him since?"

"I had. And that was why the sight of him with his ragged frock coat exchanged for a well-pressed National Guard uniform made my blood freeze."

"Had he accosted you again in the café?" Louis asked.

"No. This time the circumstances were quite different. I had gone, out of curiosity, to a Bonapartist rally which was held in the place de la Concorde on June 13th. As I looked around, my attention was caught by a familiar figure: a tall, brawny man, dressed like a juggler, with a massive head of hair rearing up a foot or so above his forehead, was standing astride a two-wheel cart, bawling his head off and handing out leaflets. I had often seen him – you probably have too – on the boulevards, selling miraculous cures for toothache, ointments to soothe rheumatic pains… that sort of thing. I pushed my way over through the crowd and took one of the leaflets, which turned out to be a fulsomely flattering biography of Prince Louis-Napoleon. As I was glancing through it, repelled by the glutinous style and disregard of accuracy, I felt a hand on my shoulder. It was Monsieur François, staring at me ironically over those rusty iron glasses, his mouth cracked open in a toothless leer.

"'You see, my good sir, you see?!' he gibbered, rubbing his hands in delight.

127

'It's beginning, it's beginning.' He pointed to the tout. 'There is the voice crying in the wilderness, the one who prepares the way.'

"I couldn't hide my revulsion. 'You mean to say,' I asked him, 'you're comparing that egregious charlatan to John the Baptist?'

"'Oh yes. It's precisely charlatans that are needed,' he replied, his eyes boring more feverishly than ever into mine. 'Hair like storm-tossed bracken, bracelets on his arms, sequined jacket, these things catch the imagination. Legends accumulate around them. And legend is what we are in need of, good sir… spectacle, wonders, miracles. At first people are astonished. Then astonishment changes to respect and respect to belief… Oh, you may smile your detached foreign observer's smile. But listen once again to what I tell you. I wasn't wrong before, was I? The serious business is just beginning. Soon we will have crossed the Red Sea, and then…'

"Unfortunately, at that moment a detachment of troops, who had been called by Lamartine to disperse the rally, charged. The crowd scattered in panic, and Monsieur François and I were separated. I never saw him again until I glimpsed that vision of dehumanized brutality charging down a Paris street. I made my way gloomily back to the Boulevard des Italiens and there I stayed for the next four terrible days."

"Because it was too dangerous to go anywhere?" Pauline asked.

"It was forbidden. Cavaignac, who commanded the army of Paris, gave orders that no one was to circulate in the streets without a permit. The soldiers and the National Guard fought. Everyone else, women, children, the old, the sick and, above all, foreigners had to stay at home and keep their windows open to forestall the possibility of ambushes. One of my neighbours told me they were shooting rebel prisoners in the town hall. Occasionally we would hear news that had been passed from mouth to mouth and window to window: the whole of the Left Bank was in the hands of the rebels, every prisoner taken was being shot on sight, mothers and daughters of bourgeois families were being held hostage and frequently raped. We had, of course, no means of knowing if any of this were true…

"By the second night, I couldn't stay in my room another minute. I had to go out, even if only to breathe a little cool air. But I had barely gone fifty paces down the street before a National Guardsman from the provinces – they were always the worst because of their hatred of Parisians – stopped me roughly and asked who I was. His suspicion was aroused because, before leaving my room, I had slipped on a daytime jacket. He interrogated me like an inquisitor. 'Where have you come from? Where do you live? Why aren't you in uniform?' I made the great mistake of telling him I was Russian. 'Ah, a spy, that's who you are. The city is full of your kind. That's why you're dressed like that, so you can mix with the rebel pigs unnoticed. I wouldn't be surprised if those pockets were full of gold to stir up even more trouble than we have already.' Trying to keep calm, although I must admit I was quite frightened, expecting any minute to be marched off to some barracks, I suggested that he search my pockets to confirm his suspicions. This only made him more angry, as he thought I was trying to cheek him. He pointed his rifle at me and said if I wasn't out of his sight and back in my house within two minutes, he'd shoot me in the back. I was very glad no one I knew was there to see me at that moment. I assure you it is not easy to walk as fast as your legs can carry you while still trying to affect an air of dignified unconcern."

"Poor Ivan!" Pauline's genuine sympathy was only slightly tempered by her amusement at conjuring up the picture he had just painted. "We had no idea things were that bad. The papers we read in England tended to play the whole thing down."

"Of course they did," said Louis. "They were reporting what they heard from the French authorities, and it was in their interest to make it all sound like a brief skirmish. I'm told the dead will have run into many thousands, although the official figures talk of a few hundred. It was of a brutality not seen in France since the Terror of '93. But what you have to understand is that, for many otherwise decent people, the vicitms were barbarians, savages, scum. Even the best of them – even good friends of ours – while perhaps regretting that so much blood was shed, consider it a necessary purging to enable France to resume its rightful course. What we in Paris forget, especially in the circles we move in – musicians, painters, writers – is that there are millions who think like that at every level of society. I tell you, France is a profoundly conservative country. And if this idiotic Constituent Assembly of ours do as they threaten and vote for election of both the Chamber and the President by direct universal suffrage, I fear we'll end up regretting the 'good old days' of Louis-Philippe.

"You mean you think the Republic is doomed?" Pauline asked.

"I fear so, yes. Not immediately, perhaps. But if the election is held under those terms, we can forget about all those reforms we were dreaming about in February. In the villages and small country towns, the *curé* and the local landowner will lead their flock to the hustings, and they would vote for Attila the Hun if they were told to. Who have we as a presidential candidate to put up against Cavaignac, a republican general who crushed the uprising of the Paris mob, and Louis-Napoleon, with the famous Bonaparte mystique somehow managing to cling even to that flimsy scarecrow? Ivan's story about his Monsieur François doesn't surprise me in the least. There are many men of intelligence and learning who look on him as 'a man of destiny'. No, the only hope is to get that election law changed. If the President were to be voted by the Assembly, it is unlikely they would choose some aspiring despot. Even if they settled for a figurehead like Lamartine, it would be better than the alternative. Tomorrow, I must go back to Paris, talk to George Sand and Leroux and see what can be done."

129

"But Louis," Pauline protested, "we've only just got back. You should rest for a day or two."

"I'm perfectly rested, my dear," Louis said. "I've done nothing for the last three months but watch you work. It's you who needs a rest, not me."

Pauline insisted. "But surely you'd like to spend a few quiet days here in the country. Why this hurry to rush off to Paris? Wouldn't you like to do a bit of shooting?"

Viardot gave his wife an affectionate smile and laid his hand on her arm. "My dear," he said, "we've been married now… how long is it?… eight years, and it still hasn't penetrated that clever head of yours that there is no shooting in August! But even if there were, I would have to leave it to Ivan for the time being. My mind will not be at rest until I've seen if there isn't some way to change that electoral law. I'm not a director of *La Revue Indépendente* any more, but I fancy I still have a certain influence. At any rate, I have to try."

Pauline pulled her full Spanish lips together into something resembling a French pout.

"But I was looking forward to inviting all our friends. We haven't seen them for such a long time."

"I'm sure they'll be prepared to wait another week. But the future of France perhaps won't."

A momentary flash in Pauline's eyes might have been followed by 'The hell with the future of France!' But she thought better of it and spread her hands in resignation.

"Are you sure you don't want me to come with you?" she asked, almost meekly.

"I wouldn't hear of it. You stay here and spend a few quiet days with Ivan. I know he'll be glad to keep you company until I get back"…

Having been starved of her presence for over three months, Turgenev would have been glad to keep Pauline company twenty-four hours a day. But she made him accept the rule that they would see little or nothing of each other until the evening. He was to get on with his writing – *Sovremennik* was still clamouring for more of his *Sportsman's Sketches* – while she had many domestic duties to attend to at Courtavenel after so long an absence. But the evenings were given over to entertainment, most of which consisted of Pauline recounting to her mother and Turgenev the highlights of her London season. Turgenev especially wanted to hear everything down to the smallest detail: how everyone had sung, what costumes they had worn, how English audiences compared with French and Russian ones, whom they had met after the performances and, above all, every shred of gossip, the more malicious the better, about other members of the troupe.

The first evening she regaled them with the story of how she had got her revenge on the jealous, scheming Grisi. "From the day I arrived, she did everything in her power – which is considerable – to spite me. She had already arranged with the management that most of the leading roles in the popular Italian operas would go to her. For a while, I naively searched for an explanation for this hostility: after all, she is a beautiful woman, which I am not, with a magnificent voice which is still in its prime. What had she to fear from me? I asked Louis one evening and his reply was a lapidary 'Ten years'. There was a whole section of the London public who adored her... particularly the young aristocrats, who know little about music but consider themselves – wrongly, I discovered – to be as expert a judge of women as they are of horses. The few I met I hated, but perhaps this was because I blamed them and their kind for Maria's death. But you'd think their idolatry would have satisfied La Grisi. Not at all! There was a much smaller group, led by Henry Chorley, the critic of *The Athenaeum*, who preferred me. And this she couldn't stomach.

"I was sure trouble was on its way after the first night of *Les Huguenots*. All the Italians, including her lover, Mario, who was singing opposite me, were expecting, at best, a tepid reaction. But they didn't know that in England, unlike Italy, Meyerbeer is very popular, and it turned out to be the success of the season. This time all the London papers, not only Chorley, talked about little else. So you can imagine my state of mind when, on the *very morning* of my benefit performance, which was going to be in *Les Huguenots*, Mario announced that he was sick and would not be able to sing that evening. Grisi had the nerve to send a note to my hotel, in which, in a language that would make molasses taste like lemons, she suggested I replace it with *Norma*, in which she would be glad, for my sake, to appear in the title role, while I could sing Adalgisa."

Turgenev hugged his knees in anticipatory joy. "And what did you answer?" he asked.

"That if anyone were going to sing the part of Norma in my benefit performance, it would be me. But that *Les Huguenots* had been announced and *Les Huguenots* it would be. I knew that Gustave Roger was in London – you remember he sang in my cantata in April? – so I traced him and he agreed to sing Raoul that night. The only problem was he knew the part in French and we were singing the opera in Italian."

Turgenev gave a wicked chuckle. "Don't tell me the English didn't notice the difference?"

Pauline laughed. "It could well be some of them didn't. But they didn't have to for long. You know I'm not on much of the time in the early part of the opera, so I swotted away in my dressing-room and learned the part in French. And we sang the last two acts, where all our big duets take place, in the same language."

Turgenev gazed at her in admiration. "There's no other singer in the world who could have done that."

"Oh, it wasn't so difficult. But it was certainly worth the effort. Most of the audience, of course, caught on and we got the longest ovation of the whole season. And Grisi and Mario were in the house, probably hoping to witness a fiasco. One of the critics the next day praised Grisi for 'the sincere delight she had shown in her rival's triumph'. Well, I have never denied that she's a magnificent actress!"

The following evening is stiflingly hot and airless. As soon as dinner is finished, Madame Garcia complains of a headache and goes off to bed. Pauline and Turgenev chat aimlessly for a while and then he asks her about Chopin, who had been in England at the same time.

"Poor Frédéric," she sighs. "He is a very sick man. Apparently his doctors say he's unlikely to last more than a year. It's not possible to believe that unique talent can be silenced so young."

"Did you see him?" Turgenev asks.

"Oh, many times. We visited him often at Jane Stirling's house where he was staying, and once we gave a concert together."

"You and Chopin?"

"Yes. Do you remember my telling you that I visited George Sand once at Nohant when she and Frédéric were still... together, and he let me arrange some of his mazurkas as songs? We used to perform them for friends in the evenings. Well, I'd sung a few at a concert at Covent Garden, and they were a great success. In fact, I had to encore them all. So when I heard he was giving a recital at Lord Falmouth's house in St James's Square, I thought if I performed too, it might bring a few more people in. He's desperately in need of money, poor soul, because he doesn't compose any more and his doctors' bills must be exorbitant. But with his Polish pride, he won't accept help from anyone."

"So how did you arrange it?"

"Through my brother, Manuel. Frédéric had told him that he would love me to sing at his concert, but he was embarrassed to ask me because of the problem with George."

"What problem with George?

"You know how desperately sensitive Frédéric is. He apparently thought that George had ordered me to spy on him in London: find out exactly what he was doing and who he was seeing. Between you and me – and I mean that, I haven't even told Louis – he wasn't entirely wrong. But of course, much as I love George, I wouldn't dream of doing anything of the sort. Anyway, we made out that it had all been a brilliant idea of Manuel's, and I sang a couple of arias and several of his mazurka settings, with him, of course, at the piano."

"And it was the talk of the whole London season!"

Pauline lays her arm on his elbow. "Yes, my most uncritical admirer, I would be lying to you if I didn't admit it was."

She's looking at me in a way she never has before. There's a different expression in her eyes… not the usual affectionate, ironic, slightly mocking look, the 'Yes, I'm very fond of you, my great big shaggy Russian bear, but you do know you must keep your distance, don't you?'… no, tonight there's something deeper, something more vulnerable, it's almost as if she's appealing to me for something… and then – it would be ridiculous to make too much of it – but that little confidence about George Sand, she has never before shared a secret with me that she has kept from Louis…

Turgenev nods towards the piano.

"Play!"

It is the nearest he has ever come to giving her an order.

She rises without a word, moves over to the piano, sits down and begins to play. As they have been talking about Chopin, she chooses his *Berceuse*, not too demanding technically, allowing her thoughts to drift in and out of the gently lilting melody…

Dear God, how refreshing it is, this palpably sincere adoration, especially after all the elaborate compliments of the past few months, usually expressed with that particularly English blend of trying to be gallant and 'continental' while being too awkward or inhibited to bring it off… Louis is devoted and loving in his way, but he's inclined to treat me like his prize possession – do you know my wife, the great singer? He knew I didn't want him to go straight back to Paris, but politics must always come first, even though I fear his friends don't think he's anything like as influential as he does, but that's not the point, this man now standing beside me as I play places me at the centre of his world, I believe he would give up writing if I asked him to – not, heaven forbid, that I ever would – but how wonderful to feel this intensity of passion, I never knew anything like that from Louis, but then – I know I shouldn't even think this – the dear man's so old, he was old when I first knew him, I think he was born old…

She touches the final D flat in the bass and lets it resound until it dies away of its own accord. The liquid beauty of the music, which seems to have cooled the oppressive heat of the night, makes speech seem redundant. Eventually Turgenev lays his hand on the top of her head, almost in blessing, then runs it down the back of her thickly-coiled black hair.

"Sing!"

This time it is no order, but a whispered plea.

After a moment's thought, she starts to play the twenty bars of piano introduction she has transposed from the end of one of Chopin's mazurkas to the beginning.

133

She didn't shrink away from my touch, she almost seemed to lean back into my hand, what is going to happen?, if I'm reading her wrong and make some move that might offend her, it will be all over, I'll lose everything, I'd probably have to leave, never see her again…

Pauline starts to sing:

Tu commandes qu'on t'oublie,
J'ai grand peine à t'obéir…
(You order me to forget you,
I find it very hard to obey…)

But if what I feel is true and I don't respond to her, she'll take it as an offence, a rebuff, she'll think I'm insensitive, cowardly, surely the way she glances at me as she's singing couldn't be mockery…

Ton désir est mon désir,
Vraiment, mon désir…
(Your desire is my desire,
Truly, my desire…)

After lightly emphasizing the repeated '*vraiments*', Pauline launches into the high trill under which the piano takes over the melody.

If he and I are ever going to make the difficult change from friendship to love, there will never be a more propitious moment than this… and how can I deny myself this immense, tender lovingness?… it is I who will have to decide… I who will have to take the first step… for most assuredly he never will…

As she sings the final strophe of the song, she takes her eyes off her hands and gazes directly into his…

…Mais quoi! des pleurs, ma belle;
Écoute, apaise-toi;
Plus de folle querelle,
Je t'adore, aime-moi.
(But why these tears, my beauty?
Listen to me, calm down;
No more of this foolish quarrelling;
I adore you. Love me.)

AIME-MOI! This is order and plea rolled into one, and it is not to be denied. Standing directly behind her, he lays his hands gently on her shoulders. She gives a little shudder and her hands, as though jerked violently by invisible strings, fly up across her chest and clamp down on his. She leans her head back and smiles up at him. He bends down, kisses her on the forehead and opens his mouth to say... who knows what? She silences him by laying a finger across his lips. Then she rises from the piano stool and moves round to stand facing him, her body close against his. With a gleam of amusement in her eyes, she reaches up to grasp his forearms, raises herself on tiptoe and kisses him lightly on the mouth. Again Turgenev tries to speak and again she shushes him, with a whispered '*Ton désir est mon désir.*' Seeing that the poor man is now beginning to tremble in an effort to contain the torrent of passion he is forbidden to express in words, she takes his hand and leads him out of the room.

Two days later Louis Viardot came back from Paris, even more disturbed by the course events were taking than he had been before he left. His discussions with his friends had not been reassuring: all of them were convinced that the gains of February were gradually being dissipated, that there was no progressive politician strong and popular enough to halt the slide, and that the future lay in the hands of the reactionaries. Louis was so despondent that he even talked about selling his beloved Courtavenel and leaving France altogether.

Pauline used all her tact and charm to try and convince him that he was taking too dark a view. And anyhow, she told him, this was no time to do anything drastic: very soon they would be moving to their new Paris house which Louis had had built in the rue de Douai, and she would begin preparing for her forthcoming debut at the Opéra. The astonishing fact that she had never sung there was due above all to the implacable enmity of Rosine Stolz, the power behind the throne at that scandal-ridden institution. A moderate singer but masterly intriguer, Stolz had rescued herself from an unpromising early career by marrying the director of the Théâtre de la Monnaie in Brussels, after which she was soon singing leading roles in two of Meyerbeer's operas. Transferring her ambitions to Paris, she became the mistress of Léon Pillet, the director of the Opéra. Nicknamed by Berlioz *la Directrice du Directeur*, she used her position to ensure that no dangerous rivals would be seen or heard on that august stage. But the previous year she had appeared in a fiasco called *Robert Bruce*, a hodge-podge of chunks of Rossini's operas cobbled together by a Swiss composer at Pillet's bidding, and had been hissed and booed at the final curtain. Not a woman to submit meekly to this kind of treatment, she had ripped her handkerchief into shreds with her teeth and shouted insults and curses back at the audience. After this, both she and Pillet had been forced to resign and now Pauline was to gain the sweetest of revenges, having been chosen by Meyerbeer himself to create the leading woman's role in his new opera, *Le Prophète*.

Turgenev noted, to his bewilderment, that Pauline's behaviour towards her husband and himself remained exactly as it had been before. Louis now required her attention, and she gave it him unstintingly. Turgenev understood that she was required to play a part, and was, of course, not surprised to see how well she did it. But nevertheless he could not refrain from hoping that at least once in a while an expression in her eyes, a touch of her hand on his sleeve, would confirm for him that the world had changed. It took only a few days for him to come to the conclusion that for her it had not. Apparently everything was to go on just as it had before. But how could it? He no longer felt at ease, either with her or with Louis, who, finding in their hunting expeditions the only respite from his political torments, redoubled his courtesy and attentions towards him. He soon decided that it was essential for him to spend some time away from Courtavenel. Following Louis's advice, he set out in October for a tour of the south of his newly-adopted country.

Shortly after his departure, George Sand came up to Paris from Nohant and immediately went round to rue du Douai to follow up a clue she had detected in a letter from Courtavenel. Pauline took a malicious double pleasure in showing her friend in great detail round her new house: the natural pride of ownership, which justified poking into every remotest corner, was enhanced by the fact that she knew very well that Sand was not the least bit interested in other people's houses and that she was consumed by curiosity to know what it was that Pauline had alluded to in her letter.

When eventually there was not another nook to admire or cranny to explore, and Sand's exasperation was becoming incandescent, the two finally withdrew to Pauline's sitting room and tea was ordered. Until the maid had arrived, deposited a tray, bobbed a curtsey and left, the conversation still had to remain anodyne. But the moment the door closed behind her, Sand leaned forward in her chair and asked for clarification of the hints contained in Pauline's letter. This was now supplied, but the result was far from being what Pauline had expected: she was astonished to hear the experienced, world-famous writer sitting opposite her, who had shocked even Paris by the *libertinage* of her youth, start to cluck at her like an apprehensive spinster.

"Be careful, be careful, Fifille, don't be rash. Don't do anything to jeopardize your marriage. Louis would be shattered if he were to find out."

"He won't find out."

"But he must surely be aware already that the man is infatuated with you."

"Perhaps, but they are the best of friends."

"They have been up to now. But if he were to suspect…"

"I will give him no cause to suspect. Remember, I am an actress as well as a singer. I shall be discretion itself."

"You may be, but will Ivan? He is not an actor, and already his position in your house is of an ambivalence…"

"His position in our house is that of a valued friend of both of us. And so it will remain. If he is not prepared – or able – to play his part, I shall send him away."

Pauline had to control herself not to betray a touch of annoyance. She had been looking forward to confiding her secret and sharing with her closest woman friend the sense of thrill and adventure she couldn't allow herself to relish to the full even with Turgenev. She had not expected to be lectured. But in fact, the lecture was by no means over.

"You should send him away in any case. This is not the moment for an adventure. This winter will be critical to your career. The most important theatrical composer of the day, in his first opera for thirteen years, has created a role especially for you. With all your triumphs, up to now you have been one of the princesses of the operatic world. After *Le Prophète* you will be the Queen. Nothing – no attraction to a man, no family responsibilities – *nothing* must be allowed to come between you and your coronation. This is the responsibility of great artists. Love is ephemeral, art eternal. Affairs of the heart cannot but distract from the total concentration you need. Believe me, I know what I am talking about. And you know I do. I implore you to send your Muscovite away. It's time he went back to his own country anyway. A writer must never be absent for too long from his roots. And devotion like his can be very wearing. If you're not careful, this Russian giant will monopolize you, body and soul."

"He won't monopolize me. He's thoughtful and tender and wonderfully sensitive. He saw that Louis needed me when he came back from Paris and immediately left on a journey so as not to be in the way. Do you want to hear what he wrote to me the other day?". She took a pile of letters out of a drawer in her desk and opened the top one. "He always writes his most personal thoughts in German. Listen to this – I'll translate it: *'May God bless you a thousand times, my dearest, best, adored angel. My most ardent greetings to your whole beloved being…'* Then there are three words he has crossed out."

"No doubt just as well," George remarked tartly.

"*'I am too excited to write to you any more…'*"

"That would explain the three words!"

"Stop being so odiously cynical and listen: *'I cannot tell you how often today I have thought of you, of happiness, of the future. On my way back here, I cried out your name with such joy, reached out my arms so lovingly towards you that you must certainly have heard and seen. Good night to you, dearest and best creature in the whole world.'*" She refolded the letter, put it back in its envelope and appealed to Sand, on whom these words seemed to have made little effect. "How can I shut a love like this out of my life? I don't expect ever to come across such passion again."

"A great artist should save her passion for her performances. Don't forget what too much of the other kind did to your sister."

A grimace of pain flitted across Pauline's features and George instantly regretted her unintentional cruelty. She hastily apologized, but Pauline's thoughts had drifted away from her companion… first to expel from her conscious mind the still too painful memories of her tragic sister, then to ruminate on why, eight years ago, the plump, middle-aged lady now sitting opposite her had practically dragooned her into marrying her old friend Viardot…

Was she concerned to see Louis finally settled down?… Could it have crossed her mind that her love for me might take a turn that she was afraid of? Would the kind of love it was rumoured she had shared with Marie Dorval have been acceptable for a 'great artist'?... Or was she just totally sincere in enumerating all the advantages it would bring to my career – Louis's knowledge of the business world of opera, his position as director of the Théâtre Italien, his solidity, reliability, his comparative wealth? 'He will allow your art to soar while all your mundane needs are taken care of', she had said. She was right about that and I'm grateful to her for it. But is it possible that it never occurred to a woman of thirty-six that a girl of eighteen might eventually find total fidelity to a man twenty-one years older than herself a little difficult? Suppose something else inside me occasionally wanted to soar!... I feel like asking her, rhetorically, what on earth I would need a dominating figure in my life for when I've got her!... But I'd better not... I can see she is upset. She is such a dear, kind person, I must say something to put her at her ease...

"You don't really know him, Ninounne. When you met him before, he still often acted like an adolescent, striking poses, trying to impress people, especially people of your fame. But he's put all that behind him now. You'll see that he's the most gentle, least monopolizing of men. He's incapable of self-assertion... almost to a a fault. I remember we were discussing our parents once in St Petersburg. His mother had come to one of my morning concerts, but refused to be introduced to me afterwards. She didn't want to meet the 'damned gypsy'. And I discovered that, whereas I had had one dominating parent and one placid one, he had had two monsters in their different ways. His mother is still tormenting him from the steppes, while his father torments him from beyond the grave.

"How old was he when his father died?"

"Fifteen, I think. But he was never close to him. From what he says, it doesn't sound as if anyone was close to his father. He must have been a very cold man. But fascinating to women, apparently."

"Is that what Turgenev told you? He can't have known too much about it if he was so young when he died. Hearsay, I suppose."

"You suppose wrong, my dear Ninounne. Personal experience."

Sand tut-tutted impatiently. "What kind of personal experience can he have had at that age? I know they're all supposed to be eccentrics in that country, but don't tell me they have razor-keen insights into sexual attraction practically before they've reached puberty!"

Pauline let this pass, merely allowing a secret smile to play around her lips as she silently refilled her friend's cup. Sand squirmed in her chair in aggravation. "There's something you know that you're keeping from me. And it's most unkind of you. I haven't travelled two hundred miles to be fobbed off with sly hints and indecipherable allusions. What are you trying to tell me? Or should I say, what are you trying not to tell me?"

139

Pauline laughed and sat back in her chair, clasping her hands behind her head. "I oughtn't to really, because he asked me to keep it to myself. But I know I can trust you... can't I, Ninounne?"

"Yes, yes, of course you can."

"And anyhow, he said that one day he hopes to make a story out of it, so then it won't be a secret any longer, will it?"

"No, no, of course it won't. Now, for the love of God, get on with it, Fifille! What was it he told you?"

"We were talking about our first experiences of love and he told me of what happened to him one summer when he was fifteen. His parents had taken a house in the country outside Moscow. Their next door neighbours were a Bohemian group of young men, guests of an impoverished and rather vulgar old princess who had a ravishingly attractive young daughter. Ivan fell head over heels in calf love with this girl, who was at least six years older than him and was busily flirting with all the young men. But she responded to his timid advances too and even made him jump from a high wall to prove his love for her. He hurt himself a bit and can still remember the girl bending remorsefully over him and giving him a kiss. She must have had strange tastes, because she also apparently told him that she could never love someone weaker than herself; she needed a man who would bend her to his will... and hoped she would never find him."

"But of course she did."

"It seems so. For a while, at least. Ivan had noticed that his parents had been quarrelling even more than usual. His mother overwhelmed his father with reproaches for his neglect of her and he, as was his habit, withdrew behind an impenetrable screen of silence. But he seemed, perhaps in compensation, to have more time for his son and Ivan seized on the rare opportunity to be a little more intimate with the father he adored, but who usually kept him at arm's length. They often went riding together, and one evening he followed him secretly, hoping to surprise him, play a trick on him, I don't know... He came across his father's horse tethered to a fence near an outbuilding of the princess's house. He crept up to the window and saw his father and the girl in an attitude which left him in no doubt that she was his mistress. As he stood there, looking in, unable to move, he saw that they were beginning a violent argument. He couldn't hear a word they said, but at a certain point his father lifted his riding whip and slashed the girl's arm. At which she lifted the arm to her lips and kissed the wound."

Sand pursed her lips and thought for a moment, her novelist's imagination savouring the possibilities. "Did the relationship last?", she then asked.

"Ivan thinks that his father continued to see the girl in Moscow that winter. But the next year, he died."

Sand shook her head gently. "Poor boy," she said. "Heaven knows our confidence is fragile enough at that age. But that experience could damage it for ever."

"So you see now why I don't share your fears. Turgenev is the least dominating of men. He has an inbuilt horror of oppression… any kind, political or personal. The chief childhood memories he talks about – at least to me – are the scenes between his father and mother, with both of them resorting to any lengths in their efforts to establish supremacy. His mother invariably lost, perhaps because she fundamentally loved her husband, whereas he was quite indifferent to her; she took her defeats out on the servants – whipping them, exiling them and God knows what else. Ivan offers us a lesson we who have children should never forget: that example is everything, words little or nothing. I believe he'll be shielding his eyes from his parental models as long as he lives…"

Shortly after returning to Courtavenel, the subject of this conversation wrote to Annenkov:

Courtavenel,
April 14, 1850

My dear Pavel Vasilevich,

Here for your consideration are a few lines I wrote last night:

'Who is it who said that only truth is real? Falsehood is just as vivid as truth, if not more so. And we solitary men are just as incapable of understanding what is going on inside us as what is happening before our very eyes. And then, would love by any chance be a *natural* feeling? Is it really natural for a man to fall in love? Love is a disease; and there's no law that governs disease. So how are we to know what's normal and what isn't?…'

These are part of the reflections of the hero of a story I am working on. Hero! He is anything but that. In fact I am thinking of calling the story The Diary of a Superfluous Man, *since that is what he is: the sort of person that it would make not a jot of difference to the world or anyone in it whether he existed or not. When I began it, I thought it would be a fairly easy thing to do – a simple tale about a man who falls in love with a girl who falls in love with someone else who flirts with her for a while and then abandons her, leaving our 'hero' to hope that she will turn to him, but no, she marries another man to whom she is entirely indifferent. In fact, I hoped to finish it very quickly and get it off to Nekrasov, as I am in dire need of money and writing is now my only income. But I find myself probing deeper and deeper into the character of this man. Don't worry, I do not think of myself yet as entirely superfluous. But there are various questions, such as the ones with which I begin this letter, which are beginning to trouble me. So I turn to you, whose advice I always value. One of the inconveniences of living in a country which is not your own is that, however kind people are, you sometimes miss the familiarity of old* acquaintances, those whose roots plunge down into the same soil and to whom it is natural to turn when you are in need. Of course I have Herzen here in Paris, who was goodness itself to me when I nearly died of cholera last spring, but he is so waspish and positively delights in criticizing me whenever he can.

Talking of criticism, some words my father said to me just before he died came into my mind the other day and stubbornly refuse to leave it. It was the only intimate conversation I ever remember having with him. Although of course I wasn't aware of it, I think he must have known he was dying and wanted to pass on to me his philosophy of life. All that counts in this world, he told me, is to express your will and take whatever you can. You must belong to yourself and never let yourself be dominated. That is the only way to be free. But, I would answer him now (of course I listened in silence then), that would be the freedom of eternal solitude. It leaves no room for love, a condition my father, I believe, never experienced. And how do you express your will if you are by no means sure what your will is!?

And here, Pavel Vasilevich, is where I need you, because I am becoming paralyzed with indecision. One day I cannot bear the thought of leaving France. The next I feel it is time I came home. The very idea of being separated from Madame Viardot lacerates my entire being. And yet I think/fear/dread that my presence may be becoming an encumbrance to her. At the moment she is in Berlin, where not a ticket is to be had for any performance of Le Prophète. But when she is in Courtavenel, she is entirely taken up with Sapho, the new opera that young Gounod is writing for her. And her enthusiasm extends to its composer. He is a handsome, charming, talented fellow, whom Madame Viardot snatched, as it were, from the altar: he was studying in a seminary and was about to take Holy Orders when she persuaded Roqueplan, the director of the Opéra, to include Sapho in next season's repertory, as long as she promised to be in it. He and his mother, to whom he is slavishly devoted, have come to stay here. In Madame Viardot's eyes he can do no wrong, but I can't help wondering if his devotion to her is not a trifle calculated. There is something almost too good about monsieur Charles: a perfume of the sacristy seems perpetually to waft around him, and his eager graciousness to everyone can't help reminding me of a parish priest's unctuous, hand-rubbing bonhomie towards his parishioners, especially the wealthy and influential ones. Oh dear! Now I am being spiteful and perhaps unfair. On the surface, we are the best of friends and I do, genuinely, admire his great musical gifts.

There… I fear I have bored you with all this superficial chatter… but I needed to test the patience of someone who comes from the same stock. Write soon and help your Hamletic friend to find some sense of direction. In a word, should he return or not? The news that arrives here from Russia gets darker all the time. We hear that the screw of censorship is being tightened to strangulation point. And yet my sketches continue to be published… perhaps Authority is too blind to see that some of them do not show the gentry in a very favourable light. Herzen, having been ordered home and refused to go, has now been exiled, and they are trying to confiscate all his property and possessions. Will they do the same to me? Or throw me into gaol if I return? I have been much less involved in revolutionary politics than Herzen, but the government must know that all the young radical exiles in Paris find a warm welcome and a ready ear when they come to see me. And – who knows? – perhaps that makes me, in their eyes, a dangerous conspirator.

I await your advice with impatience and trepidation. I fear I know what you will say, and I don't think I am ready to hear it. But don't spare me…

Your devoted,

I.T.

In the middle of May the Viardots returned from Berlin, where Pauline had repeated her success as Fidès in *Le Prophète;* but they were only able to spend a few days in Paris before setting off again for London, where she was to take part in another summer season at Covent Garden. It was with only mild surprise that they found Turgenev waiting to greet them at rue de Douai. Before they left, he had been so emphatic about the necessity of returning to Russia, had so impressed on them the personal and professional risks he would be taking if he stayed abroad any longer, that they had been fully expecting him to pass through Berlin on his way home. But he had never appeared. And now he seemed a little embarrassed; when they sat down to dinner on the evening of their arrival, he parried their questions about himself and begged them instead to tell him all the news from Germany.

What he really wanted to hear, as always, was every detail of Pauline's triumph in *Le Prophète*, which she had sung in German for the first time. But Louis chose to keep him on tenterhooks and dwelt instead on the political situation. Like practically every other European country, Prussia and its king, Frederick William IV, had felt the repercussions of France's 1848. And as Pauline had been asked to give singing lessons to the king's daughter, Princess Louise, they had become fairly well acquainted with the artistically romantic and politically vacillating Hohenzollern. Pauline's opinion had been substantially favourable; Louis's considerably more critical.

"After all," she pointed out, "compared with the rulers of most other countries – Austria, Hungary, Russia – he has gone some way towards meeting his people's demands; and he refused to call out the army to put down demonstrations."

Louis gave his wife an affectionate smile. "I'm afraid you were carried away by the king's love of art and music. And God knows that is a rare enough quality in a monarch these days. But there is another side to Frederick William. Politically, whatever you may say or hope, my dear, he is an instinctive reactionary. Do you know what he told the representatives of the Frankfurt national parliament who came to offer him the crown of a united Germany? 'I might have accepted it,' he said, 'if it had been offered to me by the German princes. But I will never stoop to pick up a crown out of the gutter.'"

Turgenev chuckled. "That will endear him to the Czar! But, my dear friends, you didn't go to Berlin just to observe the revolution. I want to hear how they took to *Le Prophète*."

"It was perhaps an even greater triumph than in Paris," Louis remarked simply. "At the first night, in the presence of the royal family and the whole court, after the fourth act Meyerbeer himself, who was conducting, led Pauline by the hand out on to the stage and the whole audience stood and cheered for ten

143

minutes. It was an unforgettable night."

"We hoped you would be there to share it with us," Pauline observed. "You wrote and told us you would be in Berlin early in May, on your way back to Russia. What made you change your mind?"

Even though he was expecting the question, Turgenev couldn't help blushing. "Well, when I wrote to you, I had just heard news that my mother was seriously ill, and I thought I would have to leave at once. Then, for a moment, knowing what she is capable of, I had a suspicion this might be just another trick to lure me back home. But when I received 6000 roubles from her for my return journey, I realized that there must be some truth in it. And my brother is also begging me to come, as he needs support in the terrible war my mother is waging against his wife."

"So you will be leaving soon." This was more a statement that a question from Louis.

Turgenev glanced at them both and grinned sheepishly. "I have recently heard that she is not at death's door, and Annenkov wrote to me the other day to warn me against returning to Russia just at the moment. So I think it can all wait until the autumn. That way I could look after Courtavenel and Gounod for you while you're away in England."

He looked at them both, expecting, at least from Louis, an enthusiastic endorsement of this proposal. But Viardot merely grunted a guarded, "Well, you must do whatever you think best."

"Has the situation in Russia deteriorated so badly?" Pauline asked.

"It gets worse every day. Particularly in the field of literature. Nicholas is terrified of his docile people being corrupted by subversive writing: especially French. We may no longer have the word 'France' inscribed on our passports. George Sand, along with many others, is banned. It has become almost impossible to publish anything. A well-known historian, Professor Bodiansky, was arrested for publishing a translation of some impressions our country made on Queen Elizabeth of England's ambassador to Muscovy. Even thoughts two hundred and fifty years old are dangerous! And you are not going to believe this, but Annenkov assures me that Count Buturlin, who presides over a secret censorship committee, said that if they weren't so popular, he would have the gospels banned because of their democratic spirit."

Pauline gave him an alarmed glance. "But how will you be able to work when you do decide to go?"

Turgenev shrugged his shoulders. "At the moment, apart from a few alterations and cuts here and there, they don't seem to find my stories dangerous. It's almost insulting, when you come to think of it. They won't put on any of my plays, of course, but that may simply be because they're no good. I will just have to find out what happens when I get back. I had a dream the other night which may have some significance. I saw Russia as the Theban Sphinx and I was Oedipus. Its huge inert mass was shrouded in mist and its stony eyes fixed me with a gloomy stare. 'Have a little patience, Sphinx,' I said to it. 'I'll come back to you and you can devour me at your leisure if I don't solve your riddle. But leave me in peace for just a little longer. You will see me again soon enough.'"

There was a short silence before Viardot rather brusquely brought the evening to a close. Rising to his feet, he stood behind Turgenev's chair and laid a hand on his shoulder. "My dear Ivan," he said deliberately, "no one can make up your mind for you. Nor would I, or I am sure Pauline, presume to do anything of the sort. And you are, of course – and here again I know I can speak for both of us – welcome to stay at Courtavenel for as long as you like. But, allow me to take advantage of the twenty years' difference in our ages to draw your attention to a remorseless fact of life: the longer we postpone difficult decisions, the harder it becomes eventually to make them. Only weak people never bring things to an end themselves, but wait for the end to come. And when it eventually does, it is often more disagreeable than it would have been if it had come earlier."

When Turgenev got back to his room, he found Diane, his piebald English terrier, curled up at the foot of the bed. She greeted him with a feeble, nice-to-see-you-but-don't-expect-too-much-enthusiasm-at-this-hour-of-night wag of the tail and Turgenev suddenly found himself shedding twenty years. As a boy, after his mother had punished him for some trifling misdeed, he would seek consolation in long conversations with the only creature on earth he felt could understand him. Now he sat down on a chair, bent forward and raised Diane's head, stroking her behind the ears and looking into those brown, mournful eyes, which seemed to gaze back into his with a sense of the deepest sympathy and understanding... *You don't want to leave Courtavenel any more than I do, do you? We have everything we want here. So why move? You want to sleep in your familiar kennel, play with that great brute of a German Shepherd, Viardot's Sultan, who knocks you flying on your back time after time, and the more he does it the happier you are. You're content to explore the same tracks and paths you've gone down a hundred times, but which always offer some new, exciting smells... but come to think of it, perhaps I'm wrong... after a couple of days you'll probably find Russian smells just as enticing as French ones... a partridge or a quail must smell pretty much the same, whether it was hatched on the steppes or in the Brie. What's important to you is that I'll be there. You'll find another Sultan soon enough... And perhaps I'll find someone to play with too, but the person I really need, the one who gives my life a direction, will not be there. And then again, the advantage of being a dog is that if I sold you or gave you away to another master, as soon as he picked up a gun and started to stride over the fields, you'd follow him just as eagerly as you follow me. You don't know how lucky you are, Diane: a kind master, enough to eat and regular sport, that's all you need. You could be happy anywhere in the world. My friends think I am like that too… the international man. But it's no longer true… it's all a façade… I've put down roots and the thought of wrenching myself free of them terrifies me…*

Diane indicated her opinion of all this by stretching open her jaws in a long, gurgling yawn…

INT. LONDON, TEAROOM – DAY

An elegant tearoom in London's West End, catering to a fashionable clientele. A three-piece band – piano, violin and accordion – plays Johann Strauss and Offenbach (neither of whom had as yet made their name, but never mind that). Waiters bustle about between the tables carrying trays bearing silver tea services, delicate Dresden china and an assortment of scones and cakes.

In an alcove, slightly apart from the main body of the room, Turgenev is sitting at an empty table, his massive frame perched precariously on a slender gilt chair. He gazes anxiously over towards the revolving doors which lead out into the street.

Pauline Viardot comes through the doors. Less self-possessed than we have always seen her before, she glances almost timidly around the room and then catches sight of Turgenev, who has leapt to his feet and is beckoning to her. She hurries over to his table, giving the impression that she wished she were invisible.

Turgenev takes her hand, holds it for a long moment between his, and then ushers her into a chair.

PAULINE

Ivan, what are you doing here? Have you gone mad? I only came because your note said it was so important.   But Louis would be most upset if he knew I were here.

TURGENEV

I had to see you again. I had to see you alone.

PAULINE

But we said goodbye in Paris only three days ago.

TURGENEV

I said goodbye to you and Louis, yes. But I couldn't speak freely then. And I didn't know for certain if I was going back to Russia or not. I still don't know. It depends on you.

PAULINE
(alarmed)

On me?...

A waiter approaches their table.

PAULINE
(forcing herself to sound matter-of-fact)
I never expected to see you in London.

TURGENEV
It's not so far away… only twelve hours or so. We forget how modern methods of travel shorten distances…

WAITER
May I take your order, sir?

Turgenev looks at Pauline who shakes her head. Turgenev glances distractedly up at the waiter.

TURGENEV
We don't want anything, thank you.

WAITER.
I am very sorry sir… madam… but it is not permitted to sit at a table without taking some refreshment. If you wish, you could move to the lounge…

TURGENEV
(impatiently)
Very well, I'll have tea… Russian tea…with lemon, in a glass, if that can be done.

WAITER
Certainly, sir.

He moves away.

TURGENEV
I was saying, my fate depends on you. I have been in agonies of indecision over the past few months. Should I go back or shouldn't I? My mother says she needs me and threatens to die if I don't come. My Russian friends tell me it would be very dangerous. Louis… I have the impression… can't wait to see the back of me. But you… you have never given any sign of what you want me to do.

PAULINE

(after a pause)

I want you to do what's best for you.

TURGENEV

(desperately)

But I don't *know* what's best for me. All I know is that I have been happier these past three years at Courtavenel than ever before in my life. But perhaps life has decided it's time to show me its darker side. At any rate, I have finally come to a decision, and that's why I had to come over and see you…

He falls silent as the waiter comes back and puts the tea down on the table. After he has left, Pauline casts a quick glance at Turgenev. She is unable to hide her agitation.

PAULINE

And what is your decision?

TURGENEV

(after a long pause)

I will do whatever you tell me to.

Pauline gives a rather harsh laugh.

PAULINE

Is that what you call a decision? To leave your fate in the hands of others?

TURGENEV

You are not others. You are everything in the world to me.

Pauline can barely conceal a slight irritation.

PAULINE

But you mustn't let me be everything to you. I belong to my husband, my daughter, my art…

TURGENEV

And a little bit to me too?

She leans across the table and touches the sleeve of his jacket.

PAULINE

More than a little to you too. But Ivan, you also have other responsibilities. From what you have told us, it seems your family needs you, and…

TURGENEV
(interrupting her)

You are my only family. You are all I love in the world. Nothing else is of any importance. Nothing! I would rather sit on the edge of your nest than share a whole nest of my own with anyone else.

Pauline can think of nothing to say in answer to this. But her embarrassment is resolved, or at least diverted, by a middle-aged Englishwoman who bustles up, pink-cheeked, to their table and addresses Pauline.

ENGLISHWOMAN

I hope you won't mind my intruding, but you *are* Madame Pauline Viardot, are you not?

(Pauline nods)

Oh, I knew it, I knew it. I said to my husband…
(she waves vaguely in the direction of the table she has left, where a stout, rubicund man dressed in a tweed suit raises his teacup in salutation)
I said, I saw her in that opera of Bellini's about Romeo and Juliet – I never can remember its name – and how could I ever forget an artist like that.
(turning to Turgenev)
Isn't she wonderful, sir?

Pauline pulls herself together and, for the first time since she has come into the tearoom, reverts to something like her usual confident manner.

PAULINE

I'm sorry, Mrs…

ENGLISHWOMAN

Lady Weymouth.

PAULINE

Lady Weymouth, this is… Mr Muraviev.

TURGENEV

(with a wicked smile)

Count Muraviev…

PAULINE

(barely able to suppress a giggle)

I'm sorry, Count Muraviev. He has come over to… to offer me a season in St Petersburg.

ENGLISHWOMAN

Oh, how interesting. Well, I mustn't interrupt you any longer than I have already. It's been *such* a pleasure talking to you. And I can't wait to hear you in this new Meyerbeer opera. *Good*bye, then.

And with a smile at Turgenev, she returns to her table.

The interruption has helped Pauline clarify her thoughts. She now leans towards Turgenev and addresses him in an almost businesslike fashion:

PAULINE

Ivan, you said you had come all the way to England to ask my advice. Well, here it is. I think the time has come for you to leave us for a while. I shall miss you terribly… you must know that. But it doesn't have to be for ever. A year or so… the time it takes to settle your affairs… and then, who knows?…

(she forces a smile)

I may really come and do another season in St Petersburg…

(seeing the desperation in his eyes, she begins to lose her hard-won self-possession)

Don't make it so hard for me, Ivan, this is not *addio*, it's *au revoir*.

TURGENEV

(solemnly)

I feel absolutely sure that if I leave you now, we will not see each other again for many years. If ever.

(she tries to intervene, but he is not to be deflected)

So pardon me if I ask you to be truer than truth itself. You are telling

151

me, are you not, as gently as you know how, that you want me to go.

PAULINE

It's not that I want you to go, Ivan. It's that I think you ought to.

TURGENEV

The truth, Pauline, the truth. You want me to go.

She lowers her head, and only after several seconds raises it again and looks him straight in the eye.

PAULINE

Yes.

Turgenev remains absolutely motionless for a moment, then, overcome by emotion, seizes her hands and is about to pull her towards him, but is stopped by Pauline's resistance and her whispered 'Ivan', as she nods in the direction of the Weymouths' table.

 He makes a fearsome effort to regain control of himself, then stands up, formally takes her hand, kisses it and, with a choked 'Goodbye', hurries away from the table and out into the street.

Pauline doesn't turn her head but remains staring at the wall in front of her. Anyone who had seen Le Prophète *would recognize her expression. It is that of Fidès, compelled to deny that she is her son's mother in order to save his life.*

FIDÈS

Oui, la lumière brille à mes yeux obscurcis. Peuple, je vous trompais, ce n'est pas là mon fils!
(Yes, the light shines on my benighted eyes. People, I deceived you, that is not my son!)

Turgenev arrived back in Paris the next day and thought it prudent to write the following letter to Mme Viardot, knowing it would be also read by her husband.

Paris,
19 June, 1850

Dear and good Madame Viardot,

A week of reflection after seeing you and Viardot off at the Gare du Nord has only confirmed my resolution. I have to tell you that it is, alas, impossible for me to put off my departure. A longer absence from Russia,

152

together with the inevitable malicious gossip about my political contacts in France (and that includes Viardot, who, Annenkov tells me, is branded as an ultra-revolutionary) could well have me put on the list of official exiles whose work, of any kind whatsoever, is forbidden to be published in Russia.

And so, in four or five days' time, I leave... but with what sadness in the soul, what a weight on my heart! One's native country has its rights, of course; but isn't the country that is really native to us the one where we have found most affection, where the heart and mind feel most at ease? In that sense, there is no place on earth I love as much as Courtavenel. I always knew that I could not remain for ever in France, but I am finding the wrench of this departure indescribably painful. I know now how a plant must feel when it is plucked from the earth; it has put down its roots in all security and suddenly, from one moment to the next, everything is shattered. Well, in my case not, I hope, everything; we shall remain friends, shall we not?... affection and memories will still bind us.

Speaking of memories, I am leaving with your concierge a little carpet I've always had beside my bed. It is of no great beauty, but perhaps you could find somewhere to put it where your eyes would be bound to fall on it at least once a day.

I must go out now to take care of last-minute arrangements. Goodbye, goodbye, my dearest friends. I plunge into my desert; every step forward I take, it stretches before me, more immense and desolate than ever.

Your

I. Turgenev.

P.S. A kiss on both cheeks to Viardot. I fear the meeting between his Cid and my Diane will never take place. Poor Diane, she's going to be very cold in Russia. Like her master...

Before leaving Paris, Turgenev received this letter in reply.

London,
21 June, 1850

My dear, good Turgenev,

Your letter took me completely by surprise and left me stunned! Are you really leaving? Well, if you must, go with the firm intention of settling your affairs as soon as possible and returning to us. You will find your friends as you left them... no, even better, since they will love you that much more insofar as your absence has made them suffer.

You will be my first thought in the morning and my last at night. I shall try not to be too miserable over your absence, because for me unhappiness and sickness are as one... if I'm upset my health suffers and I become good for nothing. But, this said, if you think the news of your departure has done me good, you are much mistaken. I console myself by thinking of your absence only as one of the many we have undergone since first we met.

Poor little Diane! I know she will be lonely and miserable in one of those cages on your ship. And she'll probably be seasick. I can see you from here, holding her in your arms and consoling her, as though she were a little child. You are so kind and good-natured.

And so, my kind, good-natured Turgenev, bon voyage et à bientôt,

Pauline.

P.S. Louis wants to add a word.

My dear friend,
I was sure that you would go back to Russia, but I didn't want to indicate that I had divined your secret! I think you are doing the right thing. Four years have gone by, and your various affairs there will demand some months of your presence and your efforts. Painful though I am sure it was, let me assure you that your decision is praiseworthy.

I would recommend that you pass straight through St Petersburg, where dangers may lie in wait for you, and go directly to Moscow or the country. There you can settle down to work, to ensure that when you come back, you will be a man of independent means. I know that you will forgive this fatherly advice, knowing it comes from one who has only your best interests at heart.

I have no doubt that little Diane will soon be giving her Russian counterparts lessons when it comes to indicating woodcock and partridges. Tell her that Cid, who has heard a lot about her, sends her an appreciative, exploratory sniff and hopes to get to know her better very soon! Remember that dogs serve also to remind us of our real friends.

I hope that family business will leave you time to write and increase your reputation. Let us know at least the titles and themes of your future works.

I send you my most cordial and affectionate good wishes,

L. Viardot.

On June 25th, Turgenev left Paris and travelled to Stettin, where he took a boat for St Petersburg. Following Viardot's advice, he only stayed there two days and then went on to Moscow. At first he was undecided as to whether to stay with his brother and new sister-in-law or to go straight to the house his mother had taken in the Ostochenka. He felt he needed to be brought up to date by his brother before confronting Varvara. But when he saw the size of his mother's house and heard that the man in charge of running it was his old friend, half-brother and Berlin companion, Porfiry, he decided he could risk staying there at least overnight without her finding out. And if she did, he could always say he wanted to spring a surprise on her.

The doorbell was answered by an old manservant, whose face lit up when he recognized the young master. But Turgenev put a finger to his lips, told him to lead him to a room as far away as possible from the mistress's quarters, to fetch Porfiry and keep his mouth shut. It was not long before there was a knock on the door and his half-brother came into the room, tall and massive as ever, but thinner in the face than when he had last seen him. Turgenev approached him with open arms and was about to envelop him in a joyous embrace. But Porfiry stepped back in embarrassment, took both of Turgenev's hands in his and kissed them rapturously.

"Welcome home, master," he said, timidly.

"Master!" Turgenev exclaimed. "Porfiry, what is this? I don't remember you calling me master when I was translating your love letters to all those delectable *fräulein*."

"That was a long time ago, master. And we were not in Russia, and above all not under the roof of Varvara Petrovna. You must forgive me, but the pleasure of calling you Ivan Sergeyevich is not worth twenty lashes."

"Has it come to that?" Turgenev asked. When Porfiry glumly nodded his head, he motioned him into a chair, sat down opposite him and began to question him.

He learned how his mother had become virtually crazed by his four year absence. Every year she would have the wing of Spasskoye which she had made over to him cleaned, renovated and sometimes completely redecorated. Last summer, having sent him the paltry sum of 600 roubles, she had felt so sure that this would entice him home that she had announced to all the local gentry that she would be giving a ball on a certain date to welcome her son back from France. When it became clear he was not coming, rather than face the humiliation of cancelling the invitations, she had left for Moscow, unconcerned that the less well-informed of her guests would arrive for the ball, only to find the house deserted. When she came back, she put up a signpost at the point where the road to Spasskoye branched off from the highway with the defiant inscription: *ILS REVIENDRONT*. For Nikolai had never set foot in Spasskoye either for the past several years – not surprisingly, as his mother refused to meet the girl he was living with and was soon to marry.

Turgenev now asked Porfiry about his brother. "I heard that at least mother has finally consented to his marriage."

Porfiry pulled a long face. "Yes, after four years. And her gracious condescension has ruined him."

"Ruined him! How?"

"She made it a condition that he would resign his commission and leave St Petersburg, in return for which she would hand over to him the running of all her estates. But after their wedding, which she refused to attend, she claimed that he had misunderstood her."

"What did she give him instead?"

Porfiry gave a sour little laugh. "She appointed him to be administrator of *one* of her properties – and not a particularly big one at that. So now he is a sort of glorified bailiff, entirely dependent on the salary she pays him. Of course I don't know how much that is, but judging by his style of life when he comes to Moscow (he's here at the moment, by the way), it can't be very much."

Turgenev considered all this gloomily for a moment and made up his mind that, before presenting himself to his mother, he would have to confer with Nikolai. But now his attention returned to his half-brother and the grotesquely humiliating situation in which he found himself. In Berlin, thanks to Turgenev's insistence, he had enrolled in the medical faculty of the university, completed the course and emerged as a fully-fledged doctor. Turgenev had begged him to stay on in Germany, especially as he was practically engaged to a charming Berliner fellow-student, but he had insisted on following his master back to Spasskoye. Feeling a certain sense of responsibility, Turgenev asked him how he was treated in this household.

Porfiry replied, with a touch of his former easy-going good humour: "Better than the serfs, not so well as the dogs." Then his brow furrowed and a momentary flicker of resentment flashed into his eyes. "I hope you won't mind me saying this, master, but I had the misfortune to be the bastard from the wrong bed."

"What do you mean?"

"You remember Varya?"

"Little Bibi. Of course I do. With great affection. My little sister. I taught her how to ride." Seeing Porfiry's lips clamped together as though terrified of letting any indiscretion emerge from between them, he continued; "Why? Is she now being badly treated too?"

The tight lips twisted into a wry grin. "Oh no. Not her. No princess could be treated better than she is. Every week new clothes. Every month new jewels. Anything she wants she has only to ask for and the next day it's hers. At seventeen, she is the little mistress of the house. And that's what I have to call her; I, who am also her brother in a way. I would be flogged if I didn't call her mistress every time I address her."

After assuring him that he would do everything in his power to see that he was treated with greater dignity, Turgenev asked him where Nikolai and his wife put up when they were in Moscow.

"Put up! Oh, I forgot to tell you about that. As a wedding present she gave them a splendid town house on Pyatnitskaya Street."

"Ah, well, they're not so badly off then."

"Worse than before. She provided them with servants, horses, carriages… all the trappings of a luxurious life. Only one thing missing: any money to keep it all up."

An hour later, Turgenev saw with his own eyes that Porfiry had not allowed personal bitterness to tempt him into exaggeration. The carriage he had hired dropped him off in front of an elegant two-storey house, standing in its own courtyard with glimpses of a garden behind. But when he was shown inside, by a manservant who wasn't even dressed in livery, he noticed immediately that the hall was practically devoid of furniture, and the little there was was of the simplest, most functional kind.

As he ran his finger listlessly along the top of a ponderous wooden table, ploughing a deep furrow in the thick layer of dust on its surface, Nikolai came out of a side door and hurried forward to greet him. The two brothers embraced with all the pent-up affection stemming from a four-year absence. Since they were small boys, they had never seen a great deal of each other and if they had, they probably would not have been very close. Nikolai, two years older than Ivan, had turned into a rather graceless man. He would have made a model regimental officer, liked well enough by his comrades and respected well enough by his men. But that career had been denied to him, and his chronic lack of initiative made him ill-suited to any other. The only strong decision he had ever made in his life was his determination to marry the woman who was now his wife – and he was paying a crippling price for that. Anna Yakovlevna Schwarz was the daughter of a German woman who had once been Varvara Turgeneva's head housekeeper. She had all the efficient, sensible qualities of her nation and was genuinely devoted to Nikolai; but during her upbringing in an aristocratic household she had not managed to acquire a veneer of style and grace which might – just – have made her acceptable to Varvara as a daughter-in-law. For the tyrannical old woman, this was a *mésalliance* which made her other son's flirtation with the 'damn gypsy' seem like a match with one of Russia's most distinguished families.

Nikolai led Turgenev back into the room from which he had emerged. He called it his 'study', but all it contained was a long oak table, two upright chairs, a couple of threadbare easy chairs placed in front of a fireplace and a few books on some wooden shelves around the walls. He rang a bell and the same servant who had opened the door to Turgenev appeared and was asked to bring tea. He departed with such a surly expression that Turgenev asked if there was something wrong with the man. Nikolai replied evasively that he thought he was having trouble with his wife, but Turgenev, remembering Porfiry, deduced that he probably hadn't been paid for some time.

"I'm sorry Anna Yaklovevna is not here to greet you," Nikolai said. "We knew you were on your way, but not exactly when to expect you. She has gone out to do a few errands, but I don't think she'll be long."

"I am very anxious to meet her," Turgenev replied, "but perhaps it is better that the two of us discuss a few things between ourselves first. I had hoped that, with your marriage – on which, by the way, you have my warmest congratulations – your life would have been set back on course again. But I gather from a few words I had with Porfiry just now that this is far from being the case."

157

Nikolai gave a hollow laugh. "Back on course?! What course, Vanichka? I have no money, no job worth the name, a wife to support... and a child to mourn."

Turgenev stared at him in disbelief. "A child? I never knew... you never wrote..."

"You were so far away. You might as well have been living on another planet. I really thought you would never come back, so it didn't seem right to torment you with our sufferings. Yes, Anna and I had a daughter. A smiling, chubby blonde little..." He broke off to choke back an involuntary sob. "Of course, Mother would never consent to see her. Who knows, if she had, perhaps some family instinct, some feminine impulse might have..." Again he had to stop, but when he spoke again his voice was calm and his words measured. "When she was just eighteen months, she caught a bad cold. Although she was a little feverish, we both thought she would soon pull through. But suddenly she took a turn for the worse. The doctor we had been seeing said there was nothing to be alarmed about, but Anna, with a mother's instinct, didn't believe him. She begged me to persuade Mother to arrange a consultation with Doctor Kosenko, one of the best and most expensive doctors in Moscow, but I..." he bit his lip until Turgenev was afraid it would bleed... "my pride wouldn't let me appeal to Mama. I convinced myself that Lyubochka would soon get better. But twenty-four hours later she was dead."

Turgenev muttered his appalled condolences. But this last revelation of Nikolai's did at least have the effect of stiffening the resolve he had formed in the carriage on the way. "We must learn a lesson from this tragedy," he said. "We cannot continue to let ourselves, at thirty-four and thirty-two, be dominated by our mother for the rest of her days. Even if those days may now be numbered. Let's take advantage of the fact that the prodigal son has returned. She must at least pretend to be glad to see me. Perhaps this is our chance to see if we can't establish some kind of normal relations with her... talk to her as equals. After all we are her sons, not her slaves. We have always shown her the greatest respect. It's ridiculous and humiliating to go on living in fear of her every word as though she were some implacable oriental deity."

Nikolai, though sceptical, agreed, on the basis that at least a frank talk could do no harm. Their outlook could scarcely be worse. "But I fear she would rather employ us as stableboys than see us truly independent." With a rare flash of humour, he begged his brother not to carry the biblical parable too far, reminding him that the prodigal son had indeed been feted and showered with gifts, but his elder brother had gone empty-handed. "In her eyes," he reminded him, "at least you didn't marry your Pauline. Whereas I have committed the ultimate sin of disobedience."

A veil of sadness momentarily clouded Turgenev's eyes. "I cannot marry her," he said, "because there is an insurmountable obstacle in the shape of a good and loving husband. Otherwise…" but he left the sentence unfinished. Saying that he would wait to meet his sister-in-law another time, he said goodbye to Nikolai and promised to arrange for the two of them to lunch with their mother the following day.

Turgenev was not prepared for the sight that met his eyes when he and Nikolai were shown into his mother's sitting-room. He had left her a vigorous, wiry, erect woman in her mid-sixties, still capable, if she chose, of spending an entire day in the saddle. Now he went over to kiss the clawed, withered hand of a frail old lady whose puffy face, protruding belly and grotesquely swollen legs proclaimed the dropsy from which she had been suffering for the past couple of years. Despite all that had happened, he couldn't help feeling pleased when she greeted him with the undisguised delight and affection she had sometimes shown him on his return from a university term.

"My dearest boy," she said, holding on to his hand and patting it convulsively, "so you've finally come back to see your old mother. She's not quite what she used to be, but now that her Vanichka's home again, you'll see, she'll soon be on the mend. Welcome home, welcome home! And now stand back and let me have a look at you." An imperious wave at Nikolai, who had been waiting in the background. "You too, you too. I hardly ever set eyes on you either. Well now," she turned to Varya, who had been standing at the head of the chaise longue on which she was stretched out, "what was I saying to you just now? There's not a mother in Moscow who could boast two such handsome sons. Wasn't I right?"

Varya nodded and smiled. "You certainly were, madame."

"Handsome they are, but thoughtless rogues as well. What is this, Vanichka? You stay away four years, and then when you come back you don't even come to greet your mother the moment you arrive. You have to keep her waiting on tenterhooks for a whole day!"

Turgenev wondered how his mother had known about his arrival yesterday, until he noticed the smug smile on the face of his half-sister. She had seen him the day before on his return from Nikolai, and they had had a brief exchange in the hall. The playful, affectionate little girl he remembered had turned into a contained young miss of seventeen, who, instead of kissing him, had coolly offered him her hand and formally bid him welcome home. Neither her long sallow face nor her awkward bony body were particularly appealing, but he noticed that she was turned out at the height of the current fashion: a long afternoon dress of patterned material with a deep falling collar set off her smooth white shoulders. Her black hair fell tightly over her ears; her necklace was studded with emeralds; and the ring on her right hand was one Turgenev remembered his mother often wearing. To his joyful cry of "Bibi!" she had returned a moue of distaste and begged him not to call her that any more. "Everyone now calls me Varya," she had said primly. Remembering that Porfiry had said she was 'the mistress of the house' he had asked her to arrange for a family luncheon the next day, but not to tell his mother that he was already here.

"It seems that somebody doesn't know how to keep a secret," he now remarked, amiably enough.

Varya's smile grew broader and without a trace of embarrassment she said: "You couldn't really expect me to keep such wonderful news to myself. This is the moment Varvara Petrovna has been waiting for for years."

"Only to have it spoiled at the last minute," the old woman grumbled.

Turgenev thought of the lecture he had been reading to himself all morning, rather like an actor going over his lines before a first night, and said to her light-heartedly: "Now then, Mama, let's not start immediately hammering away at what I haven't done. Wouldn't you rather hear what I have? I didn't come to see you earlier this morning because I had a business appointment…"

"Business!? What business are you engaged in?"

"My business… my writing…" Ignoring the 'Hrrumph' which this caused, he proceeded calmly: "I went to the *Sovremennik* office (in case you've forgotten, that's the paper which publishes my stories) this morning and spoke to Nekrasov. He encouraged me to write another two or three, and when there are a couple of dozen or so he told me he will try and get them published in book form. There may of course be some problems with the censorship, but he seemed to think it might slip by. And as luck would have it, Nadezhda Samoilova, the actress I used to know and who's quite famous now, was in the office and she asked me to write a one-act play for her and her brother, which they will put on here in Moscow this winter and next spring at the Aleksandrinsky in St Petersburg. Now don't tell me that's not quite a good morning's work!"

He looked around for confirmation and perhaps even congratulation, but nobody, not even Nikolai, seemed to be paying much attention. His mother's mind had obviously wandered far away and she now broke in with: "I hope you two boys are hungry. I've had a fine spread laid on for you. Varya, go and tell those lazy servants that it's high time we were at table."

When Varya had left the room, she turned to her sons and expatiated on the young girl's merits. "I can't tell you how good she has been to me all these years. What a contrast to you two! She couldn't have shown me more love and care if she had been my own daughter." The two brothers of course knew perfectly well that was exactly what she was, but neither would have dreamed of referring to it. On Varya's return to announce that luncheon was on the table, Turgenev leaned over to help his mother to her feet and put her walking stick into her hand. He started to slip his arm under her shoulders to support her, but she pushed it away. "I can manage perfectly well on my own, thank you very much. I have had to, for many years now."

Her claim to have 'laid on a good spread' was an understatement. The sideboard was loaded with an abundance and variety of food and wine that would have furnished a princely banquet for a dozen people. After Varya had set down in front of his mother a frugal plate of a couple of fillets of fish and a few runner beans, Turgenev, forcing himself to remember the purpose of the visit, helped himself sparingly to a slice of herring mousse, some egg mayonnaise and a crackling piece of suckling pig covered with horseradish sauce. Out of the corner of his eye he noticed Nikolai heaping two plates with stuffed goose, roast beef, spiced meat balls and sautéed potatoes, no doubt calculating, Turgenev reflected sadly, that at least twenty-four hours could now go by before he would need another meal.

Varvara was delighted to see her sons enjoying her hospitality, and she reverted to the good mood with which she had first greeted Turgenev. Most of the conversation took place between the two of them. Nikolai still had difficulty in communicating with his mother at all, and was more than content to devote his full attention to the formidable task in front of him. Varya ate daintily and spoke little; but her keen, restless eyes seemed to take in every nuance of what passed between mother and son.

Although pleased that his mother was making herself so agreeable ('this should ease what has to come later,' he thought) Turgenev was astonished that she made no reference whatsoever to the four years he had spent in France. It was as though he had never been away. She went at length into all the changes she had made at Spasskoye – the orchards she had had planted here, the deforestation that had been carried out there – and asked him countless times when he would be coming to see everything. Tomorrow? The next day? Saturday? He tried to fob her off with a vague, "Soon, Mama" and to introduce the subject of Courtavenel, starting to comment on the similarities and differences between a Russian and French country estate. But she turned to Varya in mid-sentence and told her to ring for the dessert. Varya nodded meaningfully over towards Nikolai, whose plate was still not quite empty, at which the old lady uttered a contemptuous snort and barked: "That's quite enough for him! He has a German wife who has nothing better to do all day than cook for him. *Fleisch und Kartoffeln*. She must at least be good for that!" Nikolai flushed and pushed his plate away, flashing a glance of suppressed rage at his brother, who responded with a mute appeal to keep calm or all would be lost.

Halfway through his dessert, which was the blackcurrant pudding he had loved as a boy, Turgenev decided that the time had come cautiously to draw aside the curtain of bonhomie and see what lay behind. After thanking his mother for remembering his favourite pudding and assuring her it was just as delicious as he had always remembered it, he remarked, in what he hoped appeared a casual tone: "Mother, I think you, Nikolai and I should take this opportunity to discuss a few business matters."

"Business matters!" The eyes squeezed tight from behind their surrounding rolls of yellowish fat. "You keep on mentioning that word. What have you ever known about business?"

"I'm talking about family business now. And specifically about Nikolai's and my future."

"Ah! You mean you've come begging for money. Neither of you are capable of making any yourselves, so you come crawling to me. Is that why I had the honour of this visit! Or is it that you want to dispossess me? Force me out of my own home? Take over Spasskoye? Well, if that was your intention I can answer you in one word. Never!"

Turgenev managed to remain calm. "No one wants to force you to do anything, Mama. But I think," he glanced at Varya, "it would be better if these matters were discussed just between the three of us."

Varvara hesitated for a moment and then nodded to Varya. "Very well, leave us. It's better that your young ears be spared all this. But remember, if I ring for you, bring me… bring me what I left with you this morning."

Varya nodded gravely and silently left the room. Varvara glared at her two sons, all trace of her previous good humour erased. She opened her tightly clamped lips just wide enough to spit out: "Well, what is it you want to discuss?"

Turgenev glanced at Nikolai, who nodded; it had already been agreed that the younger brother would act as spokesman. "We just think, Mama, that perhaps the time has come for you to provide us with some regular income, however small. We are both over thirty and neither of us has been a disgrace to you. Nikolai is a married man and has no regular employment since, in answer to your wishes, he resigned his commission. I have worked very hard at my writing and have managed to achieve some small success, which I now hope to build on. But it is very hard for us to go around without a rouble in our pockets. And I cannot imagine that this is what you would want for us. It's not as if we were asking for you to make a great sacrifice. It should surely be possible for you to allow us an income of a few thousand roubles a year without it impinging to any degree on your way of life."

He paused and waited for her reply, his heart, to his annoyance, thumping furiously away in his chest. The old woman looked at them both with her hard eyes and then broke into a disagreeable cackle of a laugh. "I was expecting something of this sort. You're both very good at saying what you expect of me as a mother, but you never give a moment's thought as to what I might have expected of you. I had hoped that, as befits your birth and upbringing, you would have risen to some position in the state or the armed services by now, and would find time to take some of the burden of running my properties off your old mother's shoulders. Not to mention giving me the pleasure of providing me with grandchildren." Turgenev shot an uneasy glance at Nikolai, who had opened his mouth, but now shut it again. "But no. Nothing of that sort. One of you marries a woman who might just about be fit to be his housekeeper, and the other leaves a promising ministerial job to go gallivanting off abroad in pursuit of a married actress... or singer, or whatever she is." Now it was Turgenev's turn to have to force himself to remain silent. *Is any amount of money worth having to listen to this?* "I suppose it never crosses either of your minds how much pain, how much bitter disappointment this has caused me. But fortunately for you, I am used to disappointment. I have looked into its face all my life. And as I told you, your request has not taken me by surprise. To some degree it is not unreasonable. All young men need some money to start to make their way, even when they've made the pretty poor beginnings you two have. So I will show you what I propose." She picked up a little handbell that was always beside her and rang it.

The two brothers held their breath as they waited for Varya to return. Was the humiliation they had forced themselves to accept about to bear fruit? Would they be able to look back on this evening as a watershed in their lives? It was with a feeling of guarded optimism that they saw their half-sister come back into the room holding two rolled-up pieces of paper that looked like official documents.

Varvara took them from her, studied them carefully for a moment and handed one to each of them. She gave her sons a triumphant look, as if to say, 'See how you misjudged me!' and announced: "These are deeds to two properties, which you probably remember. I propose giving Sytchovo to you, Nikolai, and Kadnoye to you, Ivan. You may do with them what you want: live off the revenue or sell them outright, if you so wish. Now, tell me, does that meet your demands?"

Turgenev, without even looking at his document, bent down and seized his mother's hands, lavishing kisses on them. But before he had finished thanking her, he heard behind him Nikolai's hesitant, embarrassed voice saying: "Excuse me, Mama, I also would like to thank you, from the bottom of my heart. But, as perhaps you realize, there is something more that needs to be done.."

"Something more? What are you talking about?" the old woman snapped.

"For these documents to be valid, they need to be drawn up in front of a notary and for each page to have an official stamp. As they are... just like this... they are quite worthless."

"Always wanting more. Nothing's ever good enough for you, is it? Very well, we'll see about this tomorrow. And now I must ask you to leave. You've quite tired me out, the two of you."

As the door closed behind them, Turgenev whispered to his brother to follow him to his room. Once there, he asked Nikolai if he didn't feel he had been too harsh. "It must surely be her intention to have these documents properly legalized. Perhaps she had just forgotten about it. After all, she is an old lady and not at all well."

"Of course I wish you were right," his brother replied. "But I don't believe it for one moment. She may be old and ill but, God forgive me, her soul will leave her body before her business sense does. And while you were thanking her, I happened to look over at Varya. I swear to you there was a look of triumphant mockery in her eyes, which it was fearful to see in someone so young. I am convinced this whole scene was staged for our benefit. The two of them are in league to make us look ridiculous."

Turgenev clasped his head in his hands and gazed at his brother in despair. "If you are right, it means that we are totally impotent. But let's not assume the worst until we have no alternative. Tomorrow morning all will be clear... one way or the other."

Nikolai nodded glumly and bid his brother goodbye. After he had left, Turgenev threw himself fully-dressed on his bed, closed his eyes and tried to bring some order to the confused jumble of ideas, sensations and impressions that had crowded in on him from the moment he had crossed the Russian border...

... *is it for this I left an existence when each hour seemed more blessed than the last? Shouldn't I have obeyed that inner voice which kept insisting I should stay in France? What did I come back for? First, to try to put my career as a writer on a more secure footing... well, this morning was encouraging, but it would be foolish to expect too much from it. Second, to regularize my financial position and afford a little pleasure to my mother, who cannot have long to live; but if what Nikolai says is true, can even the claims of motherhood have any validity in the light of such inhuman behaviour? What is my choice now? To crawl back to France without a rouble in my pocket? Or bow down and accept my mother's tyranny? Live in poverty or lose my dignity. No need to hesitate over that. Perhaps I am beginning to understand. The only right action to take is to confront my mother. If she has really played this trick on us, for the first time in my life I must stand up to her. It's not the sort of behaviour that comes easily to me, and the fact that she is so ill makes it doubly difficult. But perhaps I should admit that she, old and ill, is made of a tougher fibre than I shall ever be. And after all, I have little to lose: the worst she can do is cut me off; and that will simply officialize my poverty...* and taking some comfort from a decision made, he closed his eyes and soon fell into a deep, untroubled sleep.

Later in the evening, he had just finished dressing and was about to leave his room on his way to a supper party with friends, when there was a timid but urgent knocking at his door. He opened it to see Porfiry standing there, white in the face and visibly nervous. "Excuse me, master, but there is something I have to tell you," he almost babbled.

Refraining from begging him once again not to call him master, Turgenev led him into the room and asked him to sit down. But the young man couldn't wait to unburden himself. "I have just been talking," he said breathlessly, "to Maxim Tropakin. I don't know if you remember him, but he's now the chief administrator of all your mother's estates. He knows you're here, but he didn't dare speak to you himself. I can't blame him, I'm probably risking my life doing this, but I thought you had to know."

"Know what, Porfiry?" Turgenev asked quietly. "Don't worry, from now on you are under my protection."

"Well, Tropakin had just come from Varvara Petrovna and was leaving that moment for the country. He had had orders from the mistress regarding the properties of Kadnoye and Sytchovo…"

"Those are the properties which mama offered to Nikolai and me a couple of hours ago. Perhaps she wanted him to regularize the deeds of sale."

"Not exactly, Ivan Sergeyevich. His orders were to tell the bailiffs of those two properties to sell everything, immediately: all the grain stored in the barns, even the corn that has not yet been harvested. And if that was to prove too difficult to arrange, they were to burn all the fields. There was to be no seed left for next year's sowing. If they didn't follow her orders to the letter, she would have them both sent into exile in Siberia, along with their families."

Turgenev stood for a moment, silent, aghast. Then he took a deep breath, patted Porfiry on the shoulder and thanked him for his courage. "I shall be leaving this house tomorrow," he said. "I don't know as of this moment where I shall be going, but wherever it is, you will be coming with me."

INT. MOSCOW, VARVARA PETROVNA'S BOUDOIR – EVENING

Varvara Petrovna is sitting in a high-backed chair in front of a small, round table covered with a lace cloth, on which cards are laid out for a game of patience. She is playing slowly and methodically. Every so often her eyes flicker over towards an open desk, on which the two deed-of-sale documents are lying.

Close by, Varya, reclining comfortably in an easy chair, is working on a piece of embroidery. She glances occasionally towards her mother to ascertain that all is well. A samovar is bubbling away in a corner of the room.

VARYA

Would you like some tea, Varvara Petrovna?

VARVARA
(curtly)

No.

Surprised by the abrupt tone of voice, Varya looks over again and her face registers something between alarm and astonishment.
THE CAMERA GOES IN TIGHT on Varvara's hands manipulating the cards. They are shaking violently.
Varya raises her eyebrows, considers saying something, but decides against it and goes back to her needle.

A KNOCK ON THE DOOR

VARVARA

Who is it?

TURGENEV(O.S.)

Ivan, mother.

VARVARA

Come in, come in.

Turgenev comes into the room, closing the door behind him. He is elegantly dressed for the evening's entertainment he has been forced to forego, but his face is pale and drawn and his nervousness tangible.

It is hard to detect whether Varvara is pleased to see him or not. Perhaps she doesn't know herself. In any event, she tries to make herself agreeable.

VARVARA

Sit down, Vanichka. I wasn't expecting to see you again until tomorrow. Would you like Varya to pour you some tea?

Turgenev remains standing. He tries to suppress the tremor in his voice and to indicate that he is here on business, not pleasure.

TURGENEV

No, mother, I would like Varya to be good enough to leave us for a few minutes.

167

VARVARA

Ah, no, no! You can't always be sending Varya out of the room.
Anything you have to say, you can say in front of her.

TURGENEV

As you wish. I have come to talk about those properties you said
you were going to cede to us…

VARVARA

(interrupting)

Ah, so you've heard already! I didn't waste any time, did I?

The apparently cool effrontery of this leaves Turgenev speechless. He stands and stares at his mother incredulously as she continues:

VARVARA

I may be an old lady, but I still know how to get things done in a
hurry if the need be. Why are you looking at me so strangely?
Don't you believe me? Varya, show Ivan the deeds.

Varya gets up, takes the documents from the desktop and impassively hands them to Turgenev…
…who gazes at them in total disbelief. As he automatically leafs through the pages…
…THE CAMERA GOES IN TIGHT and we see at the bottom of each page an official stamp and a notary's signature.
Turgenev moistens his lips. He can hardly bring himself to speak.

TURGENEV

You had them notarized!

VARVARA

Of course. Nikolai was right. They wouldn't have had any value
otherwise.

Turgenev fights to try and stay calm. But then the blood rushes to his face, turning his previous pallor to a deep crimson, and the words fly equally uncontrollably from his mouth.

TURGENEV

And what value do they have now? Two properties without a grain
of corn in the granaries or the fields!…

VARVARA

(torn between surprise and rage)

How did you...?...Who told you?...

TURGENEV

Never mind how I know. It was not Trophakin who told me, at any
rate. By the way, did you remember to tell him to have the livestock
slaughtered? Otherwise, who knows?, they might fetch something
at a sale and my brother and I would have two roubles to put in our
pockets. You wouldn't want that to happen, would you?

Varvara's face is a mask of fury.

VARVARA

I forbid you to talk to me like this. How dare you? You have no
right...

But Turgenev is not to be stopped.

TURGENEV

How dare I!? The biggest mistake of my life was never to have
dared before. If I had – who knows? – perhaps you might have
discovered there are other human beings living in this world beside
yourself. But I had to go to another country to learn, away from
you, that love is not an endless series of obligations. People who
love delight in giving... even if it means making some small
personal sacrifice. There's no pain in that... only joy. But you are
afraid to give my brother and me the least little thing, for fear of
losing your power over us. We have always been good sons to you,
but you have never trusted us. But then you've never trusted
anyone or anything. The only thing you trust is your own power.

VARVARA

Ah! So I'm a monster, am I?

TURGENEV

I don't know what you are, Mother, or what goes on in your head,
but I do know that no one can be happy anywhere near you. You
inspire fear, not love. Nikolai and I would have liked to love you,
but you don't want love... you don't know what love is... you want

169

servitude… you want everyone to crawl before you and then, when you throw them a crumb, to wag their tails like grateful dogs. I can tell you one thing… my brother and I will never ask you for anything again. Our father left us a small property and we'll go and live there. Not even you can take that away from us.

Varvara fumbles for her walking stick and heaves herself out of her chair. Varya starts to move towards her, but is imperiously waved away. Hobbling to the door on her misshapen swollen legs, she passes a table on which stands a photograph of Turgenev. She picks it up and hurls it to the floor.

SOUND OF SHATTERING GLASS

Varya again moves forward, with the intention of picking it up, but the old woman turns on her, her breast heaving painfully, her eyes almost bulging out of her head in fury.

VARVARA
Leave it where it is! I… NO…LONGER… HAVE… SONS.

She goes out of the room leaving Varya, less composed than usual, gazing in speechless bewilderment at Turgenev, who is already beginning to half-regret what he has done.

The property of Turgenevo, which lay about ten miles from Spasskoye, had been given to Sergey Turgenev outright as part of his marriage settlement with Varvara Lutovinova. When his two sons, together with Anna Yakovlevna, arrived there from Moscow, they found the land neglected and the house dilapidated. No one had lived there for many years and marauders had made off with much of the furniture and anything else that they thought they could sell or use. Here Nikolai's wife came into her element. She conscripted a bevy of young men and women from the village and organized them into groups for scrubbing floors, washing china and crockery, mending broken chairs and extracting spiders' webs from every corner of floor and ceiling. Within two days, a rudimentary kitchen was functioning and two bedrooms had been prepared, one in the main house for herself and Nikolai and another in an abandoned paper factory in the grounds for Turgenev.

Turgenev watched his sister-in-law with interest. He admired her practical sense and appreciated the efficiency with which she organized his and Nikolai's lives. She took over the running of the house as though she had been doing it all her life – which was just as well, as neither he nor his brother would have known where to start. But he also noticed how sharp she could become if Nikolai irritated her in any way, and he wondered if this might not lead to acrimony in the future. For the time being, Nikolai treated her with the most loving tenderness, as she had just announced that she was expecting another baby. Turgenev went out of his way to be as agreeable to her as he could, both because he wanted to suppress any trace of sharing his mother's unworthy reasons for disliking her and because he now saw, day after day, how dependent Nikolai was on her. If there was an element of hypocrisy in the degree to which he set out to charm her, he thought it was the least he could do to compensate Nikolai for the humiliation he had suffered at their mother's hands.

Another of Anna's qualities which he appreciated was her concern for the condition of the serfs on the property. The first weekend they were there, she had Nikolai drive her round and managed to visit almost all the peasants' cottages. Wherever there was a sick child – and rare was the family without one – she would cradle it in her arms for a moment or stroke its feverish brow, advising the mother on what she should do to cure it. The peasants, who had been left to their own devices for many years, were glad to have the big house occupied again. Many of them remembered the two brothers from when they had been little boys, paddling in a canoe on the river which flowed through the property, or dangling their lines while waiting impatiently for a perch to bite. On the Sunday evening after their arrival, they all congregated outside the house to celebrate the renaissance of Turgenevo. Dressed in traditional costume, they listened solemnly as Nikolai made a speech to say how happy he was to be there and outlined his plans for a more prosperous future for all of them. The headman then said a few words in return, welcoming the 'new masters', after which, to Turgenev's embarrassment, the ceremony of cheek kissing had to be gone through with everyone present. "I realized at that moment," he confided to his sister-in-law the next morning, "after the three hundredth beard had scratched my cheeks, that I could never have been a public man."

A selection of pies and pastries, which Anna Yakovlevna and her kitchen squad had been preparing all afternoon, were now distributed, along with jugs of vodka. Three of the villagers brought out musical instruments – a violin, an accordion and a balalaika – and began to play. Then there was singing, first in chorus and then from two soloists: a burly giant in his early forties with a luxuriant black beard almost down to his waist, to match his rich dark bass; and a slim young girl, whose delicate beauty Turgenev had already noticed when her soft flesh had offered his cheek a momentary respite from abrasive hair. They sang the songs he remembered from his childhood, and for the first time since he had set foot again on Russian soil, he felt a certain sense of contentment at being home again. 'There is, after all,' he wrote to Pauline, 'something in the air of your homeland, something indefinable which seeps into you and reaches your heart. I suppose it's a sort of silent, involuntary sympathy of the body for the soil on which it was born, for all the manifestations of nature you grew up with, so that even the imperfections, the endless monotony of the steppes, for instance, become as dear to you as the faults of a person you love. I may be unhappy here, but I shall be unhappy in my own element. If only you were here to share it with me… the song that young girl sang was very like the one I taught you and you gave as an encore after a concert in St Petersburg. You held the heart of every Russian in the audience in the palm of your hand that night. Mine is still there…'

After the singing came dancing. Three chairs had been drawn up for the 'gentry', and again Turgenev felt uneasy sitting like a monarch in the royal box watching a performance put on for his benefit. He was relieved when Anna Yakovlevna asked him why he didn't go and dance himself. He got up from his chair and went directly to the young singer, whom he had already noticed dancing with a surprising grace. But his embarrassment was not over. As soon as she had accepted, with a shy smile, his offer to dance with him, everyone else stopped and formed a circle around the couple, clapping to the rhythm of the music and encouraging them with shouts and cheers… *Now I'm the performer. I almost wish I were back in the royal box… and yet how entrancing this girl is, with what natural, surely unconscious flirtation she lifts the hem of her skirt just above her ankles and then lets it drop again … four years ago I would already be thinking of seducing her … hypocrite, you're thinking of it now, but this time you won't because, after four years outside Russia, the idea of the young landlord spending one night in the arms of a peasant girl, only to forget her the next morning, is repellent… still, there is something undeniably provocative in the way, when her eyes meet yours, her lips purse into a hint of a teasing smile . ..*

A couple of days later, on paying his first visit to Spasskoye in four years, Turgenev had reason to remember these reflections. He had decided to go in order to make an attempt to heal the rift with his mother. Perhaps if he made a partial apology, she might decide that seeing even a rebellious son was better than not seeing him at all.

So he set off with Diane in a two-wheeled cart, which he left at a farm a couple of miles from Spasskoye. He had sent word to Varya that he would be arriving about midday and to try and persuade his mother to see him. Having a couple of hours to kill, he made his way on foot over the familiar countryside, finding little game to take his mind off the thought of another searing confrontation.

He found Varya waiting for him by the gatekeeper's lodge at the beginning of the long drive that led up to the main house. She seemed surprised at his appearance: dusty breeches, muddy boots, a gun resting on his elbow and an ancient leather gamebag slung at his side. She informed him in the cool, faintly mocking manner to which he was beginning to get accustomed but was far from liking, that his mother absolutely refused to see him. "I tried to persuade her, Ivan

Sergeyevich," she assured him, "but she would not budge. She even told me that if I saw you, she did not wish to hear anything about our meeting; but that I was to tell you it was useless you writing to her, because she would tear up your letters unread. I'm afraid for the moment there is nothing you can do. You should perhaps know that for all the days before we left Moscow, she refused to allow anyone to pick up the broken pieces of your photograph."

Saddened but unsurprised, Turgenev asked rather formally after her health and was told that although the journey from Moscow had tired her, her pleasure at being back in Spasskoye seemed to be having a beneficial effect. As Varya went on to express her regret at the turn things had taken, Turgenev's already wandering attention was distracted by a scene he noticed taking place in the gatekeeper's garden. A group of young children between the ages of five and ten had been half working, half playing at picking vegetables. They had apparently now finished their task and the gatekeeper's wife was ushering them over towards a pump, where they could wash the soil off their hands, knees and faces. As they were all crowded round the pump, clamouring as to who should use it first, the woman, who had not seen Turgenev, clapped her hands and called out, in a harsh, ungracious voice: "Mam'zelle Pelageya first! Don't forget your manners in front of the gentry, children!" At this, the rest of the children giggled and formed two lines, leaving one little girl to glare at them all with a furious face before hastily splashing some water over herself and turning to run away.

Noticing Turgenev's interest in this scene, Varya asked him in an expressionless tone if he knew who that little girl was. "How could I?", he replied. Varya gave him a curious glance and then called the girl, who was heading up the drive towards the house. "Pelageya, come back here a minute!" The girl walked reluctantly up to them, scowling sullenly. When Turgenev looked into her face, he felt his heart miss a beat and a dry tightening in his throat. It was as though he were looking at a photograph of himself as a boy, which had miraculously assumed flesh and blood...

... a seamstress in my mother's employ, I even remember her name, Avdotya Yermolaevna, I must have been twenty-one or so, alone and bored in the country on one of those July days when the heat arouses your sensuality, but as often as not makes you too lazy to do anything about it, she passed me in the corridor carrying a pile of linen, I bumped into her on purpose, she excused herself but gave me a bold smile, I suggested she come to my room when she'd finished her work, as I had some shirts with frayed cuffs which needed mending, she came, it was all over in ten minutes, I gave her some money, she left, and soon after I went back to St Petersburg... later, when I was at university, I heard that she'd become pregnant, but my mother arranged everything, packing her off to Moscow and keeping the girl, when she was born, at Spasskoye with the idea of her eventually entering service...

"So your name's Pelageya, is it?"

173

"Yes."

"How old are you?"

"Eight."

"And why were they all laughing at you?"

"'Cos my father's a *barin*."

"I see. And who's your mother?"

"She makes dresses in Moscow. When I'm older, I'm going to join her there and learn to sew."

"Are you now! Does your mistress agree to that?"

The little girl opened her mouth to answer, and then looked up at Varya with an expression of fear in her eyes, before muttering, "I don't know."

"Her mistress is not pleased with her," Varya said.

"Why?"

"Because she dared to stamp her foot and shout in her presence."

Turgenev turned back to the girl. "What made you do that?" he asked, but the child remained mutinously silent.

"Come on, you can tell me. Don't be afraid, Miss Varya will not tell tales."

"I was taken into a room with a lot of people and the mistress pointed at me and asked them who I looked like. They all started to laugh, and I... " she broke off and bit her lip in fury at the recollection.

Turgenev looked at her gravely for a moment and then asked, haltingly: "And where is your father?"

An indifferent shrug. "He's not in Russia, that's all I know."

"I see. Well you'd better go back in now. And if I were you, I'd keep out of the mistress's way for a few days."

The child gave him a surprised look, unused as she was to an adult taking any interest in her, let alone offering her advice. Then she scuttled away up the drive.

Turgenev turned to Varya. "Why is she allowed to go around in that state – uncombed, unwashed, her dress all in shreds?"

"She lives with the serfs now – in a swineherd's family."

"I thought my mother was bringing her up to be in domestic service."

"She was. But she changed her mind. She decided the girl was quite unfit."

"Why?"

Varya seemed rather irritated by the persistence of Turgenev's questioning. "Because she was so rebellious, I suppose."

"And when was this decision taken?"

"Just the other day. After we got back from Moscow."

Turgenev nodded grimly. "I see. Perhaps you would be good enough, Varya, to tell my mother ... "

"You forget, Ivan Sergeyevich," Varya interrupted him, "that I am not allowed to refer to my meeting with you."

Turgenev shook his head in disbelief. "Well then, I shall write to you. And perhaps you could drop the subject of my letter into your conversation one evening. I'm sure my mother will listen to you. It is obvious that she holds you in very high esteem. And I am sure," he could not resist adding, "that you have done a great deal to deserve that esteem."

Not knowing quite how to take this, Varya contented herself with a slight nod as she took Turgenev's outstretched hand. "I will do my best, Ivan Sergeyevich. You may count on that."

Would that I could, Turgenev thought, as he started to trudge back towards the farm where he had left his cart, a variety of painful emotions churning around in his mind. *I don't trust that young woman to do anything that isn't in her immediate interests. But somehow or other I must find a way of changing the direction of that little girl's life. What a disturbing sight! I can't picture the mother's features at all, I don't even remember whether she was fair or dark; her name, yes, for some reason, I remember her name, but gazing into that child's face – Pelageya, they called her, Russian for Pauline, dear God! – was like looking into a mirror and seeing myself twenty years ago… uncanny, disconcerting experience. Shaming too. Two months ago I was playing games with Louis and Pauline's little Louise, she must be just about the same age, and beginning to teach her a few words of German, and she'd be sitting opposite me in her pretty little velvet dress, swinging her legs with their white socks and shiny polished shoes, her neat curls falling across her chubby pink face when she shook her head unable to remember* liebe *for amour, and here's this little ragamuffin, filthy, skinny, ill-fed I'll be sworn, and with what looked very much like a bruise under one of her eyes… I must find a way of taking her away from that place…*

He discussed it with Nikolai and Anna that evening. His brother of course knew of Pelageya's existence, but apparently had never mentioned it to his wife who, far from being shocked, seemed to find the idea rather amusing. After describing the scene he had witnessed that morning, he asked Nikolai's advice as to what he should do. After a moment's thought, his brother suggested sending the little girl to a convent in Moscow until she was twelve or so, after which she could live with her mother and learn her trade. Turgenev had been thinking along similar lines himself, but when he saw that Anna was shaking her head, he asked her for her opinion.

"I think it would be cruel to send the poor little thing to a convent at such a young age. After all she's been through. What she needs is to be brought up for a while in a family, like any other child. Why don't we take her in here? We would have to ask you, Ivan Sergeyevich, to contribute a little more to the household accounts. It's hard enough already to make ends meet without having another

175

mouth to feed. But I would be happy to be a mother to her. We would, of course",
she added with a determined gleam in her eye, "have to absolutely forbid any
meeting between her and her grandmother. An hour with her would undo weeks
of all the good we might be able to do."

"Do you really think Mother would care?" Nikolai asked. "She probably
wouldn't even notice she had gone – unless it came into her mind to humiliate her
again in front of her guests."

Anna's lips tightened into a half-ironic, half-pitying smile. "Oh, Nikolasha,
how little you know your mother! She is indifferent to Pelageya's existence now,
because she is there for her to do what she wants with. She is in control, which is
all that matters to her. But if the little girl was taken away from her, if she knew
that her beloved Ivan's little daughter was being brought up by us – and particularly
by me – can't you see the rage she'd fly into?! I can just imagine the scene with that
little viper of a Varya." She started not very convincingly to imitate an old woman's
whine. "'They've taken away my only grandchild, Varushka. Neither of the
wretches has produced a proper one for me, and now the only delight of my old
age – poor little thing that she is – is no longer allowed to see her grandmother.'
Oh, I can hear it all!"

Turgenev's thoughts had been following another line. "If I took up your very
kind offer," he murmured ruminatively, "it would mean virtually kidnapping the
girl. Under the circumstances, the practical difficulties shouldn't be insuperable,
but, morally, I don't know how…"

"Morally!" His sister-in-law's already red cheeks flushed deeper in
indignation. "You have a strange moral sense, Vanichka." (This was the first time
she had ever called him by his diminutive. Taking a leading part in this family
discussion had given her a new confidence.) "Can you really have scruples about
taking a small child away from – excuse me, both of you – a vicious old woman
who is deliberately mistreating her in order to spite you? *Ach*, I'm glad you weren't
my father!"

Nikolai gave her a warning frown, fearing that her outspokenness might
antagonize his brother. But Turgenev had immediately recognized the truth in what
she was saying and now brought the discussion to an end by thanking them both
for their suggestions and announcing that he was going to write to Madame Viardot
and ask for her advice. "I'll present the two alternatives to her. She'll know
immediately which course would be best. And I'll do whatever she says."

Husband and wife managed to restrain the feeling of irritation that this
subordination of their opinions to an inappellable higher authority had aroused in
them. They knew by now, anyhow, that any expression of it would have passed
straight over Turgenev's head.

My dear Turgenev,

Your letter about little Pelageya left a bruise on my heart which refuses to heal. Ever since I was touring with my family in Mexico, so many years ago, I have found the sight of a child suffering, be it from poverty or ill-treatment, unendurable. It is something – to you I dare say this – that sometimes insinuates into my mind a wicked little seed of doubt as to the total truth of what we were all taught about the ever-loving nature of the Almighty.

 But enough of blasphemy! We must form a plan of attack that will enable us to give your Pelageya at least the chance that all children should have before they embark on the turbulent ocean of life. You ask me for my opinion, so I shall give it to you frankly, as I always do. I do not concur with either of your suggested solutions. To send her to a convent would be too abrupt a change for one so young – and would also brand her as a being set apart, someone to whom it was not given to experience the pleasures and pains of family life. Why, through no fault of her own, should she be deprived of these? As to your sister-in-law's idea, I'm sure her motives are of the best. But, since you have told me of their financial hardship, perhaps even in that household she might find herself being treated more as a domestic than a daughter. And also, as they live so near to your mother, there will always be the possibility that the old lady will find some way to revenge herself on them – and you – even if only by spreading gossip around the neighbourhood, which would be sure to cause the little girl discomfort and embarrassment.

 No, my good Turgenev, I think we can both do better than that. What I propose is this: Why do you not send her over to us? She could become part of our family, grow up with Louise, who is only a few months older, and then, when the happy time comes for you to return to France, you will be able to tell us if we have done well by her. I have already discussed this plan with all the family and everyone is enthusiastic, especially Louise who, as you know, adores you and would love to have a sister sent to her by her beloved oncle *Yvan.*

 Think it over and let me know your decision. If you agree, I think the sooner you could send her on her way the better. Once you have made up your mind, we can discuss the details of her journey.

 Adieu, my dear, good friend. I very much hope you will approve of my plan and start to find some way of putting it into action as soon as you receive this. In the meantime, I am happy to tell you that we are all well, the only blessing lacking in our lives being your presence amongst us.

Pauline

The sultry heat of August had given way to blustery winds and rain-threatening clouds when Turgenev and Porfiry set off for Spasskoye in a decrepit old carriage they had found in an outhouse at Turgenevo. Turgenev had taken his illegitimate half-brother into his confidence and the two of them had devised a plan to bring his illegitimate daughter back with them, so that she could spend a few civilizing weeks in Turgenevo before being dispatched to France. Turgenev had written to Varya expressing the wish to see Pelageya again and asking her to bring the little girl to the gatekeeper's lodge at a certain hour, so that he could have another opportunity to talk to her.

They had decided to take no one else with them, so while Porfiry drove, Turgenev sought to take his mind off the intense discomfort of the wooden seat and the jolting carriage by brooding on the action he was about to take – *the first time*, he mused, *that I have altered the course of a river rather than let myself drift with the current. Am I certain that what I am doing is for the best? Surely it can only be right to remove this little girl from the intolerable position she occupies in that house… but sending her, so young, to a foreign country, to a family that, however welcoming and well-intentioned, must seem totally strange to her… might this not cause her more distress than what she is already familiar with? The only action that none of us has considered – or at least voiced – is that I should take care of her as though she were my legitimate daughter. But how could I do that? With no wife to look after her, I should have to hire a governess, and she'd be much better off under Pauline's supervision than the tutelage of some desiccated frâulein. And then I certainly don't feel like a father to her. A child from Pauline… ah, I can imagine the joy that would bring me, but this withdrawn yet hostile little urchin, what does she mean to me? Nothing, if the truth be told, except an appalled fascination at that reflecting-mirror face of hers and a sadness and guilt that I might well feel towards Diane if I had hurt her by accident and saw her suffering because of my carelessness. One can never tell, perhaps I could learn to be fond of the little thing, but I cannot hoodwink myself into thinking that I am now. Pity, guilt, sense of duty, all of these… but love, no.*

The tap of Porfiry's whip against the window alerted him that they were approaching the lodge. He looked out and saw Varya waiting for them with a sullen-looking Pelageya at her side. The wind had dropped and the clouds were low and heavy with rain. He could see from Varya's expression that she was surprised to see him arrive like this; no doubt she had expected him to walk over like the last time, and the presence of Porfiry, whom she had never liked, added to her suspicion. Turgenev climbed stiffly out of the carriage, greeted her with as much affection as he could assume, and explained that he would like to take Pelageya for a drive.

To his dismay, she announced that she would come too, adding sardonically in French, so that the little girl wouldn't understand: "*Après tout, c'est une histoire de famille. La petite sera avec son père, son oncle et sa tante.*"

Turgenev replied, also in French, that he thought he had a right to speak with his daughter in private, at which Varya threw her head back in a mirthless laugh. "Isn't it a bit late to be playing the part of the concerned father?" she asked. "At any rate, I cannot take the responsibility of letting her go with you alone. I am sure Varvara Petrovna would not approve."

Turgenev was beginning to find it hard to conceal his dislike of the young

178

woman. "The last time I was here," he pointed out, "you said that my mother had forbidden you to talk about our meeting. All you need to do is again obey her command."

"And you really think she will not hear about it if Pelageya goes off in the carriage with you?" she asked, nodding towards the gatekeeper's wife who, with the excuse of pulling some potatoes, was not taking her eyes off them for a second. "No, I'm sorry, Ivan Sergeyevich, but you must make a choice: either both of us or neither." She looked up at the black cloud hovering above them and added, in Russian: "And the weather has decided for you. It is beginning to rain. Come, Pelageya, this gentleman is taking us for a drive." She took the little girl's hand, helped her up into the carriage and was about to climb in after her.

Turgenev looked helplessly at Porfiry, who had been following the exchange as well as he could, his second language being German rather than French. But he had understood all he needed to know, and was as delighted to help his friend and protector as he was to settle old scores. While Varya had one foot on the step and the other already inside the carriage, he put his huge hands gently round her waist and spoke to her in a low, respectful but adamant tone: "I am sorry, mistress," (and what a wealth of irony was contained in that 'mistress') "but I must ask you to step down."

Varya glared round at him, indignant and incredulous that this underling should be daring to give her orders. "Take your hands off me this instant, or I will see to it that you are whipped," she barked, forgetting in her fury that they were no longer living under the same roof.

Porfiry smiled broadly and continued in the same placid tone: "It will be a pleasure, my dear sister, if you will be good enough to come down from that step."

"Sister!" Turgenev was afraid she was going to spit in Porfiry's face. She even threw an outraged glance at him, as though expecting him, in fact the only legitimate member of the party, to protect the family honour. But if Turgenev managed to keep the smile from his mouth, he couldn't keep it out of his eyes, and she turned back to Porfiry, who was still clasping her round the waist. "For the last time, I order you to let go of me." When Porfiry not only took no notice but calmly shook his head, she seized hold of both sides of the carriage door and tried to haul herself in. She might as well have tried to fell an oak by pushing against its trunk. As though playing with a recalcitrant kitten, the young giant lifted her into the air, carried her a few yards away from the carriage, deposited her on the ground and sprang back into the driving seat. Turgenev had meanwhile joined Pelageya in the carriage. Porfiry whipped up the horse and the carriage began to lumber away, leaving Varya gazing after them with a scarlet face and fists clenched in impotent, silent fury.

Inside, Turgenev looked across at the little girl sitting opposite him, again almost mesmerized by the bizarre familiarity of those features. She seemed quite unperturbed by their dramatic departure. Presumably so much had already happened in her short life that she was proof against all surprises. But after a while she did ask, albeit distractedly, as though it were expected of her: "Why didn't you want Varya Nikolayevna to come with us?"

Turgenev decided there was no point equivocating with this worldly-wise little creature. "Because," he said, "we're not just going for a drive. I'm taking you away from that house."

Not even this seemed to impress her unduly. She nodded her head and gazed out of the window for a while. Then, without turning back to look at him, she asked: "Will I be staying in your house, then?"

"Yes, for a little while, at any rate." Again she nodded, but made no comment. Turgenev, finding the silence awkward, asked: "Do you like that idea?"

She turned back and fixed him with a clear, level gaze. Then, without a hint of emotion of any kind, she simply answered: "I don't mind".

Turgenev decided that for the moment there was nothing to be gained by trying to pursue any more conversation. It was natural that she was... well, not shy exactly, but needing to take stock in her own mind of what was happening to her. He hunched himself as far back as he could into the corner of the seat, trying to cushion himself against the intolerable jolting of the dilapidated old vehicle, and followed her example of staring out of the window and allowing his thoughts to drift away wherever they wanted... which turned out to be not at all where he wanted them to go, their immediate destination being... *what absurd thing have I done?... Varya will stir up my mother over this so that any slim hope that there ever was of some sort of reconciliation has now vanished... and for what? For this little stranger that I feel nothing for and that I can't even talk to... she's a savage; no, not quite that, she's been taught the rudiments of good manners, more like the offspring of a wild animal that has been half domesticated... a fox cub, perhaps, who goes through the motions of civilized behaviour, but you feel may any day slink back into the woods, nostalgic for its natural habi...*

"Excuse me."

The clear treble voice startled Turgenev out of his thoughts. Pleased that she wanted to resume their conversation, he gave her an encouraging smile.

"Yes?"

She looked at him for a moment, and with any other child he would have judged that she was trying to pluck up courage. But timidity was entirely absent from the question she now put to him – or rather the statement in the form of a question.

"You are my father, aren't you?"

Turgenev's heart leapt to his throat. He hadn't intended to reveal this until after the girl had been living under his roof for a while and a certain familiarity had been established. But it would be ridiculous to lie now.

"Yes, I am. Who told you? Varya?"

"Nobody told me. It was obvious. I've always been told my father was a *barin*, like you. And that he's been away from Russia, which is why I've never seen him. I was almost sure the other day when you kept staring at me. But now..." she shrugged her shoulders as though the rest was so obvious it was not worth saying.

Turgenev was impressed by the child's mature intelligence. *The first twinges of parental pride? I must remember to avoid talking down to her.* He smiled at her again and said: "Yes, Pelageya, I am your father and I want to try and make your life much happier than it has been up to now. We'll have plenty of time to talk about all sorts of things. But now I just want to ask you one question..." He paused for a moment, wondering how to phrase it.

"What's that?" she asked.

"Are you glad that you've finally – at, what are you? eight, I believe – you've finally found your father?"

She looked at him with what seemed like a twinkle of ironic amusement in her eyes and said: "I don't know yet, do I?"

And again she turned away to stare out of the window, although all traces of the landscape were now obliterated by the driving rain.

Over the coming weeks, the energies of the entire Turgenevo household were channelled into converting the new arrival from a wild, rebellious little creature to a demure young lady who would be able to take her place in an ultra-civilized French home. The news of Pelageya's imminent transfer to Paris had not met with the approval of Nikolai and, especially, Anna Yakovlevna; but Nikolai had warned his wife that it was his brother's and not their business, and pleaded with her not to antagonize Ivan by opposing his wishes. She had dutifully made an effort to disguise her feelings, although Turgenev was as aware of her disapproval as he was indifferent to it. Anna nevertheless threw herself wholeheartedly into the task of domesticating Pelageya.

The first thing to be done was to dress her. Turgenev didn't dare send someone over to Spasskoye to bring back her clothes – and anyway it appeared from what she told them that she had practically none. The second day after her arrival, Anna asked Turgenev for some money and took her into Orel to buy her a dress. In truth, this was partly because she genuinely wanted to give the girl a treat, and partly to try to win her over, as from the first moment Pelageya had not taken the trouble to hide the fact that, whatever she might feel about the other inhabitants of Turgenevo, she was not at all taken with the mistress of the house. Whether the second intention was achieved may be doubted, but Pelageya was certainly pleased to be the owner of the costume Anna had chosen for her: a white ribbed cotton blouse under a lilac linen bolero and a wide skirt with two front, thigh-level pockets. This, it was explained to her, much to her disappointment, was only for 'best wear' – which meant, for the time being, practically never. But Anna's training in Varvara Petrovna's household and her thrifty German temperament came into their own for the rest of the wardrobe. With a few lengths of cheap material she had bought in Orel and bits and pieces of old dresses of hers she realized she would never wear again, she ran up jackets, skirts and blouses which an inexpert eye might well have taken to have been bought in an expensive Moscow shop.

She also took Pelageya's hygiene in hand, insisting that she take a bath every day – an activity which the little girl didn't particularly object to, merely found an absurd waste of time. Table manners were insisted on: first the essential preliminaries of how to hold her knife and fork; then admonitions not to talk when her mouth was full; and finally more sophisticated nuances like when and how to ask if she could leave the table. Pelageya responded to all this with bored but patient indifference; if it all seemed to her artificial and unnecessary, she bore it with good humour and, every now and then, showed that she did enjoy being praised when she had won approval.

Turgenev soon noticed that the only moments when his daughter demonstrated the thoughtless, carefree happiness he thought should be the natural state of all little girls was when she was with Porfiry. From the very first day, the young giant and the small child behaved more like a devoted brother and sister than a man in his early thirties and a girl of eight. He would play catch or hide-and-seek with her for hours on the lawn and among the bushes in front of the house, and her screams of excitement and joy when she was caught could be heard from one end of the estate to the other. Porfiry also taught her to ride properly, and the two of them would spend long afternoons and evenings exploring the countryside on his massive cob and her diminutive pony. Turgenev came upon them once when he was out with his gun. He was walking down a path in a wood with Diane at his heel when he heard her bright chatter and shrill peals of laughter. Wanting to give them a surprise, he hid behind a tree until they were almost upon him and then, carefully so as not to frighten the horses, stepped out in front of them. He noticed to his consternation that her attitude immediately changed: her face composed itself instantly into the polite, watchful expression it always wore when he was with her. He asked her what it was that had made her laugh, but she shook her head to indicate that it wasn't worth explaining – or perhaps that he wouldn't understand. It was left to Porfiry to relate that he had been inventing a dialogue between their two horses: switching from a basso profondo to a falsetto squeak, he imitated his cob telling Pelageya's pony how lucky she was to have someone so light on her back and wishing his rider would go on a diet, so that he'd lose a little weight...

Every day, for an hour before lunch, Turgenev would give her a French lesson. She had already picked up a little from hearing it spoken around Spasskoye, but he was delighted to see how quickly and eagerly she learnt. His primary purpose was that she shouldn't arrive in the Viardot household unable to say a word to anyone; but the lesson also enabled him to talk to her alone in a natural, casual way and to try to find out something about this, to him, disconcertingly mysterious little personage. One morning Anna Yakovlevna, with that air of reluctantly performing a distasteful duty which quite failed to mask the satisfaction it gave her, told him that Pelageya had been very rude to her: having twice told her to tidy her room with no effect, she had been forced the third time to scold her; at which the girl had turned on her and shouted that she was worse than Varvara Petrovna – than which, Turgenev reflected, there was for poor Anna no worse insult.

He decided to work this incident into the lesson for the day, which would be about *comportement*. He told her, speaking slowly in French and changing into Russian whenever he saw a fog of incomprehension clouding her eyes, that Madame Pauline would love her like the mother she had never known, but she would have to return that love by obeying every request that was made of her. "You must never behave as you did this morning with Anna Yakovlevna. Or as you used to at Spasskoye. Have you ever thought about why you are sometimes so naughty?"

A rebellious shake of the head.

"You should. You're a clever girl, and you would soon work out that, apart from giving offence to other people, it is much nicer for yourself if you do what they want you to. For instance, Varya told me that after you were rude to Madame Turgeneva, you were turned out of the big house and sent to live with one of the servants' families. Now you must have said to yourself, 'I wish I hadn't done that. I was much happier where I was before.'"

She looked at him without answering.

"Well, didn't you?"

"No. I liked it better where I was."

"You mean you were happier living in a swineherd's cottage than surrounded by all the comfort of that beautiful house?"

"Yes I was. I never felt at home there. I felt like a toy – one of the toys I used to play with in my doll's house. I put them where I wanted them to be. Not where they wanted to go. I was called in when old ladies who smelt came to visit… what should I call her now, my grandmother?… and they offered me pieces of cake and chocolates and asked me stupid questions and never waited to hear my answers. I felt like a kitten that people like to play with for a few minutes and then get bored with…"

"And the family you went to live with. Did they treat you well?"

"I suppose so. They gave me a cuff if I did something wrong and they sometimes smiled if they were pleased with me. But most of the time they left me to myself. And that's what I like."

"And what do you do when you're by yourself?"

"I read. Madame… my grandmother gave me lots of books. She liked me to read. And I make up songs."

"You make up songs?"

"Yes. I love to do that. I think of the tunes first and then I put the words to them."

"Would you sing me one?"

"No."

"Why not? Don't you ever sing them to anybody?"

"Well, I sang one the other day to Porfiry. But I couldn't to you. You're a grown-up."

"So is Porfiry."

"Yes, but… well, not like you. You'd think it stupid."

"I'm sure I wouldn't."

"Well, if you didn't, it's you that would be stupid. How could a grown-up like a song written by a little girl of eight?"

Reflecting that it was easier to talk to the most brilliant minds in St Petersburg than to this child of his, Turgenev returned to the lesson. "Now remember, whenever you ask for something, *s'il vous plaît* …"

from VARVARA'S JOURNAL

September 8th … so he's taken the girl away. When Varya told me, I didn't know which emotion predominated: surprise or anger. But now that I've had time to think about it, it is surely surprise. I would never have suspected Ivan of taking such decisive action. My first instinct was to summon the chief of police and order him to bring her back. But on second thoughts, I decided it was a good riddance. She was a tiresome little brat and, despite my best efforts, was already showing signs of the vulgarity it was inevitable she would inherit from her mother. I wonder what he will do with her. He surely will not have calculated on the extra expense involved. But no doubt my dear frau *daughter-in-law will be constantly reminding him of that. He'll soon learn that sponging as a permanent guest in a foreign country is a far cry from bringing up a child in your own. And he's cut off his usual source of supply; not even he will have the nerve now to come crawling to me. Well, at least this should stop him traipsing off to France again after that damn gypsy. I don't suppose she would be entranced by the idea of her lover turning up again with an eight-year-old child in tow.*

But, dear God, what a sorry state of affairs! Shouldn't an ailing old woman be able to count on some consolation in the form of sympathy and care from the son who has always meant everything to her? There are days when I am sorely tempted to receive him – I know from Varya that he often comes over here – and let him ask my

184

forgiveness. En fin de compte, the only solace to the torments of this illness which is soon going to kill me would be an occasional visit from my Vanichka. And yet how can I forget the way he talked to me that terrible day? Should I make an effort to do so? Should I forgive him the way I used to when he'd caused me some displeasure as a little boy? Oh, how easy things were then! A good thrashing, and it was all over. Would that I could still solve things so quickly and easily! But what is the use? It isn't a question of should I or shouldn't I? I can no more do it than these idiot doctors can make my body obey me as it always has done throughout my life…

Turgenevo,
26 September, 1850.

Dear and good Madame Viardot,

I have just received your letter at the end of which you reproach me for not writing to you often enough. I can only plead guilty, but ask for one or two extenuating circumstances to be taken into account. First, there is the everyday business of running the estate which, given the state of degradation into which it had fallen before our arrival, takes up an exorbitant amount of my brother's and my time. Secondly there are the hours I spend with Pelageya, trying to prepare her as best I can for the great change which is about to come over her life. And thirdly – and indeed it does seem to have to come last – there is my work, which is beginning to acquire a certain momentum. I have never until now realized what it means to write regularly to order and deliver by a fixed date. And yet I have no choice but to do it; my friends at Sovremennik *count on me. They have just published two more of my* Sportsman's Sketches *– one a happy tale based on a peasants' singing contest I witnessed a few weeks ago, the other a sad ten pages recounting the last meeting between a young girl and the obnoxious young valet who has been her lover and is about to abandon her. I am happy to say they have met with great success. I only tell you this because I know you and Viardot are interested.*

To more practical matters. In a few days I shall be leaving with Pelageya for Moscow, where I shall only stay a couple of days. Then on to St Petersburg, where I plan to remain for the winter. I have heard from the good Annenkov, who has found there a Frenchwoman, a certain Madame Robert, who is returning to Paris at the end of the month with her daughter and has agreed, for a modest sum which I will pay her in advance, to act as escort for little Pelageya. So you may count on the child being with you during the second half of November. I will not say more about her than I conveyed to you in my last letter, except that I have become increasingly struck by her intelligence, though I fear that it has developed at the expense of her heart. But it is better that you should not have too many preconceptions. Your unique insight will soon tell you all you need to know. You ask me about her name. She will be travelling with a Russian passport under the name of Pelageya Ivanovna. I will leave the choice of a surname up to you; perhaps something French and anonymous, Durand, Dumont …

A final word about our wretched family affairs. I have had no contact with my mother, who still steadfastly refuses to see me. I gather from my half-sister that her health is steadily failing, but as I am forbidden her presence, there is little I can do about it. Perhaps to appease my conscience, I have ceded my half of Turgenevo to Nikolai. My work is beginning to bring me in a little money now and his need is so much greater than mine; until next year's harvest is in, he has no income at all. His wife is, for the most part, a good soul, but I'm afraid she doesn't spare him some reproaches on this subject. Believe it or not, she even asked for some extra housekeeping money from me because my half-brother, Porfiry, is such a huge eater! At any rate, Nikolai is now the owner of a potentially fine property, which should yield him up to twenty thousand francs in a good year. This should make him independent and free of that debilitating anxiety that comes from incessant financial uncertainty.

Ma chère amie, in all of this there is not a word of the enormous gratitude I owe you for your noble gesture in taking on this little creature. And yet, in a sense, the word gratitude has little sense between us. For you know that you can count on my entire, absolute, eternal devotion; you know that you can ask for my life and I will be happy to give it to you. I dare to say this to you – and I know you believe me …

I kneel at your feet and kiss the hem of your skirt.

Your
I.T.

The day came for Turgenev and Pelageya's departure from Turgenevo. They were to drive in their carriage to Orel, where they would catch the diligence that would take three days to convey them to Moscow. Turgenev watched to see if he could detect any sign of emotion in his daughter; she was, after all, leaving what had been her home for the past three months and where she had given every indication of being happy. He feared that this leap into the unknown might cause the carefully constructed facade behind which she hid the feelings she must surely possess to crack. But it appeared that this would not be so, and once again Turgenev marvelled at the little girl's self-sufficiency. Anyone ignorant of what was taking place would have had no reason to suspect that this was anything but an ordinary day. Except perhaps that everyone was particularly nice to her. Especially Anna Yakovlevna, whose now visible pregnancy might have stimulated genuine maternal feelings – or, Turgenev couldn't help wondering, who was unconsciously assuaging her guilt at feeling glad to see the child go. Be that as it may, she helped Pelageya into the travelling outfit she had put together for her and checked that her few belongings had all been packed in the little leather case Turgenev had bought for her.

When the time came for them to leave, the few servants gathered behind Nikolai and Anna and came forward, one by one, to wish the little girl they had become fond of over the past months a happy journey. Pelageya favoured each of them with a formal smile and thanked them politely for their good wishes. She could almost have been a queen reviewing her troops before leaving the country on an official visit. Then she came to Porfiry. She stood stock-still for a minute and then, as the young giant bent his knees and held out his hands to her, she flung herself into his arms and clung on to him as though defying anyone ever to prise them apart. Porfiry patted her shoulders and murmured a few comforting words, but she was not to be consoled. She lifted her head, which had been buried in the side of his beard and cried out: "Come with me! Come with me, Porfiry, please! Come with me!" and then sank her face into his neck again, sobbing desperately and repeating like a mantra, "Come with me, come with me!" No one knew what to do, least of all Turgenev, who gazed helplessly around, as though waiting for someone to rescue him. Eventually his eyes met Porfiry's, who jerked his head towards the carriage, indicating for him to get in. Turgenev did so and was followed by Porfiry, still holding the little girl in his arms and mouthing 'I'll come to Orel with you'. The coachman shook his reins, clucked at the horse and the carriage moved off. Only the creak of the wheels broke the petrified silence. One of the kitchen girls raised a handkerchief and started to call a feeble goodbye, but was quickly shushed by the others.

Turgenev was amazed at the dexterity with which Porfiry managed to calm the little girl down. It was as if he already had children of his own and was as used to dealing with their crises as he was at breaking in a yearling. Turgenev felt more useless than ever, indeed almost in the way. *Thank heaven I decided not to try and bring her up myself. It would have been a catastrophe for both of us.* Porfiry stroked her hair and mumbled soft, consoling words: "We're not saying goodbye for ever, my little Palachka… you'll come back for a holiday now and then… I'll keep Milka well groomed for you and not let her get too fat…" This was a mistake, as the naming of her pony brought on a fresh onslaught of tears, but he quickly veered off on a new tack: "Or perhaps your father will let me come with him when he goes to visit you. That should be possible, shouldn't it, Ivan Sergeyevich?" Turgenev nodded and gave what he hoped sounded like an affirmative grunt. It was in all probability a lie, but already Porfiry's medicine was beginning to work: sniffs and swallows seemed to indicate that the worst was over. And indeed, before long, Pelageya disentangled herself from Porfiry's arms, slid off his knees and sat in her corner looking out of the window. For the rest of the journey, Porfiry kept up a running stream of innocuous conversation, which required nothing from father and daughter but monosyllabic replies, but was preferable to the leaden silence which would otherwise have fallen.

Fortunately, the Moscow diligence was already harnessed and waiting when they reached the central square of Orel, so the farewells had to be brief. But Turgenev noted with admiration that Pelageya had obviously made up her mind there were to be no more scenes. She gave Porfiry a quick hug and then, white-faced, but with a set I'm-not-going-to-cry-again jaw, climbed briskly up into the diligence ahead of her father, who embraced his half-brother, muttered a heartfelt 'thank you' into his ear and hurried apprehensively after her.

The three day journey to Moscow was easier than Turgenev had anticipated. It seemed that Pelageya's outburst at Turgenevo had acted as a catharsis and that, externally at any rate, she was her controlled, matter-of-fact self again. Most of the time she spent with her head buried in one of the books she had brought with her. When they did talk, it amused and alarmed him to an almost equal degree to see how manipulating she was becoming. The weapons she had needed to protect herself in her grandmother's house were now being honed. Here was her father sitting opposite her, just for another two days, and feeling awkward and guilty. This was an opportunity not to be missed. Using her rapidly acquired French whenever she could, because she knew it pleased him, she had, by the time they reached Moscow, wheedled out of him a promise that she would have a pony at Courtavenel, that she would be given music lessons (this presented no difficulty) and that she would have a small weekly allowance 'so that I can give Madame Pauline lots of presents'.

For the hundredth time since that day at Spasskoye when he had first seen her, Turgenev asked himself what he really felt for this unexpected daughter of his. By now, a certain affection, undoubtedly. Something almost amounting to admiration at the way she had learnt to deal with life. But love? he could only guess that the fact that he had to ask himself so often meant that the answer was probably no. Perhaps it would come. Perhaps the swan that would surely emerge out of Pauline's care would one day melt his heart with her grace and beauty and charm. In the meantime, he could only content himself with the conviction that he was doing the best for her that lay in his power.

Only once on the journey did the fears he had communicated to Pauline about her seeming lack of heart come to the fore. It followed after an innocently playful conversation, which he had initiated by asking her what she loved most in the world. With no hesitation she answered: "Milka and Porfiry… and you, of course, Papa." He smiled inwardly at the 'of course' and went on to ask her what she hated most. This time she stopped to think and then said, with great conviction: "Having to be nice to people I think are horrid." Before he could decide whether he dared ask her to expand on this, she put the same question to him. "And what do you hate most?" "Cruelty," he answered. "The deliberate causing of pain and suffering. It fills me with a sense of hatred of the oppressor and pity for the victim so strong that's it's almost as though it were me who had been hurt."

To his astonishment, she remarked calmly: "I don't feel pity for anyone."

"That's not possible, Palasha."

"Why isn't it? No one's ever had pity on me… except you, perhaps."

"But if you actually saw someone suffer – for instance that peasant at Spasskoye who had his hand cut off at the sawmill…"

"What's that to me? I have too much pity for myself to waste it on anyone else.

I'm only eight, but I've seen the world. I've seen everything. And I know everything."

Turgenev shook his head incredulously. "How can you say such things? You must promise me not to talk like that when you're in France, otherwise everyone will think you're a very silly little girl."

"All right, I promise you. But it's true, all the same."

"It's not true, Palasha. You haven't seen the world, You've seen one world. And perhaps you may feel that you know everything about that. But soon you will see another world. And you'll find out how much you have to learn. And then, as you grow older, another and another and another. And you'll see that we never stop learning, any of us."

She gave him a look which said, clearer than any words, that she didn't agree with him, but there was no point in arguing about it, and ducked her head back into her book.

St Petersburg,
Saturday, 21 October, 1850

You have not heard from me for a week, dear and good Madame Viardot, and that is unpardonable. I can only say in my defence that I have been so busy these last days that I have not had a minute to myself, but that will not do, since all the occupations in the world should take second place when it comes to writing to you. I can, therefore, only once again fling myself at your feet, kiss them rapturously and beg you to forgive me.

My main 'occupation' has been trying to finish a story for Sovremennik. *I promised them I would deliver it by the 24th and it is still far from done. The chief result for the moment is that my back is so stiff I can barely straighten it and my eyes ache horribly from writing all night. But, in consolation, I dare to think that it is a story you might like. I will send you a copy when it is finished.*

Most of the rest of my time has been spent dealing with the formalities over Pelageya's journey. You cannot imagine how many offices I have had to visit and how many idiotic forms I have had to fill in. I shall spare you the details. But as it all took much longer than I thought, I was not able to send her off with Mme Robert on the 14th, as we had hoped, and there wasn't another boat for Stettin until yesterday.

In the meantime, she has been staying with my good friends, the Tyutchevs, who seem to have formed a high opinion of her. They said she was very quiet and very polite. I have much less doubt now than I did three months ago that she will be thoroughly educatable. I took her to the docks at six yesterday evening with Mme Robert and her daughter and put them on the steamboat. I was quite touched that she cried her heart out when I said goodbye to her. I had become so used to her self-control that I had sincerely wondered whether she had become at all fond of me in the short time we have been together. I must say that a part of me was sad to see her go. I was becoming used to our talks, and the task of trying to fashion that rough material into a finished product was beginning to intrigue me. But she was also taking up a great deal of my time, and I have so little of that at the moment. The good Mme Tyutchev was kind enough to buy her some warm clothes for the journey, but she has very little else to wear. I thought it was better to leave all that to you. Perhaps you would be good enough to pay for whatever you think she needs and I will send you 500 francs at the New Year to reimburse you.

My brother has written to me to say that our mother's health has taken a turn for the worse. She has left Spasskoye and gone to Moscow so that she can benefit from the more advanced medical care. Apparently she will receive the occasional visit from Nikolai, but not from his wife, and she will not allow my name to be mentioned. It is hard for me to know what to wish for her: for all her faults – and God knows they are many – she is still my mother and there was a time when I meant the world to her. Should one wish for a woman formerly so energetic and vigorous to be a virtual cripple for another ten years? Or would not a speedy end be more merciful? I assuredly must bear my share of the blame for not having been a better son to her, but the price she would have exacted would have destroyed me.

A week from today it will be my birthday. I shall be 32. I'm getting to be an old man! Exactly seven years ago I met your husband through the ridiculous Major Komarov. And four days later I went to the apartment you had taken on the Nevsky Prospekt and timidly kissed your hand. No other memory in my life has a fraction of the importance that moment will always have for me.

Seven years! And I am overjoyed to be able to say to you that in those seven years I have found nothing better in the world than you – that to have met you on my path has been the greatest happiness of my life. You are all that is best and most attractive and noble on this earth. I could ask for nothing better than to stretch my whole life out like a carpet for your dear feet to tread lightly over...

May Heaven bless you and all those around you...

Your devoted,
I.T.

From VARVARA'S JOURNAL

November 7th – That idiot Inozemtsev has just left. In spite of all the anodyne platitudes about beginning to detect signs of gradual improvement, the man can't control his expression well enough to hide the fact that he's convinced I'm dying – calls himself a doctor! The first requisite qualification of that profession should be acting talent – as none of them know anything or are able to be of any use, they should at least try to make their patients feel better by their mere presence. Most of them can't even do that. But who knows? Maybe I'll live to fool them yet...

November 8th ... along with everyone else, including my sons, who are no doubt counting on my imminent disappearance – they think they can neglect their mother because she's going to be gone before long – oh yes, they write to me – concerned-sounding letters – Dearest Mama... – but that's only because they're afraid I'll treat them badly in my will – so I don't answer them – but there I have an inducement to stay alive which my body no longer provides – just to know that they're living from hand to mouth, Nikolai with his hausfrau, Ivan yearning for his gypsy warbler, waiting for the moment when they'll finally be rich and seeing it always receding ahead of them like a will-o'-the-wisp – ah, quelle satisfaction!...

November 9th ... even if the doctor's right, I can still trouble the waters for them a bit – must remember to tell Varya to find my will and tear it up – I'll make another, leaving her a large legacy and all my jewellery. Damn it, I can do what I like with that, even if the sons have to inherit the properties – how it exasperates me to think of those two weaklings wallowing in a life of ease when they've never lifted a finger to help me all these years...

November 11th ... too weak yesterday to write anything – what is the use of this journal now? The need to talk to someone, I suppose, even if it's only to myself – must tell Varya to destroy it if... those last two entries were not very Christian. Any day now the priest will come to give me the eucharist – I'll have to confess – well, I don't have to tell him everything, it's better some things should remain between me and the Almighty – and then who shall decide what are sins? I sometimes feel like that old reprobate of Shakespeare's, more sinned against than sinning – I loved my husband and he loved me not – I loved my second son and he loves me not – who else have I loved in my life? Certainly not that young doctor Behrs, Varya's father. He was as stupid as he was handsome – but he loved me and I let him... Why? A whiplash in the face of destiny? A sense of playing out my last adventure? I was 46, after all, and he was only 18 – I can see the expression on his face now as he climbed on top of me – fear, desire and incredulity flitting over his face like the shadows of clouds across a summer lawn – oh God, I'm so tired ...

November 12th ... if this is going to be my private confession to God, I'd better tell the truth – revenge played its part too... revenge on my dying husband, a signal that I too could play his game if I so wished – and oh, the satisfaction, watching him watching me getting bigger every day, wondering who it was and never able to bring himself to ask... those weeks dissolved much of the bitterness of twenty years – and then when I told him I was going away for 'health reasons', but really for Bibi to be born, I knew from his face that he was longing to beg me to stay with him while he was dying – who knows? If he had been able to bring himself to ask, perhaps I would have, but of course he couldn't...

November 13th ... there, pride again, that was the poison that destroyed both our lives – but, God forgive me (will He?), what a sense of triumph when I returned to Spasskoye four months after his death, with my new dresses from Rome and Paris – and my new daughter, although of course she was not called that – my 'ward', my 'adopted child'. The expressions on the faces of the Turgenevs and their friends – I could have been the Empress Theodora! I can't stand the gloom of this room any more, I wasn't made to live like this – I shall call one of the servants and tell them to hire an orchestra to play polkas in the next door room. If I have to go, I shall go as I have lived – no one shall feel sorry for me...

14th ... God forgive me... forgive me... this fear... this terror. Nikolai was here – his eyes, like he was seeing a dead woman – I told him to call Ivan – why hasn't he come? Vanichka, your mother's dying – why aren't you here? I'll give you blackcurrant jam. Will no one stop that music? – Mother of God, pardon me, my children... and you, merciful Lord, pardon me too! For pride, that mortal sin, has been the sin that has accompanied me every day of my life...

Moscow,
Wednesday, 22 November, 1850.

Dear and good Madame Viardot,

I arrived here yesterday evening – only to find my mother no longer alive. She died last Thursday, the very day I heard that she was sinking. Because of winter conditions, the journey took me five days. My brother is here with his wife. I shall write to you tomorrow – today I am too shattered. I just wanted to give you this news and hold your hand as tight as I can.

Till tomorrow. May Heaven bless and protect you!

Your,
I.T.

A maid comes into the living room of Courtavenel, waits for a pause in the animated conversation and discreetly hands her mistress a letter. Pauline is about to replace it on the tray and wave the girl away when she sees the familiar handwriting and a Russian stamp. She excuses herself, slits open the envelope and reads the brief contents.

Louis sees her eyebrows raise and a pensive look come into her eyes. "What is it, my dear?" he asks. "Not bad news, I hope."

"I suppose it depends on how you look at it. Ivan's mother's died."

Charles Gounod makes the sign of the cross and mutters a heartfelt "Poor Ivan!"

"Well…" Pauline says doubtfully, "She was not the most loving of mothers."

"Nevertheless," there's a touch of reproof in Gounod's voice as he looks across at his own mother, who is sitting at the far end of the room with Madame Garcia, "a mother is always a mother. No one can replace her. I'm sure Ivan would appreciate our deep sympathy."

"I'm sure he would," Pauline says briskly, "and I shall write to him tomorrow conveying condolences from all of us." She turns to their guest, the only person in the room who doesn't know whom they are talking about: "I'm sorry, Monsieur Roqueplan – a friend of ours from Russia who has just returned there. But please continue with what you were saying."

Nestor Roqueplan has been since the previous year the sole Director of the Paris *Opéra*. Like most heads of important cultural institutions, he is a conservative man, who hesitated for a long time before agreeing to stage a work by the unknown, thirty-two-year-old Gounod. It was only when Pauline, her laurels still fresh from her triumph in *Le Prophète* eighteen months before, had promised to sing the leading role before she knew a note of the music, that he had finally agreed. Now the score of *Sapho is* complete, and the Viardots have invited him to spend a Sunday at Courtavenel to talk about the opera. Lunch – pheasant shot by Louis and *a* succulent *tocinillos de cielo*, which Pauline's mother had taught their cook how to make – has just finished and the Viardots, Gounod and Roqueplan are reclining in armchairs around a coffee table. The two older women, both musicians in their youth (Gounod's mother a pianist) sit at the window exchanging desultory remarks but not missing a word of the conversation.

Roqueplan draws on his cigar and tries to give meaningful emphasis to words he must have repeated a hundred times. "I'm sure you will realize that we will not be able to spend a great deal of money on this production."

Gounod asks curtly: "So where do you see the economies being made?"

The Director conceals his irritation at being interrogated by this brash young man and answers: "We have a very small budget for the costumes. I'm afraid we won't be able to allow ourselves any extravagance there."

Viardot, drawing on his experience of running an opera company, says: "There is, however, the advantage of its being set in ancient Greece. Simple tunics for both men and women. No great expense there."

"True," Roqueplan agrees. "As long as what we gain there we don't lose elsewhere."

"What do you mean?" asks Gounod, anxiously.

Roqueplan draws a deep breath and gazes ruminatively at the glowing tip of his cigar. "I can't deny," he says, "that I am a little worried about the libretto. Ancient Greece is rather out of fashion these days. It was all very well for Gluck… but that was a long time ago. And then… Gluck was Gluck!"

Gounod's handsome face flushes scarlet. "And Gounod is Gounod," he says sharply.

Roqueplan looks at the young composer through half-closed eyes and contents himself with a long-drawn-out, "Yeees…" Then he adds: "But I am sure that even if there are a few rather static moments, Monsieur Gounod will fill them in with some splendid music." He glances over at the piano in the corner of the room. "I wonder if I could ask you to play me a few passages. As I told you, I have had very little time to look at the score, and to hear it directly from the composer's hands would be a great privilege."

Gounod goes over to sit at the piano and runs his fingers over the keys. "I'll play some of the ballet music in the first act," he says.

Roqueplan lifts a hand to forestall him. "Oh dear, I forgot to tell you. I'm afraid we'll have to eliminate the ballet."

Gounod turns round, aghast. "Eliminate the ballet? But it's some of my best music. And audiences at the *Opéra* expect a ballet. Nobody knows that better than you."

Roqueplan spreads his hands in insincere apology. "I know, my dear friend, but we have decided to open the evening with a short ballet. Adam is to write the music and we hope that Marie Taglioni will…"

"You mean there is to be a another work before my opera?" Gounod splutters.

"Yes, and it will be to your advantage. Audiences will come to see la Taglioni and remain to hear Gounod."

Gounod turns to Pauline in mute appeal, but doesn't find the defender he was hoping for. She tries to reassure the disconsolate composer. "I'm sure Monsieur Roqueplan knows best, Charles. After all, it's in his interest as well as ours."

Gounod gets up from the piano stool and returns to his chair. "I don't know what to play for you then," he mutters sulkily."

Noticing that Roqueplan can barely conceal his impatience at this childish behaviour, Louis suggests to his wife that she sing an excerpt from the opera. "Of course," she agrees at once, moving towards the piano. "Come on, Charles, let's do *Tremblant à la voûte des cieux*."

"Very well. But why don't you accompany yourself... you play much better than I do."

Roqueplan turns to Louis. "Can she play all her arias?" he asks.

Before Viardot can open his mouth, Gounod answers for him. "A week after I gave her the finished score, she could play the whole opera right through. Not just the scenes that she is in... the entire score."

Roqueplan gazes at Viardot and shakes his head in bemused admiration. Pauline explains that in her first-act aria Sapho, competing for the poetry prize at Olympus, tells of the love of Hero and Leander. She starts to play the introduction, in which a hushed high tremolo, imitating violins, hovers above an ostinato murmuring in the bass. It is a moving depiction of the sighing of the sea on a still summer Mediterranean night as described by Sapho, and when Pauline's voice, in its lowest register, steals in, the undercurrent of tension that has been building up in the room is instantly stilled. Nothing else exists for all present but the sombre, classical purity of the voice dispelling any touch of over-sweetness that might be detected in the notes.

When she finishes, there is a moment of silence, then a murmur of approval. Roqueplan rises to take his leave. With practised courtesy, he thanks his hostess for the day's entertainment and adds: "But I would gladly have sacrificed all the rest for the sake of these last few minutes. I return to Paris confident in the success of *Sapho*." He turns to Gounod, who is standing beside Pauline, shakes his hand and says: "You have great talent, my dear Gounod. But, which is more important, you are a very lucky young man."

Gounod, all sores healed by hearing his music performed like this and seeing its effect on the small audience, seizes Pauline's hands, kisses them rapturously and murmurs over and over: "I know, I know, I know..." Then he looks up at her with liquidly adoring eyes and murmurs, in the words of Phaon, the opera's hero, which follow the aria she has just sung: "'*Chacun t'admire, et moi je t'aime*'". Betraying an untypical trace of embarrassment, Pauline is forced to almost pull her hands away in order to join Louis, who is accompanying their guest to the door.

Moscow,
Tuesday, 5 December, 1850

Good morning, my dear and good friend,

It is today exactly six months since I last saw you. Half a year! Who knows how long it will be

195

before we next meet. Another year? Or even longer? Well, we shall see, we shall see…

The seals on my mother's house were finally broken yesterday, and my brother and I were able to go in. We found only a few unimportant papers. No will. No letter to either of us. But the fireplace in her bedroom was choked with burnt paper; we can only assume that she destroyed every document of any importance before she died. All that has survived is a journal written in pencil during her last months – we found it on a wooden shelf above her bed. Strange that it escaped the fire. Perhaps she overlooked it. Or perhaps she meant us to read it. We shall never know. I shall start to look through it tonight…

I shall not weary you with all the intrigues that have been played out in this gloomy house. They would not seem out of place in a drama of the Italian Renaissance. Falsity, subterfuge and a desire to lay the blame on others which has opened many mouths. A veritable concert of recriminations! The chief villainess is, alas, my half-sister. The playful, if capricious, little girl of whom I had such fond memories has turned into a kind of female Tartuffe: a mixture of an almost childish anxiety to please and diabolical duplicity. It's an unusual blend and, I find, a disgusting one. Of course all this is the inevitable result of my mother's behaviour, especially in her last years. She loved to raise people to the position of court favourite, only to find even greater pleasure in dashing them down. However hard I try, I find it very difficult to clarify my feelings about her. There are moments, remembering how much devotion she lavished on me during my young years, when I feel wretchedly unfilial; but I realize that this all took place when the rules of the game were laid down by her; when I grew old enough to want occasionally to dictate terms myself, she lost all interest in the game…

Friday morning, 8 December.

I was interrupted on Tuesday and only now find time to resume my letter. But I am a changed man – the result of reading my mother's journal. What a woman! I have been walking round like a somnambulist with an obsessive dream for three days. May God forgive her everything… but what a life! Never before have I been so aware of the necessity of trying to be true and good … if only not to die like that. One day I will read you this journal – I cannot accept the idea of hiding from you anything, however painful, which concerns me intimately. You know everything up to now. You shall know everything through to the end. Unless, at a certain point, you yourself should bid me be silent. Oh, my dear and beloved friend, the thought of you at this moment is like a shaft of light reaching down to instil hope in a poor wretch who has fallen down a well. You illuminate my darkness. I stretch out my hands to you and bless you from the bottom of my heart.

To stay in the light, to move from death to life, thank you for all the particulars in your last letter about… yes, I must learn to call her Paulinette! The news that our daughter is loving and good did much to refresh my arid soul. Of course she adores you… what else could she do? Now I really feel her to be my child and am beginning truly to love her. Give her a warm hug from her papa.

And to finish with another little creature that we both love, Diane is here with me, thank God, otherwise the loneliness would be intolerable. She is very fat, because in a month she is going to give birth to a litter of puppies who are bound to resemble her, as I managed to find a gentleman who is almost indistinguishable from her. And very talented too! I intend to start a race of extraordinary dogs. I want

196

people one day to say: Do you see that setter? That's the grandson of the famous Diane. I have just asked her if she remembers Sultan. She pricked up her ears and gave a very significant wink.

I kiss your hands and embrace you all. When you receive this, it will be already 1851. Are we to see each other again during that year? Remember this: even if I am able to come, I shall do so only if you summon me.

Your
I. Turgenev.

P.S. My Provincial Lady *is to be given here in Moscow in January and a few days later in St Petersburg with Samoilova and her brother. It's a slight thing and will probably be booed off the stage; but I enjoyed writing it, so keep your fingers crossed for me!*

'*Pauline Viardot-Garcia… Pauline Viardot-Garcia…*' Turgenev sat at the back of a box at the Maly Theatre, obsessively muttering the name over and over again as the curtain went up on his one-act play, centred around the stratagems employed by a bored young wife in the provinces to rekindle the affections of a Count who had flirted with her many years before when she was his mother's ward, in the hope that he will use his influence to get her husband a job in St Petersburg.

The charm worked beyond his most optimistic expectations. At the end, the audience clapped, stamped, cheered and called out, at first sporadically, then in unison: TUR-GE-NEV, TUR-GE-NEV. '*I panicked*' he was to write a few days later. '*I was prepared for anything except this. I was so frightened by the repeated, vociferous calling of my name that I fled the theatre as though there were a thousand devils at my heels. I am now sorry that I did, because people may have thought I was turning my nose up at their enthusiasm…*'

A similar scene was not to be repeated later that month at the Alexandrinsky Theatre in St Petersburg. Although the production was better, with the brother-and-sister team giving subtly effective, played-in performances in the leading roles, the reception, as befitted the more sophisticated city, was coolly rather than deliriously appreciative. But this time there was to be no flight: Nekrasov and Panaev, joint editors of *Sovremennik,* had invited a group of friends to the spacious apartment they shared on the Fontanka embankment for a party after the performance. Annenkov was there – another couple of inches added to his girth since Paris; the Slavophil Aksakov brothers, Konstantin and Ivan, old acquaintances of Turgenev's; and a group of writers from the Moscow journal *Moskvitianin,* who brought with them the twenty-seven-year-old Aleksander Ostrovsky, whose first published play, *A Family Affair,* had just met with satisfactorily controversial acclaim. They were soon joined by Nadezhda Samoilova and her brother, radiantly gorged with backstage compliments.

197

Presiding over the celebrations was Turgenev's old *bête noire*, Avdotya Yakovlevna Panaeva; attractive, flirtatious and as spiteful as ever, she now made no mystery of the fact that she was her husband's partner's mistress. They all lived together, forming what a St Petersburg wit had called, with disparaging reference to Panaev's virility, a *ménage à deux et demi*. She took great pride in her *soirées*, at which no expense was spared; it was common knowledge that whatever meagre profits *Sovremennik* managed, from time to time, to make were immediately squandered on the choicest foods and finest champagnes.

Soon after midnight, the opening-night socialite crowd began to make their way home, leaving the literary circle to talk out the rest of the night. Turgenev himself had drunk more champagne than was his custom. After the problems with Pelageya, the less than stimulating company of his brother and sister-in-law, the still aching pangs of separation from Pauline and the conflicting emotions aroused by his mother's death, he was happy for one evening to fall back into the easy convivial social life he had once taken for granted. After yet another toast had been drunk to the evening's success, he quietened them all down and asked them to tell him, one by one, what they had really thought of his comedy. "I can't make up my mind," he said, "if I have a gift for the theatre or not. Certainly the rewards, when they come, are more immediate and temporarily gratifying. But I wonder if it is really my *métier*."

Annenkov was the first to speak up. "I certainly think you should continue in the theatre," he said. "Prose fiction may always be your front line of attack, but you should keep playwriting in reserve. Look how successful you were tonight, and in Moscow. You reach people more directly."

"When I reach them at all. At the moment I have seven plays sitting in the censor's office."

Nekrasov gave a sardonic laugh. "Their stupidity is beyond belief! They think theatre audiences are more dangerous than people sitting alone reading. If they knew anything about literature at all, they'd know that the opposite was true. The main object of attention tonight was not Ivan's text but the slender beauty of Nadezhda's waist; the men were gazing at it in admiration, the women in envy."

"That's because the play itself was essentially frivolous." It was Ivan Aksakov who spoke. "Excuse me, Ivan, but you who write those stories Nekrasov is publishing know this to be true."

"Certainly *Provincial Lady* is frivolous," Turgenev admitted. "The plays I have written which are perhaps less so are waiting on the censor's pleasure."

"And what's wrong with a little frivolity?" Annenkov asked. "Does everything we write have to be searching and meaningful? Where does that leave Molière? Marivaux? Musset?"

"Ah, always these French comparisons!" groaned Konstantin Aksakov. "I suppose you think our only concern should be to emulate Paris."

"Not at all," Annenkov replied calmly. "But you can hardly deny that their theatrical tradition is richer than ours."

Turgenev turned to Ostrovsky, who had maintained a rather grim silence up to now. "What have you to say, Aleksander Nikolayevich? I have read your play with great admiration. You are clearly a man of the theatre. What is your opinion?"

Ostrovsky, whose plump, comfortable frame and features made him look more like the Moscow merchants he had bitterly satirized in *A Family Affair* than an acclaimed young writer with fire in his belly, spoke slowly, choosing his words with care: "Since you are good enough to ask me, Ivan Sergeyevich, I will answer you with complete sincerity. My admiration for your stories in *Sovremennik* would allow for nothing else. I agree, at least on this, with Aksakov. I believe Russian writers should write about Russian life – about what they know. To hell with Marivaux! We have to create a culture of our own, building on what Pushkin and Gogol have done – not always parrot the French.

"I'm glad to hear you say that," said Konstantin Aksakov, his six years seniority allowing him a trace of condescension. "But where is it, then, that we differ?"

"We differ in *how* we write about Russia. You and your brother want the country to turn in on itself and look for its inspiration only in the teachings of the Orthodox Church and the distilled philosophy of the peasant – whatever that may be. I reject both these teachers. I believe they would leave us in a backwater of ignorance and oppression for ever."

This was too much for Ivan, the younger and fiercer of the brothers. "Instead of which you, if your play is anything to judge by, choose to write about nothing but filth and sewage. Isn't that so?"

"Essentially, yes," Ostrovsky admitted. "And the reason for that is that I hope, by so doing, to help to get rid of some of it."

"That's all very well," said Konstantin. "But you lack a sense of proportion. You *only* talk about what is ugly. I would suggest that in your next plays you occasionally touch on the good things in our society."

"I'll try to, if you'll be good enough to tell me what they are."

This provoked Ivan into leaping to his feet and starting to shout insults at Ostrovsky. He was quickly shushed by Avdotya Yakovlevna, who took the opportunity to play the experienced hostess and direct the conversation away from controversial channels. "You're all coursing your favourite hares," she said, "but not one of you except Annenkov has answered Turgenev's question. Do you think he should continue to write for the theatre? For my part, I think he should. I think his talent lies in the small amusing thing neatly and wittily done, rather than the extended seriousness which prose fiction requires."

Turgenev received this barbed compliment with an ambiguous smile. After all, he thought, this was the woman who had said of him some years ago: 'Ivan's never done anything bad, but he'll never do anything good.' Her bluestocking reputation, which she prized almost as dearly as her sexual irresistibility, would suffer if he were to write something important. But he couldn't help being delighted when Nadezhda Samoilova declared unequivocally: "You underrate him, Avdotya. I too think he should write more plays, and not only because I'm an actress and not many people write parts for us like he does. But because I think he has a great deal to offer to the theatre. There's a five-act play of his called *A Month in the Country* that I've just read which, in the unlikely event of the censor ever releasing it, could be as big a landmark as Gogol's *Government Inspector...*" With the unforced charm she wore so lightly, onstage and off, she went over to sit on the arm of Turgenev's chair and plant a light kiss on his cheek. "And don't forget, Vanichka..." she purred, playfully tapping his nose with her finger, "I play Natalya Petrovna."

A few months later, a less aesthetic, more rigorously political, discussion took place in Paris at 50, rue de Douai. George Sand had made one of her now rare excursions to the capital. With the death of Chopin and the gradual betrayal of all the ideals she had so vigorously espoused in 1848, she had sunk into a state of apathetic melancholy which only immersion in the daily tasks of country life and a disciplined schedule of writing managed to keep at bay. But she still followed every detail of Pauline's career with passionate interest and kept up a constant stream of letters praising, encouraging, advising and scolding her protégée with all her old energy. *Sapho* had opened in April to a mixed, though generally cool reception; but the minds of most Frenchmen in mid-1851 had little time to dwell on artistic success or failure. Sand's visit to Paris had two motives: to deliver to her publishers the first draft of her new novel *Le Château des Desertes*; and to discuss with her old friends, Louis and Pauline, the threat she saw hanging over France.

This took the form of the seemingly irresistible rise in the power and prestige of Louis Napoleon. Elected President after the panic of the 'June Days', the man whom everybody despised (Thiers had called him 'a cretin whom we will manage') had shown an unexpectedly sure political touch. Certainly, as Viardot had bitterly remarked at the time, the left had given him a helping hand: in June '49, with the excuse that a French army under Oudinot was about to crush the new Roman Republic and restore Pope Pius IX to his former power, the 'men of '48' had tried to stage another revolution. But France was tired of violence and bloodshed, and they found practically no support anywhere, not even in Paris. Ledru-Rollin had to flee to England and the left seemed doomed. There was a momentary flicker of hope when elections held in March '50, to replace thirty deputies who had been expelled from the Legislative Assembly after the abortive *coup,* returned twenty red republicans; but this threw the ever more conservative Assembly into a panic, and two months later they passed a law reducing the franchise, which had the effect of excluding three of the nine million voters from the suffrage.

This was the moment for Louis Napoleon to display a flash of genius worthy of his uncle. Posing as the champion of the people, he ordered his supporters in the Assembly to propose a motion abrogating this anti-democratic law. Such was his influence that the motion was only defeated by seven votes, which, in fact, suited him admirably: few of those who would lose the vote could be counted among his natural supporters; but at the same time he could bathe in an aura of democratic virtue. The constitution of the Second Republic, which had been approved in November '48, denied the President the possibility of a second term of office. But at the time, when the three friends met in the summer of '51, there was a ground-swell of feeling throughout the country in favour of the revision of the relevant clause.

Louis Viardot wasted no time in getting to the point. "The dreadful mistake we have all made," he said, "is in underestimating that man's political instinct. He may be physically unprepossessing, he may seem of below even average intelligence, but he has played his cards like a master. If we don't find some way of stopping him, we'll find that we haven't exchanged a monarchy for a republic but for another empire."

"I share your gloom," George Sand said sombrely, "but I wonder if you aren't being just a little over-pessimistic. After all, the man did swear allegiance to the constitution."

"Ah yes?!" Viardot snorted. "And didn't he also send French troops to Italy to defend the Roman Republic? And what did they end up doing? Because he feared he might antagonize the clerical party here, they suppressed the Republic and reinstated Pius IX. The man's as untrustworthy as he is glib. I was approached yesterday by someone for whom I have a certain esteem asking me to sign a petition to revoke the four-year clause which would enable Bonaparte to stand again. And I don't know what to say to him. If I refuse, I risk supporting a slide into anarchy. If I accept, I'm confirming in the first office of the state a man I completely despise. Tell me, George, what would you do?"

A sad smile stole briefly over the novelist's face. "I'm afraid, dear Louis," she said, "it's not what I would do but what I will do. I shall go back to Nohant. I shall walk my dogs and stroke my cats and feed my chickens. I shall play with my little granddaughter, and I shall write."

"And politics?" Viardot asked.

"I shall try, my old friend, to banish them from my mind. We had our moment of glory and I very much fear it will not be repeated. I shall read my newspaper conscientiously every morning, but apart from that hour, I shall neither think of nor, heaven forbid, get involved in politics. And if you will allow me to offer you a piece of advice, I would strongly recommend you do the same. You are both about to leave for England for Pauline's London season. She has *Sapho* to think of. After what Berlioz wrote in the *Journal des Débats*, both about her performance and, surprisingly enough, about the work itself, it may well be a triumph. Take your time before coming back. She told me you had been invited to Scotland. Go there. Stay for a while. Pauline can rest and perhaps compose a little. You can shoot grouse and finish your history of the Arabs in Spain. It would be better if you were out of France at this time. Otherwise I fear you will say or write something too strong, and you know how your enemies will get back at you? Through Pauline".

"They've already started," Pauline interjected. "Don't think all the reviews of *Sapho* were on a par with Berlioz's. Of course he feels music with every fibre of his body, whereas they have to rely on their dry little heads. And he speaks only for himself, while they are always looking over their shoulders at their paymasters." She pulled some clippings out of a drawer. "Escudier in *La France Musicale*…"

"Owned by friends of Morny, the President's half-brother," Louis volunteered.

"'*Madame Viardot no longer sings; every note that issues from her intelligent voice…*' thank you very much, Monsieur Escudier… '*is a piercing cry. Her wounded organ no longer has any charm, it is no more than the shadow of a fine painting…*'

Louis seized the pile from his wife's hands and extracted another one. "And listen to this," he said, his hands trembling with rage. From *La Patrie* – I don't need to tell you where its interests lie. '*… If this once talented artist would deign to accept our advice, we would suggest that she spend more time on her* vocalises *and less on dining, when she is abroad, with the exiled enemies of our state.*'… that's a reference to an evening in London when Ledru and Louis Blanc came to our house for dinner."

George beat the sides of her armchair with her fists. It's monstrous," she cried. "Just monstrous. You must do what I say. Go. Leave France for a while. Pauline can sing anywhere – Germany, Russia, Italy. Leave these ungrateful Parisians to applaud their second-rate favourites. Nothing would make them happier than if they could find an excuse to close the *Opéra* to her once again. Don't risk it, Louis, for her sake."

Viardot nodded and got to his feet. "You're probably right," he said with a grimace of distaste. "And, for my part, I would rather watch the victory of reaction in France from another shore. I shall try and look up Ledru in London. If there is nothing we can do, we can at least lament together. And now, I will leave you two alone. I have some letters to write, and I'm sure you have much to talk about, which would not be of the slightest interest to me. Come and say goodbye before you go, George."

As soon as he had left the room, George turned anxiously to her friend. "I hope I didn't say the wrong thing," she said. "But I really am worried about Louis. He becomes more outspoken every day, and he's made a lot of enemies. I don't think he realizes how ruthless these new men are. I don't want to wake up one day and read that he's been imprisoned or exiled too. But perhaps," she added, giving Pauline a keen glance, "you have reasons to keep you here that I don't know of."

"No, no, I'd be happy to spend some time away. There's nothing I'd miss here in France. Except you, and we see each other so little."

"And Gounod?"

The actress opened her eyes wide in innocent surprise. "Gounod? What of him? He doesn't need me now."

"His career may not. But perhaps he does. After all those weeks you spent closeted together in Courtavenel, don't tell me there was nothing between you but mutual artistic admiration?"

"Perhaps a little harmless flirtation. Nothing more. And you should perhaps know, Ninoune, that I fear Monsieur Gounod is not quite the other-wordly young man he likes to be taken for. He would have made a very Stendhalian *abbé*. It is my distinct impression that, with *Sapho* now produced, my presence will become much less necessary to him."

Sand couldn't resist a satisfied smile. "Well, you know I never liked him, so you won't mind my saying I'm not surprised. But what about Turgenev? With his mother dead, he must be a rich man now. There's nothing to keep him from coming back… especially with his daughter here too."

The low tone in which Pauline answered only served to heighten the conviction behind her words. "He won't come unless I tell him to," she said.

Sand was beginning to find her friend's behaviour increasingly puzzling. She waited for elucidation, but none came. Finally she ventured a timid, "And won't you?"

Pauline gave no sign of having heard her. She sat quite motionless, chin cupped in her hands, gazing out of the window as though at unfathomable vistas; but they could not have been particularly enticing as her eyes soon filled with tears, her head moved almost imperceptibly from side to side and she whispered: "No."

A less intimate, or perhaps less curious, friend might have left it there. But Sand pressed on. "May I ask why not?"

Pauline turned her head and gazed candidly at her questioner. "Because there is no room for him in my life, Ninoune. We can't go back to where we were before. We're not the same people any more – neither me, nor him, nor Louis. There's been some… I don't know… loss of innocence, perhaps. He either has to be everything for me or – for the time being, at any rate – nothing. These past months have been the most difficult of my life. There are moments when I feel nothing is more important to me than my love for him. But they are only moments. The rest of the time is taken up with… my life: my career, my marriage, my daughter. One way or another, I have to make a definitive choice. And I think he knows that I've already made it. He wrote and told me he wouldn't come unless I 'summoned him'.

And I can't bring myself to do that. Above all, for Louis's sake. I haven't forgotten the lecture you read me not so long ago. You know how good he is to me. And how much I need him. It may sound calculating – I wouldn't say it to anyone but you – but who would look after my affairs if anything happened to our marriage? Ivan couldn't take care of a vegetable garden. He's told me that, less than a year after his mother's death, his serfs are already beginning to take advantage of him. So you see, your advice to spend the winter in Scotland is perhaps even better than you thought. It will give me time, which here in Paris I never seem to have, to devote myself to my husband. He's a dear, good man and he deserves better of me." She slipped to the floor, clasped the older woman's hands and laid her head in her lap. "Oh, forgive me for going on like this." She looked up into Sand's troubled face. "And say something, for God's sake."

George Sand stroked her thick black hair and murmured in what she hoped was a soothing tone: "I'm afraid, Fifille, that you sound as though you're trying to convince yourself rather than me."

A knock on the door made Pauline scramble back into her chair. However it was not, as she had expected, Louis who came into the room, but a young woman whose erect posture and starched governess's uniform attempted to impose an air of severity on an otherwise amiable disposition.

"What is it, Berthe," Pauline said. "Do you need to see me about something?"

"I'm afraid so, madame. It's the girls. They're quarrelling again, and this time there's nothing I can do to stop them. I'm afraid they're going to come to blows. I'm sorry to disturb you, but…"

"That's quite all right. I'll be up in a minute. Tell them I'm coming, and I expect them to be sitting quietly reading by the time I arrive."

After the governess had left the room, Pauline turned to Sand and threw up her hands in despair. "What am I going to do with those two? This happens almost every day! They detest each other."

"Does Turgenev know?"

"On the contrary! I always write to him that they are the greatest of friends. He'd be distraught if he suspected otherwise. He'd be bound to do something wildly impractical … like suddenly showing up to try and put things right."

"Perhaps he should."

"Heaven forbid! He'd only make it worse. Ivan has two reactions to emotional scenes: the first is to look the other way; the second, if his head is violently wrenched back round, is to blunder in and irreparably smash what, with a little delicacy, might have been put back together." She got to her feet and smiled down at her friend. "But perhaps I'm being too pessimistic. The first year could be the worst. Who knows, in time they may become inseparable. I won't be long. I'll send Louis back in to keep you company."

"She was reading my book!"

Jealous rage rendered Louise's never very attractive little face positively ugly. She was sitting bolt upright in a straight-backed chair, an open book on her lap, her heels viciously kicking the bottom of the chair. She had never been a happy little girl; starved of her mother's company on account of her frequent absences and competing for her affections with her many admirers, she had bitterly resented the Russian interloper from the moment of her arrival.

In pointed contrast, Paulinette, as she now was, was sitting at a table, nimbly flicking a pencil over a drawing pad, the picture of studied indifference. She barely bothered to look up when Pauline came in, but contented herself with remarking casually: "I'd picked it up first."

"Well you shouldn't have. It's my book."

"You were playing with your dolls. You only wanted the book when you saw I was starting to read it."

"That's a lie. You knew I was…"

"That's enough, both of you." Pauline's authoritative intervention brought instant silence. "I've told you before, I didn't want any more of these stupid scenes. Louise, if you're not reading the book, it's perfectly all right for Paulinette to read it. Paulinette, if it's her book, you should ask her first. Now I want you both to say you're sorry to Mademoiselle Berthe for behaving so badly and then give each other a kiss and forget all about it."

The two girls reluctantly stood up, went over to the governess, bobbed a curtsey and muttered, "*Pardon, mademoiselle.*" They then stood and glared at each other.

"Go on," Pauline said, "do as I say or I shall ask Monsieur Viardot to devise some punishment for you."

The threat had its effect. Without raising an arm to touch one another, they leant forward and brushed their lips against the other's cheek. But neither the fire in Louise's eyes nor the sullen resentment in Paulinette's underwent the slightest change.

Pauline stayed a few minutes to discuss some matters with the governess. When she got back to the sitting-room, she was unsurprised by the topic her husband and George Sand were discussing. "… if he can't persuade them," Louis was saying, "to revise the constitution so that he can serve a second term, he'll feel justified in taking the law into his own hands."

"A *coup d'état*?" Sand pursed her lips and then shook her head. "No, I don't think so. I don't believe that scarecrow is made of that kind of material."…

Good morning, dear and good Madame Viardot,

My first word must be one of extreme anxiety. Yesterday brought the news of the coup d'état in Paris. I cannot imagine that such a thing could take place without bloodshed, and knowing that your house is right in the centre of the most turbulent quarter of the city, I am beside myself with worry. Please let me know, the minute you receive this, that you and all the family are safe …

7 December.

… For three days the talk here has been of nothing else but the turmoil in Paris. And still I have not had a word from you. I understand how many things there must be on your mind at a time like this, but I have to say that I find it cruel of you not to take a moment to reassure me. A friend of mine had a letter from Paris, dated the 5th, which spoke of soldiers firing into the crowd on the boulevard Poissonière and killing many innocent bystanders. That is only a few minutes' walk from rue de Douai. If you have any feeling for me, send me a line to put my mind at rest …

10 December.

…This is the third time in six days that I have written asking for confirmation that you are all safe and sound. Is it possible that none of my letters has reached you? Or yours me? Forgive me, but I can write of nothing else. Music, theatre – all those subjects on which we usually want to exchange news – what interest can they have for me at this agonizing moment? I shall not write in the old way to you again until I have heard that all is well…

It was to be some time before Turgenev's anxieties were relieved. Louis Napoleon's *coup d'état* may have been comparatively bloodless, but it was convulsive enough to bring most of France's services to a halt. His letters didn't reach rue de Douai until many weeks later, by which time the Viardots were in Scotland. But had he known of certain indignities to which they were subjected, his worries would only have increased. Although they suffered no physical danger, George Sand's prediction that Louis's stubborn opposition to the forces of reaction, whatever form they took, would cause his family trouble was soon vindicated. On the evening after drunken cavalrymen had opened fire on innocent bystanders, who had merely stopped on the boulevards to gawk, an unexpected visitor arrived at rue du Douai. Henri Martin, a distinguished historian who was also a convinced, if not particularly vocal, republican came with his two small sons and asked if he could stay the night. He had heard that the houses of certain suspect intellectuals were being searched and any kind of incriminating writing was being sequestered and the authors arrested. Fearing that his account of the 1789 revolution, on which he was working, might be considered compromising, he had locked, barred and shuttered the house, sent his wife off to her mother's in the country and was seeking asylum from his old and trusted friend. Viardot was happy to accede to his request. Pauline took the boys off to play with Louise and Paulinette, and the two men settled down for a pre-dinner smoke and a grave discussion of the events of the past few days. But they had barely had time to light their cigars before fists were heard hammering on the door and the maid announced the arrival of a detachment of police. A commissioner was shown in and announced that he had orders to search the house. Martin gazed at his friend in almost comic perplexity as Louis tried to brazen it out: did the man realize who he was, who his wife was, who his friend and guest was? But the commissioner merely thrust a piece of paper under his nose and ordered his men to carry on.

Louis and Pauline were enraged at what ensued. As the policemen clumped from room to room, opening drawers, peering into cupboards, looking under cushions, the commissioner brusquely interrogated them. Were they hiding anyone in the house? Were there weapons concealed anywhere? Did they have any letters from known enemies of the state, especially – and here the man had to peer myopically at his written instructions – a certain Monsieur George Sand? Pauline brought all her stage experience to bear and disdainfully said that she had sometimes corresponded in the past with *Madame* George Sand, but she had no idea if she had kept any of the letters.

Eventually the search party came back and demanded the key of Louis's desk. He had no choice but to hand it over, and two letters were taken out of a drawer; one was from Daniele Manin, the other from Lajos Kossuth, both of whom had led anti-Hapsburg risings in 1848, the first in Venice, the second in Hungary. The commissioner checked these names against his list and put them in his pocket. With a warning to the Viardots that they were to hold themselves available for possible further questioning, he reassembled his men and led them out of the house.

The minute they had left, Pauline rushed up to her bedroom. She had refused to be present when the room was being searched, haughtily declaring that it was disgraceful enough that a lady's bedroom should be ransacked, without the owner being expected to stand by watching. The first thing she saw was that her escritoire had been opened; from one drawer a large bundle of letters had been extracted, hastily sifted through and then flung carelessly on to the bed. They were all from George Sand. Louis and Henri Martin had followed her in, and the three of them looked at each other in bewilderment, wondering why they had not been taken away. Then Pauline, who had been idly glancing through the letters in her hand, burst out laughing. "Of course," she said, "they're all signed Ninoune!"

This upsetting episode confirmed them in a decision which they had all but taken already, namely to return to spend several months with their Scottish friends, the Hays, at Duns Castle, near Berwick. They had gone there in August at the end of Pauline's London season. *Sapho* had not met with the approval of English audiences or critics, one of whom said of it: 'A work fuller of pretension and emptier of merit we have never heard'. Only Pauline was spared, Chorley, admittedly by now a family friend, writing in the *Athenaeum* of the 'luminous beauty' of her performance. This enraged Gounod, who wrote to a friend, after hearing her as Donna Anna in *Don Giovanni*, that 'her career is nearing its end as she sings out of tune all the time'. Fortunately Pauline did not hear of this for some time, and when she did it no longer mattered. But if England did little to further her artistic career, Scotland did wonders for her domestic life. She took the opportunity, as she had intimated to George Sand, to devote time and affection to Louis, with such success that in October she was able to tell him that she was expecting another child. They had been tempted to stay on with the Hays over Christmas, but an urgent letter from Mlle Berthe forced them to return to Paris: the rivalry between Louise and Paulinette had become insupportable, and the governess was threatening to quit if some parental discipline were not forthcoming.

Pauline had no choice but to concede that the experiment had failed. With her characteristic refusal to prolong a situation which had proved unworkable, and with the added factor of a new child on the way, she acted swiftly and decisively. A place was found for Paulinette in an educational *pension* run by a Mademoiselle Renard in rue de Ménilmontant. It was explained to her that she would still be considered part of the family and would pay regular visits to rue de Douai once or twice a week. Paulinette seemed to accept this new change in her life with complete indifference. To her father, it was announced that the step had been taken as her quick intelligence required greater stimulation than Mlle Berthe had been able to provide. Turgenev was completely satisfied with this explanation; or perhaps it would be truer to say that he gave it very little thought, his mind, when he heard the news, being taken up with quite other considerations.

"Gogol is dead?!" Turgenev gazed in incredulous horror at an out-of-breath Panaev, who was standing in the hallway of the apartment he had taken on Malaya Morskaya Street. Panaev had literally run from the *Sovremennik* offices to bring him the news. "How did it happen?"

The scrawnily-built Panaev, still recovering from his exertions, needed a moment before he could reply. Turgenev led him into the room he used as a study, motioned him into a chair and sat down opposite him. "I saw him less than six months ago, and he seemed tolerably well… or at least no sicker than he usually looked."

"I know of nothing for certain. It happened yesterday in Moscow, and already the rumours are flying around. Some are saying that he had been persuaded by that priest who had such a hold over him…"

"Father Matvei…"

"Yes. He'd encouraged him to burn the manuscript of the second part of *Dead Souls*… and he then fell into such a depression he lost the will to live."

A vision of Belinsky's face, incandescent with anger, floated for a moment into Turgenev's vision. "He was only forty-three," he murmured. "Pushkin at thirty-eight, Gogol at forty-three, Belinsky at thirty-seven! How quickly Russia kills off her men of genius. What else are they saying?"

"Since you mentioned Belinsky, his old enemies claim that Gogol never recovered from his attack on *Select Passages*…"

"You mean they blame Belinsky for his death?"

"More or less, yes."

Turgenev let out a sardonic laugh. "How Vissarion Grigorievich would have appreciated that! He was the first man to proclaim Gogol's genius. His letter – I was there with him when he wrote it – was an angry, yes, but heartfelt plea for Gogol to wrest himself away from all the reactionary and clerical influences that were strangling his unique gift and return to writing as he had before, but even better. Oh, if only he were here now. He would write an obituary that would scorch the earth."

"As he is not, why don't you do it in his place?"

"It would be a poor thing in comparison. But perhaps I will try."

"Don't try. Do it… now, while your instincts are raw… before you have too much time to think what you are saying. Write direct from your grief. I must go now. I have to tell Botkin and Granowsky. Sit at this desk and start writing. It should come out on the day of his funeral, which I hear is set for next Sunday. But it would be better not to publish it in *Sovremennik*. The authorities are just looking for an excuse to close us down. Send it to one of the daily newspapers here. They would be expected to publish an article on Russia's foremost author."

As Turgenev accompanied him to the front door, Panaev offered one more word of advice. "And I would suggest that you forget Belinsky. What he would have written could never get published today. Concentrate on Gogol's literary talent. Leave what he was trying to say to those of us who know anyway…"

After he had closed the door behind Panaev, Turgenev did go immediately back into his study and sat down at his desk. But instead of starting the obituary, he dashed off a note to Paris… '*a great disaster has befallen us. Gogol has died. It seems that, a few days ago, he burnt all his manuscripts. Then, having committed this moral suicide, he lay down, never to rise again. There can be no Russian whose heart is not bleeding at this moment. For us he was more than just a writer – he revealed us to ourselves. It will be difficult for you to appreciate what this means to us. You have to be Russian to understand what we have lost.*'

As he read these few lines over, he saw that a tear had fallen on to the paper and made 'moral suicide' illegible. He copied the letter out again and then started to make notes for the obituary.

Gogol's funeral took place in Moscow five days later. Everyone belonging to the literary and theatrical worlds was there, along with an enormous crowd of ordinary Muscovites. The authorities' attempts to play down the event proved as futile as they were petty. They forbade the coffin to be placed on the horse-drawn hearse; whereupon six stout men hoisted it on to their shoulders and carried it the three and a half miles from the church to the cemetery. If anybody had thought that novels and stories only reached the wealthy, educated strata of society, that day they were radically disabused. And that only made their fear and hatred of literature more virulent.

Two days after the funeral, Turgenev visited the offices of the *St Petersburg News,* to which he had sent his obituary, to ask why it had not been printed. The editor regretted that he had had to withdraw it, hoped that his distinguished visitor would do him the honour of contributing to his newspaper on another occasion, and explained that the chairman of the St Petersburg censorship committee had not only refused to even consider Turgenev's article, but had laid down that he would do everything in his power to ensure that 'that lackey' Gogol's name would not be mentioned in public. As Turgenev walked down the steps of the building, his cheeks burning with anger and shame, he remembered that his professor of literature at St Petersburg university, Aleksander Nikitenko, had recently been appointed the Government's chief censor. On the spur of the moment, he hailed a droshky and ordered the driver to take him to the imposing building on Vasilevsky Island which housed the Ministry of the Interior.

To his surprise, Nikitenko's clerk told him that His Excellency would receive him shortly, and a quarter of an hour later he found himself seated in a luxurious office opposite his old teacher. This man was surely the most remarkable example of upward mobility in mid-19th century Russia. The son of a serf, he had been freed and befriended by some of the Decembrists, survived their débâcle and worked his way up to a university professorship and eventually to the Ministry of Education.

After a brief exchange of civilities, during which Nikitenko congratulated him on the work he had published in *Sovremennik,* he asked Turgenev to what he owed the pleasure of this unexpected visit. For a moment Turgenev was in a quandary. For all the affability of the greeting, the man sitting opposite him was now Czar Nicholas's chief censor, and he knew from Annenkov what frustration and heartache the censorship had caused a large number of writers. But he quickly decided that as he was here, there was nothing to be gained from beating about the bush. So he explained in a few words the feeling of injustice that the morning's episode in the newspaper offices had aroused in him. Nikitenko sat, resting his elbows on the arms of an ornate gilt chair, his hands joined at the fingertips, which he tapped rhythmically against his lips. He listened attentively to Turgenev's account of his meeting with the editor. When it was over, he continued for a while to gaze in silence at his interlocutor, an enigmatic, interrogative expression on his face. The question he finally asked was not at all what Turgenev had been expecting, although there was no mistaking the dry voice and slightly pedagogic manner. "Do you still write poems, Ivan Sergeyevich?"

"Not any more, no."

"And why not, may I ask?"

"Because I don't think I'm a good poet."

"Hm! And yet I remember you submitting to me some poems many years ago now which were not without qualities."

"I remember that too, Aleksander Vasilevich. I even remember your being kind enough to arrange for one of them to be published in *Sovremennik*. It is not a thing one easily forgets. It was the year after Pushkin's death, and the first time I ever saw work of mine in print."

"Yes. The poem was called *Evening*, if I'm not mistaken."

"So it was. That I had forgotten. I am astounded – and I must confess a little flattered – by your excellent memory."

"I find one usually remembers details of things that are important to one. And literature – you will not be surprised to hear – is important to me."

There was a pause, while a question hesitated on the tip of Turgenev's tongue. But his former professor let him off the hook.

"You are no doubt wondering whether you dare ask me a question. Is that not so, Ivan Sergeyevich?" Turgenev nodded. "And that question is: If literature means so much to me, how is it that I am sitting here in this office? Have I read you correctly?" Turgenev nodded again. "Well then, in deference to a former pupil who is gratifying his onetime tutor by developing and honing his gifts, I will endeavour to explain. Someone has to be here. His Majesty the Czar is quite correct in thinking that the state cannot allow anyone and everyone to publish whatever they see fit to scribble. Books, and indeed newspapers, are read not only by people of birth and education, but also by those who are in no position to judge what is valid and what is meretricious or plain scurrilous. Now I ask you, Ivan Sergeyevich, if we admit that the office of censor is necessary for the well-being of the state, is it not better that that office should be filled by someone who esteems and respects literature than by someone who is ignorant of or even indifferent to it?"

Remembering the purpose of his visit, Turgenev prayed to Belinsky's spirit to forgive him and gave his cautious assent.

"Good," Nikitenko continued. "Now let us turn from the general to the

211

particular. You will not be surprised to know that I too was shocked to hear of Gogol's death. I hadn't seen him for many years. Had you?"

"Yes, I saw him last October. It was the only time I ever had the chance to talk to him. Shtchepkin, who had played the mayor in *The Government Inspector* and was about to appear in a little play of mine, took me to see him. I shall never forget it. It was a cold day and he was standing in his overcoat writing at a high desk. Under the overcoat he had on a green velvet waistcoat and a pair of brown trousers. His feet were stuffed into some old woollen slippers, out of one of which his big toe was protruding."

"Was he pleased to see you?"

"Oh yes, he was kindness itself. He seemed to welcome our visit, which makes me think now that his work was not coming easily. When we writers don't mind being interrupted, it usually means that things are not going well. He sat me down on a sofa beside him and made some very complimentary remarks about my work."

"That must have meant a great deal to you."

"It did. The trouble was, it was difficult for me to concentrate on what he was saying."

"Why?"

"I was so struck by his appearance. He seemed to have aged twenty years since I had last seen him. He made me think of a crafty old fox, with his restless, darting eyes, long, pointed, bony nose, carelessly clipped moustache and swollen, fleshy lips. He hadn't combed his hair, which stuck up like leftover scraps of wire tossed on to a rubbish heap. And when he opened that strangely formless mouth to talk, I saw just a few stubs of rotten teeth… and with his face thrust only a few inches away from mine, I have to say, his breath…"

"In short, your hero didn't make a very favourable impression on you."

"Physically, no. But there was no mistaking his genius. It was strange… at first, when he was talking about my stories and I was daring to ask him about his, he was the old Gogol: funny, brilliant, grotesque, irreverent… Then, when I mentioned the second part of *Dead Souls*, and said how eagerly we were all waiting for it – which I now realize was a mistake – he changed completely. His eyes lost their brilliance and became vague and opaque. He uttered a few platitudes about the redemptive powers of literature, the untold riches of the Russian soul, the unique sense of honour in every Russian's heart, and how the first part of his novel had been everywhere misunderstood and not till the second part was published would its true purpose be appreciated. I asked him whether he anticipated any problems this time with the censorship… forgive me, Aleksander Vasilevich, but for us writers it's like an eczema, we cannot help scratching it."

"And how did Gogol answer you?" Nikitenko asked.

He astonished me by intoning, like a priest delivering a sermon, that, far from finding censorship inhibiting, he now considered it salutary and stimulating. I began to see the other Gogol, the new Gogol, the Gogol who had written the *Select Passages*, which many of his old admirers found so disconcerting. And then, as though he had read my mind, he reverted to the 'old' Gogol once again, laid a hand on my sleeve and pitifully asked me to retain a good opinion of him and to champion that opinion in what he called 'the party to which you belong'".

Nikitenko considered this for a moment and then, evidently deciding not to comment on it, leaned forward over the desk and asked: "Are you able to show me this obituary you have written?"

The newspaper editor had returned the copy to Turgenev. He now handed it to Nikitenko, who read it through carefully and then laid it deliberately down on the desk in front of him. "Certainly," he said, "in itself, it cannot be considered in any way inflammatory. You do justice to Gogol's great talent and do not try to draw any political conclusions from the content of his work."

"So why do you think it was turned down?" Turgenev interposed.

"That, of course, I cannot say with any certainty. But it could be that my colleague on the committee was more concerned with how Gogol had been misinterpreted in certain quarters than with what he actually wrote. Do you know whether he had read your piece?"

Turgenev gazed at him in bewilderment. "Well, no, not for certain. The editor didn't say one way or the other."

"And you didn't ask him?"

"It never occurred to me. For that matter, it never occurred to me that work could be censored without having being read."

"It does happen," Nikitenko observed imperturbably. "It must be put down to an excess of zeal. That which Talleyrand warned us against. At any rate, I shouldn't worry about it too much. Your obituary is a worthy tribute to a remarkable writer. And as no official statement has been issued – it would have to have passed through this office for my signature – I see no reason why you should not present it again."

"Then you would be prepared to allow it to be published?"

Nikitenko favoured him with a sad smile and then rose to his feet to indicate the interview was over. "Not here in St Petersburg, I'm afraid. It would be wrong of me to overturn the decision of a colleague. But... elsewhere, perhaps?"

On March 13th Turgenev's article was published in *Moskovskiia vedomosti,* the *Moscow Gazette*. It had been passed by the chairman of the Moscow censorship committee, who had not heard of the decision of his St Petersburg colleague. It was really little more than an extension and amplification of the letter he had written to Pauline – a harmless outpouring of admiration and grief by a fledgling writer over the death of a man whom he admired as a master. But it gave two people who, over the past few years, had been following Turgenev's development with suspicious disapproval, the pretext to take the kind of action they had had in mind for some time.

INT. A SMALL ROOM IN THE IMPERIAL WINTER PALACE – DAY

Czar Nicholas I sits in his office behind a massive mahogany desk. On the other side, rigid as though at attention on the parade ground, stands the Chief of the Gendarmerie, Count Alexey Orlov, a fair-haired, strikingly handsome man who is as despotic with his inferiors as he is subservient to his master. Nicholas motions him into a chair.

CZAR

Sit down, Count …

Orlov obeys, without letting his backbone sag for a second.

CZAR

Tell me more about this Turgenev business.

ORLOV

There's not a great deal to tell, Sire. Musin-Pushkin banned his Gogol obituary here in St Petersburg. Quite rightly, in my opinion. Whereupon the fellow had the nerve to get some friends of his in Moscow… pretty dubious characters, I might say… to submit it there. Not knowing of the ban, the censor passed it… wrongly, in my opinion… and it appeared in the *Gazette*.

The Czar picks up a newspaper from his desk and contemplates it for a moment.

CZAR
(slowly)

In itself, it is not particularly offensive…

He waits for Orlov to disagree, but the Count is not going to contradict his Emperor until he is sure that is what is expected of him.

CZAR

… do you find, Orlov?

ORLOV

With permission, Sire, there are phrases in it which seem to me quite out of proportion to the subject.

Nicholas hands the newspaper across the table.

CZAR

Tell me which ones you mean.

ORLOV

(scanning the paper)

Well, for instance, here where he talks of 'this man whom we now have the right – the bitter right – to call great… this man of whom we are justly proud as one of the glories of Russia…' With respect, Sire, it seems to me that the glories of Russia have been your forebears – Peter, Catherine, your brother Alexander – or our generals who defeated Bonaparte – Kutuzov, for example – not some wretched, unpatriotic scribbler.

CZAR

Yes, I see what you mean. All writers are dangerous. And this sort of posthumous praise tends to plant wrong ideas in young people's heads and encourage them to indulge in undesirable practices.

ORLOV

Quite, Sire.

CZAR

I've had my eye on this Turgenev for some time. There are elements in those stories he writes that are quite disruptive. He's not turning out well. Pity. Comes from an excellent family. His mother was a splendid woman, I've heard. Ran the estate like a man. Wonder where he went wrong. All those years in France, no doubt.

ORLOV

And the company he kept there.

CZAR

Ah! What do you know about that?

215

ORLOV

We know everything, Sire. He was a frequent guest at Herzen's house…

CZAR

Another potentially good man gone wrong.

ORLOV

Quite, Sire.

CZAR

Who else did he see?

ORLOV

It is rumoured that he met Bakunin clandestinely.

CZAR

The sooner that man's locked up the better.

ORLOV

He is, Sire.

CZAR

Is what?

ORLOV

Locked up. He's been in Königstein fortress since that trouble last year in Dresden.

CZAR

Ah! Well then, I'd better ask Frederick Augustus to hand him over. He'll be safer with us. Who else was Turgenev familiar with in France?

ORLOV

Well, the Viardot family he was staying with are intimate friends of…
(he pauses, as though fearful of pronouncing the name)
George Sand…

Nicholas leaps to his feet, instantly followed by Orlov. The Czar strides around the room, unable to contain his anger.

CZAR

That abominable woman! I don't know which is worse, the
shameless immorality of her private life or the godless anarchism
she preaches in her disgusting books. No wonder this Turgenev
thinks he can do as he likes. We'll have to teach him a lesson.
Perhaps it's not too late for him to mend his ways. What
punishment did you have in mind, Count?

ORLOV

I think we should keep him under police surveillance, Sire. One
more false move, and a period of exile or imprisonment would
then be in order.

CZAR

Too lenient, Orlov. The man tried to make a fool of the censorship.
If we allow that sort of thing, who knows where it may end? No,
he'll serve a month's imprisonment for disobedience and infraction
of the censorship regulations, and then be exiled to his estate until
further notice.

Satisfied with this pronouncement, he sits down again behind his desk.

Orlov looks ill-at-east and gives a nervous cough.

CZAR

What's the matter, Count? Do you think I am being over-harsh?

ORLOV

Not at all, Sire. It's just that…in the same issue of the *Gazette* – on
the same page, even – there was a similar obituary of Gogol, written
by Aksakov.

CZAR

Which Aksakov? One of those hot-headed boys?

ORLOV

No, Sire, their father.

CZAR

Sergey Timofeyevich? Good heavens, man, no harm in that. He's an excellent fellow… was a Moscow censor himself for many years. Don't forget, Count, it's not the act we have to be on our guard against, it's the actor. *C'est la ton qui fait la musique…*

The place selected for Turgenev's imprisonment was the Admiralty, an early 19ᵗʰ century building with an elegant needle spire which stands on the south bank of the Great Neva, not far from the ill-famed Peter and Paul fortress. There, on the morning of 16th April 1852, he was delivered by a police captain to the prison governor, a colonel from the minor nobility who treated him with a cool courtesy which barely masked his underlying disapproval that a man of his class should find himself in this position. After a few brief formalities he was taken to his cell – or shown to his room, he later thought, might have seemed a more appropriate expression – by the warder that had been assigned to him, a gnarled, limping, grey-haired veteran of the Napoleonic wars, the chest of his gendarme's uniform covered with medals. His name was Gerasim. Turgenev was pleasantly surprised by the room in which he was to spend the next four weeks: it was of reasonable size, with a wide, if barred, window letting in plenty of light, a table with two wooden chairs, a leather armchair in a corner, a washstand with a clean white china jug and bowl and a bed with a woollen mattress large enough to accommodate even this prisoner's outsize frame.

On hearing of his sentence, Turgenev's first anxiety had been how he would cope with the lack of company; for a month there would be no one to talk to and no one to listen to. Or so he thought. In fact, the news of his arrest was known to all his St Petersburg friends within twenty-four hours, and by the second day he was receiving visitors every afternoon. Moved by affection, curiosity, or simply in search of fuel for gossip, colleagues from *Sovremennik*, acquaintances from his student days, relations he had forgotten or never knew he had, all came flocking to the Admiralty to see this unusual prisoner. Men friends brought him books and tobacco; motherly ladies arrived with icons; their daughters surreptitiously slipped him unreadable romantic novels in which later, distractedly flipping through them, he would find pressed dried flowers sewn into the pages. Every second day a basket would arrive from the Panaev's house in which Avdotya, in perhaps the one act of genuine friendship of their long acquaintance, had packed cold roast meats, pastries, dried fruits and excellent wines to substitute the tedious prison fare. Gerasim would come into the cell, the basket dangling from his arm, and joyfully announce: "More provisions for us, sir", knowing that a choice selection would be passed on to him.

But the host of visitors attracted the attention of the governor, who duly reported it to the authorities in the Third Section of the Czar's Private Chancery, a bureaucratic euphemism for Nicholas's all-powerful secret police. Fearing to make the prisoner into a martyr by refusing him the right to receive visitors enjoyed by all but the most dangerous criminals, they waited for a pretext, which was not long in arriving. One afternoon at the end of the second week of Turgenev's term, the narrow street that flanked one side of the Admiralty building was so jammed with his friends' carriages that the Third Section was able to proclaim that an unauthorized demonstration had taken place. From that day on, visits were limited to a maximum of one a day.

This threw Turgenev ever more into the company of Gerasim, which suited them both. Turgenev calculated that he would have the rest of his life to converse with the aristocratic and artistic circles of St Petersburg, whereas when again would he have the chance of talking on equal terms with a man like his warder? Gerasim, whose wife had recently died and who now lived with a son and daughter-in-law, who groaned every time he started to reminisce about his experiences during the retreat from Moscow, found a captive listener who actually egged him on; the usual run of prisoners with whom he had to deal were either serfs who were flogged and soon released or young disaffected sons of doctors and lawyers, who were far too taken up with themselves to be bothered with anything their warder had to say. But here was a real *barin*, of the same stamp as the officer to whom he had been a devoted soldier-servant, and Turgenev soon found himself considering offering the man a job as his valet after his release.

"Beggin' yer pardon, sir," he said one evening, emboldened by a couple of glasses of la Panaeva's Johannisberg, "but I don't rightly understand why they put you in 'ere."

"I'm not sure that I do either," Turgenev laughed. "The official reason is that they didn't like something I wrote in one of the papers."

"But you think there's more to it, is that the way it is?"

"There could be."

"And what, if I'm not troubling your honour's patience, might that be?"

There are some other things I've written… some stories … which I think they liked even less."

"Stories? What's wrong with stories? My captain, the one I travelled all the way across Europe with, told me lots of stories. What was it they didn't like about 'em?"

"Well… they were all about the province of Orel, where I grew up as a boy, and in some of them I showed the serfs and house servants as decent, honest, god-fearing folk… and some of the landowners and local gentry as… not always having the same qualities."

"Oh, they wouldn't like that, sir, would they?"

"No, I suppose not. But tell me about this captain of yours."

"He was a fine man, sir. One of the best. Looked after me like a father. A count, he was. Count Mansurov. I was with 'im all the way from Moscow to the outskirts of Paris. He even taught me a little *parlay-voo fransay*, but I've *oobliayed* most of that. And he'd tell me stories about what had gone on in that country... the Revolution, with Robespyair and Danton and all them. I couldn't have served under a better officer."

"What became of him?"

"Can't rightly say, sir. I never saw 'im again after I got back home. I did hear he was mixed up with all those nobles what got arrested and all after the accession of the present Czar – God bless 'im! But there may not 'ave been a word of truth in it. All I can say is, wherever he may be, alive or dead, God be with 'im. There ain't many around like 'im."

One of the last people to visit Turgenev in his cell, only a couple of days before he was released, was Annenkov. He had been settling some affairs on his property near Simbirsk, a town on the Volga in the Kuybyshev region, and had only heard of his friend's arrest on his return the previous day. He had come prepared to commiserate and was surprised to find the prisoner in excellent spirits. But he couldn't resist the old friend's privilege of reminding him that he owed the situation he was in today to not having taken that old friend's advice. "Didn't I tell you you should have stayed in France? It was madness to come back in this climate. Herzen was right after all."

"Herzen? What has he to do with it?"

"I didn't tell you... I thought it would make you angry... but he was convinced you were only leaving Paris because Madame Viardot insisted you did. In fact, he actually said to me: 'Turgenev is mad to go at a time like this to die in the clutches of Nicholas, for la Garcia.'"

Turgenev gave a rueful smile. "Aleksander Ivanovich is politically one of the shrewdest men I have ever met. But I can think of no one less qualified to pronounce on affairs of the heart. You have only to look at the mess he is now in himself. Never mind, I'm sure he meant well. And I am not going to die. Far from it. I think this past month has given me a new view on life... a view which I hope to be able to carry over to my exile at Spasskoye."

"How have you spent your days? Didn't you find time hanging heavy on your hands?"

"On the contrary, I've never been busier. In fact, I've had to make a timetable to make sure I achieve everything I've set out to do." He took a sheet of paper from the table and handed it to Annenkov. "There have been so many distractions..."

"What's this?" Annenkov, who had been casting a desultory eye over the list, suddenly froze in horror. Although they were alone in the cell, he lowered his voice to a whisper. "Polish?!"

"Yes, I'm teaching myself Polish."

"The language of Russia's hereditary enemy. You really are mad. They'll take it for granted that you're in touch with the independence conspirators. They'll give you ten years, not one month, if they find out."

"They won't find out. Nekrasov brought me the books I needed wrapped in a cheesecloth, and I told Gerasim I was learning Bulgarian. They'll think I'm preparing to lead a Pan-Slav expedition against the Turks. The penitent prodigal son ending up as hero!"

"And if the governor walks in on you and you haven't time to hide the books?"

"I'll tell him I'm planning to translate Adam Mickiewicz's poetry. It could even be true. I met him at the Viardots one evening and we talked late into the night."

Annenkov looked dubiously down at the piece of paper and asked: "Mumu... what's that?"

"It's a story I'm writing... based on something that happened years ago at Spasskoye. I suppose I shouldn't be writing about my mother in this way, less than six months after her death. It doesn't show her in a good light. But it's just coming out. There's nothing I can do about it."

"What's Mumu?"

"The name of a dog. It's the story of a deaf-and-dumb serf with a giant's strength (for the moment I've called him Gerasim, who's a born talker, I hope he won't be offended), who works for a tyrannical mistress. Out of pure caprice she destroys everything that gives meaning to his life: the possibility of happiness with a laundress he has fallen in love with, whom she marries off to a drunken shoemaker; and finally his devotion to a stray dog he has adopted, which she forces him to drown."

"How does it end?"

"I don't know yet. Either, out of frustration, he'll commit some violent act and get flogged and sent to Siberia; or he'll just walk away from the city and go back to live by himself in his village. Probably the latter."

Annenkov shook his head and looked at his friend in consternation. "It doesn't sound as if this is going exactly to endear you to the authorities either. Noble serfs and tyrannical employers. Be careful, Vanichka. Gogol's death seems to have given their determination to gag us another wrench of the screwdriver. This is a moment for you to lie low. Especially with the publication of your stories in book form under consideration."

"My presence here will have buried that for good."

"Not necessarily. The ways of the censors are beyond our comprehension. And after all, they are dealing with work that has already been published. It's now being considered by Prince Lvov, which gives us two advantages: he knows both our families and he's in Moscow, where your imprisonment has made much less noise than it has here. I stopped off to see him on my way here from Simbirsk."

"What did he say?

"He had only had time to read one or two of the sketches, but he told me he was favourably impressed."

221

"Wait till he's read them all! The book will never be published."

"We'll see. At any rate, it's better that you avoid getting yourself talked about until you've arrived safely in Spasskoye. Doctor Annenkov prescribes several months of walking round your estate with a rod in your hand or a gun over your arm." He looked his companion quizzically up and down. "By the way, how have you managed to keep so fit? With Avdotya Yakovlevna supplementing the prison diet and no exercise to speak of, I expected to see you with a stomach like mine."

Turgenev smiled and got to his feet. "I've taken a lot of exercise. I'll show you how." He picked up two packs of playing cards from the table and went to a corner of the room. "Morning and evening I take each card from the pack..." he paced diagonally across the cell, "... and put it down in the opposite corner. That means, with fifty-two cards in the pack, I make four hundred and sixteen trips. I have calculated that means I cover nearly two and a half versts a day... something you probably haven't done since you were a schoolboy."

On the evening before his release, Turgenev sent Gerasim to the prison governor to invite him to take a farewell glass of champagne with him. The offer was accepted, but the occasion was not a success. Only by adhering to the strictest rules of etiquette could the colonel conceal his intense dislike of everything about his prisoner: his friends, his insouciant behaviour, his lack of any signs of penitence. And so, after exchanging platitudes for ten minutes, he made the excuse of having an appointment elsewhere. He opened the door and called for the warder. Gerasim stood in the doorway at attention.

"Sir!"

"The prisoner will be leaving first thing in the morning, Gerasim."

"Sir!"

"I will not be here, so I will leave it to you to expedite the necessary formalities."

"Very good, sir."

He turned to Turgenev and rather reluctantly held out his hand. "Well, goodbye, Turgenev. I hope I shall never see you in here again."

Or anywhere else, thought Turgenev, but contented himself with bowing stiffly from the waist.

Gerasim escorted the governor to his quarters, but a few minutes later was back in Turgenev's cell with the news that his superior had already left the Admiralty. Another bottle of champagne was immediately opened, and the two men engaged on the last of their long conversations, Turgenev plying the old sergeant with questions about his opinions of the foreign countries he had seen, especially France. It was nearly midnight before they clinked glasses for their farewell toast; as they did so, Gerasim screwed one of his purple, battle-scarred cheeks up into an exaggerated wink and muttered: "Orayvoua, your honour." Then, with a nod towards the door to indicate the absent governor, he raised his glass an inch higher and added in a confidential whisper, "To Robespyair!"

St Petersburg,
24 April, 1852.

Dear and good Madame Viardot,

I don't know when you will be receiving this letter, as I have given it to a friend who is leaving for Germany to post there. Unforeseen circumstances have delayed me in St Petersburg longer than I thought and will continue to do so until May 15th. After that I shall be going as planned to spend the summer – and perhaps the winter too – at Spasskoye. Alas, for reasons too complicated to go into at the moment, I will have to give up any idea of travelling abroad for quite some time. Admittedly I never had many illusions when I left France that I would be returning shortly; but that will-o'-the-wisp hope will insist on materializing where it has no business being. It has now been well and truly dowsed. I have eaten all the white bread; all that is left for me now is to chew on the brown.

But, shame on me, here I am harping on about my sorrows when the happy and glorious event must be taking place any time now! I think of you all the time, would dearly love to send you a carrier pigeon every hour to convey my shifting moods of mild anxiety, interfering only now and then with fervent conviction that all will be for the best. I beg V. to write to me the following day with the result. Will it be a boy this time?

An event of comparatively infinitely minor importance may be taking place within the next month or two: there is still a possibility, however slight, that my sketches may be published in book form. I never received a definitive answer from you as to whether you would allow me to dedicate the book to you, so the only dedication will be three asterisks.

Write to me, my dear friend, as often as your health and your many engagements permit. Your letters and my memories sometimes seem to be all that I have.

Your most devoted

I. Turgenev.

Pauline Viardot gave birth to another daughter, who was called Claudie, on May 21st. Within the remarkably short time of five days the Viardots received a heartfelt letter of congratulation from Spasskoye, which also included a guarded explanation of the lines he had written her from prison; he hadn't wanted to worry her just before her confinement and had only thrown out hints of his predicament in case the letter were intercepted.

⸎

"**H**ave you thought it out carefully, Ivan? Have you calculated all the consequences? I admire what you want to do, but I don't want you, in a year's time, to blame me for any financial loss you may suffer."

The man voicing these concerns was Nikolai Nikolayevich Tyutchev, a former disciple of Belinsky, whom Turgenev had invited down to Spasskoye with his family to run the estate for him. The issue at hand was Turgenev's determination to lighten the burden of being a serf-owner, a possessor of what his friend Herzen was to call 'baptized property'. His mother's death had left him a rich man; but not so rich that mismanagement and lavish spending couldn't reduce him once again to comparative penury. The amicable agreement he had come to with his brother over dividing up the inheritance had been largely his doing; Nikolai, urged on by Anna Yakovlevna, had held out for more than his fair share, but Turgenev wasn't going to embitter relations with his brother for the sake of a few thousand roubles. Like many people who live on very little during their youth, he took the arrival of money to mean the permanent end of any financial problems. And besides, he kept Spasskoye, and for that he was more than ready to give Nikolai the best of the bargain.

But it had to be a Spasskoye purged of his mother's memory, and that meant the end of both tyrannical authority and abject grovelling. His first thought had been to free all the serfs immediately; but the prudent Annenkov had warned him in a letter that that would immediately attract the unwelcome attention of St Petersburg; if he wanted an early end to his exile, this was just the sort of action he would be wise to avoid. So what he was now proposing and asking Tyutchev to oversee was to give all the domestic servants their freedom, along with a plot of land; the others were to have the choice of substituting a small service payment for the hated *corvée* and being able to buy their freedom with a discount of one-fifth on the current rate.

The two men were riding round the estate and Turgenev smiled over at Tyutchev as he jolted uncomfortably along in his saddle with a townsman's seat. "I've been thinking of little else since I arrived here, Kolya," he answered. "Many of these men you see in the fields were my playmates when I was a boy. Their fathers taught me to shoot and fish… and ride," he couldn't help adding, as a stumble of Tyutchev's horse caused its rider to lurch forward over its neck. "They'll be expecting something of this sort from me. They know how I fought with my mother over her treatment of them. When I was nineteen I was nearly arrested for trying to protect a young girl my mother had sold to a neighbour. I couldn't accept the idea that a human being could be disposed of like an unwanted chair, so I arranged for one of the herdsmen's families to hide her."

"Why should anyone want to arrest you for that?"

"Because her purchaser had already paid my mother. He arrived one day with half a dozen armed police and demanded that the girl be handed over."

"So what did you do?"

Turgenev laughed. "It was one of my very few victories over my mother. She was so anxious to avoid a scandal that she gave the man his money back... with interest. But she took it out of me for weeks after."

Tyutchev shrugged his shoulders. "Well as long as you don't take it out of me, I'll see what you want is done."

"And I think you may be surprised," Turgenev added. "Far from losing me money, it may well increase my income. I can't believe that free men won't work better than slaves."

Tyutchev pursed his lips and kept his doubts to himself.

Turgenev had arrived at Spasskoye for an indefinite period of exile on 21 May, 1852. He had travelled from St Petersburg to Moscow on the newly-finished railway and wrote to a friend about his mixed feelings regarding the journey: *The convenience is, of course, considerable, but as I gazed out of the window at the fields and towns flashing past, I wondered if travellers in the future would not, in the long run, be the poorer for all this speed; they will reach their destination sooner, but where will be those memories that go to make up the texture of all our lives? The welcome, if indigestible, meals at wayside taverns? The companionship and gradually acquired intimacy with strangers one will never see again? The crunch of the snow beneath carriage wheels? The dawn neighing of horses? The changing accents of the people as province gives way to province? The fascination of following the twisting course of a great river? The first glimpse of a mountain range and the myriad different perspectives as one approaches the peaks?*

He was happy to be back at his childhood home and secretly relished the added attraction of possession. He contemplated this new phase of his life with a sense of exhilaration he hadn't felt since leaving Courtavenel – and had wondered whether he would ever feel again. As he had intimated to Annenkov in his prison cell, he almost felt like thanking the Czar for his timely intervention in his life. It was as though fate had plucked him up and set him down on a path he would otherwise have had difficulty in finding. *A Sportsman's Sketches*, as he had decided to call the collection, was finished and, in defiance of the rigid climate of censorship, about to be published. That was the end of one road. Now to find another. In Moscow on his way down he had picked up the proofs of his book and soon devoted a day to reading through them from beginning to end. The experience left him in two minds. 'There are many things in it which are pale and fragmentary,' he told himself, 'but there are also perceptions which are exact and true – perhaps enough of them to save the book. All in all, though, it is a small thing – the work of a *petit maître*. The question is, am I capable of something bigger, something that flows calmly on like the Oka though these lands, something with clear, well-developed lines? Well, only one thing is certain: I shall never know till I try...'

His decision to employ Tyutchev as estate manager had its disadvantages. The former contributor to *Annals of the Fatherland* came with his attractive, intelligent wife, but also with his sister-in-law, a tall, cumbersome personage with a high opinion of her talent as a pianist, unshared by anyone else. Within a few months, these were joined by Tyutchev's mother-in-law, who brought a lady companion with her, and Turgenev's impoverished Uncle Nikolai, together with his new wife and her sister. The house was dominated by women, which had not been Turgenev's original intention. In a letter to Pauline, he compared the conversation at dinner to a day he had spent at Courtavenel with no company but the hens. He soon took evasive action by leaving the main house and establishing himself in one of the pavilions on the grounds. But at least he was assured of company when he wanted it, and for the time being the fact that Tyutchev took all the day-to-day business of running the property off his hands was a great relief. Not only did he know that he was useless at estate management and would be at the mercy of the peasants' cunning and his own good nature, which often toppled over into laziness; he also wanted to clear his life as far as possible of inessentials and give himself time and thought to prepare the full-length novel he already had in mind. Here was another reason to be grateful to the Czar: if it were not for his exile, he would surely be wasting countless hours on the St Petersburg social round he pretended to despise, but secretly enjoyed. Now there could be none of that. Writing and hunting: these were to be the dominant occupations for the year he thought his exile would last.

But there was another occupation which he hadn't considered, and was to take up a substantial amount of his time. On a shooting visit to one of his neighbours, only days after his return, he saw the young serf girl he had danced with at Turgenevo. Again he was entranced by her beauty: her dark hair and black eyes, the delicacy of her features, the slim frame carried with unstudied but dignified elegance convinced him that not many generations back an aristocratic shoot had been grafted on to her peasant stock. A few days later he spoke to her owner and offered to buy her. But he hadn't forgotten his clash with his mother, and instead of paying the current rate of fifty roubles, he spent seven hundred and bought her her freedom.

Inserting Feoktista Volkov into the Spasskoye household proved easier than he had feared. The young girl, having spent her life in service, had no desire to be involved in the domestic running of the house, so there was no clash of authority with the Tyutchev ladies in the kitchen. They, in their turn, found her simple, gay and easy to please; she never for a moment abused her position as *maîtresse en titre* to the master of the house. Turgenev at first was wholly enchanted by her. He never tired of her beauty and bathed in the, to him, totally new sensation of having at his beck and call another human being whose one aim in life was to make him happy. It didn't occur to him that, with one significant exception, there was little difference between his relationship with Feoktista and that with Diane. Which was why there seemed to him no hypocrisy involved in continuing to write letters proclaiming his undying devotion to Pauline while enjoying night after night of the most ardent but uncomplicated passion with his new companion.

But after a few weeks he found himself wanting more from this beautiful girl. He saw no reason why she couldn't be a companion for him by day, as well as by night. She was just able to read and write, so he set out immediately to encourage and develop those skills. He went into the great library, where the smell of dust and old leather brought back a childhood memory with a vivid clarity that surprised him. When he was only eight, he and a young serf who loved poetry and even wrote some himself, had broken open one of the locked doors to the great bookcases; balanced precariously on the serf's shoulders, he had pulled out some volumes of verse, which the young man had then declaimed to him with dramatic emphasis in a secluded corner of the garden. Now he rummaged amongst the favourite books of his boyhood until he came across Krylov's fables. Perfect, he thought: country tales told simply but poetically, with a touch of satire that perhaps would pass her by, but never mind. He gave her them to read and awaited her reactions with keen interest. These, when they came, were positive, but lacking in detail. "You enjoyed reading it?"

"Yes, very much."

"What did you particularly like about it?"

"Oh, everything really."

"How did you feel about the way the animals talked?"

"Well, perhaps that was a bit silly. I mean, animals don't talk, do they?"

He suggested she try some of Krylov's translations of La Fontaine. These, he told her, showed that no matter what language they were originally written in, fables of country life with universal morals could be appreciated in the same way all round the world. He asked her, bearing this in mind, to write down her impressions of one of them. Not even her desire to please could hide her lack of enthusiasm for this task, but she promised she would do her best...

I DON'T LIKE THE FERST STORY. I THINK ITS VERY SAD. I MEAN, IF

THE GRASSHOPER DUSN'T GET ANYTHING TO EAT HE WILL DIE. AND ALL HE'D DONE RONG WAS TO SING IN THE SUMMER AND I LOVE TO HEAR GRASSHOPERS SING WHEN IT'S HOT IN THE EEVNINGS. I THINK THE ANT WAS VERY MEAN. I WOOD HAVE LIKED THE STORY BETTER IF THE ANT HAD GIVEN HIM SUM FOOD BUT SED NEXT YEAR YOU MUST DO SUM WORK YORSELF. THATS WHAT WOOD HAVE HAPENED IN OUR VILAGE. PERHAPS THEY ARE NOT SO NICE IN FRANCE.

Compelled to admit that the chances of his cultivating a genuine enthusiasm for literature were slim, Turgenev decided to change tack. He remembered how charmingly she had sung and how gracefully she had danced the evening he had first laid eyes on her. Perhaps he would be more successful if he tried to develop a taste for music. As winter approached and the days grew shorter, nothing in his exile weighed more heavily on him than the lack of music. He thought nostalgically of unforgettable evenings at Courtavenel, and though well aware of the folly, decided to attempt to imitate them. First he had to prevail on the ladies of the house to perform, which presented a double difficulty: the one he wanted to convince was most reluctant, and the one he would gladly have done without was all too eager. Tyutchev's wife, Aleksandra Petrovna, played with a certain flair which helped to make up for a less than immaculate technique; but she was shy about performing in front of others, much preferring to spend the evening in conversation with the husband she adored. Her unmarried sister, the gawky, gushing Olga, ever anxious to please (especially Turgenev), would barely wait to be asked before sitting down at the piano, which she played with unvarying loudness and such lack of sensitivity that Turgenev once looked over to see if she had remembered to take her gloves off. To make matters worse, the less than beautiful sounds she produced were accompanied by such heaving of the breast, rapturous throwing back of the head and uncontainable sighs that it would have taken Clara Schumann to do them justice.

But to a freezing man the most threadbare coat is welcome, and Turgenev, now with the excuse that he wanted to introduce Feoktista to classical music, persuaded Aleksandra to play duets with her sister. At least, assigned the bass part, Olga's heavy-handedness could be relieved by the more delicate sounds that were going on above her. He asked them to play the four-handed arrangement of Beethoven's 'Coriolan' overture, which he had heard them practising; the introduction might almost have been written for Olga's thumps, while Aleksandra could come into her own with the sinuous lines of the sweeping D major theme identified with Volumnia.

During the performance – which was better than he had dared hope – he stood behind the two ladies' chairs and turned the pages of the music. In between times he moved to one side and went through the motions of conducting, his intense craving to be involved in music-making rendering him indifferent to any risk of ridicule. From time to time he stole a glance at Feoktista and was pleased to see that she seemed to be enjoying the music. She never tried to catch his eye, which indicated that she was not seeking his approbation. When it was finished, she clapped loudly and enthusiastically and then looked expectantly at Aleksandra, who beckoned to one of the servants and whispered in his ear. The man nodded, left the room and came back carrying a balalaika. As a surprise for Turgenev, it had been planned that Feoktista would sing some local songs. She did this with such natural style and grace that Turgenev was enchanted. Listening to the melodies, both gay and mournful, he knew so well, watching the easy, natural gestures of her delicate hands, the occasionally rhythmic stamping of her tiny feet, he was no longer compelled to make comparisons with Courtavenel, but could revel in the spontaneity which was what, after all, had been so lacking in the painstakingly studied Beethoven.

Later, when they were alone together, he kissed her and told her how much pleasure her singing had given him. Confident of her powers again, she began to tease him as she hadn't dared do since their 'lessons' had started. "I'm glad you enjoyed it because I'm afraid I made a mortal enemy tonight."

"A mortal enemy? Who?"

"Olga Petrovna. She glared at me while I was singing as though she'd like to eat me up."

"But why should she do that?"

"Because she's in love with you."

"Oh, don't be so silly, Feoktista. Perhaps she was a little jealous of your talent."

"If that's so, it's not my talent as a singer. I've noticed for some time that she's always giving you amorous looks when your back is turned, but tonight… Whoo! How she hated me!"

"This is all in your imagination. Perhaps I've been giving you too many fables to read. We could write this one together. What should we call it? 'The Bachelor and the Spinster'? No, we'll have to invent animals to represent us. What shall I be?"

"A Lion."

"Thank you for the compliment. All right, it doesn't fit me, but we'll let it pass. And what about Olga Petrovna?"

"A crow."

"Oh, that's not very nice. Poor Olga Petrovna. Why should she be a crow?"

"Because she's big and always wears black and flaps around the place and has a loud ugly voice."

"Feoktista! What's made you so cruel all of a sudden?"

"Because I hate her. I bet she was thinking of you when she was working herself into raptures over her ghastly playing of that boring music." She saw his eyebrows raise and recognized her gaffe. Flinging her arms around him, she picked lightly at the hairs on the nape of his neck and buried her face in his shoulder. "Oh, I'm sorry, Ivan Sergeyevich, I'll never be what you want me to be, but I find it so hard to lie to you."

"Never mind. When it was written, it wasn't meant to sound like that. One day I'll take you to hear it with a whole orchestra. But to get back to poor Olga, you mustn't hate her. She's a little silly, that's all."

"She's more than a little silly about you; she thinks she's going to marry you."

"Oh, come, now you're going too far. What's put that into your head."

"Something I heard her and her sister discussing. About dividing up the house between two couples. Oh yes, Aleksandra Petrovna's very nice to me, but she's in this too."

Turgenev, charmed and amused by her jealousy, put his arms round her and kissed her with a mixture of affection and desire. "My lovely little Feoktista, they're probably thinking of inviting some suitor down from Moscow for her. You don't know very much yet about the great world."

Feoktista returned his kiss with desire clearly predominating over affection and whispered in his ear: "Ivan Sergeyevich, don't be angry with me, but you don't know very much about women…"

<hr>

*H*ow much do we – can we – know about women? This was the theme that, some 25 years later, the five writers – four French and one Russian – decided to discuss during one of their '*dîners des cinq*'. The intention was not to tackle it until the customary gargantuan dinner had been despatched, but threads of it had woven themselves into the conversation long before coffee was served. The breadth of the subject demanded closer focus, and before long it had narrowed down to an analysis of fidelity and the two sexes' different attitudes to that elusive ideal.

Zola suggested that no fruitful comparison could be made because women didn't have the same opportunities for infidelity; whether they wished it or not, they were simply expected to be more faithful than men. Edmond de Goncourt retaliated by claiming that that was because if a woman admitted to having had one lover, it meant that she had had six. Flaubert chuckled his agreement, but asked whether the very conception of fidelity was not an overrated quality. "Of course I am not married, and my only long relationship with a woman was riddled with *cornes* on both sides. But it seems to me such a trivial fault in comparison with so many others. I would much rather a wife of mine occasionally gave her body to someone other than me than that she... for instance, nagged me day and night, interrupted me when I was working, ran up debts I was unable to pay, or mistreated our children. Emile, you've been married for three or four years now, wouldn't you agree with me?"

"Of course," Zola said, though with no great degree of conviction. "I see fidelity as a virtue which has outlived its time. Along with 'honour' and 'duty', it belonged to a seventeenth century 'classical' view of life which has little or no pertinence today. We might as well try and write plays in the style of Corneille or Racine. What need to be examined now are the causes which lead to infidelity."

Daudet didn't feel that that required very deep examination. "Simply the impossibility of only fucking one woman for the rest of your life."

Turgenev, as they had expected and hoped, disagreed with them. Although it irked him from time to time that he found himself always forced to play the prude, he was fond enough of them all by now to have no hesitation in voicing his disagreement. "As someone," he said, "who has been, in his way, a faithful lover all his adult life, you would expect me to sing the praises of fidelity, would you not?"

"In your way?" Goncourt queried. "A very special way! Didn't you tell us once about a girl serf you freed and lived with for a couple of years while still protesting your total devotion to Madame Viardot?

"Ah, but I do not consider that infidelity."

"You may not, but others would. What should we call it then? A concealment of the truth from your beloved's attention?"

Daudet asked if he had ever spoken of the incident since to Madame Viardot, and Turgenev had to admit he hadn't.

"Aha, Ivan," Flaubert chuckled, "it seems we have found your Achilles' heel. Have you ever asked yourself why not?"

"By the time I saw Pauline again, the girl was no longer part of my life and the whole affair seemed of little importance."

Flaubert dropped a *langoustine* shell back on to his plate, sucked his fingers and refused to let his friend off the hook. "Are you so sure that's all it was? Might it not also have been that, impenitent romantic that you are, you wanted her to think of you as the *beau chevalier* of perfect fidelity?"

Turgenev smiled and conceded that there might be something – just a little – in that.

Goncourt wanted to probe deeper. "Leaving aside the purely physical aspect of fidelity," he said, "which is perhaps its least interesting feature, think for a moment what else is involved. We started by talking about how much men can know about women. I would go further and ask how much do we *want* to know about them? I, for example, am always horrified by those who claim that each partner in a love match should know everything about the other. This, for me, would signify not the quintessence of love but its annihilation."

Again, Turgenev disagreed. "I think the opposite is true. I believe a love, a true love, can only be intensified by an ever-deepening perception of the other's qualities – be they virtues or defects, it doesn't greatly matter. I think I can safely say that I have no secrets from Madame Viardot…" Catching Daudet's malicious eye, he laughingly corrected himself and added, "except one, of course, and now I fear the result of talking to you oh-so-moral gentlemen is that I shall have to go straight home and make my confession."

Zola broke into the laughter by observing that knowing all about each other presumed there was something of substance to know. "My impression of what you have told us about your *jolie moujike,* Ivan, is that the trouble lay there. You wanted to play Pygmalion, but your Galatea refused to come to life…"

"She didn't refuse. I don't think she would have refused me anything. It was just not in her. And the fault was mine. Pygmalion prayed to Venus and his statue became flesh. Perhaps I should have prayed to Minerva and my little Feoktista, who was certainly flesh, might have become spirit. But hard as she tried, her attempts to open her mind to new stimuli stemmed only from a desire to please me, never from inner compulsion. And eventually I was forced to give up on my attempts to educate Feoktista Petrovna."

"And did that spell the end of your liaison?" Zola asked.

"No, it survived some months longer. A man in his early thirties, in exile on the fringe of the steppe, thinks twice before casting off so beautiful and amiable a mistress."

"So what finally brought it to an end?"

"Boredom, more than anything else. On both sides. On hers because I was working on a book and had less and less time for her; she and the Tyutchevs found nothing to say to each other and her fellow serfs felt awkward in her presence. For my part, I found her eternal efforts to please increasingly cloying. I am sure you will all agree that in every *rapport à deux* there is one who loves more and one who is more loved. I seem to need to belong to the first category; in this case, I found myself in the second. And it was this perhaps that led me to the discovery that sexual pleasure by itself cannot put off boredom for ever."

"So you dismissed her?" Goncourt asked.

"Not exactly. I was very loath to cause her any unhappiness. But then she was obliging enough to start sharing her favours with someone else – a carpenter, I think he was, a good enough fellow. This, of course, was reported to me, so I was able to give her some money and pack them both off to Moscow. I heard she had a child, who I think I can be reasonably sure is not mine, and that was just about the last I heard of her…"

Daudet, who had been listening to this account in engrossed silence, now asked Turgenev if he had missed her. "Or replaced her, perhaps? There must have been many pretty little serf girls on whom you could have exercised your *droit du seigneur.*"

Turgenev ignored the provocation and shook his head. "In order to avoid missing her, I replaced her, yes, but not with another girl. With work: or rather with a strict timetable of which work was the principal ingredient – a tactic you must have employed yourself in your youth, Alphonse."

Daudet shook his head ruefully. "I tried, but usually without success. I found that whenever I sat down to write, what came into my head was not the smooth continuation of the previous day's work but lascivious memories of girls I had fucked or even more lascivious desires for girls I hadn't."

"What was the remedy?" Zola asked.

"Going to some haunt of whores and choosing any one at random. Twenty minutes later, the problem was resolved."

Turgenev gave a rather stiff smile. "That solution, however desirable, was denied to me. So I had little choice but to fall back on self-imposed discipline."

"Which proves," Goncourt observed, with what degree of irony was anybody's guess, "the inherent superiority of our good Muscovite. Wouldn't you say so, Alphonse?"

Daudet spread his hands and gave a *chacun à son goût* shrug, but could not resist a final thrust: "As long as he doesn't claim to be a champion of fidelity!"

233

Dear and good Madame Viardot,

Yesterday I received my first letter from you in a month. I open your letters like a child unwrapping a birthday present – and what did I find inside today? The news that you will be coming to St Petersburg at the beginning of next year! I didn't know whether to laugh or cry. Your presence so comparatively near to me is a blessing in itself; but the impossibility of my coming to see you would drive the best-behaved little boy into a tantrum. Perhaps you and Viardot will find a moment when you can interrupt your busy programme to come and stay with me here. I can only say that there is nothing, <u>nothing in the world</u>, that could bring more joy to my heart.

And if the truth be known, my spirits could do with a lift. The high hopes with which I began my exile here have been dashed against the reality of the Russian countryside, aided and abetted by endlessly dismal weather – skies varying between drab white and leaden grey, ferocious winds which uproot trees and make the windows sound as though they are being lashed by a knout. I just opened my balcony door and Brrr! What a blast of freezing, snow-driving wind. Diane, who had followed me, retreated in horror. Poor little French girl! 'Come on', I said to her, 'let's cuddle up together under a thick blanket and dream of Courtavenel'.

You ask about details of my life here. I will give you them in a few words. I have discovered that there is only one sure way to combat boredom and that is…would you believe it?…uniformity. I'll explain: I have divided my day into sections devoted to certain occupations, always the same, and I try not to depart from this established order. I rise at eight, breakfast and go for an hour's walk. From ten to two, reading and letters. After a light lunch, I work until five, then dine with all the rest of the house's occupants. I stay with them until ten, read till eleven, and then to sleep. And so on, day after day. Not very gay perhaps, but the routine has enabled me to achieve a fair amount of work. I have just finished a fifty-page tale called The Inn, and written five chapters of the novel I am attempting.

I look forward with even more than my usual eagerness to your next letter, which will tell me exactly when you will be arriving. Remember to pass on to Viardot my invitation to you both and give Paulinette an affectionate hug from me. I enclose the lock of my hair she asked for.

I wonder if, among all the demands on your time, you remembered this morning that it is exactly nine years today since we first met at the Demidov house on the Nevski Prospekt. I remember it as if it were yesterday. And now you will soon be back in St Petersburg, singing many of the roles you sang then, and I will not be able to hear you. The tortures of Tantalus were pinpricks compared to this! Only one thing remains constant: today, as nine years ago, as in nine years' time, I am entirely yours in heart and spirit .

Your ever devoted,

I.T.

The letters Pauline wrote to him after her arrival in St Petersburg on December 29th were short, laconic, almost curt. To learn of the delirious enthusiasm with which she was once again greeted by the capital's audiences, he had to rely on the newspapers, including the French ones, which the faithful Annenkov sent him almost daily. Feoktista would find him brooding in front of a pile of them after breakfast, and all her attempts to lighten his gloom met with failure. Thinking that it might help him to share his misery, she daringly asked him to read her something from one of them. He picked up *L'Écho de Paris*, which he had just flung down on the table, and read, in a strangled voice: '*The great event of these last days has been the reappearance of Madame Viardot... welcomed back in the Russian capital with ecstatic appreciation by her old friends and admirers... a unique and exceptional virtuoso singer... although her voice sounds slightly the worse for wear*' – here a snorted disparaging interjection about the hedging proclivities of French critics – '*there is no denying the powerful, original nature of her genius... her performance at the end of the month as Fidès in Le Prophète, which has been acclaimed throughout Europe, is awaited as the culminating event of the winter season...*'

He threw the paper down again and beat his fists on the table in an agony of impotent frustration. Feoktista, who was aware of the nature, if not the extent, of his feelings for Pauline, asked him if he had never heard Madame Vyado sing in – what was it? – Leprofet. "Heard her?!" Turgenev's tone was uncharacteristically harsh. "I attended ten – or was it eleven? – performances."

Feoktista stared at him in uncomprehending bewilderment, her lips beginning to form the question: "Then why ...?" But the fury of Turgenev's expression quenched her curiosity. She made some timid excuse about having promised to help Aleksandra Petrovna in the linen cupboard and flitted noiselessly out of the room. Turgenev, staring out of the window, was quite unaware of her departure.

In every letter Turgenev sent to St Petersburg he repeated his invitation to the Viardots to be his guests for a few days at Spasskoye. In the occasional note that he received back, this was never alluded to. Not so much as a 'we would love to but...' He tormented himself in trying to decide if this was due – as he hoped – to Pauline's unavailability or – as he feared – to her reluctance to put Louis in what she might see as an embarrassing position. But even the faintest possibility of this longed-for visit evaporated when she wrote to him that Louis had been taken ill and had to return to France. From this moment on, he became so morose, even disagreeable, that, one day when he was out alone hunting, the Tyutchevs called an emergency meeting: the three of them, his uncle Nikolai and his wife, together with Feoktista, all tried to think of some way to take his mind off Pauline and St Petersburg. Nikolai, with a suggestive wink, intimated that it was chiefly up to Feoktista, but she told them how many times she had tried and failed. Every plan they considered had to be discarded: Aleksandra and Olga volunteered to play the piano more often, but music would only remind him of what he was supposed to forget; Nikolai said he would go hunting with him every day, but even that would probably bring back the lost days of Courtavenel. The only solution, they decided, was to organize more expeditions to neighbouring properties. But when they tried to put this into practice, Turgenev, with the excuse that he was too taken up by his book, refused to go.

In March, to their relief – later to be mingled with extreme apprehension – the matter was taken out of their hands. One morning he received a letter from St Petersburg from an old friend who had been one of his most frequent visitors during his imprisonment. She told him that la Viardot had announced that at the end of the month she would be going to Moscow: there would be no opera, as the theatres were closed for Lent, but she would give a series of recitals there. The minute he had finished reading the letter, Turgenev sat down at his desk...

Spasskoye,
8 March, 1853.

Good morning, my dear friend,

I have just heard that in a week or two you will be coming to Moscow. In all honesty, I cannot deny that I would have preferred to have heard the news from your hand, rather than that of Princess Meshcherskaya. But I do understand – knowing the whirlwind in which you live – that the calls on your time, not only from your public engagements but also from your many friends and admirers in St Petersburg, must leave little over to put pen to paper. As for these same friends and admirers, your references to them in your brief letters have an hallucinatory effect on me. I close my eyes, am transported back ten years and am there with you all. Matvei Wielhorski, paw number two, Stepan Gedeonov, paw number one... can you imagine how disconcerting all this return of the past is? I can only ask myself, where am I?, who am I?

Enough of that! One thing is worrying me: in Louis's absence, who will accompany you on the journey from St Petersburg to Moscow? My question is, alas, all too disinterested, as I foresee very little possibility of leaving my exile before another two or three years. I have just been refused permission to travel fifty versts (a morning's drive) to visit two of my properties which happen to be situated just beyond the borders of Orel province. From this perspective, Moscow seems as remote as Madrid. Perhaps one of the afore-mentioned old friends will be only too happy to undertake this task for you. Oh, my dearest one, what I would not give... You and I should live only in the make-believe world of the theatre: a blackout, a rapid scene change, and there I am, standing with you under the Spasskie Vorota ...

Another day of dark brooding followed, which caused the other inhabitants of Spasskoye to take the easy way out and simply leave him alone. Early the next morning he summoned his chief bailiff and made him swear not to reveal a word of the conversation they were about to have.

"You can trust me, master, you know that."

"Yes, I think I can, Semyon Yurovich, but I have never asked you to accept such responsibility as I am about to now. Are you still good friends with… what's his name?… the clerk in the permits office?"

"Pavel Ivanovich? Lord bless you, sir, yes. We sat on the same school bench together, we chased after the same girls, matter of fact he married the one I had my eye on, but I bore him no grudge. What can I ask him to do for you?"

"Procure me a false internal passport."

The man's jaw dropped and he gazed at Turgenev in almost comic dismay. "Beggin' your pardon, sir, but how could I do a thing like that? I mean, I'm sure he could arrange it, easy as pie, but what about you, sir? I mean… supposing they found out… they'd do something terrible to you…"

"They won't find out."

"Well… don't take it bad, sir, but that's easy enough to say, isn't it? I mean, I can only take it you have it in mind to go somewhere. And there's that there policeman whose only job in life seems to be to follow you around. What's he going to think if you suddenly disappear, just like that?"

"I'll leave orders that I am sick and not to be disturbed."

The bailiff scratched his head and looked at his master doubtfully. "I never thought the day would come when I'd be unhappy to do you a favour. But, blow me, I wish you'd let me out of this one."

Turgenev, warmed by the man's concern, smiled at him and softened the rather harsh, authoritative tone he had deliberately adopted up to now. "I'm afraid I'll have to insist, Semyon Yurovich. But I want to assure you and your friend that, if anything bad should come to pass, neither you nor he will be in any way involved. I shall, of course, travel under an assumed name, so both of you can always say that you had no idea it was anything to do with me…"

As Turgenev climbs the stairs to the apartment Pauline has taken on the second floor of a mansion on Great Kaluzhskaya Street, a flurry of conflicting thoughts race through his head. For nearly three years, not a day has passed that he has not conjured up the image of the woman with whom he is about to be reunited. And yet, at this moment, which he has tried to imagine so many times, his principal concern is what effect his unusual appearance will have on her. His passport is made out for an Andrey Muraviev, the name he improvised in the tea-room in London on the last occasion he had seen Pauline; but instead of being a Count, he is listed as a wool merchant, and has been forced to dress accordingly. The dandy in him that he has never quite outgrown is horrified at the idea of appearing before her with an unkempt beard, wearing baggy breeches stuffed into knee-high boots, a rough sheepskin coat and a fur cap.

The French maid who opens the door is unfamiliar to him from Courtavenel days. As he gives his false name, he thinks – or imagines? – he detects a look of surprise, tinged with disapproval. But this is nothing to Pauline's reaction when he is shown into her living room: for a moment she stands stock still, staring in disbelieving astonishment; then she brings a hand to her mouth and dissolves into peals of uncontrollable laughter. Of all the welcomes Turgenev has envisaged over the past days, this is one that never occurred to him.

When she has more or less recovered, Pauline comes forward, excusing herself and holding out her hands in welcome. "I'm sorry, Ivan, you look as if you'd just stepped out of *Ruslan and Lyudmila*! But how good it is to see you again."

All Turgenev can do is murmur her name, over and over again, seize one of her hands and cover it with kisses. For a moment she lightly strokes his hair. Then she firmly withdraws her hand and beckons to him to sit down.

"You remind me of when Bakunin came to see us in Paris in '48. Certainly you Russian noblemen don't seem to be made for disguises. I hope you won't be going anywhere where you might be recognized."

"I won't be going anywhere or seeing anyone… but you, I hope, as often as possible."

"It won't be easy, Ivan. I'm only here for a couple of weeks. I managed it today because I have a slight cold and have cancelled my concert tomorrow. So I've been able to issue strict instructions that I will not be receiving anyone. But I can't keep that up for long. People are always dropping in. You Russians are much less formal than the French, no one seems to wait for an invitation."

After a moment's uneasy silence, Turgenev asks after the maid who showed him in. "Is she new? Do you no longer have Lisette?"

"Oh, Béatrice has been with me for over a year now. But I made sure that she was in service today, because she doesn't know you. Lisette is still with me, of course, but I gave her the day off. You know how she blabs. We cannot be too careful."

Turgenev has not taken his eyes off her for a minute. As he studies her face, he remarks that physically she seems not to have changed at all. She is, as always, simply but elegantly dressed, and her face and figure are still that of a young woman. She is, after all, only thirty-two. And yet he seems to detect that twelve years of celebrity have perhaps left their mark. There is no longer anything girlish about the person sitting opposite him; no one could be in any doubt that this is a prima donna.

There is something he has to get off his chest, and he knows that if he doesn't bring it up now, he never will. Leaning forward, elbows on his knees, hands clenched, he asks: "I am, as you know, staying with Annenkov. He is, by the way, the only other person I shall be seeing in Moscow. He... how shall I say this?... gave me the impression, without ever actually saying so, that when he told you I was coming, you didn't seem very anxious to see me."

She brushes this almost impatiently aside. "It was not that I didn't want to see you. It was that I was afraid of the danger you were running in coming here. I had already tried to persuade Annenkov to tell you to stay where you were."

"And that was the only reason?"

With only the slightest of hesitations: "Of course, Ivan. Now don't start being difficult! You have come anyhow, and I'm very happy to see you, and I want to hear all your news. How was the journey? Did it take ages?"

She wants us to chat away about trivialities like two friendly acquaintances... she's holding me at arm's length... I have no choice but to go along with her, otherwise she'll get upset, even angry... very well, I'll play her game for as long as I can keep it up...

"And how is Louis? I was so sorry to hear he was ill. I was afraid it might be cholera."

"No, fortunately, it was nothing so serious. He was just run down, I think. And then he would insist on going hunting in this freezing weather. He's not so young any more, you know. But in his last letter he said he was feeling much better."

"And the girls?"

"They're both doing splendidly. Paulinette, as you know, is boarding with Mademoiselle Renard, but we see her at least once a week. She speaks perfect French and is starting to study the piano. I give her lessons whenever I can find the time. She's beginning to show real promise."

"I suppose she and Louise are great friends."

"Ye-es. They have their little quarrels from time to time. It's the age, you know... but they're really very fond of each other."

There's more intimacy in one line of our letters than this. Have I made a dreadful mistake coming here? I wrote to her that I wouldn't see her unless she summoned me. Perhaps I'm being punished for breaking the rules...

Detecting, but misinterpreting the look of bewildered dismay on his face, Pauline changes her tone. "Ivan, you're not listening to a word I'm saying. Now, pay attention to me. You're running an appalling risk, being here. If anything happens to you, I'll never forgive myself. Promise me you'll go back to Spasskoye tomorrow."

"No, I won't promise that. It's taken me three days to get here. For safety's sake I came by minor roads and in second-class conveyances. I nearly froze to death and I'm aching from head to toe from the jolting of those terrible carriages. I'd rather throw myself into the Moskva than start back tomorrow."

"How long are you planning to stay then?"

"Three or four days. No longer, or they might notice my absence."

Now Pauline's habitual self-control wavers and her large, dark eyes fill with fear. "Ivan, what would happen if they... if this madness of yours came to light?"

Turgenev's answer is almost casual: "Oh, I suppose they'd send me to Siberia."

"For how long?"

"I don't know. Four... five years."

She springs up in alarm and moves over to the fireplace; turning her back on him, she rests her head on the mantelpiece and gazes down into the glowing coals. Hearing that he is about to speak, she shakes her head and murmurs: "You shouldn't have done it..." Then she turns to face him and repeats, very slowly: "You shouldn't have done it."

Gazing up into her distraught face, he tries to find the words to reassure her. "You mustn't torture yourself, my dear, I've taken every possible precaution..." but when he sees that her eyes are filled with tears, he abandons all control and flings himself on the floor, clasping the hem of her skirt and covering it with kisses. "Just to be with you again... for five minutes... is worth five years in Siberia."

She bends down, eases him to his feet and puts her arms around his neck. For a long moment they stand there in the closest of embraces, as though the constraints of three years have fallen away in a second. Then she gently pushes him towards the chair where he was sitting and sits down again herself.

Dabbing the tears from her eyes, she starts to address him in a level tone of voice which, after the previous burst of emotion, betrays a prepared, if not actually rehearsed speech. "Ivan, there is something we have both to understand. I repeat, I cannot tell you how happy I am to see you again after all this time. But we have to be aware – both of us – that things cannot be the same as they were." Seeing his face fall, she adds: "We're not the same people..."

"I am."

The simplicity of this statement brings a touch of asperity into her voice. "Well, perhaps I'm not."

"You mean separation has killed your... whatever it was you felt for me?"

She thinks for a moment. "Killed, no. Wounded... a little ... perhaps. But, it's no use deceiving ourselves, Ivan. We haven't been able to see each other for a long time, and, from what you say, it may be a long time before we see each other again. In the meantime, my life is very full... my husband, my two children, one of yours, my career... do you realize that when I leave Russia I will be in Paris for exactly five days? Then I'm off again for a season in London, where I am to give 36 concerts in forty-two days. All this with at least two hours of vocalizing every day, new scores to be learnt all the time... don't you see?, I have no time for any other distractions..."

Turgenev's eyebrows lift above eyes filled with pain, and his lips mouth the word 'distraction'?

She stretches her arms out towards him, but when he reaches forward to take her hands she holds them up in an arresting and, it cannot be denied, somewhat theatrical gesture. "My dearest Ivan, you have your place in my heart. It will always be there. But it's a small corner, and it has to be shared with others… as, I am sure, I have to share your affection with others…"

"There are no others." She gives him a quizzical look, which he returns with steadfast conviction. Feoktista, in this context, is simply an irrelevance.

"Well, perhaps there should be. You're thirty-five," (a half-hearted attempt at one of her old giggles) "your hair is turning grey. You must be thinking of marrying, having a family…"

Turgenev interrupts her. "Every time I think of having a family, I can only see it as a barrier between you and me."

"But only one of so many barriers!"

"The rest, for me, are insubstantial as air. You know all the sentiments I have dedicated to you. I don't think I need to underline them. They will end only with my life."

Pauline lowers her head and closes her eyes. After a few seconds, she looks up at him. She tries to keep her voice cool and decisive, but can't entirely eliminate an underlying tremor of emotion. "Ivan, I must ask you to leave now. There is a reception at Prince Golitsyn's and I must go and prepare myself. Come again tomorrow, about this time. But in the meantime, think about what I have said to you. You are not only one of the most intelligent men I know, you are also one of the most sensitive. Use your intelligence and your sensitivity and I am sure you will see that I am right. So tomorrow, we'll talk like the old friends we have always been and will, I devoutly hope, always remain. No bickering. No impossible demands. I want to hear all about what you are writing. I'm sure you'll be interested to know how the season went in St Petersburg and what I'm singing here. We'll have a chance to… catch up on each other. Will you do that? For me?"

Turgenev gazes at her in silence for a few seconds, then nods, kisses her hand with formal brevity and leaves the room.

"Now tell me about this novel you are writing. You've been very mysterious about it in your letters."

"Only because it is something of a mystery to me. It is the first time I have tried something on a large scale, and I'm having difficulty finding my way…"

Turgenev is making a superhuman effort to remain within the limits of the part he has been asked to play. Pauline has taken pains to create a domestic atmosphere as close as possible to that of Courtavenel. The two of them are sitting opposite each other in comfortable armchairs, and Lisette has served them tea and cakes. She has obviously been meticulously instructed by her mistress; when she opened the door to Turgenev, she bobbed a curtsey and, with as near a wink as her impeccable training would allow, greeted him with: "*Bonjour,* Monsieur Muraviev." At first, Pauline regaled him with a selection of the gossipy backstage stories he loved, including another attempt by Grisi's husband, Mario, to undermine her popularity with the public, which she had once again contrived to convert into a triumph for herself. Now she is questioning him about his life at Spasskoye.

"Can you give me some idea as to what it's about?"

"Well, its general theme is the conflict of generations; in fact, as a provisional title I'm calling it *Two Generations.* The older characters are a large landowner, Glafira Ivanovna, who is roughly modelled on my mother, and her estate manager, who has some of the characteristics of my uncle Nikolai. The younger ones are her son, an indecisive youth who's resigned his commission but is bored by provincial life, and a young girl in her mid-twenties, who comes down from Moscow to act as companion to the old woman."

"And falls in love with the son."

"Not really. He falls in love with her – or at any rate desires her. So does the estate manager. There's also a sort of ne'er-do-well, a hanger-on who's a vague relation of Glafira Ivanovna; he makes gross advances at Elizaveta and then insults her when she rejects him."

"She can't have a very good opinion of men!"

"No. And she becomes increasingly unsure of her position. She comes from a much lower social background than the others, who all, to a greater or lesser extent, take advantage of her. She's bullied by her mistress and treated with varying degrees of disrespect by the men."

"Dare I ask how it ends?"

"I'm not sure yet. I've only written twelve chapters. The book will be in three parts and I've just finished the first. But Elizaveta will have to get away. I think I'll have her go back to Moscow. The son and the estate manager will follow her there after the old woman dies and they're no longer afraid of her whims and caprices. The girl's absence will have made them both realize her true value, but it's too late. She'll reject them both and perhaps take a job with a family who are leaving Russia to live in Paris."

Pauline sinks her chin into her cupped palm, gives him a long, interrogative gaze and then utters a dubious "Hmm!" Turgenev, without a trace of resentment, asks, almost eagerly: "You don't like it?"

"It's not that I don't like it. It will all depend on how you write it, and I'm sure you will write it beautifully. It's just that I feel... you've done it all before. Your mother, for instance. You've used her in a couple of the *Sketches* and most recently in *Mumu.* It's time you broke free of her, Ivan. And even the humble position of the girl *vis à vis* the rest of them; you've treated that theme too in some of your stories. Although the girl herself sounds as if she could be interesting. As you're attempting a novel, shouldn't you try something different? For what it's worth, I think you should now dig deeper into your characters. You have such insight, it's time you went beyond the few quick lines with which you've sketched them up to now, and started to paint a full-scale, three-dimensional portrait. That story of yours about the superfluous man, for instance; that's the sort of line you should develop. By the time we'd finished the story, we really knew that man."

Turgenev nods enthusiastically. "You're right of course… as always. As soon as I get back, I'll tear it all up."

Pauline clutches her brows in despair. "You mustn't do that! I'll never open my mouth again if you do. Of course you must finish the novel. But then, when you're thinking about your next book, perhaps you might consider what I've said. Besides, you told me you were working on other things too. But I have to ask you something. After all this trouble you got into over a harmless obituary article, will the censor ever allow anything you write to be published?"

"Quite possibly not," he answers with a rueful laugh. "You don't know what happened over *A Sportsman's Sketches*. I couldn't write to you about it, but it was a quite surprising success. The first edition was sold out in less than six months. I cannot tell you how many letters I received paying me the most exaggerated compliments. Plus a few bespattering me with insults."

"Who were they from?"

"The nobility, of course. I was 'a traitor to my class'".

"Oh, never mind them. It's wonderful that you had such a success. Are they reprinting now?"

Turgenev shakes his head and smiles. "How lucky you are to come from a country where that would seem the most natural of questions! No, they are not reprinting and, in all probability, they never will. The book came out in August last year. Immediately the Minister of Education ordered an investigation into how it had come to be published. Somebody – probably an ambitious young functionary in the censorship office – wrote that it was a dangerous piece of work which would do more harm than good. Is it useful, he asked, that literate peasants can read about themselves being oppressed by landowners who act like vulgar savages, village priests who grovel before the landowners, and police chiefs who take bribes from all and sundry? His report ended – and these were his exact words: 'I do not think that all this can bring profit or even pleasure to any right-minded person; on the contrary, all writing of this kind leaves behind a disagreeable taste in the mouth.'"

"How did you find this out?"

"Annenkov heard it from Prince Lvov, the chief censor of Moscow, who had originally passed the book for publication. The moment Nicholas received the report, he dismissed Lvov and annulled his pension."

"That must have distressed you."

"It did, until I heard from Annenkov that he had sent a personal message to me to say that under the circumstances he was proud and pleased to no longer hold that office. There is *noblesse* in the nobility, after all."

"Well, I'm afraid you've answered my question… about your chances of being published." She gives him a mournful look and sighs: "My poor Ivan. And you're stuck here and can't even move. When will it ever end?"

"Not while this Czar is alive, you can be sure of that. I have some hopes of the Czarevich, the Grand Duke Alexander. I wrote to him asking if he would put in a word for me with a view to a pardon. So far I've heard nothing, but…"

Unintentionally, Pauline now breaks their pact. "All the more reason why you shouldn't be here in Moscow."

"Everyone has a right to one act of rebellion. This is mine. There won't be another."

"Good. Well, perhaps then we'll see you in France sooner than you think."

Turgenev shakes his head. "Even if they relax my exile, they won't let me leave the country. I may never see Courtavenel again."

"Don't be so gloomy."

He leans forward, gazing at her imploringly. "I won't be if you'll tell me that you'll find time – make time – to come and see me at Spasskoye. Just for a day or two."

Her answer is sad but decisive. "I can't, Ivan. For one thing, it would be badly looked on by people here. And I may want them to ask me back some day. But apart from that, I really don't think Louis would like it. It would not look good. You must see that."

He is reluctantly forced to agree, but can't help adding: "Then when will we see each other again? You know that my life has no meaning without you."

"It will have to have. You will have to give it some. I can never be for you all you want me to be. Never. Take what I am able to give you and don't ask for more. If you can't do this, you'll leave me no choice: even our friendship will have to come to an end. And that would be as painful for me as for you."

He starts to expostulate, but she restrains him. "No, Ivan, there is nothing more to say. Or rather, anything either of us might say now would only hurt the other. Your coming here has meant a great deal to me. Especially knowing the risk you are running. I've had many honours in my life, but never one that came at so high a price. But now you must go. And tomorrow return to Spasskoye. It would be unwise for us to see each other again. Don't look so downcast. You have to think that you and I don't only belong to each other. I don't only belong to my husband and children. There is the promise I made to Maria, remember? I have to travel all over the world to express my art. You are much better off being forced to stay in one place. You have so much work to do. Not just for yourself, but for your country. I remember you telling me something your friend Belinsky said: in Russia, change for the better can only come about through literature, not through politics. And who else is going to do this if not you?"

"If it meant I could be with you, I would take a solemn oath never to write another word."

She jumps to her feet. "No, no, this won't do." Holding out her hand, "Goodbye, my dear friend. Have a safe journey home. And God be with you." He ignores her hand and envelops her in a smothering embrace from which she physically has to fight herself free. She pushes him away, muttering a choked, "Go! Go!" He turns and rushes blindly out of the room. She stands quite still for several seconds, then sinks to the floor and abandons herself to the all-engulfing misery of a child who has lost something infinitely precious, retching up sobs of a lacerating violence the like of which she has not known since the news was brought to her of the death of her sister.

INT. A SMALL ROOM IN THE WINTER PALACE – DAY

The Czar and Count Orlov are winding up a discussion about the international tensions arising from the disintegration of the Ottoman Empire, which will eventually lead to the Crimean War.

CZAR

… It's time the Turks were put in their place. I've told Menshikov I want a signed guarantee from Constantinople recognizing our right of protection over all their Orthodox subjects.

ORLOV

And if the Sultan refuses?

CZAR

Menshikov has orders to cross the Pruth and march south.

ORLOV

A bold decision, Sire. And a just one. I only wish we could be more sure of our allies.

CZAR

So do I, Orlov, so do I. It's time young Franz Josef and that upstart vulgarian Bonaparte, who has had the effrontery to proclaim himself Emperor, showed me a little more respect. To that end, I have a mind to send my son on state visits to Vienna and Paris. What would you say to that?

ORLOV

An excellent idea, Sire.

Nicholas nods his head and ponders for a moment. His fingers fidget with a sheet of paper that is lying on his desk. Then he gives his minister a piercing glance.

CZAR

Tell me, Count, what is your opinion of Grand Duke Alexander?

Orlov's obsequious compliments falter under the scrutiny of those intense blue eyes.

CZAR

You may speak quite frankly.

Perhaps he may or perhaps he may not, but Orlov has no intention of taking the risk.

ORLOV

I have no doubt he will prove a worthy successor to you, Sire.

CZAR

Hmm!
                              (after a pause)
You don't think he's sometimes a little too… liberal in his ideas?

ORLOV

If that should ever be the case, I would put it down to his youth.

CZAR

He's thirty five, man! At that age I had been on the throne for six years. No, it's his lack of backbone, not years, that troubles me. Where there should be steel, too often there seems to be only sponge. We know who's to blame, of course.

ORLOV

Who would that be, Sire?

CZAR

Why, that tutor of his. Zhukovsky. Worst mistake I ever made. Should never have entrusted the boy's up-bringing to a poet. Especially one with a Turkish slave-girl for a mother. Should have been a military man. But the Czaritsa was so insistent. She had a soft spot for Zhukovsky. He'd taught her Russian when we were first married. She adored him. And he repaid our trust by stuffing the boy's head with a lot of pernicious nonsense.

ORLOV

Most of which he has now grown out of, Sire.

CZAR

Has he? I'm not so sure. Only the other day he asked me if I didn't think it was time the teaching of philosophy was brought back into

the university curriculum. I reminded him of when and why I had
banned it: in 1848, after the French had thrown out their rightful
sovereign. That's what uncontrolled speculation among the young
leads to.

ORLOV

And what did he say to that?

CZAR

As glibly as though he'd learnt it by rote, which no doubt he had,
he was good enough to inform me that education was authority's
strongest support. That an uneducated nation was a nation without
dignity. Pure Zhukovsky, I'll be bound.

ORLOV

Nevertheless, Sire, I have little doubt that when the time comes for
the Grand Duke to sit on your throne – and may it be many years
from now! – he will have put aside all that nonsense.

*Nicholas gives a sceptical grunt. He picks up the sheet of paper he has been playing with
intermittently throughout the entire conversation and tosses it across the table.*

CZAR

What do you make of this letter he sent me, then?

Orlov picks it up and starts to read passages out loud.

ORLOV

'Ivan Sergeyevich Turgenev… a year and a half … paid for his
misdemeanour … would Your Majesty consider … in the light of
… revoking his exile …'

*Orlov looks up, hoping to find in the Czar's expression some guide as to what line he's expected
to take. But Nicholas's face remains impassive. This puts the minister in a quandary. The
Czar is 57 and ailing. He himself is 70, but in the best of health, and has no desire to relinquish
power under a new ruler. He wants to keep a foot in both camps, but knows that the Czarevich
surrounds himself with a group of liberal-minded advisers. If he convinces Nicholas to refuse
Alexander's request, the Grand Duke's faction will hear of it.*
*Still hoping for a sign from the Czar, he nods his head pensively as though giving the matter
intense thought.*

CZAR
(impatiently)

Well?

ORLOV
(hesitantly)

I don't think there could be any harm in acceding to the Grand
Duke's request, Sire. We can presumably assume that Turgenev will
have learnt his lesson by now.

CZAR

How has he behaved all this time?

ORLOV

Oh, impeccably. He hasn't stirred from his estate, except to visit a
few neighbours. We've kept a very close eye on him, of course.

Nicholas takes his son's letter back from Orlov and gives it a final glance.

CZAR
(reluctantly)

Very well, then. But continue to keep him under surveillance here
in St Petersburg and in Moscow. I want a report on the company he
keeps …

He crumples up the letter and throws it violently into a wastepaper basket.

CZAR

… and there's to be no question of a foreign passport. This damn
travelling habit has corrupted him enough already. The biggest favour
we can do that man is to ensure he never leaves Russia again…

Turgenev's return to St Petersburg had something of the irrepressible ebullience
of a colt let out into a spring paddock after a long winter immured in a cramped
stable box. After sixteen months, the exile on which he had embarked with such
admirable intentions had become almost unendurable. Not only did he miss the
intellectual stimulation and social variety of the city, but it was also forced upon
him how ill-equipped he was to deal with the practical demands of country life. In
the late summer, suspecting that his estates were being mis- or perhaps just

unmanaged, he had forced himself to go over the books with his bailiff. Even his impractical mind could see that his fears were well grounded: the two years of Tyutchev's stewardship had been disastrous. Total expenditure had amounted to seventy-five thousand roubles, of which a mere ten thousand had found their way into his pocket. Tyutchev had been systematically outmanoeuvred by the peasants; his only answer to all their well-rehearsed grievances was to raise their wages. He had hardly ever set foot out of Spasskoye, so the revenues from the other properties had fallen by over a third. And he seemed to have had an unhappy knack of buying at the highest price and selling at the lowest. There was no question of dishonesty, and Turgenev realized that the fault was chiefly his own in thinking that a literary man and disciple of Belinsky was a suitable person to run a large estate. He was forced to tell his friend that he would have to let him go, but Tyutchev took it in good part and was perhaps relieved to be rid of a task that he must have known was beyond him.

Turgenev decided not to replace him; as he had no choice but to remain at Spasskoye, he might as well manage the estate himself. After all, his mother had done so all her life, and had still had plenty of time for other activities. For the next few months he had many occasions to remember his mother, usually with grudging admiration. How had she done it? He plunged into his new occupation with every good intention, but soon began to feel it was strangling him: bills, invoices, receipts – all of them inaccurate, most of them fiddled – when to sow, when to reap, arable or pasture, cattle or sheep, serfs complaining about bailiffs, bailiffs complaining about serfs, everyone asking for instructions when they knew far better than he what should be done… this was not the way to spend what remained of his youth. And yet any more agreeable work was out of the question. When darkness brought an end to his activities, he was lucky if he still had enough energy to read a book, let alone write one. For the first year since he had started to contribute to *Sovremennik,* he had published nothing except for an appreciative article on the *Memoirs of a Shooting Man* by the Aksakov brothers' father, Sergey Timofeyevich.

By now Feoktista had gone, and with the departure of the Tyutchevs he felt, for the first time, the full heart-shrinking misery of loneliness. There had been bleak moments when he first returned from France, but then he had at least had the regular, frequent arrival of Pauline's letters to look forward to. Communication, however unsatisfactory, had been maintained. But after the Moscow expedition, the flow had almost dried up. And no amount of protests, pleas and even reproaches on his part seemed to be able to get it started again.

And then, in the last week of November, Orlov's letter arrived, telling him that he was free to go to Moscow or St Petersburg as he pleased. That same afternoon he wrote to his uncle Nikolai, suggesting that he come to live at Spasskoye and manage the estates. He had little doubt that the offer would be taken up: relations between uncle and nephew had always been affectionate, and he knew that Nikolai, with his young wife and two children, was extremely hard up. Besides, he had run the estate for Varvara for a while, and though she had dismissed him for incompetence, Turgenev now knew from personal experience that incompetence in her eyes might be adequacy, if not actually skill, in anyone else's. And he remembered that, when Nikolai and his family had been staying with them, his uncle would often give him a wink when Tyutchev was outlining a plan as if to say: 'This fellow doesn't have an idea what he's talking about'. He was sure that with Nikolai installed at Spasskoye, he could return to spending most of the year in St Petersburg with a light heart. He was, of course, wrong...

For the first few months after his return to the city, he indulged in almost uninterrupted social activity. It was as though he had overnight shaved off fifteen years of his life. Gone were all the pious resolutions he had made at the start of his Spasskoye exile. Gone, at least on the surface, was the adoring, pining lover. Gone the disciple of Belinsky seeking to redeem his country. He seemed to be proclaiming to the world – or at any rate to his world: 'These are the last moments of my youth and I am going to live them to the full.' Although focusing his attentions chiefly on the literary coterie, he also gladly accepted invitations from those noble houses that were prepared to accept back the prodigal son who had incurred the Czar's displeasure. After so many months of rough country clothes, he again dressed like a dandy. He flirted indiscriminately with every member of the female sex he encountered, from bashful young girls making their first appearance in society to crusty old dowagers, to whose rheumy eyes he brought back the occasional twinkle. He also reverted to his youthful habit of composing scurrilous puns and epigrams, whose victims often found it hard to forgive him. To a new acquaintance at this time, he would have seemed like a charming, clever, somewhat vain and totally inconsequential social butterfly.

He received a hero's welcome. Annenkov had found him a small furnished apartment in Povarskoy Lane, where he quickly settled in with his cook, Stepan, and valet, Zakhar, both brought from Spasskoye. Two days after his arrival, Nekrasov gave the most lavish *Sovremennik* dinner anyone ever remembered. Every major contributor was there: Panaev and his wife (the only woman present), Annenkov, Ostrovsky, the poet Maikov, the novelists Goncharov and Grigorovich, the critic Druzhinin and Vasily Botkin, another member of the Belinsky circle, now an essayist and translator. Glasses were raised to innumerable toasts: to the guest of honour, of course; to the glorious future of *Sovremennik*; to Belinsky, Pushkin and Gogol; to former comrades in exile – Herzen and Ogarev – or in jail – Bakunin; to the good health of the Czarevich, of whom great things were expected; to the ill health of censors, government committees and spies; to the falling of the scales from the Slavophils' eyes; to a return to the ideals of 1848; and to the downfall of all despots, especially the parvenu of the group, the recently self-proclaimed Emperor Napoleon III. By the time this name was reached, there was scarcely a sober head in the house and Turgenev had to shout for silence; despite, or perhaps inspired by, the presence of Avdotya Panaeva very close to him, he took huge delight in relating a scurrilous story he had read in a letter from – of all people – Louis Viardot. "As you probably know," he said, "before his marriage earlier this year to his Spanish Eugénie, Louis-Napoleon, as he then was and should still be, had a notable reputation as a *tombeur de femmes*. His favourite conquests were well-known actresses. One of these was a sharp, quick-witted minx called Augustine Brohan, who took the soubrette roles in Molière at the *Comédie Française*. He had quite a long liaison with her and one night, seeking a bit of variety, he placed her on all fours and started to try and sodomize her. 'Ah no, prince,' she said, 'not there; that's the artists' entrance.'" La Panaeva wagged an admonitory finger at Turgenev, but made a point of laughing conspicuously louder than anyone else.

But by early spring, the profound monotony of the social round had gnawed away most of the euphoria. The shallowness of the gossip at the aristocratic gatherings was to be expected. As much as the Parisian equivalent had irritated him, with every Frenchman determined to show that he was cleverer than anyone else in the room, at least they *were* clever. But even the company of his fellow-writers, with their two or three eternal preoccupations, began to pall. It was not long before he drew the appropriate conclusion: he was not in his early twenties any more, and it was time to stop living as if he were. He could hear in his mind's ear the dry, mocking reproach in Belinsky's voice: 'Oh, my poor *gamin*! Is this what you are going to turn into after all? A creature of the salons, a charmer of old ladies, an amateur 'literary man', who is too busy doing the rounds of society to devote real time to serious work?'

He felt swamped by a creeping sense of inertia, and it all came bursting out in a midnight confession to the ever-faithful Annenkov. He had remained behind after a dinner party Turgenev had given in his apartment for some of the *Sovremennik* group. On the face of it, the evening had been a success. Stepan's roast suckling pig with horseradish and sour cream had been eulogized, his curd cheesecakes declared incomparable. Wine and words had flowed freely, and this time the insidious parochialism that Turgenev had begun to dread was absent: much of the conversation had abandoned the printed word and ranged around the likelihood of France and England declaring war on Russia over Turkey, and what the probable consequences would be. But as his friends started to leave, a familiar aching feeling of dissatisfaction induced him to ask Annenkov to stay and smoke a last cigar.

With the perception of long friendship, Annenkov had noticed that Turgenev had recently lost much of the sparkle that had been so evident during the first weeks after his return from exile. So when the last guest had left, he wasted no time in prevarication; easing his bulk into a comfortable armchair, he asked directly why, after so enjoyable an evening, the host seemed plunged in gloom.

"If only I knew," Turgenev groaned, striding restlessly around the room. "Life seems to have lost all its savour. I suppose it's just that I'm growing old." He paused in front of a mirror and ruffled a hand through his hair. "Look at that! Grey as a rat! I'm an old man."

"You're thirty-six," Annenkov replied imperturbably. "I am forty-two and I barely consider I've reached middle age."

"You've always been middle-aged", Turgenev retorted, unable to resist a smile.

"Perhaps that's why I don't moan about it. At any rate, your problem is not age. May I hazard a guess as to what it is?"

"You may. Indeed, you must."

"I have no evidence for this, but I have a feeling that your relationship with Madame Viardot is not what it was."

"Your feeling is correct. She seems to have erased me from her life. Since she was here last year, I have had only four letters from her. Four letters in thirteen months!"

"Do you write to her?"

"At first as regularly as ever. Now, a little less often. It's hard to know what to say when there's nothing to respond to. It's only half a conversation. Perhaps that's better than nothing. Perhaps not."

Annenkov leaned forward and abandoned the light tone he had adopted up to now. "You know, Vanya," he said slowly, "it is perhaps time that you… how can I say this?… that you began to wean yourself from the power that this woman – this very remarkable, extraordinary woman – holds over you. For ten years now, your almost every move has been conditioned by what effect it will have on her."

"I know, I know," Turgenev cried in desperation. "But how? She really means more than life to me. Or anyhow my life seems purposeless without her. I talk to her all the time, as if she were in the room with me. I'm beginning to fear for my sanity. And yet when I write to her, I have nothing to say: I cover pages discussing trivial details of my daughter's education. Tell me, my old friend, what am I to do?"

"One thing you could do would be to find some other object for your affections…" He paused as Turgenev flung himself on to a sofa and buried his face in his hands. "It doesn't have to be as dramatic as all that, you know. I mean, it has been done before. Or do you think that no one has ever loved as you have loved?"

Turgenev said nothing for several seconds. Then he slowly lowered his hands from his face. "I cannot imagine the future without her," he said at last.

Annenkov was merciless. "But can you imagine the future *with* her? You are not allowed a passport to leave the country. If, as seems certain, war breaks out with France, you will not be able to go there for God knows how long. Nor is she likely to be invited to St Petersburg. She is one of the most famous women in Europe, married with two children. And on top of all this... I'm sorry, but you suggested it yourself... she doesn't seem to feel the same way about you as she once did. What, in the name of heaven, *is* your future with her?"

As Turgenev simply gazed into space without answering, he went on: "This is the moment for you to fulfil your real potential as a writer. For that you need time and tranquillity. Why haven't you finished your novel? I know Botkin and I were critical of some of the chapters that you showed us, but that was only to encourage you to continue... to look at it in a fresh light. But you've done nothing. And you know why? Because you can never find the time to concentrate. You're always running after diversions to keep your mind off la Viardot."

Turgenev finally turned his eyes on his friend and said, in a dead voice: "What am I to do, Pavlochka?"

"Find some girl you can grow fond of – that shouldn't be difficult; you are what the French call *un parti*, you're handsome, most people, especially women, find you charming, you have plenty of money and you're beginning to be well known. What else can a young girl ask for? When you've chosen her, marry her, have children and write. There! That's the Annenkov recipe. You asked me. I've told you. And you will not take a word of notice of anything I've said."

Turgenev couldn't suppress an ironic smile. "It is more or less exactly what Pauline told me to do when I was with her in Moscow."

Annenkov smiled back. "That doesn't label either her or me a genius!"

"The trouble is," Turgenev remarked thoughtfully, "that I wouldn't know where to begin to look for this unfortunate young lady."

It was out before Annenkov could stop it. "Oh, perhaps I could help you there."

Turgenev shot him a keen glance. "You have someone in mind, don't you?" Annenkov's pink cheeks flushed slightly. "You've prepared all this, you scheming Pandarus! You were just waiting for the moment to bring it up. All right, out with it! Who is your Cressida?"

Annenkov was now thoroughly embarrassed. He cleared his throat nervously and almost stammered: "It's not like that at all. It's just that... oh, the other evening I was dining at the house of your cousin, Aleksander Mikhailovich Turgenev, and your name came up... he asked after you... said how long it was since he had seen you... and their daughter, Olga... do you remember her?"

"Why yes, but she's a child."

"She's no child. She's eighteen ...

"Great heavens! Already? You see, I have grown old."

"She's eighteen and a very charming young woman..."

254

"I see. So she's your intended victim! Well, what did she have to say?"

"Nothing in particular. She had read most of your work, and seemed very interested in it. And she's a fine musician. She plays the piano quite beautifully."

"Knowing your ear for music, I shall prefer to judge that for myself."

"Then you will pay them a visit?"

"After all this hard work you've put in, it seems I should be an ungrateful wretch not to. As a matter of fact, I was intending to look up Aleksander Mikhailovich. I remember him with great sympathy." His tone became suddenly serious. "But, swear to me, Pavlochka, you have not given any intimation to them – least of all to her – of what's been brewing in that witch's cauldron of a head of yours."

Annenkov gave him every assurance to the contrary and Turgenev led him to the door. After showing his friend out, he threw himself down on his bed and lay there, fully clothed, hands behind his head, staring at the ceiling. It was many hours before sleep finally gave his teeming thoughts a temporary rest.

St Petersburg,
23 April, 1854.

Dear Madame Viardot,

I was delighted to receive your short note telling me of your and Louis's happiness at the safe arrival of little Marianne. My warmest congratulations to you both. Unfortunately you did not take the opportunity to tell me something of yourself. For a long time now I have had almost no idea of what you are doing. I am very much afraid we are only holding on by our fingertips – and it seems to me I can feel yours slipping away altogether. Certainly it is difficult to maintain the tenacity of one's affection in the face of so dark, so uncertain a future. And yet we must try to find a way. In any case, it will not be me who lets go of your hand…

Lacking all knowledge of your doings, I will merely sketch in a few of my own. I am writing a longish story, which I think I will call 'A Backwater', an ironic title in that I show that the most violent emotions – love and despair, leading to death – can occur in the kind of environment about which people say: 'Oh, nothing ever happens here…' In the meantime, Mumu finally got passed by the censorship and was published by Sovremennik earlier in the year. I am glad to say it seemed to meet with general approval.

I have been seeing a certain amount of a cousin of mine, a man of my father's generation of whom I have grown very fond. He has a charming young daughter – blonde, fresh and innocent, but by no means insipid. She is very much what I would like Paulinette to grow up to be: a young lady of modesty and discretion, and yet with a mind of her own. She has quite a talent at the piano – and as you know, my standards there are of the highest! We have long conversations about music and literature, about both of which she is remarkably knowledgeable for her age. Otherwise, I see the usual people, do the usual things…

Turgenev had immediately been made welcome in his cousin's house and in no time at all became intimate with the whole family. After a week or so he had quite forgotten that it was Annenkov who had 'sent' him there. Aleksander Mikhailovich, a very distant cousin, was eighty-two years old. Once a general, he had been close to many of the Decembrists. Grief and bitterness at their fate had caused him to retire to civilian life. A bookish man, he had lived a contented existence as a cultivated country bachelor on his estate until, at the age of sixty-three, he had been captivated by the beauty of a sixteen-year-old orphan, Pelageya Litke, who had just come out of a convent. They had married and the following year Olga was born; but only a matter of days later the mother had died. In the short time of their marriage, the old man had quickly come to adore his wife, and from the moment of her death, he lived only for his daughter. She had been educated at home with the aid of the best foreign tutors, in turn German, English and French. As a constant companion, she had had the tireless devotion of a spinster aunt, Nadezhda Mikhailovna Eropkina. Tante Nadya, as she was known to everybody, was a remarkable woman: devout, but with no respect for the priesthood; a convinced democrat, who had followed with disappointed enthusiasm the declining fortunes of the various revolutions of 1848; a woman of impeccable behaviour herself, she had an easy tolerance of all so-called sins, except those involving unkindness or cruelty. Possessed of a wide culture (before dedicating her life to Olga, she had given private lessons in music and literature), she had chosen to conceal her true value under a veneer of superficial, chattering busybodyness.

Olga herself was surrounded by limitless love and attention, but showed not a trace of the spoilt self-absorbtion which frequently characterizes the only child. Like many children raised in exclusively adult company, she appeared older than her age. Tall and slender, conventionally pretty without being in any way beautiful, her most striking attribute was a pair of large hazel-grey eyes which seemed to look out on the world with quiet, if as yet untested, confidence. She had read widely in Russian, German and English literature, and could play all but the hardest Beethoven sonatas well enough that Turgenev never found himself making invidious comparisons. Her devotion to music was such that, if nothing else required her attention, she would start to practise after breakfast at nine and continue until lunch at two.

Turgenev was captivated by Olga's simplicity. It was not, in truth, a quality he was used to. Even Feoktista, for all her lack of sophistication, had had deep reserves of feminine cunning to call upon when, by calculation or instinct, she had felt it was required. Olga spoke little, but when she did, he found her invariably worth listening to. It was true that her opportunities to talk were limited by the almost continual presence of Tante Nadya, who bubbled away like a samovar. But during the rare moments when they were alone, he never felt she was thinking, 'Ah, now it's my turn!' He also could not fail to be aware that he had made a strong impression on her. Often when he was talking with her father he would sense that those eloquent eyes were fixed on him with an expression that combined admiration and something almost akin to pride.

Early in May, Nekrasov and Panaev suggested he take a house for the summer at Peterhof, some thirty miles west of St Petersburg, on the south coast of the Gulf of Finland. The two *Sovremennik* editors had made the habit of establishing their headquarters there for the summer, and Turgenev needed very little persuading. He knew that Aleksander Mikhailovich had a house at Oranienbaum, just a mile or two away. As soon as he moved in, accompanied by the indispensable Stepan and Zakhar, his spirits lifted. Freed from the entanglements of St Petersburg society, he began to work regularly, producing some critical articles on poets and poetry and finishing *A Backwater*, the longest work – with the exception of his unfinished novel – he had yet attempted. His leisure hours were spent in the ways he enjoyed most: long days in the marshes with Nekrasov, shooting duck and snipe, and long evenings at his cousin's house where the conversation flowed as agreeably as the wine. Friends from St Petersburg would come to visit him and give him the excuse to repay Aleksander Mikhailovich's hospitality. And almost every day he would go for evening walks along the shore with Olga, usually, but not always, accompanied by Tante Nadya. Their talk ranged over a wide variety of subjects and he found himself increasingly attracted by the young girl's artless sincerity and appetite for knowledge.

In mid-June there was a big dinner party at the house in Oranienbaum, to celebrate Aleksander Mikhailovich's birthday. When Turgenev arrived with his guests, Annenkov and Druzhinin, he found Nekrasov and the Panaevs already there. Together with their host, Tante Nadya and Olga, they were standing on the terrace in front of the house, which stood a hundred feet or so above the level of the water, admiring in near silence the multi-coloured shafts of light dancing over the rippling waters of the gulf. The two cousins exchanged a warm embrace and Turgenev offered his congratulations and a pup of the ageing Diane, which he had brought as a present. The admiring hush was now broken by the shrill yaps of the puppy and the screams of delight from Olga, who immediately started playing with it. Turgenev remarked on the splendour of the view at that twilight hour. "Yes, Ivan," the old man remarked, "it provides at least partial consolation for the idiocies of our kind." The reference was all too clearly to the war which had now broken out in the Crimea and was to dominate the conversation for the first part of the dinner.

Turgenev himself took little part in the discussion, preferring to watch Olga and note her reactions to the various arguments put forward. She was wearing a pale blue dress trimmed with white flowers which, he considered, admirably reflected her frank, simple nature. From time to time her eyes would meet his, and, realizing that he was watching her, she would blush slightly and look down at her lap.

"One had hoped…" this was Aleksander Mikhailovich, "that the carnage that ended in 1815 might have finally convinced our obtuse race that no territorial advantage is worth the hellish obscenity of war…"

… she is such a graceful creature, the delicacy of a fawn, quite without artifice, I cannot imagine her ever being obtrusive or demanding…

"…the Czar's slippery grasp of reality…" Nekrasov's turn now, "huffing and puffing over a handful of Greek priests when millions of his own countrymen are desperately clamouring for…"

… and yet she is no empty vessel, there's content there already and room for more, she is a canvas on which so far there are only a few sketches, there's much still to be filled in…

"…no one taken in by that pretence…" Druzhinin was especially bitter, "least of all our 'ally' Austria… naked aggression… the Principalities… the generals like to claim Wallachia and Moldavia are essential to Russia's security!…"

… how challenging, how rewarding it could be to be the one to apply the broad brushstrokes, to complete the already well-defined outlines…

"It's all rhetoric… expansion south… fulfilling the historic will of Peter… the only result will be to antagonize the rest of Europe…"

… I can see her at Spasskoye, I know already from our walks that she is responsive to nature, to trees and flowers and birdsong…

"… tragedy is that the army will swallow the rhetoric… even the lower ranks… 'spirit of 1812'…"

… I can imagine our travelling together, with her languages she would fit in anywhere I wanted to take her…

"… European countries all have their interests… England – sea-route to India… Napoleon – posing as champion of the Roman church… Austria – influence in the Balkans…"

… am I in love with her? I have to answer no, at this moment no, because love for me has only ever had one meaning, one direction, but perhaps, in time, certainly if ever I…

"And you, Ivan?" His cousin was eyeing him keenly. "You have been untypically silent. What are your thoughts on this war?"

"I can only go one further than Mercutio and say, a plague on all their houses. At a time like this I know personal considerations should take second place, but I had been hoping that, with the help of the Czarevich, I might be allowed to go abroad again soon. But now…!"

"Were you thinking of leaving Russia then, Ivan Sergeyevich?" There was no more than polite curiosity in Olga's tone of voice, but was there a flicker of apprehension in her eyes?

"Not permanently, Olga Aleksandrovna. I should pay visits to London and Paris. But these are now enemy capitals."

"And what would be the reason for these visits?" For those who knew him, there was no doubting the veiled sarcasm behind Annenkov's question. He remembered Salzbrunn.

"Some of my work is being translated, and I would like to oversee it. To avoid what has just happened in Paris, where a certain Monsieur Charrière, without my permission or knowledge, has made a corrupt version of the *Sportsman's Sketches*, calling it *Memoirs of a Russian Nobleman* or *A Picture of the Present Situation of the Nobility and the Peasants in the Russian Provinces*. With an introduction which made it seem that I was calling for instant revolution. I had to write an open letter to the *St Petersburg Journal* denying all responsibility, otherwise Orlov would have had me thrown back into the Admiralty... or worse. But never mind all that! We are all being too serious this evening..." He pushed his chair back, got to his feet and proposed a toast to 'the many long and happy years ahead of our honoured host' and after that had been drunk, another to 'the ladies of the house, our irreplaceable Tante Nadya and our beautiful young Olga Aleksandrovna, whom we very much hope is now going to enchant our ears with her ravishing piano playing'. As Turgenev raised his glass in her direction, accompanied by the vociferous approbation of all the other guests, he fancied her eyes smiled back at him a little less bashfully than usual.

When everyone was seated in the drawing room, Olga took her place at the piano and, after a moment's thought, began to play Beethoven's *Les Adieux* sonata. Turgenev could not help but wonder if this was her way of alluding to his frustrated desire for travel, but these reflections were soon swept away by the real skill of her performance; and after the delicacy of her *Poco Andante* had given way, in *Le Retour*, to a final brilliant flourish of arpeggios, the whole company rose to their feet to applaud her. An encore was insisted on, and she played a Schubert *Moment Musical*, knowing it to be a favourite of Turgenev's; but all the time she was playing it, and even after she had finished, she never looked in his direction.

Everyone left soon after and Aleksander Mikhailovich pleaded tiredness and went up to bed, leaving Turgenev, Olga and Tante Nadya to play the post-party game of discussing the evening's guests. Turgenev suggested a variation on this: each of them should decide which Shakespearian character would most resemble one of their departed friends. Having settled on Prince Hal for Nekrasov, Goneril and Albany for the Panaevs, Ulysses for Druzhinin, Horatio for Annenkov and Duke Theseus for Aleksander Mikhailovich, they were left to consider themselves.

"Well I know whom I am going to propose for Tante Nadya," Turgenev said: "The Nurse in *Romeo and Juliet*."

"Lord a'mercy," squawked the good lady, unwittingly immediately in character. "With all those improper remarks she makes! How could you suggest such a thing?"

"No, no," Olga laughed. "Ivan Sergeyevich is right. The Nurse is perfect for you."

"Well, I'm sure I don't know, but if the two of you agree, what can I say? But now it's your turn. And each of you must choose the character for the other. Ivan

Sergeyevich, who is your choice for Olushka?"

Turgenev had already made up his mind. "Imogen, in *Cymbeline*."

Tante Nadya, who hadn't read the play, asked why.

"Suffice it to say that at the end of the play her husband, who had earlier wanted to kill her, called her a 'temple of virtue'".

Olga gave a little laugh of embarrassment mixed with pleasure and wagged a finger at Turgenev: "You overrate me so shamelessly that I simply don't dare choose a character for you. Tante Nadya, you'll have to do it for me."

The old lady had no doubts. "Oh, for me it has to be Hamlet. I mean… you mustn't be offended, Ivan Sergeyevich … after all, it's a compliment in many ways, but you always seem so undecided about everything. I mean, just now, at dinner, there was everybody holding forth about this war… they all knew exactly what they thought… but you didn't seem to have any opinion. It was as though your mind was somewhere else. And then, this constant desire to travel. Isn't that another way of saying you never want to stay long in the same place? Of course, I understand very well. And then, who am I to judge? An old lady who talks too much and would love to travel herself, but doesn't have the means."

She stood up, went over to the window and clapped her hands enthusiastically. "What a beautiful night! And bless me if it isn't a full moon… or as near as makes no difference. Why don't we go out and fill our lungs with a little fresh sea air before we go to bed?" Turgenev and Olga were happy to agree, but the moment they opened the front door and stepped outside, Tante Nadya clasped her elbows and shivered. 'Oh no, it's too chilly. I'd catch my death of cold! You two young things go on. I'm going up to bed."

Smiling to himself at the thought of how readily she was immersing herself in the part of the nurse, Turgenev took Olga by the arm and led her over to a garden seat which commanded a superb view over the gulf. The two of them sat for some time in silence, lost in the magic of the night and both a trifle awkward at having been left so abruptly alone. Feeling her give a little shiver, he thought about putting his arm round her, but instead took off his jacket and draped it over her shoulders. She gave him a sweet smile. 'Thank you, Ivan Sergeyevich. May I ask you what have you been thinking about while we have been sitting here'?

Turgenev cast his mind around for some plausible answer; the truth was inadmissible. Fortunately it didn't take him more than a second: "As we have been so involved in Shakespeare," he said, "I was thinking of one of my favourite passages in all his work: the scene between Lorenzo and Jessica towards the end of *The Merchant of Venice*. And he began to quote: *How sweet the moonlight sleeps upon this bank* … To his delight, she immediately joined in: *Here will we sit, and let the sounds of music creep in our ears…* They went on together: *Soft stillness and the night become the touches of sweet harmony…* They looked at each other and regretted, almost in unison, that there was no music for them. "But," Turgenev added, "I am fortunate enough to have Schubert, beautifully played, still creeping in my ears."

Olga drew his jacket closer round her shoulders and asked, timidly: "When you write, do you feel that your love of music influences you?"

"I try very hard not to let it."

"Why?"

"Because if I thought of the creative power of Gluck, Mozart and Beethoven, I should never write another line."

Olga let a moment pass before finding the courage to speak her mind. "Tante Nadya is right," she said, "you really are like Hamlet. Perhaps a little *too* like Hamlet. You don't have enough confidence in yourself. Forgive me, I know it's no business of mine to say this… my only excuse is that I think so highly of your work. I believe you have it in you to be a very important writer. Not Shakespeare, of course, who could be? Not at the same level as Gluck or Beethoven perhaps, but nevertheless an artist of the front rank. But surely to achieve that, you can't always let your… your…"

Turgenev smilingly helped her out: "*Resolution be sicklied o'er with the pale cast of thought?*"

She nodded and raised her eyes in mock despair. "However hard we try, he always said it better, didn't he?"

"He did. On my twentieth birthday, my friend Granovsky gave me the complete works in English. And on the card that accompanied them he wrote: 'Approach this with fear and with faith'. But you're right, Olga Aleksandrovna. In fact you've touched on something I've been thinking about for some time now. I even have half a mind to write an essay about it. The difference between the man of thought and the man of action. And how rarely the two can combine. Hamlet is the perfect representative of the first. I'm casting my mind around who to choose for the second. The temptation is to use an historical figure: Alexander the Great, Napoleon, some great leader of men. But I'd rather oppose Hamlet with another literary creation. I was thinking of one of Homer's heroes: Achilles or Odysseus. But even they had their contemplative sides. Now I'm considering Don Quixote."

Olga's eyebrows went up in surprise. "Don Quixote?"

"Yes. Have you read Cervantes?"

"No, I haven't learnt Spanish, although I want to."

"You mustn't let that stop you reading the novel. It has been translated – very well – into French by… by a friend of mine."

"I will, then. But in my ignorance, I thought Don Quixote was a purely comic character… someone who never achieved anything. 'Tilting at windmills' has become almost a proverb, even in Russian."

"Ah, it's not the achievement that matters, it's the intention. When Don Quixote felt there was something that needed to be done, he went ahead and tried to do it. Whether he succeeded or not, which, of course, he seldom did, was of no importance…"

She started to get up. "I think I must go in now. I'm getting a little cold. But I really hope you will write your essay and I look forward to reading it."

Turgenev sprang to his feet and helped her up. "If I think it's any good at all, may I have the pleasure of dedicating it to you."

Even in the moonlight, her blush was visible. "I should be honoured, Ivan Sergeyevich. But…" she looked down at the ground, "I am quite unworthy…"

A little tentatively, he put his hands on her shoulders and kissed the top of her forehead. "It is my work that will be unworthy of you, Olga Aleksandrovna." She gave him a quick, quizzical look and he smiled: "You see? I am irredeemably Hamletesque!"

Turgenev walked home through the moonlit night enveloped in a rare sense of contentment. The sea air had not yet acquired its early morning chill, and when he breathed deeply to savour its salty tang, his nostrils also caught the sweet, elusive scent of the nearby lime-trees. *How far away*, he thought, *from Spasskoye winters… there I was always dreaming and wishing myself back at Courtavenel. But this evening was Courtavenel à la Russe: a place blessed by nature – friends with common interests but divergent views, leading to passionate argument without rancour or scorn – the pleasures of the table – the enchantment of music – and then?… Ah then!… The one fundamental difference: Olga Aleksandrovna instead of Pauline. Take that quiet ruminative talk just now, where surely our words were screens drawn across thoughts neither of us ventured to express. Certainly there were screens present the last time I saw Pauline, but those tonight were hiding a possible future, whereas the screens in Moscow were erected to blot out too painful a memory of the past. Annenkov was right, Olga is just the sort of person I should marry… I'm never likely to find anyone who would make a better wife for me or mother for my children… And yet, with all that, I have to ask myself: am I in love with her? And the answer is… I don't know. Love her as I loved Pauline, surely not… but then, what was that? Loved Pauline, the past tense. Dear God, is it possible the passion I was convinced was eternal is dwindling? Has this recent indifference of hers shaved away so relentlessly at my adoration that there is nothing left but the numb conviction that I* must *love her because I always have? A terrible, fearful kind of habit? No, this is not true … one kind word from her and I'd be back at her feet… but if that word doesn't come? I am 36! If I let this chance slip away from me, what awaits me for the rest of my life? A grovelling attachment to a woman who feels nothing for me but a mostly intellectual friendship based on shared happy times? A bleak prospect, my friend, and, in the eyes of all who know me, a ridiculous one, since I have the opportunity to rectify it. Of course, I may be flattering myself… Olga's interest in me may not extend as far as wanting to be my wife… but I don't really believe that, there was a banked-down spark inside her this evening that it would only have taken a word from me to fan into flame. Am I to say that word? And when? Before the summer is over, if at all. By then I must have made up my mind…*

His sleep that night was profound and dreamless. On the breakfast tray which Zakhar brought him in the morning, a letter was propped against the coffee pot.

Paris,
18 May, 1854.

My dear Turgenev,

I was pleased to receive your letter of 23 April and to hear that you seem to be writing prolifically and successfully.

You complain that I don't give you news of myself, but really there is little of any interest. Marianne's birth, easy as it was, has meant that I have enjoyed – and I mean enjoyed! – a long period of undisturbed calm. And calm, agreeable as it is for the one who experiences it, is very boring for everyone else. The baby is the sweetest, most good-natured little thing and I am now slowly beginning to resume my normal life. I am preparing for a two-month season at Covent Garden and have been studying the very powerful role of a gypsy woman in Verdi's new opera, Il Trovatore, which had a triumphant opening in Naples. I think this work may cause you to review your poor opinion of Verdi; it may lack the dignity of your beloved Gluck, but my goodness, what energy, what brio! This is the modern world, my friend, and we must learn to live in it.

I was glad to hear of your friendship with your cousin, and also for his daughter. She sounds a charming young girl. But I am far from pleased with, and a little suspicious of, your reticence: you cannot expect such an old friend as myself to be content with this scanty morsel tucked away at the end like an insignificant afterthought. Let me hear more! She has read some books and plays the piano. Good for her! But so has and does practically every budding young plant that is pushing its way up in the herbaceous border of polite society. And, presuming on our long friendship, allow me to sound a faint note of warning: you say she is fresh and innocent. These are admirable qualities, of course, but often not accompanied by the strength and resilience the young plant needs to fight its way through the rocky soil and choking weeds of life. Be careful, my dear friend, that you do not, even involuntarily, take advantage of this vulnerability. I know you well enough to be sure that you would never willingly hurt anyone, even people you are not fond of. But, with your disarming modesty, you might forget how attractive you must appear to any inexperienced girl eager to make the match of her life. And remember your age. If she is as young as she sounds, you must be some twenty years older. No one knows better than I how wide a gap twenty years represents. It can be bridged, but it requires very special qualities on both sides, and these are qualities I am not sure you possess. Of course, I cannot speak for her. I know so little about her, but I expect after your next letter to know much, much more!

Forgive these random, inconsequential observations from

Your devoted friend,

Pauline V.

Almost every morning, Turgenev used to take a midday walk in the gardens of the palace in Oranienbaum that Peter the Great had given to his favourite, Aleksander Menshikov. Everyone in the small community of summer visitors from St Petersburg was familiar with each others' movements, so it was no big surprise when, a day or two after his cousin's birthday, he saw Tante Nadya walking towards him along one of the box-flanked gravel paths. She, however, threw up her hands and trilled her delight at this chance meeting. Having ascertained that his walk was as aimless as hers, she suggested that they proceed together for a while, and Turgenev was happy to comply. They soon reached the large circular lake and Tante Nadya, exclaiming at the heat although it was in fact a relatively cool day, suggested they sit down on one of the wooden seats that surrounded it. Here, fanning herself vigorously, she chattered away, barely pausing for breath, favouring him with comments about their fellow-strollers, which to Turgenev seemed far from inaudible to their subjects.

"There, you see that man with the drooping grey moustache, don't you think he looks *just* like Grand Duke Constantine?" Turgenev agreed. "Isn't that that actress who was playing at the Maryinski last season? What was her name?... Markova?... Malkova?... She's not as pretty as she looks on-stage, but I really think it's her." Turgenev assured her that it wasn't. "Oh, I do so enjoy Oranienbaum, don't you, Ivan Sergeyevich? It's such a lovely place, and then one sees everyone one knows in St Petersburg, but without having to make any effort." She stopped and reflected for a moment. "Everyone, that is, except the poor, of course. What a pity that they aren't able to take a little holiday in the summer. Perhaps the time will come one day when they will. I do hope so, don't you?" Turgenev shared her hope and thought perhaps it was time he contributed something himself to this one-sided conversation.

"And how is Olga Aleksandrovna?" he asked, not congratulating himself on his originality.

But the old lady seemed delighted, almost relieved, by his conventional question. "She's very well... very well indeed. She would be with me now, but of course nothing short of a thunderbolt from heaven would make her miss her practising." She gave him a sideways glance and added: "Especially now."

"Why especially now? Is she preparing a concert?"

"Well, we do have something in mind for the end of the season, but that's not what I meant. No, it's because of you, Ivan Sergeyevich. She knows how much you know about music... what an expert you are... and when you're there she only wants to play her very best."

"I'm no expert. Just a lover. And lucky enough to have heard a lot of beautiful music superbly performed..." Was it his imagination, or did she look away at a passing couple to hide a momentary embarrassment? "But it is rare to find anyone who is not a professional play as well as Olga does."

Tante Nadya flicked her fan shut and tapped him on the knee with it. "She thinks very highly of you too, you know. She is always telling her friends that they must read your work. And she confessed to me the other day that she had never taken such pleasure in anyone's company as she does in yours."

"That can only be because she is very young and her acquaintance is therefore necessarily limited. There are a great many more interesting people than me around."

Another tap of the fan. "There you go again, Ivan Sergeyevich! Always so modest! Olushka says that's one of the things she likes most about you: everyone is always bragging about their talents, but you make so light of yours."

"I'm afraid that is because they really don't weigh very much. But I am truly flattered that Olga Aleksandrovna has so high an opinion of me. Flattered... and a little frightened."

"Why frightened?"

"Because I may not be able to live up to it. I would hate to disappoint her. Perhaps from now on I should see her less often. Otherwise my many vices may become thrown into relief and my few virtues get lost in the shadows."

She shook her head so vigorously that her bonnet slipped down over one eye. As she adjusted it with trembling fingers, she cried: "Oh, I think that is the last thing she would want. She looks forward to your visits with such eager anticipation. Indeed, she... she..." The poor lady didn't know how to continue and tried to hide her embarrassment by fanning herself vigorously.

To alleviate her misery, Turgenev rose to his feet, offered her his arm and suggested they continue their walk around the lake. But her former garrulity had deserted her. From time to time she would look up at him and open her mouth, only to lower her head again without having uttered a word. Finally he decided that the most merciful course would be to force out whatever it was that she was so desperately holding back.

They were now crossing a bridge leading to a little island. When they reached the middle, he stopped, leant back against the railing and looked at her steadily. "Nadezhda Mikhailovna," he said, slowly, "I think there is something you want to say to me..." Her hands flew to her mouth and she blushed crimson, but he continued imperturbably: "Have no fear. Whatever it is, coming from you, it is quite impossible that it will give me any offence... if that is what worries you."

She looked up at him gratefully and nodded her head. "Oh yes, Ivan Sergeyevich, there is... and it was... Dear me, how can I put it?... Well, it's just that I'm frightened in case Olushka may be treasuring hopes that are not realistic..." Turgenev tried to intervene, but there was no stopping her now... "She's so young, and she's had so little experience of the world, and I don't think I could bear... I've had my share of tragedy in this life... but I just couldn't bear to see her suffering the pangs of… dear Lord, it's so silly of me, I'm ashamed to say it, but after that game we played the other evening – you know, comparing ourselves to Shakespearian characters – I lay in my bed and couldn't stop thinking that if Turgenev is Hamlet, heaven forbid that Olushka should end up like Ophelia… oh, the Lord have mercy on me, what have I said?…" She half turned away from him and hid her face in her hands. Turgenev let a moment go by and then tried to offer some soothing words, but again she cut him off: "I should never have said that, she'd never forgive me if she knew. Of course, it's really none of my business, but…" She turned back to him and clutched his hands: "You must promise me one thing, Ivan Sergeyevich; even if you never speak to me again, you must promise me never ever to tell her what I have just said to you."

Turgenev gave her hands a reassuring squeeze and gazed into her imploring eyes. "You have my word, Nadezhda Mikhailovna," he said, "although I hope you don't need it, that everything that passes between us today could as well have been said in the confessional. But I must tell you that I think you are under the impression that relations between Olga Aleksandrovna and myself are more… how shall I say?… more developed than they actually are."

She wagged a finger in front of his face. "That's one subject that I know more about than you. You know how Olga is … she's a very private person, she doesn't broadcast her feelings to the world… but I've known her all her life, I've brought her up since she was a baby, and I can read her like a muzhik scanning the evening sky. Believe me, Ivan Sergeyevich, she is very much in love with you."

Turgenev greeted these words with a silence which she misinterpreted. "Now I have made you angry. You think I'm a meddling old woman. Well, of course you're right, that's just what I am, but this time at least my meddling is in a good cause: that of Olushka's happiness. Nothing in the world means as much to me as that. For its sake, as you can see, I will risk even your anger."

Turgenev took her arm and they walked back across the bridge. "Far be it from me to be angry with you, Nadezhda Mikhailovna. On the contrary, I am grateful for what you have told me. But as of this moment, I am at a loss for words. I must think this over very carefully. And in the meantime, perhaps it would be better if I saw less of Olga… at least until such time as my mind is clearer."

She looked up at him with a certain alarm, perhaps having hoped that her indiscretion might have provoked a passionate declaration of love on his part. But her good sense got the better of her, and for the first time since she had broached the subject of Olga, her face resumed its usual expression of quiet serenity. "I'm sure whatever you do will be for the best, Ivan Sergeyevich," she said. "And thank you for your patience in tolerating the whims of a foolish old woman."

Over the next days, Turgenev stuck to his intention and avoided Oranienbaum.

The only time he did go was for a brief luncheon, at which his cousin didn't fail to comment regretfully on his absence. Turgenev pleaded the writer's eternal excuse – that he had no time for anything but work – but justified it to himself by determining to finish a story he had begun almost a decade earlier, soon after he had broken off with Tatyana Bakunina. It was called *A Correspondence*, and charted a relationship between a man and a woman exclusively through an interchange of letters. He had still not made up his mind how it would end, and although the female protagonist bore little resemblance to Olga, he nursed a superstitious hope that the development of the story might help him solve his own personal predicament. Of course he mentioned none of this to his cousin's family, but, having previously enjoined Nekrasov not to let him down, blamed his absence on his tyrannical editor, who was insisting he finish the story for the next edition of *Sovremennik*.

At no time at the lunch were he and Olga alone together, but even in company she seemed as reserved and timid as when he had first known her. It was as though their talk the night of her father's birthday had never taken place. Or was it that she felt she had been too free with her thoughts that night and was now compensating for what she considered her undue boldness? The other alternative, that Tante Nadya had told her of their talk, he immediately rejected as unthinkable. Nevertheless, the old lady made up for Olga's silence by chattering away with even more vigour than usual. With Turgenev himself feeling vaguely ill-at-ease and Olga rarely opening her mouth unless she was asked a direct question, she probably felt herself responsible for ensuring that any awkward silences were avoided. Only once did her attitude to Turgenev reflect their walk in the palace garden. When all the guests rose at the end of the meal and started to drift out into the garden, the two of them came face to face for the briefest of moments. And in Tante Nadya's eyes was a beseeching look which could only mean one thing: "For the love of God, say something soon!"

He walked back to Peterhof, determined not to return to his cousin's house until he had made up his mind. And it was his 'tyrannical editor' who came to his aid. Dining with Nekrasov and Panaev that evening, the two men begged him to leave the next day and spend a few days in St Petersburg. One of their occasional contributors, an elderly writer by the name of Snetkov, who considered – and expected everyone to consider – his writings as sacred texts, was outraged at a few changes they had requested, some to avert possible censorship, others to avoid long-windedness. Nekrasov said he simply didn't have time to go, and anyhow his abrasive character would make the old man more stubborn than ever. "But you, Vanya, have such patience. You can listen to him for hours and then drop one word in and he'll lap it up and soon be unable to express his gratitude for your inestimable help. Besides, he's a great admirer of your work and thinks very little of mine. So you see, you have to go for me. A week in Peter will do you good too. Sharpen your perceptions. All these long, rambling walks of yours make for long, rambling sentences…"

If Turgenev had thought that his sentimental involvement with Olga was known only to the two of them and Tante Nadya, twenty-four hours in St Petersburg were enough to disabuse him. The first evening he was there he dined with the few friends who had remained behind in the capital and was dismayed when several of them asked him if it was true that he would soon be getting married. Alone in his room, he lay awake most of the night in a state of extreme agitation. If so many people knew, perhaps shreds of gossip had reached Aleksander Mikhailovich. Even Olga herself. He cursed the restricted society in which he moved, where everything was known to everyone. In the cloudy zone between wakefulness and sleep, his imagination began to circle around the idea of the world as a vast prison; he had spent a short time in an actual jail, but he had felt almost as confined in Spasskoye, and now even in St Petersburg the walls seemed to be closing in. How much freer he had felt in France! Not, God knows, that gossip wasn't rife in Paris, but as a foreigner he hadn't felt so much a target… or at any rate had been able to ignore its existence. And this brought him back to his dilemma. Was he ready to marry and settle down in Russia: summers in Spasskoye, winters in St Petersburg and Moscow, occasional trips abroad, such as he had taken when he was four with his family: Germany, Austria, Italy, France, accompanied by nannies, maids, valets, cooks and even a doctor? Wasn't this not only entering prison voluntarily but fastening the straitjacket round you? And then he listened to another voice which told him he was thinking like an adolescent… *You're nearly forty, it's high time your* Wanderjahren *were over. Even as a writer you need stability, time to concentrate on your work, free of all the incidental preoccupations which harass the eternal traveller…* By the time sleep finally brought a truce to this internal warfare, he had even, to his shame, begun to toy with the idea of visiting a fortune-teller.

The next day he paid a visit to the writer and discovered, to his relief, that Nekrasov had been right: the old man greeted him with every courtesy and listened patiently while Turgenev explained the reasons why changes had to be made before his piece could be published in *Sovremennik*. He made great use of the censorship argument and very little of the stylistic one, so artistic pride was barely ruffled. When the time came for him to leave, Snetkov thanked him for his suggestions, promised to rework his piece, and they agreed to see each other again in a day or two to settle on the final version. This left Turgenev with time to kill, and he decided that evening to go to the theatre. He had noticed a poster announcing that his old friend Nadezhda Samoilova was appearing in a play of Ostrovsky's, and it was the last night before the theatre closed for the rest of the summer.

He found the play lacking in Ostrovsky's usual mordant wit, but the evening was saved by a glowing performance from Samoilova. She was overjoyed to see Turgenev when he went round to congratulate her in her dressing-room and insisted he come with them to the cast party, which was being held to celebrate the last night. "It's not in the usual sort of place," she whispered in his ear. "Rather risqué, in fact. Now don't start making excuses. You're coming and it'll be good for you. None of your aristocratic or intellectual friends will be there. So you'll have nothing to worry about. No one will recognize you."

Remembering, with an inner smile, that only last night he had been lamenting the suffocating limitations of the society he moved in, Turgenev assured her that he would be happy to join them. And as he entered the tavern after a long drive into the suburbs, he felt as if he had shed twenty years. Not since his Berlin university days had he been anywhere even similar; and the Prussian sense of order and cleanliness had penetrated even into their nocturnal haunts. But not so here. Turgenev's first impression was of almost total darkness. His second was of ear-splitting noise: voices raised in anger or merriment, hard to tell which; glass and earthenware being thumped down on wooden tables; and a furious thrumming of balalaikas, with here and there a drunken voice trying unsuccessfully to capture an elusive thread of melody. The tavern owner, who had been expecting them, came over carrying a candlestick, and after much bowing and expressing his humble delight at the presence in his poor establishment of such distinguished visitors, led them over to a cluster of tables which by now Turgenev could identify as being next to a small stage. Samoilova, who had taken his arm – perhaps fearing that at the first sight of where he had been taken, he might turn tail and flee – this time shouted in his ear that the gypsy singers who would be performing later on were the finest in St Petersburg. "They bring dancers with them too. Not great artists, but all the men like them. But it's for the singers that we come here. You'll never have heard better."

The theatre party took their seats and immediately began consuming quantities of wine. Turgenev was a little more abstemious, but drank more than he usually did. Samoilova soon slipped away to join her current love, and as soon as his eyes grew accustomed to the darkness, he looked around at the other tables, only some of which were lit by a single guttering candle. He guessed the customers to be mostly students, with a sprinkling of failed or rejected doctors and lawyers. Cards were being thumped down with confidence or desperate bravado; howls of triumph or anguish denoted wins and losses. Prostitutes moved hopefully from table to table, sometimes received with a casual welcome, more often dismissed with obscene insults. A gypsy came over to the newcomers and offered to read their palms. Most of the actors waved her impatiently away, but Turgenev beckoned her over. Last night he had seriously considered going to see a fortune-teller. Now one had come to him which – ridiculously, he thought – lessened his sense of guilt in giving any credence to such spurious nonsense. Samoilova noticed and gave him a surprised glance, but then smiled and turned away.

The gypsy pulled up a chair next to him and took his hand. A swarthy-faced woman in her middle thirties, of Circassian stock, Turgenev guessed, she ran her long nails over the lines in his palm with a practised efficiency more intended, he thought, to arouse his sensuality than demonstrate interest in his future. But when she looked up, her glittering eyes scrutinized his with a seriousness which contained no hint of seduction. Assuming a sardonic cynicism he was far from feeling, he asked her if what she saw was too tragic to convey to him.

"Tragic, no," she said, with no corresponding smile. "But I do not see an easy life. Quite a long one, yes, but with some illness…"

"Cholera?" Turgenev had a morbid terror of the disease.

"I don't think so. People usually die of cholera, and, as I say, you will not die young. But although people will think of you as a fortunate, happy man, much of the time it will not be so. I see a restlessness… whether physical – travelling all the time – or interior – continual dissatisfaction – it is hard to see. Perhaps both." A quick look down and then an interrogative glance. "You are not married, I would say."

"No." *Oh, where's your courage, this is why you called her over?* "Will I be?"

She opened out his palm with the fingers of both her hands, as though trying to capture the least nuance of what might be written there. "I cannot be sure. There is a woman there, always with you, and children; you love the children very much, and they love you, but…" She shook her head and pulled a greasy scrap of paper out of a pocket in her skirt. "If you come to this address tomorrow, I will read the cards. Then I will be able to tell you more exactly what I see." Turgenev paid her much more than she was expecting, but, after a quick start of surprise, she controlled her pleasure and repeated in a grave voice: "Come tomorrow morning. I will expect you."

As she moved away, Samoilova called out: "What's it to be, Vanya? Health, wealth and imperishable beauty?"

"Nothing less," Turgenev replied, grateful to the actress for immediately dispelling the vague sensation of melancholy that the gypsy's words and attitude had instilled in him. He called the owner over and ordered champagne for the theatre party, "to celebrate my brilliant future!" When the wine arrived, they all turned to him and clinked glasses, and Turgenev was able for the first time to study his companions. He recognized the ones who had been in the play and had been introduced to some of their husbands, wives and lovers. But his attention was particularly caught by a strikingly beautiful woman whom he had not seen backstage at the theatre. Surely an actress, she was dressed as if she had just come offstage after playing a breeches part. A deep blue silk blouse was stretched tight across the upper part of her breasts and over it she wore a dark jacket of an almost military cut. Her jet-black hair was drawn tight back from a wide, high forehead, under which two mocking eyes of a colour Turgenev could not make out surveyed her surroundings and especially, or so it seemed, him. The man she had presumably come with, who was not one of the actors in the play, was already very drunk and rapidly becoming drunker. She noticed that Turgenev was finding it hard to take his eyes off her, and looked back at him with a bold, appraising stare that may or may not have contained a note of invitation, but was certainly neither modest nor maidenly.

But now his attention was distracted by the gypsy performers who were coming on to the stage. The musicians stood at the back while the dancers, all girls, sat cross-legged on the floor, listening intently to the singers. As ever, Turgenev was entranced by the plangent, melancholy melodies which first hushed, then completely stilled the clamour that had hitherto reigned. One song, which from the oft-repeated refrain, he presumed was called *Is That All?*, especially captivated him. It was started as a solo by a young girl who couldn't have been more than sixteen or seventeen, but whose husky voice seemed imbued with all the joy and sorrow known to humanity. After a verse or two of a long-drawn-out unaccompanied melody of almost unbearable slowness, a guitar stealthily began to pluck a rudimentary accompaniment; other voices stole in, a violin and an accordion wove arabesques, the rhythm grew faster, the dancers began to click their fingers, the customers to clap their hands. A furious accelerando, a crescendo to fortissimo, and the song came to an end amidst scenes of tumultuous enthusiasm.

Other songs followed and Turgenev let his mind wander… *this is the real Russia, ironic that it manifests itself in places like this, in the middle of smoke and drunkenness and carnality and dirt, and yet if the 'Russian soul' so beloved of the Slavophils is anywhere to be found, it is in these songs, which can first silence a brawling drunken crowd and then, raising them above themselves and their surroundings, bring them shouting and cheering to their feet. And anywhere this song were sung – nobleman's palace or village inn – the effect would be the same. This is the one unifying theme. This is something, at least, of what Gogol wanted to express in the later volumes of* Dead Souls *– the unique spirituality of Russia – but he found he couldn't do it. Words conjure up substantial images, and the reality his words evoked was the squalid, unjust, grotesque reality of everyday Russia. Only music can reach men's hearts in a totally uncontaminated way. And music can change nothing on a practical level. Books can do a little – not much, but a little – but books, by their very nature, are contaminated. That was what Gogol discovered, and what killed him. And this is what the Slavophils fail to see: they feel Russia can be redeemed by something inherently noble in the Russian soul, as expressed in songs like these. But it can't. If redemption is to come it can only be through gradual political reform, decade by decade; a depressingly prosaic process, far removed from the emotions this*

271

music is arousing in this heterogeneous crowd here tonight, but in the end the only hope for this country…

"Wherever you are, come back. You're missing something." The voice in his ear belonged to the woman who had caught his attention, now sitting in the chair vacated by the fortune-teller. She spoke in a throaty drawl with a slight foreign accent, and her eyes, which he could now make out to be grey-blue, raked his face with bold, amused interest.

Turgenev's surprise rapidly gave way to an almost automatic coquetry. "What am I missing?" he asked. "Apart from the privilege of your company."

She looked past him over his shoulder and nodded. He turned round and noticed for the first time that the floor was now occupied by the dancers, one of whom, a fiery-eyed young savage of startling beauty, was directing all her energies and exclusive attention to him. Turgenev looked her up and down with intrigued fascination. A large silver medallion in the middle of her forehead glittered in the reflected candlelight; her black eyes flashed unmistakable signals into his, and her full, bright red lips were drawn back into something between a smile and snarl, revealing two perfect rows of dazzling white teeth. Her slender arms, rising from a tight-fitting black bodice, corkscrewed sinuously above her head while the lower half of her body, encased in a full, multicoloured skirt, gyrated with sensual abandonment as her feet drummed out the wild rhythm of the music.

When he turned back to his new companion, the mockery in her eyes was even more pronounced. "I really came over to protect you," she said. "But you weren't even conscious of the danger."

"I think I would have come out alive," he replied. "It's a routine for them. She'll soon turn her attentions to another table."

The woman shook her head. "Oh no, not this one. She has seen that you are the only man in the room dressed with a certain care. The rest are penniless students, dregs of the professions and actors. None of them is going to make an assignation with her afterwards… or at least not the sort of assignation she is interested in. An artist herself, she will avoid other artists."

Turgenev couldn't resist. "I might be an artist too."

An instant's uncertainty was effortlessly swept away. "You might indeed," she said. "But not, I think, a theatrical one."

At this moment, the dance came to an end and the gypsy, stung that her quarry was paying attention to someone other than herself, gave a final flourish of her arms, a final stamp of the feet, picked a glass off the table, flung it to the floor and plumped herself down into the startled Turgenev's lap. She twined her arms around his neck, thrust her lips to within an inch of his and asked him if he had liked her performance.

"It was magnificent. Thrilling and magnificent. Thank you. But now I must ask you to get off my knees. I have company."

The black eyes flashed with an extra brilliance and she turned to look at Turgenev's mysterious companion, whom she had barely noticed up to now. But what she saw evidently won her professional respect; after planting a full kiss on Turgenev's lips, she treated the two of them to a dazzling smile, wished them a happy evening and went to rejoin the troupe, who were about to start another dance.

"Perhaps you were right", Turgenev said to the woman. "I think you did rescue me."

"And perhaps you won't forgive me. She's an enchanting creature."

Turgenev filled her glass with champagne and murmured: "She quit the field because she'd met her match. I think I had better introduce myself. My name is…"

"I know who you are. I have made enquiries. I have known Nadezhda Vassilievna for many years."

"You must be an actress too. How strange that I have never seen you. I certainly wouldn't have forgotten."

"There is nothing strange. I am not an actress."

"That is a great loss for all of us who love the theatre."

She gave the rather obvious compliment a faint smile, with a touch of the *I hope you can do better than that* to it. "It is no loss at all. I would have made an execrable actress. I am incapable of being anything but myself. And my name is Nadezhda too."

"Nadezhda?"

"Nadezhda. That's enough, isn't it?"

"It would be, except that at the moment I seem to be surrounded by Nadezhdas." *Although poor Tante Nadya would be a little out of place in this company.* "For me you will be Polish Nadezhda."

"Ah, you have discovered my secret. You have a good ear."

"Not particularly. There is no accent in Russian more charming than the Polish one."

The same smile, but this time a real hint of reproach in the eyes. *I'm on trial here! This is no frequenter of Petersburg salons and country house gatherings. She is of a sophistication that I haven't encountered since I left France. And in those days I…*

"I am very reluctant to bring this up, but, earlier in the evening, were you not with somebody?"

"There was a gentleman who accompanied me here, yes. I sent him home. He was drunk."

"Aren't we all?"

"I am not. And you…" a quick, analytic glance, "only a little. But he was boring drunk. And that's unforgivable. Alternating champagne with vodka. Unfortunately he's the type of person who is boring when he's sober, knows it, gets drunk, thinking he'll be less boring and becomes more so. But why are we wasting time on him? I think it is time I claimed my reward."

"Reward?"

"Well it was you who introduced the chivalric terminology. 'Quit the field', didn't you say? I know that conventionally it is the knight who gains the reward from the fair damsel that he has rescued. But as, in this case, it is the fair damsel who has rescued the knight…" she glanced across at the gypsy dancers, who were still in full fury, "from a fate worse than death, he will surely not refuse her the favour he was compelled to bestow on the evil temptress."

The mockery in the expression was ever more blatant. But there was something else there too. Challenge? Desire? She placed her elbows on the table, leant her chin on her hands and waited with eyebrows expectantly raised. Turgenev leant towards her and kissed her lips, which were surprisingly soft and yielding. After a few seconds he pulled away, sensing that her tongue was just about to slip between his teeth. She casually snuffed the candle in front of them between thumb and forefinger, leaving them in total darkness, pulled her chair alongside his so that their legs were touching and seemingly gave her full attention to the dancers who were working up to a climactic finale. But within moments he felt her hand gliding up the inside of his trouser leg and a second later his whole being was engulfed by a tidal wave of sexual desire. Her lips brushed against his ear: "Take me somewhere. Anywhere." He glanced round and saw that none of the theatrical party were paying any attention to them. One of the actors had borrowed a guitar from the gypsies and was singing songs in which several of them joined in. The two of them left the tavern quite unobserved and were soon in a carriage on their way to Turgenev's apartment. He gave silent thanks that he had decided to leave Zakhar and Stepan behind in Peterhof. Few words were spoken, their mouths being, for the most part, otherwise occupied. At one moment of truce, Turgenev, almost overcome with desire, stammered out his disbelief that a woman of her beauty was at that moment reclining in his arms. Her eyes sparkled with amusement. "After what I may have deprived you of back there," she said, "it is the least I can do to try and make it up to you."

"I hope the duty will not prove too onerous."

She laughed outright. "We Poles are famous for two qualities, are we not? Gallantry and self-sacrifice!"

The following hours opened up to him, at 36, areas of sexuality beyond anything he had ever known or imagined. While their lovemaking lasted – and it was well past dawn before they finally fell into an exhausted sleep – nothing grazed his consciousness beyond the imperative demands made upon his body by his insatiable companion. As his everyday self might have expressed it, it was as if, after a lifetime spent listening to young girls playing their family pianos, he was exposed for the first time to Liszt performing on a Bösendorfer grand. On reflection the next day, the memory of what he had done, and had done to him, left him with a sense of shock, almost disgust. But he could barely wait for evening to come, when they had agreed to see each other again.

He determined to extend his stay in St Petersburg. When he kept his appointment with the *Sovremennik* contributor, he claimed to have thought things over and suggested a few further changes which 'will turn what you have written from a story into a masterpiece. Think about it and we'll see each other again in three or four days'. Snetkov grumbled, but happily consented. Turgenev sent word to Peterhof, knowing that within hours it would be in Oranienbaum, that he had been delayed and would not be returning till the following week.

He and his Polish *lorette,* as he called her, after the compliant ladies who frequented the Paris district around the church of Sainte-Marie-de-Lorette, spent every evening and night together. He would have welcomed her company during the day too but she refused, saying that she was a bat who only emerged after dark. His attempts to find out something about her were entirely unsuccessful. She refused point-blank to talk about herself. She was not even forthcoming over her name. "My concierge knows me as Nadezhda Nikolayevna Glebova. I tell you that because you can find it out anyway. Will that do?"

"I suppose so. Who is Glebov? Your husband?"

"None of your business."

And there it ended.

He thought of making a few discreet enquiries around St Petersburg, but the only person he could ask was la Samoilova, and, childish though he knew it was, he couldn't bring himself to do it.

For several days he lived in limbo. Rarely rising before one, he spent the few hours before their evening rendez-vous trying to find some occupation which would extricate him from the torment of thinking about Olga. But this frenzied, foredoomed attempt to blot out reality received a sharp setback in the unexpected form of a letter from Paris, which he found waiting for him when he got home after a particularly energetic night…

London,
July 15th, 1854

My dear, good friend,
NO…
My dear ~~good~~ friend,
How can I call you good when you so deliberately ignore my most emphatically declared wishes? Your

275

letter, which – perhaps ashamedly aware of what a poor thing it was – took an unconscionably long time to reach me, contained little of interest. Above all it contained nothing on the subject about which I had so specifically asked for enlightenment: your little friend, or cousin, or whatever she is. This is really most inconsiderate of you. After all, you must realize how anxious those of us who like to think of ourselves as your second family are to hear of any sentimental interest in your life. To be told nothing at all makes it hard not to construe your silence as a deliberate attempt at concealment; it's almost as if you were ashamed of something, were trying to conceal some hole-and-corner mésalliance.

As this surely cannot be the case, I can only assume that your silence is due to the, perhaps, too personal remarks I ventured to make in my last letter. If that is so, you must forgive my saying that this is rather stupid of you. All I was attempting to do was, as an old friend, warn you of possible dangers in the situation which you – and perhaps even she – might not be aware of: that whereas to an unfledged girl, a man of your age and experience is bound to seem an uncommonly alluring prospect, for you the very youth and freshness you now find so appealing might, if not reinforced by other, more substantial qualities, eventually, with the passage of time, pall. Surely, for one of your sensitivity, it is not necessary to underline what I alluded to in my letter: that nobody could be a better qualified judge on these matters than I...

There now, I've been scolding you! But to show you that my affection for you is undimmed (if this were not so, why should I go to all this trouble in the middle of a busy London season?), let me end by telling you that Louis and I drank a toast the other evening to the end of this most stupid of all wars and the return of our good Turgenev to Courtavenel where, alone or in company, he will, as always, be welcomed with open arms ...

Affectionately yours,
P.V.

He threw himself down on his bed, fully dressed, the letter in his hand, the odours of his mistress's body still clinging to his skin like dew to a cobweb... *was I really, only five or six days ago, giving serious thought to marriage with Olga?... I have no right even to entertain the idea... up to now I've been contemplating it exclusively from my point of view (Would she make a good companion for me? Would she be a good mother to my children?), not a moment's consideration as to what it would mean for her... perhaps this week in St Petersburg was a gift of destiny... the serene atmosphere of holiday life in Oranienbaum and Peterhof clouded my sense of reality... now, drugged as my body is, my brain can see all too clearly: I am no longer a young man who can expect to mature and develop as life goes along... I'm a middle-aged dissolute voluptuary, the offering of whose corrupted body to a young virgin would be an offence against nature... vis-à-vis Pauline, my conscience can justify this. She is a married woman and I cannot be expected to live like a monk for the rest of my life... but to Olga, the way I have lived the past few days would seem an enormity. And I certainly don't want to imitate those despicable men who appear in society with their wives posing as the* ne plus ultra *of respectability, while creeping off to mistresses and brothels* to satisfy their ever more depraved lust. Try as I might (and I was trying too hard in Oranienbaum, trying to make myself believe something I didn't really feel), I don't see myself as a happily married man. I'm sure it would be the end of me as a writer, the essential tension, the stimulation of variety would be missing… an unhappily married one, ah, that perhaps yes, but I can hardly ask a young girl to be my wife and then sit there for a couple of years drumming my fingers on the table waiting for the quarrels and resentments to start. And now, this letter from Pauline – the first time since Moscow that she has mentioned the possibility of my rejoining them in France… that means that if peace were declared tomorrow, the next day you'd be applying for a passport, wouldn't you? Of course the Czar would make sure you didn't get it, but you'd try all the same. And where would poor Olga be in all this? She is a young person of the highest merit and she deserves the very best, and what you have to offer her is soiled and shabby and fatally compromised. No, you have no alternative. You know what you have to do…

St Petersburg,
23rd July, 1854.

My dear Olga Aleksandrovna,

This is the most difficult and painful letter I have ever had to write. I wish I could avoid it, but that would be adding cowardice to irresponsibility. Yes, it is of irresponsibility that I must above all accuse myself, never ill design or cruel intent. But it is best that I get straight to the point. I have let relations between you and me reach a stage that I should never have let them reach. These are very delicate matters, but I have such admiration for the intelligence and sensitivity of which you have given me abundant proof over the last months, that I do not think or fear that I shall be misunderstood.

I must say immediately that I and I alone am to blame. I am considerably older than you and that gave me the responsibility – the duty – to think for both of us. I had no right to let myself be swept along by sentiments that I did not stop to analyze. I had no right to forget that, for you, a great deal was at stake, whereas I risked nothing. I do not wish to say that I took advantage of your youthful inexperience, because that would intimate that there was some degree of conscious thought behind my conduct; but I did not force myself to maintain a proper guard. Recently it has become clear to me that my feelings for you are only of the deepest respect and friendship, and at that point I should have immediately communicated this in some way to you. That I did not do so is my great fault and I can only ask you to forgive me for it.

In spite of all that has happened, I consider the brief period of my association with you as one of the happiest events of my life. For now, as you will immediately appreciate, my only course must be to avoid frequent meetings with you and any kind of intimate exchanges. Only thus will we be able to still the rumours and the gossip which, I realized when I came to St Petersburg, I had brought into being by my culpable behaviour. When all that has quietened down, it is my fervent hope that we can continue to enjoy a friendship which, for my part at least, has brought such rich rewards.

May I ask you to convey my most affectionate greetings to your father and Nadezhda Mikhailovna.

I pray that they will not look upon me with too much disfavour, as I hold being in their good report almost as highly as being in yours.

Your devoted,
Ivan Turgenev.

St Petersburg
29th July, 1854

I have in my hand, dear and good Madame Viardot, your letter of 15th July which I was very happy to receive – not so much for its content as for the evidence it provided of the continuation of our correspondence. It has, alas, been flying on one wing, this poor correspondence of ours. Yet God is my witness that never have my friends been more dear to me. It would be unbearably painful for me to think that I am beginning to fade from the memories of all of you over there. So I am especially grateful for the affectionate words with which you end your letter.

As to the 'silence' with which you reproach me, here is what I have to say in my defence: the affair in question was of an extremely vague nature, and nothing demonstrates this better than its sudden end. So what was the use of talking about it to you? That, at any rate, was the way I saw it – and saw it wrongly – since even my most secret thoughts should belong to you. Nevertheless, I would ask you to take into account that it was from me that you heard about it, not anyone else.

Now it is all in the past and what can I tell you more than I already have? The young person, as you know, bears the same name as myself. Her first name is Olga. She is blonde, graceful and intelligent; she turned my head for a month or so, but it didn't last and now, while doing full justice to her qualities, I am very happy to be a hundred miles from Peterhof on a two-week hunting expedition with Nekrasov, Panaev and Botkin. But she deserves the best, and my dearest wish is that she will soon make a happy marriage. There you are! It came and it went like a puff of wind. And it's over…

Throughout the autumn and winter, which he divided between St Petersburg and Spasskoye, Turgenev continued to see his *lorette* whenever he was in the capital. In the country he would make iron resolutions to break off with her, but as soon as he reached town he was unable to resist paying 'one last visit', which was inevitably renewed at regular intervals until he left again for Spasskoye. Witty and provocative as he found her at the beginning of the evening and tirelessly inventive at the end, he soon perceived that the excitement of their meetings was becoming numbed by routine. By mutual, if unspoken agreement, they never went out in company. He would go to her small but tastefully furnished third-floor apartment in an imposing classical building on Kazanskaya, always bringing a present: jewellery, articles of clothing or household bric-a-brac if he was feeling inventive, otherwise armfuls of flowers or hampers of food and wine. After an hour or so they would go to a restaurant always chosen by her, as in all his familiar haunts they would be bound to encounter someone he knew. Occasionally they would visit some tavern similar to the one where they had met, but usually they would go straight back to her apartment, where he would remain until early morning.

One evening he asked her if she wasn't getting bored with their tête-à-têtes. "Wouldn't you prefer once in a while to go out with friends?"

The corner of her lip curled in an ironic smile. "You know as well as I do that there are no friends of yours we could meet without you being embarrassed; and no friends of mine without… both you and they being embarrassed."

"And which would be more embarrassing for you?"

"I am never embarrassed."

His eyes twinkled and he took her hand. "You know, I think I believe you."

There was a hint of threat in her voice as she answered: "You had better!" But immediately her tone lightened and she ran her fingers over the palm of his hand. "Aren't you flattered that I am always content in your company?"

"Very. But you do, I hope, see other people from time to time."

"Oh yes."

"Tell me about them."

"Oh no."

He had no choice but to shake his head in amused bewilderment and let the matter drop.

As the months passed, Turgenev became more and more determined to end the relationship. The only person he had confided in was the pleasure-loving Botkin (Annenkov being out of the question, as he was still hoping there would be a reconciliation with Olga), who couldn't understand why his friend should turn his back on this enviable liaison. "Why stop seeing her unless you have stopped liking her? Have you?"

"No."

"Does she make demands on you?"

"Never."

"You mean she has never complained that she hasn't seen you for… two months, three months…?"

"Not once."

"She sounds a paragon of virtue… as well as of vice, from what you lead me to believe. But are you really telling me that all this time you've never had a quarrel?"

"Well, yes, once. But it was my fault."

"What had you done?"

"I had completely forgotten to think of some present for her. I was late and none of the flower stalls had anything left worth buying. She said nothing, but at the end of the evening I handed her some money and suggested she buy something for herself."

"What did she do?"

"I thought she was going to hit me. So did she. I saw her fists clenched tight. But she drew in a long breath, stared at me with eyes that bored through my head and said: 'If you ever do that again, Ivan Sergeyevich, it will be the last time you ever see me.'"

But Turgenev couldn't bring himself to tell Botkin the real reason why his enthusiasm was dwindling. It took him some time before it became clear even to him that the relationship was essentially sterile. For all her wit and iconoclastic dazzle, their evenings, lacking any variety in the form of interchange with others, were simply a way of killing time before the true purpose of their being together could be reached. And although the intensity of their lovemaking never faltered, he found that it was beginning to pall on him. The first time he realized this was when, one evening after dinner, he found himself wishing that he could think of an excuse to go home alone. Once they were in bed, her inexhaustible skill and fantasy won him over, but the episode marked a turning-point: he decided the experience must either be broadened or brought to an end. It was with this in mind that, knowing he was risking her fury, one afternoon he went round to her apartment unannounced.

When he asked the concierge if the lady was in, the old woman nodded and then gave him a rather strange look. He thought she must be wondering what he was doing here at this hour. But he soon realized that that was not the reason. When he knocked at the apartment door, it was not his *lorette* who opened it but a woman in her early forties, who looked as surprised to see him as he was her. In the moment of awkward silence that followed, he had time to take in thick auburn hair coiled up into a chignon, puffy rouged cheeks and a full, pouting mouth, which now opened to venture: "Monsieur Turgenev?" After his bewildered acknowledgement, she introduced herself as Svetlana Yegorovna, pulled the collar of the robe she was wearing across her throat in a gesture of instinctive prudery and invited him to come in. As he followed her into the sitting room, he noticed that the peach-coloured silk robe in which her tall, tending to plump figure was swathed was one he had given Nadezhda several weeks ago. She was a handsome woman, he thought, but with something unappealing about her: she reminded him of a rich merchant's wife in a play by Ostrovsky.

But she smiled at him with practised graciousness, indicated the sofa, settled herself in an armchair and asked him if he would like tea. She was expecting Nadezhda back at any moment. His curiosity getting the better of his unease, he accepted and she rang a bell. A maid appeared, whom Turgenev had never seen before but who seemed to take it as the most natural thing in the world to be asked by this woman to serve tea. As his mind struggled to make sense of all this, he heard her ask him: "Is Nadezhda expecting you?"

"No," he answered. "I thought I'd give her a surprise."

The smile acquired a touch of malice. "Really! She doesn't usually take very well to surprises. Well, well, we shall see, shan't we?"

They exchanged a few platitudes and even under those Turgenev couldn't rid himself of the feeling that there flowed a current of underlying hostility. The samovar must have been already lit, because in no time at all the maid reappeared wheeling a trolley on which he immediately recognized a Finnish hand-chased silver teapot he had bought for Nadezhda and Meissen chinaware, which his mother had picked up on the family visit to Dresden so many years ago; he had always found the design over-elaborate for his taste, so he had taken the opportunity to bring it round only the previous week. As the maid handed round glasses of tea and plates of cakes, Turgenev glanced appraisingly around the room at various other presents he had brought Nadezhda over the course of the last few months: a bronze figurine of Poseidon, an onyx vase, a small French travelling clock. His companion must have read his mind, because, as soon as the maid had left the room, she remarked in honeyed tones how fortunate Nadezhda had been in meeting him. "Your generosity is prodigious. Not to mention, of course, your taste."

Fighting down a desire to ask what business it was of hers, Turgenev took a sip of tea and remarked that she and Nadezhda must be close friends.

"Very close, yes. We have no secrets from each other."

"That puts you in a very privileged position. She has nothing but secrets from me."

"How clever of her! I'm convinced that all men love mysteries."

"Perhaps they do. But they also like to believe there's a remote chance of clearing them up. And Nadezhda does not hold out that chance."

She contented herself with an enigmatic smile, so he was forced to press his case – a little clumsily, as he soon had to admit. "So perhaps, while we are waiting for her – and as long as I don't pry into anything too private – you could give me an idea, for instance, of how your friend spends the day."

Her eyebrows shot up. "I am surprised at you, Ivan Sergeyevich. You surely cannot think I would be so indiscreet as to impart information to you which Nadezhda has, for her own best reasons, chosen not to reveal."

Turgenev cursed himself for having so ingenuously placed the weapon in her hand which she had been only too happy to use against him. He extracted himself as best he could. "You would only be anticipating the discovery by a matter of minutes. My purpose in coming here was to ask her that question… and one or two others."

A withering glance of contempt. "Then you will have to hear it from her own lips. Or not at all. I strongly suspect the latter."

He leant back in the sofa, crossed his legs and, after studying his shoes for a second or two, looked across at her again. "Very well," he said, in his gentlest, most disarming voice: "If we can't talk about Nadezhda, perhaps you would tell me something about yourself."

"What do you want to know?"

"For instance, do you live here?"

"No, I live with my husband." For the first time, he noticed she was wearing a wedding ring. "Why do you ask?"

"I suppose because you seem so very much at home here."

"Well, in a sense, I am."

"In what sense?"

She seemed to be considering the question very carefully, but Turgenev was not taken in. He could see she was intent on telling him.

"The apartment belongs to me. Together with the two floors above." The mouth smiled but the eyes did not. "That is why I so much appreciate all the beautiful gifts you have lavished on Nadezhda. It has given this place a certain… style."

But Turgenev was by now well beyond appreciating compliments. His questions no longer had the veneer of polish. They were terse and lapidary. "So you divide your time between your husband's house and here?"

"You could say that."

He now understood everything, but still wanted confirmation. "And your affections?"

The smile drifted up to the eyes. "You could say that too."

The moment of silence as they both stared at each other, he troubled and confused, she confident and derisive, was broken by the sound of the door opening. Nadezhda came into the room, but stopped abruptly when she caught sight of Turgenev. With all the other thoughts that were racing through his brain, he couldn't help admiring her presence of mind: apparently not the least disconcerted, let alone annoyed, she said calmly: "Good afternoon, Ivan Sergeyevich. To what do I owe this honour?"

All he could manage was a weak "I was in the neighbourhood and thought I would drop in."

"How unusual!" She seemed to make a swift calculation before asking: "For any particular reason?"

"Oh, perhaps because I thought our meetings were beginning to resemble a railway timetable... you know, depart at six, arrive at eight. Sometimes it's good to leave things to chance ... unforeseen circumstances... the element of surprise..."

"I don't like surprises."

"No, so Svetlana Yegorovna was telling me."

For the first time since she had come in, Nadezhda turned to look at the other woman, who hadn't moved from her chair. "She told you that, did she?" This in any icy tone as she glanced down at the half-drunk tea glasses and the plates covered with crumbs. "It looks as if the two of you have had a long talk." She finally addressed Svetlana directly. "What else did you tell him?"

This was met with a noncommittal smile and a reductive shrug. "Nothing special. We talked of this and that. He asked me a few questions, most of which I didn't answer. I said he should wait for you."

Nadezhda turned back to Turgenev. "Questions? Did you come here to spy on me?"

Turgenev fought down his indignation and answered calmly enough: "Until half an hour ago I didn't know of Svetlana Yegorovna's existence. So spying can hardly have been my intention. I came here, as I said, to see you."

For a moment she was at a loss for words and stood looking interrogatively from one to the other, seeking an explanation. Svetlana seemed to feel she needed to fill the silence, although Turgenev had no doubt her innocent words concealed deliberate malice. She picked up one of the Meissen plates, twisted it around in her hands and murmured: "I mentioned to Ivan Sergeyevich how grateful we were for all the beautiful things he has brought us."

"**WE! US!?**" Two pistol shots.

Another smile from Svetlana, patently false this time. "Oh, I meant you, of course, dear." She allowed herself a slight pause. "But it comes to the same thing, doesn't it?"

"**IT … DOES … NOT!**" Three pistol shots. The lips were pressed so tightly together that the mouth disappeared. Then she spat out: "Did you tell him…?", but she couldn't finish. She didn't need to.

"That this little place belongs to me? Well, yes, I did." She turned to Turgenev in appeal. "It sort of slipped out, didn't it?"

Turgenev watched as Nadezhda, who hadn't moved since she came in, took three rapid strides over to the chair and glared down at Svetlana, her fists opening and closing, her slim body tense as a drawn bow. He was convinced she was about to strike her, and prepared himself to intervene for the first time in his life between two fighting women. Instead she opted for verbal abuse and a stream of insults issued from her mouth which left him aghast; no accidentally overheard quarrel between vodka-soaked Spasskoye serfs, no gutter brawl in midnight city streets, could have contained more brutal, violent profanities than issued from the lips of this woman, whose poise and sophistication he had so much admired. The only thing that kept him from getting up and leaving was his astounded fascination at the attitude of the target of all this vituperation. For all the notice she took of the obscenities that were being hurled at her, Svetlana Yegorovna might have been totally deaf. Or being harangued in a language she didn't speak. She never looked up at her persecutor. Not a muscle of her body moved. She simply gazed ahead of her with a strangely absent-minded expression. Either, Turgenev thought, she has heard this sort of language so many times before that it no longer has any effect. Or she knows that she is so effortlessly in command that she will wait for the avalanche to run its course and everything to go on as before.

Nadezhda finally fell silent, her body still trembling with a rage she was unable to control. The other woman remained quite motionless. Without a word, Turgenev stood up and started to go out. Nadezhda quickly came over to stand between him and the door. Willing herself into a calm she couldn't possibly have been feeling, she asked, in a quiet voice: "When shall we next see each other?"

Turgenev looked at her gravely for a moment and then answered: "You know the answer to that question."

She surprised him to the last, her face betraying a sense of loss, of almost childish vulnerability that he would never have expected to see there. Was there even the hint of a tear? He forced himself to ignore it.

"Adieu, Nadezhda Nikolayevna."

Her answering 'Adieu' was an almost inaudible whisper.

He had not got half way down the stairs before he heard the sound of china smashing. "Poor Meissen!" he thought ruefully. "After surviving my mother, you might have expected eternal life. But it was not to be."

For several days after this, Turgenev lived in his own person a Platonic dualism of mind and body that took him back to the days of his philosophy studies in Berlin: evening after evening he had to invent some occupation – a course of reading, visits to friends he had no great desire to see – in order to prevent himself from jumping into a carriage and paying his *lorette* a surprise visit. Work was hopeless: his concentration, usually immune to distraction, was in shreds and his thoughts, already involved in an uphill struggle trying to resume work on the novel he had put aside, strayed inexorably from the rambling provincial country house of his book to a small cluttered apartment on Kazanskaya. Despairing of ever being able to grope his way out of this fog of indecision on his own, he enlisted the help of the one friend he could count on to be both sympathetic and firm. Botkin was still the only person who knew the true story, though rumours had not been lacking in the hothouse atmosphere of St Petersburg society…

> *'Why do we see so little of Ivan Sergeyevich these days?'*
> *'They tell me he's working very hard on a book.'*
> *'That's never stopped him having dinner before!'*
> *'Perhaps he hasn't got over that business with his pretty little cousin'*
> *'More likely she hasn't got over it, poor dear. They tell me he dropped her from one day to the next… without a word of explanation.'*
> *'That can only mean one thing!'*
> Sighs and headshakes…

In Vasily Petrovich Botkin, Turgenev had the perfect confidant. The son of a rich tea merchant, he had never lacked money nor the readiness to spend it. His natural generosity and charm had eased the way into many love affairs. He had shared with Belinsky an unrequited passion for one of Bakunin's siren sisters, Aleksandra. A seasoned European traveller, he was a self-styled expert on Spanish bullfighting, Roman baroque sculpture and French cuisine. Now in his early forties, the critic and aesthete had begun to supplant the pleasure-loving dilettante; but his experience of starting, and especially ending, love affairs was far greater than Turgenev's. He was in no doubt as to how his friend should resolve his dilemma.

"Your only way out," he urged, "is to make a complete change. Change everything… except friends. Change houses…" he looked around Turgenev's, by now rather overcrowded lodgings. "It's time you bought a house of your own anyway. Change women… well, all right, that's already been taken out of your hands. Change the way you work: if you write in the morning, try the afternoon.

Or night. Change *what* you're writing. You've started on your novel again? Put it back in the drawer. I told you a year ago, there are some good things in it, but it's too like what you've already done. And the characters don't really *live.* Try something new. Use your experience with that woman – and perhaps with Olga Aleksandrovna too – to look at love from a new angle. I know it's not for me to tell you what to write, but you have so much talent, I hate to see you repeating yourself…"

Delighted, as ever, to have someone make the decisions for him, Turgenev took his friend's advice to the letter. He wasted no time in buying a spacious apartment on the Fontanka, not far from the Anichkov bridge, and happily spent the next few weeks acquiring furniture, supervising the hanging of curtains and re-upholstering of chairs and sofas, and entertaining a multitude of friends to lavish meals. The woman issue he was happy to shelve. The *lorette* had satisfied his requirements for some time to come. If it were not to be her, he preferred it to be nobody and, as he wrote to Botkin from Spasskoye during a brief visit a few weeks later: 'My life is of a chastity to gladden the heart of Augustine and, all in all, after my recent excesses, I have no quarrel with that.'

It took longer to absorb and decide how to act on Botkin's suggestion regarding his work. Re-reading the chapters of *Two Generations*, he became increasingly dissatisfied with it. He agreed with all his friend's strictures and added several of his own. But what to do instead? Had he written himself out? Perhaps he had nothing more to say. While still in Spasskoye, after a dismal day going over the accounts with his uncle and sensing that the estate's affairs were faring little better than they had under Tyutchev, he wrote a gloomy letter to this effect to Nekrasov, who replied by return: 'There is only one person in Russia who thinks your career is over and that is you.'

On returning to St Petersburg, he shut himself up in his new apartment, avoided seeing anyone and covered page after page of notebooks with ideas which might serve to rekindle his enthusiasm for writing. The first theme he tackled was, unsurprisingly, love. More and more it seemed to him that this endlessly analyzed emotion had never been properly understood. Love was not, as the idealists liked to depict it, a free union of souls. On the contrary, it demanded – presupposed – a stronger and a weaker element. The equal distribution of virtues and failings was an illusion. And, as often as not, the one who loved was not loved in return but was the object of someone else's passion to which he/she was indifferent. Here, perhaps, was a theme he could use. He had touched on it in *A Backwater*, but there it had been incidental. Now to bring it to the forefront and create four or five characters, all suffering from a more or less unrequited love. He played with the idea of basing it on his own experience: he in love with Pauline, whose recent indifference, for all he knew, might well be due to a transfer of her affections elsewhere; Olga in love with him, though surely some young man was already trying to take his place. And the *lorette*? Was she in love with that monstrous woman? Quite possibly. In this field, no explanation, however irrational, implausible or unnatural, could be discarded.

To bind these ideas together, Turgenev chose to weave the story he wrote, *Yakov Pasynkov*, around the figure of Belinsky. He had long had it in mind to pay some kind of literary homage to his dead friend. As always, he pared away various characteristics of his real-life model and used only what served him. In this case, gone were Belinsky's abrasiveness, his impatience and intolerance, everything that had led to him being called 'the furious Vissarion'; what remained were the qualities only his close friends had known: the sweetness, the gentleness, the single-minded pursuit of the ideal. Turgenev's long period of reflection bore fruit; once he started, he wrote with fluency and completed the first draft of the fifty-page story in twelve days. Anxious as ever to know the opinion of his friends and colleagues, he invited them to come to his apartment on the 4th of March for a reading. They all came to his apartment. But the reading never took place...

The event that cancelled, not only the reading of *Yakov Pasynkov*, but virtually every other activity over the vast expanse of Russia was the death, three days previously, of The Emperor of All the Russias. His illness, surely exacerbated by the catastrophic news from the Crimea, had been brief and unknown to all but the innermost court circle. So when the news broke, it had the effect of a thunderbolt. Nicholas was only fifty-nine, and before the disastrous war had rarely known a day of ill health. His thirty-year-long reign seemed to many to have lasted three hundred years. He had had one overriding concern: that nothing should change. And, on the surface at least, nothing had. To the majority of educated Russians, the event was a cause for celebration, the removal of a malignant boil from the body of the state. But as Turgenev was to find out, there were those who felt differently...

As he related to the *Sovremennik* circle gathered at his apartment, he had been invited that afternoon to watch the funeral cortège from a balcony on the first floor of the Stroganov Palace. Though unable to resist the opportunity of being a firsthand witness at such a historic moment, he had gone along with mixed feelings: mingling with the other guests in the staterooms as they waited for the procession to pass on its way to the Peter and Paul fortress, the solemn reflections automatically aroused by the advent of sudden death were continually being elbowed aside by an elemental, irrepressible feeling of euphoria. On looking round the assembled company, with most of whom he was on familiar terms, he received the impression that he was not alone in this. Everyone was of course dressed with the utmost sobriety and wore a suitably grave demeanour; but did he not read in many eyes, especially those of his generation, the sense of excitement, only momentarily veiled, over the new dawn that so many hoped would follow this momentous event?

The wait seemed endless; Turgenev moved listlessly round the great rooms, joining one group after another in the vain hope of hearing something other than endless murmured platitudes. When the muffled drumbeat of the procession was finally heard, the windows were flung open and everyone hurried to try and gain a place on the balcony overlooking the Nevsky Prospekt. Turgenev had been standing by one of the windows, so had no trouble gaining a favourable position. No one spoke as selected detachments of crack infantry and cavalry regiments filed past with faultless precision. Turgenev's mind began involuntarily to stray from the mechanical perfection of the marching figures below to thoughts of the appalling privations and suffering being endured by their fighting comrades in and around besieged Sebastopol; but it was soon brought back to the matter in hand by the behaviour of his neighbour on the balcony. Looking down on the immense avenue, he saw that the gun carriage, drawn by a pair of magnificent black stallions, on which the Czar's velvet-draped coffin had been mounted was now passing directly beneath them. The lady on his right, crushed almost indecorously against him by the ever-swelling crowd on the balcony, suddenly began, as Turgenev related to his friends, "to emit a series of hysterical shrieks which might have seemed exaggerated coming from a mother learning of the death of her only child. Then she crossed herself and raised her hands to the heavens in imploring supplication: 'God rest Your Majesty's soul!'" Turgenev gave gleeful vent to his well-known falsetto and marked gift for mimicry. "'Look down on your faithful subjects, most Merciful Father, give them strength to bear their terrible loss!' Well, my friends, the abyss between the narcissistic ostentation of the grief and the unworthiness of the subject so revolted me that I squeezed my way off the balcony and left the palace without a backward glance."

The reading of *Yakov Pasynkov* was only postponed for a day or two and Turgenev's self-appointed jury passed a very favourable verdict. To Nekrasov's annoyance, it was published a month later in *Annals of the Fatherland,* to whose editor, Andrey Kraevski, the author had often promised a contribution, and it met with popular, as well as a critical, acclaim. In the meantime, Turgenev had decided to celebrate the hoped-for new dawn to which he and his friends had drunk many a toast during their 'wake' for Nicholas I, by again centring a story, of about the same length as *Pasynkov*, around one of the 'men of the forties', before all memory of those undaunted seekers after truth should be swept away by the remorseless tide of history. As he had drawn from Belinsky for his selfless idealist, Pasynkov, so now he turned to Bakunin... but not the anarchist agitator who, after his participation in the February uprising in Paris, had taken his inflammatory oratory to Germany, where a year later it had landed him first in a Dresden jail, then in an Austrian jail, and now in the Peter and Paul Fortress in St Petersburg. No, the Bakunin he wanted to write about was his friend Michel, whom he had known and loved in Berlin, the charmer whose leonine head was crammed full of Hegelian idealism which he would expound for hours on end, preferably to an audience of wide-eyed, open-mouthed young girls whose lives, they were convinced, from that moment took on a meaning they could never previously have suspected.

But Turgenev had changed in these last seven years, as well as his unwitting model, and the title he chose for his story was an ironic one: *The Man of Genius*. He had gone to Spasskoye in June with the intention of dividing his time between hunting and writing; but a violent outbreak of cholera in the Orel region kept him confined to the house, and after a mere seven weeks he had completed the first draft. As he wrote, the pessimism to which he was becoming increasingly prone flowed through his fingers, into his pen and onto the page. Almost despite himself, other qualities of Bakunin's began to surface in the character of the protagonist, Rudin: the determination always to be the dominant figure in any conversation or relationship; the essentially cold heart that lay beneath the dazzling exterior; the habit of borrowing money with no intention of ever repaying it. Gradually both the author and the other characters in his story began to see that behind the charm of Rudin's conversation, under the surface of his seemingly original, probing, even brilliant ideas lay... a void. Once again the man seemed, both to others and eventually to himself, superfluous. But this time Turgenev went to pains to limit his superfluity: if Rudin is destined to fail himself, he thought, the sheer force of his enthusiasm may lead some of his listeners at least to try, to dare, if not to succeed... *I will be accused again of not taking sides, of sitting on the fence. But despite my conviction that the Rudins of this world – or at least of this country – will never achieve anything (look at poor Michel, languishing in what looks like life imprisonment), better their prodigal impetuosity than the indifference of those who accept that everything, however bad, is the way it is and nothing can be done about it. And for the first time I will leave the reader with the possibility that my protagonist might have learnt a lesson: disgraced as he is in both the other characters' and the reader's eyes, he may just have taken to heart the perception that, from now on, he must sometimes act and not just endlessly talk. My thoughts on Hamlet and Don Quixote may be relevant here: although Rudin is quintessentially Hamletesque, I will leave him with a dash of the mad knight's folly/wisdom; when he leaves Darya Mikhailovna's superficial, self-consciously sophisticated little provincial circle on which he has been sponging for months, he will quote the Don's words on liberty: 'Happy is the man who has a crust of bread for which he is obliged to no one'.*

In the autumn of the previous year Turgenev had received a visit from Count Valerian Petrovich Tolstoy, who lived on the nearby estate of Povrovskoye and was as keen a sportsman as himself. Intrigued by the ambiguous character of the author of *A Sportsman's Sketches,* Tolstoy had invited him to be his guest for a week. For Turgenev, he and his wife and distant cousin, Marya Nikolayevna Tolstoy, were ideal friends: with the husband he could happily spend the daylight hours roaming the countryside with rod and gun, only to return for delightful evenings with his hostess, with whom he soon found himself having to make a great effort not to fall in love. Marya Tolstoy was not a beauty, but she had an open-hearted, unaffected charm which many men found irresistible. She was small and delicate, with a high, smooth forehead and a pair of pale grey eyes, which she kept fixed on her interlocutors with an inquiring steadfastness which could be either disconcerting or flattering. She usually dressed like a young girl, in a simple white dress with a pale blue belt. Her thick, shoulder-length chestnut hair was pulled back and held in place by a broad velvet band. The illusion of extreme youth was maintained by the childish timbre of her voice, which sounded more like that of a seven-year-old girl than a twenty-five-year-old mother of two. She protested she had little interest in novels – though she had read more than she liked to admit – and none in poetry. Her preferred reading was history, both Russian and European. But she was very proud of her favourite brother, that Leo Tolstoy whose memoir/novel *Childhood* Turgenev had read with unstinted admiration during his Spasskoye exile.

Immediately after finishing *A Man of Genius,* Turgenev paid another visit to Povrovskoye and decided to try his story out on his hosts before sending it to the usual critical panel of friends. He read it to them over a series of evenings and was encouraged by the reception it met; Marya, especially, was gratifyingly enthusiastic. "There's something new and fresh about it," she told the happy author. "Of course there are echoes of Pushkin and Lermontov. But what you've done so well is to look at your main character from so many different points of view. We see Dmitry Rudin through the eyes of his friends, his enemies, those who are infatuated with him, those who are jealous of him… and then through his own eyes too, and those of his author. The total effect of this is to give the man a three-dimensional quality which you hardly ever find in a novel – only, occasionally, in plays. And at the end of the story, I really didn't know how I felt about him: Was I sorry for him? Did I despise him? Did I understand him? Did I wish him well? Did I think he deserved everything he got? Well, a little bit of all those things. And isn't that how we feel about almost everyone we know?"

Only her husband's presence prevented Turgenev from seizing her hands and covering them with kisses. "You leave me speechless, Marya Nikolayevna," he said. "Coming from such a reluctant reader of fiction, this is flattery indeed. But you must have found some weaknesses too. Please have no scruples about telling me. It is, after all, only a first draft. There is much I shall want to rewrite before it is published."

Marya glanced at her husband, thought for a moment and then said: "There were a couple of things Valya and I discussed: one was the title. We thought *A Man of Genius* was perhaps too laboriously ironic. You make your point so well in the book there seems no need to underline it in the title."

"What would you suggest?" Turgenev asked.

"Why not just *Rudin*?"

"*Rudin* is the story's name. What other criticisms did you and Valerian Petrovich have?"

Again Marya looked towards her husband, but from the depths of his armchair he waved his pipe towards her, indicating that he was happy to let her speak for him. "Well, we were wondering," she began hesitatingly, "about the length. What is it?… about a hundred and twenty pages. It seems a little long for a story and a little short for a novel. We thought perhaps you could flesh it out a bit – without padding of course – and make it into a real novel. I'm told that is what your readers are expecting from you. And Rudin is so intriguing, we'd like to know more about him. About his past, for instance. How did he become the way he is when your story starts?"

"This I will have to think over," Turgenev said. "But I thank you both for your suggestion and I'll see what my friends in St Petersburg say."

Marya gave a deep sigh and put aside the skirt she had been embroidering. "Oh, if only we could have my brother read it. I'd give anything to know Lyovochka's opinion." The conversation turned to the 24-year-old artillery officer, who was now fighting in the Crimea. Since *Childhood*, Turgenev had read with equal admiration its successor, *Boyhood*, which Nekrasov had also published in *Sovremennik,* along with articles on the siege of Sebastopol and a number of stories, one of which Tolstoy, a great admirer of the *Sportsman's Sketches,* had dedicated to him. Marya was terrified for the safety of her beloved brother: his battery had been posted to a position little more than a hundred yards from the French lines and even the official casualties among the Russian troops were alarmingly high. Realizing that this talented young writer was risking death every day, Turgenev wrote to Tolstoy expressing his desire to make his acquaintance, if only, for the time being, by correspondence. 'You can have no idea,' he wrote, 'how painful it is for me, with the high opinion I have of your talent and your future, to think of where you are. Your impressions and experiences have no doubt been of great value to you, but enough is enough… From now on your weapon should be the pen, not the sword.'

He begged him to look him up the next time he was in St Petersburg on leave, and was taken at his word. On November 21st, 1855, the young officer, dressed in a crumpled, mud-stained uniform, his weathered face bursting with rude health, appeared unannounced at the door of Turgenev's apartment on the Fontanka. The two writers flung themselves into each others' arms in an emotional embrace that neither seemed to want to interrupt. Finally it was Turgenev who pulled away and, brushing the dust off his bottle-green velvet jacket, ushered Tolstoy inside. An hour's animated conversation was enough to induce an invitation to stay and the offer was immediately accepted.

For the first day or two, even though there was only an age difference of ten years, they could almost have been taken for father and son. The older man couldn't wait to introduce him to the literary clique centred round *Sovremennik*, and the younger was only too happy, after months of the Spartan rigours and dangers of camp life, to bask in the genuine admiration of established writers a generation older than himself. A couple of days after his arrival, Turgenev gave a dinner in his honour. It was a bizarre occasion: here was a selection of the top intelligentsia of St Petersburg confronted by a young officer of twenty-seven, who knew nothing of literary life; and yet he was unquestionably the dominant personality there. All the civilians, except possibly Turgenev himself, couldn't entirely suppress feelings of guilt, even inferiority, vis-à-vis this tough, battle-hardened veteran, who was happy to bask in their compliments but made no attempt to hide his conviction that he knew more of life than they did. When Panaev held forth on the circle's most frequent topic of conversation, the battle between the Slavophils and the Westerners, Tolstoy gazed at him with a blank, indifferent stare, later telling Turgenev that he thought the matter about as important as whether you started shaving the left hand side of your face or the right.

It was not long before this intolerance, this impatience began to rub off on Turgenev. After the first flourish of mutual admiration, small slivers of contrast began to manifest themselves: Tolstoy, who took no care of his personal appearance, was irritated by Turgenev's fastidious attention to dress. And Tolstoy's brusque outspokenness, which sometimes spilled over into a delight in being offensive, became distasteful to Turgenev. Hating emotional scenes as he did, he tried hard to conceal his irritation at the boorish behaviour of his guest, whom he privately (and, at first, affectionately) referred to as 'the Troglodyte'. But Tolstoy, who soon sensed a weaker character (did he ever meet a stronger?), would needle away at his host, testing to the limit, and sometimes beyond, Turgenev's deep reserves of patience.

During these last weeks of the year, Turgenev was hard at work revising *Rudin*, a task he found much harder than the original writing of it. One complicating factor was the news that Bakunin had been transferred from the Peter and Paul, where he had recently enjoyed a considerable relaxation of the harsh regime he had had to endure in the early years of his imprisonment, to the grim, dank Schlüsselberg fortress on an island on Lake Ladoga, whose gruesome conditions had caused the death of innumerable prisoners. Everyone who had read *Rudin* had commented on the similarity between the protagonist and Bakunin, and it was now unthinkable that the heroic victim of Czarist oppression should be shown in a negative light. In following Marya Tolstoy's suggestion that the story be extended to novel length, Turgenev wrote a new central sequence, laying emphasis on how eloquent and inspiring an influence the young Dmitry had been in his university days, and added an epilogue emphasizing the man's qualities, minimizing his defects and holding out a hope that it might not be too late for him to make some sense of his life. Dmitry Rudin emerged from these additions not, certainly, as 'a hero of our time' but at least without the total hopelessness of most of Russia's 'superfluous men'. The changes met with Nekrasov's approval and he inserted an announcement in the forthcoming edition of *Sovremennik* that the next issue would contain a new 'novella' by Ivan Turgenev, to be published in two parts. The result was an increase of some twenty per cent in the journal's sales. There could no longer be any doubt that Turgenev's work was followed by a faithful body of readers.

In the middle of February, 1856, Nekrasov gives a dinner to celebrate an agreement he has made with what can now be called his three 'main authors': Turgenev, Tolstoy and Ostrovsky. *Sovremennik* is to gain the exclusive right to their work in return for a small share of the profits, if any. A private room in Donon's luxurious restaurant is hired and the company includes the lyric poet, Fet, the Panaevs, Annenkov, and Druzhinin. The invitation is for seven, and a quarter of an hour later everyone is present except Tolstoy. At first no one takes much notice, but when eight o'clock arrives and he is still not there, Nekrasov asks Turgenev if he has remembered to tell his guest of the appointment.

"Oh, he knows very well," Turgenev tells them, in his most languid drawl. "But I have learnt that it is no use counting on Lev Nikolayevich for anything. Above all for consistency."

"Why do you say this?", Avdotya Panaeva asks, scenting gossip. "I thought the two of you were like brothers."

"So we are. But I am never sure when we're David and Jonathan and when Cain and Abel."

"In what way is he so inconsistent," Panaev asks. "Whenever he's promised us a contribution, it has always been ready more or less on time."

"As a writer he may have certain standards which, as a man, he cannot live up to. I know why he is late this evening." To a chorus of 'Why?'s he goes on to explain. "You, all of you, remember how happy Lev Nikolayevich was to be welcomed by us when he came here three months ago. Well... how can I put it? ... Much of this happiness seems to have worn off. For the last several weeks he has been continually preaching to me about how pampered we all are, how self-indulgent, how detached from what he calls the real business of living. At the same time, mind you, he spends four or five nights a week at the gaming tables, gypsy taverns and brothels. Last night, for instance, he came home at three in the morning and, as he often does, woke me to tell me how stricken with remorse he was, how disgusted with himself. Never, he swears, will he hold a card or buy a woman again. I eventually calm him down and persuade him to go to bed, whereupon he sleeps till two in the afternoon. If I have visitors in the morning, I have to ask them to whisper so as not to wake him up."

"And yet," Nekrasov says, "he still manages to produce fine work. He gave me a tale called *Two Hussars* last week, which is as good as anything he's done."

"God knows", Turgenev growls, "when or how!"

"Tell me, Ivan Sergeyevich," Avdotya purrs, "could it be that you are just a little bit jealous of him?"

Turgenev stiffens and glares at her for a moment. Then he gives a good-humoured laugh. "If you mean am I jealous of how productive he is, of course I am. But he'll have to find somewhere else to produce. My nerves won't stand it any more. Nor will his. We are constantly on edge. I seem to provoke him into provoking me! I'm sure that when we're no longer at such close quarters, our very real friendship will be able to thrive again."

Nekrasov, ever the editor, scents a danger of losing one of his best contributors. "Break it to him gently, Vanichka. He's hot-headed, yes, but we must remember his age. We don't want him taking his work to Katkov for the *Russian Herald*.

"It wouldn't surprise me in the least if he did. In many ways he has more in common with the Slavophils than with us. He's always rhapsodizing about his peasants. And he's so proud of his title. I think he would like to see a Russia composed entirely of aristocrats and muzhiks. We are all categorized as bourgeois and intellectuals, neither of which he has any time for."

Avdotya Panaeva is not easily going to be denied her opportunity to sow trouble. "You're growing more bitter by the minute, Ivan Sergeyevich. It sounds to me as if there's going to be a complete rift between the two of you."

Turgenev ignores the malice. "I most sincerely hope not," he says sadly. "I love and admire Lev Nikolayevich. But, great heavens, he can test that love to the limit. One day... no, one minute... he is charming, friendly, anxious to talk... and even to listen – though that, more rarely. The next, he is hurling insults at me. And then relapsing into silence. A sulky, obstinate, hostile silence. And staring at me. He has a stare that would... "

But he is interrupted by the arival of the subject of all this speculation, who comes in, resplendent in full-dress uniform. He makes no apologies for being late, but greets everyone with a benevolent smile. He seems especially pleased to see Turgenev, who looks him up and down in surprised admiration. "You're always taunting me about the way I dress," he says, "but you've certainly outdone me this evening. We are honoured indeed!"

"Oh, I didn't put this on for you," Tolstoy remarks, offhandedly. "In fact, I will not be able to stay very long. I'm going to a ball at the Obolenskys."

"In that case," Avdotya remarks, "we had better start dinner. We wouldn't want you to be late for the Princess!"

Tolstoy either misses, or chooses to ignore the irony. After attacking his soup with gusto, he looks around the table and blurts out, ingenuously: "I hope I didn't keep you waiting, but I have to tell you that I had very little sleep last night."

Remembering what Turgenev has told them, none of the company feel it necessary to make any comment. Avoiding each others' eyes, they go on with their soup. Tolstoy glances keenly around and puts down his spoon. "What is this? Is no one going to ask me why?"

Annenkov placidly volunteers: "Why, Lev Nikolayevich?"

"Because I spent the whole night reading."

Turgenev conspicuously raises his eyes to the ceiling, but remains silent.

"And what was it you were reading," Annenkov murmurs, "that kept you so wide awake?"

"Turgenev gave me the first draft of a story he is working on. A series of letters. From one man to another. You don't even see the replies. But take it from me, it will be one of the best things he's done."

Nekrasov looks suspiciously at Turgenev. "You haven't talked to me about this! You're not going to offer it elsewhere, I hope."

Turgenev twiddles the stem of his wineglass awkwardly and mumbles... Tolstoy being too kind, work only at a very early stage, not ready to be read, but Tolstoy had seen it lying around and insisted so vigorously... But if and when he is satisfied with it, he will, of course, submit it to *Sovremennik*. "After all, that is what we are here to celebrate, is it not?"

Nekrasov nods in a not entirely convinced way, and Panaev, assuming the editorial mantle, asks Tolstoy to tell them something about this story. Turgenev waves his hands in front of his face in horror, but Tolstoy is happy to take up the invitation. "The basic idea is very good: a young girl who has been forbidden by her mother to read poetry or novels. So she has grown up without any of the fanciful romantic notions that flutter around most young women's heads. If I ever have daughters, I'll be tempted to do the same thing myself. She marries a nonentity, but then re-meets a man who courted her, not very ardently, several years previously. He, in the meantime, has become ever more wary of engaging with life. For any meaningful action, he substitutes love of nature, animals, literature..." his lips twist into a mischievous grin, "a bit like the author, you might say..."

Turgenev starts to expostulate, but Tolstoy takes no notice. "His way of wooing her," he continues, "(of course he writes to his friend that he hasn't fallen in love, but we know that he has) is to read her Goethe's *Faust*. Can't you see Ivan Sergeyevich doing that?"

He's enjoying himself immensely. Annenkov tries to put in a word for his friend, but Tolstoy drives remorselessly on. "It has all been very well done up to there. But then – I suppose I shouldn't spoil it for you all – there's some supernatural rubbish which…" he turns to address Turgenev directly, "I'm sure you'll eliminate when you rewrite." He picks up a leg of mutton and starts to gnaw at the bone. "There, have I done your story justice?"

Turgenev gives him a patient smile. "More than it deserves," he says. "But…"

"Ah," Tolstoy bursts in, "I forgot to mention one thing. One very important thing…" He waves the bone, half-playfully, half-threateningly in Turgenev's direction. "The heroine, Vera Nikolayevna, bears a strong resemblance to my sister. A *very* strong resemblance. You seem to know her through and through. She might almost *be* Masha. And, like my sister, she is married. And like my sister she is an incorrigible coquette. Far too much so for her own good… although Masha will not, I hope, die… oh, there, now I *have* spoilt it for you. Never mind, you'll all be reading it soon enough… she will not, I say, die from remorse for having declared her love to her suitor, who is a weak and immoral numskull." He throws the depleted bone down on his plate, plants his elbows firmly on the table and stares meaningfully into Turgenev's face.

Turgenev is torn between embarrassment and irritation. "If you see a resemblance between Vera Nikolayevich and your charming sister," he says, "it is no doubt there. But we all in this room know that a fictional character is never taken exactly from life. I spent some delightful days last summer with Marya and Valerian Petrovich at Pokrovskoye, and she did once happen to mention to me that she had always been indifferent to poetry. We had a long, animated discussion about this, and it certainly provided me with an element of my story. But beyond that…" he shrugs his shoulders and looks reproachfully at Tolstoy, who now seems to have lost interest in the whole business and has started talking with Ostrovsky about the theatre.

As the meal progresses, the literary men worry away at their favourite topic: literature. Familiar lamentations about censorship lead to a discussion of George Sand, whose books are banned in Russia, although clandestine copies are readily available. Fet asks Tolstoy if he has read any of her novels.

"One. And that was quite enough. It only confirmed my opinion about women novelists."

"And what is that?" Ostrovsky asks.

"That they should leave novel-writing to men."

This is greeted with a chorus of protestation, but Tolstoy continues unperturbed: "What a fruitless waste of time it is to read about some spoiled woman's fluctuating state of mind… How can I love this one when yesterday I thought I loved that one? The best thing she, along with her author, could do would be to stay at home and look after her children. If writing is to be of any value it has to be about life. And what do women know of life?"

This is too much even for Avdotya. "Different aspects of it, Lev Nikolayevich," she says sharply. "I doubt if even you, with all your experience, have known the pangs and joys of childbirth."

"I have not, Avdotya Yakovlevna. But nor have I read a stimulating book about that experience. But what I am saying does not only apply to women. I would ask the same question of all you gentlemen here. How many of you have really *lived*? How many of you, for instance, have been able to analyze how you felt when a bullet whistled by, an inch from your ear?"

Turgenev has heard this line of argument before. "Are you suggesting," he asks, "that no writer can produce anything of value unless he's served as a soldier. That would eliminate Gogol. Not to mention Shakespeare."

"Gogol is a law unto himself," Tolstoy answers. "But Shakespeare's reputation is universally overrated. Take him all in all, he was a windbag. A phrase-maker!"

Turgenev can hardly find the breath with which to reply. "You can only be saying that with the intention of provoking us. Have you read *Coriolanus*?"

"No."

"Read it. When Shakespeare writes about war, you feel he might have been a soldier all his life. It's conviction that counts. Not just experience."

"But that's what all of you lack. What is conviction without experience? An empty shell. And your experiences are so limited. You, Ivan Sergeyevich, are always carrying on about the artistry of your cook and how he cost you a thousand roubles. I say you'd appreciate him more if you'd lived on army rations for six months."

Annenkov now comes to the defence of his friend. "You forget," he says acidly, "that Turgenev has suffered prison and exile for his convictions. Up to now the same cannot be said of you."

Two angry red spots appear in the middle of Tolstoy's cheeks. The bantering, deliberately provoking tone he has been using gives way to a harsh rasp. "I do not have to demonstrate my convictions. I can stand here, a sword in my hand, and say: 'As long as there's breath left in my body, no one will enter this room.' That's a conviction. Whereas all of you go out of your way to keep your deepest thoughts hidden behind a veil of 'literary' verbiage."

Turgenev, in his distress at the turn the conversation has taken, has started to stride nervously up and down the room. Now his patience cracks. "If that's what you think," he hisses, gesticulating wildly, "why do you waste your time with us? Your place is not here! Go to Princess Obolensky's."

Tolstoy's eyes, now blazing with fury, follow the ambulatory figure. "I do not have to ask you where I should go," he roars. "And neither my presence nor my absence will transform your futile chatter into deep convictions."

Nekrasov, scenting calamity, tries diplomacy. "Come now, Lev Nikolayevich," he says soothingly, "don't lose your temper. You know how much Turgenev loves and admires you."

Tolstoy still doesn't take his eyes off Turgenev for a second. "A fine way he has of showing it!" he snarls. "He does everything in his power to infuriate me. Look at him now! Pacing up and down on purpose, waggling his democratic 'literary' buttocks in my face. But for once I will give him the satisfaction of following his advice." And he springs to his feet, seizes his sword-belt and hat which he had flung over a chair when he came in, and without a word of salutation to anyone, strides out of the room.

On his return home, Turgenev waited up in the hope of intercepting Tolstoy when he came back from the ball. He wanted to make the quarrel up before, like many quarrels, it grew so out of proportion that neither party any longer had a clear recollection of what had been actually said. He was quite prepared to be conciliatory and to admit to his share of the foolishness; all he wanted from his antagonist was a smaller – given his character – helping from the same dish. But by four in the morning there was still no sign of Tolstoy, and he went to bed counting on having it out with his cantankerous guest in the morning.

But when Zakhar woke him at nine, he brought with him a note which, he explained, "The Count handed me an hour ago on his way out. He told me to give it to you as soon as you were awake." Turgenev opened the envelope, already guessing its contents:

> *Dear Ivan Sergeyevich,*
>
> *I wouldn't want to leave your house without thanking you for your hospitality. I was anxious to make your acquaintance and am glad to have done so. But I think we would both agree that the differences in our outlook are too large to permit any intimate friendship. Better respect from a distance than insincerity at close quarters.*
> *In haste,*
>
> *Cordially yours,*
>
> *L. Tolstoy.*

Turgenev spent the last months of winter in St Petersburg, preparing and writing a preface for the first publication, in three volumes, of a collection of his work, under the title 'Tales and Stories, 1844-1856'. On March 30th the Treaty of Paris brought the Crimean War to an end; it was a humiliating setback for Russia, whose terrible expenditure of money and men had not achieved one of the causes for which she had fought. But all this was overshadowed by relief that the suffering was at last over, and for Turgenev in particular it meant that it was again potentially possible to visit western Europe. More because he had been thinking and talking for so long of his desire to travel, than from any compelling desire immediately to do so, he submitted a humble application for a foreign passport with very little hope that it would be granted.

In the spring he moved to Spasskoye, taking with him Nekrasov, Botkin and Annenkov. For the first few weeks they lived a happy, carefree life, shooting snipe in the morning, working – a little – in the afternoons and writing, rehearsing and performing one-act plays and skits in the evenings to a delighted audience of country neighbours, who revelled in this invigorating injection of metropolitan sophistication. But soon their bucolic serenity was ruffled by an event that, only a few months earlier, would have sent their host into transports of joy: a letter from His Imperial Majesty's Chancery indicating that it had pleased Czar Alexander II graciously to grant Ivan Sergeyevich Turgenev a passport permitting him to travel wherever he wished.

In the evening, champagne was called for and toasts drunk to the released prisoner. Turgenev beamed with satisfaction throughout the first bottle, but half way through the second, he sat down heavily and, with furrowed brow, gazed at his guests in almost comic perplexity.

"What's the matter, Vanya?" Nekrasov called out. "Are you beginning to feel homesick before you've even left?"

Turgenev shook his head. "No, it's just that I'm suddenly asking myself if I really want to go."

There was a sudden silence. Nekrasov and Botkin looked incredulous, Annenkov sympathetic. It was he who suggested that they let the matter rest for the night; tomorrow Turgenev would be able to see things in a clearer light, and they would be better placed to offer whatever advice they might deem helpful.

But the matter was not cleared up in a day. Most of the following week was taken up with anguished debates back and forth. Very few birds were shot; work was shamefully neglected; and the neighbours had to swallow their disappointment when it was conveyed to them that a one-acter featuring a comic debate between Oedipus and Antigone, programmed for that week, had had to be postponed, if not cancelled, owing to an unforeseen emergency.

Instead, another play, broken up into any number of short scenes, was improvised by the four author/actors themselves. The settings were those of their daily life: the dining room at mealtimes; the countryside during walks; and the drawing-room for long smoky evenings that often lasted until the early hours. The entire play would demand more of the reader's patience than any author has the right to ask; but here are some extracts, which should convey adequately enough the general drift…

NEKRASOV: Before we can be of any help at all, can you clear
              up one point, which I think is baffling all of us?
TURGENEV: What's that?
NEKRASOV: If you didn't want to go, why did you apply for a passport?
TURGENEV: Well, for a start, I never dreamed they'd give me one. And anyway,
              I *thought* I wanted to go. In many ways I still do. I'm just not so
              sure anymore.
ANNENKOV: The only way to resolve this is to weigh up the
              pros and cons: why you *do* want to go, and why you
              don't want to go. We'll put them on the scales and
              see which way they tip.
BOTKIN: Wise words! Will you collaborate, Vanichka?
TURGENEV: Do I have any choice?
BOTKIN: None at all. We'll start this evening…

★ ★ ★ ★

BOTKIN: Right, first question. Why do you want to go to Western Europe?
              Reasons one, two, three, as many as you like…
TURGENEV: Well, the first is simply my love of travel, of which I've been
              deprived for six years. Call it my *Wanderlust*; it's been part of me
              since I was a boy.
NEKRASOV: (*looking round at the others*) Any objections to that, gentlemen?
              (*The other two shake their heads*)
              Reason unanimously accepted. Next!
TURGENEV: I think I owe it to my daughter to see her after all these years and
              find out how she has developed.
              Now that I have the opportunity…
BOTKIN: Excuse the interruption, but you make this sound very much like

300

TURGENEV: a duty. Is it only that, or does the parental instinct also play a part?

TURGENEV: (*hastily, and with some embarrassment*) Oh, of course, it would give me the greatest pleasure to see the little thing… well, not so little any more, quite the young lady, I hear she's become…

ANNENKOV: Forgive me, Vanya, but you don't sound too convincing…
(*The other two nod*)

TURGENEV: No, no, no, you're all mistaken. I want to, and I think I should, see my daughter as soon as possible. There, will that do?

NEKRASOV: Gentlemen?

BOTKIN: Reason accepted… with slight reservations.
(*Annenkov nods*) On to the next!
(*A long pause*)

TURGENEV: Well, it's no secret to any of you that I have a desperate longing to see Madame Viardot again… I cannot accept that the… intense feeling we had for one another is over until I hear it from her own lips.
(*A longer pause*)

ANNENKOV: This is surely your most compelling reason… and the most delicate for us to make any comment on.

BOTKIN: I think we should wait until Ivan Sergeyevich tells of his doubts about going. That may put us in a better position to offer him some unwanted advice on something which is, of course, absolutely no business of ours.
(*Turgenev smiles his assent and the debate is adjourned*)

★ ★ ★ ★

NEKRASOV: Very well then, Vanya, let's hear the reasons for your doubts.

TURGENEV: Reluctantly, I have to admit that going to France would involve a certain interruption of my work…
(*As his friends nod vigorously in agreement, he immediately starts to backtrack*)
… but not, I think, necessarily a damaging one.
It might provide me with fresh perspectives… a more objective, distanced way of looking at my country and people.

ANNENKOV: Aren't you afraid of cutting yourself off from your sources? Of losing touch with what's happening here?

TURGENEV: My dear friends, I'm going to France, not Japan, like Goncharov. Nor, like Herzen, am I going into permanent exile. I have no idea how long I will stay. I may be back before you even begin to miss me.

NEKRASOV:	*(looking around)* Gentlemen?
BOTKIN:	Qualified approval…
ANNENKOV:	Not from me. You'd work much better here, I'm convinced of it. There will be far more distractions for you in France. And we all know how easily you're distracted!
NEKRASOV:	Jury divided. I tend to side with Annenkov. Next reason why you might choose not to go?
	(Turgenev draws a deep breath)
TURGENEV:	The only other reason is the personal one. I realize I might be making a grave mistake. Mme Viardot may not take any pleasure in seeing me again – except perhaps for a short visit – and I may be laying myself open to atrocious suffering and humiliation. But, I ask you, what is the alternative?
	(Annenkov opens his mouth, but Turgenev anticipates him)
	Oh, I know what Pavel Vasilevich wants me to do: marry a nice Russian girl, settle down to domesticity and produce a child every two years and a masterpiece every three. But life doesn't seem to want to offer me this idyll. And I might add… *(looking at Nekrasov and Botkin)*, as we're stripping our souls bare, that you two seem in no hurry to follow that path either…
	(Nekrasov, who lives openly with his friend and co-editor's wife, and Botkin, who married a French adventuress in Kazan cathedral and abandoned her a month later, find nothing to say)
TURGENEV:	Some men may be masters of their fate, but I am not one of them. It would seem that a family life is not for me; I must live as a gypsy. Over the last two years I have experimented with the Annenkov formula, been charmed by an eminently eligible young girl and drawn back at the last moment; I have plunged into a cauldron of eroticism and emerged gasping but, I hope, unharmed; and now I am digging my nails into my flesh to avoid falling in love with… with whom? With the wife of my neighbour and good friend! Who, I venture to surmise, may not be indifferent to me. So what am I to do? Nekrasov's solution is, I fear, not feasible in the provinces!
ANNENKOV:	From what Lev Nikolayevich said at that eventful dinner, you are referring, I presume, to Marya Tolstoya.
TURGENEV:	I am.
BOTKIN:	You are aware, of course, that her husband's infidelity is the talk of St Petersburg?
TURGENEV:	I have heard something of the sort. I have no idea if it's true. I

have been a guest at their house several times and have noticed no blatant lack of harmony. But even if there were, what use is that to me? *(to Botkin)* Are you suggesting I wait around for God knows how long *in case* their marriage might break up? And *in case* she might be prepared to marry me? While in the meantime..

NEKRASOV: In the meantime you want to travel and you want to see Madame Viardot… and your daughter. Vanya, for what it is worth, you have my blessing… I speak as your friend, not as your publisher. In your place, I should surely do the same… even if for all the wrong reasons.

BOTKIN: I second that.

ANNENKOV: And I'm in a minority, so I'll have to concede. But be sure you come back. You need Russia and Russia needs you.

TURGENEV: Don't worry, my friends. Despite what they say of me, my Russia is dearer to me than anything else in the world. And I never feel that more than when I am abroad. Even gypsies can have deep feelings for their roots, you know…

Grateful to his friends for having helped him make up his mind and fearful lest he should again start to fall prey to doubts, he excused himself and went straight up to his room to write a letter to his daughter, which would irrevocably commit him to departure…

Spasskoye,
25 May, 1856.

Dear Paulinette,

In your last letter you gave me a scolding for not having written to you in such a long time. And you were right to do so. The fact that I have been very busy is no excuse. But you must always remember that, even if my pen is shamefully lax in your regard (it has so many other calls on its attention!), my thoughts do their very best to make up for it.

And now I have a piece of news for you which I hope will make you as happy as it makes me: and that is that, if all goes well, this summer we shall finally see each other again after these long six years. With the war finally over, I have been able to get a passport and plan to leave Russia some time in July. I may have to go first to London, but in August we can all have a big family reunion at Courtavenel. How you will have changed! You are thirteen now, and Mme Viardot wrote to me some time ago that you are nearly as tall as she is. But I know I shall recognize you all the same. And I hope that you will recognize your old papa, grey hair and all!

I am glad to hear that you have settled down well in your new pension and that you are doing your best to please Mme Harang. The more you please your Directrice, the more you will please me. And I can only presume you want to do that, as Mme Viardot tells me that you are still very fond of me!... Believe me, dear daughter, I am of you too and can't wait for the day when I can put my arms around you and replicate in happier circumstances the long, tight hug we shared six years ago before you and Mme Robert boarded the steamboat for Stettin.

Your loving father,
Ivan Turgenev.

One early June morning, Leo Tolstoy rose at five, saddled a horse and rode the fifteen miles or so that separated his estate at Yasnaya Polyana from Spasskoye. He was bored with the sole company and masochistic adoration of his 62-year-old 'Aunt Toinette', a distant cousin of his father's, who had looked after him and his brothers since the early death of his mother. He was also fuming at his failure to come to an agreement with his serfs, whom he had tried to liberate under conditions that they had found unacceptable. The company of his neighbour and fellow-writer was bound to provide some sort of relief. If all went well, perhaps they could make up their differences and establish a solid friendship; if the other man's bland, pampered manner and high-pitched, oversensitive protestations got on his nerves, at least he could relieve his frustration with a good quarrel.

He had sent no advance warning of his arrival, and when he reached Spasskoye he found that Turgenev was away for the morning. He had no difficulty in convincing the major-domo of his intimate friendship with the master and was given the freedom of the house until such time as he should return. Wandering round the spacious downstairs rooms, he was gradually invaded by a smarting sense of nostalgia. The original wooden house at Yasnaya Polyana in which he had grown up had had to be sold; a neighbour had dismantled it piece by piece and reconstructed it on his own property several miles away. He and Aunt Toinette now occupied one of the small stone houses that used to flank it and had none of the lived-in charm of the original. Here everything brought his happy childhood back to him: the large, rumpled sofas and chairs, the host of little tables cluttered with dusty bric-à-brac, the creak of the floorboards under his feet, the smell of beeswax, the dark corner where candles flickered in front of tarnished silver icons, the portraits of ancestors on the walls in their tilted frames ... how familiar it all seemed to him! All of a sudden, his whole being was flooded with an immense sense of warmth and affection towards the owner of this house. He walked out of one of the French windows and into the garden, where he was joined by a dog who saw an opportunity for the walk his master had denied him. Plunging into the birch trees which skirted the drive, Tolstoy felt more and more at home. *Nothing can stop Ivan Sergeyevich and I from becoming fast friends now.*

We come from the same stock, all that is fundamental to us is rooted in this earth. We may feel differently about certain aspects of art, but what is art? A man-made contraption with all the weight of gossamer, in comparison to the solidity of this land. In the cities – those monstrosities created by man – our opposing points of view may fly to the surface, but here, in a life which is elementally more congenial to us, it should be easy to heal all divisions...

Half an hour later, emerging from the trees, he saw Turgenev, who had obviously heard of his arrival, striding towards him with a broad smile of welcome. Without a word, the two men fell into each others' arms, and when Turgenev drew back he was moved to see that the visitor's eyes were moist. Throwing an arm around his shoulders, he invited him in for lunch. They spent the rest of the day together in an intimacy they had never enjoyed in St Petersburg, not even in the early days. Neither mentioned their quarrel at the *Sovremennik* dinner. In the afternoon they went for a long walk and Tolstoy poured into his host's interested ears the whole story of his dealings with his serfs.

"I was determined to give them their freedom," he explained. "I know word has it that emancipation is in the air. They even say the Czar was converted to it by reading your *Sportsman's Sketches*. But now they've appointed a committee, and knowing some of the people who are sitting on it and the time that any committee takes to reach a decision in this benighted country, I decided I'd go through with it on my own. I worked out the terms and summoned a meeting the moment I got back to Yasnaya. I offered to lease out to them the land on which they worked for a small rent, which they'd pay me for thirty years. After that, the land would be theirs. I couldn't believe their attitude. I wasn't asking for their gratitude, but at least I thought they would be pleased."

"But they weren't," said Turgenev, with a knowing shake of the head.

"Ah, you're not surprised. Have you been through something of this yourself?"

"I freed my domestic serfs immediately after my mother's death. But as for the others, I decided, after a few inquiries, that it was better to wait for the state to take some action. I made it possible for them to buy their freedom at a very favourable rate, but few of them did. Tell me, how did yours respond to your offer?"

"At first with great appreciation. Kissing my hand and bowing and scraping. Of course, they just wanted to discuss a few things amongst themselves, and I said, 'Certainly you must, come back when you're ready to talk.'"

"And when they did?"

"They started demanding ridiculous terms: halving the rent I'd suggested they'd pay me and asking for outright ownership in five years. I told them that would ruin me."

"And what did they say to that?"

"Oh, you know, they scratched their heads and shuffled their feet and grinned as if they were shyly taking part in some great joke."

305

"And in the end?"

"In the end, after five – I'm not exaggerating, *five* – meetings, during which I had reduced the rent by a little and made it twenty-four instead of thirty years that they'd have to pay it, I smelt a rat. I became convinced that they weren't really trying to negotiate at all. They had no intention of accepting my offer, and simply didn't know how to say it. And then I discovered I was right."

"How?"

"In a fit of total exasperation one evening (I felt like taking one of their chief men and flogging the truth out of him), I confided in my steward, Yakov. I started to relate to him the whole sequence of events, but he just smiled, shook his head and said: 'You don't have to tell me, sir. I know all about it.' 'You do?' I say. 'Well, tell me then, why don't they want what's good for them?' 'A very simple reason,' he says. 'Rumour has got around that during the Czar's coronation in August, there's going to be a proclamation announcing the unconditional liberation of all serfs. They think you're just trying to hoodwink them. But they don't bear you any grudge. In fact, they sort of admire you. One of them said to me – you must excuse me, sir, – "E's a cunning young rascal, that one! You've got to hand it to 'im. If we hadn't known better, 'e'd 'ave stolen the money right out of our 'ands."'" Turgenev nodded pensively. "You should bring this up with our extreme Slavophils," he said. "The Aksakovs, for instance, who believe that all the virtue and wisdom in the country resides in the peasant communes."

Tolstoy gave a derisive snort. "I don't know about virtue and wisdom," he said. "Greed and cunning, I'd call it. And if something isn't done soon, the Aksakovs, along with the rest of us, will wake up one morning with their land stolen from them and their throats cut. There's a dangerous air abroad. You know what Yakov also told me? Apparently one of the chief troublemakers said to him: 'It's time the *barin* understood something: we may belong to him, but the land belongs to us.' With this false expectation about the Czar's intentions, it would only take a few firebrands here and there to set off a rebellion that would make Pugachev's seem like a spring shower."

When they returned to the house, Tolstoy was about to take his leave and ride away, but Turgenev persuaded him to stay and have a nap. In the evening, sunk in wicker armchairs on the long front terrace, the conversation turned to the more controversial topic of their work. But here again the days of polemics seemed to belong to the past. Tolstoy was working on a book he would eventually call *The Cossacks,* and gave a rough outline of what he was aiming at: by drawing on his experiences in the Caucasus, to embroider his favourite theme of the contrast between (over-)civilized man and the simple, healthy life of a primitive, if sometimes barbaric, community.

Turgenev told him he was beginning to consider a not dissimilar subject, but, both psychologically and geographically, from the reverse angle. "I'm turning over the possibility of a story about a man who returns to his estate around here from Paris, disgusted with the artificiality of life there; he meets and falls in love with a young girl, loses her, but remains convinced that life on his own soil, even if limited, is preferable to any other."

This occasioned a peal of laughter. "And you're writing this just as you're about to leave Russia for Paris!"

Turgenev gave an apologetic shrug and hastened to add: "I still don't know whether I shall write it or not. At the moment I have just finished correcting my Faust story, which you read in St Petersburg."

"Ah, the one with Masha in it…" Tolstoy burst out and ignored Turgenev's attempt at a self-justifying interruption. "You know what we'll do? I'll stay the night here, and tomorrow we'll ride over to Pokrovskoye and give them a surprise. I haven't seen Masha since I came down here."

Turgenev's mild objection that perhaps they should at least announce their arrival, was tempestuously swept away. "No, no, that'll be the fun of it. I can't wait to see their faces when we show up together." And he added, with no trace of fraternal disapproval: "I know at least one of them will be overjoyed to see *both* of us!"

In fact both Valerian and Marya Tolstoy were delighted to see their unexpected visitors. When marriages are under strain, the distraction of company is often welcome. Soon after their arrival, with the Tolstoy cousins deep in discussion of the ubiquitous serf problem, Marya took the opportunity to slip her arm familiarly through Turgenev's elbow and glide away with him on the excuse of showing him that part of the garden which she insisted on tending herself. "I have a new rose to show you," she told him, "I had it sent over from England. It is a beautiful deep red, with a wonderfully delicate scent.

Turgenev duly admired the rose, although with the mental reservation that many in his mother's garden were of greatly superior quality. They then walked on, trapped in a silence which Turgenev eventually broke by mentioning that he was on the point of finishing *Faust*. She blushed slightly, as it was no secret that many of the characteristics of the heroine had been based on her. Then she asked: "Does it still end so sadly, I mean with Vera's death?"

"I'm afraid it does. Perhaps even more sadly, because after Vera dies, Pavel loses all taste for life. He reflects that once the first flush of youth has passed, nothing is left to us but resignation. Life is no longer a game or even a pastime; it's a hard task, a stern duty."

"And is that your conviction too?"

"Most of the time, Marya Nikolayevna, I'm afraid it is. Oh, there are moments when the rash enthusiasms of youth flare up again, but they happen more and more rarely."

Marya thought about this for a moment and then stated simply: "You have changed much, Ivan Sergeyevich, in the two years we have known each other. When I first met you, if I had been forced to say what I thought was your greatest fault, I would have said a certain superficiality. If I were asked now, I think I would have to say a perhaps unwarranted pessimism."

"Unwarranted? I wonder. The fact is that these have been two very difficult years for me. And the result is I really no longer expect happiness for myself... not what the young think of as happiness anyway – which is chiefly foolishness." He looked around at the garden and then beyond to the woods and fields stretching to the horizon. "We should all try to imitate Nature's pace, her tranquillity, her sense of submissiveness to time."

Marya now allowed herself a ripple of a laugh. "Oh, come, you are beginning to sound like a man of sixty, and you are not yet even forty. I'm sure there's a little bit of foolishness left in you yet."

Turgenev gave her a keen glance. Did she know about his decision to go to France? Probably. Very little remained secret in their environment. But he responded to her touch of humour with a shaft of his own. "Of course, we're all wise when we talk; but the moment our nostrils catch a scent of some intriguing piece of folly, off we go in pursuit of it."

She stopped to let that sink in and then, without lifting her eyes to his face, poked the stones in the path they were walking down with the tip of her parasol and murmured: "I hope you find what you are looking for in Paris."

He heaved a deep sigh, of which he was probably unconscious, but she was certainly aware. "Do we ever find what we are looking for?", he finally asked.

A veil of melancholy clouded Marya's habitually clear gaze. "I suppose we think we do," she answered. "But then we discover that it isn't what we imagined it would be, so we start looking all over again."

Turgenev impulsively reached out and put his hands on her shoulders. "Marya Nikolayevna…" he began but she did not let him finish. She laid a finger on his lips, then took down his hands and held them in her own. The eyes which looked steadily into his had now regained their customary candour. "Nevertheless," she repeated, "I hope you find what you are looking for in Paris."

They walked back to rejoin the other two, who were just about to sit down to a late lunch. Leo Tolstoy was refilling a large tankard with *kvass* and seemed in boisterous good humour. He eyed his sister and Turgenev as they sat down at the table and made a rather gross comment on how long it took some people to admire a rose.

Marya gave her brother a cool glance and remarked that they had had other things to talk about.

"I have no doubt that you had," Tolstoy said. "What would it have been now? The use of the rose as a literary symbol, from Virgil to Victor Hugo?" He turned to his cousin. "You know, Valerian Petrovich, if I were you I should keep an eye on this Turgenev. Inside that well-groomed salon dandy lurks a hidden tiger ready at any moment to spring into action. And Masha has always had a yearning to play the sacrificial lamb."

Valerian's only response was a nondescript smile, but Turgenev's lips tightened in suppressed anger. Marya seemed quite unmoved; she helped herself from a dish of vegetables and remarked to her brother that as he was no longer a serving soldier, he should have learnt to leave barrack room conversation behind. This in turn irritated Tolstoy, who sarcastically begged pardon for his rough tongue. "It may take me a little while," he said, "before I can manage to spend half an hour dissecting a line of Pushkin with the precious subtlety of Ivan Sergeyevich and his friends."

Sensitive to his position as guest in another's house, Turgenev ignored the provocation and abruptly changed the subject by asking the two men what they had been talking about. The other Tolstoy, happy to defuse the situation, told them that he and his cousin had agreed that discontent among the serfs was spreading rapidly and immediate action had to be taken. "I have convinced Lev Nikolayevich to address the government directly."

"Someone has to take this matter in hand," Leo Tolstoy said." Otherwise, like everything else in Russia, nothing will ever get done. I'm going to write to Bludov, who's a minister and whose family I know. I'm going to tell him that if some precise legislation is not implemented in the next six months, a conflagration could break out which would destroy our whole society. They have four precise questions to answer: How much land will each peasant receive? What will be the landowner's compensation? What form – rent or government grant – will this compensation take? And over what period of time will it be paid? I shall write this letter from Yasnaya this evening." He turned to Turgenev. "And it would do no harm, Ivan Sergeyevich, if you did something similar yourself."

Turgenev's eyes wandered to some far corner of the ceiling. He seemed to be searching for inspiration, and soon found it. "I don't think it would serve your cause, Lev Nikolayevich. You must remember that I am under surveillance as a dangerous man with a criminal past. There may be a new Czar, but the commission appointed to look into the emancipation question is presided over by Count Orlov. My signature on a piece of paper would be enough to delay the whole process by ten years."

"I think you rather overestimate your importance," Tolstoy remarked gruffly.

"Perhaps I do. But I don't think it's a chance worth taking."

Marya now intervened. "You forget, Lyovochka, that you have been away from the centres of power for over five years. Ivan Sergeyevich knows more about these matters than you do."

Turgenev tried to signal with his eyes that this was not the right tack, but it was too late. For all that she was his dearly loved sister, she might as well have been a picador goading an already irascible bull. "I am sure," he said, carefully articulating every syllable, "that Ivan Sergeyevich knows more about these matters than I do. But then Ivan Sergeyevich is also *above* such matters. Ivan Sergeyevich believes that an artist should not sully his hands with such grubby practical considerations, does he not?"

Turgenev could no longer conceal his anger. "No, he does not," he said. "I do not believe that it is in the capacity of art to change the face of the world. That does not mean that I deny to the artist *as a man* the right, indeed the duty, to protest against injustice and to strive to combat it. It is just that I do not consider the move that you suggest to be the right one for me at this time. Especially," he added rather lamely, "as I shall be leaving for Paris in a matter of weeks."

Tolstoy leapt on this. "Ah yes, I had forgotten," he crowed. "And Paris is of course the best place from which to resolve the problems of Russia!"

This was enough for Turgenev. He rose to his feet, insisted that he must be getting home, thanked his hosts, gave Tolstoy a curt bow, and stalked out of the room, leaving Leo Tolstoy very pleased with Leo Tolstoy, Marya Tolstoy very angry with Leo Tolstoy and Valerian Tolstoy quite pleased with Leo and quite angry with Marya.

On 21 July, six years to the month after disembarking from the Stettin-St Petersburg steamship, Turgenev set out on the return journey. He had come back to his native land with a heavy heart. But, contrary to what he would have thought at the time, he didn't leave it with a light one.

Not, at least, until his first night at sea…

On his way to St Petersburg, he had spent two days with Botkin at Kuntsevo, just south of Moscow, where he followed his friend's suggestions and made a few changes to *Faust*. He then went on to join Nekrasov and Panaev at Oranienbaum, where he hardly left the house for fear of meeting someone from his cousin's circle. Nekrasov teased him that he was reviled locally as an 'unscrupulous seducer', but Turgenev, who was usually the first to laugh at his friends' jokes at his expense, looked so forlorn that Nekrasov had to admit that it was only his malicious invention.

On the second day Turgenev's spirits were temporarily lifted when he spent the afternoon reading *Faust* to his hosts. Both the editors were lavish in their praise and Nekrasov declared it the best thing he'd done. Panaev, after promising he'd publish it before the year was out, gave Nekrasov a wry glance and said: "I wonder what Chernyshevsky will think of it."

Turgenev looked puzzled. "Why should it matter?" he asked.

"At the moment, it doesn't," Nekrasov replied with a smile. "But we've decided to make him a sub-editor – partly to make up for your absence, as a matter of fact – so from now on he'll have something to say about what we publish. But not too much, for the time being."

Turgenev had only met Nikolai Chernyshevsky, a young contributor to *Sovremennik,* once or twice, but had formed a high opinion of him. "You've made a good choice," he told them. "I read that treatise he wrote on aesthetics. I didn't agree with everything he said, of course, but he has a penetrating mind."

Nekrasov laughed. "You may find it penetrates a bit too far for your taste. He's beginning to go even further than Belinski at his most Grand Inquisitorial in condemning all art that doesn't have a social purpose. I can see the two of you coming to loggerheads one of these days."

Turgenev murmured something to the effect that on a paper like *Sovremennik* there should room for broad differences of opinion and then gazed sadly at his companions and lamented how much he was going to miss them and their little world.

"Don't tell me you're having doubts again!" Nekrasov made no effort to hide his impatience.

"I swear to you that if it wasn't for my daughter, I would tear up my ticket and spend the rest of the summer here with you all in Oranienbaum. How happy we were two years ago! Perhaps even Olga and her family would forgive me. Or perhaps she and I might…" His voice tailed off and he relapsed into a broody silence which even the quick-witted Nekrasov was at a loss to know how to break. He eventually fell back on platitude and remarked that, if the worst came to the worst, he could always spend a month or two with his daughter and then return. "You'll see, Vanichka, you'll be back in Peter carving turkey for us before the year is out…"

Turgenev shook his head with a weary smile, but not even his mercurial friend could lighten the gloom that still enveloped him as he walked across the gangplank to board the SS *Morgenstern,* which plied between St Petersburg and Stettin. As soon as he was on board, even before being shown to his cabin, he leaned on the guard-rail, gazed disconsolately down at the docks and over towards the city and shook his head in disbelief. Was it only six years ago that, with his elbows resting on the self-same guard-rail, he had looked down into Diane's mournful brown eyes and, with a lump in his throat, offered up a prayer that within no more than a year or two they would both be making the return journey? And here he was, finally embarked, and the lump was back again. *Only one explanation: those six years had marked the passage from youth to middle age. Youth is above all hope; endless possibilities stretch ahead, and if all of them will not lead to happiness, well… most of them will. But by forty this is reversed: costs are counted, traps anticipated, setbacks guaranteed…*

After he had arranged his things in his cabin and eaten an indigestible meal with the captain, who claimed to be a great admirer of his work (though after only the briefest of exchanges, it became clear that at most he might have read a couple of the *Sketches*), he went up on deck to breathe the night air, which he hoped might induce the sleep that he foresaw eluding him. And then… was it the warm summer night, was it the diamond brilliance of the stars, the harsh, monotonous cry of the seagulls, the acrid smell of smoke from the funnel, the rhythmic sway of the deck beneath his feet, transmitting through every fibre of his body the pulsing, irregular motion of the sea?… the years peeled away as though an invisible hand had stripped him naked and he was the young man of twenty, bound for the University of Berlin, thrilled by the adventure of standing alone in the prow of a ship which was taking him out of the reach of his mother's tentacles towards a future of incalculable promise. *I'm off again, and I feel buoyant, transparent, weightless… I know I shouldn't be going, I'm leaving behind duties and responsibilities which, if the truth be told, I'm ready to shake off with the insouciance of a spaniel splattering the air with a thousand drops as he emerges from a river… I'm in search of love again, my love, my one love. And if she rejects me? Well, perhaps I prefer rejection by her to adoration from any other woman. And at least I know there is one person who will greet me with unfeigned pleasure… and that poses a tantalizing question; who will be the happier to see me, big Pauline or little Pauline?…*

W hen Turgenev arrived in Paris he found a note from the Viardots saying they were in London until the following week and inviting him, as soon as they returned, to join them at Courtavenel. The next afternoon he went to Paulinette's *pension* without alerting the *directrice*. Madame Harang was at first not too pleased by this unannounced visit; but Turgenev, instinctively sensing the humanity beneath the conventionally severe appearance and manner of her trade, took an immediate liking to her and had little difficulty in charming her out of her pique.

"You will understand, madame, that after six years, I can't resist giving her a surprise. But perhaps she is already expecting me?"

"She has talked about nothing else for days, monsieur. I have never seen her so excited; she is usually an undemonstrative young lady, almost too much so, I sometimes feel. But she wasn't sure of the exact day, so it will be a surprise just the same. If you will be so good as to follow me, I will take you to her. I believe she's practising the piano just now. There was a piece she wanted to perfect before your arrival. But I'm afraid she'll have any old clothes on; I would have liked, the first time you saw her, for her to have been looking her best."

Turgenev assured her that that was of no importance and followed her out of the room. They walked down a number of corridors, passing doors muffling the sound of girlish chatter and laughter. A pupil, tearing round a corner and nearly bumping into them, pulled herself up, bobbed a slight curtsey, muttered an '*Excusez-moi, madame*' and continued more circumspectly on her way. Turgenev was gratified to discover that his daughter had not been immured in one of the virtual institutions of correction that Cassandra-like acquaintances had told him about. Eventually they came to a door behind which could be heard the unmistakable sounds of the *Pathétique* sonata. Mme Harang had her hand on the doorknob, but Turgenev restrained her and put a finger to his lips. The third movement was being played, for a while quite competently; but during a rapid downrushing staccato scale passage for the left hand things went amiss, and a jarring discord, unsanctioned by Beethoven, was followed by an explosive howl of frustration. Turgenev smiled at his companion. "It's not as easy as it sounds", he remarked. "Shall we go in now?" The pianist had gone back a few bars to try again and did not hear the door open and her unsuspected audience slip into the room. Mme Harang waited until another, more minor mistake, brought a brief pause and then said quietly: "Paulinette!"

The girl who was playing gave a start and whipped round in her chair; when she saw who was standing beside the *directrice*, her face flushed a deep crimson and she uttered a strangled "Papa!" This was followed by a bellowed "Papaaaa!" and she hurled herself across the room and into Turgenev's arms, practically knocking him off his feet. Turgenev, touched but a little embarrassed by this rapturous reception, stroked her hair and smiled at Mme Harang, who tactfully slipped out of the room to leave father and daughter alone. Instinctively, Turgenev's first words came out in Russian, but Paulinette shook her head: "I hardly understand a word of Russian any more, Papa. I'm sorry."

"You don't have to be sorry. I don't mind at all. I... I... oh, my dearest girl, I don't know what to say. You're so changed. I was expecting it, of course, in my head, but to see you transformed into this young lady... it's left me speechless. I tell you what, you talk to me for a bit while I recover. Tell me about yourself, your studies, your friends, your hobbies, and give me a little time to come back to my senses."

And so she did, but Turgenev took in very little of what she was saying. He kept his eyes on hers, seemingly attentive, but a multitude of images raced through his mind... *she's almost as much a stranger to me as when I first saw her at the Spasskoye gate, if I'd passed her in the street I'd never have recognized her, she's charming but won't be a beauty, the resemblance to me is still striking though, the same broad Slav forehead, the same strong 'Orel nose', you could wander the Paris streets for hours and never see its twin... she's tall for her age and is going to have a good figure, there shouldn't be any problem in finding her a husband when the time comes... but don't be ridiculous, she's only fourteen, for heaven's sake!... her voice is low and pleasant, even though she's so excited at the moment, and her French is excellent, you'd never believe it from the way she writes it...*

"... and the Herring's all right"... a little giggle... "That's what we call her when her back is turned. She's awfully strict, but if she's pleased with our work she gives us little rewards, takes us to the theatre, that sort of thing... But now I want to hear about you, Papa. How was your journey? You must be terribly tired."

Turgenev promised he'd tell her everything in good time: "We're going to be seeing a lot of each other, Paulinette, we'll have all the time in the world to talk. In fact, I must leave you now – I have to change for dinner with some friends – but first I want to give you an exciting piece of news: you start your holidays next week, and we've been invited to Courtavenel to spend August and September there with Monsieur and Madame Viardot. And you'll be able to see Louise again and the two little girls, who sound like the dearest things... Won't that make a marvellous summer holiday?"

Paulinette replied with a smile and a "Yes, Papa," but no great show of enthusiasm; and she followed it with: "but we will be able to be alone a bit too, won't we? The Viardots are very kind to me, but I haven't seen you for so long and I'd love it if we could do things together sometimes, just the two of us."

Turgenev assured her that they would, and then asked her, before he left, to play the famous *adagio cantabile* of the sonata. She dutifully went back to the piano and played it through, every note in the right place, he granted, but without much feeling. *All right, she's not going to be an extraordinary pianist, but she will have a lot of other qualities. I'm really very pleased with these first impressions...*

But the first impressions he was waiting with long pent-up anguish to gauge were those awaiting him at Courtavenel; and here again the reality exceeded his most optimistic expectations. As the carriage containing him and Paulinette crossed the moat and drew up in front of the familiar facade, he saw that the whole family was waiting for him, some sitting on the semicircular flight of steps that led up to the front door, others scattered around on the lawn. As soon as he alighted, Pauline tripped down the steps, her eyes sparkling with delight, and kissed him on both cheeks; then she took his hands in hers, stood back to get a better look at him and exclaimed with the most artless sincerity: "Welcome, dearest Ivan. Welcome back!" Louis then came up and shook his hand as though he never wanted to let go of it. Pauline welcomed Paulinette with an affectionate kiss, as Turgenev greeted Louise: "I thought I was going to pick you up in my arms and toss you in the air as I used to do, but you're too big for that now." As he turned to examine the two little girls he had never seen before, Claudie and Marianne, five and three, each clinging on to their nursemaid's hands, the habitual observer in him, even at this moment of high emotion, couldn't refrain from glimpsing out of the corner of his eye the cool, formal kiss that his daughter and Louise exchanged. But that was soon swept to the back of his mind as he was ushered into the house and began exploring the rooms he had held so accurately in his mind's eye all these years. And when he was finally shown into his old bedroom with the willow-green wallpaper, and remained there alone, he felt no shame in letting the tears course down his cheeks. He went over to the window, looked out over the smiling Brie countryside and thanked the god he didn't believe in for allowing him to return to the one place he associated with perfect happiness.

In fact, over the next several weeks, Turgenev felt he had been granted admittance to his own personal heaven. The clock seemed to have been turned back to 1847. His friendship with Louis Viardot grew in strength and depth. The older man perhaps found time beginning to lie a little heavy on his hands: the days of editing a newspaper were long gone, as were those of administering an opera house; he still managed his wife's career, but even that, given her eminence, demanded less of his energies than before. He made little secret of his bitterness about the state of France and none at all about his loathing of Mister Louis-Nap, as he called the Emperor; at times he lapsed into the mannerisms of an ageing, disillusioned and grumpy cynic. "It is hard for me to love my country," he confided to his foreign friend. "I hardly believe I belong in France any more. I have no place here, my opinions are anathema to my fellow-countrymen. I can give nothing, and I receive nothing…" But if political action was now a closed door, that gave him more time to indulge in his other two passions, hunting and literature, and no companion could better share these occupations with him than the Russian. When they weren't out with their guns and dogs, they could often be found closeted in Viardot's study, discussing plans for collaborating on translations into French of Pushkin, Gogol, and some of Turgenev's stories.

Turgenev also took great pleasure in playing with the two little girls, who could never have enough of his company. 'Didie', as Claudie was always called, and Marianne were instinctively drawn towards their mother's giant friend, who was so much more approachable than their loving but stern and rather distant father. Uncle 'Tourgel' would often play with them for an hour before their bedtime, imitating animals and their sounds, carrying them piggyback around the nursery until their screams of delight brought an anxious nanny running in and respectfully begging Turgenev 'not to get them too excited, please Monsieur, otherwise they'll never go to sleep', and above all telling them stories, which they never tired of. Sometimes, exhausted or genuinely drained of inspiration, he would tell them that he couldn't invent any more stories that evening; whereupon they would climb on the back of his chair and pound their fists against his back, screaming: "Think, Uncle Tourgel! Think!"

The evenings were true family gatherings. Often there was music: Pauline would sing, accompanied by Louise, who had inherited her mother's talent at the keyboard; sometimes the two of them would play arrangements for piano duet of Beethoven's symphonies. Paulinette, to her father's secret relief, refused to play, but would turn the pages at the piano and occasionally sing duets with Louise. The other great occupation was rehearsing and eventually putting on plays in the *Théâtre des Pommes de Terre*, a little theatre at the top of the house, complete with raised stage, curtain and footlights, which owed its name to the admission fee of one potato.

Only two disappointments occasionally cast a shadow over this, for Turgenev, otherwise idyllic existence. One was his gradual realization that he was hardly ever able to see Pauline alone. Her behaviour towards him radiated warmth and affection but, whether by design or because of her endless, round-the-clock activity – he could not be sure which – they were always in company. The other was his discovery, hard as he tried at first not to see it, that Paulinette was considered, both by the others and by herself, as an outsider: a familiar family guest, yes, but not one of them. She and Louise never played spontaneously together – indeed they shunned each other's company unless they were specifically thrown together. With Pauline, whom she resolutely refused to call *Maman*, she was on glacially good public terms, but, try as he might, Turgenev looked in vain for any evidence of real

316

affection. As the weeks went by, signs of strain appeared and he began to fear a possible explosion; ironically, the occasion was provided by an event which might, under different circumstances, have provided the chance for his daughter for once to feel really integrated into the family.

It had been decided that the main dramatic performance of the autumn would be a drastically shortened version of Racine's *Iphigénie*; Louis had been at work for several weeks cutting the play by over a half and reducing it to about an hour's playing time. Pauline and Turgenev had been responsible for the casting, and he was delighted when she suggested that Paulinette should play the lead. He had only one doubt: the part of Iphigeneia's rival, Eriphyle, could only be played by Louise, and as the two characters exchanged the most mortal of insults, with Iphigeneia usually on the receiving end, he wondered whether this might not exacerbate an already delicate situation. But as Pauline seemed quite oblivious of the problem, he kept his mouth shut. And so the following cast was decided on:

AGAMEMNON, King of Mycenae	Ivan Turgenev
CLYTEMNESTRA, his wife	Pauline Viardot
IPHIGENEIA, their daughter	Paulinette Turgenev
ERIPHYLE, daughter of Helen	Louise Viardot

Louis refused to take part, so the roles of Achilles and Ulysses were taken by two enthusiastic neighbours, whose local reputations enjoyed an impressive boost when it was heard they were about to appear on stage with 'la Viardot'! All the other parts had disappeared under Louis's rigorous pen.

Rehearsals, although enjoyable, were a serious business: Pauline was an exacting director, the chief target of her impatience being Turgenev, who was awkward on stage and not very good at remembering his lines. And gradually tensions began to emerge. The potential clash between Paulinette and Louise never materialized, since both were able happily to sink themselves into their parts, relishing such lines as…

IPHIGENEIA: You burn with desire for me to be gone…
or…
ERIPHYLE: If Fate joins me in my hate for her,
              I shall not weep alone
              Or die without vengeance…

Sublimation, *avant la lettre!*

But both Pauline and Turgenev, as the days went by, found there were moments in

317

rehearsal that were embarrassing for them personally, particularly in regards to their relationship with Paulinette. The crux came in Act II, Scene 2, between Agamemnon and Iphigeneia, when he knows he is going to have to sacrifice her and she can't understand her beloved father's cold behaviour towards her after their long separation. Here is an extract from Louis Viardot's cut-to-the-bone version of this scene…

IPHIGENEIA: Whither do you hurry, my lord?
                  What pressing errand tears you from our embraces?
                  To what must I attribute this sudden flight?
                  After the Queen's transports of elation,
                  May not my respects detain you for a moment?
                  May not my joy explode before your eyes?
                  May I not…

AGAMEMNON: Very well, my daughter, embrace your father.
                  He loves you still.

IPHIGENEIA: What rapture to be the daughter of such a father!

AGAMEMNON: You merit one more fortunate.

IPHIGENEIA: All Greece regards you with reverence and love.
                  To what greater fortune can a king aspire?

AGAMEMNON: Kings sustain burdens you know not of.

IPHIGENEIA: My lord, forget your rank when you're with me.
                  A long separation awaits us. Can you not
                  Bring yourself for one moment to be just a father?

AGAMEMNON: For some time now the gods have been cruel to me.

IPHIGENEIA: I hear Calchas is preparing a solemn sacrifice.
                  Will it be offered soon?

AGAMEMNON: Sooner than I would wish.

IPHIGENEIA: Will I be allowed to attend?

AGAMEMNON: *(aside)* Alas!

IPHIGENEIA: You do not answer.

AGAMEMNON: You will be there, my daughter. Goodbye.

With its cruel dramatic irony, this is one of the finest scenes in the play; but given the personal circumstances of the actors, it was a minefield. Pauline was unhappy about a daughter talking about her mother's 'transports of elation' (wasn't there a suggestion of an exaggerated 'show' of affection in greeting her 'husband' after a long separation, as compared to the daughter's more dignified – and more sincere? – 'respects'?). And Turgenev felt uneasy when his daughter gazed directly into his eyes and asked: 'Can you not bring yourself for one moment to be just a father?'

He would have done nothing about it, but Pauline, noticing that Paulinette was putting more and more emphasis on these lines, and other similar ones which could refer to her own particular position, finally decided to put her foot down and asked her, the day before the dress rehearsal, to cut both the 'transports of elation' and 'just a father' lines, along with several others. The reason she gave was that the play was running too long and a few cuts were necessary to avoid overstraining the audience's patience. But Paulinette was not fooled for an instant and asked, a little defiantly, why it was only her part that had to be cut?

"You're playing the lead, my dear," Pauline pointed out gently. "It's only natural that the longest part should be the one to be shortened."

"But it's so difficult to change things at the last moment," Paulinette moaned. "It's going to confuse me completely, and I've taken so much trouble to learn my lines." This was no less than the truth: she and Pauline were the only members of the cast who did not have frequent recourse to Louis's heavily whispered interventions from the prompter's box. But Pauline was adamant, and Paulinette seemed to have no choice but sulkily to obey.

But on the night of the performance, which took place before an audience largely composed of distinguished friends of the Viardots who had come all the way from Paris, Turgenev was reminded, for the first time since his arrival, of the stubborn determination of his illegitimate daughter. At first, as the cast gathered on stage before the curtain went up, he was taken by surprise by a flush of parental pride at how striking Paulinette looked in the simple long white Greek tunic that Mme Garcia, who had been responsible for the costumes, had run up for her. With her tall, slim figure and confident, poised carriage, her hair swept back from her high wide forehead and kept in place by a broad gold band, she looked everyone's idea of a classical Greek heroine, in unavoidable contrast to the – no doubt historically more authentic – shorter, more Mediterranean figures cut by Pauline and Louise. She negotiated her early scenes with grace and ease, but when she reached the confrontation with her father, he was startled to see that she put back every line that she had dutifully omitted during the dress rehearsal. And when it came to saying, 'Can you not bring yourself for one moment to be just a father?', it was delivered to him with such intensity that he completely forgot his next line and had to glare at Louis in mute desperation.

The performance was a great success, the audience applauded with un-Parisian enthusiasm and naturally nothing was said during the lavish supper the Viardots had laid on for their eminent guests. But the next morning, a tense Pauline took Turgenev aside and, in one of their rare tête-à-têtes (and one which Turgenev could very well have done without) demanded that he speak severely to his daughter about her disobedience.

Turgenev tried to minimize. "But surely it's nothing to make a great fuss about.

It didn't make any difference. And anyway, it may not have been deliberate."

"Of course it was deliberate." Pauline was in no mood for charitable interpretations. "Perhaps it's time I spoke frankly to you about her, Ivan. She's a dear girl in many ways, but at times she can be very difficult. I must tell you that when I decided to send her to a *pension* it was not only because, as I wrote to you, I thought it was best for her. It was also because she was becoming a quite destructive element in the family."

"Destructive?!" Turgenev looked surprised and upset, but there was no comfort in store for him.

"I'm afraid so. When she wants to get her way nothing will deter her – a characteristic she certainly hasn't inherited from you! And if she's thwarted, she can become really quite unpleasant. It hasn't been easy for me, as I'm not her mother, but now that you are here, you really must speak to her and try to get her to be a little less self-centred. Otherwise she's storing up a lot of unhappiness for herself... and others."

Turgenev promised to do his best and, knowing that the iron unstruck would cool very rapidly, went straight to Paulinette's room, where he found her sitting in a chair by the window reading. When she saw him she jumped up and looked so pleased to see him that he was quite unable to come straight to the point. He started by congratulating her again on her performance, which he had, in fact, found surprisingly good.

Her face lit up. "Do you really mean it, Papa? Or are you just saying it because you're my father?"

"No, no, I mean it. Absolutely."

"Oh, I'm so glad. I was beginning to wonder if I'd been just terrible."

"How could you think that? After all the applause and everybody congratulating you afterwards..."

"Everybody but Madame Viardot."

"Didn't she...?"

"She didn't say a word to me."

"Oh." *This has got to be my cue.* "Well, I'm afraid she was a little upset with you."

"Why?" *Ingenuity or defiance?*

"You must know why, Paulinette. You put back all those lines she'd asked you to cut."

"Yes, I did." *Defiance, then.*

"Let me ask you something. Did you do it on purpose, or..."

"Yes." *Well, she's not a liar, anyway.*

"Why?"

"Because they were important to the part. Leaving them out weakened the scene."

Artistic integrity! How am I going to answer that?!"

"If you felt that strongly about it, you should have reasoned with her."

"Reasoned with Madame Viardot?!" A sardonic laugh.

"Now don't be rude, Paulinette. You know very well there's no one in the world with more experience in the theatre than she. Don't you think she should know what's best?"

The grey eyes bored into his, just as they had at that moment on stage. "Papa! Do you really think I don't know why those lines were cut?"

Now what am I to do. Lie myself?!

"That's none of your business. Madame Viardot decided they should be, and she's an adult and you're a young girl. Besides, she was the director. It was your job to do as you were told. Now…" *it's time to cut this short…* "I want you to go to her and tell her you're sorry. I'm sure she'll be happy to accept your apology, and then we can all forget about this silly little episode. Will you do that for me?"

She lowered her head, and for a moment he thought she was going to burst into tears. Then she looked up at him and said, simply: "Yes, Papa."

"There's a good girl." He gave her a warm hug and was about to leave the room, thankful that an ungrateful task had been accomplished; but she kept hold of his sleeve, and with downcast eyes asked timidly if he minded if she asked him something.

"No, of course not." *What now?*

"How much longer will we be staying here at Courtavenel?"

Pretend to be surprised. "Why do you ask that? You surely can't mean that you're not happy here?!"

Her eyes evaded his. "Oh, I'm happy enough. It's just that… well, we seem to see so little of each other."

"But, Paulinette, we see each other every day. And usually, if I don't go hunting, all day."

"Yes, I know. But always with other people. I wondered if… I mean… couldn't we, before I go back to school, spend a few days in Paris together. Then you could show me all those things you know so much about and teach me how to appreciate them; we could go to museums and concerts and theatres together."

"We'll do that in the winter, my little one. I can't think of anything I'd enjoy more. And I'm very happy that you asked me. But while the good weather lasts, with all this wonderful countryside around us, it would be a shame to waste it in a crowded, dirty city. Don't you think?"

"I suppose so." *Which means, of course, "No, I don't". Poor little thing, she's lonely, she'd been waiting with huge excitement for my arrival, and the way it's worked out has been a great disappointment to her. I'd better communicate to her now the plan I've been mulling over in my mind. I meant to wait until I'd discussed it with Pauline, but she looks so miserable…*

321

He sat down and took her on his knee. "Now, I'm going to let you into a secret. I don't want you to tell anyone else about it until I say so. It must remain between us, agreed?"

"Yes, Papa."

"When we get back to Paris, I'm going to look around for an apartment for the two of us… and possibly a governess to help look after you. That way, on Sundays and during your holidays, we can be together and do all those things you were talking about. How do you feel about that?"

She squirmed round in his lap, threw her arms around his neck and pressed her lips to his cheek. "Oh, that will be wonderful, Papa. I can't wait, I can't wait…" and she bounced off his knees, clapped her hands and did an excited little dance on the floor.

"But you must remember, when I work I mustn't be disturbed."

"Of course not. You're a famous writer, Mme Viardot told me so, and you need to spend a lot of time alone. Whenever you're working, I won't make a sound. I promise."

"There's a good girl. I'll leave you now. But remember, for the time being it's our secret…"

The next day Pauline drew Turgenev aside and suggested the two of them go for a walk in the garden. It was an unusually warm autumn day, and they soon settled down on a bench under a chestnut tree that Turgenev, on his first visit to Courtavenel, had named *Hermann* after Goethe's epic poem (he had always meant to find a *Dorothea* to plant next to it, but the opportunity had never arisen). Pauline laid a hand on his sleeve and gave him a grateful smile. "Thank you, Ivan," she said, with the familiar tilt of her right shoulder which had always melted his heart. "Paulinette came and apologized so sweetly to me this morning. I really think the dear little thing was very sorry for what she had done."

"I know she was."

"Anyway, it's all over and done with now. I really thought, by the way, that she was very good as Iphigeneia. She seems to have a feel for acting. Perhaps we should see if Mme Harang could take her to the theatre from time to time."

"She does, once in a while, as a reward for her best pupils."

"Really? That's funny, Paulinette never mentioned it."

"But of course it's not very often. I shall be able to take her myself more regularly now."

Pauline seemed surprised. "Well, yes… regularly as long as you're here. But I meant… the older she gets…"

"I may be here for longer than you think."

"What do you mean, Ivan?" Was there a touch of hardness in her tone?

"Well, how long did you think I was staying in France?"

"I don't know. We never discussed it. Two or three months, I suppose. Perhaps until the spring…"

"That was my original intention… insofar as I had one. But I've changed my mind over the past few weeks. I've decided to take an apartment in Paris, work here and keep an eye on Paulinette."

"And never go back to Russia?!" The hardness had given way to something approaching panic.

"Never?! Of course not. I shall always be going back to Russia. But for the time being, I mean to make Paris my principal place of residence."

There was a short silence, then Pauline muttered: "But you've always said you don't like Paris."

"In many ways I don't. But perhaps once I live there I shall see it differently."

She jumped to her feet and began to walk away, agitatedly twirling her parasol. Turgenev followed her, bewildered by her attitude. "You obviously don't approve," he stammered.

For a moment she didn't answer him, but walked rapidly on, her lips pressed tight together. Then she stopped abruptly and turned to face him. "It's not for me to approve or not approve of what you decide to do, Ivan. But I can't help wondering if your decision is wise."

"Why should it not be wise?"

"Wouldn't you be turning your back on your career? Wouldn't you be trampling on the success which is finally coming your way?"

"I can still write in Paris."

"Oh yes. And I could still sing in Guadeloupe!"

Turgenev shook his head. "You're beginning to sound like Annenkov," he said mournfully.

"Am I? I'm glad. He's another one who knows you and loves you."

They walked on in silence until they came to a low stone wall on which they propped their elbows and leant, gazing thoughtfully over the patchwork green and gold of the autumnal countryside. It was Turgenev who forced himself to speak first. "You must understand, Pauline. I've just found my daughter again. It won't be easy for either of us, but I think she needs me. I can't just walk away from her after all this time."

She shrugged her shoulders. "She's thirteen, you know. If anything, it was seven years ago that she needed you. But then you weren't able to look after her…" He started to protest, but she silenced him. "That was not meant as a reproach, just an observation… to illustrate that now she has had time to settle down and is turning out very well. She has her faults, of course, as I've told you. But so does Louise. What I'm trying to say is, her life has been steered into a regular channel: she still has her schooling to finish, she's getting on well at Mme Harang's, and she can spend her holidays with us here or in Paris. What I'm afraid of is you may be making a great personal sacrifice in order to introduce a whole new element into her life which may prove more upsetting than stabilizing."

"So you think I should just abandon her again?"

"Oh, 'abandon'! It's not like you to use these big words. You stay with her for a month or two, you write to her regularly and you come and see her every now and then. In the meantime, you meet your obligations to your talent, and to your country, by – you'll forgive me being so frank – going back where you belong."

Turgenev shook his head in disbelief. "If I didn't know better – or perhaps even if I did – I would say you were trying to get rid of me."

This brought a flush to her cheeks, but the protagonist of so many melodramas did not miss her cue. "Perhaps I am, Ivan. Perhaps I am. But only in your own best interests. After all, apart from Paulinette, what does Paris have to offer you?"

He needed only a second to find the courage to reply: "You."

She sighed, then straightened up, turned round and leaned back against the wall. "I was afraid that was where we were going to arrive. Now listen to me. It's hard to describe how… content I've felt these past few weeks… as though a hole in my life had been filled in. I've been so happy to see you…"

He couldn't help interpolating, "We have hardly seen each other at all."

She gazed at him, close to despair. "What did you expect? Surely I don't have to remind you again. We are not twenty any more. And six years cannot just be erased as though they had been a forty-minute interval between acts. We are people in the public eye. We have families. You talk about doing what is best for your daughter. What favour would it be doing her if she thought we were anything but dear friends?"

Turgenev couldn't help muttering, "Who knows what she thinks?"

"She may think whatever she likes, as long as we don't give her any genuine cause for grievance. At any rate, you now know my opinion. You will of course do whatever you think best, but I firmly believe, for your own sake, you should go back to Russia before the winter is over. And now we'd better be getting back to the house, or they'll begin to wonder what happened to us…"

A few days later Turgenev took his daughter up to Paris and, while he left her with his friends, the Trubetskoys, went in search of a suitable apartment to rent, which he soon found at 210, rue de Rivoli. During the ten days before she started school again, he tried to do as she'd asked and take her round the museums and concert halls. But he soon discovered he was not a very good cicerone for an almost totally ignorant schoolgirl: he either wrongly assumed she knew some of the essential background and ended up talking over her head; or took it that she knew nothing at all and seemed to be talking down to her ('Jacques Louis David was court painter to Napoleon Bonaparte, who was Emperor of France at the beginning of the century.' 'I know <u>that</u>, Papa!'). After a few excursions, he was secretly rather relieved when she often expressed a preference for going to tea parties at the houses of her school friends.

Soon after, the Viardots left Courtavenel and moved up to their house on rue de Douai. Pauline had no engagements at the opera for that season but had been booked for a number of concert appearances. For once she had some time to herself, but the friend who reaped the benefit from this rare availability was not Turgenev but the painter, Ary Scheffer, whose house and studio were in rue Chaptal, only a few minutes' walk from rue de Douai. Hearing that his wife had died early that autumn, she paid him a visit of consolation the day after she arrived back in Paris. As she was leaving, he begged her to come and see him often, and soon rarely a day passed that she didn't spend an hour or two with him.

She had known Scheffer as long as she had known her husband, and had had her portrait painted by him at nineteen, immediately after her marriage. Louis liked to tell the tale of how, after first introducing his then fiancée to the artist, he later asked him his opinion of her. Scheffer replied that she was fearfully ugly, but half-seriously begged his friend to keep them apart, otherwise he would indubitably fall in love with her. This turned out to be less of a joke than he had intended, but he kept his passion well hidden for sixteen years.

Born in Holland, Ary Scheffer had lived and worked in France since 1811. For many years his small, exquisite house at 16, rue Chaptal had been a meeting-place for the most talented men and women of Paris and as often as not his *soirées* ended with music. Having sired in his youth an illegitimate daughter, whom he doted on, he had finally, at fifty-five, married a widow. He had been fond of, if never in love with, his wife, but she had been the victim of poor health, and the last years had been clouded by illness and suffering. This had enhanced his misanthropic tendencies, and he had recently become something of a recluse, confining his social life to a very few close friends. Pauline, quite unaware of his never-wavering love for her, had always valued him as a wise counsellor; it was largely on his insistence that she had so drastically reduced her correspondence with Turgenev during the years he was in Russia.

Although the initial reason for her frequent visits to rue Chaptal was to comfort him in his bereavement, the roles were soon reversed: she began to treat him as a lay father confessor, pouring into his ever-sympathetic ear the troubles she could confide in no one else now that George Sand could rarely be persuaded to leave her beloved Nohant. For his part, Scheffer found a certain relief from his sense of loss at being able to indulge his partiality for imparting stern but affectionate moral guidance; and he was probably not averse to dwelling on the disadvantages to

Pauline of an affair with a man so much younger and more attractive than himself.

No one who had seen the confident, smiling, revered mistress of Courtavenel during those summer months could have guessed that Pauline was experiencing the first real crisis of her adult life. The reappearance of Turgenev had rekindled feelings which had lain dormant for six long years, coinciding as it did with a period when her professional life was less time-consuming and she had occasional moments of leisure in which to take stock. Thirty-five, mother of three, with an eminence in her profession so firmly established that her problem was not what offers to accept but which to refuse, she couldn't help asking herself whether the sense of adventure that ran in her family's blood – less tempestuously than in her sister's, but there just the same – was from now on forever to be smothered. Her devotion to Louis was constant, but there were times when she found it hard not to be exasperated by his pedantry, and his ever-increasing pessimism made her aware, more than ever before, of the twenty-year gap in their ages.

One afternoon, she arrived in Scheffer's studio unannounced and found him working on the face of Jesus in a *Temptation of Christ* and therefore unable to talk. He asked her if she would play to him until he could move to another part of the huge canvas which required less concentration. She went over to the piano he kept in the smaller of his two studios and, after a moment's thought as to what would be appropriate to the work he was engaged on, started to play the mysterious *adagio molto* of the *Waldstein*; but when she reached the moment when the C major theme of the finale steals in – a passage which Turgenev always proclaimed to be one of the most magical in all music – tears filled her eyes, her throat was convulsed with sobs and she had to stop playing.

Scheffer hurried over to her and anxiously clasped her hands: "What is the matter? What is it?"

"Nothing, Ary. Just a moment's weakness. I don't even know myself…"

"I don't believe you. Come over here and sit down and tell me what's troubling you."

"No, no, you must work. I'm interrupting you. I'll go home and come again tomorrow."

"You'll do no such thing. I'm ready to take a rest anyhow." He rang for a maid and told her to bring tea, then led her over to a chair and sat down opposite her. "Now, tell me everything. I've noticed since you came back from Courtavenel that you've not been yourself. Don't hold anything back. You know you can trust me. No one, not even Louis, my oldest friend, will hear a word of what you tell me."

Pauline was about to start, but another fit of sobbing robbed her of speech. Scheffer leaned back and looked at her with quizzical sympathy, as she shook her head in disbelief, blew her nose, dried her eyes and forced a smile. "I'm sorry, I'm making a complete idiot of myself."

"There's nothing idiotic about suffering. It's Turgenev, isn't it?"

She nodded, still unsure whether she dared risk words.

"He should never have come back. I suppose he's been pestering you again."

"No, no, he's been sweetness and gentleness itself, as always. It's just that I…"

"You?"

"I seem to have learnt that I love him more than I thought. And I don't know what to do about it. All these years I succeeded, often with your help, in almost expelling him from my life. I didn't allow myself to think how much I missed him. And then I was always so busy, travelling, performing, having babies… And now, suddenly here he is again, with his charm and his devotion and his kindness and his wonderful mind and his sensitivity to music and his sense of humour and his sweetness with the children and his… oh, what can I call it?… that quality he has that means you can never be bored in his company…"

Scheffer's voice now had a slight edge to it. "Will he never be content just to accept your friendship? Not to mention that of your husband?"

"That's what I am continually telling him he must do. You should hear me! I'm so cold to him sometimes. Almost cruel. But he's like one of his beloved dogs. He puts his tail between his legs for a while and then comes back with an adoring smile on his face. Tell me what I am to do, Ary. I'm at my wits' end."

"You must see as little of him as you can, and sit it out until he leaves Paris and goes back to Russia."

"Yes, but that's just it. He's not going back to Russia. He's decided to stay. He's taking an apartment for himself and his daughter… whom I have less and less patience with (he'll probably ruin her, but that's another story). He's going to be here all the time, and I have to find a solution. I can't go on improvising for ever."

Scheffer rested his chin on his clasped hands and assumed the demeanour and tone of a judge delivering a sentence. "In that case, Pauline, your task is relatively easy. You have two quite clear alternatives: one is that you leave your husband, abandon your children, jeopardize your career and cause a scandal that will make it difficult for you to remain in Paris; the other is that you stop seeing him… or, at the very least, convince him that that is what will happen unless he is content to accept your friendship and nothing else. But my advice to you would be to break it off competely."

She gazed at him for a while with sightless eyes that can only have been looking into a future they didn't want to see. Then she asked, in a crushed whisper: "But the pain, Ary? How will I bear the pain?"

"There are antidotes."

"Antidotes!?"

"Yes, my dear, antidotes. Especially for an artist like you. And believe me, I know what I'm talking about. Above all, work. Challenging work, of the kind that you, like your sister before you, have flung yourself at all your life. Recently you've been resting on your laurels. It's time for you to break down barriers again!"

She considered this for a moment and then asked: "And what other antidotes can you prescribe?"

"Your husband. And your children. Especially Louis. I don't have to tell you how much he adores you. Perhaps after… how many years of marriage is it, fifteen?…"

"Sixteen."

"Sixteen… the risk of staleness is always there. I wouldn't know. But… how can I put this?… turn to Louis again, not just as a wife but as a woman, and *you* could find happiness in making *him* the happiest man in the world. Perhaps you might even give him a son."

"Another child! Oh no. Three is quite enough. And then…" For the first time since she had arrived she allowed herself a hint of a smile, "childbearing hardly goes with breaking down artistic barriers."

"Wouldn't you like a little boy?"

She didn't answer at first, subjecting him to a long, penetrating look. Then: "Did he ask you to say this to me?"

Scheffer also took his time to answer. He finally came out with: "Not in so many words."

She nodded, appreciating his tact, and gave a deep sigh. "Ah, Ary, what would I do without you to turn to?" She leant forward, put her hands on his knees and gazed into his eyes. "I sometimes think I depend on you more than anyone else in the world."

Only an involuntary twitch of his cheek muscles betrayed the emotion these words caused him. He cleared his throat, took her hands and rose from his chair, drawing her up with him. "Then you will forgive me if I ask you to leave now. I must get back to my painting."

As he led her to the door, he reminded her to come to a *soirée* he was giving the following week. "It will be the first since poor Francès-Sophie left me. It will be a great help to me if you can be there." She assured him that she would, and he added: "Shall I invite Turgenev too?"

She thought for a moment and then said, perhaps a little reluctantly: "Why not?"

It was a particularly large and distinguished group of guests that gathered that evening at 16, rue Chaptal, to celebrate both the resumption of Scheffer's *soirées* and the beginning of the autumn season. Knowing that Viardot avoided social events involving more than eight to ten people, Turgenev had offered to accompany Pauline, but she had said it was so near she would just walk over with her maid. As

Turgenev passed through the little gate and made his way up the path that led to the house, he noticed that both the main studio on the ground floor in front of him and the smaller, separate atelier giving off the courtyard to his left were already crammed with guests. He also realized to his dismay that, Pauline not having yet arrived, there was hardly anyone he knew there, except by sight or reputation. Rossini was sitting back in an armchair looking very old and surrounded by such a throng of admirers that he didn't feel like presuming on his one meeting with the maestro so many years ago. He recognized Berlioz by the leonine mane of hair he had often seen tossing around above the conductor's podium, and Delacroix, who had been a fellow-pupil with Scheffer at the studio of Pierre Guérin. Resisting the temptation to slip away before anyone noticed him, he went to pay his respects to Scheffer, who courteously thanked him for coming and introduced him to the man he had been conversing with, who turned out to be Daniele Manin. Turgenev was happy to meet this attractive Venetian, one of the earliest champions of Italian unity, who in 1848-9 had been President of the Venetian Republic before being compelled, after a heroic six-month siege, to capitulate to the Austrians. But before they could exchange more than a few words, Scheffer brought up a short, plump young man with the pale, delicate features of the seminarist he had once been, and introduced him as Ernest Renan, who was writing some essays for the *Revue des Deux Mondes* based on his experiences in Italy in 1849. He immediately began to bombard Manin with questions about the ill-fated republic, but, like many men of action, the Venetian, who had been answering the same questions for seven years, seemed much more interested in acquiring new, than imparting old information, and started sounding out Turgenev as to what could be expected of the new regime in Russia. Turgenev, whose admiration for Manin's reputation was only enhanced by the man's personal charm, was in the middle of expounding his hopes that the new Czar would gradually release his country from his father's stranglehold, when he happened to glance out of the window and see Pauline walking up the path. Within seconds she was surrounded by admirers and, almost without knowing what he was doing, he broke off his conversation with a muttered apology and moved off towards her.

A baffled Manin looked after him for a moment, frowned slightly and asked Renan: "Who is that man? I didn't catch his name."

Renan brushed the question aside. "I don't know... one of the crowd of Russian scribblers that you trip over all the time in Paris these days. Since the war ended, they've been migrating like wild geese. But tell me, signor Manin, when you were negotiating surrender terms with the Austrians..."

When Turgenev eventually managed to fight his way through the crowd surrounding Pauline and reach her side, which is where he felt he belonged, he found her engrossed in laughing conversation with a number of young musicians, each trying to outshine the other in dazzling the diva. On seeing him approach, she called out, "Hullo, Ivan," waved her hand in his direction, muttered his name and those of some of her companions, and then caught sight of Rossini at the far end of the room. "Ah, there's Gioacchino, I haven't seen him for ages, please excuse me," and without paying any more attention to Turgenev than to her coterie of admirers, she made her way over to the grand old man, whose tired eyes, one of which was plagued by a constant tic, lit up when he saw her coming…

As the evening wore on, it was forcibly borne in on Turgenev that, whereas at Courtavenel he was, to the Viardots' friends, practically a member of their household, here in Paris he was an unknown nobody. He drifted around aimlessly, hovering on the fringe of groups of people who all knew each other and often seemed to be continuing arguments that had begun elsewhere. He wondered whether it was his imagination, but it seemed to him that every time he got close to Pauline, she would turn away and engage someone else in conversation. Only at the end of the evening was there a small consolation. Yielding with only the most perfunctory resistance to a universal plea that she sing for them, she dragged over to the piano in the garden studio one of her previous group of admirers, who couldn't have been more than twenty and whom she introduced as Camille Saint-Saens, "A young composer whom maestro Rossini, no less, says you're all going to hear a lot of very soon." She enchanted everyone, especially the old maestro, by singing his *La regata veneziana*, three songs in which a passionate Venetian girl fiercely urges a gondolier taking her to her lover to row faster; then a couple of *mélodies* by her young accompanist; and finally, searching the audience for his tall frame, her eyes alighted on Turgenev and she announced: "And now, in honour of my old friend, Ivan Turgenev, the Russian writer, who honours us this evening with his presence, and whom I hope you've all had a chance to talk to…" And she sang, in almost faultless Russian, a song written for her by Glinka, to lyrics taken from an aubade by Pushkin.

The evening at Scheffer's atelier was, for Turgenev, like a prelude to a tragic opera, hinting at various themes that were soon to be fully developed. In writing to Botkin, he had ascribed his happiness at Courtavenel to an observation contained in a short Pushkin poem:

> 'The last flowers of the season
> Mean more to us than
> The firstborn of the fields…',

but he didn't refer to the poem's bittersweet conclusion:

330

which he would have found it hard to endorse during what he would refer to as his 'black winter' of 1856/57. The first symptom of the misery to come was a violent outbreak, four days after moving into the rue di Rivoli apartment, of an old physical problem, a neuralgic disease of the bladder. He had had a mild attack before leaving Paris six years ago, but of nothing like the virulence with which it now returned, causing frequent bouts of stabbing pain, blood and pus in his urine and even occasional incontinence. Although he had drawn up a rigorous programme for his Paris winter – work in the morning on what was to become *A Nest of Gentry*, reading and correspondence in the afternoon, dinners with friends and visits to the theatre in the evenings – he soon found he was almost incapable of writing, and much of the time the pain and embarrassment of his disease made all kinds of social life, even with his closest friends, out of the question. Fortunately Paulinette had returned to Mme Harang's, as he would have found it difficult to explain to her what was wrong with him, but impossible to conceal his suffering for any length of time. It was perhaps a mixed blessing that when Pauline Viardot paid her first – and as it turned out only – visit to the apartment on a Sunday, when Paulinette was there, it happened to be one of those rare days when he was almost free from pain.

It is a cold, sharp January afternoon and Pauline is already forty-five minutes late. Turgenev paces nervously up and down the long rectangular sitting-room, frequently consulting his watch. Eventually he goes over to the window and stands gazing moodily out at the stern bare trunks of the lime trees in Le Nôtre's Tuileries gardens, before craning his neck to try and peer down into the street. Paulinette is sitting in a chair, engrossed in a book, pointedly uninvolved in her father's agitation. When the bell rings, she barely looks up as he hurries into the hall to open the door. He greets Pauline, who is wrapped in a Siberian sable given to her in Moscow, and reaches out to help her off with it. But she only draws it tighter across her chest, shivers a little and asks if it is always this cold. "The hall, yes, I'm afraid," he admits. "I'll have to find some way of heating it. But come in here," he gestures towards the sitting-room, "there's a good hot fire."

As he ushers her in, Paulinette gets up, carefully puts a marker in her book, and bobs a minimal curtsey. Pauline kisses her on the forehead and asks how she is.

"Very well, thank you, madame. And you?"

"Oh, well enough. A little out of breath after all those stairs. Did you really have to take an apartment so high up, Ivan?"

"It's only the fourth floor." Turgenev shares a smile with his daughter. "The climb keeps us warm, doesn't it?"

"Well, that's one advantage," Pauline says. "You'd better show me everything straightaway, because then I'm going to sit by this fire and not move from it until I leave."

Turgenev leads her round the apartment, which has three bedrooms, all at the back: his own, Paulinette's and a smaller one which he intends to use as his study. After a quick look at the kitchen (which he is told needs repainting) he asks his daughter to make them tea before taking Pauline back into the sitting-room. "Well, what do you think?"

"It's very nice," she says, drawing up an armchair to the edge of the fireplace. "But a bit small, isn't it?"

"I don't think so. I'm here alone most of the time. During Paulinette's long holidays, I'll have to give up my study for the governess. But I don't mind that."

"Where will you work?"

"I'll set up a table in here. I shall probably enjoy it even more. In spring, summer and autumn, the view over the Tuileries will be superb."

"Superbly distracting, I should say. I think you would do much better to keep your study where it is, and the governess could share Paulinette's room. It's quite a good size. What do you think, my dear?", she adds as an afterthought, seeing Paulinette coming in with a tea tray.

"It depends what she's like. If Papa chooses a really nice one it would be all right, I suppose. But I do rather like having a room of my own. One sugar or two, madame?"

"One, please." She takes a sip of tea, then looks round the room, at first distractedly then with ever-increasing attention. She interrupts some inconsequential remark of Turgenev's with: "Oh dear, Ivan, I'm afraid I'm going to have to take charge here. There are several things that must be changed. That, for instance…" she points at a massive Empire table with Egyptesque ormolu mounts at the far end of the room.

"Oh, it's all right," Turgenev says, with a shrug. "I can live with it."

"It's hideous. You couldn't serve a dinner on that monstrosity."

"I shan't be serving dinners. I shall entertain in restaurants. I don't have Stepan here."

"Nevertheless, it will have to go. A simple Louis Seize table is what you need there. I'll keep my eyes open. And then you must have a piano for Paulinette."

"I agree with you there. And for you too, I hope, from time to time. I'll look into that next week."

"You must go to Diefenthal's. He has a very small shop on the Île de la Cité, but every piano there is of the highest quality. Tell him I sent you. No, come to think of it, I have to go and see him myself anyway. I'm not happy with the tuner he sent me. I'll pick a good instrument out for you."

"An upright, of course."

"Well, yes, there isn't room for anything else, is there?" Another cursory glance around the room. "And, dear Ivan, really, these paintings!"

The objects in question are an ill-matched assortment of small bust portraits of anonymous French provincial ladies and large landscapes after – a long time after – Claude Lorrain.

"Yes, they're not very beautiful, but…"

"They're dreadful! We must find something else. I know… I'll ask Ary to lend you a few of his."

"Oh no, I wouldn't want you to bother him."

"It'll be no bother. On the contrary, it could be to his advantage… give your friends an opportunity to see his work. Not everyone is prepared to go all the way to Pigalle to visit an artist's studio."

"Really, Pauline, thank you, but…"

"I won't take no for an answer. The next time I see him, I'm going to ask him."

"I would really rather you didn't."

"Stop being so stubborn!" She turns to Paulinette, who has picked up her book again. "Paulinette, tell him to stop being so stubborn."

The young girl looks up, gives the two of them an appraising glance and says: "I don't think it's for me to tell my father what to do, madame."

Pauline throws her arms in the air. "Oh, I despair of the pair of you. Here I am, offering to brighten up this rather dreary room with work of the greatest artist in Paris, and you try to refuse. What's the matter with you, Ivan?"

Turgenev draws a deep breath. "The fact is, my dear," he says slowly, "that for once, our tastes differ. Not only do I not think Scheffer is the greatest artist in Paris, I do not even – charming though he is personally – like his work very much. I find it – forgive me – cold and insipid." As this leaves Pauline temporarily speechless, he goes on: "I happened to be in Delacroix's studio not so long ago. I was thinking about it when I saw the two of them together the other evening. What a difference! What passion there! What life!"

Pauline shakes her head sorrowfully, as though in grief at her friend's blindness and, with a wave around the walls, contents herself with: "Very well, if you prefer to live with these masterpieces…" She turns again to Paulinette. "Would you be a dear girl and leave us alone for a moment. I'd like to have a few words with your father in private."

After the girl, with no pretence at reluctance, has slipped out of the room, she turns to Turgenev and says: "Well, Ivan, I have a surprise for you."

"What is that?"

"Guess!"

"Er… Meyerbeer's writing a role for you in his new opera."

"Wrong."

"Berlioz wants you for his *Trojans.*"

"Right, but that's not what I was thinking of. More personal. I do have a life as a woman as well as an artist, you know."

"I don't think you need to tell *me* that."

A momentary pause, with a hint of embarrassment, then she says simply: "I'm expecting another child."

Between astonishment at this announcement and an obscure sense of pain at its implications, it is a while before he can bring himself to stammer out the obligatory congratulations, ending with a conventional, "What exciting news!"

"Yes. It's particularly exciting for Louis of course. He's hoping very much that it will be a boy this time."

"When will we find out?"

"In July." The subject seems to have exhausted its interest. "By the way, talking of children, I have to tell you that I'm afraid I was not very taken by your latest offspring."

"I'm sorry…?"

"Your story, *Faust.*"

"Oh! You didn't like it."

"I didn't think it was really worthy of you. There are some fine things in it, of course. But you seem to lose your way towards the end."

"Can you be specific?"

"Yes, I think I can. It's particularly the last page that doesn't ring true to me. Pavel's homily to his friend about the virtues of resignation and devotion to duty seems to be stuck on him like a label by *you*. It's the author talking there, not the character. You're preaching at us a bit. That's not like you. What made you do it?"

Turgenev gives a wistful smile. "As always, you're right," he says. "I had been reading some essays of Schopenhauer, especially one on transcendental fatalism, and what he said so chimed in with my mood at the time that perhaps I transferred it undigested to the finale of my story. In a later edition I'll change it."

"I think you'd do better to move on to something else," she says, standing up and holding out her hand. "Goodbye, Ivan, I must be going. Take care of yourself. You're not looking all that well. There's nothing wrong, I hope."

"No, no, no… just a little tired perhaps."

"Well, don't work too hard and try to keep warm…" She gives an exaggerated shiver. "Easier said than done in this place!" As she leaves the room, she can't resist stopping in front of one of the paintings, shaking her head and giving him a reproving look. Then she calls to Paulinette, who comes out of her room to say a polite goodbye, and leaves.

Half an hour later, father and daughter are in a cab together on their way to take Paulinette back to Madame Harang's. Turgenev takes her hand in his, gives it an affectionate squeeze and says: "How lucky we are, are we not, to have Madame Viardot to look after us! For such a busy person, she's extraordinarily generous with her time."

There is a short silence, broken only by the creak of the carriage and the clatter of the horse's hoofs. Paulinette turns her head away and stares out of the window at the Sunday evening crowds in the streets. When he asks her rather sharply if she's heard what he said, she doesn't turn back towards him but answers: "I'm sure it's very kind of her, Papa, but…"

"But what?"

"Well, it's just that she seems to decide everything for you… as if she was your wife. But she's not your wife, she's someone else's wife, and I don't see what right she has to…"

"That's enough, Paulinette. It's not a question of right, it's a question of the goodness of her heart and her unselfish desire to be of as much help to me – and to you – as she can. Now I don't want to hear any more of that sort of talk from you."

She looks back at him and forces a smile. "I'm sorry, Papa." Then she gently releases her hand from his and resumes gazing out of the cab window.

'My only hope of salvation is to bury myself in my work,' Turgenev had written early in January to Nekrasov, who had announced that he would be coming to Paris the following month. But he was soon to discover that that hope was to prove illusory. As long as Paulinette had been with him for the Christmas holidays, he had managed to use, as an excuse to avoid regular work, his paternal duty to accompany her round Paris and introduce her to some of his Russian friends – the Trubetskoys, the Nikolai Orlovs and yet another branch of the Turgenev family – who lived there. But after she went back to school, he sat at his worktable, morning after morning, trying in vain to recapture the smooth flow of composition for his new novel that he had found in Spasskoye for *Rudin*.

The main framework of the story was as he had outlined it to Tolstoy that afternoon at Spasskoye, but all his attempts to flesh it out ended in dozens of sheets with two or three scribbled lines crumpled up and tossed into the wastepaper basket. His frequent attacks of atrocious pain rendered extended concentration impossible. The only passage of any length he managed to sketch out was a heartfelt description of the hero's disgust at the frivolity of life in Paris with his superficial and faithless wife, and his longing to return to his homeland. Nothing else he wrote seemed to him of any value, and after a while he gave it up and forced himself to write a story he had promised Druzhinin for his new journal, *The Reader's Library*.

This was, he regretfully had to admit, a return to the format of the *Sportsman's Sketches* which he had determined to leave behind him, but the mood was very different. Whereas in his early stories nature had usually been portrayed at her most beautiful and benign, in *Excursion into the Great Woods* the great coniferous forest seems to say to man: 'I have nothing to do with you. I am in command here. You just occupy yourself with not dying.' The author's pessimism and despair were reflected in the protagonist's vision of the forest as a place where '*I felt the breath of death, I sensed its continual proximity. If only a single sound had broken the silence, if only a furtive leaf had dared to rustle in the immobile abyss of the forest which surrounded me! I lowered my head, almost in fear; it was as though I had cast a glance somewhere where man was not supposed to look...*' This latest incarnation of the 'superfluous man' tells his heart, if it wants rest, *to learn the resignation of the last separation, become familiar with the bitter words 'goodbye' and 'forever'... not to look where happiness, faith and strength were, that was not our place...*

Turgenev's intention had been to end the story on a more positive note, but his illness militated against any lightening of tone: never one to minimize his maladies, he became convinced that he was suffering from gallstones, which had been the cause of his father's death. He consulted doctor after doctor, who all prescribed different remedies, the only feature in common being their inefficacy. When one of them recommended cauterization, he cancelled all his subsequent appointments. Only quinine seemed to offer some slight relief, and he drank excessive quantities of it every day. His mood was not improved when, dining with friends, a man he had not met before referred with relish to the scandal that was now titivating *le tout Paris*: Pauline's frequent visits to rue Chaptal could only be accounted for by the affair she must be having with the elderly Scheffer. Turgenev immediately made an excuse and was starting to leave, when the gossip-monger, who may well have known exactly what he was doing, asked him if he had found the news so upsetting. Turgenev replied acidly that he was not upset by the rumour, which bore every mark of malicious, envy-inspired invention; it simply disgusted him that such filth could be bandied around a dinner table in what was commonly considered the most civilized city in the world.

Although his immediate reaction in public had been to dismiss the scandal out of hand, he nevertheless, for several days, couldn't stop himself brooding over whether there might not be some atom of truth to it. *Why has she ignored me so completely after those blessed weeks at Courtavenel, where we were all as happy as trout in a sunlit stream? She has never paid another visit to rue de Rivoli, nor invited me to rue de Douai. And she certainly seemed almost to be playing hostess that evening at rue Chaptal. Is it conceivable...?*

It was in this mood of extreme dejection that one morning, shivering with cold from trying to work in his unheated study, he found himself unable to finish urinating because of the pain; he dragged himself back to his desk, failed to add a word for an hour and started to read over the ten or so pages he had written. Then he got up and opened a cupboard where he kept all his unfinished manuscripts and notebooks full of jotted-down ideas; seizing a pile at random, he picked up a pair of scissors and went into the bathroom, where he began systematically to cut the pages into shreds and stuff them into the water closet. The first extracts to go, he noticed, were some pages he had written with the vague intention of possibly completing *Two Generations*. When the bowl was sufficiently full, he poured a pitcher of water into it and watched, with grim satisfaction, as the results of so many hours of work disappeared on their way down to the Paris sewers… *This is the end of my life as a writer. I will finish* Excursion *because I have promised it to Druzhinin, but after that, no more. I have said the little I have had to say, I have no desire to continually repeat myself. I had a small poetic gift, but it has run dry. In compensation, I have gained a certain technical command of my language which I may use for collaborating with Viardot on translations of French and Spanish literature. But another line of my own? Never! Goodness, how long it takes to flush down all this trash. It would be quicker to burn it, but that might look as though I were trying to emulate Gogol…* He would have carried out his intention to destroy everything had Parisian plumbing been more robust, but after the fifth flush the pipe became completely blocked and, to add to his physical miseries, the closet was unusable for several days until he was finally able to secure the services of a plumber…

"Let us raise our glasses to the three ladies without whom we would not be sitting here: Gentlemen, I give you Avdotya Panaeva, Valerya Arsenyev and Pauline Viardot!"

The man proposing the toast was Nekrasov; the friends he was addressing were Tolstoy and Turgenev. The three of them were sitting at a window table in the Vefour, the restaurant in rue Beaujolais that occupied the site of the former café of the Palais-Royal. Turgenev had invited them there in the hope that the elegant surroundings, exquisite food and wine and the company of his compatriots would succeed, at least for an evening, in raising his spirits.

Nekrasov's ironically grateful reference to the three ladies was not unapt. He himself had come to Paris to escape from the ever more demanding attentions and ruthless ambition of his mistress. He was just about ready to sever the relationship, but the wily Avdotya never forgot the status that being the mistress of St Petersburg's most influential literary figure afforded her; she read the danger signals well, judging perfectly the moment to draw back and deploy her considerable charms whenever an outright break seemed imminent. Tolstoy, having resigned from the army, had been embroiled since the early summer with a twenty-year-old orphan, Valerya Arsenyev, who lived with an old aunt and a French companion on an estate only five miles from Yasnaya Polyana. He had blown characteristically hot and cold, one day giving her every indication that he was irresistibly in love with her, the next telling his diary she was stupid, narrow-minded and trivial. On receiving a letter in which she complained that she was bored by his continual preaching, he finally gathered the courage to break with her. But the reaction of the local gentry was so disapproving that he decided he had no choice but to flee abroad. He had arrived in Paris on 9 February, and two days later rented an apartment in a *pension* on the rue de Rivoli, two doors down from Turgenev, who had of course welcomed him with open arms. At their first meeting, he hadn't been able to resist taunting Tolstoy by referring to the last words he had heard from him: "I'm glad to see that you too find Paris the best place from which to resolve the problems of Russia." But Tolstoy, feeling perhaps a little uncertain of himself in this new country, had taken it in good part and even allowed himself a sheepish grin. By now, however, after several weeks in Paris, during which he had become one of the main repositories of Turgenev's woes, he was often his old overbearing self, and indeed at this moment was looking around the luxurious restaurant with ostentatious disapproval.

The *bon viveur* Nekrasov, on the other hand, had studied the menu with the keenest appreciation. Having finally made up his mind and given his order (Tolstoy absent-mindedly told the appalled waiter to bring him whatever he liked), he proposed his toast and then turned to Turgenev. "I mentioned your lady last, Vanichka, but perhaps I should have put her first. Lev Nikolayevich and I are trying to escape from ours. Yours, I gather, is trying to escape from you. Or is that too harsh a judgement?"

"I wish it were," Turgenev said with a grimace. "But I fear it's not."

"If I remember our talks in Oranienbaum correctly, this is not something for which you were totally unprepared."

"No," Turgenev admitted. "Deep inside, I knew before I left Russia that I should not go. But I came all the same, and fate is punishing me in the way I expected... and in a couple of ways I wasn't."

"Are you still as much in love with her as you were before?" Tolstoy asked bluntly.

Turgenev gave a bitter smile. "If she were here now and ordered me to strip naked, paint myself yellow and dance on the table, I would immediately do so. Never before has it been so clear to me that she is the only woman I have ever loved and will always continue to love."

Tolstoy and Nekrasov looked at each other in mute, who-goes-next enquiry. Tolstoy grasped the nettle. "I cannot understand that kind of love," he said. "If a woman were indifferent to me, I should quickly lose all interest in her. I have even heard a rumour that she is carrying on with someone else – some painter or other."

"That is all untrue."

"Because you know it to be, or because you want it to be?"

Turgenev hesitated for a moment. "Let us say that if I believed it, I should lose whatever remaining faith I might have that decency and nobility have a place in this world."

Tolstoy shook his head in disbelief. "How can you lay all that responsibility on the shoulders of one person – and a woman, at that?"

Nekrasov tried a more diplomatic approach. "I'm not sure how fair it is to her either. You will end up putting yourself, body and soul, into her hands. Perhaps she doesn't want that responsibility."

"I'm sure you're both right," Turgenev admitted sadly. "But there is nothing I can do about it. I have to submit to this woman's will. When I tell you I have no choice, you must believe me. She is literally more important to me than anything else in this world... my daughter, my work, my friends, everything. And this being so, I deserve what I get. Perhaps I can only be happy when a woman puts her heel on my neck and grinds my face into the mud!"

Tolstoy let out an impatient snort and threw his knife and fork down on the table. "It's time you went back to Russia, Ivan Sergeyevich. You'll waste away if you stay here. Come back with me this summer. I'll drag you away, by force if necessary, from this Paris you love so much."

"I don't love it at all. I don't even like it very much. And what's more, it's ruined my health."

Tolstoy's patience was at an end. "Then why in God's name…" he groaned, and then gave up and clutched his head in his hands.

"Why indeed, Lev Nikolayevich!" Turgenev felt he owed his friend, not only an explanation but an apology. "I can only tell you that there are days when I feel I'm decomposing in this foreign land like a frozen fish during a thaw. I'm too old not to have a nest of my own and be content to stay in it. But it seems I have condemned myself to a gypsy's life, so I shall probably never build a nest anywhere. But rest assured, I shall return to Russia one of these days, even if, in doing so, I shall be saying goodbye to my last dream of happiness."

Nekrasov took a sip of his Burgundy, held the glass up to the light, gazed at it appreciatively and then put it down and tried to tease his friend out of his misery. "It is not like you, Vanichka," he said, "to be such a bad host. You invite us to this superb restaurant and then make it impossible for us to enjoy all the delicacies they put in front of us. Instead of going home slightly drunk and full of bonhomie, Lev Nikolayevich and I will be hard put not to seal a suicide pact." Turgenev spread his hands and muttered an apology. "Fortunately," Nekrasov went on, "for us writers there is a golden rule: nothing heals the wounds of the heart like a prolonged period of work. Let me give you some good news. Chernyshevsky, who, to my surprise, is turning into a great admirer of yours, told me before I left that he had been reading your completed chapters of *Two Generations*; he is very taken with it, and told me to insist you finish it in time for publication for the Christmas issue. So there's your salvation: sit at your desk, forget Madame Viardot and complete your novel."

After Nekrasov's light-hearted recriminations, Turgenev couldn't bring himself to confess that he had determined never to write another word, and that most of *Two Generations* was now in all probability floating down the Seine; he simply nodded his head and said that, as soon as his bladder stopped tormenting him, he would try to get back to serious work. Then, anxious to steer the conversation away from himself, he asked Tolstoy how the third part of his trilogy, *Youth*, which had just been published in *Sovremennik,* had been received. "Everyone read it, but no one liked it," was the answer. "No one of the critics, at any rate…" Nekrasov started to protest, but was airily ignored. "Druzhinin, who's the only one who knows what he's talking about, indicated that I had something to say but didn't know how to say it. He's probably right. And some champion of manners and morals on the *St Petersburg News* wrote that if my protagonist was supposed to be typical of Russian youth, it was an insult to both Russia and youth!" This led Nekrasov to relate some gossipy anecdotes of St Petersburg literary life; and as, with the passing of the second bottle of wine, they became increasingly scabrous, even Turgenev's afflictions relaxed their stranglehold on him for a merciful couple of hours.

When they left the restaurant, he and Tolstoy, after hailing a *fiacre* for Nekrasov who was staying at a hotel on the Champ-de-Mars, started to walk back to the rue de Rivoli through the gardens of the Palais-Royal. As they passed under the arcade of the Comédie-Française, the tall, slim figure of a woman, dressed entirely in black, materialized from behind one of the columns and whispered, *"Bonsoir, messieurs"*. The two men threw her a cursory glance, and both took in her remarkable beauty. There was none of the vulgarity of her trade: no gaudy make-up, no exaggerated, hip-swaying walk. She might have been one of the customers of the Vefour, abandoned by her escort. An actress, Turgenev supposed, trying to supplement her meagre salary. With a pang, he couldn't help thinking that if it were not for his wretched malady... Tolstoy, after one fierce, intense glance, looked away immediately, as though his attention had been momentarily distracted by a stray dog; but he seemed unable to recapture the gist of their previous conversation, responded to his companion in monosyllables and, when they reached the door of his building, muttered that he was not ready for bed and would go on walking for a while. Turgenev tactfully didn't offer to accompany him, but wished him good night and, fighting down an absurd stab of envy, climbed the stairs to his apartment, mentally praying that he wouldn't be subjected to a torrent of anguished 'mea culpas' the following day.

As it happened, the unpredictable young count had another use for him. Their relationship had by now resumed the familiar Russian pattern: one day they might have been inseparable brothers, with no topic, however intimate, too personal to share or confide in; the next, the most seemingly anodyne opinion could threaten a permanent rift. To Turgenev's surprise, Tolstoy proved to be an indefatigable tourist: not a monument, museum or church in Paris escaped his scrutiny; he made expeditions to the surrounding châteaux, Versailles, Fontainebleau and Vaux-le-Vicomte; a morning was devoted to walking round the Père-Lachaise cemetery, the afternoon to its southern counterpart in Montparnasse; he even inspected the racecourses at Longchamp, Auteuil and St Cloud. Now deciding it was time to move further afield, he asked Turgenev if he would like to accompany him.

"I want to go to Dijon. Why don't we spend a week there together?"

"Why Dijon?"

"I had an idea the other day when I was in the Bibliothèque Nationale. It will probably come to nothing, but I might as well tell you. I've been thinking for some time of trying a long historical novel. Up to now, everything I've written has been based on my own experience. It's time I risked something else. But as I'm not

341

interested in purely imaginary work, the idea of blending an invented story with historical people and facts rather intrigues me. I was looking at some books in the library on the great Burgundian period of the 14th and 15th centuries, and just the names of the Dukes – Philip the Bold, John the Fearless, Philip the Good, Charles the Bold – the 'Grand-Dukes of the West', seemed to clamour for my attention. I want to go and look into the background. Will you come with me?"

Turgenev, who had never been to Burgundy, agreed, and the two of them set out a few days later. They stayed at a 17th century coaching inn ten minutes' walk from the centre of Dijon, and every day Tolstoy went off to explore a different aspect of the town. At first Turgenev accompanied him, but after a day or two, discouraged by the cold, drizzly weather, he preferred to spend most of the day in his room, trying to finish his story for Druzhinin. He had hoped that a change of scene would bring on a renewed enthusiasm for the work, but although his health improved and he was almost free from pain, he couldn't find a way to switch from the gloom with which the story began to a more positive, or at least less nihilistic ending. It was not until towards the end of their stay that a possible solution dawned on him, and the clue was accidentally provided by Tolstoy in the course of a dinner conversation.

They had been discussing once again the eventual emancipation of the serfs, able, it seemed, now that they were away from their country, to do so without quarrelling. Tolstoy, more ambivalent than ever (Turgenev suspected that what he really wanted was for the serfs to be freed to satisfy his conscience, without him being deprived of any of the advantages he derived from their services), was harping away on the lunacy of treating all the peasants as though they were the same. "They range from honest, hardworking, splendid fellows to the most drunken, ignorant, idle scum of the earth," he intoned. "I don't have to tell you this: your *Sketches* corroborate it on every page. But in the eyes of our myopic lawgivers, they are all identical. The result will be that the best will get the worst treatment and the worst the best. And then there are the really exceptional ones – for better or for worse. Let me tell you of a peasant I ran into just before I left. I'd heard about him for years, but he lives in the woods on the neighbouring estate and I'd never met him. He's a thief, the cleverest there's ever been. He lives off what he steals, but he's only been caught two or three times. On those rare occasions, he spent a few months in jail and then went free… when he hadn't already escaped. Everyone, but everyone, is frightened of him. They think he has the evil eye. But when he attends the rural assemblies, which he does assiduously, he's listened to in silence and his suggestions are nearly always followed. And rightly so; he's apparently far more intelligent than all the others, including the elders and headmen.

"Well, I was driving with my steward through those woods, we pulled up in a clearing and there was this Kuzya. He started speaking to Yakov on completely equal terms, if not downright cheekily. When asked why he wasn't in jail, he grinned and snapped back: 'You know as well as I do, Yashka, there are some people it's better not to keep locked up.' He went on to tell us the brigadier had begged him to quit the district, had even offered him a passport to go wherever he wished. And do you know what he said? 'I wouldn't do that to you people. After all, you'd never find another thief like me.' And he's right. Apparently, when business has been good, he invites everyone to his house to eat and drink as much as they want. He turned to me and asked me, quite politely, if I was going hunting. When I said I was, he told me to be careful, he could tell from the way the woodcock were flying there was a forest fire some twenty versts ahead. This turned out to be the exact truth. He then asked me for a tip for the information. Yakov was appalled. 'How dare you behave like this before a gentleman?' he cried and whipped up the horses. But Kuzya just called out 'Ho!' and the horses stopped. Nothing Yakov could do could get them going again. I couldn't resist throwing the fellow ten kopecks. He touched his cap, swivelled his quicksilver eyes round to Yakov and cackled with merriment. 'Learn one thing from Kuzya, Yashka,' he cried. 'If you're scared, you lose; if you dare, you win!' Another 'Ho!', which sounded identical to me, but obviously not to the horses, as they set off without as much as a flick of the reins. Yakov told me on the way home that the man is training his ten-year-old son to take after him. He put several five kopeck pieces in a pot and hid it in a large clearing. He then told the boy to find it: he wouldn't get anything to eat or be allowed back in the house until he had. And he kept his word, even though the poor devil had to spend a whole night out in the woods until he found it. Now I ask you, Ivan, if a man like that, starting from the bottom of the heap, can, relatively speaking, flourish because of the extraordinary strength and resilience of his character, what would he not do if he'd started as a free man with no social bonds to tether his ambition?"

"He'd end up like one of Ostrovsky's merchants and we'd all be hopelessly in debt to him," Turgenev replied, deliberately veering towards the facetious, as his thoughts had swerved away from emancipation towards the more immediate, if less weighty, problem of how to finish his story. It occurred to him that there might be a way of using this Kuzya. But how? The tantalizing but elusive possibility remained with him throughout the following day, when he decided to abandon Tolstoy, hire a vehicle and drive out to the little village of Gevrey-Chambertin to spend a day among the vineyards.

To his delighted surprise, the morning dawned bright and sunny and, after lunching at an inn in the village, he decided to walk off the rich meal. He struck out along a road which threaded through the geometrically perfect parallel rows of vine stems. Crossing a bridge, he paused to look down on a stream which came tumbling down from a hill crowned by a small spinney. He left the road and made his way up, remarking ruefully to himself that months of near immobility in Paris had sapped his hunter's physique. By the time he reached the spinney he was glad to stretch out on the ground by the side of the stream and catch his breath. He soon became aware that, for the first time in months, he felt utterly at peace. In the drowsy state induced by the full-bodied wine he had drunk with his lunch, he might have been back at Spasskoye, lying in a summer meadow with the warm smell of the mown hay in his nostrils. Nature, no longer the blind indifferent force that had oppressed the protagonist of *Excursion* at the beginning of his story, seemed once again like an intimate companion, murmuring wise advice: 'Rest, my friend: breathe lightly, cast off your agitation, be at one with me.' He made a half-hearted attempt to find a place for Tolstoy's Kuzya in his story. But his attention was soon diverted from any consideration of an anarchic Russian peasant by the extraordinary sight so early in the year of a dragonfly perched, motionless, on the last twig at the end of a thin branch. He couldn't have said how long it was that he watched it – twenty minutes, half an hour? – as it basked in a totally contented lethargy interrupted only by an occasional flick of its emerald green head, over half of which was taken up by huge darting eyes. Once in a while the two pairs of transparent wings, held at an angle away from the long, graceful body, would quiver slightly as though in acknowledgement of what the *demoiselle*, as the French charmingly call this miraculous insect, clearly considered a thoroughly satisfactory state of affairs.

Contentment… acceptance… this is what we should try to imitate in nature, even though it is all one to her whether we do or not. If we could only repeat this stillness, this equilibrium, how much suffering we could spare ourselves! A mysterious rhythm is its immutable law, its unshakeable foundation. Everything that departs from this mean, be it up or down, transgresses. Insects – not this one, but others – die at the sublime culminating moment of the sex act; they have aimed too high. A sick animal hides away in a thicket to die alone; it feels it no longer has the right to warm itself in the sun, to breathe the air that is common to all; in a word, it no longer has the right to live. And a man who has fallen on bad times, be it through his own fault or that of others, should at least know how to keep silent.

These thoughts continued to occupy his mind as he made his way back to the village; and gradually Tolstoy's Kuzya, unbidden by him, began to insinuate himself among them. *On my narrator's second visit to the woods – to a less forbidding section… birches, say, rather than pines – he could run into a similar character who would personify instinctual man living in harmony with indifferent nature, in contrast to the educated narrator with his moral doubts and self-lacerating dissatisfactions. While he is tormenting himself with reproaches and regrets that he has never achieved any of the fine goals he dreamed of as a young man, the other is as unconcerned about all that as my dragonfly: at ease with himself and his surroundings, he lives each day as it comes, exploiting all the opportunities he can seize without a thought for their rights or wrongs. For the narrator, the impact of meeting his opposite could*

344

be a soothing influence, putting a more positive slant on his resignation, which he could now see in the light of an acceptance of fate for good as well as for ill…

The two men decided to benefit from the unexpectedly warm, dry evening and take their last dinner before their return to Paris at a celebrated restaurant near the Gothic church of Notre-Dame in the centre of Dijon. At first they walked through the narrow cobbled streets of the old town in silence. Tolstoy's glowering manner might have indicated that the day had been marked by some setback. But Turgenev, still basking in the afterglow of his earlier sense of contentment, took no notice; he glanced appreciatively at the cross-timbered facades of the houses on either side, which brought back memories of other night-time strolls with the friends of his student years through the lime-scented towns of southern Germany. This instilled a desire for eager, open-hearted communication, which he was able to hold in check only until they had sat down for dinner. Forgetting that his brooding companion was not Bakunin or Stankevich, he dared to voice some of his afternoon's reflections. They were greeted, predictably, with withering scorn. "All you would be doing," he was told, "would be giving immorality an intellectual justification. Kuzya doesn't *represent* anything other than himself. And you can't put men and insects on the same level. Man has an immortal soul…"

"Does he?" It slipped out involuntarily, and he immediately regretted it. Tolstoy slammed his fist down on the table with such force that all the other diners turned to look curiously at the two Russians.

"When you talk like that, Ivan Sergeyevich," he raged, oblivious or indifferent to the effect he was creating, "you make me question the basis of our friendship. I don't believe you say those sorts of things out of conviction. You simply do it to provoke me. And you succeed. Your fine free-thinking phrases may make a stir on the Faubourg Saint-Germain, but they're wasted on me."

Turgenev, cursing himself for his intervention, was all conciliation. "Let us not quarrel on our last evening," he said, gently. "I had no intention of provoking you. It is just that you are lucky enough to have strong convictions, while I find it hard to be sure of anything. Never mind about your Kuzya, I probably won't use him at all. Indeed, I probably won't finish the story – or any other, for that matter. But enough of me. Did you have a satisfactory day? Do you feel you've absorbed enough of the background here to be able to begin your novel?"

"I have absorbed enough to put all thoughts of writing the novel out of my head," was the curt answer.

"But why? The idea was promising."

"I thought so too, until I went today into the *Salle des Gardes* in the Ducal Palace. I stood in the gallery looking down on the black marble tombs of John the Fearless and Philip the Bold. I gazed for half an hour at their effigies, the joined hands raised in prayer. I looked into their sightless eyes and they said to me: 'Leave us alone!' I felt annihilated by my own mediocrity. The Dukes of Burgundy are *there*. Nothing else needs to be said about them. Never have words seemed to me so futile."

Turgenev, who had brought *Youth* with him to Dijon, shook his head reproachfully. "When you speak, your words say one thing, Lev Nikolayevich; but when you write, they say another. I finished your book last night. You have a rare talent. And I tell you as a friend, you have no right to neglect it. You should curtail all your other occupations and devote your life to writing."

Tolstoy gave his familiar snort. "This comes strangely from somebody who's just said he won't write any more."

"I don't have your talent. And besides, I have done what I had to do. You're only just starting."

Tolstoy threw himself back in his chair and stared at the ceiling in silence. Then, after a heavy sigh, he said plaintively: "There must be more to life than scribbling. I do it as a hobby; from time to time it quite amuses me, but the thought of becoming like some of those St Petersburg literary men fills me with horror. They're so preoccupied with style at the expense of content. The position of a comma brings on a migraine. I write the way I write, I'm driven to dig towards the truth, but the deeper I dig, the more the truth seems to elude me. You're just the opposite, your writing is elegance personified, but I sometimes feel – don't be offended – that you're almost content to stay close to the surface, for fear of uncovering anything that might unsettle you…

These words had come back to Turgenev in Sinzig, a placid little spa on the Rhine, halfway between Bonn and Koblenz, where he had gone early in July to take a cure. He had, in fact, thought of them frequently over the peripatetic five months he had spent since leaving Dijon. His precarious sense of well-being didn't survive his return to Paris. The weather was at its February worst: leaden skies, gusty winds and driving rain often turning to sleet. He had forgotten to ask anyone to come in and light the fires while he was away, so the apartment was unbearably cold. No inquiring, let alone welcoming, message from Pauline awaited him. And within two days, he had an attack of his malady which drove him to take to his bed, under every blanket in the house, until he felt strong and free of pain enough to drag himself up. He forced himself to finish *Excursion into the Great Woods* along the lines he had mapped out in Dijon and sent it off to Druzhinin. Resolutely resisting any temptation to glance at the surviving notes for his novel, he dabbled from time to time with his 'Hamlet and Don Quixote' essay, which had won the surprising approval of Tolstoy; but it was more to fill in the empty hours than with any thought of publication. Spiritual inertia induced physical restlessness, and between early May and his arrival in Sinzig, he had been continually on the move.

In May he went to London, where he took a room in the Sablonnière Hotel in Leicester Square; but much of his time was spent in Putney, where Herzen was living. His old friend was happy to see him, but unless their conversations were conducted late at night, they were rarely able to talk without interruption for more than a few minutes at a time. The house bore more resemblance to one of the great new railway stations than to a private dwelling. The coming and going was incessant. Aleksander Herzen had just emerged from five years of debilitating dejection: the failure of the 1848 rebellions had shattered his faith in the efficacy of political revolt; and the affair between his wife and his intimate friend, Georg Herwegh, ending in Natalie's death, had put a terrible strain on his normally buoyant nature. His recovery was triggered by the news of Nicholas I's death. Everything seemed possible again: the journalistic work which recently he had been producing fitfully, more out of habit than enthusiasm, was now fired with the urgency of a crusade. The magazine he had founded, *The Pole* Star, printed in Russian and surreptitiously circulating in his homeland, had met with a certain success, but its literary slant and price of eight shillings mitigated against any possibility of widespread circulation, let alone commercial success. Recently he had received fresh stimulation with the arrival from Russia of his childhood friend, Nikolai Platonovich Ogarev, known to his intimates as 'Nick'; the two of them had been in their early teens when the Decembrist rising had been bloodily suppressed, and they had sworn a romantic oath on the Sparrow Hills outside Moscow to dedicate, and if necessary sacrifice, their lives to the struggle against tyranny. Now they were preparing a much more ambitious journal which would become *Kolokol* (*The Bell*), an exclusively political pamphlet to be published monthly at a cost of sixpence. The first issue was planned for July, and no one except Herzen seemed to believe it could ever be ready. He drove himself to exhaustion, never refusing to see anyone. And when word of the new venture began to spread, Laurel House, High Street, Putney became an essential port of call for the numerous colony of political refugees who had found in London their only permitted place of refuge: exiles from Russia, Poland, Italy, Hungary, Germany and France, plus sympathizers (few in number) from England, all poured into the house at any hour of the day or night, together with printers, typesetters, messenger boys and a host of fanatics and eccentrics convinced that *their* contribution to the new publication was the only guarantee of its success.

What Herzen, who had just published a violent pamphlet attacking serfdom under the name of *Baptized Property*, wanted from Turgenev was a report on the progress of emancipation. Turgenev recounted the conversations he had had with Tolstoy, and reiterated his conviction that it was better for the reforms to come from the top rather than the bottom. Herzen cautiously agreed with this, "as long," he stipulated, in a rare moment when the two were left alone, "as our reactionaries

347

don't convince the Czar to water them down so drastically that very little changes."

"That is the danger," Turgenev agreed. "But I believe Alexander to be totally committed to substantial reform."

Herzen permitted himself the grin of long familiarity. "Is that belief," he asked, "founded on hard evidence or on your passionate desire that it should be so?"

Turgenev could only smile back: "If only I could answer that question… But one thing I *am* sure of, and that is that no workable solution can ever come from the local peasant assemblies."

Herzen gave him a keen, questioning glance. "You have no faith in the *mir?*"

"To adjudicate in a minor land dispute, to be sure, or weigh up the merits of a charge of chicken-stealing. But never to resolve problems of this complexity. Here, I have to say, I agree with Tolstoy… although that would be quite enough to make him change his opinion. And you? Don't tell me you're turning into a Slavophil – the sacrality of the peasant cap and the long homespun coat!"

"I haven't gone as far as that. But after '48, I perhaps have a higher regard for them than I did before. We have seen the complete futility of the bourgeois leaders of Western Europe and the brutish mobs they are unable to lead or control. Perhaps, after all, there might be something more… dare I say 'noble', in our muzhik…" But before he could enlarge on what that might be, Ogarev put his head round the door and announced that Ledru-Rollin had arrived for what he claimed to be an appointment, and was getting tired of being kept waiting. Herzen shook his head a little wearily and, as he moved towards the door, wondered aloud if, for a while, it might not be more productive to conduct their conversations by letter…

But Turgenev had not come to England only to talk to his countrymen. Armed with letters of introduction from his Russian friends in Paris, he gained access to Thackeray, Macaulay, Disraeli and Carlyle. During these weeks he conceived a rather bemused but affectionate respect for England and the English; he went to the Derby to observe them at play, and to St Paul's, where he was enchanted by a concert given by the boys' choir. Just before he left, he was surprised and flattered to hear he had been elected to the Athenaeum, the literary club founded thirty years before by Sir Walter Scott. He was tempted to stay on: his health was much improved; he found the easygoing social life, which his letters of introduction had opened up for him, far more to his taste than the more formal, stratified French equivalent; and although he wrote regularly to Pauline without receiving one reply, distance even took some of the sting out of that. But the exiled Herzen, anxious to buzz vicariously around the Russian beehive, persuaded him that it was time he went home, and Turgenev began to make preparations. He would spend only a day or two in Paris, chiefly to say goodbye to his daughter, then go to Berlin, where a doctor had been recommended to him, and finally on to St Petersburg. But the

Berlin doctor sent him to a colleague in Dresden, who swore that a patient of his with a condition identical to Turgenev's had been completely cured after a month taking the waters at Sinzig. And to Sinzig he had gone.

Before he had been there a week, he was joined by Druzhinin, who had always been sickly and had now developed a recurrent cough which brought back disquieting memories of Belinksy. Aleksander Vasilevich Druzhinin, six years younger than Turgenev, had also been Belinsky's protégé; when he was only twenty-three, *Sovremennik* had published a novel, heavily influenced by George Sand, deploring the subservient state of women in Russia. After that he had renounced fiction, read widely in foreign literatures, especially English, and become one of the journal's most respected critics. But he had recently fallen out with Chernyshevsky over the relative merits of artistic quality and political significance, and had left *Sovremennik* in order to try and revive another literary journal whose circulation had dwindled to vanishing point.

He and Turgenev spent most of their days together, taking the waters in the morning and ambling through the town and surrounding countryside in the late afternoon and evening. The citizens of Sinzig were used to foreign visitors, but heads were often turned as the two Russians, engrossed in their conversation, walked by. Druzhinin was almost as tall as Turgenev, but his awkward, portly frame lacked the other's natural grace. He too dressed with fastidious care in, as it seemed, a vain effort to compensate for his unprepossessing appearance. His pale, bland face, with its bushy triangular moustache gave no clue to the keen intelligence that lay behind it, the pale watery eyes hinting at an indecision which manifested itself occasionally in social life, never on the printed page. To combat his natural myopia, aggravated by constant reading, he had, just before leaving St Petersburg, acquired a pince-nez; but it had not been adjusted correctly to his long, thin nose and was continually falling off.

Druzhinin was enthusiastic about *Excursion into the Great Woods*, which he was publishing in October, and made no secret of the fact that he was after more material for his *Readers' Library*. Having written to most of his friends that he was done with fiction, Turgenev felt a little foolish discussing hypothetical future works; but the attitude of nonchalant detachment he consequently tried to assume cut little weight with his shrewd companion.

One afternoon the two of them hired a boatman to row them up the Rhine. At first they both remained silent, passively observing the tranquil scenery to either side: the vineyards reaching in places right down to the river bank, the stone walls and crumbling towers, the sailboats, steamboats and barges making their way up and down the great river. Rousing himself eventually from his drowsy contentment, Turgenev asked his friend if he felt the cure was doing him any good. "I think so,"

Druzhinin replied. "It's too early to say yet, of course, but I certainly feel better than I did the last weeks in St Petersburg."

"You were wearing yourself out. Trying to revive a moribund paper is harder than starting a new one. Couldn't you have stayed with *Sovremennik?*"

"Not with Chernyshevsky there. He despises any art that isn't strictly utilitarian. It was him or me. And Nekrasov is giving him an ever greater say in the paper's policy. He's now brought in a disciple of his, a certain Dobrolyubov; he's only twenty-one, but – take my word for it – one day he'll make his master seem like an otherworldly aesthete."

"I'm surprised at what you tell me. I had the impression that Chernyshevsky was beginning to mellow. I have to admit he wrote me a charming letter in Paris, paying me all sorts of compliments, far above my deserts."

"What did he say?"

"Oh, I couldn't possibly tell you. Too embarrassing."

"Come on, I want to hear. You can't be embarrassed in front of me." Druzhinin, who was sitting in the stern, leaned back suddenly, resting his elbows on the gunwales; the boat started to rock and the boatman, a grizzle-faced old fellow wearing a blue serge cap, gave him a surly glance.

"Oh, it was a lot of exaggerated nonsense about Nekrasov and me being the only real Russian writers and how any criticism of my work was an offence to the Russian people who worshipped me! I think he'd drunk a bottle of vodka before he wrote that letter."

"Not at all. It was finely calculated to separate you from the rest of us, because we don't always see eye to eye with him."

"Nor do I."

"I know, but he wants to keep you attached to *Sovremennik*, because you're the readership's favourite contributor; and anyway, you're always abroad, so you don't get in his way. Did he say anything about me?"

Turgenev deceitfully shook his head; he couldn't bring himself to tell his friend that Chernyshevsky had referred to him and Botkin as 'insipid scribblers'.

Druzhinin looked sceptical. "I'm surprised," he said. "But I suppose he no longer considers me a threat. He can go on his way, turning the paper founded by Pushkin into an organ of political propaganda. You're the only person now who can hold out against him. But I doubt whether you have the strength. He'll grind you to dust. Which brings me to the question you asked me: how is *your* health responding to the waters of Sinzig?"

"Oh, I feel better than I did in Paris… but then I feel better anywhere than I do in Paris. I wonder, though, how much this is due to science and how much to psychology… to being so happy in this simple little place. I feel at home here. I've realized I belong in a German-Slav environment… if I belong anywhere at all. It reminds me of my youth. To me there is something surprisingly similar about the Russian and German countrysides. Though everything here, of course, is on so much smaller a scale. And so orderly, so civilized. Don't you love it when all those flaxen-haired *fräuleins* we pass in the street at night call out *Guten Abend* just because we are foreigners? You wouldn't get a *bonsoir* from a French girl if you walked all night... except from the whores."

Druzhinin reached over the right hand gunwale and let his hand trail in the water. "When I came into your room last night before dinner," he said, keeping his eyes on the little wake this caused, "you were at your desk writing. But not on the hotel stationary, so presumably it wasn't a letter. Taking notes, perhaps? Setting down thoughts like these?"

Turgenev flushed like a guilty schoolboy. "Something of the sort," he stammered. "Every now and then one has to remind oneself there's more to life than drinking and bathing."

Druzhinin still didn't raise his eyes from the river. "Any idea of working them up into a story"

"No, no, no, no, no! Absolutely not!"

Druzhinin now looked up with a mocking smile. "The gentleman doth protest too much, methinks."

Turgenev's confusion was comical. "Well, I... I had a sort of little glimpse of an idea the other day. Before you arrived. But it was just to pass the time. Nothing will come of it."

"In that case, there can be no harm in sharing the 'glimpse' with me."

Turgenev gave it a moment's thought, then relaxed and smiled back. "You're wasting your time, Sasha," he said. "But all right. You can't talk away a book that is never going to be written. The fact is... I've been thinking a lot, since I've been here, about Paulinette, my daughter. And about her being illegitimate. In spite of everything that I can do for her, it will always be a handicap. And people born with a handicap have to fight twice as hard as the rest of us. If it's physical – a limp, or a stammer – people make allowances. But illegitimacy... it's a sort of curse that very few are ever able to shake off. It's hard for us to imagine, but it probably affects them in one way or another every minute of every day."

"And you were thinking of a story with an illegitimate girl as heroine."

"It crossed my mind, yes. How a love affair between two young people could come to nothing because of the man's inability to cope with this stigma."

"It's a subject you would handle very well. Don't dismiss it."

"Tolstoy told me last winter that I was afraid to dig too far below the surface. I think he was right. This would probably require too deep an excavation for me."

Druzhinin shook his head and wagged a finger in Turgenev's face. "Don't take too much notice of Lev Nikolayevich's sermons. You and he are very different types

351

of artist: your work may seem superficial, but on closer examination, it isn't. Tolstoy is a very powerful writer, and I expect great things from him. But a little of your lightness of touch wouldn't do him any harm now and then. Tell me more about this heroine of yours."

"Well, I can't exactly put a face to her. It certainly wouldn't be Paulinette's, who *looks* very calm and strong. I've been thinking also of Anna, an illegitimate daughter of my uncle's, who was brought up by my mother. She was a charming, idiosyncratic little thing, half woman half child, but she never found a place for herself: one day she'd be taking tea with the local gentry, the next playing and flirting with some of the young serfs. If I'd left Paulinette at Spasskoye, that's probably how she'd be now. Asya, as we used to call her, had a more *gamine* look – a mop of dark hair and a round, mobile little face with two bright black eyes – which would be more right for... but what am I talking about, I have no intention of writing this story. And look, it's beginning to get dark, it's time we started for home."

He spoke to the boatman, who turned round and began to row back to Sinzig. Before they reached it, the sun had sunk behind one of the two high hills that dominated the little town and both men were content to gaze pensively at the shimmering play of light – red, green and gold – on the barely rippling surface of the river. Nothing broke the silence but the regular plash of the oars and the occasional plaintive voice of a nightingale. The boatman was now rowing close to the bank and Turgenev's attention was struck by the strange appearance of one of a cluster of houses, most of them semi-ruined: built of wood and adorned with heavy carvings, each of its three stories jutted out a little further than the one underneath it, making it resemble a huge squatting bird. At first sight it too had an abandoned air, but when they drew opposite he saw two heads looking out of the second and third floor windows: on the lower floor, the wrinkled face of an old crone; above her, the delicate features of a young girl – somewhere between seventeen and twenty – gazing into the distance with what seemed to him a desolate sense of melancholy longing. As the boat passed directly under the house, he drew Druzhinin's attention to it. The old woman looked down at them without a trace of interest, but the girl's faraway gaze never shifted.

"What do you make of them?" Turgenev asked.

Druzhinin seemed surprised by the question. "Well, mother and daughter, I suppose. No, grandmother and granddaughter more likely. Why?"

"I don't think so at all," Turgenev mused. "The girl is of a different class to the old woman... who's some kind of nurse, I would say, left in charge. Or, better still, a casual acquaintance who is the only person in the world she can confide in. Because the girl, of course, is hopelessly and miserably in love."

Druzhinin's sallow features lit up with a gleam of amusement. "And you've found the face for your heroine."

Turgenev's eyes, which had been raking the house as though trying to divine its soul, now turned in perplexity to his friend.

"What?... Oh no, what nonsense!" Druzhinin said nothing, but simply raised an eyebrow and allowed himself a sardonic smile. Turgenev glanced back at the house, which was now receding behind them. "Well..." – he gave an embarrassed little laugh – "there is something there which..."

He tailed off and Druzhinin finished the thought for him. "...which, *if* you were thinking of writing the story, you *might* be able to use."

"Oh, a little picture was beginning to form in my mind, but tomorrow will tell me it's ridiculous."

"Let tomorrow make up its own mind. And you jot down a few notes this evening."

"It's a waste of time. What's the point?"

"The point is to write your story. Promise me you'll try."

"Sasha, it's no use, I..."

Forgetting where he was, Druzhinin leaned clumsily forward, causing the boat to rock violently from side to side and the boatman to catch a crab. Ignoring the man's growled, *'Passen Sie doch auf!'*, he grabbed Turgenev's elbow and stared into his eyes. "Promise me!"

With half of his mind still back at the house, Turgenev gazed abstractedly at his friend, then finally shrugged and smiled: "All right. I promise to *try.*"

Druzhinin leaned back, tension released and muscles relaxed, and the pince-nez fell off his nose. He picked it up from the bottom of the boat and saw that one of the lenses was broken. Laughing off Turgenev's concern, he reminded him that broken glasses, unlike a broken mirror, meant good luck. "Your story," he assured him, "is born under the best possible auspices."

Hurrah! Ypa! Lebehoch! Vivat! Evviva! *<Ζητω>! Long live little Paul! Long live his mother…
his father… his whole family! Brava! I told you all would go well and you would have a son. I congratulate
you all and embrace you all. And now I want (as soon as your condition permits, of course):*

*1) A detailed description of the young man's features, colour of his eyes, etc., etc.; if possible, also a
little pencil sketch.*

2) An account of all the wittiest words he has uttered up to now.

*I'm drivelling a bit, I know, but that's pardonable at my age, and given the joy the great news has
caused me.*

*The postman has received some money to enable him to drink a glass of Rhenish wine (not beer, I
insisted) to the health of young Paul-Louis-Joachim; I shall do so too, of course.*

*You must be happy, are you not? You devour him with your eyes, this little being who only yesterday
was part of you and who now has his own life, his own thoughts, his own individuality. I will be a
prophet, I will read into the dark night of the future, in the* Almanach National *of 1950:*

*VIARDOT (Paul, Louis, Joachim), famous (for what, I leave blank), born at Courtavenel-en-
Brie, etc., etc., son of the celebrated Pauline Garcia, etc., etc., and the learned writer and translator of* Don
Quixote…

I won't quote the whole article.

*You will write me a short note, won't you, as soon as you have the strength? Did you ever enjoy a
sweeter moment than waking up on the morning of the 21st? Is there any music to compare to the little
one's cries?*

*There, there, all has gone well. I will write to you tomorrow or the day after in a more reasonable
manner; today, I go back to shouting:* Hurrah! Vivat! Allons, enfants de la patrie! Alaaf Köln!
(that's a cry of joy used only in Cologne, but it will do very well).

*I embrace you all again, starting with Mr Paul, and I kiss your dear, but (when it comes to putting
pen to paper) oh such lazy hands,*

Your old friend,

I. Turgenev.

He waited with even more than his usual trepidation to see how this letter would
be received. But no reply ever arrived.

Towards the end of the month Druzhinin was summoned back to St Petersburg
on urgent editorial matters and Turgenev began to find time lying heavy on his
hands. He kept his promise to his friend and tried to work on the story that was to
become *Asya*, but once again his health made concentration difficult. Eventually he

was reluctantly compelled to admit that, far from improving his condition, the cure was worsening it. Relief came in the unexpected form of a letter from Tolstoy who, after leaving the 'Sodom' of Paris, had spent three months in Switzerland and had then been lured by a 'moral abortion' of a French banker to the Black Forest gambling haven of Baden-Baden, where he had lost all his money at the roulette tables. He was now desperate to return to Russia, but lacked the means to do so. This was all Turgenev needed. Their parting in Paris had been one of the peaks of their tormented friendship: Tolstoy had almost reduced him to tears by telling him that he loved him like a brother; he had even thanked him for having made a different and better person of him. Delighted to shrug off the suspense of waiting for the post every day, Turgenev booked a passage on a steamer going up the Rhine, assuring himself that the moment he left, word from Paris would surely arrive. He even gave his landlady the name of Tolstoy's hotel as a forwarding address.

Arriving at Baden-Baden in the evening, he found Tolstoy in a dreadful state. Unshaven, his clothes looking as though they hadn't been changed for at least three days, he was not only lacerating himself over his gambling losses; he was also full of self-disgust at having caught crabs from 'a plump Swiss chambermaid, who forced herself on me in the most depraved fashion. But who am I to blame her? If it hadn't been for my revolting lust...!' Turgenev tried to comfort him by pointing out that it was the sort of thing that could happen to anybody. What was more to the point were his gambling debts. "How much did you lose?"

"Three thousand francs."

Turgenev opened his mouth to give vent to his astonishment, but seeing Tolstoy's little-boy-caught-in-the-act expression, shut it again. "Three thousand francs! Well, I can just about let you have that, but not a sou more. Tomorrow you must go straight away and book your ticket."

"What else do you think I would do with it?"

Treating this as a rhetorical question, Turgenev suggested they go somewhere for dinner, but Tolstoy pleaded exhaustion – with some plausibility, as he did in fact look as though he hadn't slept for a week – and they agreed to have a late breakfast together. But the next morning Tolstoy was nowhere to be seen. He didn't appear in the hotel dining room for breakfast, and when, at eleven, Turgenev asked the concierge to send someone to wake him, he was told that the count was not in his room, nor had the bed been slept in.

This could only mean one thing, and Turgenev, suppressing his irritation, decided he must find him, all too aware that Tolstoy would be making himself as inconspicuous as possible. Fortunately Baden-Baden in those days was a compact little town and the Russian count had attracted a certain attention. An Englishman who was picking up his keys had overheard the conversation and volunteered the information that, on returning from his early morning walk, he had seen someone he took to be 'the chap you're looking for' making his way rather unsteadily towards the station. Turgenev thanked him and hailed one of the pony traps waiting outside the hotel, promising the driver to double his fare if he would get him there in the shortest possible time. At the station there was no sign of Tolstoy on either of the two platforms, nor in the waiting rooms; he asked the stationmaster how many trains had left that morning, and was told two: one for Frankfurt and one for Basle. It seemed unlikely that Tolstoy would have left for either of these places without luggage or, if Turgenev's suspicions were correct, money; but no hunter knew better how unpredictable his quarry could be. As he walked out of the station, wondering what he should do next, he saw his driver coming out of a café on the other side of the square. Thinking it might be worth a look, he asked the man to wait for a moment before taking him back to the hotel.

The sight that met his eyes as he entered the café revealed the reverse side of the cosmopolitan spa: no elegant ladies and gentlemen here, sipping their coffee while comparing their 'cures' and chuckling over the 'little flutter' they had indulged in last night. An air of hopelessness hung over the large, dismal room. Class differences had evaporated: officers' uniforms and evening tails were as much in evidence as rough country jackets and shabby woollen shirts. The men – and occasional woman – slumped around the not very clean tables were, apart from the odd traveller waiting for a train, either drunks trying to chase away last night's excesses or unsuccessful gamblers postponing the moment when they would have to contemplate a bleak future. And sure enough, Turgenev soon made out Tolstoy, hunched over a corner table, a half-empty glass of schnapps in front of him, a cheap cigar between his fingers.

As he walked over to join him, Turgenev wondered how he would be greeted: with pleasure or resentment. The moment Tolstoy looked up, he knew which it was going to be.

"Ah, you found me!"

"Yes. Just by chance."

Tolstoy gave a mirthless hoot and drew heavily on his stinking cigar.

After a heavy silence, Turgenev sat down and muttered awkwardly: "I'm sorry but I have to ask you… How much did you lose?"

No reply.

"All of it?"

A minimal nod.

Turgenev drew a deep breath, then got to his feet again. "Come on, let's get back to the hotel. We'll talk it over there."

As Tolstoy drained his glass, Turgenev reached into his pocket and drew out some coins. But Tolstoy held up his hand. "It's all right. It's paid for. I kept back a hundred francs. Sense of responsibility!…"

356

The short journey back in the trap took place in silence. But just as they were drawing up to the hotel, Tolstoy took an envelope out of his pocket and, tapping it against his knuckles, said: "When I got back here last night, I found this. That's why I went out again. I knew I wouldn't sleep."

"Bad news? Who's it from?"

"My brother, Sergey. Masha's left Valerian. Taken the children away. Another failure in the family!"

Uncertain how to take this disquieting news, Turgenev sent Tolstoy up to his room. "Have a bath, shave, and lie down and sleep for an hour or two. Put on some fresh clothes and everything will seem less black. We'll talk it all over at lunch." He laid a hand on his shoulder and ventured a smile: "But don't think of running away again. I shall tell the concierge to let me know if you try and leave the hotel."

"What am I to do? Masha will need me now. She's all alone in Pokrovskoye with the three children. It won't be easy for her. Apart from the scandal, Nikolenka in particular will be missing his father. If I were at Yasnaya Polyana, I could be over there all the time, helping in one way or another. But after last night... oh God, I don't how you can sit at the same table with me, I should go out and shoot myself... how am I ever going to get out of this accursed place?" He slammed his fist down on the table and Turgenev glanced uncomfortably round at the other guests eating quietly in the luxurious dining room.

"Let's leave that aside for a moment," he said. "Tell me more about Marya. I'm astonished by this news. We still write to each other from time to time. I had a letter from her only a month or so ago, and she never alluded to anything of this sort."

"Well, she wouldn't to you. But it didn't come as all that much of a shock to me. That idiot Valerian has pushed even her sainted patience beyond the limit. Listen to what she says..." He pulled out her letter. "'I have finally realized that it is not enough for me to be the favourite sultana in his harem.'"

Turgenev couldn't resist a wan smile. "At least her wit hasn't deserted her."

Tolstoy's eyes lit up with a gleam of enthusiasm. "I have an idea, Vanichka. You've always admired her. Why don't we go back together? She'd be so happy to see you again, and... who knows?..."

Turgenev shook his head. "That's impossible. To begin with, my cure at Sinzig having been a complete failure, I am now on my way to Boulogne to see if sea bathing and some kind of electrical treatment will do any good. But apart from that, I don't think this would be the moment for me to force my attention on Marya Nikolayevna."

"Who's talking about 'forcing your attention'? You can't deny there's always been something... special between you two, and now, with him out of the way..."

Turgenev held up his hand. "Please, Lyovochka! I shall not be coming with you… for a number of reasons. I have my responsibilities in Paris too. What is important now is to work out how we are going to get you home. And, after thinking about it all morning, I think I may have come up with a solution."

"I can't accept any more money from you."

"Even if you could, I have no more to lend you. But there's someone here who undoubtedly has."

"Who?"

"Don't look round too obviously, but do you know our fellow-countryman sitting over there by the fireplace, opposite that charming woman?"

"Prince Smirnov? I know who he is, but to the best of my knowledge we've never met. And yes, she certainly is charming! Who is she, his wife?"

"By no means. I know his wife very well… or rather I used to. Aleksandra Smirnova was, for a while, the main literary hostess of St Petersburg. An impossibly pretentious, insincere person. She had known Pushkin and never let anyone forget it. When I knew her, poor Gogol was her prize exhibit."

"Why are you telling me all this?"

"Because I have it in mind to do something very immoral. The Prince is extremely rich. And I intend to ask him to lend me the money you need to return to Yasnaya."

"Why should he give it to you. Do you know him well too?"

"Hardly at all. But he knows I know his wife. And, as we are agreed, that lady with him is exceptionally charming. If word were to get back…"

"Blackmail! Vanichka, I can't let you…"

"Oh, of course I would never breathe a word. But he is not to know that. And anyway, it's only a loan. I will be back in Russia by the end of the year and will arrange to repay him then. No, the moral side of the affair doesn't worry me in the least. Only a certain aspect of the practical side."

"What is that?"

"Well, do you remember Darya Mikhailovna in *Rudin*?

"The young girl's mother. Of course. One of your most achieved characters. A truly abominable woman."

"Hmm! Yes, well a great deal of Aleksandra Smirnova went into her. As a number of people recognized."

"Including herself?"

"I think not. I count on the fact that she fancies herself far too lofty a soul to see any resemblance. But suppose he did!"

"I would exclude that. For one good reason. Look at him! Does he strike you as the sort of person who has ever read a book in his life?!"

The loan was negotiated, the two friends parted the next day, Tolstoy swearing eternal gratitude, and Turgenev made his way first to Boulogne and then back to Paris. The treatment in Boulogne was scarcely more effective than that of Sinzig. As he wrote in a despairing note to Nekrasov, 'It used to be that I only really suffered when I was in Paris. But now the pain seems to follow me everywhere. I cannot work, I am loath to accept invitations, as I never know whether I will be well enough to attend… I am sick of my company and unable to enjoy that of others… there really seems little point in continuing to live.' He announced his intention of going to Paris to settle his affairs and take leave of his daughter, and then returning to Russia for the winter. 'Perhaps the air of my homeland will have a more benign effect than all the doctors of Germany and France.'

Nekrasov wrote back, welcoming his decision to come home, and issued a specific warning: 'When you are in Paris, do not yield to temptation and go to Courtavenel… saying to yourself it will just be for a couple of days. Dispatch your business in Paris and board the train…'

Courtavenel,
23 August, 1857.

Dear Nikolai Alekseyevich,

I have to confess to a certain embarrassment in writing you this letter. As you can see, I am here… that is to say I have committed the very blunder you rightly warned me against. But it was impossible for me to do otherwise. You have heard my attempts at explanation before, and I suspect you are, quite understandably, beginning to tire of them. But I will try once more.

Despite my initial pessimism, the treatment at Boulogne did afford me some relief. I arrived back in Paris feeling a little more at ease with life and spent a pleasant week, much of it in the company of my daughter. It was she who dissuaded me from leaving for Russia immediately, as had been my intention. She clearly took such pleasure in roaming around the city with me that it would have been cruel to tear myself away so soon. We also made little excursions together out to some of the châteaux around Paris and generally made the best of the warm, but not stifling, summer days.

I was about to start making plans for my return journey when, as some would have it, fate took a hand. One evening, after a day that for once had been disagreeably hot, we went for a stroll in the gardens of the Palais du Luxembourg… and who should we meet but Louis Viardot, up in Paris to conclude some business for his wife. He invited us to take a sorbet with him and, during the course of the conversation, asked – you could almost say begged – us to come and spend some days at Courtavenel. After observing the scene here for some days now, I think I can say that he is beginning to find time lying rather heavy on his hands; Mme Viardot has made a lightning recovery from childbirth and is dividing her remarkable energy between caring for the newborn son, planning a concert series for the autumn and taking on one or two young neophytes to whom – lucky things! – she is preparing to impart her incomparable knowledge of the art of singing. Not surprisingly, she has very little time for anything – or anyone – else.

Believe it or not, Nikolasha, at the moment Viardot made his invitation, I thought of you. I even heard your voice in my ear. But what can I say? Mme Viardot acts like a magnet on my will; if I am anywhere within range, I cannot avoid being drawn to her presence. So here I am. Paulinette decided to remain in Paris; she has her life there now, with her piano lessons and her studies and her school friends. I pass my time agreeably enough, but it is not like it was a year ago. I spend much of the day with Louis; we are translating some of my stories, which he has arranged for Hachette to publish under the title of Scenes of Russian Life. *I provide him with a rough French version, which he polishes. I see very little of Madame Viardot, whose engagements require her to be in Paris much of the week. And I have to confess that when she is here, I sometimes feel my presence is not altogether welcome to her.*

I'm afraid the little story I conceived in Sinzig is making no progress. But for that, no doubt I need to get home. And as things stand here, I shall probably be back in Peter earlier than I thought. To go on living like this is impossible! I have had enough of being on the edge of someone else's nest. If you haven't got your own, it's better to do without completely.

So sharpen that knife! I hope to be carving a turkey for you in a month or less. The rice, I will leave to you…

Your irredeemable???,

I.T.

But Nekrasov had to carve his own turkey. Turgenev stayed on the edge of the Viardots' nest for all of two months, seeing more and more of Louis and less and less of Pauline. And when he did leave, in the middle of October, it was not for St Petersburg but for Rome. Botkin had arrived in Paris and persuaded him, with little difficulty, that the mild Mediterranean winter would be better for his health. He had also added slyly that he had heard from Druzhinin that there was a promising story in gestation; in Rome he would be able to give it his full attention, undisturbed by all the calls on his time which would have been accumulating over the past year in St Petersburg and Spasskoye.

Turgenev spent the whole winter in Rome, not leaving until the following March. He was glad to be back in the city which he had last visited seventeen years ago. But its impact on him now was the reverse of what it had been on his twenty-two-year-old self. Then he had been young, it was summer, and like many another idealistic, Goethe-imbued young man from the north, dazzled by its beauty and the artistic treasures of its past, he had felt an almost mystic identification with the place. Now he felt old, it was winter, and yet once again he found in Rome something that suited his mood: this time it matched his melancholy. Like him, he felt, all its glories were in the past. After centuries of papal rule, interrupted only for a few republican months in 1848, the city slumbered on, gorged on its own self-satisfaction. Intellectually, artistically, spiritually (he didn't relate that adverb to the Church of and in Rome), it was a dead place. The Romans knew it, but felt no urge to do anything about it. Stagnation was quite acceptable. For, just look! How beautiful everything was!

The first few weeks were spent agreeably enough sight-seeing with Botkin in the autumnal splendour of the Roman *campagna*. But he soon realized that if he was going to conquer his melancholy, or at least tame it to suit his purpose, he had to resume disciplined hours. He promised himself, as he told Botkin, 'to pour whatever remains of passion are left in me into my writing'. He returned to *Asya* and at first found the sensations Sinzig had aroused so vividly in him hazy and hard to recapture. But with persistence – and more deletions and false starts and arrows and corrections than he had ever employed before – the story began to take shape. And this contributed to his gradually shaking off the worst legacy of the last terrible winter: the sense of the purposelessness of everything. His natural conviviality began to reassert itself. Helped by the gradual improvement in his health, he felt a need to emerge from his Parisian isolation, a desire, after a day's work, to seek out company.

It didn't take him long, however, to discover that the local variety was not going to be satisfactory. One of his Parisian acquaintances had written to a Prince Corsini who, shortly after his arrival, sent him an invitation for an evening reception at his *palazzo* in Trastevere. But having admired Ferdinando Fuga's graceful neo-classical facade, and been graciously welcomed by the prince, he was thereafter left to his own devices, which were to prove quite inadequate. Introduced to nobody, and hampered by his scant knowledge of Italian, he drifted from group to group, finding no one who took the slightest interest in him. Knowing that everyone there would speak perfect French, he once or twice tried to initiate a conversation in that language; but after a few perfunctory replies, they all reverted to talking in Italian and, to his intense annoyance, exclusively about themselves. After less than an hour, he slipped away without, he reflected wryly, anyone being any more aware of his departure than they had been of his presence.

After that he felt no compunction about falling back on his own countrymen, of whom Rome was almost as full as Paris. He soon found himself living the mirror image of his life in St Petersburg after his exile, dividing his time between artists and aristocracy. Introduced by Botkin, he began to frequent a group of Russian painters and sculptors, who met regularly in the Caffè Greco opposite the Spanish Steps; when he visited their studios, he could not help finding their work pitifully inept, and his patience was tried by their vociferous scorn for the Italian High Renaissance painters he admired so much. Raphael and Leonardo were dismissed, with almost Slavophil intensity, in favour of academic Russian artists whose work had never travelled – and never would – beyond their city limits, let alone their national frontiers. But they were a cheerful, warm-hearted group and he found their company agreeable and undemanding. One topic they were constantly reverting to eventually aroused his curiosity: it concerned one of their number, a certain Aleksander Ivanov, who never joined them at the café, indeed rarely ventured outside his studio. He was apparently an artist of unusual eccentricity in that he had been engaged, or so they assured him, on the same painting for twenty-five years. In the face of Turgenev's scepticism, they arranged for one of their number to accompany him to Ivanov's studio to see for himself.

Expecting to be confronted with a wild-eyed, long-haired misanthrope, he was instead greeted by a small, tubby, balding man in a paint-stained smock, who spared no pains to make him feel welcome. He soon realized that his friends had not been exaggerating; the studio was dominated by a colossal painting, propped up on three easels, of Christ appearing to the multitude. Piled up around every inch of the walls were stacks of sketches, almost all depicting the face of Christ. Turgenev couldn't resist asking him how many he had made. "The last time I counted there were over two hundred," was the almost apologetic reply. "You see, each time I look at my Christ when I think he's just about finished, I say: 'No, that's not him. That's not him at all.' So I have to go on searching"

Although suspecting that he was slightly mad, Turgenev found this confusion far more appealing than the blinkered certainties of the Caffè Greco group, and Ivanov soon became his and Botkin's frequent companion. The three of them would go on long excursions to the hill towns around Rome – Frascati, Albano, Rocca di Papa – where Ivanov would spend hours in dark churches peering at indecipherable fragments of frescoes, while Botkin examined a series of trattorias before making up his mind which they would patronize, and Turgenev perched happily on a stone wall, soaking himself in the benign rays of the winter sun and marvelling at the shifting play of light on olive groves, cypress alleys and grey, weather-beaten bell towers. He tried to drench himself in the hedonistic pleasures of the south, hoping thereby to alleviate his lurking guilt at not being in Russia at such a momentous time. But if he were ever in danger of forgetting, there were always friends ready to remind him. Old Sergey Timofeyevich Aksakov, whom he loved and admired, wrote him a stern letter exercising the privilege of age to dispense with any equivocation: 'One cannot', he pronounced, 'live on foreign soil when the fate of one's country is being decided.' Other conscience-keepers were nearer at hand: Rome that winter harboured a number of his influential countrymen who had come south in search of warmth, but did not for a minute forget the topic which obsessed the minds of all educated Russians, whether in Rome, Paris or St Petersburg: the forthcoming – or was it? – emancipation of the serfs...

INT. ST PETERSBURG, A SMALL ROOM IN THE IMPERIAL WINTER PALACE – EVENING

Sovereigns pass, ministers remain. It is now Alexander II sitting behind the massive mahogany desk, but it is still Aleksey Orlov standing rigidly in front of him. The new Czar, aged 38, is a soft replica of his father: he has inherited the handsome Romanov features, but is shorter than Nicholas and beginning to run to plump; a drooping moustache gives a vacillatory cast to his amiable but weak face. Orlov, who was awarded the title of Prince in reward for his efforts at the Treaty of Paris, where Russia failed to gain one of the objectives for which she had fought the ruinous Crimean War, is now 79, but still a superb figure of a man: not an ounce of flesh has been added, nor a flicker of discernment. He is now President of the Council of State, an amazing appointment considering the hopes that all enlightened Russians had placed in the new reign, but in line with Alexander's policy of choosing his ministers indiscriminately from extreme reactionaries and inveterate liberals, presumably in the hope of arriving at safe, middle-of-the-road solutions. One of Orlov's principal duties is to act as Deputy Chairman (under the Czar) of the committee set up to study the best means to effect the abolition of serfdom. To say that his heart is not in it is an understatement of truly epic proportions...

CZAR

I know, Prince, how much store my father set by your wisdom and loyalty. I trust that I may count on them too.

ORLOV

After the honour of serving Your Majesty's father, God rest his soul, I would feel privileged indeed, Sire, if my humble abilities could be of any service to yourself.

CZAR

Thank you, Orlov. Let us waste no more time, then. As you know, this question of emancipation is very close to my heart. If serfdom is not abolished from above, the peasants may begin to liberate themselves from below. And that must be avoided at all costs.

ORLOV

Indeed, Sire.

CZAR

Yes, but I don't see much progress being made. Can you shed some light on this?

ORLOV

Committees are being set up all over the country. The nobles will be discussing the various schemes put forward, and we shall be receiving their reports…

CZAR

(interrupting him)

When?

ORLOV

(taken aback)

Well, these things take their time… It would be a mistake to rush matters…

CZAR

It would be a mistake to procrastinate too long, too. The whole country is expecting action. And soon. I have heard rumours that the muzhiks are ready to take things into their own hands if they lose faith in me.

ORLOV

That would be most inadvisable of them. The Army…

CZAR

(again interrupting)

God forbid, the Army! My father's reign began with bloodshed. With the Decembrists, of course, he had no choice. But now times have changed. The nobility is with me, is it not?

ORLOV

Heart and soul, Your Majesty.

CZAR

I believe so, I believe so. And that encourages me to outline to you my intentions… But sit down, Prince, make yourself comfortable. Would you care for a glass of wine?

ORLOV

(taking a seat)

Thank you, Sire, never on duty.

CZAR

Of course, of course. Well now...as you know, soon after my accession, I asked the provincial nobility for suggestions as to ways and means. At last, over a year later, I have had one reply. From Lithuania. You have seen it, no doubt.

ORLOV

I have, yes.

CZAR

Your opinion?

ORLOV

I thought it had much to commend it.

CZAR

Perhaps. But it had one unacceptable proviso.

ORLOV
(knowing full well)

What was that, Sire?

CZAR
(indignantly)

It proposed a scheme whereby the peasants would be freed without acquiring the right to own land.

ORLOV

Ah yes, so it did.

CZAR

How dare they! I have always insisted that there shall be no liberty without land. Otherwise the peasants would be worse off than before. What is freedom worth if they lack the means of subsistence?

ORLOV

Would that necessarily be so?

CZAR

Not necessarily. Not always. But sometimes, yes. The great
majority of the serfs are well treated by their masters, are they not?

ORLOV

Indubitably.

CZAR

But we have to allow that some are not. There are landlords who
fall short of their responsibilities. And in those cases, if self-interest
no longer induces them to feed and clothe their peasants, the poor
devils starve. I saw that for myself on the journey I took with
Zhukovsky when I was nineteen. In bad winters they were reduced
to eating acorns and the bark of trees.

ORLOV

Terrible, terrible…

CZAR

Indeed. And, in general, they are such splendid people. You know
who sees them as well as anyone…that writer fellow, Turgenev. Did
you ever read any of those sketches of his?

ORLOV

No, Sire.

CZAR

You should, Orlov, you should. They open our eyes to things we at
court are not aware of. Besides, the chap's a friend of your son's, isn't
he?

ORLOV
(stiffly)

I believe so.

CZAR

Fine man, that boy of yours! Behaved like a hero in the Crimea…
badly wounded… lost an eye, if I remember correctly.

ORLOV

You do, Sire.

CZAR

You must be very proud of him.

ORLOV

As a soldier, I am. In civilian life, Nikolai Alekseyevich and I have
our disagreements… amongst which I have to include his intimacy
with Turgenev.

CZAR

That's why you don't read him, eh? Bit too advanced for you?
Come now, Prince, mustn't let your mental joints stiffen up… got
to allow us youngsters a loose rein now and then, eh?…eh?…

He laughs uproariously. Orlov attempts an appreciative chuckle, but it emerges more like the
groan of a man on the rack.

CZAR

Now, where was I?

ORLOV

You were about to tell me how you were going to reply to
Lithuania.

CZAR

Yes, indeed. Well, I intend to send an edict to every provincial
governor, stipulating that there shall be no liberty without land.
And I shall then have it published, so that anyone who wishes may
read it and know what his Emperor has in mind for his people.
(a pause)
You are silent, Orlov.

ORLOV

(feigning hesitancy)
I was humbly wondering whether it was a wise move for Your
Majesty to publish his edicts.

CZAR

Why should it not be?

ORLOV

It might look as though Your Majesty was inviting debate on his decisions, which should instead be final and unalterable. You know there are certain publications which would seize any opportunity to foment discord.

Alexander rubs his chin as he ponders the import of this. Then:

CZAR

I appreciate your misgivings, Prince. But this will be an exception. I do not intend to make a habit of publishing my edicts. In this one case, however, I want my intentions to be known to every one of my subjects who cares to inform himself. Does that allay your fears?

ORLOV
(unconvincingly)

Entirely, Sire.

Late in January, Turgenev received an invitation from the Grand Duchess Elena Pavlovna to attend an evening reception in a wing of the Palazzo Altieri that she had rented for a couple of months. This took the form of a handwritten note from one of her ladies-in-waiting, a certain Julia Fedorovna Stubbe, who specified that dress would be informal and added a P.S., declaring that she herself was particularly looking forward to making his acquaintance, as she had at one time had the honour of being a pupil of Pauline Viardot's. Turgenev, assuming that there would be a large crowd, arrived, in accordance with Roman custom, nearly half an hour late, and was chagrined to discover that there were only two other guests. The Grand Duchess swept aside his apologies and told him that it was to be a Russian evening. "It is really I who should apologize, Ivan Sergeyevich," she said. "I have brought you here under false pretences. You were no doubt expecting a convivial social gathering; instead, I have invited you for a very specific purpose. I am an admirer of your work and have been looking forward to making your acquaintance for some time now. You never seem to be in Russia these days, so I have had to come to Rome to meet you! I don't think you know these two gentlemen: Prince Cherkassky and General Rostovtsev. Now, let us sit down close to the fire, because, despite its reputation, it seems that Rome in January – at least in these palaces – is almost as cold as St Petersburg, and get down to business."

The Grand Duchess Elena Pavlovna was the German-born widow of Czar Nicholas's younger brother, Michael. A fearless and outspoken champion of reform, she had been many times on the verge of being banned from court by her inflexible brother-in-law. But her force of character (she had founded and run the first organization of nursing sisters in the Crimean War) and friendship with the Czaritsa (who had arranged for her beloved Zhukovsky to teach her Russian) had seen her through and, with the new reign, she was now, together with Alexander's brother, Constantine, at the forefront of the emancipation movement; her *salon* in St Petersburg had become the meeting place for all that was most enlightened and cultured in Russian society. A short, stocky woman in her early fifties, she dressed with what could well be taken for studied negligence; although tirelessly energetic, she moved with some difficulty now, having suffered for years from arthritis; but her brilliant, piercing eyes, which missed nothing, lent an air of indomitable youthfulness to her sharp, wizened face. She was never at a loss for a word and could sometimes stray into garrulity, but, despite a reputation to the contrary, she knew how to listen. She now ushered the men into their seats, sat down next to her companion, a slim, attractive woman in her late twenties, who had greeted the new arrival with a shy smile, and, after calling on a footman to serve champagne, reverted to Turgenev.

"These gentleman," she said, indicating Cherkassky and Rostovstev, "know you from your books, but I should perhaps say a word or two about them. They are both devoting themselves unsparingly to the cause of emancipation. Prince Cherkassky edits the review, *Russian Conversation,* which you may know of; it has slight but not excessive Slavophil tendencies. But," this with a twinkle, "despite all your travelling, I sometimes think that's true of you too. The Prince is a member of the Editorial Commission, whose job it is to sift through all the suggestions that arrive from the provincial councils and tabulate the most worthwhile proposals to set before the Emperor. General Rostovstev has, if possible, an even more difficult task: he is the mediator in what, I believe, is still called the secret committee, although all Russia knows about it, which the Czar has appointed to make the final decisions about ways and means. Unfortunately Alexander has seen fit to pack this committee with some of the most reactionary nobles in the Empire: Prince Orlov, with whom I believe you are familiar, is the effective chairman. Count Panin, his right-hand-man and the Minister of Justice, once announced that whoever first put the idea of emancipation into the Emperor's head deserved to be hanged! So you can see what they're up against."

"But surely, Your Highness," Turgenev asked, "if the Emperor has declared so forcefully that emancipation must come about, there is no one in the land who can stop it."

The Grand Duchess shook her head. "Stop it, perhaps not," she said. "But delay it until it loses all propulsive force, that is a very real danger. Yes, Alexander made his proclamation and he means it. Most of the time. But he is easily swayed by whoever manages to catch his ear. And he is all too ready to lend that ear, as I have said, to deplorable counsellors who assure him that any action that would really liberate the serfs would mean disaster for the nobles. This is, of course, not true, but the thought frightens him. He remembers December, 1825. He was only seven, but he remembers. I shouldn't say this, and let it not go outside these four stone walls, but if his brother Constantine were Emperor, emancipation would already have taken place."

Rostovstev leant forward. "The problem, Ivan Sergeyevich, is this. When we heard His Majesty's proclamation, there was almost universal rejoicing. But now everyone is sitting back and waiting for something to happen. And this is just what the reactionaries want. Because if everyone waits, *nothing* will happen. We have the whole of Russian history to attest to that. The Czar has put responsibility for advancing the cause wholly in the hands of the nobles. And they, with some exceptions like yourself, have every interest in slowing the momentum until the whole machinery grinds to a halt. And with the expectations of the peasants so aroused, what would happen then does not bear thinking about."

Turgenev turned to Cherkassky. "But are ideas and suggestions not coming into your Commission?"

Cherkassky smiled. "Let us say, we don't risk being buried under an avalanche! And most of those that do arrive rule out the cession of land to the peasants, which the Czar has insisted is non-negotiable. There are two fundamental questions that have to be resolved: how much land is the peasant going to get, together with how will the landowners be reimbursed for what they lose; and what will replace the landowner's previously autocratic authority. On neither of these issues are we getting any positive suggestions at all."

"Which is where you come in, Ivan Sergeyevich," the Grand Duchess said briskly.

"Me! What can I do from Rome?"

"Aha! More than you think. I made some enquiries about you before leaving St Petersburg and everyone expatiated on your modesty; but some of your more sardonic friends hinted that you sometimes exploited this to extricate you from unwanted involvements. Be that as it may," she waved an imperious hand to stifle Turgenev's expostulations, "we are going to ask you to give us a little of your time. You are writing a novel here in Rome, I believe."

"I am working up some notes I made over a year ago," Turgenev said diffidently. "But I don't know whether they will lead to anything."

"Just the sort of answer I had been led to expect! Well, now you will have to earn the time to write your novel. Or rather, to put it more graciously, we would be grateful if you would lend us a little of it."

"If there is anything I can do to be of service…" Turgenev began.

"We think there is." She cut him short and waved a hand towards Rostovstev. "General, outline your idea to Ivan Sergeyevich."

"What we have to do," Rostovstev began slowly, "is to try and keep the momentum going, in spite of all the attempts to slow it down. I think of the emancipation process as a mule, and of us who support it as muleteers; we have to keep prodding and pricking the lazy beast, otherwise he'll just come to a halt. None of us is under the illusion that it will all be over in a few months. There are too many awkward details to be worked out and too many influential people only too happy to block the mule's path. But one way, we thought, of preventing the whole business being drowned in a bog of bureaucracy is to keep it constantly in the public eye. And to that end, it seemed to us that a journal might be useful: a weekly publication keeping a record of every development, every advance, every setback; and in which supporters and opponents alike could air their thoughts. An ever-present forum for discussion, in other words."

Turgenev intervened. "Would you ever get permission to publish it? I can't see our censors warming to the idea. The paper my friend Herzen puts out in London, which has recently been devoted almost exclusively to the emancipation question, is rigorously banned... although I've heard that copies do circulate clandestinely."

His companions exchanged a look of conspiratorial amusement, which left Turgenev in no doubt that they were regular readers of *Kolokol*. Cherkassky answered his question.

"The problem has of course occurred to us, but we have reason to believe that it can be overcome. Her Highness tells us that Grand Duke Constantine has taken a great interest in the idea; he has asked for a memorandum to be drawn up setting out the aims and methods of the journal; if it convinced him, he would show it to the Emperor and recommend that it should go forward."

Turgenev smiled round at his companions. "I had never realized," he said with a contented sigh, "until this minute, how things have changed since I left Russia." And then, directly addressing Rostovstev: "But how can I be of help to you?"

The general returned his smile: "We have read your books, Ivan Sergeyevich. And we remember how you freed your domestic serfs immediately after your mother's death. We are in no doubt that your heart is with us. We wondered whether we could enrol your pen."

"You mean you would like me to draft this memorandum."

"Exactly."

Turgenev hesitated. "You honour me with your trust, but, with the best will in the world, I wonder whether I am qualified to do this. I have taken a great interest in the question, of course, but the details..."

Cherkassky intervened. "Naturally we will be available to give you any help you may need."

The Grand Duchess let out a raucous chuckle. "I think at this point we had better come clean: these two gentlemen, Ivan Sergeyevich, have made a list of everything they believe should go into the memorandum. All you will have to do is look it over, add anything of your own which you think appropriate and make it look elegant."

Turgenev gave a relieved smile. "In that case, your Highness… gentlemen… I shall be proud to be of service. It seems that the moment I have been waiting for with such eager anticipation is now at hand. I count myself lucky to have lived to see it."

Elena Pavlovna clapped her hands. "Excellent, excellent," she cried. "Now let us go into the dining room, defy the draughts and have something to eat." She offered her arm to Turgenev. "And talk about something other than politics. Here I am in this legendary city and I haven't heard a note of good music yet. I know you are a connoisseur. You and Mademoiselle Stubbe must tell me what to look out for."

"To tell the truth, I have heard very little since I came here. I was taken to listen to some sacred music in St Paul's, where they have a first-rate choir and a famous soprano named Mustapha: no doubt he sang very well, but I have to confess that that sort of timbre of voice gives me goose-flesh."

"And the opera?"

"Oh, I hardly ever go. It's always Verdi, Verdi, Verdi. The screaming from the stage only matched by the screaming from the audience. But I hope that, later on, I may have the pleasure of hearing Mademoiselle Stubbe sing for us."

"I'll see to it that you shall. She has a delightful voice and, what's more, knows how to use it. But then, so she should…" She gave him a light tap on the wrist with the fan she always carried, whatever the temperature. "She has, after all, studied under someone of the highest competence!"…

The moment was well chosen. *Asya* had, on Nekrasov's insistence, been dispatched to Russia and was to appear in that month's edition of *Sovremennik*. He still had not found a satisfactory form for *A Nest of Gentry*, and the temptation to put it aside and go treasure-hunting with Botkin and Ivanov was beginning to wear away at his newly acquired disciplinary habits. Instead, he launched himself enthusiastically into his unusual assignment. Consulting almost daily with Cherkassky and Rostovstev, in little more than a month he had completed his task. 'Memorandum on the publication of the journal: *The Economic Indicator*' was a remarkable document in that it anticipated most of the features of the eventual Act of Emancipation, which was still three battle-scarred years away. His chief concern was to strike the right balance; never far from his mind were some words Cherkassky told him Koshelyov, a fellow-collaborator of his on *Russian Conversation,* had written to the Czar: 'This reform is more necessary for us than it is for the serfs themselves; until now we have been the victims of a system that destroys our human qualities more surely than it does theirs.' Consequently the chief appeal in the memorandum was not only to the conscience of the nobles, but to their self-interest. Turgenev himself was convinced that even though the abolition of serfdom might cause the landowners a temporary financial loss, the eventual result of free men working the land would eventually be bound to be more profitable. Hence the memorandum urged the more recalcitrant nobles to speed up the process, already underway in many parts of the country, of changing from *barshchina,* fixed service on the land, to *obrok,* a form of quit-rent, or payment in lieu of service; this would prepare the peasants for a large degree of autonomy. It recognized that they would have to own their own land and that the government would need to pay compensation to the landowners. Heeding Elena Pavlovna's warning that Alexander would furiously resent any specification of details, which he considered his unique prerogative, no suggestion was put forward of either the amount of land or the extent of the payment. But the nobles were encouraged to believe that, despite their fears, they would, in the long term, be better off.

Turgenev ended his memorandum with a heartfelt appeal to the censors. The *Economic Indicator*, he assured them, would not be a dissident, anti-governmental publication; on the contrary, it would be loyally serving the government which, by setting up the provincial councils, had demonstrated that the reforms, although originally pronounced from above, would need, to have any real effect, to be supported from below. He ended with an appeal that the Palazzo Altieri group felt alone justified their having co-opted him. 'We are ready,' he wrote, 'to move towards this government to which we have always been subject, but which only recently we have begun to love.'

Prince Cherkassky returned enthusiastically to St Petersburg to consign the memorandum to Grand Duke Constantine, who happened to be in Poland at the time. Whether he read it on his return, or whether it was somehow kept from him, was not known. The impatient prince probably made the mistake of handing it over to one of the members of the 'secret committee'. Turgenev later let it be known to a close circle of his friends that it had apparently been considered 'premature'. Not one issue of the *Economic Indicator* ever saw the light of day.

Hôtel d'Angleterre,
Roma.
15 February, 1858.

Dear Paulinette,

I was very happy to receive your letter, even though the spelling mistakes took a slight edge off my pleasure. Try and correct this fault, dear daughter; it gives such a bad impression, however charming or interesting the actual content may be. I was delighted to hear of your progress, both with your studies and at the piano; I can see I am going to have a well-educated and talented daughter. I hope I will be able to live up to her!

I have been much taken up the past few weeks with the movement to free the serfs in Russia. I know this will not be of great interest to you in detail, but I'm sure you will be glad to know your papa is not forgetting those who are so much worse off than we are. Apart from that, I am at last getting down to serious work on a new novel I have had in mind for some time.

I would like to think I could finish it by the end of the year. But soon I shall be on my travels again. I intend to return to France, after a short visit to some of the most beautiful cities in this endlessly beautiful country: Naples, Siena, Florence, Pisa and Venice. I shall then stop off in Vienna to see a Doctor Sigmund about this malady of mine, which is still troubling me, though less so than last winter. After all that, I shall no doubt be relieved to arrive finally in Paris, where I must be at the latest by the third week in May when my friend, Prince Nikolai Orlov, has kindly asked me to be best man at his wedding. So we shall be seeing each other again before very long.

And now I must ask you to do something for me, and do it immediately, please. And that is to give me all the news about Madame Viardot and her family. I had hoped to receive a letter from her, but nothing has arrived in the past few weeks. Perhaps it has got lost in the post… or perhaps absence is an unforgivable crime. At any rate, I want to hear everything. Is Madame Viardot going to London, or is she perhaps already there? That might account for the absence of news. How is poor Monsieur Scheffer? I have heard that he was quite seriously ill. Madame will be sure to keep informed as to his condition. On these questions, and anything else that may come into your mind, please reply giving full details. _And soon_.

Goodbye for now, my dearest daughter. Work hard! I send you an embrace as strong as my love.

Your father,
I. Turgenev

"**Y**ou remember Molière's Monsieur Filerin, doyen of the medical profession, exhorting his fellow-doctors?"

Turgenev was talking to Herzen in front of a welcome coal fire on a chilly mid-May evening in London. "'Men's greatest weakness is their love of life; and we, with our pompous gibberish, know how to take advantage of the veneration for our profession which the fear of dying inspires in them. With our patients, therefore, let us agree always to take credit for successful cures and blame nature for our blunders.' The illustrious Viennese Doctor Sigmund, whom I went well out of my way to visit because of his exalted European reputation, belongs firmly in that tradition, differing from his Parisian and Berliner colleagues only in the extent of his verbosity. He told me in five thousand words what I could have told him in fifty: without a life-risking operation I am never likely to be totally cured of my bladder condition, but if I go on frequenting spas every year for the rest of my life, I may be able to control it so that the agony of that Paris winter will not have to be endured again."

Turgenev had gone straight to London, instead of Paris, in order to give Herzen a first-hand account of his meetings in Rome. He was received in Putney with all his old friend's customary warmth, and this time the two of them had more time to talk uninterrupted. *Kolokol* had now had two years of life and was read around Europe; its founder, whose eyes gleamed with satisfied amusement when he heard of the Grand Duchess Elena's hint that it was surreptitiously read even in the Winter Palace, still spent long hours every day in some branch or other of the business of getting the paper out; but he usually managed to keep his evenings clear. And Turgenev's horse's-mouth news of what was actually happening in St Petersburg and the rest of Russia was of invaluable importance to him. Not that the two men's interpretation of events always coincided…

"And you still believe Alexander's heart is really behind emancipation?" he asked his guest.

"I do. As the Grand Duchess indicated, he needs to be prodded from time to time. But there are plenty of determined prodders in Peter, the most determined of all being his own brother."

"I'm glad to hear it. But I suspect that there are also many good enough souls who liked the idea when it could tickle their liberal self-esteem, but are beginning to have doubts now they see the process might lighten their pockets. Your friend Tolstoy, for instance…"

"Oh, I think Lev Nikolayevich's afterthoughts have quite a different origin."

"Namely?"

"When we discussed the matter less than two years ago, he was seriously considering freeing all his serfs immediately. But they were suspicious of his motives, and thought they would get better terms from the government. Then came the Czar's proclamation, the emancipation movement got under way and Lev Nikolayevich's enthusiasm waned. It's part of his intractable nature: if he can think of an idea as his exclusive invention, it will be brilliant and must be realized instantaneously; if its origins lie elsewhere – let alone if he gets the faintest suspicion it is being imposed on him – it immediately loses validity."

"You're hard on him. I thought you were good friends."

"We are the best of friends… and the best of enemies. There are moments when I feel in perfect harmony with him. There are others – more frequent, I fear – when his chronic inability to be at ease with himself destroys any possibility of normal intercourse with anyone else. Only one aspect of his personality is unquestionable: his talent as a writer. As I've told him many times, if he perseveres and doesn't let himself be distracted by the thousand other whims he picks up and discards like a miner sifting for gold, he will produce exceptional work. As for the rest, he is an anthill of contradictions."

Behind his bushy moustache, the corner of Herzen's lip lifted in an ironic smile. "According to the natives of this country that has generously granted me its hospitality," he said, "that simply identifies him as our compatriot. We are not famed for our consistency. And with good reason, as I have recently had occasion to discover. You remember Chicherin?"

"Boris Nikolayevich? The lawyer?"

"Yes, and one of the more liberal of our noblemen, we always thought. He has stayed with me here in London, and with his trained legal mind gave me one or two good ideas for the launching of *Kolokol*. And now, in a letter which I printed in last month's edition, he claims that because the paper calls for extreme change in Russia, irrespective of the level of society that initiates that change, I am actively calling for revolution."

"That could do a lot of damage to our cause. Have you received any letters of comment, one way or the other?"

"Yes. That's why I brought up the unpredictability for which we are famous. I had a letter only yesterday from Kavelin, Professor of Philosophy of Law at St Petersburg University."

"I know him slightly. He contributes occasionally to *Sovremennik*. What does *he* say? Don't tell me he supports Chicherin's position."

"On the contrary, he defends mine better than I could have done myself. He says Chicherin, who is an old friend and colleague of his, might as well have gone over, body and soul, to the reactionaries. Aleksander Herzen, he writes, is, as I am,

376

an advocate of change – radical change. But he is no revolutionary."

Turgenev raised an interrogatory eyebrow. "I wish I were as sure as he is about that last part," he murmured.

"You can be, as long as the Czar keeps the momentum moving forward. But if he weakens under pressure – and, God knows, the pressure will be strong – then there may be only two choices for Russia: stagnation or revolution. And in that case I hope I know which side I should be on."

Turgenev replied affably: "I suppose I must be content with that as reassurance. Alexander may take his time – the legislation involved is extraordinarily complicated – but I have no doubt about his determination to succeed. And to help him along, I shall go to see the Grand Duchess as soon as I get back and arrange for a lot of prominent people to co-sign a letter I shall write, supporting Kavelin's position. When that appears in *Kolokol,* who knows? Chicherin's attack may prove a double-edged weapon."

"You are invaluable to me, Vanichka. I think of you as a spy in the enemy camp – my eyes and ears in St Petersburg. Will you stay there for the rest of the year."

"No, for as short a time as possible. I must hurry down to Spasskoye."

"For the shooting?"

"For that too, but not only for that. I have a book I want to finish before the end of the year and I intend to free my serfs as soon as possible. I don't have to wait for the government to tell me how to dispose of my 'baptized property'."

"Have you thought how you're going to do it?"

"I'll have to discuss the final details with my uncle Nikolai. He is, after all, managing the estate… although whether in my interests or his, I'm never quite sure. But I've worked out the general lines. I shall abolish *barshchina* and transfer all my peasants to *obrok*. They shall own their own houses and enough land for them to feed their families; in return, they'll pay me about one rouble an acre."

"Many of them will not have it."

"They can make the payment over a number of years – with no interest. After all, I have to have some compensation. From now on, I shall have to hire labourers for all the work on my estates. I have calculated that it will cost me between a quarter and a third of my income. But nobody will have to call me *barin* again."

Herzen smiled as he leaned forward to throw another log on to the fire. "They'll go on calling you *barin* just the same. And unless the muzhik has changed in the twelve years since I left Russia, a lot of them will be none too enthusiastic about your offer of *obrok*. They'd rather do a little – as little as possible, of course – work on your land and know that their bread and vodka is guaranteed, than suddenly become independent and responsible for their own welfare."

Turgenev looked surprised. "I thought you were almost on a par with the Aksakovs in believing in the inherent wisdom of the Russian peasant."

Herzen chuckled. "I am, Vanichka, I am. I simply believe it may take some time for that wisdom to manifest itself after centuries of slavery. But don't misunderstand me: what you are doing is good. I just hope you won't be disappointed by the results. You still believe in an enlightened class of educated liberals like yourself gradually leading the exploited of this earth into democratic contentment. I had that dream too. 1848 killed it. And not just once. Many times. In Paris, Naples, Vienna, Frankfurt, Berlin…"

"So what hope is there?"

It was a while before Herzen replied. When he did, the animation had drained from his face. "There is the hope that Russia will find its own way out of tyranny and repression. The western European way has proved a failure: all the ideals we believed in before 1848 have been commuted into the pursuit of material objects. Look at France and its petit-bourgeois Emperor and Empress. What a dismal sight! The middle classes genuflecting before property and the poor with only one ambition: to become middle class. Morality has been reduced to the have-nots trying desperately to clutch what the haves try equally desperately to preserve. Envy on the one hand, avarice on the other. How can we want Russia to copy the West?"

"We must revive the ideals of 1848, but realize them better. You and I are old, but that is what we should try to instil into the young and idealistic."

"Perhaps you and I should agree to go our different ways – with the same aim in mind. You believe in improvement gradually filtering down from the top; I rather see it swelling up from below, yes, even from those muzhiks I was being cynical about a few moments ago. This Czar will never grant a constitution, with a freely elected government. So let the local assemblies, with their specialized knowledge of what is needed in each part of the country, become a model for local government, and that spread to provincial level and on up."

Turgenev shook his head. "I'm afraid twelve years away has cast a rosy glow over your memories of the reality of our country."

Herzen smiled again and leaned over to pat his friend's knee. "The important thing is for us not to quarrel. We both want the best for our poor country, even if we sometimes differ as to how to bring it about. Let us go on working in our own ways for those who, in the past, have worked so hard for us – and with such scant reward."

Herzen was not the only person Turgenev had come to see in London. Pauline Viardot was appearing at Covent Garden in *Don Giovanni;* but this time the most famous Donna Anna of her day was taking the role of Zerlina. The universally spiteful tongues of opera-lovers had wagged to the effect that playing a girl of eighteen was a risky venture at thirty-seven, and Turgenev had decided not to announce his presence; if the unthinkable were to occur and her performance not to be up to her usual standard – let alone a downright embarrassment – he would spare himself the agony of having to assure her she had been as wonderful as ever. A useless undertaking, anyhow: she would know he was lying before he had uttered two words. But he need not have worried: once again she astonished the discerning London audience by her totally convincing assumption of a part. And when, in 'Batti, batti' (which would have turned the most sternly unforgiving of Spanish males into a cuddly teddy bear), she told Masetto that she would submit to his blows like a little lamb, an inexperienced opera-goer would have wondered how so young a singer could possess so impregnable a technique.

But it was no girl of eighteen who greeted Turgenev with some surprise when he went round to her dressing room after the performance. On knocking at the door, he was disconcerted to feel his heart thumping absurdly away in his chest. It was six months since they had laid eyes on each other, and her failure to reply to almost all his letters from Italy was not encouraging. And now, seeing he had been preceded by a couple of her admirers, he cursed himself for not having announced his presence. Her stare of incredulous astonishment gave way instantaneously to the warmest of smiles; but did this reflect the practised delight of an actress, or the spontaneous happiness of – at the least – a dear friend?

"Why didn't you tell us you were coming?" She gestured to Louis who was standing beside her and had shaken Turgenev's hand with unusual warmth. "We could have had supper together. But tonight, I'm afraid…"

Turgenev, to avoid having to hear her excuse, immediately said that he had a prior engagement. He couldn't help noticing she looked rather relieved, but immediately turned to the silver-haired gentleman with a monocle she had been talking to before he came in and asked him to excuse her: "A very old friend I haven't seen for ages…" Then turning back to Turgenev, with an affectionate arm on his sleeve: "But what brought you to London?"

Turgenev couldn't resist remarking that he had told her in his last letter that he had been invited to the annual dinner of the Royal Literary Fund, but immediately added: "No doubt it didn't catch up with you, wherever you were."

"But how interesting. And how flattering. Tell us about it. Who was there?"

"Well, it was presided over by Lord Palmerston, a most impressive, self-assured man, and a great champion of freedom. Then there was Dickens, words pouring out of his mouth as irrepressibly as they seem to on to the page, who told me he had had a delightful dinner in Paris with you and Madame Sand a couple of years ago. Thackeray, whom I don't think I like very much: a little too determinedly jolly for my taste. And Macaulay, who has no time for any opinion except his own…"

"A distinguished company," Viardot remarked. "The pillars of English literary society. You must have enjoyed yourself."

"I did, to a certain extent. But I rather had the impression that everyone was trying to compete. Fortunately my pedestrian English absolved me from that task. But it was more than just a social engagement. The dinner was given to launch a plan to raise funds for authors who find it hard to make ends meet. I was most impressed by this, and intend to copy the scheme as soon as I get back to Russia." He wondered whether she had taken this in, as her eyes had wandered to the door and, the moment he drew breath, she excused herself: "I'm sorry, Ivan, what you are saying is very interesting, but that man who has just come in is Sir Henry Plumpton. I just must have a word with him. Please excuse me. Give Louis all your news and he'll pass it on to me." One second's intense gaze from those luminous black eyes. "And then we'll see each other very, very soon, I hope." And she was gone.

Louis, looking a little uncomfortable, explained: "Plumpton is an important entrepreneur; he is organizing a concert tour for Pauline this summer in the North of England. But tell me, Ivan, how can you manage to stay away from your country at this momentous time?"

"I am on my way back, and I shall remain there for the rest of the year. Just a day or two in Paris and I shall be off."

"Do you have business in Paris?"

"Ambassador Orlov is to be married next week, and he has asked me to be his best man."

"What an honour!"

"Indeed it is. We are old friends, and when I demurred, he told me it was the least he could do to make up for his father's having sent me to prison. So I shall perform that function, say hello and goodbye to Paulinette and obey the call of my fatherland."

"I'm sorry we shall miss you at Courtavenel this summer. But, to make up for our loss, we shall have the pleasure of Paulinette's company. She is turning into such a charming young lady." He gave a thoughtful puff on his cigar. "I am glad to hear that you will be in Russia, Ivan. I'm sure you will have a great influence on events, in general by your writing and in particular by your example. We are all waiting with bated breath to see whether emancipation will indeed come about."

"You may have to release your breath now and again to avoid suffocation," Turgenev said with a smile. "Nothing is going to happen fast. But happen, sooner or later, I am convinced it will. And when it is all over, I shall come back to Courtavenel, if I may, and we will shoot some game and continue our translation work with our consciences clear."

"Ah, your conscience will be clear," Viardot sighed. "But as long as that upstart impostor is lording it over France, I shall never feel at home there. But I see Pauline signalling to me. I too must go and pay my respects to Plumpton. *Au revoir*, my dear friend. And continue the fight; you at least, in your country, can still do so."

On May 21st, Prince Nikolai Orlov was married to the young Princess Ekaterina Trubetskoy at a lavish ceremony attended by the entire Russian aristocratic colony of Paris. Word had got around of the best man's close relations with the Grand Duchess Elena Pavlovna, and Turgenev was bombarded with questions about the attitude at court to the emancipation question. But as many, if not most, of the questioners were firmly against any concession to 'the Reds', Turgenev favoured them with his most benign smile and remarked that it would be a pity to spoil such a happy occasion by discussing politics.

The next morning he went to see Madame Harang to ask her if she minded if he removed Paulinette from the school for a day. "I have seen so little of her recently," he told her, "and I shall be away again for another seven or eight months, so I would like, just for once, to spoil her a little." The good lady was entirely sympathetic and told Turgenev that, on the whole, she was well pleased with Paulinette's progress. "She works hard and gets on well with the other girls," she told him. "Her only faults are a tendency to lend too much importance to trivialities – earrings, bracelets, ribbons and so forth – but that's not unusual in girls of her age and will probably soon pass. The only other defect I need to reproach her with from time to time is a stubborn, almost mutinous streak she sometimes displays; she can be oversensitive and feel she is being persecuted when she is simply being corrected."

"She has had that tendency since she was a child," Turgenev observed. "We must try to eliminate it as far as possible, because it could cause her a lot of misery later on."

"Certainly. But I don't want to make too much of it. You have told me she did not have an easy childhood, and it would be surprising if some effects of that had not remained. But I have to tell you," and she gave Turgenev her best attempt at a roguish smile, "she is so devoted to you. I think all the efforts she makes are above all to please you. She practises very determinedly at the piano – although she is not especially gifted – and when you were in Italy last winter, she asked me if she could study Italian. She may surprise you with some verses of Petrarca, which she has learnt by heart. I think it is absolutely right that you should make your short visit a real treat for her."

The next day, Turgenev took his daughter for lunch at a celebrated restaurant surrounded by a beautiful garden in the Bois de Boulogne. After they had consulted the voluminous menu and made their choices, Paulinette looked around her as Turgenev studied the wine list. "I think the occasion calls for a glass of champagne," he said. "You won't disgrace me by getting tipsy, will you?"

"No, Papa, I promise. I'll make it last all through the meal." She leant forward and almost whispered to him: "Have you noticed that everyone is staring at us?"

Turgenev, having surreptitiously ascertained that this was in fact so, commented, rather smugly: "Well, you know, your father does have his little reputation, even in Paris."

"I'm sorry, but I don't think it's anything to do with that."

"What do you put it down to then?"

Paulinette blushed slightly and gave him a naughty smile. "I think they think I'm your *petite amie*."

"Paulinette!" He flung the wine list down on the table and gazed across at her as sternly as he could manage. "What a thing to say! You shouldn't be thinking like that, let alone talking like that."

She gave a little giggle. "Oh, come on, Papa, don't forget I'm sixteen. You can't expect me to stay a little girl for ever. And anyway, look at the company we're in. Almost all the ladies here could be the daughters of the gentlemen they're with – but I don't think any of the others are."

Turgenev couldn't resist smiling back. "You seem to be learning more at Madame Harang's than literature and languages. I see I shall have to be more careful about where I take you in future."

"Oh no, you can bring me here any time you want. It's a lovely place… and I'm so happy to be here with you."

The radiant smile on his daughter's habitually composed, almost expressionless, features brought a lump to Turgenev's throat, which thickened and swelled as it was rapidly replaced by a hint of tears, her face clouding over as she said: "I wish you weren't going away so soon. I haven't seen you for nine months and now you're off again, goodness knows for how long. Most of the other girls see their parents every week. Couldn't you stay a little longer?"

"I'm afraid I can't, my dear. You have to believe me, I'm needed back in Russia. You know there are great changes in the air, and it's important that your father is there to do what he can to influence them."

Paulinette considered this gloomily for a moment and then her eyes lit up. "Papa, I have a wonderful idea. School will be over soon. Why don't you stay just another few weeks and then take me to Russia with you?" As her father just gazed at her in silence, as though he had hardly understood what she had said, she continued: "Oh, don't say no until you've given it some thought. Just think, I'm sure there are ways in which I could be useful to you. I don't know… I could help you entertain your friends… I'm much more grown-up than you think, you know. The Herring says I've made big strides this year. There are all sorts of things we could…" She broke off, seeing him avert his glance from her desperately appealing eyes. "Oh why not, Papa? I'd so love to go back. And see Spasskoye again. After all, I am Russian. What reason can you have to say no?"

For a brief moment Turgenev let himself consider this totally unexpected proposition… *could it do so much harm for her to come for three months, before going back for her last year at the pension? She would keep me company at Spasskoye and wouldn't get in my way. And if she became as fond of the place as I am myself, she might... But no, I can already hear the voices, both in Peter and in Orel.. Have you heard? Ivan Sergeyevich is back, and instead of one of his mistresses he's brought his illegitimate daughter!... No, no, it would never do...*

"There are many reasons, Paulinette. First of all you must finish your studies before we can think of your making the trip to Russia. Secondly, I shall be very much involved in a whole number of matters: the political situation, settling affairs with my serfs, and trying to finish a book by the end of the year. I would have no time to be with you. And then, what would you do at Spasskoye, where I shall be spending most of my time? You don't remember a word of the language, and not many people around Spasskoye speak French.

Paulinette hadn't quite given up. "But I'm sure it would come back to me," she pleaded. "After all, if I can learn new languages quite easily..."

Her father cut her short. "Perhaps it would, perhaps it wouldn't. But there's another thing you haven't thought of: Monsieur and Madame Viardot are expecting you at Courtavenel for the summer."

The tears that had been lurking now cascaded down. "Oh, do I *have* to, Papa?"

"Have to?! What a way to put it. Of course you will go. You're very lucky to have such an enchanting place to spend your holiday. Most other girls your age would give anything to be in your place."

And there was the mutinous expression detected by Madame Harang, lips clenched together, eyes cast down.

"Let *them* go, then."

Turgenev repressed an angry retort. "Paulinette, don't spoil our nice lunch. Now tell me, calmly, what possible reason you could have for not wanting to go."

"I can't."

"Of course you can. It may be difficult, but remember, I'm your father. You can say whatever you like to me. I may not agree with you, and I may rebuke you if I think you are being unreasonable. But I will not rebuke you for speaking your mind. Now, tell me why you don't like the idea of going to Courtavenel."

Sniffling, she blew her nose and dabbed at her cheeks before answering, tentatively: "Well, there are lots of things, but especially it's Louise."

"You don't get on any longer?"

"We've never got on. We hate each other, and always have. You just didn't notice. And when you were there a lot of the time, she didn't dare to be too beastly. But now..."

"Now what? What does she do?"

"Oh, it's dozens of little things that seem trivial but all add up to trying to spite me whenever she gets the chance."

"What sort of things?"

"Well, like always telling Madame Viardot that it's my fault if anything goes wrong, or gets broken… or barging in when I'm playing with the two little girls – they're the sweetest little dears, I adore *them* – and trying to interrupt whatever we're doing and take my place, because she's their *real* sister. She even spites me when I'm playing the piano. She plays better than I do, so when we perform a duet for Madame Viardot – who, heaven knows, is critical enough anyway – she plays much faster than we'd rehearsed it, so sometimes I can't keep up and feel really silly…"

"All the more reason to practise harder, so you'll become as good as she is."

She opened her mouth as though to give him a sharp retort, then dropped her head and muttered dumbly: "Yes, Papa."

That was a stupid remark: pompous and unhelpful. I must do better… but I feel so out of my element… what do I know about what goes on between two almost grown-up young girls? I must remember to write to Pauline about this… but does she ever read my letters any more?…

"He reached across the table and tenderly took her hand. "If what you say is really true, and you're not exaggerating, as you often do, my advice to you would be to maintain a certain distance from Louise. Sometimes it's better, in family life – and not only in family life, for that matter – to stand aside and not participate too actively. I'm not preaching indifference, just the art of trying to acquire a sense of when to advance and when to retire. Do you understand me?"

"I think so. I'll try."

"That's a good girl. It's not easy to be your age: you're no longer a little girl and not quite yet a grown woman. And I appreciate that for you it's perhaps particularly difficult, in that you are not quite a member of the family in the way the others are. But everyone treats you as though you were, so you're really a very lucky girl, aren't you?"

This only elicited a resigned nod.

"There is one other thing I should say to you, though. I am sure a lot of what you say about Louise is true. But you are sometimes too touchy about other people's behaviour towards you. I've noticed also from your letters that if something doesn't go exactly the way you want it to, or someone doesn't behave exactly as you think they should, you turn what is essentially a quite trivial little matter into a catastrophe. So let's not make a tragedy out of spending a summer at Courtavenel… and see instead what the waiter recommends in the way of ice-cream?"…

As soon as Turgenev arrived in St Petersburg, early in June, he was given a lavish welcome-home dinner party at Dusseau's, the capital's most fashionable restaurant. Botkin was there with Ivanov; the two of them had come back together from Rome with sketches of the now almost completed painting, and Botkin was hoping to help him find a buyer. Ivanov greeted Turgenev with effusive pleasure, hoping, no doubt, to renew the free-flowing conversations the three of them had enjoyed in the Roman campagna. But seeing the guest of honour receiving the prodigal son treatment, with everyone trying to catch his attention, he soon relapsed into a gloomy silence, punctuated only by occasional bouts of talking to himself. Nekrasov and the Panaevs were hosts, and proposed endless toasts to the hero of the evening; even Avdotya Panaeva embraced him and told him how greatly he had been missed. Turgenev noticed that the guests belonged exclusively to the 'old guard'; it might have been the same party as that which had welcomed him back two years ago. Annenkov was there, of course, and Druzhinin, who no longer contributed to *Sovremennik*. Towards the end of the evening, Turgenev drew Nekrasov aside and asked him why there were none of the new men there; he had expected at least to see Chernyshevsky, having heard what an important position he now held on the paper. Nekrasov, showing what in anyone else might have seemed a trace of embarrassment, put his arm around his shoulders and murmured confidentially that he had wanted this evening to be a purely social event: "We are all here with no other intention but to welcome you home," he said. "There will be plenty of time to discuss work over the coming weeks. "Not so much," Turgenev told him. "I'm only planning to stay in Peter four or five days. Then I leave for Spasskoye. My uncle is expecting me: we have much to discuss. I'm proposing, against his will, of course, to free all my remaining serfs. I can no longer wait until the government has finally made up its mind how it wants to do it."

"Well, we must grab you before you leave, then," Nekrasov said. "Come and see us tomorrow afternoon. Chernyshevsky will be there, and our new literary critic, Dobrolyubov. You haven't met him, have you?"

"No, but I've heard about him."

"He's a very bright young man. Don't be put off by his manner, which can be rather abrupt. It's mostly shyness. When you get to know him better, I'm sure you'll be impressed by his brilliance."

Turgenev agreed that he would meet them all there the following afternoon.

But when he arrived at the familiar apartment on the Fontanka, which served both as living quarters for the Panaevs and Nekrasov and the *Sovremennik* offices, he was greeted by Chernyshevsky with the news that Nekrasov had been called away on a matter of vital urgency – 'some tedious financial business' – but had insisted that the two of them talk things over with the greatest frankness. It had been almost three years since they last met, and Turgenev noticed a certain change in the man. Not in his physical appearance: with his mop of reddish-brown hair and thick brows, ill-kempt beard and awkward, shambling manner, he still would be taken rather as a muzhik who had made his way up in the world, than the only son of a village priest. But his new position of authority on the editorial board of *Sovremennik* had, at least in appearance, softened him; he no longer seemed to find it necessary to inject every opinion with the maximum aggression; in conversation, if not in print, he was now sure enough of himself to be able to express himself with quiet conviction.

"We are very pleased to have you back, Ivan Sergeyevich," he began, after waving Turgenev into a chair. "Your contributions have been slender indeed over the past year or two. We don't have so many writers of your quality that we can afford to dispense with you."

Turgenev found it hard to repress an insidious feeling of resentment at being talked to *de haut en bas* by a man ten years younger than himself, who had been a poor scholar in a seminary when he had first started contributing to *Sovremennik*; but he fought it back and replied, with his most gracious smile: "As you probably know, Nikolai Gavrilovich, I was, for various reasons, unable to write very much for a certain period. But I hope that my return home will revivify my pen. I am working on something which I hope to be able to submit to…" (he was about to say 'to Nekrasov', but thought better of it)… "to you all by the end of the year. And then there was that little story you published in January."

"Ah yes… *Asya*, wasn't it? The piece you wrote in Rome…"

Turgenev gave an even broader smile. "You say that as though anything written in Rome would inevitably be of inferior quality."

Chernyshevsky, ignoring the lightness of tone, considered this with full seriousness. "It's perhaps a case that could be argued… at least for a Russian writer. But that's probably not the trouble. You would, no doubt, have written *Asya* wherever you had been."

"I take it you didn't like the story."

"There has been much of your work that I have preferred."

"And what was it that you felt let me down. Speak freely, Nikolai Gavrilovich, I always welcome criticism… especially from someone as discerning as yourself."

"Well, it goes without saying that it was finely written. There is nobody who writes descriptive prose as elegantly and evocatively as you. Your portrayal of the little riverside town and the country round it made us feel as though we were there. But the trouble lay with the narrator."

"What was the matter with my poor narrator?"

"You may have answered the question yourself. You call him 'poor'. Perhaps he is that, in other senses than the one you intended…

He broke off as the door opened and a young man in his early twenties walked in and was introduced as 'my invaluable colleague, Nikolai Aleksandrovich Dobrolyubov'. The first thing Turgenev noticed about him was that he was dressed even more shabbily than Chernyshevsky. His black sack-like jacket was frayed at the elbows, his tie had been knotted round his neck like a shoelace and his trousers looked as though they hadn't been pressed nor his shoes cleaned since they'd been bought. He was tall, skeleton-thin with a pinched, sallow face and a bony nose on which perched a squat pair of glasses. His already thinning hair was uncombed, his fingernails dirty. He quickly grasped and immediately released Turgenev's proffered hand and stood there, fidgeting nervously, as though not feeling enough at ease with himself or the company to wish to remain in the same place for any longer than necessary.

"Ivan Sergeyevich and I were just talking about his story, *Asya.*"

This elicited nothing but an uninterested, "Oh."

Chernyshevsky turned back to Turgenev. "We felt that you expected your readers to take a sympathetic attitude towards him. We didn't."

"You disliked him?"

"We despised him. And we think our readers should too. Because we see him, not just as a superficial, dithering young man, but as representative of all that is blocking Russia's path towards progress."

Turgenev couldn't resist a protest. "My dear man, aren't you making much ado about really very little. It was a slight, harmless tale for people to enjoy…"

"Our readers have changed since you started writing for this paper. They want more now than a mild divertissement to pass an empty evening. And they are not all, as they used to be, from the same comfortable background as you. They are looking for signs pointing to the way ahead. And your narrator points directly back into the past. His indecision – about even so banal a problem as whether or not to declare his love for the girl – his incapacity to come down on one side or the other of the fence is a symbol of all that is preventing any real improvement in the state of Russian society.

"There I have to disagree with you. There have already been real improvements in Russian society in this new reign: censorship has eased up, passports are granted for foreign travel, university restrictions have been relaxed, the Decembrist survivors have been recalled from Siberia. All this may not mean much to you young men, but to those of us who lived through the forties, it opens up a new world. You must, however reluctantly, give the Czar some credit. And soon there will be the emancipation of the serfs.

387

"Soon?! But when? And how? The way things are going, it looks as though the serf may become technically free, but with such crippling financial burdens that he will remain a slave in all but name. We praised the Czar when he first made his pronouncement: you may remember I myself wrote an article comparing him to Peter the Great; I even reverted to my religious education and called down blessings on him as a peacemaker. But what a false spring that turned out to be; now everything is in the hands, at worst, of diehard reactionaries, at best, of people like your narrator: should we do it this way, should we do it that way, should we do it all? Another year or two of this, and it will be time for the peasants to take matters into their own hands with axes and pitchforks."

Turgenev spread his hands and murmured, knowing he was being provocative: "The impatience of youth!"

Dobrolyubov sprang to his feet and strode over to the window. "That's just what Nikolai Gavrilovich was talking about! Another woolly generalization, typical of you people." He turned back, leaning against the window, his hands thrust into his pockets. "We find no virtue in a patience which justifies wrong being protracted *ad infinitum*. In cases like that, patience itself becomes a wrong."

"Oh dear. We seem to be drifting rather far from my little story. Which, unlike some of my other work, I believe, had no political purpose whatsoever. It only asked the reader to take a moment and reflect on the vagaries of human nature. Is there any harm in that?"

If he thought of this as a rhetorical question, he was to be quickly disillusioned. "Yes," Dobrolyubov snapped, "there is. The time has passed for 'reflecting on the vagaries of human nature'. Any art which doesn't in some way further the cause of human progress is as useless as a china ornament on a table which no one ever looks at."

"With respect, Nikolai Aleksandrovich, quite a lot of people seem to have looked at my humble ornament. Nekrasov told me it was one of the most well-liked pieces the paper had published in quite some time."

The young critic opened his mouth to retort, but thought better of it, turned and gazed moodily out of the window. Chernyshevsky took up the cudgel, but wielded it with marginally greater delicacy. "It had some success with our older readers, yes. But we are now trying to attract the younger generation. And they are seeking something very different... something your *Asyas* cannot give them. Because there's another quality which your characters are always promoting; it's an offshoot of patience I suppose, but it's even more negative. And it's the last thing young people want to hear about."

"And what is this terrible vice?"

"Resignation. Most of the men in your recent work end up gloomily resigned to their fate. You seem to be telling us that is the best we can ever attain. But we think those days are over. We believe new men and women will appear – are appearing – who will be *im*patient, who will *not* resign themselves, who will accept nothing just 'because it is there', but will fight to replace it with something better. And that's what we at *Sovremennik* want – and intend – to encourage our contributors to provide."

Turgenev gave the impression he was taking time to let this sink in, although it was only the medicine (albeit in a rather stronger dose) that Botkin and Druzhinin's accounts had led him to expect. Then he said slowly: "That may well be, Nikolai Gavrilovich. But what they will be providing will be propaganda, not art. It is not art's job to change things. The most it can do is perhaps create a climate in which things may be more easily changed. But poetry and music never by themselves changed anything."

Chernyshevsky returned his gaze. "That," he said, "is why I have no time for poetry and music."

"Whereas for me they are as necessary as life itself, *'più del pane ch'io mangio, più del aria che spiro'*."

"What does that mean?" Dobrolyubov almost yawned from his window.

"It means they are for me what women were for Don Giovanni – more necessary than the bread I eat, than the air I breathe. They are the great consolations for the disappointments and disillusion that make up so much of life."

"And there's your third negative quality – and the worst of all." Dobrolyubov walked forward, hands still plunged into his pockets, and stared down at Turgenev who looked up at him with, by now, a certain discomposure. "Pessimism. It exudes from your pages. Nothing is worth striving for, fighting to achieve. It's all a waste of time. Nothing good can ever come of it. Look at your Rudin. You parody your friend Bakunin, who happens to have been languishing in Peter and Paul for something he *did* believe was worth fighting for, and make him out to be completely ineffective. All his words empty air. But don't you see, you've created your 'superfluous man' in your own image... and in that of your friends and contemporaries... perhaps it's the result of your circumstances: it's easier to be miserable in comfort than when your stomach's empty and your teeth are chattering with cold... but he's totally out of date now. We want *Sovremennik* to inspire young people to positive action. But if you go on and on about the uselessness of everything..."

"Not everything." Turgenev's tone sharpened for the first time. "You are both putting too much weight on a slender tale I wrote in Italy. And forgetting that I have done other work. You will certainly never have heard me talk about the uselessness of Gogol. I'm sure I don't need to remind you that I even suffered for my humble championing of his genius. But what he wrote was literature, not propaganda."

"And that's what we want you to do, Ivan Sergeyevich." Chernyshevsky reduced his voice to a purr and even attempted a smile, but Turgenev had the feeling that this was a habit he had when preparing to stick the knife in even further. "Let's forget *Asya*. It had its charming moments, and no doubt helped you to while away your days in southern climes. But now you are back, we hope for a long time. And we want you to engage your unique talent in the cause of something more substantial; something that will concern itself at least partially with the ills of your country and what can be done to remedy them. I remember you wrote, a few years ago, that there were certain periods of history when it was impossible for literature to be an art alone. Surely you must agree that this is one of them."

"I do. And I believe the work I am currently engaged on will reflect this."

"Good! Would you be prepared to say a word or two about it?"

To have you and your fellow hyena sink your teeth into it before it's even written? You must take me for an even bigger fool than I thought!

"I think for the moment that would be premature. I still haven't seen clearly myself the exact direction it's going to take. But it will certainly be a work of more substance than *Asya*, and I hope it will not disgrace the pages of *Sovremennik*."

Chernyshevsky got to his feet. *He's telling me the interview is at an end.* "We have no fear of that, Ivan Sergeyevich."

"I'm glad to hear it. But, however it comes out, it will not, I am sure, tell the readers what to think. That I must leave to them."

Turgenev heaved himself out of his chair, bestowed a gracious smile of farewell on Dobrolyubov, who replied with a curt nod, and let himself be accompanied to the front door by Chernyshevsky, who took leave of him with a long, cordial handshake. "You are one of our glories, Ivan Sergeyevich," he said. "We will never expect you to abandon completely your poetic vein. We can count on the 'new men' for that. But don't forget the lesson of your revered master and friend, Belinsky…"

"He dared to throw Belinsky in my face!…" was Turgenev's first outraged comment to Annenkov and Druzhinin, when he dined with them that evening. "I'd give my immortal soul, if I believed I had one, to hear what Visya would have had to say to those two."

"Like all fanatics," Annenkov observed, "they see only one side of an argument… and that's the side they want to see. They remember that Belinsky insisted that the artist was connected organically with the issues of his society and his era. But they forget that he also wrote that he was proud and happy to call himself a *littérateur*. How many times have we heard him say: 'Russian literature is my life and my blood.'

"The crux of the question, it seems to me," Turgenev said, "is to what extent Nekrasov is going to give those two a free hand. Is he going to relinquish all responsibility and let them have their heads. Because, if so, there is no room for us on the paper."

As you know," Druzhinin said, "that is a conclusion I came to over a year ago. I'm afraid Nekrasov has changed since you were last here. He's been involved in some murky financial transactions and unfortunately, from what I hear, has not always acted very scrupulously. Many of his old supporters are keeping a certain distance from him; I think that's partly why he is so obsessed with attracting young people."

Annenkov agreed. "Yes, he told me the other day that the readership of *Sovremennik* has become creaky-limbed, and we're just spoon-feeding them pap for easy consumption. Young people have become impatient with the slow progress of the reforms – and you can't blame them for that – and they want to hear new voices. For him, that means Chernyshevsky and Dobrolyubov."

Druzhinin gave a wry grin. "And you were thrown naked into the lions' den! You can be sure that it was no accident that he left you alone with them. How did they treat you? Were they at least amiable?"

"Chernyshevsky, yes. He coated the pill with almost too much flattery. The other one could barely conceal his contempt. He looked at me with eyes that would turn a hot soup cold before you could get the spoon to your mouth. But there's something about him that fascinates me. I suppose it's his certainty; he seems more sure about everything at twenty-two than I am about anything at forty. But my personal opinion of them is of no matter. What I have to ask myself is, will I be able to collaborate with them."

Annenkov was in no doubt. "You must, Vanichka. Otherwise the whole tone of the paper will become unbalanced. There'll be nobody of any authority to oppose them. Apart from all other considerations, even with the relaxed censorship, six months of being a mouthpiece for their convictions, and *Sovremennik* will be no more."

Druzhinin demurred. "Too late, Pavlochka. *Sovremennik*, as the paper founded by Pushkin and revived by Belinsky, is already dead. The best thing Vanichka could do – and I don't say this only for selfish reasons – is to come over to me and write for *Readers' Library*."

Turgenev thought for a moment, looking from one friend to another. "Perhaps my choice does not have to be so drastic," he eventually said. "I signed an exclusive deal with Nekrasov and Panaev two years ago, but under these new circumstances, I don't feel bound by that any more. Tolstoy has ignored the agreement for months. So I will present them with a test case. Let's see what they will do with my *Nest of Gentry*. I think it will turn out less 'political' than *Rudin*; it may even find some favour with the Slavophils. If they can accept that, so much the better; if not, I'll have to try and peddle my wares elsewhere... with a preference of course for you, Sasha. And then there's always Katkov... we had a quarrel three years ago over my

Faust, which he thought I'd promised to him, although I hadn't. But he's started asking me for material again, so…"

Annenkov chuckled. "If you go to him and publish in his *Russian Herald*, that will be a declaration of war on *Sovremennik*."

"Why? Has he quarrelled with them too?"

"It's more than a quarrel. It's an ideological gulf. Over the emancipation dispute, he's begun to take the side of the reactionaries as vehemently as they take that of the liberals. The young Mikhail Katkov, who sat with us at Belinsky's feet, would not give much joy to his master now."

Turgenev stretched his legs, clasped his hands behind his neck and gave a rueful laugh. "My God, how things change in this hothouse of a city. You're away for a little less than two years and you don't know who your friends are any more. You can't even be too sure of your enemies! Next week I'm going down to Spasskoye for the summer. At least there are a few things I can count on there. Diane, old as she is, will recognize me and go into contortions of joy as always. My servants will still call me *barin* – though not for much longer – and will be affable to me, at least to my face. Tolstoy and I will see each other from time to time, enjoy our hunting and argue about everything else. And the woodcock will have come up from North Africa in March, will be breeding in the birchwoods and will give me good sport until they take off again in November. And when they go south, I'll come north and be back here with a finished book. I'd be delighted, of course, if you'd pay me a visit… but in a couple of months you'll both have probably decided you can no longer stand the sight of me!"

Soon after reaching Spasskoye, Turgenev set off with Tolstoy to attend a committee meeting of the nobility of the Orel and Tula provinces. At Tolstoy's request, he had already paid a couple of visits to Yasnaya Polyana, where he had tried to resume his former close friendship with Tolstoy's sister. But he had found her much changed: where before she had compensated for an unstable marriage by cultivating arts of every kind, she now, as a single woman, was consumed by a bitter fury against her ex-husband which dominated her life, leaving little time for any other interest. He paid her conventional little compliments whenever the occasion arose, and she behaved as though she were suitably flattered by them. But he had the depressing feeling that they were like two puppets going through the motions dictated by an unseen presence, with no volition of their own.

The two men had decided to share a carriage to take them to Tula. Turgenev picked up Tolstoy at Yasnaya Polyana and was immediately greeted with an ultimatum: "I don't want to talk with you about the serf question until after the meeting. I want to keep an open mind. If you can't agree to this, it's better that we travel separately."

Turgenev was perfectly happy to fit in with this strange demand, although he couldn't help reflecting on how 'open' his companion's mind could be after all the years the subject had been on everyone's lips, in addition to his own very forthright views of a couple of years ago. However, he himself was content enough not to get entangled in Tolstoy's passionate but inconclusive ideas on the issue; he turned the conversation instead to the direction *Sovremennik* was taking. Tolstoy immediately told him he wanted nothing to do with the publication any more. "Nekrasov has given in completely: I had a letter from Panaev the other day containing a little lecture to the effect that even the finest work of art would attract no attention today unless it concerned itself with current events and problems. And he added, idiotically: 'Sad but true'. Apparently one of the 'new men' – probably that scarecrow Dobrolyubov – had told him that no one would ever read Homer and Goethe again."

"What did you reply to him?"

"I told him that was the most arrant nonsense I had ever heard, but dangerous nonsense all the same; if someone tells you every day that the sky is black, after a while you begin to have doubts about the state of your eyesight." He chuckled. "I also thanked God in my letter that I hadn't taken my friend Turgenev's advice and become a full-time writer. Otherwise by now, I would be no better than a journalist!"

"And what are you, then? A butcher? A philosopher? A prophet?"

"I'm a Russian nobleman who supervises the running of his estate and frequently takes an active part in it. I plough, I scythe, I stook. I am thinking of opening a school and becoming a teacher. As a part-time occupation, I write when I feel I have something to say. There, will that satisfy you?"

"It will have to, Lyovochka. As long, at least, as you always find something to say. And, at the risk of breaking our agreement, I am greatly looking forward to hearing what you will have to say at this meeting... if these carthorses they've put between the shafts ever manage to get us there..."

INT. TULA, TOWN HALL – AFTERNOON

On a dais at one end of a large, rectancular room sit the four men appointed to chair the meeting: two chosen by the provincial governors and two elected by the local nobility. It is they who will send a report to the Editorial Commission in St Petersburg, which will then make its final recommendations to the Czar.

The main body of the room is taken up by a hundred or so landowners from all over the provinces of Tula and Orel. The place is thick with smoke and the noise level high: when someone has obtained permission to speak, he is supposed to step up to the platform and address the ensemble from there; but as often as not, he merely gets to his feet and shouts a few sentences to his neighbours. *All except those within a small perimeter around him continue to talk, argue and yell at each other. It is rare that any speaker has the authority to compel silence and enable everyone to hear what he is saying. Turgenev and Tolstoy sit near the back of the hall, the one resigned and ironic, the other making no attempt to disguise his disgust.*

A noble known for his spendthrift habits in the capital and his complete indifference to his serfs' welfare on his estate is presently holding forth…

REACTIONARY NOBLE

… this will be the end of everything. The next thing you know, they'll be demanding to take part in our assemblies…

Heads nod in sage agreement.

REACTIONARY NOBLE

… they'll be claiming the right to sit in judgement over us…

VOICES

That's right… you'll see…

REACTIONARY NOBLE

… they'll be asking our daughters' hands in marriage…

VOICES

Never… Shame!…

REACTIONARY NOBLE

I tell you this, my friends. If these measures go through, I shall sell my estate and my palace on the English Quay and leave this country… for ever!

Cheers, shouts, protestations…

A tall man in his late fifties, wearing a light brown caftan, rises from his seat and begins to make his slow, dignified way towards the dais. When he reaches it, he bows to each of the four presiding nobles, then turns to face his still jabbering colleagues who quieten down a little as he starts, with almost paternal authority, to address them.
Tolstoy leans over and whispers in Turgenev's ear:

TOLSTOY

That's Aleksey Stepanovich Gorchakov, a near neighbour of mine.

TURGENEV

A good man?

TOLSTOY

Too good. Very pious, very long-winded. We'll never hear the end
of him.

*Gorchakov holds up his hand to request – and surprisingly obtain – silence. He fixes his
audience with a glittering stare from steel-grey eyes under bushy steel-grey eyebrows, and draws
some sheets of paper out of a leather pouch.*
Tolstoy gives an audible groan.

TOLSTOY

It's a prepared speech, God help us!

Some disapproving shushes…

GORCHAKOV

My friends, you must not let yourselves be carried away by Vasily
Borisovich's rhetoric. The world will not cease to turn if the serfs
get some measure of freedom…

He lifts and wags an admonitory finger.

GORCHAKOV

But 'some measure', I said. Complete liberty, no! That would go
against the divine order of things. Look at it this way… Our
peasants look after their animals, and they know that if they treat
them well, give them enough food and keep them warm in winter,
their efforts will be repaid and they will derive benefits from their
good stewardship. Just so do we know that, by looking after our
muzhiks, they will serve us better and themselves be content in the
knowledge that they are performing well the tasks that the Good
Lord ordained for them…

Nodding of heads and murmurs of agreement…

TURGENEV
(in an undertone, to Tolstoy)
Perhaps they'll wag their tails in appreciation!

395

GORCHAKOV

It is God's will that we should treat them like our children – which
in many respects they resemble: when they're good, we reward
them; at other times we have to punish them. It is the only
behaviour they understand. Total freedom would leave them lost
and bewildered. Therefore I urge you all to follow my example. I
never ill-treat my peasants, I never send them into exile. If they
wish to move elsewhere, they are free to go. But as long as they stay
on my property, they must recognize me as their lord – and also as
their protector.

*He gravely replaces the sheets of paper in his pouch and walks slowly back to his place amidst
murmurs of agreement mingled with head-shaking and suspicious mumbling…*
*Before he has regained his seat, a bullet-headed, thick-necked man jumps to his feet and
harangues the company at the top of his voice. Those close to him can smell the vodka on his
breath.*

LANDOWNER

What Aleksey Stepanovich says may be all very well, but what I
think is this: we're wasting our time here. Those bureaucratic
swine in Peter aren't going to take any notice of what we say. This
is all a farce to try and get our support for what they're going to do
anyway. Nothing we say is going to change anything… and I, for
one, have better things to do with my time than sit here listening to
a lot more useless verbiage…

*He stumps out of the hall, followed by a few like-minded cronies. The ensuing uproar (a few
vociferously agreeing with the last speaker, the rest venting their indignation at his boorish
behaviour) is of such intensity that the senior of the two chairmen appointed by the governors
has to thump the table and shout for order. His colleague – one of the two elected by the nobility
themselves – tries to sweeten the atmosphere with an appeal to reason.*

PRESIDING NOBLE

As you have done me the honour, gentlemen, of choosing me to
represent you, allow me to make a suggestion. The only grain of
truth in that last unfortunate intervention is that we do not know
exactly what St Petersburg has in mind. Why, therefore, do we not
wait and see what the final proposals are, then meet again and
decide if we can accept them?

Karsakov, a neighbour of Turgenev's, with whom he is on friendly terms, intervenes:

KARSAKOV

I have a better idea. Let's make our own conditions, and if they're not largely met, we reserve the right to turn down the proposals.

This suggestion is greeted with general approbation, but the Presiding Noble spots the flaw...

PRESIDING NOBLE

But how are we to agree on our conditions? Nothing we have heard today would suggest there is any unanimity. Can anyone put forward a programme which everyone in this room would be behind?

At this point, Turgenev attracts his attention and requests permission to speak. He goes to the dais and describes the measures, already outlined to Herzen, that he intends to adopt at Spasskoye. This provokes frantic debate, with angry glances cast in his direction and comments only just under the breath along the lines of 'what does that fellow know? he spends all his time abroad'... The senior chairman has again, with some difficulty, to restore order, and he proposes a motion that Turgenev's plan should be generally adopted. The vote is taken: 65 per cent vote against, 34 per cent for. Tolstoy abstains. It is agreed that two reports – a majority one and a minority one – will be sent to St Petersburg. The meeting is adjourned.

For several minutes after their carriage had rumbled off towards Yasnaya Polyana, neither man uttered a word. Tolstoy stared ahead of him with that set, grim expression which signalled: 'Speak to me if you dare!' Turgenev, who knew it so well, feigned for a while an unconvincing interest in the suburban streets of Tula, but at last, finding the silence ludicrous, ventured to break it. Unfortunately, in an attempt to lighten the atmosphere, he slipped into his St Petersburg man-of-the-world manner, which always grated on his companion's nerves.

"Well, Lyovochka, you didn't want to reveal your thoughts about emancipation to me on the way here. Could it be that the return journey might loosen your tongue? Your contribution to the debate didn't give me much to go on."

Not a muscle on Tolstoy's face moved, as he growled: "I'd rather be struck dumb than speak in such company."

"Well may I at least ask you what you thought you were achieving by abstaining?"

"It was the only means I had of disassociating myself from that farcical procedure and the blockheads and rascals who attended it... yourself excepted, of course."

"Thank you. But, you know, even though some of them may be blockheads or rascals, it is on these assemblies that the serfs' future depends. If all the reports from all the provinces of Russia are unanimously against emancipation, it is going to be very difficult for the Czar to proceed." A further silence began to nettle Turgenev. "I don't want to offend you, but it almost seems as though if everything can't be done one hundred per cent your way, you would prefer nothing to be done at all." It was now Tolstoy's turn to stare out of the window, but the other man was not to be stopped. "You once told me that if the serfs weren't freed – and freed soon – there would be a revolution. Assuming that you are not in favour of a revolution, what steps do you believe should be taken?"

Tolstoy finally replied, but without turning his head. "Emancipation should take place tomorrow. The existence of slavery in this country is a disgrace. But the land question is very complex and should be studied by the best brains in the land, not the worst."

"My solution for Spasskoye may not be the fruit of the best brains in the land, but it could, surely, serve as a basis for further discussion."

Tolstoy flung his arms in the air and glared across at Turgenev. "Your solution! Your solution! That's all you can think of. It may be all very well for you, but it may not suit me. That's what I'm talking about. It is very hard, perhaps impossible, to legislate for every circumstance. You're a rich man, you can afford to give away your land and wait for the peasants to pay you… if they ever do, which is far from certain. But I am always short of money, I find it hard to make ends meet, I have Masha and her children on my hands now too, and perhaps I can't afford to give my land away."

"But if we don't make a start somewhere, the whole process will come to a stop. And think how happy that will make your rascals and blockheads. This is a time for solidarity, not individualism…"

Tolstoy's face flushed a deep red. "Will you stop preaching at me," he shouted. "You're almost as self-satisfied as those other preening turkey-cocks we've just been listening to." He sat back in his seat, folded his arms and gave every indication that he had no further wish to speak. Turgenev, overcome with irritation compounded with frustration, was happy to comply, and not another word passed between the two men until they reached Yasnaya Polyana.

In spite of the late hour, Turgenev had every intention of proceeding on to Spasskoye; but as they drew up, the servant who came out to open the carriage door informed them that Marya Nikolayevich had left express orders that Turgenev was expected for dinner. "You'd better come in," Tolstoy growled, ushering him into the house with a show of cordiality which was perhaps intended to compensate for his recent brusqueness. But this didn't last long into the meal itself. As soon as

Marya, who was an enthusiastic proponent of emancipation, asked for news of how the meeting had gone, her brother cut her short: "I'd rather not discuss it now. We've had enough for one day." She glanced at her guest, who mutely signalled his assent.

Despite Turgenev's habitual skill at keeping a conversation going under difficult circumstances, the atmosphere at dinner was not convivial. All three were ill-at-ease, and the moment Tolstoy had gobbled down his apple pie, he muttered something about having business to attend to, excused himself and left the table. Turgenev, in the meantime, had been covertly studying Marya and noting the effects her domestic misfortunes had had on her. She was only 28, but there was no missing the physical changes that had taken place since she had left her husband: two sharp lines now ran down and outward from the corners of her mouth, the frown wrinkles had deepened and the candid expression in her grey eyes often clouded over. The childish treble of her voice had moved down the scale, and even though she still dressed in simple, girlish frocks and wore her hair long and swept back down to her waist, this now seemed less natural and more the affectation of a woman no longer in her first youth trying to cheat time.

But she still seemed to take great pleasure in his company, and it was with one of her old shy smiles that she now asked him: "Do I dare ask, Ivan Sergeyevich, if you would tell me a little about your new book?"

"I usually try to avoid doing that," he said, "but you were so encouraging and helpful over *Rudin* that I can make an exception with you. I've had the idea in my mind for a long time now. My first interest was to examine a man who, for various complex reasons, has led a drifting life, makes a bad marriage, wanders abroad and returns to Russia to work out his salvation. At first he thinks he's found it in his love for a young girl, but when that proves impossible he goes back to his estate and devotes his life to running it well."

"Does he find his... salvation, as you call it?"

"He finds, if not happiness, at least a certain resigned contentment and satisfaction."

"And your second interest?"

I find I'm becoming more and more involved in the girl – Liza, I think I shall call her. She has points in common, I suppose, with Vera in *Faust*..."

"Who had points in common with me."

"Yes, and Liza probably does too. But she's very young..." detecting a shadow flicker momentarily across Marya's face ... "no, no, *very* young... 18 or 19, and devotedly religious. I have to work on this, as profound faith is something I have never been blessed with... perhaps it has to do with her fear of life; she's had a difficult childhood, her religion may be a sort of refuge, I don't know, we shall see... When we first meet her she's about to marry the family friend because she thinks that's what's expected of her, but then the protagonist arrives on a visit and they fall deeply in love…"

"Why does it prove, as you said, impossible?"

"Because his wife, whom he had believed dead, turns up."

"Isn't that a bit *diabolus ex machina*?"

Turgenev thought for a moment. Then he smiled at her. "Yes, you're right. As usual. I'll have to try and find a way of making that more convincing."

Marya, encouraged by his ever-open ear for suggestions, reverted to her old role of friendly critic. "So, your hero… what's his name?…"

"Lavretsky."

"Lavretsky goes off to cultivate his garden. And what becomes of her?"

"She takes the veil."

"Oh no! How sad! Does she have to?"

"I hope it won't seem too sad. Sad that their love couldn't blossom, yes. That is always sad. But not sad that she goes into a convent. For her it is a kind of fulfilment. She feels she has sinned in loving another woman's husband, and this is her way of making reparation."

"That could only be said by a man… especially a man who admits he's never been overburdened by faith. I think you're going to find it hard to make this girl credible."

"Perhaps. But I have someone who is helping me."

"Some deeply pious, beautiful young virgin, I suppose!" For all the teasing intention, there was an acid undercurrent.

Turgenev chuckled. "Not exactly," he confessed. "Rather a grey-haired lady in her late thirties married to the Czar's aide-de-camp, Count Lambert. She hopes to make a good Orthodox Christian out of me one of these days. In the meantime, she is helping me with Liza."

"Oh dear. I was hoping I could persuade you to keep her out of that convent. But it seems I don't have a chance.

"What would you have her do?"

Marya emitted a raucous laugh. "Oh, I'm not the one to ask." He noticed her nails digging into her palms and a new, rough quality to her voice. "But I'll tell you, all the same. I would have her marry a decent, honest man – perhaps the family friend – and then take lover after lover without making any effort to conceal it. But that would be a different book, wouldn't it?"

"It would indeed. Perhaps you should write it."

This time a deprecatory laugh. "Oh, I think one scribbling Tolstoy is enough!"

"You could write it under a male pseudonym. I would pass you off as a young protégé and get Nekrasov to publish it."

She shook her head. "As you know, I don't even read much fiction, let alone wish to write it. But I will read yours. I always do. And now, as it looks like Lyovochka is not going to come back, I had better show you to your room. Why is it you two are always quarrelling?"

"You had better ask him. It gives me no pleasure. I admire, esteem and love Lev Nikolayevich. But it seems there is nothing to be done. I have only to eat a plate of soup and pronounce it good to be absolutely certain that he will, there and then, declare it disgusting…"

The next morning brother and sister came into the hall to see their guest off. The night didn't seem to have improved Tolstoy's mood, but Marya, with perhaps a touch of malice towards her brother, made no attempt to hide her affection. After kissing Turgenev three times, she clasped his elbows. "Come back very soon, Vanya. Your company is one of the few pleasures left to me." She leaned forward and murmured confidentially in his ear: "And thank you for honouring me with a glimpse of your book…"

Turgenev bent low, pressed his lips to her hands and kept them there for several seconds. As he straightened up, he murmured in his most urbane drawl: "Thank *you*, Marya Nikolayevna. Only someone of your intelligence and charm could have winkled it out of me." His smile penetrated deep into her eyes and he pressed her hands warmly, seeming loath to relinquish them, before finally moving away with her brother towards the door.

The carriage was waiting and Turgenev turned to Tolstoy before climbing in. "Thank you for your hospitality, Lyovochka," he said, reaching out to shake his hand.

Tolstoy barely touched the hand before letting it drop. "Yes, well, it's better you don't come back here until you make up your mind how you're going to behave."

Turgenev froze with one foot on the carriage step. "I beg your pardon. Behave about what?"

"About Masha, of course. You play her like a fish on the end of a line. The poor girl's suffered enough from men's swinish behaviour. She doesn't need to be tortured by you in order to feed your self-satisfaction at thinking yourself irresistible to women."

Turgenev turned his back and climbed into the carriage. Just before it drove off, he spoke out of the window: "Until you apologize for those words, Lev Nikolayevich, we have nothing more to say to each other.

For the rest of the summer and autumn he was able to keep his word to Annenkov and Druzhinin and work steadily and productively on his novel. The only distractions came from the life he had left behind in Paris…

Spasskoye,
23 June, 1858

My dear friend,

I write by return in reply to your letter informing me of the death of Ary Scheffer. I knew, of course, that he had been very ill, but forced myself to believe that all could still be well. And now he is no more. I shall miss him for his own sake, and I participate to the depths of my being in the cruel sorrow this loss will have caused you and Viardot. He loved you both. It is not consolation that I offer you, just a friendly hand held out, and a devoted heart on which you can count as you counted on the one which has just ceased to beat.

Here in Russia we are also in mourning. Aleksander Ivanov, the painter I mentioned to you in my letters from Rome, has just died of cholera. Poor man! After twenty-five years of work, of poverty, of voluntary isolation, at the moment when his painting was finally exhibited, before he had received any remuneration, before he could even begin to gauge how this work, to which he had dedicated his entire life, would be received, death snatched him away in an instant. A cruel newspaper article, full of abusive language, was all his country offered him in the short space of time between his return and his death. He did not, in all truth, belong in the empyrean. He saw the promised land from afar, but was not destined to enter it. In order to depict his John the Baptist, he copied both the head of the Belvedere Apollo and that of Christ Pantocrator in the cathedral of Monreale, near Palermo, some thirty times. Not the way great painters create. And yet in his dedication, his asceticism, his unsparing search for the truth, there was much to admire in this kind, honest, unhappy Russian artist…

Spasskoye,
11 October, 1858

Dear Paulinette,

All your letters begin with complaints about the infrequency of my letters. In fact I write to you fairly often, but whether I do or not, you must not get it into your head that I forget you when I am in 'my' Russia, as you call it. That is just foolishness. I love you and think of you very often. So chase these ideas from your head.

I thank you for your long letter, but I have to say that once again it was far too full of misspellings and grammatical errors for a young woman of your age. But this is not what I have to take issue with you about today. It is something else altogether... namely your excessive over-sensitivity, of which there are several examples in your letter, and which sometimes makes you sulky, bitter, even obnoxious. Mme Viardot forgot to invite you to a musical soirée. What a catastrophe! Did it occur to you she might have had other, perhaps a trifle more important, things on her mind?! You risk storing up a lot of suffering for yourself by this wretched prickliness, which, in reality, is an unhealthy form of pride. You must make a big effort to correct this ugly fault, my child. You lead me to believe that you gratuitously spoilt for yourself this summer's holiday at Courtavenel. Let that be a lesson to you.

As for myself, I have finished my novel, except for the inevitable little last-minute adjustments, and will soon be taking it to St Petersburg to lay before the lions. The saddest news, which you would want me to share with you, is that my poor Diane died the day before yesterday. We buried her yesterday morning and I have no shame in admitting that I couldn't stop crying all day. It was a friend who was leaving me, and good friends, whether with two legs or four, are a rare species.

Your promise to work hard and practise the piano diligently fills me with joy. My dream is that when I come back to Paris you can give me a fluent performance of a Beethoven sonata, write a long letter without a single fault and, above all, never again be oversensitive. Then you would see how much I would love you!

Not that I don't love you a great deal – I mean a great deal – already. I wish you the best of health and all good fortune with your exams.

Your loving father,
I. Turgenev

A Nest of Gentry being the longest and most ambitious work Turgenev had so far attempted, he had decided to read it to a selection of his friends before officially submitting it for publication. He arrived in St Petersburg early in November, having spent a few days in Moscow, where Katkov had tried to poach the novel from *Sovremennik* for his *Russian Herald*, offering half as much again as Nekrasov. Turgenev held firm, on the grounds that he had verbally promised the novel to Nekrasov; but with Chernyshevsky and Dobrolyubov in mind, he didn't close the door on the possibility of a future collaboration. He deplored Katkov's recently acquired conservative ideas, but for the time being they remained on personally good terms.

The reading had been supposed to take place soon after Turgenev's arrival in the capital, but a cold he had caught in Spasskoye developed into a bad case of bronchitis, which left him voiceless. The event had to be continually put off until, with Christmas only a few days away, he resigned himself to his condition and asked Annenkov to read for him. Nekrasov had assumed that they would all gather as usual in the *Sovremennik* offices, but Turgenev unexpectedly dug his toes in: "Any amount of *friendly* criticism will be more than welcome," he told the editor. "That's why I want you all to hear it. But I'm not yet ready to face the venom of those two snakes."

"Snakes?" Nekrasov raised a hypocritically inquiring eyebrow.

"Yes. You know who I mean."

"Oh, come now, Vanichka, you exaggerate."

"No, I don't. As a matter of fact, I minimize. One's a snake, the other's a rattlesnake."

For once Turgenev was adamant, and it was eventually decided to hold the reading in his new apartment on Great Stable Street near the Moyka embankment. This also had the advantage of avoiding his having to expose himself to the winter cold. It took place over two long evenings and represented the real celebration of his return to Russia and Russian literature. Almost all his friends were there, including his old teacher, Nikitenko, the former censor, together with a number of artists, young actors and writers, gathered to hear the latest work of the man they loved and had feared they had lost. The book was received with virtually unanimous praise, an opinion which would be echoed by the wider public and the majority of the critics when it was published in the January edition of *Sovremennik*. Even the 'two snakes' held their tongues, or at least sheathed their pens. The lyrical and sad, but not hopeless, autumnal quality of the story appealed to almost everyone. Lavretsky's hard-won acceptance of his fate, as beautifully expressed in the epilogue, and the portrait of Liza, whom many saw as the most touching exponent of Russian womanhood since Pushkin's Tatyana, won universal acclaim. And the varied delights of the subsidiary characters – especially the pathetic displaced German composer Kremm and Liza's sharp-tongued, indomitable great-aunt, Marfa Timofeyevna – were incidental, but not minor delights.

The publication of *A Nest of Gentry* marked a turning-point in Turgenev's life. He was now the leading figure of Russian literary life and his fame quickly spread abroad. A French translation soon appeared, and although it took ten years for an English one to follow, word of mouth celebrity was his before people had actually read his work. Wherever he went – and he travelled extensively for the next three years – he experienced the sweet and sour taste of success: as he wrote to Pauline: 'I often find myself in the position of what in Russia we call having to play the goose. Everyone feels obliged to favour me with a stupid smile, and I find myself returning a satisfied, idiotic simper. But I suppose if success has no worse inconveniences than this, I can learn to live with it.'

It is hard not to see in Turgenev's new dedication to his writing (the man who less than two years ago had announced his determination to write no more was to publish over the next three years *On the Eve, First Love and Fathers and Children*) some equivalent to Lavretsky's renunciation of any hope of love and consequent dedication to *his* self-appointed task: 'Unhurriedly to hack out one's path as a farmer traces a furrow with his plough.' Although he was still made welcome at Courtavenel during the summer months, he had understood by now that his position was that of family friend and absolutely nothing more. He wrote from there to his new confidante, Countess Lambert: 'My health is good but my soul is sad. Around me is a regular family life. Why am I here? Why, having broken with everything that was dear to me, am I busy looking behind me? You will have no difficulty in understanding what I mean and what my situation is here. But having said that, I do not torment myself. They say that men die many times before their real death. I know what has died in me. So what's the use of looking at a sealed tomb?'

The three years leading up to the proclamation of emancipation also marked for Turgenev the ever-widening rift between himself and the journal in which he had made his name, and whose reputation he had done so much to enhance. For a time, after the publication of *A Nest of Gentry*, Chernyshevsky and Dobrolyubov lay low, though the latter especially made no attempt to hide the annoyance the older man's manner caused him. But they held their fire, secure in the conviction that, in one way or another, he would soon expose himself. Ironically enough, it was his determination to bear witness to the social and political currents of his time – the very action they were demanding of him – that bared his back for their knives.

A day or two after the reading, when Turgenev had recovered a croaky use of his voice, he dined alone with Annenkov. He'd had a suspicion that his old friend's congratulations and compliments had been a little less spontaneous than those of the others. Sensitive as ever to the opinions of those closest to him, he wanted to discover if his intuition had been accurate, and if so, why. But, as at all the best social occasions, gossip took precedence over more serious matters and Annenkov could hardly wait to take off his coat and hat before blurting out the news.

"Guess who's getting married."

"I have no idea. Who?"

"Olga. Your cousin."

For a long moment, Turgenev was speechless. Pleasure struggled for predominance with a nudging tinge of regret. Then: "Who to?"

"Ilya Arkadyevich Somov. Do you know him?"

"No."

"A good man. Something at the Ministry of Education. Has a largish estate near Kalinin. I've seen them together now and then. She seems quite happy. I don't think she's in love with him. But he seems devoted to her, and he'll treat her well."

"I pray God he does. No one deserves better of life. If I didn't feel I had behaved so badly towards her, I would try to renew our friendship."

"You could do so any moment you like. We often talk about you, and I can promise you she has no resentment. Not a trace. She takes a great interest in what you do, and has always read your latest work. I think seeing you again would give her nothing but pleasure – especially now."

"In that case, I must make a point of it. You know who also wants to bring us together?"

"No. Who?"

"My daughter. Olga was in Paris last spring, when I was in Italy, and arranged with the Trubetskoys to see Paulinette. It seems that the two of them took to each other immediately. I know at any rate that Paulinette adores her. Olga took her with her when she went shopping and bought her all sorts of presents – probably spoiled her terribly."

"Well, it won't do her any harm to be spoiled once in a while. Yes, Olga told me she'd seen her and found her delightful. She was a little worried about her though. Your daughter confided in her that she didn't think Mme Viardot treated her very well, that she always felt an outsider in the family."

Turgenev signalled to the waiter to bring them another bottle of wine and made little attempt to conceal that this was a conversation he wanted truncated. "I'm afraid that's just an attempt to gain sympathy. It's a fault she has and she must rectify. Mme Viardot is goodness herself to her. But to get back to Olga, she's been in my mind a lot recently."

"Why is that?"

"Well, it has to do with my work. And, *à propos*, Pavlochka, look me in the eye and tell me something. You weren't very impressed by *Nest*, were you?"

"What makes you say that? My God, the book has achieved something which no other writer in Russia today could even contemplate. It has established a literary truce in this most litigious of countries. It has been praised with equal fervour by Westerners, Slavophils, reactionaries and radicals. It is a marvel of our age."

"You're being devious. I didn't ask about the effect of the book, I wondered about your opinion of it. You didn't like it as much as most people, did you?"

There was a moment's silence, and then: "Perhaps not." "Why?"

Annenkov, whose plate was empty, while Turgenev's had hardly been touched, leaned back in his chair, patted his stomach and glanced around the room, as though searching for inspiration. Then he looked back at his friend and smiled. "It's a beautiful book, Vanichka, we all know that. If I think it lacked anything, it was perhaps a sense of adventure. You were doing what we all know you can do superbly well: analyzing the behaviour and psychology of the Russian *rentier* class, and enchanting us with your loving descriptions of the beauties of the Russian countryside. I can't help feeling that there's a danger that the Slavophils will now start to claim you as their own. But apart from that, I hope in your next book, you'll take a risk or two… perhaps describing the present, or even projecting into the future, instead of always analyzing the past."

"Hm! That's precisely what I hope to do. And that's also where Olga comes in. I remember, one happy evening we spent together, talking to her about an idea I had to write an essay on Hamlet and Don Quixote, as representing the man of thought and the man of action. She was intrigued by the idea, and it's been at the back of my head all these years. But now I think I see my way to doing it, and connecting it with the novel I have in mind. Did I ever tell you about Karateyev?"

"I don't think so."

"He was a neighbour of mine. When I was confined to Spasskoye in 1855 he used to come and see me from time to time. A strange, taciturn man, with vague ambitions to become a writer, but no talent to match them. He would show me things he had written, and I never knew what to say. Then, one day, he announced his intention of going to fight in the Crimea, and told me he had a premonition he would never come back. So he entrusted me with a manuscript, asking me to read it only in the event of his death, in which case I could do what I liked with it. He was indeed killed at Sebastopol and one evening, when I was at a bit of a loss, I took a look at it."

"What was it, a draft of a novel?"

"No, it was a factual account of a love affair he had had with a girl who eventually left him for a Bulgarian patriot. She had accompanied the man to Bulgaria with the idea of fighting by his side, or lending whatever support she could, but before he had been able to engage in combat he had died of tuberculosis."

"And you think you can use this?"

"Yes. I've been gathering my thoughts on my *Hamlet and Don Quixote* essay, because I promised it to Panaev and, sooner or later, I must deliver. And then I thought, there, I have it! The hero will be the man of action who wills his own fate; he's prepared to give up everything – would give up the girl if need be – in order to go off and fight for a cause. And I will surround and contrast him with a group of Russian friends – charming, intelligent people – with their inevitable, Hamletesque, doubts and reservations."

"And he'll be a Bulgarian?"

"Perhaps. Not necessarily. I don't know yet. He could be Italian, fighting for the freedom of *his* country. Like Garibaldi is doing now. I sometimes think if I were younger I would yield to impulse and go to Italy to experience and absorb this *enthusiasm* for liberty. I fear it's a plant that will always wither and die here. But it's probably just as well I won't. I'm a born spectator; people like me only get in the way."

"And you exclude his being a Russian."

"I don't exclude it, Russia does."

"You mean we're incapable of breeding men of action?"

"I mean, above all, that they – the extreme form, that is, the Don Quixotes – are not what we need. We don't have an exterior enemy to fight, we have an autocratic apparatus to dismantle, and that needs wise, patient men, not heroes."

Annenkov nodded, with less than total conviction. "And the girl? She will be Russian."

"Oh yes. I see her as a development of Natalya and Liza. But for her, political idealism will take the place of Natalya's intellectual curiosity and Liza's religious faith. *She* will do what I would never have dared do – renounce everything for an ideal."

He drained his glass of wine and looked quizzically at his friend. "Well, does that sound more like what you were hoping for?"

Annenkov answered cautiously: "I think it sounds promising. Of course, it will depend on how you treat it. Your young Russian girl leaving home and country to follow a foreigner will not go down well with some of your more faithful readers. But that is probably just as well. I look forward to reading it."

"And I to writing it. I have never begun a book with a clearer idea of what I wanted to do than this one. Let's hope the act of writing it doesn't muddy the waters."

He wrote the book wherever he found himself, in bursts of concentrated energy, finding in work alone some relief from the unhappiness that emanated from every other aspect of his life. His relationship with some of his friends, especially Tolstoy and Nekrasov, had sharply deteriorated. The advance towards emancipation, hampered by attempts to slow it down or eviscerate it, seemed to be losing momentum. Paulinette's erratic development gave him cause for frequent anxiety. Pauline, taken up as she now was with her family as well as her career, had virtually no time for him at all, answering his letters, on the rare occasions that she did, with a few scribbled lines. And he viewed with growing resentment the stranglehold the radicals had by now obtained over control of *Sovremennik*. In March, 1959, Dobrolyubov reviewed the last volume of the memoirs of old Aksakov, who was already a dying man. After paying a passing, condescending compliment to the old man's gracious style, he ripped into the book's content, using it simply as a pretext to air his by now familiar views: '*Once again,*' he wrote, '*we are regaled with syrupy nostalgia for the 'good old days' of Catherine's reign, when the principal preoccupation of the nobility was making a 'good marriage' for their daughters and preventing their sons from making 'bad' ones. Meanwhile the peasants knew their place, were duly grateful for gifts of a sack of corn or permission for their children to marry the person of their choice, and shouted loud hurrahs on their benefactor's name-day. When will these outdated relics of an era which we can only rejoice is bygone, stop smothering us with their rose-tinted regrets for a way of life which we utterly condemn?'* Turgenev was appalled by the insensitivity of this review. When Aksakov died only a month later, he sat down the following day to write two letters: one to Sergey Timofeyevich's son, Konstantin, apologizing on behalf of the paper; the other to Katkov, offering him his new novel for the *Russian Herald*, an offer that was instantaneously and enthusiastically accepted.

He spent the first three months of the year at Spasskoye, experimenting with preliminary drafts of his book. Then he left again for the west, stopping first at Vichy in the hope that the waters there would do more for his still recurring complaint than those of Sinzig. With next to no hope of receiving a reply, he wrote, out of force of habit, to Pauline…

Vichy, Hotel du Louvre,
20 June, 1859.

So here I am at Vichy, dear and good Madame Viardot. I have a pleasant room and have already seen my doctor, drunk two glasses of water, made appointments for my baths at 3.45 every afternoon and taken out a subscription at the local library. My life, you see, could not be more regulated.

Vichy has nothing of the flirtatious charm of its German equivalents: it is rather dirty, rather sad and at the moment rather empty. A horrible barrel-organ is presently grinding away under my window… this would never be allowed at Karlsbad or Ems. A large river, the Allier, flows hectically but unpoetically over a gravel bed, the water a grubby yellow. There are poplars everywhere and it's raining.

None of this, as you can imagine, contributes to inspire in me a great gaiety; but at least I should be immune from distractions. There are, fortunately, very few Russians here, so I hope to be left alone and able to work.

I beg you to write to me, and soon. If you only knew what joy a letter would bring me! But you do know. Goodbye – au revoir. I add two lines for Viardot.

My dear friend,
Now that Asya has been translated into French under the title of 'Annuchka, souvenirs of the banks of the Rhine', I won't absolve you from reading it and giving me your opinion. I have too high a respect for your taste not to want your criticism, even while fearing it a little! You will soon be going to Courtavenel, so you will not lack the time. If, as in the past, you would feel like offering me your hospitality after I have done with Vichy, I could perhaps show you my last published book, A Nest of Gentry… or we could start translating some of Pushkin's lyric poems.
In the warmest friendship,

Jean Turgenev

The letter to Pauline went unanswered, but a note he wrote to his daughter received a reply he could well have done without…

Hotel du Louvre, Vichy,
22 June, 1859.

Here I am, my dear Paulinette, installed in a decent enough hotel. Now you know my address, I look forward to hearing from you. I shall not be staying as long as I first thought; apparently they won't keep you here more than 25 days, so I shall be in Paris on July 15 – we can spend a nice day together – and then I shall go to Courtavenel (if, as I hope, I am invited!). I shall, of course, come back to Paris for the great day of your prize-giving and will be all prepared to play the proud father.

I drink litres of water, take a bath a day and walk a great deal; so if I am not cured, it won't be my fault. The weather is terrible…

Paris,
24 June, 1859.

Dearest Papa,

I am glad to hear that you are working hard on your cure and that we shall be seeing each other again soon.

I have very little news for you, except that I went for my first lesson with Father Vassiliev, who Mme Trubetskoy arranged to give me instruction in the catekism of the Russian Orthodox Church. He was very nice and said he thought I would make a good pupil.

Please forgive me, dear Papa, if I talk to you <u>seriously</u> about something that may make you angry. And that is, wouldn't it be possible for you <u>not</u> to go to Courtavenel this year? When you say you hope you will be invited, it sounds so humiliating. You're a wunderful writer and a famous man and yet you seem to depend on the Viardots for everything. I sometimes wonder if you come to France to see me or just Mme. Viardot. It seems she can ignore you for ages and then bekon with her little finger and you come running. She hasnt been so nice to me recently either. She had Mme Harang change my singing teacher from one I liked very much to one I hate, and without even asking me. I sometimes think she does these things just to spite me.

While I'm making you angry, I might as well go on. I'm afraid I bought a rather expensive dress last week. I fell in love with it and it cost 200 francs, but the Herring says it looks very nice on me. I look forward to showing it to you in July. I hope you like it.

Hoping the cure is doing you lots of good and that this letter won't make you <u>too</u> angry,

Your loving daughter,

Paulinette Tourgueneff

My dear daughter,

As you see, I am replying to your letter by return. I am glad to hear you went to the church and got on well with Father Vassiliev. But, to talk to you 'seriously', as you ask, I am very unhappy with the rest of your letter. You adopt an attitude towards Mme Viardot that I can neither admit nor permit. You unforgivably forget everything you owe her. And please realize that I forbid you to try and pit me against her – which, in any case, would be quite useless, as ten times out of ten I would be in agreement with her. For example, since you mention it, how can you expect me to imagine that she, of all people, was not right about your singing teacher? And what could she have had in mind except your interests? I repeat, you owe her complete obedience and, believe me, it would be a very bad thing for you if she stopped taking an interest in you and abandoned you to certain instincts of yours which <u>must</u> be curbed. You are self-centred, touchy and you tend to love not those who deserve it but those who show particular attention to you or spoil you.

So, my child, no more of this. No more injunctions not to go to Courtavenel: on the contrary, it is most probable that it is there that we shall spend our holidays, instead of hanging aimlessly around who knows where?

As for the 200 francs for your dress, if you are happy with it, I am delighted you bought it. It is not that sort of behaviour on your part that will make me angry.

This letter will not bring you much pleasure. But if you reflect on what I have said, it could be very useful for you. If I don't tell you the harsh truth now and then, who will? I do so because I love you with all my heart.

Goodbye for the moment, my child. I send you a fond embrace… and no ill will.

Your father,

I. Turgenev

Quick, my dear child, let me kiss you on both cheeks! Your last letter gave me the greatest possible pleasure. It proved once again – what, in fact, I already knew – that you have a good heart and that you are glad to receive sound advice. Don't worry: I know very well that you love me because you love me, and not because I spoil you. My remark was not meant to refer to us. We both love each other, and there's an end to it!…

Your letter only reached me yesterday because you left out of the address an important word: Vichy! So it went for a stroll around Moulins before arriving at my hotel. Next time, you'd do well to read the address on your letters.

I haven't heard from Mme Viardot, so I don't know if she has moved yet to Courtavenel. Write to me if you know something about this. Otherwise you can expect me in Paris on the morning of Thursday, July 14th – fateful date!

Your loving father,

I. Turgenev

Before he left Vichy, Turgenev received a note from Louis Viardot, warmly inviting him and Paulinette to stay with them for the rest of the summer. He gladly accepted, but spent a few days in Paris first with his daughter. Unable totally to dismiss from his mind her lack of enthusiasm regarding Courtavenel, he set out to make her enjoyment his principal concern – with less than total success. Her exam results had not been distinguished, and she had failed to win any prizes. He forced himself to conceal his disappointment, but she couldn't hide hers and was continually telling him that she felt she had let him down. Having checked with Madame Harang that she had worked well during the year and that the meagre results were due more to lack of exceptional ability than to idleness or lack of interest, he tried to console her by reaffirming his conviction that the attempt was more important than the result.

On one occasion, however, it was his turn to disappoint her. Just before they were due to leave for Courtavenel, she rushed into his room in great excitement: the Emperor was to review an imposing military parade as it marched past him in celebration of the French victory over the Austrian army at Solferino; the parents of school friends of hers had invited them to watch it from their balcony on the Champs-Elysées as it proceeded down from the Arc de Triomphe on its way to the Invalides.

"I'm sorry, my dear, but I shall have to ask you to thank them but say we will not be able to go."

"But why, Papa? Everybody says it will be the most splendid show."

"I'm sure it will be. But that splendid show will be to commemorate a battle in which, in return for a very slight territorial advantage, over 15,000 Frenchmen lost their lives. And for what cause?"

"The Herring says that it's to support the Italians in their struggle for independence from Austria."

"I would like to think Madame Harang was right. If it were so, I suppose it would be a good enough cause. But I fear the true reason is to try and invest the Emperor with a shred or two of his uncle's military glory." Upset by seeing the enthusiasm drain away from her face, and remembering his resolution, he went on: "But I won't stop you from going, if you're so set on it. I'll put you in a fiacre and we'll make up a good excuse for my absence."

412

"No, Papa, I agree with you. I don't want to go now. I didn't know about all those horrible deaths. What could we do instead?"

"How would you like to go and watch the horse racing at Longchamp?"

Paulinette clapped her hands and was all smiles again. "Oh, I'd love that. Could we really?"

"Of course. We'll probably have the place practically to ourselves. All the people who normally go there will be watching and cheering the parade…"

The rest of the summer passed very much like the previous one, although Turgenev kept a closer eye on his daughter and tried to spend more time with her. He worked for two or three hours a day on his novel, which he had decided to call *On the Eve*, and wrote to Katkov promising that it would be finished by the end of November, and guaranteeing him the right to publish it in *The Russian Herald*. This move was provoked by his ever-increasing sense of alienation from all that *Sovremennik* was coming to represent. His anger at Dobrolyubov's treatment of old Aksakov had hardly died down when Annenkov sent him a series of articles in which the same critic cast scorn on the 'wise old men' who tried to silence the young with their abstract philosophic ideas and their attachment to 'principles' which they never applied to real life. It was time, he wrote, for them to stop pillorying petty, corrupt provincial officials and '*wasting their and our time in sterile, if beautiful, phrase-making. We need fresher and prouder words which will stir the hearts of the determined citizen and inspire him to independent, far-reaching action. Who will unleash the crowds with the all-powerful word: Forward!: the word which Gogol dreamed of and for which Russia has been waiting so long, with such impatience and such suffering?*' It was not hard to guess to whom, in particular, the young critic was addressing these words, and they swept away any scruples he might have felt about possible disloyalty.

When he was not with Paulinette, he collaborated with Viardot on translating *Rudin* into French, invented games for the children and lost his heart to Didie, who was growing up fast and flirted with him as only seven-year-old girls can with men their fathers' age. He saw even less of Pauline than last year: she had been approached by Berlioz with a view to reviving Gluck's *Orphée* in a version he was preparing for the *Théâtre Lyrique*, whose enterprising director, Léon Carvalho, had asked him to revise the French version of the opera with a mezzo soprano replacing the tenor in the title role. Berlioz lived close to the Viardots' house in Paris, and the composer and singer spent long hours together studying the score. For Pauline, who had enjoyed a triumph earlier in the year in Dublin, creating the role of Lady Macbeth in the British première of Verdi's opera, it was a welcome opportunity to sing again in Paris, where she had not appeared since her performance in Gounod's *Sapho*, eight years before. For Berlioz, now a sick and embittered man, it provided a respite from his Herculean labours on *Les Troyens*, and in Pauline's company he found some consolation for his wretched relationship with his shrewish second wife, the Spanish soprano, Marie Recio.

In the rare intervals when Pauline was able to spend a day or two in the country, she was as gracious to Turgenev as she was to any other guest who might be staying. No more and no less. Only once did she exceed the self-imposed limits of the perfect hostess: one warm evening he had taken his manuscript out into the garden and was sitting in the shade of Hermann, his favourite chestnut tree, idly scribbling a few notes; she came up, unheard, behind him, took the manuscript and the pencil out of his hands, wrote something and handed it back to him with a quick, conspiratorial half-closing of the eyes and a ravishing smile. Before he could say a word, she had moved away; when he looked down, he saw that she had written on the top of the first page: 'May I bring you luck!' He was hard put to it to stifle the involuntary sob that burst up unbidden from the pit of his stomach.

Apart from this epiphanic moment, he had to content himself with sinking into the role of old family friend and resigning himself to looking on Courtavenel as a pleasant place to spend the hot summer months, rather than the earthly paradise it had once seemed to him.

In the middle of September he took Paulinette back to Mme Harang for her last year at the school and proceeded straight on to St Petersburg. He had no intention of staying there, but the night of his arrival he received a note from Nekrasov asking him not to leave for Spasskoye before talking to him. Now, he thought to himself, the masks are going to be removed. Word will have arrived from Moscow that I have given my new book to Katkov, and the two snakes will have seized the opportunity to convince their editor that all relations between me and *Sovremennik* should now be terminated. As he walked across the Anichkov bridge over the Fontanka on his way to the house that had been like a second home to him, he was annoyed to notice that his mouth was dry and his heart fluttering; for a moment he was a small boy back in Spasskoye, summoned for an interview with his mother over some issue where he knew he was in the right. Looking up at Pyotr Klodt's statues of wild horses that adorn each corner of the bridge, he asked for some of the mental toughness of the men who are taming them.

But on his arrival, he found no sign of the 'wild horses' he was expecting. Only Nekrasov at his most silkily charming: after a bear-hug of an embrace, he asked concernedly after his health and diplomatically after 'your two Parisian ladies'. Receiving only a conventional assurance that all was well with both of them, he neglected to press the point and passed on to inquiring about the progress of his book.

"I think it is going well," Turgenev told him, obviously happier on professional ground. "I hope to have it finished by the end of the year."

But the editor couldn't resist. "Do I detect signs," he asked, "that the lure of France is less strong than it was. Can we count on your spending more time with us here?"

"Perhaps. You know the proverb from my part of the world? When the strawberry season is over, what's the use of going to the woods?"

Nekrasov let this sink in for a minute and then gave his friend a tentative smile. "You have all my sympathy, Vanichka," he said. "But understand and forgive me if I say that we here can only be grateful to Mme Viardot. When all is well between you and her, you write practically nothing. When the opposite is true, you turn out a book a year."

Turgenev gazed at the surface of the table that separated them and said, in a sad, low voice: "And yet she need only snap her fingers and I would agree never to write another word."

"Then may God keep her fingers on the piano, where they so divinely belong! You are finally working like I always hoped you would. We published *Nest of Gentry* in the first issue of '58, and we'll be able to publish *On the Eve* in the first issue of '59."

No point in beating about the bush. "I'm afraid you won't. I've promised it to Katkov."

"You can't be serious!" Nekrasov sat bolt upright in his chair and looked flabbergasted. *He's pretending he doesn't know. I don't believe it for a minute. Word like that gets from Moscow to Peter in days, not weeks. But how convincing he is!* "You've said this before, Vanichka. What are you trying to do? Get a better price from me? All right, I'll pay you more. How much is Katkov offering?" Receiving no answer, he reached into a drawer underneath his desk and pulled out a couple of little sacks; the resounding clink they made as he put them down on the table left no doubt as to their contents. *My God, he's really prepared himself for this meeting!* "There's five thousand roubles there. Whatever Katkov has offered, I'll give you half as much again."

Turgenev, who had accepted four thousand from Katkov (a far larger sum than he had ever received for any previous work), forced himself to take his eyes off the sacks. "It's not a question of money," he said. "I gave *Nest* to you, even though Katkov offered me more, because I'd promised it to you. This book I've promised to Katkov."

Nekrasov shook his head in disbelief. "But why? All our readers are waiting for a new book from you."

Turgenev tried to smile, but it came out more like a grimace. "Well, you'd hardly think so by what your chief literary critic was writing while I was away."

"Like what?"

"Like, for instance, his references to the wise old men with their beautiful, sterile phrase-making."

"But I'm sure that wasn't directed specifically at you."

Turgenev looked at his old friend with a raised eyebrow and didn't even bother to comment. "Let us just say, Kolya, that your main collaborators and I do not agree on what we mean by literature. I feel I no longer belong on the paper founded by Pushkin and revived by Belinsky."

Nekrasov looked almost distraught. "You mean you won't write for us any more?"

"I didn't say that. In fact, I hope to finish my essay on Hamlet and Don Quixote in time for your January issue. I promised it many years ago to Panaev. After that, we'll see. It's really up to you, you know. I presume you still have control over what is published in your paper. You might cast a slightly more critical eye over some of the stuff those two churn out."

"Despite what you say, they make a brilliant team. But perhaps you're right. Maybe I should rein them back a bit... if only not to lose you."

Turgenev seized on this slight advantage. "Yes, Kolya, make them an *element* of *Sovremennik*, not the only voice. There should be room for differences of opinion. And would you mind taking those sacks off the table?"

Nekrasov tossed them back into the drawer, then got up and threw an arm round Turgenev's shoulders. "I have to go now. I'll try and do as you say. But you could also try a bit harder with them. Every time you talk to them you seem to ruffle their feathers." *I ruffle* their *feathers?!* "Use some of your famous patience and charm. You'll see, they'll roll over on their backs like one of your beloved dogs and let their stomachs be tickled."

As they moved together towards the door, Chernyshevsky came out of one of the offices. Nekrasov gave Turgenev's arm a meaningful squeeze and called out gaily: "Look who's back, Nikolai Gavrilovich. I have an appointment with my lawyer, will you entertain Ivan Sergeyevich for me? Give him tea and some of those lemon curd tarts Avdotya baked yesterday." He shook Turgenev's hand with a tight grip, gave him a long, intense look and hurried out into the street.

Chernyshevsky ushered Turgenev hospitably enough into the room that was used for meetings and told a boy to fetch Panaev and Dobrolyubov, who soon joined them. As they drank tea, Turgenev tried to put Nekrasov's advice into practice. With Panaev there was no difficulty: he was as pleased to see him as ever and delighted to hear that he would finally be getting *Hamlet and Don Quixote*. Chernyshevsky was outwardly amiable, but glanced frequently and openly at his watch. Dobrolyubov, having greeted Turgenev and given him a curt handshake, remained glumly silent. Responding to Panaev's inquiry as to the quality of the literary life in Paris, Turgenev painted an unflattering picture which to a large extent mirrored his views, but was also calculated to win the approval of his nationalistic-minded listeners. "They're a petty, prosaic, squabbling bunch of mediocrities," he told them.

"We have far more talent here in Russia: Tolstoy, Dostoevsky, if he can start to write again now that he's back from Siberia. And Goncharov... I hear Ivan Aleksandrovich has just had a big book serialized in *Annals of the Fatherland*. How is it?"

There was a silence as the other three looked at each other to decide who was going to answer. Eventually it was Dobrolyubov who spoke: "*Oblomov* is both the celebration and the death knoll to your way of life, Ivan Sergeyevich. It purports to be a satire on the superfluous man, at the same time wrapping its arms around itself in cuddlesome self-appreciation. You and Goncharov could write each other's books.

"Ivan Aleksandrovich says we do." Turgenev couldn't resist interrupting. "He has twice accused me of plagiarism."

"I don't know about that. But whether it's true or not, it might as well be. All right, let us admit that there is something of Oblomov in every Russian: the aspiration to spend as many hours as possible lying on a couch in a dressing gown; but it is something we must not congratulate ourselves on but devote every energy we have to extirpate."

Turgenev smiled and stretched out his legs. "You should hear my friend Herzen on this subject," he drawled, but Chernyshevsky immediately interrupted with a sardonic chuckle: "Another one!"

Turgenev looked from one to the other. "Ah, you don't approve of him either! A man who was twice exiled for his radical views at a time" – and he gave the two younger men a penetrating stare – "when it was dangerous to hold them..." He broke off as Dobrolyubov began impatiently drumming his fingers on the table. "You are a brilliant young man, Nikolai Aleksandrovich, but like many young men, you lack a sense of perspective. It will come to you, if you are fortunate. All in good time."

Dobrolyubov got to his feet, thrust his hands in his pockets and gazed down morosely at Turgenev. "You must excuse me, Ivan Sergeyevich. Talking to you bores me. I suggest, for both of our sakes, we stop doing it." And without a glance at the other two, he left the room.

Turgenev almost relished the embarrassed silence that ensued. *Let one of them be the first to find something to say.* Panaev was gnawing his lower lip and staring anxiously at his companion, clearly indicating he thought it was up to him to account for his protege's behaviour. Finally Chernyshevsky too stood up and smiled vaguely at Turgenev. "You must forgive him, Ivan Sergeyevich. He told me he had coughed all night, and that leaves him with dreadful migraines. I am sure he will regret what he said. I shall ask him to make you an apology."

He was about to leave the room, but Turgenev stopped him. "Please do nothing of the sort. I don't think he will in any way regret what he said, and I think he's quite right not to. He spoke sincerely, and that is a small merit in itself. To tell the truth, I feel rather the same way myself, but I would not have had the courage to say so. Nikolai Aleksandrovich has cleared the air. He knew where he stood before. Now I know too."

Chernyshevsky nodded and went out without another word, leaving poor Panaev to congratulate Turgenev on his sang-froid. "You behaved beautifully, Vanya," he said. "But all the same, I shall tell Kolya to reprimand him."

Turgenev held up his hand. "I beg you not to," he said. "If you have to mention the incident at all, just tell him that I didn't dare try to tickle his stomach for fear of getting my hand bitten off".

Panaev stared at him blankly, but Turgenev assured him that Nekrasov would understand, gave him a fond embrace and went his way. As he passed back over the bridge, he looked up again at one of the statues and said, half to himself and half to the superbly muscled man wrestling with the rearing horse: "If you can't tame them, I suppose the only alternative is to let them run wild."

On his way south, Turgenev stopped off for a couple of days in Moscow, in order to see Katkov who wanted to sign an agreement for the publication of *On the Eve*. The editor of the *Russian Herald* was eager for gossip about his competitors on *Sovremennik*, but Turgenev kept his thoughts to himself and made no mention of his recent disagreements. On a sunny autumn Sunday afternoon, their business done, Katkov suggested they hire a droshky and go for a walk in the Neskutchny gardens in the suburbs of the city, near the Kaluga Gate. Turgenev agreed enthusiastically: it was here that, when he was fifteen, his family had rented a large house for the summer, and it amused him to see if he could find it again. They drove round the pleasant leafy area for what seemed to Katkov an eternity; Turgenev, in constant discussion with the driver, would shift from one side of the carriage to the other, poking his head out of the windows in an attempt to spot a familiar landmark, each time digging his elbow into some different part of his companion's anatomy. Katkov had had something very different in mind: a leisurely stroll, accompanied by a frank exchange of views on political and literary matters and perhaps an attempt, post-*Nest of Gentry*, to gauge the extent of Turgenev's seeming swing to a more conservative, pro-Slavophil position. But none of this was to be: just as he ventured a piercing question about Herzen, with whom he had had a bitter quarrel, Turgenev gave an excited shout and called out to the driver: "Turn right here, I think I recognize this beech avenue." A few seconds later he let out a boyish whoop of joy and pointed to a large house set slightly back from the road, with a garden in front. "That's it! Stop! That's it!" he cried, and leapt from the droshky almost before it had come to a halt. Katkov, following slowly and reluctantly behind him, saw him ring vigorously at the bell but no one came out to open the gate. For a moment Turgenev was downcast; then he started walking along the fence that separated the road from the garden and at a certain point came upon a small wooden wicket gate that was just ajar. "This will lead into the wing that Princess Chakovskoy rented that summer," he explained to his bemused companion, and started to push it open.

"You can't go in without permission," Katkov cried. "It would be trespassing."

But Turgenev was already through and striding up a narrow path under the bare trees, the leaves, russet and yellow, crackling under his boots. "There won't be anyone here," he announced blithely. "These houses are only rented in the summer. And this one was so shabby then, nearly 30 years ago, that I shall be surprised if it's still standing." He rounded a thick straggly clump of acacia and came out in front of a low building which was indeed in an advanced state of disrepair. All the windows were boarded up, many of the tiles on the roof were missing and most of the paint had been washed off the pinewood front. But from the way Turgenev gazed at it, it might have been a palace designed by Rastrelli. After a long while, he turned round to Katkov and pointed: "That was her bedroom window", he said in a hushed voice.

"Whose window?", asked the ever more perplexed Katkov.

"Ekaterina's. Ekaterina Chakovskoy, the first girl I ever loved. Here, I'll show you something else." He seized his arm and dragged him away down another path overgrown with brambles which caught on the fastidious, city-bred Katkov's trousers. Ignoring his protestations, Turgenev didn't let go of him until they reached a rotting wooden fence, part of which, succumbing to the years, had collapsed to the ground. Beyond it, through the trees, the outline of the main part of the house could just be distinguished, also clearly uninhabited, though in a better state of repair. But Turgenev paid no attention to that; stepping over the fence and pulling Katkov after him, he turned back towards the dilapidated wing and pointed in front of him: "This is where I first caught sight of her. I'd come out in the evening with my gun in the hope of shooting a pigeon; I was creeping along this fence when I heard voices; and there on the other side was this enchanting girl of about twenty surrounded by four or five young men; she was tapping their foreheads with those little greyish flowers – what are they called? – which pop when you bang them against something hard. I just stood there, unable to take my eyes off her. I think I fell in love with her in that instant."

"And did you see her again?" Katkov asked, looking around him as though quite indifferent to the answer.

"Oh yes, many times." But the enthusiasm to communicate his memories ceased as abruptly as it had begun and he gave his companion a long gaze, seeming barely to recognize him. "Mikhail Nikiforovich, will you do me a favour?" he asked, in a dreamy voice. Katkov nodded. "Will you go back to the droshky and wait for

419

me for a moment? I won't be more than five minutes." Katkov assented willingly enough, but had to pass an impatient quarter of an hour before he was finally rejoined by Turgenev, who still looked and behaved as though in a trance. And for the rest of the afternoon, during their walk in the Neskutchny gardens, he remained wrapped in a broody silence which only Katkov's persistent questioning and his own good manners induced him from time to time to break.

His desire to start as soon as possible on *First Love* fuelled his determination to finish *On the Eve*, and he arrived back in St Petersburg with the completed manuscript at the beginning of December. He made the mistake of showing it first to Countess Lambert, whose sense of convention and pious conservatism was shocked by the idea of a young Russian girl of good family abandoning everything to follow a Bulgarian adventurer with whom she had fallen in love. She and her husband made a personal call on Turgenev to try and dissuade him from submitting it for publication. "It's a horrid book," she told him. "And it would have a most nefarious effect on young girls. After reading about your Elena Nikolayevna, they will all feel perfectly justified in flinging themselves at the first man that takes their fancy, behaving in the most immoral fashion and thumbing their nose at their families and all decent society. You would bear a heavy responsibility, Ivan Sergeyevich." Turgenev was so discouraged that he considered consigning it to the flames, but fortunately called on Annenkov for a second opinion. Annenkov came over the moment he received the summons and found his friend gazing mournfully – and perhaps a little melodramatically – into a blazing fire. "You see, I've kept it alight, just in case…" Annenkov, a fast reader, read undisturbed for a couple of hours, after which Turgenev brought in some cold beef and a bottle of wine and asked the inevitable question. Annenkov's grave look induced him to lean over and give the fire a vigorous poke. But then his friend spoke: "I'm only half way through, but it may be the best thing you've done." He raised his glass and then lowered it again. "Tonight we have a double toast to drink, Vanichka. To your book and my marriage."

Turgenev gazed at him dumbstruck. "You don't mean it?"

"I do, I do. Glafira Aleksandrovna has been unwise enough to accept the proposal of an old bachelor like me. I must try and make sure she will not live to regret it"

Turgenev, who had known the lady in question for many years and knew how devoted she was to Annenkov, gave his old friend the warmest of embraces. "She will not regret it," he assured him, "and neither will you. You're made for each other. And I demand – and I brook no contradiction – to be your best man. I am becoming an expert in the role."

"You will do me a great honour."

"And I have another idea. I shall dedicate my next book – and I'm already starting to write it – to you. It will be called *First Love*. What could be more appropriate?"

"Except that knowing your love stories, it will surely end badly."

Turgenev couldn't help smiling. "Not as bad as some. But hardly 'they lived happily ever after', I'm afraid. But it is the title I shall dedicate to you. Not the content."

"Very well, then. I am honoured again. And now, enough of this orgy of sentiment. Let me do what I came here to do and finish your book."

Annenkov remained enthusiastic, and the following morning Turgenev sent it off to Katkov, who soon confirmed that he would publish it in the next issue of the *Russian Herald*.

St Petersburg,
30 December, 1859.

Dear and good Mme Viardot,

It took almost a month for your letter to arrive, but how welcome it was! I was especially intrigued by what you told me about Berlioz. I only met him that one time with you at Courtavenel, but to me he is a man of mystery… as is his music. A startlingly original voice that can produce works of the greatest beauty and others whose wildness of harmony and rhythm bewilder my conventional old ears. But it is music to those same ears to hear of your triumph in Orphée. *Oh for some magic machine that could transport me to the Théâtre Lyrique for one evening and then deposit me back here! And how good to hear that you have such a high opinion of his grand opera and that he has offered you one of two roles in it – Cassandra or Dido, what a choice! I cannot, however, agree with the hint you let slip that he might want you to sing both. Surely an artist should content himself with one impersonation an evening. Even God only created one world at a time.*

I have read and reread your letter at least a dozen times and each time can only conclude how extraordinarily good you are to him. You lend a sympathetic ear to his endless woes. You make piano transcriptions of his orchestral scores. And now what has happened? What else could happen? He has fallen in love with you. We could all have foretold that – I above all. I appreciate how difficult it must be for you: there is so much that draws the two of you together – the great interpreter and the great creator – that it is a thousand pities that something should intervene, like a stick caught in the wheel which prevents the smooth running of the carriage. But I have no doubt that your immense tact and goodness will find a workable solution.

While swallowing my disappointment over not being able to hear your Orpheus, I must now take a line or two to tell you about my forthcoming performance. You remember, perhaps, that for many years I have been working on the idea of an essay on Hamlet and Don Quixote. I finally finished it at more or less the same time as I finished my novel, and have been asked to read it before publication to an audience of no less than 500 paying guests to raise funds for the charity Druzhinin and I have set up to help writers and scholars in financial need. I am of course quite terrified – it is the first time I have ever done anything like this in public – and to make matters worse, my throat trouble of last year has returned, and there are some days when I can hardly croak. I have till January 10 to recover, so please do all the things you theatre people do for each other in the cause of your

Ever devoted

I.T.

Early in February, *On The Eve* appears in the *Moscow Herald*, and three days later Annenkov, Druzhinin and Botkin receive an urgent summons from Turgenev. The three of them go to his apartment early in the evening and find him unusually flustered. Barely giving them time to take off their coats, he explains that he has received from Nekrasov a draft copy of Dobrolubov's critique of his book, which is due to appear in the next issue of *Sovremennik*. "He asks me if I have any comments to make," he tells them. "Let me read you some of what the rattlesnake has written – I've underlined what seem to me the most significant passages – and tell me what you think I should do." The three of them settle in their chairs and Turgenev begins to read from six or seven closely handwritten pages. "First of all, it's headed: '*On The Eve*: But When Will The Real Day Dawn?'…"

"A tendentious title," Druzhinin remarks.

"But an eye-catching one," Botkin says.

"Oh, he's out to catch a lot of eyes. And I have no doubt he'll succeed. But listen…" There is an unusual note of irritation in his voice which surprises his friends. "He starts with a few conventional compliments: '*Turgenev presents us with as convincing a picture as always of the provincial gentry, with several well-drawn, well-rounded characters…*' He goes into some details of these, which I won't bother you with. Then: '*But is it enough? Certainly we must give him credit for placing at the climax of his story a political action: the attempt to liberate a country from a foreign yoke. This is a new departure for a writer who, in his previous work, has limited himself to analyzing individual behaviour. But there is a snag. He has to make him a Bulgarian! This leads us to think that he considers that unfortunate people to have, in their struggle for liberation from the Turks, a cause worth fighting for – as indeed they do – and that Russia does not – as indeed it does.*"

"This is inexcusable," Druzhinin interjects. "He's reviewing a novel as though it were a political tract."

Turgenev holds up his hand and continues reading: "'*The trouble is that Insarov, the Bulgarian, is more an embodied idea than a living creature of flesh and blood. Could the reason for this be that Insarov's creator himself never really believes in him? That he has tried to portray a 'man of iron' out of a sense of what was expected of him, rather than from any deep-seated conviction? A close reading would support this hypothesis. We know little about Insarov's deepest motivations because the author never lets us in on them. His omniscient authorial voice gives us all sorts of insights into the innermost sentiments of his heroine (even producing extracts from her diary) and those of her Russian suitors. All we know about the hero's sterling qualities derives from what these and other characters are continually telling each other – and us: namely, what a magnificent fellow he is.*'"

Druzhinin explodes. "This isn't criticism. It's butchery!"

The other two nod their agreement and Annenkov asks: "What does he say about Elena?"

Turgenev shuffles the pages around, looking for the relevant passage. "I'm trying to find it. He starts off being quite complimentary and then… Ah yes, here it is. *'Elena, his heroine, is one of Turgenev's more successful creations, a far cry from the limp Liza of his previous novel. Despite her conventional restricted background, she is filled with a restless desire to make her mark by some act of self-abnegation, at the cost of renouncing all the privileges of the position into which she was born. "To be good," she says, "is not enough; to do good, yes, that is the essential thing in life." Although her spoilt-little-miss persona may irritate us at first, she engages our sympathies as the book proceeds… which is more than can be said for Insarov, despite all his qualities – or rather despite his one quality (he is singularly lacking in any others), which is to dedicate his life to the liberation of his native land. But being Bulgarian, we are inevitably distanced from his cause – and therefore from him too. Why couldn't he be Russian? Because, of course, that would not agree with our author's outlook, which only envisages one method of combating our country's ills: the half-hearted proposals of timorous reformers from the privileged class, who don't want to take an axe to the tree they are sitting in. What they are blind to is that the social heroism Russia needs makes greater demands than its patriotic equivalent. And who is there to meet these demands? The final words of the letter Elena writes to her parents after Insarov's death, bidding them goodbye for ever, are: 'What is the use of returning to Russia? What is there to do in Russia?' Allow us to tell her: there is everything to do, Elena Nikolayevna. We need a 'man of iron' to fight the internal enemy, a much more insidious foe than an occupying power. And perhaps his time is coming sooner than any of us think. Perhaps Russia is 'on the eve' of finding its Insarov. Could this be the message that surreptitiously, oh so circumspectly, the author is offering us?'"*

Turgenev throws the pages down on the table and looks round at his friends. "Well, what am I to do?" he asks.

The three men exchange glances. Annenkov is the first to speak: "I suggest, nothing. If you write a letter of protest, it will simply draw attention to the article. If you ignore it, any interest it may at first attract will soon melt away."

"I don't agree," Druzhinin said. "Those two won't let it. They'll go on twisting the knife till it draws blood. This is part of a concerted campaign against Ivan Sergeyevich. They are frightened that his moderate approach may appeal to some of their younger readers more than their own radical one. *On The Eve* represents a real threat to them. This review is their counter-attack."

Botkin offers a suggestion: "Would it be worth while talking to Dobrolyubov and asking him to modify certain aspects?"

Turgenev is adamant. "That I could never bring myself to do. And besides, it would be useless. I can hear him…" He imitates the critic's high-pitched, squeaky voice: "'I'm very sorry, Ivan Sergeyevich, but I have to write what I believe.' No, I don't want the article to appear at all. There's a very real danger it could put me in a compromising position with the authorities. After all, I'm still under a cloud of suspicion in certain areas of St Petersburg."

"That occurred to me too," said Druzhinin. "What Dobrolyubov is insinuating is that your novel is a thickly veiled call for revolution. He's putting *his* thoughts into *your* mouth, while writing a generally negative review of your book. The man's diabolically clever, you have to admit."

"The only person who can sort this out," says Annenkov, "is Nekrasov. Either he demands that Dobrolyubov makes some alterations, or he doesn't print the article."

Druzhinin agrees. "Pavel's right. You can make this a defining moment for your relationship with *Sovremennik*. Force Nekrasov to show where he really stands. If he's not prepared to listen to you, of all people, a friend and collaborator from the very beginning, then your place is no longer there."

The other two nod their heads, and Turgenev finds himself in reluctant agreement...

19 February, 1860.

Dear Nikolai Alekseyevich,

I thank you for sending me a draft copy of your colleague's review of my book. You ask me to let you know if there is anything I would like changed. I'm afraid the answer is: everything. Apart from a few palliative commonplaces, it is a poisonous review, which I would resent coming from anywhere, let alone from Sovremennik. I must ask you most urgently not to publish this article; it can bring me nothing but unpleasantness; it is unjust and brutal; if it appeared, I wouldn't know where to hide. I beg you, in the name of our old friendship, to respect this request of mine. I will come to see you in the next day or so to be apprised of your decision...

After discreetly leaving a few days, during which he hoped he would hear directly from Nekrasov, he reluctantly made his way once more to the house, where he was informed by a servant that Nekrasov was away, he believed in Moscow.

"Did he leave a message for me?"

"Not as far as I know."

"Perhaps you'd be good enough to ask Panaev."

"Ivan Ivanovich has gone to Moscow too. I can ask Chernyshevsky if you like."

"That's all right, I'll wait until Nekrasov returns."

As the days went by, his time and thoughts became monopolized by his involvement in *First Love*. His attempt to recreate – and refashion – his adolescent memories afforded him greater delight than any of his previous work. Gradually

425

his irritation faded into the background; surely Nekrasov would have spoken to him if he had not been prepared to comply with his request. He had probably had to leave for Moscow in a hurry...

It was Druzhinin, to whom he had promised *First Love*, who brought him back to reality. He came round early in March to read the first draft and brought with him the current issue of *Sovremennik*. He could hardly refrain from gloating as he pointed out that Dobrolyubov's piece had been printed with various cuts, quite obviously made not by Nekrasov but by the censor. The implications that the book was a coded instigation to revolution were still there, although many references to the country's grievances had been omitted. There could scarcely be clearer evidence that Nekrasov had thrown down the gauntlet: he was standing side by side with his critic, daring Turgenev to do his worst.

"I have something else to show you," Druzhinin told the stupefied Turgenev, taking another slim publication out of his greatcoat pocket. It was a copy of *The Whistle*, a satirical supplement of *Sovremennik*, which came out every three or four months. He opened it at a page headed *Around the Salons*: a number of short paragraphs made more or less scurrilous references to well-known but unnamed figures, the author remaining anonymous. One of the paragraphs had been underlined and Turgenev read about a leading light of the St Petersburg literary world who was rarely to be seen in the nation's capital, as he spent most of his time *'ploughing doggedly along in the wake of a vagabond songstress, organizing claques for her on the stages of provincial theatres.'*

Turgenev covered his face with his hands and moaned: "Who would want to write a thing like that?"

"Any number of people. But it doesn't really matter. What does matter is that they are clearly determined to attack you from every possible front. It's time you saw Nekrasov again and made it plain that you have had enough. You're fighting from a position of strength. After your last two novels, you are universally recognized as Russia's greatest writer, and he's not going to want to lose you if he can possibly help it."

"You are right, Sacha, but the one thing I cannot do is go back to that house again. I feel like I'm walking into the lion's den. Nekrasov's all smiles, but I don't believe a word he says; Chernyshevsky conceals his malice under a veneer of unctuous bonhomie; and that other one admits it bores him to exchange the time of day with me. Even the servants are supercilious. I'll tell you what I'll do: I'll write again to Kolya and get Annenkov to deliver the letter to Panaev. Let's see what the two diplomats can hammer out between them."

"Very well, if you think that's best. But make your letter strong, otherwise it will have no effect at all."

Turgenev's letter was strong... *my relationship with your paper has become* *intolerable… I can no longer write for a publication like that… either there is a complete change in the attitude of you and <u>all your staff</u>, or I shall have to ask you to consider my association with you at an end…* but it never reached Panaev. Annenkov, the master of fence-sitting, hoped that a softer approach might have better results. So instead of delivering the letter, he had a long talk with Panaev, trying to convince him that only he could work on Nekrasov to avoid their losing their most illustrious contributor. Panaev agreed and did his best, but the only result was another letter from Nekrasov, begging Turgenev to stay, but repeating that he was prepared to take any steps to bring this about, short of dictating what his journalists should and should not write.

By the time he received this, Turgenev had finished *First Love*, given it to Druzhinin, who published it immediately in his *Readers' Library,* and left for the small German spa of Soden, near Frankfurt. Here he was joined by Tolstoy's eldest brother, whose ravaged, 37-year-old body was a battlefield, where tuberculosis and cirrhosis competed as to which would carry him off first. Nikolai, the most loveable of all the siblings, clearly had very little longer to live. But he carried his illness with the lightest of touches, and Turgenev found him an excellent companion. 'He practises,' he wrote to Herzen, 'the simplicity and humility which his brother preaches.' That brother was not in fact very far away: he had come with Marya and her children, all in varying degrees of ill-health, to Berlin to seek expert medical advice. By chance the lung specialist they consulted had recommended Marya to take a cure at Soden; Tolstoy refrained from accompanying her, officially because, having just opened a school for 22 peasant children in a third-floor bedroom at Yasnaya Polyana, he felt it incumbent on him to study teaching methods in the German capital; but Nikolai confided in Turgenev that he was sure Leo was still haunted by the death of his other brother, Dmitry. He had never forgotten the sight of the mortally sick man, holding the hand of the prostitute he had rescued from a brothel, coughing blood and stammering his disbelief that he could be dying before he reached thirty. "Lyovochka couldn't even bring himself to attend the funeral," Nikolai told the incredulous Turgenev. "His excuse was that he couldn't extricate himself from a previous engagement at the theatre."

As long as Tolstoy stayed in Berlin, Nikolai accepted his absence with a good grace, even making light of it with Turgenev. "Poor Lyovochka," he smiled. "He has a constitution of iron, which allows him never to be called to account for his excesses; whereas with Dmitry and me, the bill was presented in double quick time… and with no margin for payment." But not even this gentle, suffering man could hide his sorrow when he heard that his brother was visiting the Harz mountains, midway between Berlin and Frankfurt. "It would be only a five hour journey from there," he murmured to Turgenev. "Perhaps I shall have to go and see him. I wouldn't want to leave without saying goodbye to my brother. I've always believed he'd be the one of us who might make a mark in one way or another."

Turgenev, whose own guilt over his neglect of the dying Belinsky never lay far below the surface, had planned to stay with Nikolai until his brother arrived; but with the uncertainty emanating from Leo's letters, which one day announced his imminent arrival and the next offered a florid bouquet of reasons why it would have to be delayed, he was in a quandary of his own. He had enjoyed the company at Soden of an exceptionally pretty young German girl, infatuated with literature, who adored him 'as though,' he wrote to Annenkov, 'I were the reincarnation of Sophocles, Virgil and Shakespeare in one human form. She would lie down in the mud and beg me to walk over her body to avoid getting my feet wet. This devotion is very appealing for a short while, but I have to confess that in time it can become a little wearing.' Nevertheless, with no remission of the silence from Paris, he would have basked in Ilse's veneration for a little longer if he had not heard from Nikolai that Marya was on her way to Soden. This convinced him that he must leave. Her presence there could only cause him embarrassment: he could hardly ask Ilse to disappear out of his life from one day to the next; and the thought of Marya, with whom he had once been so intimate, gazing with her now embittered eye on the uncritical worship lavished on him by the languishing *fräulein* was unbearable.

Salvation came from the most unexpected source. A week before Marya's expected arrival, he received a letter from Pauline: her little son Paul had fallen seriously ill of scarlet fever; they feared for his life; she was distraught with worry and was terrified of spending even a minute alone. She was continuing to give performances of *Orphée* to provide her with momentary distraction (spectators were later to say that her final aria over the dead Eurydice was almost impossible to watch), and Louis, of course, was there; but he was too overcome with grief himself to provide her with any comfort. Could her old friend spare her the time to pay a visit and share the vigil with her? Wherever he had been, whatever he had been doing, Turgenev would have been at the little boy's bedside as fast as carriage or rail could carry him. Her wish, as ever, was his command. In this case, it also extracted him from an invidious position. Marya's arrival acquitted him from guilt about abandoning Nikolai... and Leo was still assuring everyone that he would soon be coming. He took a rather relieved farewell of the tearful Ilse, and by the middle of July was taking turns at Paul's sickbed.

Before leaving Soden he received from Druzhinin the June issue of *Sovremennik*, which contained the final indignity. While still in St Petersburg, he had prepared a four-volume collected edition of his work for the Moscow publisher, N.A. Osnovsky. In the course of revision, he had written the second epilogue to *Rudin*, where the eponymous hero, carrying a red flag in one hand and a blunt, curved sword in the other, dies a gratuitously futile death on the barricades of 1848 Paris. This had stemmed from his reflections on the figure of Don Quixote for his essay, with a hint too, post-Insarov, that a Russian could also make a heroic, if useless, gesture. He had thought, rightly or wrongly, that it would make a more sympathetic figure of his protagonist. As he was leafing through the journal, he was surprised to notice that Druzhinin had underlined a passage in a review by Chernyshevsky of Nathaniel Hawthorne's *Tanglewood Tales,* a collection of stories for children adapted from Greek mythology. With growing incredulity he read that the critic had managed to drag *Rudin* into this, calling the book 'not the tragedy it purports to be, but a mixed salad of pages, now sweet, now sour, now ironic, now hotheaded.' He went on to accuse Turgenev of having added the epilogue to ridicule the character of Bakunin, now languishing in Siberian exile in Irkutsk, in order to make a good impression on his rich literary friends, 'in whose eyes every poor wretch down on his luck is essentially a scoundrel'.

One quiet afternoon at Courtavenel, when the baby boy was clearly out of danger and life had resumed its even flow, Turgenev sat down and, with a heavy heart, took up his pen…

Dear Nikolai Aleksandrovich,

The contents of this short note will surely not come as a surprise to you. They are, in fact, no more than the seal on a door that has already been closed. It has now become abundantly clear that certain of the collaborators on the paper which you edit, and to which I have had the honour to make some small contributions over the years, are in league not only to criticize my work in the most destructive manner possible (which professionally, of course, they have every right to do), but also to level attacks on me of a personal nature which have nothing to do with the function of literary criticism. We have thrashed over these matters on many occasions in recent months; but after the totally gratuitous attack made on me in the course of a review of a children's book by an American author, I have no wish or intention to add one more word to what I have already said and written. Consequently, I would ask you to consider, as of receipt of this letter, my collaboration with Sovremennik to be at an end.

It is my sincere wish that you may find a way to correct the mistaken course I consider the journal to be taking, and restore it to the honoured position it held under its illustrious founders.

I regretfully add that, along with the severance of my relationship with the paper, it seems to me disingenuous to delude ourselves that our personal friendship could continue.

With precious memories of the many good moments enjoyed during that friendship,

I remain,

Yours, in sorrow,

Ivan Turgenev

To Nekrasov's answering letter, expressing the hope that he would change his mind, but reiterating the impossibility of his interfering with the work of his collaborators, Turgenev made no reply.

During his fortnight's stay at Courtavenel, Turgenev and Pauline spent more time alone together than they had for many years. For the first week, no one in the house could think or speak of anything but the condition of baby Paul: the degree of his fever, the hours he had slept, his appetite or lack of it – any conversation that veered away from these topics seemed heartless and out-of-place. But after the crisis had passed, the two of them often found themselves in each other's exclusive company. Pauline only went to Paris for performances of *Orphée*, of which she had now given over seventy, returning the next morning. For once there were no other guests in the house and, in the evenings, Louis usually went to bed the minute they had finished their supper; the very real fear of losing the only son he had waited so long for seemed to have aged him ten years in as many days. Pauline was less physically marked by the ordeal, but she clearly found it a relief, after all the strain, to spend long evenings conversing with her old friend on any number of topics. Because of the scarcity of their recent correspondence, they knew little about each others' lives over the past few years, and she seemed anxious to fill in the gaps.

One evening he inquired after Berlioz, wondering if, after the triumphant success of their collaboration on the Gluck opera, they still saw each other regularly. "Oh, I think we've reached a sort of agreement," she told him. "We had it all out one afternoon here at Courtavenel. He had come down with the finished score of *Les Troyens,* which he wanted to discuss with me; we went for a walk after lunch and suddenly the poor man seized my hand and went down on his knees, pouring forth his love as passionately, if less beautifully, as he did in his *Romeo and Juliet.* I meant everything to him, he couldn't live without me… and all the rest of it. It was quite painful to listen to."

"How did you extricate yourself?"

A gleam of amusement flashed into her eyes. "I reneged on my Mediterranean heritage and became pure British. I remembered when Louis and I were staying with Henry Chorley – the music critic, I think you know him – at his house in Lancashire, we visited some friends of his who had a small boy, looked after, of course, by a governess. At some point the boy fell over on a gravel path and grazed his knees, quite badly in fact. When he started to bawl, the governess simply wiped off the blood, dusted down his shorts and said: 'Now, Master Robert, we're not going to make a fuss in front of all these people, are we?' And believe it or not, the boy immediately reduced his howl to a snivel, looked around at us and said: 'No. I'm sorry, Miss… Pritchard, I think her name was.' I'd heard a lot about Anglo-Saxon phlegm, but I'd never realized it started at such an early age."

"And you applied it to Berlioz, of all people!"

"Yes, and with great success. I pointed out to him that I had been married for 20 years, that he was married too… he tried to break in there, but I stopped him before he could begin to pour out his woes about his wife, who is truly dreadful, I have to say… that we had a valuable friendship and an invaluable professional collaboration, both of which could only be damaged by anything more… intimate. So, not of course in so many words, I suggested he stop making a fuss. I think Miss Pritchard would have been proud of me."

Turgenev smiled, but had difficulty in disguising the sorrow these disclosures caused him. Hearing the woman he loved refer so lightly to another man's infatuation with her confirmed that for her, now, he was a reliable old friend with whom to share the vicissitudes of her romantic adventures. You didn't confide in people you were still even a little bit in love with. He switched, with some relief, from the personal to the professional and asked her about *Les Troyens*. She told him that she had agreed with his advice not to play both of the main roles, and was to sing excerpts from the opera that autumn at the Baden-Baden festival, with Berlioz conducting. "I shall do one duet as Cassandra," she told him, "and another as Dido. That will help me to make up my mind… though I still think it very unlikely that anyone in Paris will take the risk of putting on the whole work, beautiful as much of it is. It would last all of four hours, you know. Can you imagine the Parisians sitting still – and more or less silent – for four hours?!"

Another evening he announced that, unless she still needed his presence, he would be leaving soon for England. She took his hand and thanked him for having come to her rescue: "It meant so much to me, your being here. I think without you the strain would have been too much for me. Poor Louis… it was almost more difficult looking after him than little Paul. He's the dearest of men, but sometimes his dependency on me becomes a bit of a burden. I hardly dare confess it, but to you perhaps I can…" the twinkle of complicity in her eyes brought back times past so forcefully he was hard put to it not to leap out of his chair and into her arms… "those little trips I have been making alone – to Leipzig, to Baden-Baden, to Birmingham – have been like the holidays I never take… I come back feeling so refreshed! There, now you know my guilty secret! But tell me, why are you going to England?"

He explained to her that a number of his countrymen were congregating at Ventnor, on the Isle of Wight, to discuss various issues arising from the imminent emancipation of the serfs. He had also been advised by his doctors to resume the sea-bathing that had seemed to benefit him at Boulogne. He would be going to London first, to give Herzen the latest news from St Petersburg and also – and here he became hesitant – perhaps to look for a governess for Paulinette. "She's finished with school now, and I have to start thinking about her future." His hesitancy had been due to a vague hope she might suggest taking his daughter back into her family,

431

but she seemed to have read his mind and soon disillusioned him on that score. "I've been thinking of Paulinette recently too. You know I personally would love to have her with us again, but I'm afraid it would not be a good idea. For her, particularly. She needs to develop her own personality, and that's not easy in a big family. It was different when she first came over, because then there was only Louise. But now there are four of them. She might find herself swamped. No, I think your idea is a good one. You must find a Miss Pritchard, so that when you are not in Paris you can feel confident that she is being well looked after. And then you will have to start looking for a husband for her."

Turgenev raised his eyes to heaven and groaned. "That's not a task I look forward to. Nor one that I believe I have the slightest talent for. I was hoping you might give me a hand."

Pauline shook her head. "I am the last person to do that. Paulinette resents any decision I make on her behalf. I don't blame her entirely, of course. The poor dear is dreadfully jealous of you. Which is entirely natural. But unfortunately, it makes it impossible for me to help her over the least little thing."

"I have hopes for my cousins, the Nikolai Turgenevs. Or the Trubetskoys. She's staying with them now at Bellefontaine. They're very fond of her and quite take her under their wing when I'm away... which is just as well, as I may have to spend many months in Russia soon. But there's no great hurry to marry her off. If I succeed in finding the right governess, they could travel together, see a bit of the world... she's very anxious to join me at Spasskoye, but I'm not so sure it's a good idea..."

Pauline sensed his awkwardness and cruelly let him tail off without coming to his rescue. Then, instead of giving him the opinion he was waiting for, she gave him a searchingly direct look and asked: "Tell me truthfully, Ivan, what are your exact feelings for your daughter?"

He looked at her askance for a moment, then cleared his throat and answered: "I am very fond of her. I think she is a kind, thoughtful girl with many qualities and a few defects... which I never tire of pointing out to her. But I suffer sometimes from the fact that we have so little in common. She does not like music, poetry, nature or dogs... and I like little else. She is a much more practical person than I am... and I hope that will make a her a good wife. But she's a little like my character Insarov: I respect her, but I find it hard to love her as wholeheartedly as a father should love his daughter. Is that a terrible confession? Of course, I would make it to no one but you."

She reassured him with a smile. "If you had said anything markedly different, I would not have believed you. But don't torment yourself. She will be all right. You have two duties ahead of you now: first to find her a suitable governess; then, an even more suitable husband!"

Predictably, the first duty was to prove much easier than the second. After

432

interviewing three applicants sent by a London employment agency, Turgenev had no hesitation in choosing a handsome middle-aged widow by the name of Mary Innis. Her husband, a naval lieutenant, had died at sea and since then she had been the companion of a wealthy brewer's daughter who had just got married. Her chief appeal to her new employer stemmed from a quality he had not been expecting: a great admirer of the down-to-earth empiricism and dependability of the English, he had never credited them with much sense of humour. But when, having explained that Paulinette had only a smattering of English, he asked her if she spoke any French, she replied: "Only what I learned at school; and most of that I'm afraid I have forgotten. I did once try to brush it up a little by reading a French novel in my last position; but my employer saw it and gave me to understand that he did not wish to find such objects in his house, especially in the vicinity of his daughter. But never mind, Mr Turgenev; if you decide to hire me, your daughter and I will be able to help each other: I will teach her English, and she will teach me French. I will have to keep my head below the battlements in France, though; you have been so courteous as not to ask me my age; but I should perhaps tell you that I was born in 1815 – Waterloo, you know!"

Turgenev hired her on the spot and made arrangements for her to come over to Paris as soon as he had found lodgings for the three of them. In London he had been staying with Herzen, who had moved from Putney to a house just off Regent's Park. Now the two of them travelled down to Ventnor, where they joined a miscellaneous group of their fellow-countrymen. The visitors were all staying in a boarding-house standing on a pleasant flower-strewn terrace overlooking the small fishing-port. The landlady, a severe matron more used to the cowed, complaisant behaviour of British tourists than this anarchic group of Russians, some of whom spoke little or no English, read them the rules the moment they arrived: no ladies, liquor or smoking allowed in the rooms and mealtimes at fixed hours, with no form of sustenance available at any other time. Herzen, whose long familiarity with the ways of this strange island race designated him as the spokesman of the group, did eventually charm her into allowing a loaf of bread and a hunk of ham to be left in the pantry – 'there will be an extra charge, of course' – at the disposal of the 'foreign gentlemen'.

These included Annenkov, who had made the trip even though he was due to be married in September; and General Rostovstev's son, whom Turgenev took to as instinctively as he had to his father. There were representatives of most of their turbulent country's multifarious shades of opinion: Westerners, Slavophils, landowners, merchants and writers. Turgenev was pleased to see that there was no one from *Sovremennik* ("Surely because they knew you were going to be here," Herzen remarked), although a young doctor by the name of Bazhenev, who had published some inflammatory articles on the serf question, reminded him of a slightly less uncouth version of Dobrolyubov.

It had been only three months since Turgenev had left Russia, but so delicate was the balance of powers around the imperial throne that he and Herzen were anxious to hear from Rostovstev where the latest lines had been drawn. The evening they arrived, the three of them walked down to the port and sat in an inn listening to the young man's report. His father had died in February, literally worn out by his struggle to keep the reformist cause uppermost in Alexander's mind. The reactionaries, led by the dangerously attractive, utterly ruthless Count Peter Shuvalov, had let no scruple impede them from blackening, if not poisoning his reputation with the Czar. The Grand Duchess Elena Pavlovna had insisted that he go off to his country estate for a rest, but, deprived of the daily stimulus of fighting for his cause, he had caught a bout of influenza which had proved too much for his weakened physique. The Czar, to the despair of the reformists, had proceeded to replace him with Count Panin. "But how can this be possible?" Herzen exclaimed. "This is the man who said that whoever first put the emancipation idea into Alexander's head (and it was surely Zhukovsky) should have been hanged." Rostovstev nodded grimly. "Yes. And this is the man who is now President of the Final Editing Commission. Poor Father! Perhaps it was better for him that he died when he did."

"But isn't this a major setback?" Turgenev asked.

"Almost certainly not," was the comforting reply. "It is too late for Panin to reverse the whole process – much as he would no doubt like to. The final draft has already been drawn up. The Grand Duchess told me just before I left that there are only the most minute details left to settle." He allowed himself a smile. "And I don't think His Majesty, even coming directly from a tête-à-tête with Shuvalov, would dare to face Elena Pavlovna and Grand Duke Constantine with an announcement that the whole process was to start all over again."

"Nevertheless," Herzen growled, with a sideways look at Turgenev, "what you tell us doesn't reassure those of us who are less than confident about Alexander's genuine desire for reform."

"He wants reform," Rostovstev said, "but on his own terms. My father often emphasized how tormented he was by the idea that the sacred aura of the Czar's authority would be damaged if he were seen to submit to any pressure from the reformist nobles. Five of them sent him an address promulgating elected local government, an independent judicial system and the public's right to denounce administrative abuses."

Herzen gave a sardonic laugh. "Where are they now? In Siberia?"

"Not quite. But they received the severest of official rebukes, and were warned against any other such insolent meddling in the future. Perhaps that is the background to the appointment of Panin: the reactionaries will feel reassured and the more advanced of the reformers will not dare step out of line."

Herzen shook his head gloomily. "It doesn't augur well for the future," he said. "Emancipation by itself isn't enough. If it isn't followed by real reform, the peasants may well end up worse off than before. Free, yes… to starve to death."

"Everything will depend," Turgenev put in, "on how the final recommendations are carried out. And that is something none of us can foresee. All we can do is try and anticipate some of the measures we think will be necessary. And that, more or less, is what we're here for, isn't it?"

When the whole group – about twenty in all – met the following morning, they started discussing a post-emancipation plan Turgenev had put forward to provide elementary education to as many of the newly liberated serfs as possible. He and Annenkov had already drawn up a draft proposal to form a 'Society for the Diffusion of Primary Instruction'; if official permission were forthcoming, funds would soon be needed to cover the initial costs: converting huts into reading rooms, providing text books and finding teachers prepared to work for a pittance. He now asked the wealthy among those present to guarantee contributions and solicit the same from their friends; the others he exhorted to try and extricate some money from the local authorities. The Society would then approach the central government and ask them to match the funds that had already accumulated. But he was to be disappointed at the lukewarm support he and Annenkov received. Young Rostovstev was enthusiastic. But many of the others, including, to Turgenev's disappointment, Herzen himself, were sceptical. And the doctor, Bazhenev, was scathing in his opposition.

"Whatever money there is," he said tersely, "will have much more urgent priorities."

"Such as?" Turgenev inquired politely.

"Medicine, for example. Hospitals, sanitary equipment, proper training for doctors, nurses…"

"These are certainly important," Turgenev agreed. "But we must hope that these will be forthcoming anyway. The Grand Duchess is already thinking along these lines. And you know, I suppose, what she achieved during the Crimean War?"

"No. Tell me."

"She enlisted, trained and sent out 250 nurses, including her own lady-in-waiting."

"Very admirable. But war creates urgencies which mysteriously melt away in times of peace."

Rostovstev intervened. "Then it will be our business to bring them back to public attention."

The doctor shook his head. "You will have a hard time. An arm hacked off by a sabre inspires pity. Thousands dying of cholera is considered an act of God."

"Nevertheless," Turgenev insisted, "it will always be easier to find people prepared to spend money on men's bodies than on their minds."

Herzen gave the young doctor a confidential wink. "Ivan Sergeyevich envisages our muzhiks reading Pushkin to their wives and children around the evening fire."

Turgenev was not to be deterred. "And why not? Eventually, why not?"

Bazhenev gave a short laugh. "What use would it be to them? What use is Pushkin to anyone?"

There was a murmur of disapproval from the rest of the company, but Turgenev answered calmly: "What use? None, I suppose, in a practical sense. But then neither is the song of a thrush any use. Or the miracle of an autumn sunset. But wouldn't you miss them if they weren't there?"

"I don't suppose I'd notice."

This did pull Turgenev up short. All he could say, after a minute, was: "Then you have my deepest sympathy."

Bazhenev laughed quite naturally. "I really don't need it," he said. "I suspect rather that you need mine... and that of those of us who think like I do. And there are many of us."

A journalist from Katkov's journal, the *Moscow Herald,* which took an ambiguous stance towards emancipation, asked, aggressively: "And why should Ivan Sergeyevich need your sympathy?"

"Because he..." he looked round at Herzen, Annenkov and several others, "and many of you here, are men of the past. You've played your parts and the curtain's come down." Turning back to Turgenev: "I have read some of your stuff, Ivan Sergeyevich. I've even quite enjoyed bits of it. It's like reading history. Homer told some good stories, but what relevance does he have today?"

"Perhaps more than you think. But let's leave Homer aside. As a man of the past, I would like to return to the future of our country after emancipation. You see it, if I've understood correctly, purely in terms of scientific improvements – medicines that will prolong people's lives, for example. Which, of course, we would all welcome. But if you consider what millions of these lives actually amount to, one might wonder if they themselves would want them to be prolonged."

"Wouldn't you, if you were one of them?"

Turgenev thought for a moment. "If I was a woman tied up and beaten half to death every Saturday night when her husband came home drunk, perhaps not. If I was a young girl of fifteen forced into the bed of the father of the man who had been chosen, not by me, to be my husband, perhaps not. If I was a serf torn from my wife and children and sent into exile because I had forgotten to remove my hat in my mistress's presence, perhaps not. I might think the reward promised me in Heaven would be preferable."

"There you demonstrate the gulf that separates you liberal intellectuals from us. We intend to go step by step, improving the day-to-day conditions of life. You can see progress only in terms of changing the entire sociological structure of the country. And as it is clear to the dimmest mind that several generations must pass before this can be achieved, you will just go on talking – and writing – as you have for the past twenty years. And *nothing* will change."

"We are talking today about trying to change something: illiteracy."

"Ah yes, I forgot. Pushkin is the answer to all our ills!"

"So you have no interest in trying to change, not only the conditions, but also the quality of people's lives?"

"By giving them the chance of a change of bed linen every now and then, yes. By forcing Pushkin… or Beethoven… or whoever else you had in mind down their throats, no. Especially because you'll never succeed."

Herzen smiled across at his friend. "He's right, Vanya. There are too many of the likes of us around anyway. Especially in Russia. What are needed are good cobblers, tailors, carpenters…"

Annenkov came to Turgenev's aid. "But they wouldn't be any less good if they could also read and write."

Bazhenev gave a half smile. "That could be true. Perhaps it is our priorities that are different. Ivan Sergeyevich mentioned the future of our country after emancipation. As he said, all will depend on what happens then. If it heralds the dawn of a blessed era of enlightened progress, so much the better. We can even start thinking about schools for all children. But if, as we believe, all the old evils will still be there – an aristocracy concerned only to maintain its privileges, an intermediate class of cowed clerks, sycophantic bailiffs and corrupt lawyers, and a peasantry that can't think beyond its next glass of vodka… then, to change all that no amount of Pushkin will suffice. A whole way of life will have to go… and with it, inevitably, I fear, many people like yourselves, personally charming as I find you all. And now, if you'll excuse me, I have a book to finish." He turned on his way to the door, forestalling the question on Turgenev's lips. "No, no, not Pushkin, I'm afraid. A dissertation on the digestive tracts of rodents…"

A day or two later, Turgenev left Ventnor, as he had urgently to find lodgings in Paris. He asked Annenkov to draw up a document outlining the intentions of the 'Society' and to get as many signatures of support as possible. He was then to return to Russia and circulate it to everyone who might look favourably on its proposals. Then, and only then, he jokingly added, could he devote a little time to the business of getting married. He himself would canvass amongst the Russian community in Paris for adhesion to the scheme and would write to Annenkov with a list of names as soon as he had done so. But it was to be several weeks before Annenkov received the letter.

On returning to Paris, Turgenev found a copy of *Sovremennik*, sent to him by Druzhinin:

SOVREMENNIK

Editor: N.A.Nekrasov

September, 1860

We open this issue with an item of information we wish to bring to our readers' attention: namely that Ivan Sergeyevich Turgenev will no longer be contributing to this journal. While we, and surely many of you, will regret that the work of the distinguished author will not appear any more on our pages, the total divergence in our political views that has recently manifested itself has left us with no choice but to dispense with his services. We nevertheless wish him a luminous future as one of Russia's foremost men of letters.

For once, Turgenev did not procrastinate: the following morning he composed a letter which he sent back to Druzhinin, who was only too happy to publish it in his journal…

THE READERS' LIBRARY

Editor: A.V.Druzhinin

October, 1860

<u>Letters:</u>

Sir,

May I beg the hospitality of your pages to correct a misconception that will have been implanted in many people's minds by the editorial in the September issue of Sovremennik. *In correctly stating that the paper and I have decided to part company, it is incorrectly implied that they were the instigators of this rupture. As we say where I come from: 'The geese have eaten the fox!' May I take this opportunity to state in the most emphatic terms that it was I who broke off relations with that publication, despite their almost begging me to remain. Only a certain sense of fastidiousness prevents me from enumerating the series of provocations that led me to take this painful step; but I believe those of your readers who also scan the pages of* Sovremennik *will have some idea of what I am talking about.*

Respectfully yours,

Ivan Turgenev.

He also finally wrote the long-promised letter to Annenkov…

210, rue de Rivoli,
Paris.
30 September, 1860.

Dear Pavlochka,

I will spare you the excuses for the delay in this letter, as you will soon gather how busy I have been. Ventnor seems a year, not a month away. As you see, I have found an apartment just two doors away from my old one in the rue di Rivoli; it is pleasant enough, with plenty of room for three – I say 'three' because the splendid Mrs Innis has arrived; I am happy to say that Paulinette took to her immediately, which was an enormous relief to me. Our little family is beginning to 'settle down'.

And you, of course, are now a family man too. Please convey once again my congratulations to Glafira Aleksandrovna; I deeply regret not having been able to be present at your wedding, let alone be your best man, but, as you will soon find out, we 'family men' are not as readily available as we used to be.

Domesticity apart, much of my time since my return has been taken up with pondering over an idea for a new book. I have not decided on a title yet, but might even go back to the old 'Two Generations', as that is the general theme. My mind has been harping for some time now on the radically different ways we 'of the forties', as they call us (as though we were already in the dustbin), contemplate trying to grapple with our country's problems and envisage its future, compared with people 20 years our junior. Of course, this is as old as history – think of all those Roman senators lamenting their sons' lack of moral fibre! But I do not believe there has ever in Russia been so drastic a divide between one generation and the next. We often hardly seem to be speaking the same language. My book would be an attempt to explore the nature of – and the reasons behind – this divide. It would of course only have any value if I strive valiantly to give both sides their due. Although the idea has been rambling around in my mind for some time, you will not be surprised to learn that the igniting spark was provided by our conversations with that young doctor on the Isle of Wight. I have in my mind as a protagonist a character with elements of him and others like him I have talked to in recent years; there would be something of Dobrolyubov too, but I will have to avoid letting any personal animosity get in the way. Contrary as the opinions – they would call them convictions – of these young men are to just about everything we hold dear, there must be some validity in what they say; and it is that which I must try to winkle out, as they instructed us to do with those – what were they called? – was it 'whelks'? – in Ventnor. I hardly need say it would be so much easier if they weren't so extreme in their dogmatism.

I have worked out a detailed plan of the book, which Botkin has seen and approved. I have also made sketches of the principal characters and am writing an imaginary diary of my protagonist, in an attempt to get into his head and discover how he would comment on daily events – not just political ones, but all the items one reads in the papers. Its a salutary exercise, believe me. At any rate, I shall soon be sending all this to you for your advice and suggestions which, along with those of Madame Viardot, I value above all others. But as this book will have so specifically Russian an atmosphere – geographically it will move very little, if at all – I must depend above all on your habitual shrewdness and perspicacity.

So, there now. Enjoy the rest of your honeymoon, as there will be work for you to do as soon as you get back. Don't let up with your efforts to propagate our educational proposals, and give me your honest opinion of my idea as soon as you can. I would like to think I could get the major part of the book written over this winter.

Your devoted,

I.T.

Turgenev saw nothing of Pauline for three months. She was embarked on an exhausting operatic tour of most of the principal English cities and repeating her Lady Macbeth in Dublin. But he did, from time to time, spend a few days at Courtavenel, as he and Viardot were working on a translation of *On the Eve*. Once he took with him a French version he had made of *First Love* and asked Louis at lunchtime to read it and tell him if it were acceptable or needed reworking. He had been approached by Buloz, editor of the *Revue des Deux Mondes*, who was anxious to publish an example of his work. Seeing nothing of his host for the rest of the day, he allowed himself the pleasant suspicion that Louis had been so taken with it he hadn't been able to put it down. To some extent this was true, but not for the reasons that the author had assumed. They met again for dinner and Viardot wasted no time in giving his opinion.

"The French is perfectly acceptable, Ivan," he said. "A few changes here and there, but nothing radical. What I find unacceptable – and I have to be truthful with you over this, in honour of our long association – is the story itself."

Turgenev was genuinely surprised. Always ready to listen to criticism and sometimes over ready to accept it, he had found his feeling that the novella was one of the best things he had done confirmed by all members of his usual 'jury'. "What didn't you like about it?", he asked, placidly.

"Virtually everything," was the uncompromising reply. "If I were Buloz, I would certainly turn it down."

"On what grounds? Is it so badly written?"

"Nothing you do can be badly written. You know that. It is the content that is offensive. It belongs in the ranks of what I call 'unhealthy literature'. What a wretched cast of characters! The vulgar, grasping old princess; the young girl flirting outrageously with the clear intent of putting her attractions up for sale; and her wretched little court of admirers, none of them with any qualities to interest or amuse us. And who is this current version of *La Dame aux camélias* going to choose? A married man. Of course. Adultery, adultery, always adultery! Romanticised and glorified. Like that Flaubert fellow, with his *succès de scandale*. If there hadn't been all that legal kerfuffle, very few people would probably have bothered to read the book…"

"Have you read it?"

"No. Have you?"

"Yes. To me, it's the most remarkable novel of contemporary French literature."

"Indeed?! Then I suppose I shall have at least to dip into it."

"Perhaps you shouldn't. He goes into much more adulterous detail than I do."

"Well, at least your adulterer is a man. That's something, I suppose. But I've said what I had to say. And, I repeat, it's only because of the immense respect I have for your work that I forced myself to bring it up. One last word. Whatever you do with this story, let me beg you to return to what you do so well: casting a caustic eye on Russian society, with a subtle touch here and there of comedy. For the love of God, don't fling yourself, along with all the others, into the sewer of the 'modern novel'.

In February, Tolstoy passed through Paris on his way to London from Hyères in the south of France, where he had sat for two weeks at his brother's deathbed. Not since their first meeting in St Petersburg six years ago had the two men taken such unruffled pleasure in each other's company. The tragic experience he had lived through seemed to have skimmed off all Tolstoy's abrasiveness. He spent his days visiting Parisian schools, where he was shocked by the old-fashioned disciplinary methods, and buying every book he could lay his hands on that dealt with education. He warmly greeted Turgenev's and Annenkov's venture and promised to further it when he returned to Russia. Avoiding theatres and music-halls, he was happy to spend his evenings with Turgenev's friends in the Russian colony, where he would sit listening but rarely participating in the conversation, and never taking violent issue with anybody. Turgenev wrote to Herzen, who would be meeting him for the first time when he went to London, that 'if good can come from bad, Nikolai's tragic death seems to have metamorphosed his brother.'

The evening before Tolstoy left for London the two men dined alone together. Knowing how fond his brother had been of Turgenev, Tolstoy finally let himself go and searched for words to describe the void that Nikolai's death had left in his soul. "As I sat there day after day, taking turns with Marya, watching the life gradually ebb out of him, I came face to face with the utter futility of everything. I tried to resist my memory, but it was too strong for me; scenes from my childhood flashed before me, and always there was Nikolenka, the one we all looked up to, admired and tried to emulate. I remembered the green stick on which, he told us, was carved the secret which would banish all evil from the earth. It was buried somewhere in a deep gorge on the edge of the forest of Zakaz, and anyone who found it would be able to fill the hearts of men with everlasting love. I think all my life will be a search for that stick. And when I die, I would like to be buried in Zakaz forest."

Turgenev, who had not dared mention the matter before, now plucked up the courage to ask about Nikolai's end.

"It's difficult to gauge the extent of his suffering, because he was so determined to conceal it from us. He even used to try the hide the handkerchiefs he had been spitting blood into. But I could tell from his eyes that it was not so much pain he was struggling to overcome, but fear. And the day he died – I was alone with him, Marya was looking after her children – he had relapsed into unconsciousness, then suddenly came round, stared at me with something resembling panic – whether he recognized me or not I shall never know – and stammered: 'What is it?' A moment later he was dead."

"'What is it?'", Turgenev repeated.

Tolstoy nodded, and the two men relapsed into a pensive silence. Then Tolstoy resumed: "Those three words have become so firmly lodged in my mind that I have come to the conclusion that, if I am to go on writing, the only justification for churning out more and more words would be the attempt to answer their question. Everything else that goes by the name of art is a lie."

Normally Turgenev would have challenged this assertion, but now he let it pass. "And have you had time to think of the form this search might take?" he asked.

"To try and take my mind off Nikolenka, I scribbled down a few chapters of a possible novel about the Decembrists."

"Beginning in 1825?"

"No. It would start with a man like Prince Sergey Volkonsky, who was a cousin of my mother's, returning to Moscow after thirty years' exile in Siberia... looking around him with both the dispassionate objectivity of a foreigner and the passionate concern of a Russian patriot. What he has hoped to find, what instead he sees... and then it would go back to the experiences of the men who defeated Napoleon... their hopes, their dreams... oh, but it won't come to anything..."

"No, no." Turgenev beat his hands on his knees with excitement. "That's what you should be doing: a big book with a historical sweep to it. Like the idea you had in Dijon about the Burgundians."

For the first time Tolstoy waved his arm in his characteristic gesture of impatience. "If I couldn't do it then, what chance is there now? Where can I find the patience to put useless words down on sheets of paper when I have stared meaninglessness and emptiness in the face?"

"Perhaps by allowing yourself to think – to hope – that those words might relieve meaninglessness and emptiness for other people."

"Ah, there you go again!" The reproach was familiar, but now there was regret rather than contempt in the tone. "The healing mission of the artist. You are

442

convinced of it, but you haven't just watched the person dearest in the world to you as, day by day, he slides off into nothingness. And so young. Younger than you."

Turgenev nodded. "I have no argument with you, Lyovochka, about the futility of life. There is hardly a day when I don't feel the clutch of its cold fingers round my heart. I can only suggest, from the vantage-point of my extra ten years, that we have only two choices: either we carry our despair to its logical conclusion, or we pursue... how shall I say it?... those activities which seem to us less futile than others. Continue with your school, improve it, start others... and force yourself – if only for Nikolai's sake, who thought so highly of you – to exploit your great gift and write the works that we are all expecting from you."

Tolstoy stood up to go; there was an unusual warmth in his farewell embrace, and a rare tenderness in his words. "Goodbye, my friend," he said. "Come and see me at Yasnaya as soon as you get back." He held Turgenev at arm's length and looked him straight in the eye. "And let us vow never to quarrel again."

The day after receiving this telegram, Turgenev read in the *Journal de Paris* that a *Te Deum* would be celebrated in the Russian Orthodox Church. This was where Paulinette went regularly for instruction from Father Vassiliev, and Turgenev asked her if she would like to accompany him to the service. She gave him a surprised, almost challenging look. "But why do you want to go, papa? I thought you didn't believe in anything like that."

He repressed the instinctive urge to scold her for her cheek. Since she was no longer a schoolgirl and with the arrival of Mrs Innis, he had made a point of trying to treat her as an adult. "I believe," he replied, "it is good to show gratitude to someone or something on the rare occasions when good triumphs in this world."

"But you could do that by yourself, here in this room."

He glanced at Mrs Innis, almost seeking support. "I could. But I would like to be in the presence of some of my fellow-countrymen who feel the same way as I do. After all, I don't have to accept every tenet of the Russian Orthodox Church in order to say thank you for the freeing from servitude of some twenty-three million fellow human beings. Don't forget that I have longed for this, and in a small way worked for it, since I was younger than you. But Mrs Innis has a different creed. Let's hear what she has to say on the subject."

"Oh, I absolutely agree with your father," was the comforting contribution. "The differences in our beliefs, which are, after all, not as frightfully important as all that, pale into insignificance in the light of a great event like this. The only thing we should ask ourselves is whether it would find favour in the eyes of Christ. And no one can have any doubt as to that. I might even attend the service myself."

Paulinette mounted a not very convincing rearguard action. "Yes, but it's different for you, Mrs Innis. You're a Roman Catholic. Papa doesn't believe in anything."

"Oh, I'm sure that's not true," Mrs Innis asserted stoutly.

Turgenev laughed. "Put it down to the exaggeration of youth," he said. "Certainly I do not have the sort of faith that sweeps away all doubts. Paulinette makes that sound like a crime. Perhaps it's just my misfortune." He put his arm round his daughter's shoulders. "At any rate, my dear, if my presence would be an

444

embarrassment to you, there is no obligation on you to accompany me. I can very well go alone… or even with Mrs Innis, if she would do me the honour."

The lady in question looked as if she would have been only too delighted, but, perhaps sensing this, Paulinette decided to relent. "No, no, Papa, I'm sorry, I was just being stupid. It would be lovely to go together…"

And go they did. On the way, in the carriage, Paulinette glanced at his face and was struck by his serious expression. "You don't look as if you're going to a celebration, Papa. More like a funeral."

Turgenev smiled and patted his daughter's hand. "There are so many thoughts going through my mind. Of course it's a moment of rejoicing. But the joy might feel more spontaneous if it had all happened four years ago. Sometimes when one waits too long for something, when it finally comes about it has lost a little of its savour. We're living in a world where all the old certainties are crumbling. Down they fall… one by one. And it's probably right that they should do so. But it is all happening so fast. And can we be sure that the new will be better. Who knows… who knows?…"

When they joined the hundred or so members of the Russian colony in Paris who had come to the little church in the rue de Berri, many with young children in their arms, it was soon clear to Turgenev that two moods were on display: the majority of the faces he scrutinized glowed with a sense of deep inner joy; others exuded bitter resentment… and many of these made no secret of their feelings towards him. One of them, a Count Vasilchikov, barred his way and almost spat in his face: "Well, I hope you are content now, Ivan Sergeyevich; you may not have ruined yourself, but you have certainly ruined us!" Turgenev ignored him, tightened his grip on his daughter's arm and led her over to where he saw his old friends Nikolai Turgenev and Prince Trubetskoy talking to a very frail, white-haired man, down whose furrowed cheeks tears were coursing without his making the slightest effort to control them or even wipe them away. On being introduced by his cousin, he realized he was standing in front of a legend: Prince Sergey Grigoryevich Volkonsky, scion of one of the oldest and wealthiest noble families of Russia, had paid for his involvement in the Decembrist insurrection by serving thirty years of exile in Siberia, from which he had just returned. On hearing Turgenev's name, he enveloped him in an emotional embrace and told him: "One of my happiest memories is that of reading your book, your *Sportsman's Sketches*. It gave me hope, and that was the most important commodity we had… and sometimes the most difficult to obtain." Before Turgenev could reply, a hush fell over the vociferous crowd as Father Vassiliev started his sermon. It was an impassioned homily, its basic theme being the great-hearted munificence of the Czar. When he achieved his peroration with a full-throated, passionate cry of 'God bless Alexander! Long live

445

the Czar!' it was replicated with a great answering shout. And now it was not only Volkonsky but the majority of those present, including Turgenev, who wept unashamedly.

When they left the church, they found Princess Trubetskoy's companion, Marianne, waiting outside for them. The Trubetskoys were a living example of the successful marriage of opposites: Nikolai Ivanovich was extremely devout, had converted to Catholicism, which he didn't let interfere with his Slavophil leanings, held spiritualist sessions and was politically a high-minded liberal; Anna Andreyevna, a declared atheist, spent much of her time reading philosophical works, always dined alone and was an ardent republican. She rarely moved from a horizontal position, asserting that a childhood disease had left her legs paralyzed; but one of her grandchildren claimed he had once gone into her boudoir unannounced and found her walking swiftly around the room. Her husband used to say of her: "I adore her, but she's crazy"; she of him: "He has a heart of gold, but he's an idiot."

The Princess had taken a liking to Paulinette and was looking out for a husband for her. Marianne explained to Turgenev that a possible fiancé was expected at their house in rue de Clichy that afternoon, and her mistress had asked her to bring his daughter back with her. Paulinette was less than enthusiastic: she loved being at her adored father's side when he was in the company of his friends. But Turgenev, who hoped she would make a happy and advantageous marriage at the earliest opportunity, urged her to go, and she reluctantly obeyed.

The four men strolled through the winter streets in search of a café, which they soon found round the corner in the rue du Faubourg St Honoré. They were about to order coffee, but Volkonsky insisted on a bottle of champagne. "If ever a day calls for celebration, it is this." After they had drunk their toast, he turned to Turgenev. "Give me your opinion of how this great change will work," he asked. "These two haven't been back in Russia for over thirty years. They don't know anything. And although I have now been allowed to return to my homeland, I can't go near Moscow or St Petersburg to feel on my own cheek which way the wind is blowing. Besides, I'm a leftover dish from a previous feast. I was born in the Great Catherine's reign, you know. But you are a landowner and a writer as well. No one can answer my questions better than you? What are we to expect?"

Turgenev sipped his champagne and answered thoughtfully: "I'm afraid I can only foresee hard times ahead. The reactionary element amongst the Czar's advisers will not give up easily. In that context, the death of General Rostovstev was more than a personal tragedy. I am in frequent contact with his son: he tells me that Panin, at the last moment, managed to make the terms of the settlement considerably less advantageous to the peasants than they would have been under the proposals put forward by his father. They will get less land than originally intended and will have to pay more for it. It's not a good beginning. Especially considering many of the peasants had been led to believe they would get all the land for nothing." The silence that followed these observations brought home to Turgenev that this was a darker diagnosis than his companions really wished to hear. He tried to make amends. "But I believe absolutely in the sincerity of Alexander's determination to see these reforms through, and we must hope that after a few years the initial difficulties will be ironed out."

"With God's help, may it be so!" Trubetskoy murmured.

Old Volkonsky roused himself from the meditative mood into which he had slipped. "After a few years, I will surely not be there to see, one way or another," he said. "But that's of no great consequence. The important thing for me is to have lived to see this day. It has made every minute of my thirty years of exile worth while. God bless the Czar!" The other three lifted their glasses and drained the last drops of the wine. Then Volkonsky turned back to Turgenev. "I presume you will be hurrying home now."

There was an uneasy pause. Then: "Yes, indeed. As soon as I can get away. Unfortunately I am not able to leave Paris just now. I have some unfinished business…"

Over the next few weeks he was to produce this or some similar vague formula to many of his Russian friends when they wondered, many rather bitterly, why he was still lingering on foreign soil. Herzen had written a sharp letter to this effect, to which he had replied: 'Why do you have to twist the knife in the wound? I am not a free man. I have a daughter to marry. That is the main reason I must stay for a while in Paris. But with all my thoughts, with my whole being, I am in Russia.' This was taken by many who knew him best with a fair degree of scepticism. Whether they knew it or not, among the factors that kept him away from Spasskoye was a request from Pauline. After their momentary rapprochement following Paul's illness, she had seemed again to withdraw into indifference. She had only paid one brief visit to his new apartment on rue di Rivoli, and there had been no invitation to Courtavenel since the autumn. But now, after many weeks of silence, she asked him to lunch at rue de Douai. When he arrived, he found that Louis was not there. Surely a *tête à tête* meant he had been invited for a purpose. And so it was. She was in an artistic dilemma and wanted his opinion. *Orphée* was finally drawing to the end of its three-year run and Carvalho, hoping, like every impresario down the ages, that by following it with something similar he would repeat its phenomenal success, had suggested she revive another Gluck opera: either *Armide* or *Alceste*. She had consulted Berlioz, but he had not been as encouraging as she had expected. He was totally immersed in the final revisions of *Les Troyens* and desperately trying to persuade Carvalho to stage it at the *Théâtre Lyrique*. Anything that distracted him

447

from this was a source of irritation. So, with a suitable show of reluctance, he declined Carvalho's offer to renew the *Orphée* collaboration.

As Pauline had made up her mind that this would be her last performance on the operatic stage, the decision as to which role would be more suitable for her farewell had assumed a supreme importance. To help make the right choice, she had arranged to sing a selection of arias from *Alceste* at the Conservatoire, and a few weeks later perform the third act of *Armide* at the *Théâtre Lyrique*. Would her dearest Tourgel, whose opinion she valued above all others, attend both and tell her which she should do?... And from one moment to the next, the need to return to Spasskoye lost all urgency. After all, what difference would a couple of months make? Weren't most of his serfs already freed? And wasn't there always uncle Nikolai to deal with immediate day-to-day business?

Turgenev stayed in Paris until the end of April. He dutifully attended both performances and pronounced in favour of *Alceste*; in this he was influenced, not only by his innate musical taste, but also by Carvalho, who took him aside and intimated that his audiences would have difficulty in accepting Pauline Viardot, with all her accomplishments, as the sorceress, Armide, on whose unearthly beauty all the other characters are continually remarking. Whereas Alceste, the heroically virtuous wife and mother of several children, could have been written for her. So *Alceste* it was. Six months later, Pauline opened to the expected triumphal reception. And though Berlioz the musician had refused to be involved, Berlioz the critic made handsome amends, writing in the *Journal des Débats* of 'the consummate actress, the inspired non-pareil of an artist', whose Alceste was 'a paragon of grief and tenderness... yet another triumph for Mme Viardot and perhaps the hardest ever for her to achieve...'

Turgenev left for Russia at the end of April with his new novel, which he had now decided to call *Fathers and Children*, about half completed. The possibility of arranging a marriage for Paulinette had evaporated, as she had taken an instant dislike to the suitor produced by Princess Trubetskoy. Before leaving he took steps to enrol another potential matchmaker, whom he had met through his friendship with Prosper Mérimée. He had known Mérimée since the 'black winter' of 1857, and found him the one member of the Parisian literary scene whose company he was glad to seek out: he was as impressed by the sense of tragic irony in the author's tales as he was intrigued by the studied air of cynical indifference of the man who wrote them. The two men had continued to see each other whenever Turgenev was in Paris, and Mérimée had often suggested he should come to the Thursday salon of his friend, Valentine Delessert.

This remarkable lady of aristocratic birth had married at 18 the son of a wealthy banking family twenty years older than herself. As intelligent as she was beautiful, as ambitious as she was charming, she had been Mérimée's mistress for fifteen years. When she was 45, her son had introduced her to the 29-year-old Maxime du Camp, Flaubert's friend and companion on their voyage to the eastern Mediterranean. She promptly seduced him, broke brutally with Mérimée and embarked on a tempestuous affair which lasted, seasoned with bitter quarrels, for nearly ten years. She eventually convinced herself, perhaps wrongly, that du Camp was resuming his old habit of trying to seduce every woman he met and then bragging about it to his friends, and sent him packing. The patient Mérimée was taken back into favour and was a regular presence at her salon in Passy, one of the most distinguished in Paris, frequented over the years by politicians, writers and artists of the eminence of Thiers, Stendhal, Musset and Delacroix.

The prospect of mingling with another group of chattering Parisians had not appealed much to Turgenev; but eventually, intrigued by the fact that, despite everything, the chronically misanthropic Mérimée still liked the woman, he had yielded to his friend's insistence and been charmed by her. She had drawn Turgenev out on the subject of his daughter and eventually asked him to bring her with him one evening. The two women had immediately taken to each other, and Turgenev now allowed himself a small hope that someone with so wide and varied a selection of friends might find the right man for his not particularly eligible daughter. After arranging for Mrs Innis to accompany Paulinette on a trip to Switzerland and northern Italy in the hope of broadening her cultural interests, he felt his paternal duties had been accomplished for the time being, and finally left for Russia.

Throughout the spring and early summer he resumed regular work on his book, which he had indicated to Katkov he hoped to finish by August. The only major interruptions he had to allow himself were caused by the need to make administrative decisions. He was unsurprised to learn that his uncle had taken virtually no steps to put the measures required by the emancipation act into practice. He had found Nikolai Nikolayevich, now sixty-six, not improved with the years. Communication with his wife, who was thirty years younger than himself and had been his mother's housemaid when he had married her, had been reduced to an almost permanent shouting-match. She was said to seek consolation in the arms of much younger men, and he most certainly found it in the bottle. He had become flabby and arthritic and this made him lazier than ever; he rarely left the house, and when he did it was only to order up the carriage and drive into Orel for a day of drinking and cards with his cronies. Turgenev was still fond of the old man, but he found it hard to hide his exasperation at his constant evasions when it came to discussing estate business. He would hide behind a pretended interest in his nephew's literary career, or, having once in his youth spent a winter in Paris, quiz him on his putative amorous adventures. "I am an old man," he had told him the day after his arrival, "and I don't understand a word of what it's all about."

Turgenev could hardly blame him, even though he knew that no effort had been made. He found the situation even more complicated than he had expected. Certainly, the euphoria of February had not survived the winter. Part of the problem was that the manifesto had been worded in such a way as to make it incomprehensible to almost everyone, not just the illiterate peasants. On the same Sunday that Turgenev had attended the thanksgiving service in Paris, the proclamation, drawn up by the Metropolitan of Moscow, had been read out by the priest from every pulpit in the land. But, as Turgenev had mentioned to Viardot before leaving, it might have been composed in French and revised in Greek before being translated into Russian by a German. It was no surprise that it had been greeted with fury by a majority of the landowners; but neither had the peasants welcomed it with any enthusiasm. The chief responsibility for this lay in the time the whole process had taken. After waiting for five years, the serfs were convinced that everything would be theirs: they would at last be free men living in their own houses and farming their own land. But that was not at all the way it turned out. When they gradually realized that for many of them nothing would change for another two years, while the 'arbiters of the peace', chosen mostly from the nobility, examined claims and counter claims as to how much land they were entitled to, disenchantment rapidly set in. And when it was explained to them that they would either have to rent their new land by continuing to work it or with cash payments, or else buy it with the help of a government loan to be paid back over a period of forty-nine years, their dissatisfaction changed, in many cases, to mutinous anger.

On the surface, Turgenev noticed very little difference in their attitude to him. As always, they gave him a warm welcome back. They continued to call him *barin*, so that he had to beg his bailiff to ask them to stop. But he sensed that behind the outward bonhomie lay a wary watching and waiting to see what he was going to do. Despairing of getting any helpful advice from Uncle Nikolai, he decided to sound out his old hunting companion, Alifanov. Abandoning his desk for the day, the two of them set off at dawn to pursue snipe in the marshy land around the river Ista. The sport was poor, but as soon as he had taken a nip or two from a flask he now carried attached to his belt, Alifanov became his usual garrulous self. He himself felt disdainfully above all the post-emancipation turmoil. Having been freed by Turgenev so many years ago and possessing his own smallholding, he and his wife earned enough for him to be independent and indulge in his two passions, hunting and drinking. Turgenev, on whom a sedentary life in Paris had also had its effect, noticed with amusement that, after walking for an hour or so, the once indefatigable Afanasy would puffingly invent an excuse to sit in the shade and rest for a while. 'We'll get better sport in 'alf an hour,' he announced knowingly, as if his companion had never been out with a gun before. But Turgenev was happy to comply, as it gave him the chance to talk. He discovered that Alifanov, from the height of his long independence, had little time for most of his fellow-muzhiks. "You'll 'ave to be careful, Ivan Sergeyevich," he warned his old master. "Them's going to trample all over you, if you don't look out. Don't give 'em everything all at once. I know you and your kind 'eart. Let 'em 'ave things bit by bit, like."

"Well what are they expecting?"

"Everything. Don't get me wrong. Most of 'em think the world of you. And they reckon that all in all you've done pretty well by them. As far as giving them land, that is. Trouble is, when it comes to paying for it. They don't like that. And that's where the mischief-makers come in. There's some rotten apples in the barrels, you know that as well as I do. No need to name names. From the moment the news broke, some of 'em's been stirring up trouble. They say the Czar – God bless 'im! – said one thing and the *barins* are doing another… behind his back, like. Countin' on no one understanding anyway. 'What right does any *barin* have to the land?' they say. 'He doesn't know what to do with it. He couldn't plough a field any more than he could fly. So how can he call it his? We've worked the fields all our lives and that makes them ours by right.'"

"I can see their point," Turgenev couldn't help saying.

"There you go. I knew it. You'll end up with nothing but your bed to sleep in if you go on like that. You know that bit of woodland you gave to them villagers near Zheltukhina, just after you got back?"

"Yes. I thought they could chop a few of the trees down and use the timber."

"Know what they did with it?"

"I've no idea. What?"

"Sold it the next day. They've been drinking on the proceeds ever since. I ought to know. Lot of the time I'm drinking with 'em."

Despite his disappointment, Turgenev tried to make the best of it. "Well, there's a lot of woodland where that came from."

"At the moment there is. But if you're not careful, there won't be a tree standing. Timber fetches a lot these days. But that's not all. You know what I heard one of them say the other day… in the tavern, when they were talkin' things over?"

"What?"

"They said, seeing as 'ow, when all's said and done, you'd been a pretty good master, they'd let you stay in the big house for as long as you live. But after that… " he took a swig from his flask and let Turgenev complete the thought. "And, beggin' your pardon, that's no thanks to your uncle. If there were only 'im to think of, I shouldn't wonder as to 'ow they'd be in there already."

"Is he so disliked?"

"It's not for me to speak out of turn, Ivan Sergeyevich. All I can say is, he and

Varvara Petrovna – God rest her soul! – may not have had the same blood in their veins, but he sure as eggs is eggs learnt a thing or two from 'er…"

Turgenev decided he'd heard all he needed to hear, and proposed they resume their search for snipe.

Before confronting his uncle, Turgenev decided to hear what Porfiry had to say. He knew that his half-brother no longer held any official position on the estate. Since running the Moscow house for Varvara Petrovna and then supervising the stables at Spasskoye for her son, the gentle giant had drifted, in Turgenev's absence, into an inconclusive sort of life, now and then doing the odd job, all ambition to better himself apparently quiescent. Recently he had started down a new path, utilizing the medical instruction he had received in Berlin to become an itinerant doctor. Alifanov had told Turgenev that he was greatly loved by everyone; he would harness his pony trap and turn up at a bedside at any hour of the day or night, stay as long as his presence was necessary or desired, and request only the barest minimum for his services… or nothing at all if the household was too poor.

Turgenev had imagined he would present himself as soon as he heard he had returned; but when days passed with no sign of him, he decided to seek him out, riding over alone to the little house, little more than an *isba*, on the road to Mtsensk where Porfiry lived. Not wishing to barge in unannounced, he pulled up in front of the house and, seeing the door open, called out. If he had been unsure of his welcome, he was soon reassured. A second later Porfiry, recognizing the voice, ran out of the door, seized the bridle as Turgenev dismounted and enveloped him in a smothering embrace. He led him inside and poured out *kvass*, ignoring his visitor's protestations that he would prefer a glass of water. While exchanging the conventional greetings, Turgenev noted sadly that here was another strong country body on its way to ruin… and from surely the same cause; but whereas on Alifanov's thin, wiry frame the physical difference was as yet barely noticeable, Porfiry's neck, waist and thighs were now unmistakably bulging. He was only two years older than his half-brother, but a stranger might have put the difference at ten.

As soon as he could, Turgenev brought up the subject of the former serfs, and immediately a weary smile crept over the bloated face. "You have all my sympathy," he said. "Those wise men in the capital may have thought they were acting for the best, but they botched the job, that's for sure. And the results are going to be with us for a long time. But what is anyone to do?"

"There is a great deal for us all to do. And this is one of the reasons I came to see you. My uncle is incapable of handling a question like this and has no desire to try. I wanted to ask you if you would work with me while I am here and act for me when I am away."

452

"Porfiry shook his his head. "I'm sorry, Vanya, I'm afraid I'm not the man for you. Let me tell you something. Immediately after the proclamation, I made a mild suggestion to Nikolai Nikolayevich that, if he needed any help, perhaps I could be of some use to him... having been brought up here and knowing almost everybody. He turned me down flat. You know what he said?" He imitated the old man's fruity voice. "'I know you, my boy. You'll give everything away. You won't leave Vanichka and me with two kopeks to rub together.' What he really meant was that *he* wouldn't give *anything* away unless it was physically torn out of his hands."

"Is it as bad as that?"

"I'm afraid so. I know the commune elders have several times tried to make an appointment to talk to him, but they've always been fobbed off with excuses and procrastinations. There's a lot of ill-feeling building up. But I'm sure it will be better now that you're here."

"I will do what I can. But I won't be able to spend very much time here. I have a book to finish, a daughter to marry off and..."

Porfiry's mottled cheeks creased into a delighted smile. "To marry off, eh? That much time has passed! How is my little Palachka? How I would love to see her again!"

"She is charming and beautiful. And she often asks after you." This was a lie, as Paulinette had never once mentioned Porfiry's name since the day she left Spasskoye. "Some day you must come to Paris and see her." Porfiry nodded with the fatalism of one who knows that that day will never come. "But, as I say," Turgenev continued, "I will need someone to handle these matters when I am away. Never mind what Uncle Nikolai says. If I appoint you my representative, he will have to accept it."

"I appreciate your trust in me. And perhaps ten years ago I would have said yes. But you see, Vanya, I'm not the man I was. Too many things have happened to me since we were in Berlin. And I have to tell you that I watch what goes on here with growing despair. We were all holding our breaths that the liberation of the serfs would take place. But I'm now wondering if it isn't going to cause more problems than it's solved. Under the old ways, there may have been a lot of grumbling, and God knows there was fearful injustice, but at least everyone knew his place. Now, no one is satisfied: the landowners think they've been robbed of what belonged to them by divine right, and the peasants feel cheated because they were expecting the land to be given to them free. If I were a writer like you, perhaps I could make something of it." He offered to refill Turgenev's glass, and, meeting a refusal, topped up his own. "But I am useless... and, worst of all, I know my uselessness. I belong nowhere, you see. I am neither gentry nor peasantry. I tried for a while to rise above my station, but Varvara Petrovna put paid to that."

"From what I have heard, you are anything but useless. I hear your skill as a doctor is the talk of the region."

"My skill!" This time the smile was weary and self-deprecating. "I try to dredge up from my memory some scraps of what I learnt in Berlin to help people who are often beyond help. But I sometimes wonder if I haven't killed as many as I've cured."

Seeing there was no chance of persuading him to change his mind, Turgenev, after extracting an assurance that he would pass on any information he picked up about the peasants' wishes and intentions, soon took his leave, reflecting sadly, during his ride home, on the waste of a life that had seemed at one time to hold out so much promise. Now, he told himself, there was nothing for it but to beard his uncle, and he determined to do so at the earliest opportunity.

The following morning this resolution was strengthened when he took a short stroll before breakfast and discovered five or six farm horses grazing in the garden, showing, it seemed, a particular penchant for his favourite dahlias. He saw a peasant whom he knew loitering not far away and called him over. "Good morning, Fedya. Is there no grass left in the fields? Has the drought come so early this year? After all, we're in April, not August."

His irony was wasted on the peasant, who showed neither embarrassment nor guilt. "Beggin' your pardon, *barin*," he said. "I didn't expect to see anyone around this early. Nikolai Nikolayevich never shows 'is face before ten. But if the 'orses are botherin' yer, I'll take 'em somewhere else." And after touching his cap, he turned away and with a loud series of 'HOUAH's, drove the reluctant beasts out of the gate and away.

Turgenev decided to broach the subject with his uncle after the midday meal, when he could be expected to be in a mellow mood. They each lit one of the Spanish cigars he had brought from Paris and he light-heartedly related the morning's episode in the garden as a pretext for asking what steps had been taken since emancipation that might help avert such incidents. The only surprise about the response was its predictability. "Oh, come on, my lad, let's not spoil a good lunch. I'm sick to death of hearing about the muzhiks. Nobody ever talks of anything else these days." But this time Turgenev was not to be deterred. He pointed out that they had not had any serious discussion on the subject for two weeks, and it could no longer be avoided. The old man heaved a sigh and grunted: "Well, what do you want to hear from me?"

"For instance, what do you think would be the best way of getting the peasants to pay for the land I'm about to make over to them? Money or labour?"

"The easy answer to that is you lose either way. You choose *obrok* and you can whistle for your money, because you'll never get more than the odd kopeck now and then. They will choose *barshchina*, and you'll see that, without a bailiff to hold a big stick over them, they won't do a stroke of work."

"So what is your suggestion?"

"My only suggestion is that you consider it as money thrown out of the window. Give them as little land as you can and write it off. Serves you right, anyway. It was you liberals who wanted this reform, so I suppose it's only just that you lose by it."

Turgenev forced himself to remain calm. "It might have helped if you had had some discussions with the elders before the measure was passed. After all, uncle, I pay you to administer this property."

Nikolai didn't turn a hair. "And what would these 'discussions' have led to? Engagements on their part which they would never have kept. You've lost touch with the reality of life here, Vanya. It's all very well for you, gallivanting around Europe writing your books and pursuing your lady friends. Those of us who have to stay here are convinced the whole emancipation business will bring ruin on us and no great benefit to the muzhiks. The hard-working, sober ones had a good life under your mother and have had a good life under me. Now they'll find they have to put in more work for less gain. The lazy ones – and that's, near as makes no difference, every mother's son of 'em – won't even survive; if there's no one there to make them work, they'll do nothing but drink themselves to death." He leaned back in his chair and waved his cigar at his nephew. "There you are, my boy, you wanted my opinion and now you've had it. But you must go ahead and do what you want. Soon you'll be off again, no doubt, leaving me to pick up the pieces. But that's what we old people are for. I sometimes envy your father, dying when he did. Prime of life. Before it all starts to go wrong. They say he put that last little conquest of his – little more than a child, she was – in the family way. (It would seem that Nikolai Nikolayevich had not read *First Love*.) But Varvara Petrovna covered it all up. Of course, he had the sense to marry a rich woman. Whereas I…" his voice tailed off and he blew a couple of pensive smoke rings before shaking off the moment of gloom. "Damn good cigar. Brought them from Paris, I'll wager. Now tell me about your life there, and the hell with these damn peasants. Got a little *couturière* tucked away somewhere, have you? I know all about your singer friend, but you can't live only off a diet of high art, eh? You need a sweet little bit of *pâtisserie* to get your teeth into every now and then, what?"…

Despairing of obtaining any positive collaboration from this source, Turgenev spent the greater part of his non-writing hours over the coming weeks trying to settle affairs with the peasants he had not already freed. In yet another attempt to exorcize his mother's ghost, he gave away much more land than he was required to by law. Even so, he couldn't persuade many of the suspicious muzhiks to sign, or more often affix their mark to, the agreements he laboriously arranged to be drawn up. Nothing could dent their conviction that if they stalled for long enough they would eventually get more, if not everything. He wrote to Annenkov: 'My concessions to the peasants verge on cowardice. But you know what a strange bird our muzhik is. Having any expectation that he will pay you what he owes is sheer folly. And you might as well batter your brains out as try to explain to him why he should…' But his fervent desire to prove, if only to himself, that the 'new dawn' in Russian affairs he had so long hoped for should not prove a false one led him to lay down plans to build a new church, a hospital, an old people's home and a school. And remembering Tolstoy's enthusiasm over his educational experiments at Yasnaya Polyana, he sent a letter inviting him to come and spend a few days at Spasskoye. He was anxious to cement their rapprochement, having heard from Botkin that Tolstoy had written to say the two of them had become 'very close' in Paris. And after his recent inconclusive discussions on his own estate, he hoped to receive some practical suggestions from the man who had been appointed 'arbiter of the peace' for the Krapivna district in the province of Tula.

When Tolstoy arrived, the two men greeted each other with a warmth equal to that with which they had taken leave of each other three months ago in Paris, and Turgenev led his guest immediately in to lunch. He had ordered his favourite dish, a tender suckling-pig, and opened a couple of bottles of fine Burgundy he had brought back with him. Tolstoy, while eating and drinking with evident pleasure, expatiated on the impossibility of his task, given the intransigent positions taken by landowners and peasants alike. "Before long," he mused grimly, "I shall be equally hated by both parties. The nobles are divided only between those who would have me flogged and those who would prefer to see me hanged. Some of the peasants appreciate what I try to do for them, but when I have, in all fairness, to decide against them, they give me black looks and start to whine and mutter about being cheated of their rights. Solomon himself would never succeed in satisfying everyone."

Turgenev wondered instead whether it was ever possible to satisfy anyone. He recounted a dream he had had a few nights before. "I was sitting on the back porch on a warm evening, drinking tea. A group of peasants came in through the garden, took their caps off and bowed low. 'Good evening, my good friends,' I said. 'And what can I do for you? Would you care to join me for a glass of tea?' 'No thank you very much, *barin*,' they said. 'I hope you'll excuse us, and please try not to be angry. You've been a good master and we are fond of you. But we've come to hang you.' 'Hang me?! What are you talking about?' 'I'm afraid so, yes. A decree has been issued to that effect. But take your time. If you want to say your prayers, we can wait a little…' And one of them, with a curious, shy smile, produced a large coil of thick rope and started looking up at the trees. At which point, I'm glad to say, I woke up." Tolstoy growled that after the mess 'those idiots' in St Petersburg had made, it would be no surprise to him if blood didn't soon start to flow. Then, unpredictable as always, and perhaps wishing to please his host, he abruptly changed the subject. "My mind is choked from dawn till dusk with half acres of pasture-land and fifty roubles of *obrok* and six per cent on redemption payments. For God's sake let's talk about something else… anything, even literature. How is your book progressing?"

Turgenev, who would have been hesitant to bring the matter up, was delighted. He told his guest that he had all but finished the first draft and would be most grateful if he would cast an eye over the early chapters and give him his opinion. He himself had some business to do that afternoon, so he left his guest stretched out on the couch in the library with a jug of lemonade and the manuscript. When he returned three hours later, he looked into the room and saw Tolstoy sound asleep with the book on his lap. Tiptoeing over, he gently picked up the manuscript and saw that it had remained open on page three. 'I gave him too good a lunch,' he thought ruefully, but could not entirely overcome his disappointment. However, he didn't bring the matter up during the rest of the evening, and Tolstoy surprisingly – or perhaps not – made no reference to the book at all. Turgenev presumed he would take another look at it before going to sleep, but the following morning, again not a word was said.

They had decided to go and spend a couple of days with their friend, the lyric poet Afanasy Fet, who lived with his wife on his estate of Stepanovka, about forty miles away. The evening they arrived they enjoyed an excellent and convivial dinner, with Turgenev's favourite Roederer champagne, and everyone went to bed in the best of spirits. The next morning Turgenev was the last down to breakfast; he took his place at the table next to Fet's wife, who was involved in a conversation with Tolstoy about the upbringing of children. "I was just telling Lev Nikolayevich," she told him, "how important I think it is that the offspring of comfortably-off families should be made aware that other children are not so fortunate."

Turgenev glanced across at Tolstoy, who kept his eyes fixed firmly on his plate. Sensing that the night had altered his mood and knowing that he found Madame Fet vacuous and gushing, he slipped into his tactful, diplomatic persona, forgetting that this never failed to infuriate the 'troglodyte'. "How I agree with you," he remarked smoothly. "And I am glad to say the English governess I have engaged to look after my daughter is of exactly the same opinion."

"Is she really? How interesting! I have to admit, Ivan Sergeyevich, I always forget you have a daughter."

"So does he, most of the time," Tolstoy blurted out. "And no wonder, as he keeps her hidden away in Paris."

Turgenev bit his lip and forced himself not to be provoked. Fet, sensing the underlying tension, asked him if he was satisfied with the governess.

"With Mrs Innis? Absolutely. A remarkable woman. I couldn't have found a better person to look after Paulinette." He turned to his hostess. "And as to what you were saying, you know what she did? Quite of her own initiative, she asked me to set aside a small sum every month for Paulinette to give to the poor."

Tolstoy put down his coffee and glared across the table. "Presumably to remind her that there, but for the grace of God…"

Turgenev flushed and kept his eyes fixed on Madame Fet's face, as though trying to eliminate Tolstoy not only from his field of vision but from his consciousness. "And she goes further. She makes my daughter collect the tattered clothes of poor children and orphans, mend them herself and then personally take them back."

Madame Fet clapped her hands in front of her chest and flashed her husband a smile of rapt admiration. "How splendid!" she declared.

Tolstoy had never taken his eyes off Turgenev's face. "And you approve of that?" he now asked.

"Of course I do. It makes charity not just an abstract giving of money but a way of bringing the benefactress face to face with the reality of poverty."

"As far as I'm concerned," Tolstoy said, "a well-dressed little madam holding in her lap a pile of smelly, dirty clothes is simply acting out a hypocritical farce."

White in the face, Turgenev asked, in an ominously quiet voice: "Will you please take that back?"

"I will do no such thing," Tolstoy answered, equally quietly. "I have every right to say what I think."

"So you think I am bringing up my daughter badly?"

"I am simply expressing my opinion. If you choose to take it personally…"

Fet, seeing the blood now rushing into Turgenev's cheeks, tried desperately to steer the conversation into safer channels. "Of course, there are more ways than one to help the poor. For instance, a neighbour of mine…"

But Turgenev was past all mollifying. He sprang to his feet and beat his fists on the table, rattling the china and sending a plate crashing to the floor. "Who are you to talk about hypocrisy?" he shouted. "You preach one thing and practise another. You sow the countryside with your bastard children and never give them a second thought."

Now it was Tolstoy's turn to leap to his feet and clench his fists. "How dare you…?" he yelled, but Turgenev was not to be interrupted. "If you say another word, I'll punch you in the face. You, of all people, have no right to… to…" But words failed him completely. He clutched his hands to his hair, gazed around him with eyes rolling like a madman, and rushed out of the room.

Before the other three had time to do anything but exchange bewildered, and in Tolstoy's case, enraged glances, he was back again. He stood by Madame Fet's chair, gave a half bow and stammered: "I ask you, Marya Petrovna, to accept my apologies

458

for my disgraceful behaviour. I shall leave your house this minute." He looked wildly across at Tolstoy and added, in a tone which belied the import of his words. "And you, sir, I crave your pardon for anything I may have said which offended you."

He rushed out out again, and within ten minutes they heard his carriage rolling away down the driveway.

There then followed a series of mishaps and misunderstandings that would have seemed excessive in the most far-fetched of those feuilletons which were just becoming the rage of Paris. Tolstoy also immediately stormed out of Stepanovka and, on his way back to Yasnaya Polyana, stopped off on the estate of his friend, Ivan Petrovich Borisov, where he gave orders to one of the servants to gallop after Turgenev with a note demanding an instant letter of apology which he could show the Fets; failing this, he was to present himself at the posting-station of Bogoslovo ready to fight a duel. On receiving the missive, Turgenev, who, from the calmer perspective afforded by distance and time, was beginning to see the whole affair as faintly ridiculous, immediately sat down and wrote a reply: 'I can only repeat what I thought it my duty to say to you in front of the Fets: carried away by a feeling of involuntary animosity, the reasons for which it is not the moment to go into, I offended you with little or no provocation on your part, and apologized immediately afterwards. I herewith repeat my apology in writing and ask your forgiveness a second time. What happened this morning clearly proves that all efforts at reconciliation between two natures as contrary as yours and mine can never come to any satisfactory end. I perform this duty towards you all the more willingly in that this letter will very likely be the last communication between us.' This would probably have mollified the irascible count, but Turgenev sent it to Borisov's estate and Tolstoy had already left for Bogoslovo. After waiting twenty-four hours, his fury increasing with every instant, he sent another letter insisting on an immediate duel at the edge of the forest of Bogoslovo – 'and not one of those travesties masquerading as an affair of honour when two writers fire a few shots at each other from a safe distance, each taking good care to miss, and end the evening with their arms around each other drinking champagne'. He enjoined Turgenev to present himself at dawn and bring his pistols. The next morning Borisov's servant brought him Turgenev's reply to his first letter, but an hour later came the answer to his second: 'I wish to tell you in the plainest manner possible that I would willingly expose myself to your bullets if I could thereby cancel out my absurd outburst. The fact that I spoke to you in the way I did is so contrary to the habits of a lifetime that I can only attribute the incident to irritation provoked by the excessive and perpetual antagonism of our opinions on every subject. This is why, in separating myself from you for ever – one cannot forget such incidents – I believe it my duty to repeat to you that, in this affair, it is you who are right and I who am wrong. I would add that, for me, it is not a question of showing or lacking courage, but of recognizing your right to call me out, and also your right to forgive me. You have made your choice, and I comply with your decision.' At this point a duel seemed more than possible, but Tolstoy drew back and contented himself with sending a scornful letter, ending: 'You are afraid of me; I despise you and wish to have nothing more to do with you'.

Turgenev, who was by now feverishly engaged in rewriting parts of *Fathers and Children* in accord with suggestions from his friends, was relieved to let the matter drop. But the following September, when he was already back in Paris, he was told that Tolstoy was denigrating him in the presence of mutual acquaintances and depicting him in a contemptible light. This was too much. The correspondence started again. 'Sir, I have heard that you are showing a copy of your last letter to me around Moscow and are calling me a coward because you claim I refused to fight a duel with you. After all I have done to try and erase the unfortunate phrase which escaped me, I consider this behaviour offensive and disloyal, and warn you that I shall not let the matter rest here. On my return to Russia in the spring, I shall demand satisfaction.' By the time this reached Tolstoy, he was immersed in one of his periods of all-forgiving Christian love. He replied: 'Sir, You call my letter and my behaviour disloyal. Once, you threatened to punch me in the face. For my part, I ask you to excuse me, I recognize my guilt and I refuse your provocation to a duel.' Feeling that at last they had reached a satisfactory compromise, Turgenev wrote to Fet saying that Tolstoy had also renounced resorting to arms. 'From this day on, for the love of God, *de profundis* on the whole miserable affair'. But Fet, who by now was closer to Tolstoy than to Turgenev, perhaps because of critical judgements the latter had made on his poetry, passed on the content of this letter to Tolstoy who, in the meantime, had emerged from his angelic cocoon. He wrote to Fet: 'Turgenev is a scoundrel who deserves to be thrashed. I beg you to convey that to him with a fidelity equal to that with which you convey his charming remarks to me, although I have several times begged you <u>never to mention his name to me again</u>.' And as the bearer of bad tidings had become as unwelcome as the tidings themselves, he concluded: 'I also ask you to desist from writing to me, as I shall no longer open your letters, any more than I do those of Turgenev.'

It was to be seventeen years before the two men met again. They circled around each other's literary products like two fighting cocks sizing each other up before the feathers start to fly. Turgenev never stinted in his praise for Tolstoy's supreme gifts as a novelist, although he was not sparing in his criticism either. But, as he said to a friend, on a personal level there was nothing to be done: "We must live as though we inhabited different planets or different centuries."

By the end of the summer he had finished *Fathers and Children* and was ready to leave Spasskoye. The endless procrastinations of the peasants had worn him out:

he had come to a mutually satisfactory arrangement with a few, and was happy to leave the claims of the more recalcitrant in the hands of the local 'arbiter of the peace', whose judgement he trusted. With a final admonition to his uncle to abide by the arbiter's decisions, whatever these might be, he left for Paris, stopping only to drop off his manuscript with Katkov in Moscow and Annenkov in St Petersburg.

After allowing himself a week of relaxation at Courtavenel, most of which he spent shooting with Viardot (Pauline was rehearsing *Alceste*), he settled back in rue de Rivoli with his daughter and Mrs Innis. He was looking forward to a restful winter after his strenuous efforts of the last few years. Since the cooling of Pauline's affections in 1856, he had written three novels, two major stories and the long essay, *Hamlet and Don Quixote*. It was surely no coincidence, as Nekrasov had shrewdly noted, that this prolific output coincided with a period of personal unhappiness. Now, he felt, it was time to lay his pen aside for a while: he had no idea for a new book; perhaps *Fathers and Children* had emptied the well. At any rate, with the concentrated work of the novel behind him and the feeling that he had done the best he could at Spasskoye, he was ready to make himself more available for his daughter, help her find a husband, strengthen his ties with his friends in Paris… and even let his mind linger over the possibility that Pauline's imminent retirement from the operatic stage might leave her with more time for him.

That had been his intention; it was not to be his fate. He would say in later years that he worked harder during the winter of 1861/2 than at any other period of his life. The actual writing of *Fathers and Children* turned out to have been the relatively easy part of the creative process; the revision became a gruelling ordeal. His 'juries' in the past had always been predominantly favourable; this time they were divided as never before – reflecting the conflicting opinions that were to cascade down on him after publication. Controversy raged primarily around the figure of Bazarov, the rough-tongued, strong-willed 'nihilist'. The two 'cores' of the book were his confrontations with Pavel Kirsanov, the dandified representative of the older generation, and with Anna Odintsova, the cool beauty with whom he falls in love, thus shattering his conviction of his monolithic self-reliance. Turgenev knew that the success of the book would depend on the credibility with which he had depicted his protagonist. He was open, as always, to critical advice, but perhaps received more than he was bargaining for.

The first opinion he heard was that of Botkin, to whom he read the novel in Paris. His shrewd, worldly friend professed immediate admiration, but feared that Bazarov's boorishness might antagonize the young readers whom Turgenev was so anxious to address. Annenkov, whom Turgenev had asked to represent him in all dealings with the *Moscow Herald*, went further: writing from St Petersburg, he pointed out that Bazarov seemed to regard his own intimate feelings with the same withering scorn that he directed on those aspects of society that he so despised. 'You must soften him up a little,' he wrote, 'otherwise what could be taken for inhumanity will make the 'Children' think you are denigrating instead of sympathizing with them.'

Katkov, to nobody's surprise, came from the opposite direction, but arrived at a similar conclusion. He detested Bazarov and all he stood for. At first, not wishing to alienate the author whose last work, *On The Eve*, had sold a record number of copies of the *Moscow Herald*, he addressed his strictures to Annenkov. 'I could understand it,' he wrote, 'if Ivan Sergeyevich had intended this repellent youth to be the villain of the novel; but alas, it is quite clear that he actually admires at least some aspects of his character. In your capacity as representative of Turgenev's interests, I beseech you to confront him with what he has done. How can he not be ashamed not only to grovel before an out-and-out radical but to pay homage to him as though he were a valiant warrior? Think it over: this Bazarov scoundrel wins every round without ever encountering a real obstacle. Even his death becomes a triumph… it is made to seem some kind of sacrifice, even though the cause of it is totally involuntary. No, no, this time Turgenev has really gone too far. I beg you to use your influence over him and make him reconsider this character. He must be shown up for what he is… which is exactly as Pavel Kirsanov describes him: an 'insolent scoundrel'.

Turgenev tried to give all these and many other observations their due, while remaining true to the character as he had envisaged him. But after a particularly harassed day's tinkering, he confessed to Botkin that sooner, rather than later, Bazarov would have to stand as he was. "Otherwise I shall end up pleasing no one, least of all myself. I'm worried that in trying to listen to all of you I'm only succeeding in watering Bazarov down. It's little exaggeration to say that it was he who wrote me, rather than I him. In rubbing off some of his rough edges and tempering the virulence of his political pronouncements, I fear I may be tilting the delicate balance, which is the *raison d'être* of the book, away from the 'Children' and in favour of the 'Fathers'. If anything, I would prefer it to be the other way round."

Botkin had seen the changes that had been made and generally approved them. He advised his friend to stop rewriting there and then. "Katkov is never going to like this book anyway. But he's committed to publishing it, so what does it matter? If he had his way, Bazarov would murder his father so everyone could see he was no better than a common criminal. But there's something I've wanted to ask you ever since you first read me the book. What are *your* feelings about him? Except perhaps at the moment of his death, it's very hard to make out."

"It's just as hard for me," Turgenev said with a smile. "All I can tell you is there are days when I love him and days when I hate him."

"We must hope that is the way readers feel too," Botkin said. "If it is, the success of the book is assured."

Prophetic words. The appearance of *Fathers and Children* in the March issue of the

Moscow Herald constituted a literary and political event of a scale hitherto unknown in Russia. Avdotya Panaeva was to say that it had been read by people who hadn't opened a book since they left school. But the voices raised in anger and hostility – from whichever part of the political spectrum they came – all but drowned out the quiet murmurs of approval. The Right took Katkov's line that Bazarov, a repulsive insect crawling over the skin of Mother Russia, had been idealized; the Left found him a grotesque travesty. The first blast came from *Sovremennik,* whose entire editorial staff saw the book as nothing but a spiteful polemic against the journal which had dispensed with the author's services. Their mouthpiece was a certain Maxim Alekseyevich Antonovich, who had been brought in by Dobrolyubov; they had attended the same seminary, and Turgenev liked to remark that 'whatever else they taught them at that institution, Christian charity seems to have been absent from the syllabus.' Antonovich's article was entitled *The Asmodeus Of Our Time* and made Dobrolyubov's piece on *On The Eve* seem a panegyric...

'This Bazarov, whom we have to believe the author is holding up for our admiration, is not a living personage but a caricature; and principally a caricature of an esteemed contributor to this paper, with whom the author has had well-aired personal differences. Turgenev's claims in the past to propound a liberal outlook can now be seen for what they were: juvenile posturings to shock his peers. He has now shaken all that off, along with his youth, and retreated back into the caste into which he was born... His self-styled 'nihilist' shows no interest in those in Russia who are anxious to promote progressive ideas. His pride leads him to preach destruction, but he scornfully brushes away all allusions to rebuilding. He is not a man but a monster, a demon, or to put it in Biblical terms, an Asmodeus...

'The purpose of the novel is laudable, if hardly original: the time-honoured generational struggle, when old ideas lose whatever value they may once have had and are replaced by vital new exigencies. This struggle will always end with the the victory of the 'Children', but Turgenev has only considered the most superficial aspects of this perennial war. His concern for the older generation is everywhere apparent, as is his fear and ill-concealed dislike of the younger...'

Some relief came in the form of an article in *The Russian Word* by Dmitry Pisarev, a brilliant young critic of only twenty-one; although in many ways as intransigent as the *Sovremennik* team and a thoroughgoing materialist who saw no value in art except as a means to further social aims, he wrote what amounted to a refutation of Antonovich. Coming from a family of minor nobility, he saw reform in Russia proceeding from an alliance of the liberal gentry and the radical intelligentsia, rather than the result of violent revolution from below. Entitling his article merely *Bazarov,* he commended Turgenev for having, albeit reluctantly, understood that the future belonged to young people like his protagonist, a prototype of the 'new man' who would 'promote freedom in all its forms, destroy obstacles and prejudices and exalt the dignity and emancipation of the individual'. Where Antonovich had seen Bazarov as a caricature, Pisarev recommended him as a model...

'He is what we are waiting for: an independent aristocrat of the spirit, who will lead the passive masses towards an ideal which, by their own efforts, they could neither envisage nor attain. He cares little if they fail to heed him now, knowing that, when the time comes, they will follow him... For now, all that can be done is to denounce the ills of our time. Realism – honest realism – is what is required and this is what we find in Bazarov. His author may be too deeply rooted in the mores of the previous generation to accompany us along our path; but in his way he gives us his blessing. He resists the temptation to hold the 'Fathers' up as an example to follow: although he paints them lovingly, in gentle pastel colours, he leaves us in no doubt that they belong to the past. They have had their day. Bazarov is the future...

This divided opinion on the hated left was gleefully mocked by the right, and by no one more eagerly than Katkov himself, who wrote an anonymous critique in his own paper, repeating and reinforcing the arguments he had used to Annenkov. Ignoring the literary merits of the novel, he vented his sarcastic hostility on Bazarov, *'an insolent scoundrel who is only assuming the persona of scholar in order to disseminate his iniquitous and dangerous political propaganda...'*

Individual judgements were similarly extreme. Botkin and Annenkov considered the novel to be indisputably Turgenev's masterpiece. Countess Lambert and the Slavophils, with Ivan Aksakov the most vociferous, had not a good word to say for it. Only Herzen was uncharacteristically ambivalent: he admired the novel for its literary qualities and the sharply-etched delineation of character; but he reproached Turgenev for not having, in a work of fiction, sufficiently suppressed his desire to settle scores with the staff of *Sovremennik,* and Dobrolyubov in particular. He found Bazarov's 'boastful, coarse materialism' an unfair reflection on the serious, reasoned positions of the best of the young Russian radicals and feared that his old friend was in danger of sinking back into an easy, sterile, liberal pessimism.

One of the most gratifying responses came from an unexpected quarter. Turgenev's early relationship with Fyodor Dostoevsky had been a chequered one. He had shared the enthusiastic admiration with which Belinsky and Nekrasov had greeted the 25-year-old's *Poor Folk* in 1846 and welcomed his admittance into the *Sovremennik* circle of those days. But the initially timid, tongue-tied young man, dazzled by success and recognition, soon became absurdly arrogant and opinionated, and Turgenev took the lead in teasing him with sometimes exaggerated cruelty. Dostoevsky at first admired and looked up to the polished older writer, writing to his his brother: 'Turgenev is quite in love with me. What a man! I am not far, myself, from falling in love with him. A talented poet, an aristocrat, a handsome fellow, rich, intelligent, cultivated. I truly believe that nature has refused him nothing.' But soon the realization that he was being led on and encouraged to make a fool of himself began to penetrate even his blinkered self-regard, and 'love' quickly turned to animosity and rage. After hearing of the wicked verse skit that Nekrasov and Turgenev had composed beginning:

> 'Knight of the mournful countenance,
> Dostoevsky, you amiable braggart,
> You glow on the nose of literature
> Like a ripe pimple...'

he never again returned to the Panaev's apartment on the Fontanka, even though his head had been turned by Avdotya and he had almost convinced himself that she had fallen for him.

But then came his involvement with the Petrachevsky group of intellectual revolutionaries, the sentence of death, the mock execution and the ten years of exile in Siberia. In 1860 he had been allowed to return to St Petersburg and had met Turgenev again, having in the meantime read and admired both *A Sportsman's Sketches* and *A Nest of Gentry*. The occasion of their meeting was a reading of Gogol's *The Government Inspector,* in aid of the Russian Literary fund. Neither of them could pretend to take great pleasure in each other's company, but circumstances impelled them to paper over their differences: Dostoevsky was in the process of trying to found a monthly journal, *Vremya (Time)*, and was well aware of how advantageous a contribution from Russia's leading novelist would be; and Turgenev had appreciated a couple of articles Dostoevsky had written, taking his side in the quarrel with *Sovremennik*.

In fact, Dostoevsky himself had wasted no time in crossing swords with the same journal. He had written an article attacking the 'utilitarian' position of Chernyshevsky and Dobrolyubov and passionately defending the right, the duty of art to insist on absolute freedom of expression. This had drawn down on his head the anathema of the 'seminarists', who now attacked *Vremya* with the same vigour they had used against *Fathers and Children*. Dostoevsky replied with two articles in his journal, one by his close associate, Strakhov, and the other from his own hand: after sarcastically trouncing the *Sovremennik* staff for their overweening complacency (*'Turgenev has dared to refuse to accept our extraordinary selves as an ideal. Indeed, he even seems to be searching for something better. Better than us?! Great Heavens, how could such a thing conceivably exist?'*), he launched into an eloquent defence of 'the restless, yearning Bazarov, who displays, despite his 'nihilism', all the signs of a great heart.' Grateful for this support from so unexpected a source, Turgenev visited the *Vremya* offices when he returned to St Petersburg and invited Dostoevsky, his brother, Mikhail, and Strakhov out to dinner. During the course of the meal, he mentioned a couple of stories he had in mind and indicated that he would be happy for them to appear in *Vremya*. Dostoevsky accepted the offer enthusiastically.

Another figure from his youth had already claimed his attention. In January he received a letter from Herzen telling him that Mikhail Bakunin, after a rocambolesque escape from his Siberian exile, had arrived at his house one morning, flung open the door and bellowed: 'Can one get oysters in London?' He had promptly moved in and one of his first queries had been as to the whereabouts of his former fellow-student at Berlin. 'He wants you to come over,' Herzen wrote. 'I am sure he is genuinely anxious to have a reunion. He is also very short of funds, and I have lent him all I can afford for the moment.' Turgenev wrote back, regretting he was unable to move from Paris for the time being (he was just about to send the revised manuscript of *Fathers and Children* to Katkov). But he sent money, undertook to raise more by organizing a collection among his Russian friends in Paris, and promised he would make the journey as soon as he could. He was indeed curious to see Bakunin after so many years, but it was a curiosity mixed with apprehension: would their friendship survive the different directions their lives had taken since the shared Hegelian dreams of their student days?

It was early May before he, together with Botkin, travelled to London. They spent only three days there, but each, on leaving for St Petersburg, confessed to the other that it had been quite long enough. Herzen, with his mania for changing lodgings, had moved again, this time to the five-storey Orsett House in Westbourne Terrace. The space was necessary, as Herzen now presided over a large and unconventional ménage. Natalie, the wife of his oldest friend and collaborator, Nikolai Ogarev, had fallen in love with him and finally won him over. They now had a three-year-old daughter, who for propriety's sake was called Elizaveta Nikolaevna Ogareva, and infant twins, which necessitated an English governess by the name of Miss Reeve. On top of that there was 'Poor Nick', official husband and father, who accepted the situation as best he could, and the three children of Herzen's first marriage, who made no secret of their hostility to their 'stepmother'. Add the usual stream of visitors from every part of Europe, come to pay their respects to or cadge some money from the editor of the widely-read *Kolokol*, and there was little chance of Turgenev finding in Orsett House the atmosphere conducive to the calm airing of political and literary differences that he had had in mind. And into this already turbulent household had now breezed the whirlwind Bakunin.

At their first meeting, Turgenev had difficulty in hiding his shock at the man's appearance. Eight years of solitary confinement, most of them in a dank cell of the grim Peter and Paul Fortress, followed by four of exile, had taken a terrible toll. The strong, athletic physique of the handsome young aristocrat was now a quivering mass of blubber. He had lost all his teeth, and Turgenev was glad to be finally released from the all-enveloping embrace with which he was greeted, in order to escape the combined stench of unwashed body and sour breath. Imprisonment had obliterated the need for even the most elementary form of grooming; hair and beard grew wild, neither having had any recent truck with scissors or razor. The only feature that had not changed were the eyes; these still glittered and flashed in perpetual witness to the man's impatient, irrepressible energy.

In contrast to Bakunin's physical transformation, it took Turgenev only a few minutes to detect that the intervening twelve years since he had been arrested by the Saxon police had not in any way tamed the hot-headed agitator, nor even minimally modified his views. The long period of laborious preparation for emancipation had passed him by, as had the significance of a reforming Czar succeeding the adamantine Nicholas. He had not absorbed the failure of all the 1848 revolutions and the restoration of autocratic governments. He was like a wild beast, long held captive in a dark cage and suddenly unchained, glaring around for some victim to dig his claws into. And as always, he had no money and little prospect of obtaining any, except from his long-suffering friends.

Turgenev was not at ease in Orsett House. After the ruptures with Nekrasov and Tolstoy, he saw the beginning of the end of another two friendships dating back to his youth. With Bakunin it was immediately clear that, as he had anticipated, there was little but memories to bind them now. The firebrand had not emerged from twelve years isolated from one of Europe's most eventful decades in order to support the gradual, constitutional transformation of his country from despotism to democracy. And the visitor could sense already the change that was to come over *Kolokol*. The cautious, sceptical Herzen was now in a minority at the head of the paper he had founded. Ogarev, in his bullheaded, opaque way and Bakunin, bursting with pent-up revolutionary zeal, were going to force the pace; passionate but lucid denunciation of social wrongs was about to be replaced by direct incitement to the use of force. And that left Turgenev more estranged than ever.

But the first evening there was no trace of the shadows that were to darken the bright simplicity of youthful friendship. Turgenev, Herzen, Bakunin, Ogarev and Botkin had all known each other in Moscow in the late 1830s. This improbable reunion after more than twenty years was first of all an occasion for reminiscence, for forgetting past quarrels and exchanging affectionate memories of those of their group who, like Belinsky and Stankevich, had died so tragically young. Then Bakunin, whose lifelong relish for holding an audience spellbound had only been reinforced by the years of solitude, recounted every detail of his escape from Siberia; exceptionally, he had no need to embellish anything, so extraordinary were the events themselves. Having received permission from General Korsakov, the Governor of East Siberia (whose cousin had married his brother), to make a commercial journey to the east coast on condition that he was back before navigation on the Amur river closed for the winter, he had broken his word, left the young Polish wife he had married three years previously in Irkutsk, his imposed place of exile, and transferred to an American trading ship bound for Japan. When the ship was obliged to remain a day or two in the port of Olga, Bakunin put up with the Russian general in charge of the local troops, charming him with his conversation and assuring him that he was only waiting for a few days before returning to Irkutsk by a different route. At Hakodate, his first Japanese port of call, he found another American ship, the SS Carrington, bound for San Francisco. On the night before sailing, the captain asked him to join him for dinner, mentioning that he was expecting a very important guest. Only after coming on board did Bakunin discover this was the Russian Consul-General, who recognized, with some surprise, the notorious political exile. As there was a small Russian squadron in the harbour about to sail for Nikolayevsk, the Consul presumed that Bakunin would be returning with them, but his fellow-guest corrected him: he had only just arrived and wanted to see a bit more of the country. This the Consul found quite understandable. The following morning, as she sailed out of the harbour, the Carrington passed the Russian squadron, to which Bakunin, standing on deck, gave a friendly wave. He soon made friends on board with a young English clergyman, from whom he managed to borrow $300. After writing to Herzen, begging another $500 for expenses involved in crossing the Atlantic, he reached New York via Panama, and after visiting Boston and Washington, set sail for Liverpool, where he arrived two days after Christmas and immediately made his way to London.

His peroration had the others uncertain whether to admire the indomitable spirit or shake their heads at the ingenuous optimism. "So here I am," he declared, slopping vodka into his glass, "a living refutation of the old adage that only cats have nine lives. I lived one life, was dead for twelve years, and am now about to embark on another." He raised the glass and beamed round at the others. "Let us drink, my dear friends, to a new Mikhail and a new world, to which we will all in our various ways contribute."

The toast drunk, he turned to Turgenev. "And none more notably than you, Vanichka. You have become a famous man since I have been away. But of course I always predicted that. I read all your books with great joy… and sometimes with a certain irritation. But we know that has always been the case. You're still so careful to hide your feelings; we must never know what your real thoughts and emotions are, must we? That Rudin, for instance. Some people have said he was modelled on me… but we'll let that pass for the moment. What annoyed me about the book was, at the end we couldn't make out if you admired your protagonist or despised him. Are you ever going to get off that fence?"

Here Botkin put in a word. "Wait till you read his new book. It's going to set Russia ablaze."

"Because he climbs down off the fence?" Bakunin asked.

It was Herzen who answered. "I've only read the first draft," he said, "but unless Vanichka has made radical changes, he's going to be accused of coming down on both sides at once. Our enemies will either damn him for sympathetically portraying a man they would like to crush under their boots, or praise him for exposing the iconoclastic barbarity of the new young men they are so afraid of."

"And our friends?"

Herzen thought for a moment about how to put into words a doubt he had been nursing since reading the book. "Our friends," he said gravely, looking steadily at Turgenev, "will also, I believe, be divided: there will be those who will hail the protagonist as a prototype of the hard men they are waiting for, the future saviours of Russia; and there will be others, and I suspect they will be in the majority, who will condemn Vanichka for throwing in his lot with the enemy and creating a negative protagonist who, in the long run, he fears more than he admires."

"And where do you stand?" Bakunin asked.

Herzen smiled. "I won't answer that until I have read the final version."

Turgenev was about mildly to remind them that the book was intended to be a novel not a political tract, that there were other characters in the book besides Bazarov, that it was also a love story... but Bakunin had grown tired of an argument in which he was unable to participate. "I will read it as soon as it appears," he declared distractedly. "If I can bring myself to read anything published by that wretch, Katkov..." (Bakunin and Katkov had quarrelled bitterly in those far-off Moscow days, exchanged vitriolic insults and nearly fought a duel... although this had not stopped Bakunin writing to Katkov from Siberia asking for a loan – which had not been not forthcoming.)

"... But enough of literature and politics for this evening. Tell me, Vanichka, how is the lovely Mme Viardot, of whom I have such charming Parisian memories?..." Without waiting for an answer, he went on to inform the company: "I am married myself, you know? I believe I mentioned it. A charming young Polish girl, Antonia, only... let me see, how old is she now? She was 18 when I married her, that must have been 4 years ago...22, yes, 18... I met her when I used to teach her and her sister French in Tomsk. The dearest little thing, pretty as a picture..." While he continued to expatiate on her charms, the others speculated on what had caused the pretty-as-a-picture 18-year-old to marry a man over twenty years her senior, an exile with no money, no prospects and no teeth. But the enamoured husband had not paused: "I am already trying to think of how I can arrange for her to join me. The first step would be for her to travel to my family at Premukhino. They would all love her. And then she would have to get a passport. The trouble is… journeys, passports… they all require money, and my brothers have followed me into the Peter and Paul – for rather less time, I hope – and just for the moment, I…"

Seduced by the mention of Premukhino and the memories it conjured up of the happy summer blissfully submitting to the spell of the fascinating family in general and Tatyana in particular, Turgenev suppressed the guilty feeling of irritation and slight distaste which Bakunin had aroused in him and undertook to do what he could to help the penniless exile. Before he left for St Petersburg, he had promised to 'lend' the Bakunin brothers money, and even attempt to obtain permission to visit them in the fortress to discuss the possibility of arranging for the young wife to rejoin her husband. But all this was only of subsidiary interest to him; his chief purpose in coming to London had been to try to clarify where he and Herzen now stood. Were they still travelling, even if in different conveyances, down the same road, or had the path forked and each chosen a different route? He couldn't deny that Herzen's less than enthusiastic reception of his novel had disappointed him. Having drawn on all his philosophical reserves to shrug off the virulent attacks he had received from both Right and Left, he had counted on his depiction of the generational conflict at least finding favour with his contemporary and friend. If this were not so, was it for political or artistic reasons? A long talk was required to clarify this, for Turgenev, vitally important question. It could be that nothing less than the survival of their friendship depended on it. But when, given the feverish activity that filled every waking minute of the day at Orsett House, were they ever going to manage even five minutes alone together? To his gratified surprise, the occasion was provided, the day before his departure, in an unexpected way.

Ogarev, to console himself for having made over his wife to his oldest friend, had become involved with a prostitute called Mary Sutherland. She had drifted into the trade in order to keep a five-year-old son, whose father she had been unable to identify. The penurious Ogarev ascertained how much she needed to maintain herself and her little Henry without recourse to the streets, and, with the ever-generous Herzen's assistance, set them up in lodgings in Mortlake. He now announced that a theatrical troupe she was familiar with were giving a performance in a music-hall and had asked her to bring along a few friends for the opening night; admittance would be free on condition that every turn would be greeted with thunderous applause, and every joke with infectiously raucous laughter. Bakunin accepted enthusiastically and even the fastidious Botkin was intrigued by the chance to compare the lowlife entertainments of London with the Moscow gypsy taverns he had always loved to frequent. Turgenev declined, pleading the need for a good night's sleep before his departure and patiently bearing with the others' taunts of artistic snobbery. In fact, the moment he heard Herzen declare that he had no intention of going, he realized that his opportunity had come.

Once they were alone, Herzen himself confessed that he had stayed behind because he too wanted an undisturbed dialogue. But neither seemed to want to be responsible for opening Pandora's box. During a sparse dinner, they behaved like two boxers sizing each other up during the opening minutes of the first round, unwilling to risk any overtly aggressive move for fear of laying themselves open to a counter-punch. They settled on the subject of Bakunin for their preliminary discussion, rightly guessing that here their views would more or less coincide. Herzen admitted that his initial delight at his arrival was now under some strain: the boyish impulsiveness of the young man had lost much of its charm with the passing of the years. As had his chronic nonchalance regarding money. "He assured me," Herzen confided, "that it would be no time before he would be able to repay all his debts from the large sums he was certain to receive when his account of his Siberian escape would be published. The problem is that it is now five months since he arrived in England and not a word has been put to paper."

"And rest assured it never will," Turgenev interjected. "Michel's pen is for writing interminable letters to his friends, exhorting them, cajoling them, bullying them, not for calmly setting facts down on paper. Besides, essentially I believe he considers it beneath him; he would agree with my mother – on this if on nothing else – that it is undignified for a Russian aristocrat to write for money. And as long as we all go on supporting him, why should he ever think differently?"

"Those letters are a much greater worry to me," Herzen said with a frown. "You cannot imagine how many he writes... sometimes up to fifteen or twenty a day, to almost every country in Europe: Italy, Austria, Germany, Serbia, Moldavia, Bohemia... his energy is inexhaustible. My little daughter Liza is learning geography from him. She's hardly ever out of his room. She even sits on his knee when he's at his desk and asks him about all the places he's writing to. They adore each other..."

"Little baby and big baby..." Turgenev murmured.

Herzen chuckled. "You don't know how true that is. I heard the other day that my older children refer to Mikhail behind his back as 'big Liza'. She's just beginning to learn to spell, and she astonishes her governess by suddenly asking: 'Please, Miss Reeve, where's Semipalatinsk?' Yes, it's the ones he writes to Russia that worry me most. It's a very risky business. He won't have seen many of his correspondents for some fifteen years. They may have completely changed their opinions; they may even be in government service. And then he entrusts delivery of the letters to any compatriot he meets who is about to set off somewhere. They could be spies, or just the usual penniless exiles who wouldn't think twice about selling the letters to any government prepared to pay a few pennies for them. *Kolokol* is just about accepted in Russia now, but there are signs of a post-emancipation reaction setting in, and there's nothing that Shuvalov and his coterie would like better than to be able to brand me as a fanatic calling for revolution."

Turgenev saw his opening, but exploited it cautiously. "Then you had better make sure you don't play into their hands," he said.

Herzen raised an ironic eyebrow. "I think I can guess what you mean by that. But before you elaborate on it, let's go where we can argue more comfortably." They moved into his small study, where Turgenev took up his usual position on the divan, while his host filled brandy glasses and opened a box of cigars. "And how do you think I might play into their hands?" he asked eventually, easing himself into an armchair.

"By gradually yielding to pressure from Bakunin… and also, forgive me, from Nikolai Platonovich." Herzen gave a slight frown, but made no comment. "I'm afraid that they'll keep nudging you towards taking an ever more radical line. We all know Michel's old war cry: destruction for the sake of destruction. It doesn't seem as if he has seen cause to alter it in all this time. And Ogarev will be like putty in his hands. They'll force you to become more intransigent, and that will be the effective end of *Kolokol* as we know it… or at least of any influence it may have inside Russia."

Perhaps because he scented a danger he feared but didn't want to acknowledge, Herzen defended his weak position by attacking. Swilling the brandy around in his glass, he addressed his friend without looking at him: "I thank you for your advice, Vanichka. Coming from you, I will consider it carefully, even though at first sight I don't think I am that malleable. But you must allow me to give you a warning in return."

"Of course."

"If you are worried that I may be becoming too radical, I fear you are drifting into an attitude of stagnant immobility, which could easily be taken for indifference. Hence my doubts about your novel. I am not in complete disagreement with Mikhail here. I appreciate, as he does not, that an artist is not obliged to take an unyielding political stand. But the ground bass of your book is a search for the way forward for Russia. So you cannot blame your readers for asking: 'Yes, but what does *he* think?' All they could answer would be: 'Well, he paints the old-style landed gentry as agreeable but ineffective nincompoops, and his 'new man' is a surly young beggar who batters everyone's ears with what he is against, but is much more reticent about what he is for.' The natural deduction – at least from a less sympathetic viewpoint than mine – would be that the author is in danger of resembling one of the 'superfluous men' whose futility he so scathingly showed up in his earlier work."

"The difference being," Turgenev suggested, "that, unlike the superfluous men, I *do* see a way forward. That does not mean I feel the need to trumpet it out in every paragraph of my novel – not in this one, at any rate… the next, who knows?… but let that pass, it may never come to anything. The trouble between us, Sashenka, stems from a truth we can no longer avoid: our ways forward differ. Radically. I am as convinced as ever that Russia must follow a western European pattern; preferably without any more revolutions, but through democratic procedures, piecemeal reform…"

"So that we may all end up good little petit bourgeois," Herzen broke in impatiently. "With a nice little house with nice little windows looking on to a nice little street, a nice school for the son, a nice dress for the daughter, and a servant – who doesn't have to be so nice – for the hard work! We've seen the dismal effect this has had on developed countries like England and France. Are we to have no higher aim for ours?"

"Would it have to be so dismal?" Turgenev retorted. "And even if it were, would it not be preferable to the ignorance, drunkenness and crippling poverty that we have now?"

"If these were the only two alternatives, yes. But why should Russia be put in a straitjacket and frogmarched into a predisposed future?" He stood up to refill the glasses and looked down for a moment on Turgenev with exasperated affection. "What puzzles me about you, Vanichka, is how, with your love of art, you can still have such respect for western European institutions. To me the two concepts are antithetical."

"Why? Most of the masterpieces that are just about our only consolation for the bleakness of life were created in states in which those institutions were either established or evolving."

"They *were*. But will they ever be again? You must see that the petit bourgeois tone of Western Europe, which since 1848 has become the predominant tone, is quintessentially hostile to art. The supremacy of bourgeois values, with their celebration of decorum and moderation, represents undoubted progress for humanity. Henri Quatre's chicken in every pot has become an achievable aim. Everything is striving up towards bourgeoisie from below and sinking down into it from above. Even poetical Italy discarded her fanatical lover, Mazzini, to become the mistress of Cavour, the fat little man in spectacles, the petit bourgeois of genius. What we are witnessing is a radical conflict of interests: as man grows richer, art grows poorer. Art is far more at home with the whore selling her body than with the respectable woman selling dresses in her shop for three times what she pays starving seamstresses to make them. You and I revere Dante, Shakespeare, Mozart. But where are their peers today? Art can grow out of almost any soil; it can derive inspiration from a Virgin and Child or from pockmarked peasants brawling in a

Flemish tavern. But can it sprout out of bourgeois vulgarity? Look around you and tell me where you see true creativity? Who's your new Beethoven? Gounod? Your new Rembrandt? David? Your new Shakespeare? Scribe? I'm afraid your defence of Western civilization may just be a threnody for a vanishing phenomenon. Which is why Nick and I want Russia to look towards a new future, rather than back to a dead or dying past. Why should Europe's end not be Russia's beginning?"

Turgenev swung his legs off the divan and spoke with unaccustomed vivacity, occasionally jabbing his half-smoked cigar at Herzen to emphasize his points: "For two reasons: first, because I'm not as convinced of Europe's end as you are; and second, because I don't agree with the way you see Russia 'beginning', as you call it. On the first point, yes, we are passing through a period of mediocre artistic creation; that has happened before and will happen again; it doesn't mean the end of civilization as we know it. In the meantime, democratic evolution has brought about notable improvements in the daily lives of vast numbers of people. Of course you know all this. But it's as if the failure of '48 and the triumph of the petit bourgeois, especially in France, has blinded you to virtues that have survived. Doctor Herzen lists all the symptoms of the chronic disease which afflicts modern man, and then, in his carefully considered diagnosis, pronounces that the root cause of the malady is that the patient is French! You well know that I am no great admirer of the Parisians: I find most of them shrill, shallow and superficial. But I don't go as far as you; and here we're touching on my second point, and reaching the heart of what divides us. You ruthlessly expose every defect of Western civilization, but what do you propose as a substitute for Russia? You, whom I have always considered to be the personification of scepticism, are now setting up a new idol: not a golden calf, but a sheepskin coat. I'm afraid that soon you'll be making obeisance to it and demanding that everyone recognize it as 'The One Omnipotent Sheepskin, Eternal And Indivisible!'"

Herzen's amused chuckle encouraged Turgenev to press his point: "You and I used to laugh a little at our Slavophil friends, but I wonder if now you wouldn't feel more at home in their company; although I can't help feeling that it's easier for you from the safe haven of Orsett House than if you were spending the summer at Abramtzevo with the Aksakovs."

"It could be so," Herzen admitted; but instead of developing the thought, he fell silent, gazing at his companion as if he were not quite in focus and stroking his beard pensively. Turgenev allowed himself a moment of optimism… *perhaps, after all, our friendship is not at risk… all will be as before, we'll bicker over details but agree on fundamentals.* Encouraged, he essayed a summing-up that he thought might bring the evening to an amicable end. "When all's said and done, Sashenka, we Russians belong to the European species; we are physiologically bound to follow the same path. Ducks and fish spend most of their time in or on water. But a duck belongs

474

to the breed of ducks, not of fish. Have you ever heard of a duck breathing through the gills?"

Herzen's eyes now regained their usual ironic alertness as he saw the chance to score a point over his opponent. "No," he said briskly. "But that is only due to evolutionary chance. There was a moment when the duck's aorta might have branched out in the direction of gills; instead it took what we might call the more sophisticated route and chose the superior respiratory form of lungs…"

Turgenev waved his hand to indicate that this abstruse scientific piece of knowledge didn't invalidate his argument, but Herzen was not to be deterred. "No, Vanichka, this is all- important. You talk about the 'European species', but within that species there are people who have never developed a bourgeoisie: the southern Italians, for example, or the Celts. These are my ducks. While there are others, the majority certainly, for whom the bourgeois system seems as natural a habitat as water to gills. What I ask you is why there should not be a European nation for which the bourgeois system would prove to be a transitory, unsatisfactory phase, as gills were for ducks? By what immutable law should Russia either strive towards attaining a bourgeois society, or even feel obliged to pass through a bourgeois phase? There are no monopolies in nature to prevent new political systems. The future is a variation improvised on a theme of the past. Since Peter, Russia's themes have been West European. Perhaps the time has come to look around for alternatives. Why should we wear European shirts when we have our own, with the collar buttoning on one side? America has deployed old themes, borrowed from Europe, but with them she has created some remarkable new music. Who is to lay down that we must settle for the old bourgeois model when every day we are brought face to face with the most dispiriting examples of what it leads to?"

"The only thing," Turgenev said, rising to his feet, "that I am going to lay down is that I am going to lay down on my bed and catch a few hours of sleep. We have reached stalemate. I understand your point of view, I hope you understand mine. But, tonight at least, neither of us is going to convert the other. And I have to leave the house tomorrow morning before you'll be awake."

Herzen, though reluctant to bring the evening to an end, made no protest and accompanied his guest up to his room. "There are so many details we haven't touched on," he said, as they climbed the stairs to Turgenev's fourth floor bedroom. "We must go on thrashing them out by letter. But in the meantime, I want you, as soon after your return as possible, to send me a full report on the mood of the country; especially in the circle around the Czar. Are the reactionaries or the reformers in favour at the moment? 'Who's in, who's out?' This is important to me. I depend on you as much as anyone to help me judge how far I can go in *Kolokol* without having effective censorship restored."

When the two of them, puffing heavily, reached his room, Turgenev, sensing that it might be a long time before he saw his friend again, embraced him with especial warmth. "I will do what you ask," he said. "But it will not be easy. Much will have changed in the eight months I've been away. I will need to talk to all my friends. And the first thing I will have to find out is if, after *Fathers and Children*, I still have any friends…"

In the event, Turgenev only spent ten days in St Petersburg, and much of his time was taken up with honouring his promise to Bakunin. It was not going to be easy to convince the authorities to allow Antonia Bakunina to leave Siberia and join her escaped criminal of a husband in London. First he would need the intercession of a 'friend' in high places for permission to visit the imprisoned brothers. He decided to consult Aleksander Nikitenko, remembering his wise, dispassionate advice over the Gogol obituary affair. Nikitenko, now sixty, gave him an affectionate welcome and spoke of his high regard – with a few professorial reservations – for *Fathers and Children*. He had retired from public service and was writing his memoirs; but he believed he still had some influence with the newly-appointed Minister of the Interior, Count Valuyev. When Turgenev, thinking of Herzen's request, asked him whether the holder of this all-important office was likely to further or impede the progress of reform, Nikitenko gave him a quizzical look. "Between you and me," he said, "he will do whatever he thinks is the Czar's will at that particular moment. No more and no less. But he doesn't want to be thought of as another Shuvalov. He will enjoy appearing to grant liberal concessions as long as there is not the slightest danger of their making any dent in the autocratic edifice." When Turgenev explained that he needed to talk to the Bakunin brothers, Nikitenko was cautiously optimistic. "That's just the kind of gesture he would like to be seen to make. My only fear is that the very name Bakunin at the moment is likely to bring on a fit of apoplexy." Turgenev pointed out that Aleksey and Nikolai shared little with their brother beyond the name; they were loyal, model landowners without a revolutionary thought in their heads. "You and I know that," Nikitenko replied. "But not everyone at court is that clear-sighted." However, he assured Turgenev of his wholehearted support. The man who had been born a serf on the Sheremetev estate had been horrified by their arrest and at Turgenev's request he explained the exact circumstances that had led up to it.

A year after the Emancipation Act a group of thirteen landowners from the province of Tver, led by the two Bakunin brothers, had sent a petition to the Czar, lamenting the unsatisfactory conditions of the newly liberated serfs and offering to contribute themselves towards the excessive compensation payments the peasants were sometimes obliged to make for their meagre allotments of land. Unfortunately, this rare act of generosity was accompanied by a call for the establishment of an elected national assembly to deal with the various issues arising from emancipation. The governmental reply was to incarcerate all thirteen in the

Peter and Paul fortress; the original sentence was two years, though no one expected they would have to serve the full term. Shortly after that, a Ministry of the Interior edict stipulated that assemblies of landowners must confine their petitions to the strictly local requirements of their area.

Thanks to Nikitenko's intervention, Turgenev was immediately granted access to the two Bakunins. The meeting got off to an uneasy start: the last time he had seen them they had been little more than boys, in awe of their brilliant elder brother and his distinguished, cosmopolitan friend. Now the elder brother had brought disgrace upon the family and the friend was visiting them in gaol to discuss a matter of scant concern to them. At first, both Nikolai and Aleksey were curt to the point of rudeness; torn between incredulity and despair at finding themselves locked in a dark cell for having performed what they had seen as their duty, their minds were occupied with quite other matters than the problem of transporting the penniless daughter of a Polish merchant from Siberia to London. But gradually Turgenev's persuasiveness won them over; he painted a moving, if a trifle overcooked, picture of how distraught Mikhail was at the thought of never seeing Premukhino again, how his one consolation was the idea of being reunited with his adored wife. Turgenev tactfully let it be known that he had guaranteed their brother 1500 francs a year until 'such time as he will be able to take care of himself', and promised to provide a further 200 roubles towards the cost of Antonia's journey. Before he left, the two brothers had assured him that, once they returned home, they would make her welcome at Premukhino until such time as she could obtain permission to make the journey to England; they also promised to organize a family collection to defray her travel expenses.

The fate of the Tver thirteen was not the only indication that Turgenev's response to Herzen's request was going to be a simpler task than he had foreseen. The day after his visit to the Peter and Paul, he spent the evening with Annenkov. His newly-married friend, while revelling in the constant attention lavished on him by his adoring wife, was gloomy about the prospects for his country. "Only a year has passed since emancipation" he observed, "and reaction is already beginning to set in. The Shuvalov faction is in the ascendant. They are experts at playing on Alexander's morbid terror of relinquishing even the smallest shred of his authority."

"Does that mean that all hope of further reform is doomed?"

"Not necessarily. There are still good men around the Czar who will not give in easily. Golovnin, for instance, the new Minister for Education, is preparing a law which would give the universities some form of autonomy. Nikitenko was one of his advisers. But they are dealing with a petulant child. At the first sign of the initiative coming from anyone but himself, he stamps his foot. That's why I fear our education proposals are a lost cause."

"What point have we reached? Has the programme been brought to his attention?"

"Who knows? We had nearly two hundred signatures at the end and everyone I spoke to gave us their enthusiastic support. I delivered the petition myself to the Ministry of Education. I might as well have dug a deep hole and buried it. I've been back a couple of times and made enquiries. The first time the clerk said it was passing through the regular channels; the second time, a different clerk said he could find no record of it. We must resign ourselves to the likelihood of having devoted a great deal of time to a chimera. Perhaps if Golovnin hears of it, he might take it up. But in the present climate, I am not at all hopeful…"

Annenkov's pessimism was immediately to prove well-founded. On May 26, two days before Turgenev was to leave for Spasskoye, a number of fires broke out in several central areas of the city, particularly in the Shchukin and Apraksin markets; the wooden stalls went up like bales of straw, and in a few minutes the flames, driven by a gusty spring wind, were devouring much of the surrounding area; the Apraksin palace itself was gutted. It was three days before the conflagration was finally brought under control. The death toll was proclaimed, with probably deliberate exaggeration, to be in the hundreds; the amount of property damaged or destroyed was considerable, though this too was certainly not minimized in the official reports. It was what the reactionaries had been waiting for: although there was no evidence to indicate if the cause of the fires had been accidental or deliberate, it was put out that they were the work of disaffected students and professional troublemakers. In the wake of the uproar *Fathers and Children* had caused, an irate nobleman accosted Turgenev on the Nevsky Prospekt with the accusation: "You see what your nihilists have done. They've burnt St Petersburg. I hope you're proud of them!" Repressive measures followed immediately. Several independent schools were shut down, Golovnin's measure to grant the universities more autonomy was temporarily shelved, and *Sovremennik* was forbidden to publish until further notice.

Dismayed by the polarization of attitudes he detected in the city, Turgenev was happy enough to set off for Spasskoye. As he climbed into his carriage on the St Petersburg-Moscow train, he discovered the only other occupant to be Nekrasov. They had not laid eyes on each other since his break with *Sovremennik*, but he knew that the intervening period had not been an easy one for the paper. The previous November Dobrolyubov, at only twenty-five, had finally succumbed to his tuberculosis, and just two months ago the gentle Panaev had died. Turgenev felt it incumbent on him to say a word about his former rival and told Nekrasov in all sincerity: "God knows we had our differences, but the death of so brilliant a young man can only leave one bewailing once again the senseless idiocy of fate." With Panaev, the two of them shared so many memories that comment seemed superfluous. Turgenev forbore from asking him if he now intended to marry

Avdotya, and Nekrasov matched his tact by avoiding any mention of Pauline. Instead, almost as if holding out an olive branch to his former contributor, he groaned about the difficulty of filling the gaps made by death in his editorial board. Turgenev, remembering Antonovich and 'Asmodeus', kept silent.

"I fear very much for Chernyshevsky too," Nekrasov continued gloomily. His fellow-editor, as Turgenev knew, had published an inflammatory article in which he had advised the peasants not to take up arms until they were fully prepared and organized. This was the first time the the concept of 'revolt' had been considered as a serious practical step in an official publication. "I expect every day to hear that Nikolai Gavrilovich has been arrested. You know that they've – I hope temporarily – closed our paper down?" Turgenev nodded. "The trouble is that after those fires, they're beginning to win the people's sympathy. The poor idiots don't realize that it was they who started them."

"Do you know that?" Turgenev asked.

"Well they didn't actually tell me," Nekrasov replied, with a flash of his old acerbic wit. "But I would have known if our people had been responsible, and fires don't break out in four or five different parts of a city at the same time by accident."

"What troubles me," Turgenev said, "is the lack of any moderating voice. The whole city seems in the grip of hysteria."

"And many people," Nekrasov remarked with a provocative grin, "put that down to the influence of *Fathers and Children*."

"And others," Turgenev retorted, "blame it on the ever more inflammatory articles published in *Sovremennik*."

It seemed they were about to fall back into one of their old embittered arguments; but surprisingly it was Nekrasov who retreated. "Ah Vanichka," he sighed, "we've moved far apart politically; but it should still be possible to while away a train journey without coming to blows. Let us, for the sake of our old friendship, talk about the things we used to enjoy together: pretty women, fine wines, beautiful music, plump pheasants…"

Turgenev was only too happy to comply.

On parting at the station in Moscow, they vowed to be sure not to lose sight of each other again.

But it was to be eighteen years before Turgenev was next to see Nekrasov. And then he was on his deathbed.

THE LAST MEETING

We were once close, intimate friends. Then came an unfortunate moment and we parted like enemies.

Many years went by. One day I was visiting his city and learned that he was hopelessly ill and wished to see me.

479

I went to his house, entered his room… Our eyes met.

I scarcely recognized him. God, what havoc sickness had wrought! Yellow, shrivelled, with a completely bald head and scanty grey beard, he sat there in his nightshirt, which had been torn on purpose, as he was unable to bear the slightest pressure from clothing. Jerkily he stretched out towards me his appallingly thin arm, which looked scarcely more than bare bone. Making a great effort, he uttered a few unintelligible words – impossible to tell whether they were meant for a greeting or a reproach. His emaciated chest heaved and from the contracted pupils of his eyes rolled two solitary tears of suffering.

My heart sank. I sat down on the chair by his side, involuntarily dropping my eyes before such a picture of horror and disease. I also stretched out my hand.

But I had a feeling that it was not his hand which grasped mine. It seemed to me that a tall, quiet, pale woman sat between us, enveloped from head to foot in a long shroud. Her deep, pale eyes gazed into space, her stern, pallid lips uttered no word… That woman had joined our hands… She reconciled us for ever.

Yes… Death had reconciled us.

The two summer months that Turgenev spent at Spasskoye passed uneventfully enough, though rarely a day went by without a confrontation with a group of discontented peasants: having realized it was useless bringing their problems to his uncle, they welcomed their *barin* back by lining up most mornings to air their grievances. With many of these, Turgenev felt largely sympathetic: more often than not, moved both by his innate sense of justice and his desire to be rid of them, he ended up granting everything they asked, at considerable cost to himself, and earning no gratitude from them… only the scornful reproaches of Uncle Nikolai. He roamed the countryside with his gun, delighting in the prowess of Bubulka, one of Diane's progeny who had taken her mother's place in his heart; she slept in his bedroom under a blanket, and would wake him if the blanket slipped off her and nudge him until he got out of bed to replace it. From time to time he jotted down notes for the new novel he had in mind, without any conviction that he would eventually write it.

But this time the bucolic life brought him little serenity. In the country his inherent pessimism, fuelled by an absorbed reading of Schopenhauer's *The World as Will and Idea*, was harder to suppress than in the city, where social activities could, at least temporarily, distract him from his gloomier thoughts. With more time for reflection and discarding the shield of pride he had used to protect him from disappointment, he brooded on how deeply the reception of *Fathers and Children* had wounded him. The dark looks and occasional snub or insult that had come his way in the St Petersburg salons left him unmoved; not so the continuing, often vicious attacks from the young intellectuals, so many of whose aims he shared. His lifelong conviction that emancipation would herald a new dawn for Russia was being daily eroded. The St Petersburg fires had provided a catalyst for both extremes; the right viewed with growing suspicion the mere mention of any kind of representative assembly; the left coalesced into small radical groups with ever more violent aims. 'Where,' he wrote in despair to Annenkov, 'is there a place for me in this country? I risk being imprisoned a second time by the authorities or torn to pieces by the maenad young. If I am to be despised by everybody, would it not be better to spend my last years in a land where the most I shall have to fear is indifference?'

But it was with no great enthusiasm that he viewed the prospect of returning to Paris in the autumn. All that awaited him there was the prospect of finding a husband for Paulinette, who, he learnt from Mrs Innis's regular letters, was busily turning down one suitor after another. He wrote to his daughter making light of this, and assuring her that the decision was hers alone to make. But he couldn't help hoping that she would soon find someone acceptable. The apartment on the rue de Rivoli was going to seem very cramped after Spasskoye. And then, one morning, he opened a letter which was to change the course of the rest of his life...

Villa Montebello,
Tiergartental,
Baden-Baden.
6 July, 1862.

Dear Ivan,

I have heard nothing from you since you left Paris for London and St Petersburg and hope that is because your work and your friends have left you no time for correspondence. I seem to remember your telling me you would be in Spasskoye for the summer, so am taking the chance of finding you there.

Louis and I are back in Baden-Baden where, as you know, Berlioz has been directing a summer festival since 1856. He is rather distant to me now, I think because he no longer wants me to sing in his Troyens, and doesn't know how to tell me. He has approached Anne Charton-Demeur, who has no doubt breached the hardly impregnable fortress of his heart (she is to open in his Béatrice et Bénédict here in August) and will now be, for him, the only person who can ever do justice to his masterwork... that is, of course, if he ever persuades anyone to stage it. Be that as it may, I have sung for him in a couple of concerts which obtained a great success, and enjoyed the very high standard of musical life which he has succeeded in creating in this charming little town. The other day we heard an extraordinary young – only 18 – violinist called Sarasate, who is surely going to astonish the world.

Now to my chief purpose in writing this letter: if your many engagements permit, why don't you come and spend a few weeks with us here? You would enjoy the cultural life and Louis assures me that there are excellent opportunities in the Black Forest for your expeditions of slaughter. I mentioned it to the girls too, and Didie and Marianne whooped with excitement at the idea of seeing their uncle Tourgline again. (You will find enclosed a few lines from Didie.)

While on the subject of daughters, I'm afraid I saw very little of Paulinette before leaving Paris; she seems to prefer the company of your compatriots to that of her family and there is little that either I or the excellent Mrs Innis can do about it. I have to say that on the few occasions we have been together, her attitude towards me has not encouraged further efforts on my part.

But let me not dwell on disappointments. If you have nothing better to do, come. We shall be here until the middle of October, and would greatly welcome your company. Let me know soon.

Affectionately yours,
Pauline.

'*If you have nothing better to do!*'… Was there a trace of teasing, a touch of malice in those words? Or was it a noncommittal way of conveying her need, after renouncing the adoration of operatic audiences, to recover the lost security of *his* adoration? He didn't hesitate for a moment. Not long ago he had written to Countess Lambert: '*All my life belongs to the past. All that is dear in the present is a reflection of the past. And what, after all, was the best thing about the past? Hope… the possibility of hoping… in other words, the future…*' Was there now, perhaps, a future for him again?…

Spasskoye,
10 July, 1862.

Dear and good Madame Viardot,

I arrived home yesterday evening after a visit to one of my estates to find your letter waiting on my desk. It's mere presence had the effect of illuminating my empty old nest. Thank you a thousand times; I think you would have been happy to see how joyful it made me. I hasten to accept your and Viardot's kind invitation. I don't think I need add that I will remain here only as long as is strictly necessary. You can expect me, God willing, no later than the end of August, perhaps earlier.

It is a relief to be back here. Apart from the incessant, and often justified, grumbling of the peasants, all seems to be reasonably well. The garden is fresh and green, the harvest promises to be a good one and the house servants gave me a touchingly warm welcome. I wish I could say the same for the situation in St Petersburg, which threatens to turn serious. Wild heads are everywhere in the ascendant. One can only hope that the Czar will resist the pressure put on him by the reactionary element and prove to be an anchor of safety. But more of that when I see you… how wonderful it is to be able to write these words!

The fact that I am only here provisionally will probably prevent me from working (by which I mean writing). My last novel has caused an uproar, thanks to the moment in which it appeared. I have earned a remarkable collection of epithets: Judas, poisonous toad, spittoon... to mention only the most complimentary. I have been struck by hands I would have liked to clasp and stroked by hands whose touch repelled me. Young people are, in the main, irritated with me: I fear they are like beautiful women who expect to be found flawless from head to foot! But you will judge for yourself when I have the opportunity to read it to you. As ever for me, against your judgement there will be no appeal.

I am expecting some visitors, without, I have to admit, a great deal of enthusiasm. I have to be bored in order to work, and I have to work not to be bored. A vicious circle, I fear!

That is enough for now. Please thank Didie for her little note, you will find one from me to her enclosed. And would you be good enough to send me a photograph of her. That young person has a power over me of which she is not, I believe, totally unaware; she could put a collar round my neck, like she does to Flambeau when she takes him for a walk, and I wouldn't mind at all. I don't dare tell her that I kiss her hands, but I do all the same. As for you, that's another matter. I do it and I tell you.

My blessings on you all. Be well and happy, as happy as I am at the thought that in a few short weeks I shall be with you all again.

Your,

I.T.

Turgenev arrived in Baden-Baden on the 9th of August and stayed for two months, during which, as he wrote to Annenkov, 'I did nothing, with the utmost pleasure'. There were occasional moments of awkwardness with Pauline, neither being at first quite sure on what basis their once so intimate friendship could be revived. But she was unreservedly pleased to see him and clearly welcomed the presences of someone always ready to listen and give sympathetic advice when she speculated about her future life. The Viardots had practically decided to leave Paris the following year and move to Baden. She was considering organising a series of concerts in Berlioz's wake and setting up a singing school for rich young pupils; she also wanted to publish an album of songs she had written to the lyrics of Russian poets, and the coupling of her name with that of Russia's most famous literary figure could only have a beneficent effect on sales. He worked with Viardot on a French translation of *Evgeni Onegin* and the two men resumed their shooting expeditions with unabated enthusiasm. He delighted in the presence of the two little girls and invented a variety of new games to play with them.

But the realities of his homeland broke in even on the carefree life of the little Black Forest spa. In June, an attempt had been made by a Polish fanatic on the life of the Grand Duke Constantine, Alexander's liberal brother, who had been appointed Viceroy of Poland; he made light of his injuries and insisted on continuing to promote the reforms he had already inaugurated; but the attempt provided fresh fuel for the reactionaries in St Petersburg and a full-scale Polish rebellion seemed imminent. A month later the danger that Herzen had foreseen finally and inevitably materialized. One of Bakunin's casually encountered emissaries, a certain Vetoshnikov, to whom he had entrusted a number of letters, was seized as he entered Russia; as there was nothing to link him with any of the subversive groups, the notorious Third Department of the Chancery, responsible for state security, had clearly benefitted from the services of an informer. The letters were not only from Bakunin himself, but from Herzen, Ogarev and others involved to varying degrees with the group around *Kolokol*. At almost the same time, Chernyshevsky was finally arrested and investigations began in the Senate regarding the links between the proto-revolutionaries in Russia and the London *émigrés*. The inquiry into what came to be known as 'The Affair of the 32', after the number of the accused, began its lengthy, cumbersome deliberations.

Turgenev followed these events with concern, but with no premonition that they would in any way involve him. He was not aware that his name appeared in many of the letters, particularly in connection with his efforts to reunite Bakunin with his Polish wife. The first indication that he was once again subject to governmental suspicion came when he was drafting a reply to three letters Herzen had published in *Kolokol,* summarizing and developing his arguments from their last conversation in London. He was astonished to receive a curt note from the Ministry of the Interior, which had him for a moment wondering if they hadn't guessed his intentions.

> *Ivan Sergeyevich Turgenev is hereby advised that it would be considered most regrettable if any writing of his were to be published in the scurrilous journal published in London under the name of 'Kolokol'. If he chooses to ignore this warning, he is advised that he and he alone will be responsible for any consequences that might ensue.*

Offering up silent thanks that his amiable, busy life in Baden had prevented him from finishing the letter as soon as he had intended, he stuffed the observations he had already written into an envelope and sent them to Herzen with the admonition that on no account were they to be published. In only answer, he received a letter containing an 'Address to the Czar' which, from its turgid style, he immediately recognized as the work of Ogarev; it called on Alexander to summon a representative assembly to pass legislation to ease the burdens under which the peasants had been struggling since emancipation. His signature was requested, but he wasted no time in writing back and refusing to append it, specifying that, as everybody knew that Alexander would never agree to this, it was simply a hypocritical device intended to blacken the reputation of the Czar in the eyes of those who were already his enemies. Exasperated by what he considered Ogarev's baleful influence on his friend, he added a paragraph to this effect, blaming *Kolokol's* now declining circulation on Ogarev's cerebral, impractical socialist ideas, his total ignorance of what was actually taking place in Russia, and his unreadable prose. He received no reply from Herzen.

He hoped the matter would end there, but was to discover otherwise when he returned to Paris. At the beginning of February he received a summons to present himself in St Petersburg in order to be interrogated by a senatorial Commission of Inquiry in connection with his association with the dangerously eversive elements in London. In some alarm, he consulted his friend Baron Budberg, the Russian ambassador to France, who advised him to address a personal letter to the Czar; at the same time Budberg himself wrote to Dolgorukov, the Chief of Police, assuring him that Turgenev was an artist not an activist, and his political opinions in no way resembled those of Herzen and Bakunin.

Your Majesty,

May I presume to take up a few minutes of your time and ask you to cast a benevolent eye on the unfortunate position in which I find myself. Last week I received a summons to appear before the Senate Commission in connection with relations I am supposed to have entertained with persons who, unmindful of the immense benefits bestowed on the country since your accession, seek to undermine Your Majesty's supreme authority. That their motives may often be of the best, I am prepared to believe; that the course of action they propose is mistaken, I am deeply convinced.

Your Majesty is not unaware that, since my earliest youth, I have been a member of the writing profession. I have even had the honour of hearing from a reputable source that some of my work has found favour in your Majesty's eyes. I am a writer and nothing else. My life is expressed in my works and it is by them that I should be judged. I dare to hope that anyone prepared to pay them a little attention would recognize that I have never attempted to conceal my opinions, which are independent, moderate and, above all, sincere.

I therefore ask Your Majesty to believe me when I say that, if I do not come immediately to St Petersburg, it is not because I have anything to hide; His Excellency Baron Budberg will reassure you as to that. My reluctance to travel at this moment is due, above all, to the poor state of my health; my doctors have advised me that it would be most imprudent to undertake a journey to Russia at this time of the year. I am also detained here by certain family responsibilities with which I wouldn't dream of bothering Your Majesty. Might I therefore, in all humility, ask if it would be possible for the Senate Committee to send me a questionnaire, which I will be only too happy to complete in every detail and which, I have no doubt, will demonstrate my complete extraneousness from any charge that might be brought against me?

With all good faith in Your Majesty's wisdom and understanding, I beg to remain,

Your humble, loyal and faithful servant,

I.S. Turgenev

The questionnaire duly arrived a month later and requested information on nine points. Most of these were matters of detail and easily answered: where, when and why he had met such radical elements as Chernyshevsky and Serno-Solovievich, founder of the 'Land and Liberty' movement, to whom several of Bakunin's letters had been addressed. He could truthfully reply that his dealing with such people had simply been part of his professional life: the former had been one of the editors of the journal to which he had contributed for thirteen years, and he took pains to point out that he had parted with it when he no longer agreed with its political viewpoint; the latter he had only met a couple of times while trying to interest him in publishing a friend's manuscript. But the main demand for elucidation concerned his connections with the London *emigrés* and it took him many attempts before he produced answers which, while not strictly inaccurate, fell some way short of the whole truth…

On Ogarev: I first met Nikolai Platonovich in the early 1840s in Moscow, but never frequented his circle. We have met from time to time since in London during my occasional visits, but there has been no intimate friendship between us; on the contrary, I have once or twice indicated how strongly I disagreed with most of his political views.

On Bakunin: in our youths, Mikhail Aleksandrovich and I were bound by close ties of friendship. But after attending the University of Berlin together in 1840, we lost touch with each other until I saw him again last year in London. I cannot sufficiently emphasize how strongly I disagree with his political opinions, but I couldn't forebear to take pity on his sufferings, however much he may have brought these on himself. I therefore arranged for a collection to alleviate his immediate financial need and undertook to try and arrange for his wife to join him from Siberia; but all these dealings have been carried out in the light of day, as witnessed by the permission I obtained last year from the gendarmerie to visit his two brothers in the Peter and Paul fortress. Regarding our current relationship, I might add that he wrote recently to a mutual friend: 'Turgenev is a talented writer and a charming man, but in politics he is a buffoon'.

On Herzen: Aleksander Ivanovich and I first met in the middle 1850s and we have remained on friendly terms ever since. But whereas, at least until recently, the ties of friendship have remained unbroken, there has been a gradual divergence in our political views. In the course of many conversations over the past five years, we have aired our differences frankly and I recently became aware of how far apart we had drifted; but I never deemed it necessary to break off relations with him, as I always believed his superior intelligence would eventually have the better of his extremist position, which I take to be largely the result of the negative influence of Ogarev and Bakunin… As for his present opinion of me, I respectfully refer you to a recent sentence in Kolokol: 'Turgenev is an epicurean, a man who has remained behind and who has had his day.'

Although it might be thought that Turgenev had exculpated himself for the benefit of the Russian authorities somewhat at the expense of his friends, his answers still did not fully convince the Senate Committee: in September he received another communication summoning him to present himself in person, this time with the threat that if he did not put in an appearance he risked the confiscation of all his properties and possessions in Russia. Thoroughly alarmed, he again fell back on Budberg and his doctors and managed to postpone his appearance until January of the following year.

In the meantime, the Viardots had, as expected, decided to make a permanent move to Baden-Baden. Louis, unable to pursue even a peripheral political life, felt stifled under the outwardly benevolent but fundamentally oppressive regime of Napoleon III. Pauline, aware that her voice was showing signs of strain, preferred to take her leave of the world's major theatres with her triumphs in *Orphée* and *Alceste* at the Paris *Opéra,* rather than wait for her enemies to gloat over her decline. There were plenty of German opera houses which would be overjoyed to have the occasional services of the great *diva* in works of her own choosing. Accordingly, not without a certain regret on their part – and a wrenching sense of loss by Turgenev – they sold Courtanevel and bought a spacious villa just outside the town in the Tiergarten area, at the foot of the Sauersberg. And here, in May 1863, they installed themselves with the whole family except Louise, who, the year before, had married a French diplomat in Berne. In the same month, Turgenev arrived with Paulinette and Mrs Innis and took lodgings in the Schillerstrasse, only a few minutes' walk away. The two families were once again united in a replica of the Courtavenel days of the fifties; and once again the only one who felt no enthusiasm for the arrangement was Paulinette.

A casual observer would have found Turgenev happier than he had been for years; his health was good, he worked and shot with Viardot and immersed himself in all Pauline's plans and activities. The only work of his own, however, that he toyed with at the time was the searingly bleak story *Enough*, which could be read as an extended apologia for suicide: its final image of '*a world where, stopping our ears to block out our own cries, we hurry convulsively towards an end which is unknown and incomprehensible to us... No... No... Enough... Enough... Enough...*' would seem to indicate that the carefree life of the little spa had not entirely dispelled his melancholia. He also, try as he might, could not fail to notice that Paulinette was more of a misfit than ever. Louise, fiercely though they had quarrelled, had at least been her own age and was company for her, of however abrasive a nature. But ten years separated her from the eleven-year-old Didie, and Marianne and Paul were still small children.

Her father treated her with his usual careful affection, but how could she fail to notice the difference between his dutiful behaviour towards her and the joy he took in romping with the two other girls? She drew ever closer to Mrs Innis, thereby arousing all that good lady's protective instincts. She became, at least to her employer's eyes, almost too defensive of her charge; she was even heard from time to time to allow herself a sharp retort to Pauline when she felt she had been too hard on Paulinette – occasions which occurred with ever-increasing frequency as the summer wore on. Turgenev noticed with growing perturbation the tell-tale signs of his daughter's discontent: the sullen expression, the tightening of the mouth, the resentful glare in the eyes. The only times she seemed entirely happy were when he took her by herself to the *Konversazionhaus*, the elegant meeting place beside the casino where fashionable habitués of Baden congregated to listen to the music played in the nearby pavilion, and gorge themselves on cakes bulging with cream. On one of these occasions he brought up, not without a certain embarrassment, the subject of a potential suitor he had heard about from Anna Andreyevna Trubetskoy. This was Monsieur Pinet, an official receiver, who apparently had been paying assiduous court to Paulinette.

"Tell me a little about this young man. Do you like him?"

"He's all right."

"That isn't saying very much."

"Well, what do you want me to say?"

"I'd be interested to know how you feel about him. I understand you've been seeing quite a lot of each other."

"Yes, he's always calling round."

"And does that give you pleasure?"

"Oh, Papa, what is all this about? Are you asking if I want to marry him or not?"

"Something of the kind, I suppose. These are things that fathers are interested in."

"Well, I don't know. I don't think so, but... well, I'm not sure, I mean... oh I find it so difficult to talk to you about these kind of things."

"I quite understand that. To tell the truth, I find it rather hard too. I tell you what, why don't you have a good talk with Madame Viardot. I'm sure she..."

Paulinette didn't let him finish. Unable to conceal an emotion she rarely exhibited before her father, she glared at him and hissed between clenched teeth, "She is the last person I'd dream of talking to!"

Turgenev could no longer maintain the easy bantering manner he had imposed up to now. "Paulinette, once again I have to forbid you to talk in that tone of voice about Madame Viardot. Do I have to remind you..." He was about to embark on his now familiar reprimand about her attitude to Pauline when, to his surprise, he found himself, for the first time, mildly rebuked by his new grown-up daughter.

"Papa, I do the best I can. She resents my presence here and, clever as she is, is often unable to conceal it. The best I can do is keep my mouth shut, and I don't know how much longer I will be able to do even that." Turgenev started to expostulate, but before he could say a word, she laid a hand on his arm and looked at him with a pleading expression he was quite unable to ignore. "Please, Papa, let me enjoy just these few minutes with you. It's such a beautiful place. And I love this music. What is it?"

This was a clever move, as it gave Turgenev a convenient justification he was only too happy to exploit to switch to a more congenial topic. "It's a potpourri from *La Traviata*," he told her. "An opera of Verdi's. He's not a composer I admire greatly, but I have to admit there are some agreeable melodies in this one"...

It was the custom of the distinguished denizens of Baden-Baden to take an early evening stroll along the Lichtenthaler Allee, the fashionable avenue running parallel to the river Oos, through a park containing a wide variety of magnificent trees. It was here, one hot August day, that Turgenev recognized, hurrying towards the Kurhaus, a familiar figure dressed in an unseasonably heavy, shabby black frock-coat, in marked contrast to the elegant lightweight male attire on display around him. It was Dostoevsky who, raising his black hat from his thinning hair, seemed uncertain as to whether he was glad or not to see his famous compatriot. There was an evasive expression in his eyes that Turgenev immediately construed as saying, 'I am here to gamble, but I don't want anyone to know.' Turgenev invited him to join him for an aperitif, suggesting a café in the nearby Sophienstrasse rather than the Konversazionshaus, where he feared his oversensitive compatriot might feel out-of-place. Determined to avoid mention of the casino, he asked Dostoevsky if he was here alone. After a moment's uneasy hesitation, Dostoevsky replied he was. "My wife is not at all well, I fear, and I find it very difficult to pay all the doctors' bills." It was more than Turgenev could manage to refrain from asking: "Why then are you in Baden-Baden and not St Petersburg, publishing your journal?" "For two reasons, Ivan Sergeyevich. One, because I want to consult European specialists about my wife's health... and my own too, as I'm here. And the other – perhaps you have not heard, it must be difficult for you to stay abreast with everything in our country when you spend so much time abroad – *Vremya* was closed down last May."

Turgenev had of course heard, but feigned surprise and expressed commiserations. "I'm very sorry to hear that. But why? I would have thought your views, unlike mine it appears, would not have been displeasing to the government."

"They misunderstood an article of Strakhov's about the Polish question. They took it to be pro-Polish, when it wasn't anything of the sort. In fact, they have now realized their mistake. I heard from my brother Mikhail the other day and it seems we may soon be allowed to restart the paper under a different name. But in the meantime, we have lost a lot of money."

"I repeat, I am very sorry. And just think, not long ago I finished the story I promised you. But perhaps it's just as well. It's a strange tale, quite unlike my other work. It deals with the supernatural. You might not have liked it. And then you would have been afraid of offending me by refusing it. And probably rightly. It may be no good at all."

But Dostoevsky was eagerly interested. "No, no, you must show it to me. As I say, any time now we may be publishing again. We're thinking of calling the new journal *Epokha (Epoch)*. It would make me very proud to be able to include your story in the first issue. What's it called?"

"*Phantoms.* There you are, you see, I give everything away in the title! But I'll let you have it. I think I brought it with me. I'll look as soon as I get home. If I find it, I'll send it round to you." He got up from his chair and threw some coins down on the table. "And now I must ask you to excuse me. I have an appointment. Where are you staying? The Europe?"

I would be likely to be staying at the most expensive hotel in the town, wouldn't I? But then, it's probably the only one he knows! "No, at the Pension Müller. It's just behind the station."

"I'll have it brought round there. Goodbye for the moment, Fyodor Mikhailovich. And don't forget, if you don't like it, don't be afraid to tell me so."

He shook Dostoevsky's hand, but was unable to withdraw it. His companion drew him towards him and with a furtive glance around whispered, "Excuse me, Ivan Sergeyevich, but I wonder if you could lend me 100 thaler? I'm in a little difficulty. Just temporary, of course. I'll pay it back as soon as Mikhail and I get started again."

"I'll see what I can do. I'll send something round with the story. And now forgive me, but I must be on my way."

By the time he described this meeting to Pauline in the evening, there was a flourish in the tail. "I sent a messenger boy round with the manuscript and an envelope with fifty thaler. I would have given him the hundred he asked for, but he's only going to lose it at the tables and then he'll be back for more. I know the boy who went. He's a cheeky rascal, and I couldn't resist giving him 50 pfennigs and asking him to make a few inquiries."

"That was naughty of you, Ivan. Why did you do that?"

"Oh, I've never been able to resist teasing Dostoevsky, ever since I first met him. He's so earnest. Poor fellow, he's suffered a lot, but he treats himself and the whole of life with such unyielding seriousness. If only he possessed a grain of humour! Perhaps he does, and he's reserving it for his books. If that's so, he could become a fine writer. But without it!…"

"All right, then, what did you find out with your disgraceful spying? I can see you're dying to tell me."

"Disgraceful or not, the gods were on my side. It seems the boy has known one of the servant-girls at the *pension* all his life – pretty intimately, so he led me to believe – so he had no trouble extracting the information. It's as I had guessed. He's here with a startling, attractive young girl – only just over twenty, apparently, and Dostoevsky must be in his forties by now – but he's desperately trying to keep her hidden."

"Well, if he's married and his wife is very sick, that's understandable, isn't it?"

"Yes, but it seems that's not the only reason. Apparently she treats him very badly, always flying into rages, more like a wife than an exciting young mistress. And she insists on getting her own way over everything, otherwise she blackmails him."

"How can she blackmail him, if they have no money?"

"By withholding her favours, of course. When they first arrived, he had registered them as man and wife in one room. But after one of their quarrels, the girl – her name's Apollinaria Suslova, he calls her Polina – insisted on moving into a separate room. Ah well, it will give him more time to read my story, I suppose…"

But there Turgenev was wrong. Dostoevsky lost almost everything he had at roulette, and three days later continued on to Italy with his Polina without seeing Turgenev again. He eventually read the story in Rome and later wrote to the author about it in glowing terms, assuring him how proud he would be to publish it in the first issue of *Epokha* in March 1864. To Mikhail, on the other hand, he wrote that there was, 'a lot of rubbish in it – something grubby, unhealthy, senile, tainted with impotent disbelief… in short, all of Turgenev. But the poetry will make up for a lot…' His letter to Turgenev ended with a postscript asking for a loan, which he promised to repay within three weeks: 'I feel most ashamed at bothering you, but you are so much more intelligent than all the others, which makes it morally easier for me.' There was no mention of the Baden-Baden loan.

INT. BADEN-BADEN, VILLA MONTEBELLO, LIVING ROOM – EVENING

An evening like many others at the Viardots' villa. Didie and Marianne are standing by the piano, singing a duet written by Pauline, who accompanies them. Turgenev lounges in an armchair, entranced. A drowsy Louis listens appreciatively. The six- year-old Paul, sitting in the lap of the children's governess, Fräulein Arnholt, beats time, remarkably accurately, to the music. Paulinette and Mrs Innis sit next to each other on a sofa some way from the piano, both busy with embroidery; their palpable sense of detachment from the others cannot be explained by distance only. By the way she digs her needle into the material, we deduce that some incident that day has caused Paulinette to feel more than usually rebellious.

The duet comes to an end and Pauline rounds it off with a brilliant virtuoso flourish. Everyone claps except the two on the sofa, who do have the excuse that their hands are occupied. Pauline stands up from the piano, gives the two girls an affectionate pat on the head and pushes them off towards Turgenev. Each jumps on one knee and blissfully receives kisses and compliments. Pauline turns to Paulinette.

PAULINE

Now, Paulinette, your turn.

Paulinette looks up from her embroidery and shakes her head.

PAULINETTE
(very politely)
No, madame, not this evening, if you don't mind.

PAULINE
Oh, come on, just one piece.

PAULINETTE
(firm but still polite)
No, really. I'm sorry, but I'd rather not.

TURGENEV
Don't be so silly. We'd love to hear you. Play that piece from
Schumann's *Kinderszenen* I heard you practising this morning. You
were doing it very nicely.

PAULINETTE
(with some irritation)
Papa, I don't want to play.

PAULINE
Why not?

*Paulinette keeps her head bent over her embroidery and doesn't answer. She's trying to control
herself, but the violent heaving of her breast shows how difficult she is finding it.*

PAULINE
(sharply)
Paulinette, I asked you a question!

The girl now looks up, eyes flashing.

PAULINETTE
Because I don't want to, that's why. I don't feel like it.

PAULINE
But perhaps *we* feel like it. Perhaps it would give us pleasure.

PAULINETTE

(sarcastically)

Oh I'm sure it would. So you could all say to yourselves, 'She really doesn't play very well, does she? I mean she's not really one of the Garcia/Viardot clan, is she?'…

TURGENEV

(horrified)

Paulinette!

But she is not to be stopped now. The dam has burst.

PAULINETTE

And there's another reason, if you really want to know. And that is, I'm fed up with music. I HATE music…

She throws her embroidery to the floor and stands up, first gazing wildly round her, then fixing her eyes on Pauline.

PAULINETTE

And I hate this place, and I hate being here… and…

PAULINE

(very quietly)

And you hate me! That's really what you're trying to say, isn't it?

No answer. Paulinette stands stock still, biting her lips and digging her nails into the palms of her hands.

Turgenev also stands up, distraught. All he can do is repeat:

TURGENEV

Paulinette!

She would love to fly into his arms, but doesn't dare. As she stifles a sob, Mrs Innis also gets to her feet and takes her in her arms, uttering soothing noises. At this Paulinette breaks down and sobs wildly… The other children's governess gathers her charges together and ushers them towards the door.

FRÄULEIN ARNHOLT

Come on, children, time for bed.

They go out in a deathly silence, broken only by Paulinette's sobbing.

Pauline addresses Mrs Innis in as matter-of-fact a tone as though she were suggesting a morning walk:

PAULINE

Mrs Innis, I think it would be better if you left us too, please.

Mrs Innis looks her straight in the eye.

MRS INNIS

Excuse me, madam, but I am employed by Mr Turgenev.

TURGENEV

Do as you were asked, please, Mrs Innis.

For a moment, rebellion threatens. England stands its ground. Then the habit of obedience takes over; she pulls away from Paulinette, pushes a stray curl back over the girl's forehead, pats her lightly on the cheek and leaves the room, head high, back defiantly straight…
A short pause, then Turgenev speaks sternly to his daughter:

TURGENEV

Now, Paulinette, will you please apologize to Madame Viardot.

His daughter has now controlled her sobs, and looks back at him defiantly:

PAULINETTE

For what? For not wanting to play the piano?

TURGENEV

You know very well for what. Now do as I tell you.

A long silence indicates the effort this is costing her. Finally she addresses her father through clenched teeth:

PAULINETTE

I'm sorry.

Only now does she turn to look at Pauline.

And now, if you don't mind, I'd like to go to bed, please.

PAULINE
(sweetly)
Of course, my dear. You must be tired.

She holds out her arms and Paulinette forces herself to go over and give her a peck on the cheek.

PAULINETTE
Good night, Madame.

PAULINE
Good night, Paulinette. I hope you sleep well.

Paulinette gives a bobbed curtsey to Louis, who has watched the proceedings with evident discomfort…

PAULINETTE
Good night, monsieur.

… and then stands in front of her father. Her quivering lips show that any second she may burst into tears again. We feel that Turgenev would like to take her in his arms and press her tightly to him, but can't bring himself to do it. Instead, he cups her face in his hands and kisses her on the forehead.

TURGENEV
(in a low voice)
Good night, my daughter. We'll have a talk in the morning.

She nods.

PAULINETTE
Good night, papa.
(almost imperceptible)
I'm sorry.

She leaves the room.

Another silence while everyone collects their wits. Then Turgenev starts to apologize, but is silenced by Pauline.

PAULINE

No, no, it's much better that it all came out now. It had to happen sooner or later. And now we all know where we stand.

LOUIS

Do we? Where do we stand?

Pauline looks at Turgenev.

PAULINE

She'll have to go, won't she? For everybody's sake, hers above all. She's not happy in our family, and never really has been. We've all done our best, but it hasn't worked out. It's no use pretending any more. She's grown up and luckily she has Mrs Innis. She must go back to Paris and you, Ivan, must take more trouble to find her a husband. You agree, don't you?

A moment's pause. Then:

TURGENEV

Yes, of course. She could come out here to visit us from time to time. But...

PAULINE

No, I'm sorry. It's time to make a complete break.

LOUIS

Oh come, my dear, I don't think we have to be that extreme.

PAULINE

Yes, we have. What happened just now has been building up for weeks. And I don't want Didie and Marianne growing up with someone who's always dissatisfied. Always sulky and sullen. I would rather not have to say it, but, from now on, my house is closed to her. After all...
         (with a nervous little laugh)
...she all but said that she hated me!

497

Turgenev woke up the next morning dreading the confrontation with his daughter. But the tears and tantrums he had feared were nowhere to be seen. Mrs Innis and Paulinette had obviously spent much of the night discussing what had happened, and both had reached the same conclusion. To her father's relief, she greeted the news that she would be returning immediately to Paris with undisguised joy. Before leaving for Baden-Baden she had been invited to stay for the month of September with the family of Nikolai Turgenev at their château of Bellefontaine near Fontainebleau; she and their daughter Fanny being great friends, she had longed to go, but hadn't dared risk upsetting her father. Now the way was cleared.

For the rest of the morning she kept to her room, packing and preparing for her departure. After a frigid lunch, she took formal leave of the Viardots: a cursory exchange of kisses with Pauline and exclamations of how much they were both looking forward to seeing each other again one of these days in Paris... a more genuinely tender farewell to Louis, who had always been good to her in his gruff, unemotional way... quick embraces for Didie, Marianne and little Paul, and she and Mrs Innis climbed into the carriage that was to take them to the station. Turgenev went with them to see them off. He assured his daughter he would be back in Paris by October, and made her promise to behave herself. Not a word was said about the previous evening's incident. After a warm hug on the platform and a cordial handshake with Mrs Innis, he helped them up into their compartment and stood watching as the train drew out of the station. He had guiltily to admit to himself that sadness at his daughter's departure was mingled with a certain sense of relief.

Only a few days after Paulinette had left he received a letter from the indefatigable Valentine Delessert, suggesting that her matchmaking would be made much easier if the potential young bride were closer at hand; a small apartment had just become available at 10, rue Basse, in Passy, the next house to hers. It was a much more healthy neighbourhood and she thought it would suit Mrs Innis and Paulinette to perfection. Turgenev was in grateful agreement: the idea of his daughter being next door to her benefactress relieved him of the responsibility of spending long periods in Paris. With the Viardots no longer there, there was no other reason for him to leave the little spa where he felt so content for the city he had never much liked. He accordingly made a flying visit to Paris to establish the couple in their new quarters and then returned to Baden, from which he was due to leave in early December for St Petersburg and his appearance before the Senate Committee. But the fates exacted their revenge for his rather spurious plea of ill-health to avoid going the previous winter, by bringing him down with quite a severe attack of gout – a complaint that he was to suffer from regularly for the rest of his life. Once again he had to ask for a delay – this time of only two weeks – and he finally arrived in the Russian capital in the first week of January.

Before he left, Pauline, sincerely anxious about the outcome of his interrogation, asked him to write to her every evening with an account of the day's events. He told her this would be unwise, as his letters would certainly be censored before leaving Russia. He undertook, instead, to write a diary setting down his experiences, which she would then be able to read at her leisure. To while away the tedium of the long journey, he sketched out an introduction in which he tried to dispel his very real sense of misgiving by coating it with a layer of comic invention…

'When I arrive in St Petersburg, on my way to the Hôtel de France where I have arranged to stay, I shall pass the Admiralty; and as I admire once again the golden spire (Pushkin's 'needle'), my mind will go back to the month I spent there as a prisoner. Who knows, the experience may be repeated, although, if all goes badly, I am unlikely to be honoured another time with such a comfortable place of incarceration. I can envisage the whole scene. My friends coming to visit me, Annenkov gravely reproaching me for my imprudence in getting involved in Bakunin's marriage problems, Botkin whining about how he had always warned me that I should keep out of politics, and who was he to dine with now? My dear ladies – Madame Viardot and her daughters – will be leaning over the rail of one of those charming little wrought-iron bridges in the Lichtenthaler Allee, looking sadly down at the Oos bubbling gaily over its bed of paving-stones and swelling its shallow waters with their tears. The editors of Sovremennik will publish an article intimating how close their links still are with their one-time collaborator, who has now assumed the glorious mantle of martyrdom. Like my fellow-scribe, Fyodor Dostoevsky, I shall write a memoir of my life in prison, expatiating on the triumph of the sprit over the travails of the body, and musing on the Russian people's insatiable need for suffering. Viardot will translate the book into French and it will be read by the finest minds in Europe. They will admire it prodigiously but neglect, for reasons best known to themselves, to make any diplomatic effort with the St Petersburg authorities to obtain its author's release. Upon which my 'ladies' will smuggle a saw into my cell, wrapped in a long scarf knitted by their own dear hands. I shall make an escape as daring and dramatic as Casanova's from the Piombi prison of Venice. Once I am out of the country, the government will decide that I was, after all, innocent and I shall be appointed Governor-General of Bukhara…'

The diary proper then begins:

SATURDAY 4 JANUARY: Arrive at the Hôtel de France where am met by Annenkov and Botkin, who has reserved two comfortable, warm rooms for me. Exhausted after my journey, I exchange a few brief words with them and take to my bed.

SUNDAY 5 JANUARY: Wake refreshed. A preliminary interview with Karnioliny-Pinsky, president of the Senate Committee which is to 'try' me. We were slightly acquainted as young men, when he had literary aspirations. He was even for a while under Bakunin's influence! He could not have been more civil, and simply put one or two questions to me of so general a nature that I feel he only asked them because he felt he had to. My first 'hearing' will be on Wednesday. Already dare to feel that this whole absurd business will soon be over in the best possible way.

In spite of this, I find myself prey to an insidious sense of sadness. Am beginning to feel out of place in my own country. Events since my arrival have taken on a dreamlike quality: the people and objects I encounter seem somehow insubstantial. I keep thinking any minute I shall wake up in Baden, sitting perhaps in a café on the Leopoldsplatz, sipping a glass of Rieslingsekt and letting my glance roam appreciatively over the neat, brightly-painted houses – pink, green and ochre – that surround the square. I know that I shall not be content again until I have returned to that charming town where I left the best part of myself.

WEDNESDAY 8 JANUARY: Am led into a vast room, empty except for a long table at the far end, behind which sit six elderly gentlemen in full uniform, their chests covered with medals. They keep me standing, which is thoughtless of them, but compensate by otherwise treating me with the greatest courtesy. They read out the answers I have given to their questionnaire and ask if I have anything to add. When I say no, they send me away, telling me to come back on Monday, when I will be confronted by another gentleman. I leave in good spirits. No one had raised their voice, they were all exceedingly polite, which I believe to be an excellent sign.

In the evening go to a concert and then on to a sumptuous reception at the Italian embassy, given by the ambassador, Marchese Pepoli, now married to Marietta Alboni, the elephant with the melodious voice whom some tried to set up as a rival to P.V.. Many familiar faces. Just as I am leaving, am approached by a hugely fat man, whom I don't at first recognize. Turns out to be Aleksey Arkadyevich Venevitanov. I'd known him and his brother Dmitry, the poet, when I first went to university. Dmitry was an ardent Decembrist and they both were friends of Pushkin and Gogol. He is one of my judges! He assures me that my case is a mere formality.

MONDAY 13 JANUARY: My second hearing. There is no 'confrontation' with anyone else. Only the same six judges. They give me the complete dossier on the whole affair (in itself, I think, a sign of great trust), indicating the pages where my name appears in the various letters. (Almost exclusively, I am relieved to see, in connection with the business of arranging for Bakunin's wife to join him in London.) I write a few additional explanations to those I had included in the questionnaire and this seems to satisfy them entirely. Not one of them puts a single question to me. On the contrary, they start to chat about other matters altogether – literature and music for the most part – and we end up on the best of terms.

When I consider the contrast in the tone of the missives summoning me to St

Petersburg and the impeccably courteous way in which I have been treated, I can only surmise that His Majesty, after receiving my letter, sent word that I was to be handled gently. I have no doubt now that I can consider the whole silly business over and done with.

TUESDAY 28 JANUARY: Receive permission to leave the country any time I wish. IT IS OVER! For me, at least. The committee is not expected to reach its final conclusions until June, but it appears that several of the 32 may face severe sentences...

The next issue of *Kolokol* contained an article signed by Herzen himself, who had obviously heard of Turgenev's letter to the Czar. After mockingly commenting on those 'far-sighted fainthearts who are beginning to abandon the red camp, people ready to accuse themselves and repent of all possible and impossible crimes', he drew his readers' attention to 'a grey-haired Mary Magdalen, albeit of the male sex, who had written to the Czar to inform him that he had lost his appetite, hours of sleep, a few white hairs and several teeth through worrying that the emperor did not yet know of his repentance, which had led him to break off all relations with the friends of his youth.'

Turgenev considered sending a reply to *Kolokol*, but settled for a direct response, enclosing a copy of his letter to Alexander. Sadly accepting that, for the time at least, their friendship had come to an end, he gave his reasons:

"... *That Bakunin, having borrowed money from me and placed me, by his female tittle-tattle, in a very disagreeable position, should have busied himself in spreading false, ugly rumours about me belongs in the natural order of things; indeed, having known him most of my life, it came as no surprise. And this despite his letter to me of less than a year ago, thanking me for my efforts on behalf of his wife and ending: 'You are the only one of our political opponents who has remained our friend; only with you can we talk with sincerity and an open heart.'*

"*But I would never have imagined that you, of all people, would fling mud at a man who had been so close to you for twenty years, and do so simply because he no longer shared your opinions. But I fear this is wasted ink. What is the point of going on irritating one another? I do not propose from now on to continue our correspondence.*"

But Herzen could not refrain from one final salvo: after ascribing Turgenev's 'volte-face' to his resentment at the young generation's hostility to *Fathers and Children*, he suggested they leave the final decision to posterity. "*The time will come when the 'Children' and not the 'Fathers' will judge. I know, in all conscience, that you are not and never have been a 'political animal'; but for God's sake, don't meddle any more in politics! I wish with all my heart that you become what you have always been: an independent writer, showing no political bias; just a writer, pure and simple.*"

Turgenev might well have been happy to take that advice, but he was not allowed to forget that he was a father as well. Only allowing himself a stopover of a couple of days in Baden-Baden after leaving St Petersburg, he went straight on to Paris, where he was expecting to meet his future son-in-law. According to a letter he had received from Klara Trubetskaya, the match with Mr P., as Monsieur Pinet was now known, was as good as made. The Princess spoke highly of the young man: perhaps his employment as receiver was not everything that might be hoped for, but he seemed very taken with Paulinette, he had indicated that he had some private means, and in any event a reasonable future was assured: there would never be a dearth of bankrupts.

On arriving at the new apartment in Passy, the first person he saw was Mrs Innis; Paulinette was spending the afternoon at the house of Valentine Delessert. In answer to his first inquiry, the Englishwoman informed him with tight-lipped economy that Mr P. had been sent packing. When pressed for more information, she made it clear that it was not her business to furnish him with any details; those he would have to hear from Paulinette herself.

"Allow me to ask you just one question, Mrs Innis. Are you yourself pleased that this match has been broken off? You know I place the highest value on your judgement, in all matters concerning my daughter."

The request was carefully considered, and eventually she decided that she could allow herself just this much liberty. "I think Paulinette made absolutely the right decision, Mr Turgenev."

And not another word was he able to extract from her on the subject.

But he didn't have long to wait. Paulinette soon came running into the house, overjoyed to see her father again and seemingly in the highest spirits. She overwhelmed him with questions about his weeks in St Petersburg, insisting on hearing every detail of his brush with the authorities. For her part, she told him how happy she was to have moved to Passy, how kind to her Madame Delessert had been and how many interesting people she had met at her house. This, Turgenev reflected, was certainly not the behaviour of a girl disappointed in love. As he was thinking of asking Mrs Innis to leave them alone, that good lady read his mind and excused herself. Turgenev started to lead up to the question that was uppermost in his mind, but Paulinette read it and forestalled him.

"Please don't ask me about Monsieur Pinet, Papa. I never want to hear that man's name mentioned again."

Turgenev was somewhat taken aback by the violence of this declaration, but quickly decided he should accept his daughter's plea. "Very well, my dear," he said gently. "As you wish. I have always told you that I never wanted anything for you other than a marriage based on affection; if that is lacking, the rest is nothing. So there goes another suitor! So much for him. We will talk no more about him."

She flashed him a grateful smile, but he held up a finger to indicate that he hadn't finished on the subject. "There is one thing I think I must tell you, though," he said. "You are now… how old are you?"

"Twenty-two, Papa."

"Twenty-two. Yes. You're no longer a child, you're a young woman. And I think – and I hope you will agree – that it is time you started living as such. I am glad that you are happy here and that Madame Delessert is so good to you. But things can't go on like this indefinitely. By the end of the year we must make a decision. What I would suggest is this. Let us, of course, hope that you meet the right man; it would be a great joy for me to see you happily married. But if it doesn't happen, I think you should start looking around for some kind of employment."

Paulinette's eyes opened wide in surprise. "But what on earth could I do? I'm not trained for anything."

"I didn't have anything in mind that needed training. You have many accomplishments: you are conversant with several languages; you have studied the piano all your life. You could exploit these advantages and pass them on to some young children. Perhaps the children of families you know. That would surely be a very pleasant occupation. I wouldn't want you to do anything that you wouldn't find agreeable."

She thought about it for a moment and then nodded her head in agreement. "All right, Papa, if you think so. But perhaps I had better start immediately. It doesn't look as if I'm ever going to find the right man. I'll surely die an old maid."

Turgenev smiled and stroked her hair. "'Ever' is too big a word for someone your age. No, no, we'll do as I said. Enjoy yourself for another year and then we'll talk about it again. And in the meantime, let's see what Paris can offer us in the way of entertainment; I don't have to be back in Baden for a day or two…"

In contrast to the restlessness of the preceding decade, the six years that Turgenev was to spend in Baden-Baden were relatively tranquil. Gone was the incessant travelling. He would go to France for a week now and then to see Paulinette, and always tried to attend the performances which Pauline gave in various German cities. But he never spent more than a month or two in Russia, and then only when driven there by the need for money. And he had not been in Baden long before he decided, with the enthusiastic support of the Viardots, to build his own house there. He bought several acres of land almost adjacent to the Villa Montebello, immediately engaged a French architect and began planning the construction of a large three-storey mansion – or perhaps small château would be nearer the mark – in the style of Louis XIII; it was to have a grey slate roof and turrets, French windows leading from spacious ground-floor drawing rooms on to a semicircular terrace with steps that led down to an ample garden, in which he planned to construct a small theatre where Pauline and her daughters and pupils could give public performances.

His excited announcement of this purchase aroused various emotions in Russia, ranging from disappointment amongst his friends to ill-concealed malice from those who were already hostile to him. Countess Lambert sent him a scolding letter of reproach for abandoning his country, and warned him that his work would suffer. In reply, he wrote: 'It is in no way indispensable for a writer to live in his homeland in order to capture the changes that take place there; at least it is not necessary to do so permanently. In short, I see no good reason to prevent me from settling in Baden. I do so, not from a foolish pursuit of pleasure (that is for the young), but merely to build myself a nest in which to await the inevitable end.' The attitude of Russian friends more worldly-wise than the pious countess on receiving similarly unconvincing justifications ranged from the smilingly tolerant to the dismissively scornful. Common to them all, however, was lack of surprise: as soon as he had had the opportunity to be near the woman he loved he had, apparently without a moment's hesitation, wrenched up his Russian roots and sunk them down in Germany. Annenkov and Botkin, who came to visit him, were of two minds: they agreed it would be churlish to resent his evident delight in his new surroundings; but at the same time they couldn't help wondering if he would ever write again. One thing at least was certain: apart from the occasional attack of gout, he had little reason to complain about his health; and as Annenkov remarked, no man's physical condition was more dependent on his psychological well-being.

Much of his time was taken up with his devoted involvement in all aspects of Pauline's life: he advised her on whom to invite for her concert seasons; he often attended her singing classes (the young pupils, while respectfully in awe of their teacher, were entranced by her elegant, grey-haired companion lounging on a settee in the corner, his half German Shepherd, half English sheepdog, Pegasus, curled up at his feet); and he tried to arrange for the publication of her song albums in other countries as well as Russia. For his own part, he had three principal private concerns: his relationship with his daughter, the building of his house and the writing of a new novel.

After the ignominious end of Mr. P., Turgenev had become pessimistic about his daughter's chance of ever finding a suitable husband. In the forefront of his mind was an issue he was unable to discuss with her that had troubled him ever since she had left school. His aristocratic Russian friends, particularly the family of his cousin Nikolai Turgenev and the Trubetskoys, wanted to introduce her into the best Parisian society. But he was emphatically opposed to this. Before leaving Paris he had confided in Valentine Delessert, in whom, as a woman of the world, he found a sympathetic listener. It could, they agreed, lead to her finding herself in an embarrassingly uncomfortable position. Paulinette was now an attractive young woman, and when the mood was on her, could be entertaining company. Suppose some young sprig of the French nobility were to fall in love with her. Sooner or later the truth about her birth would have to come out, and the repercussions of that could be much more damaging to her than any loss of social status involved in becoming a children's tutor. "I don't want her to marry beneath her," Turgenev explained, "and be unable to live the kind of life for which she has been educated. But even less do I want her to be humiliated when the story of her parentage became known." La Delessert, born Countess de Laborde, was in complete agreement and promised to redouble her efforts. It came as an unexpected and welcome surprise, therefore, when one mid-December morning in Baden, he received two letters from Paris: one from the matchmaker, telling him that she thought her search had come to an end; the other from Paulinette, announcing that after all the false alarms, she was sure she had at last found – written in English – 'the right one'.

This was a certain Gaston Bruère, a young man of 29, manager of a glass factory in the Loire district, owned by Valentine Delessert's son-in-law, the Marquis de Nadaillac. To Turgenev it sounded like the ideal match. On the one hand, the 'right one' was seemingly assured of a reliable, lucrative future. (la Delessert wrote that he was so smitten that he had indicated to her in a casual way that, having talked it over with his family, they would not be over-concerned about the size of Paulinette's dowry. 'An unusual attitude in this country,' she added, 'where it is more common for there to be little concern for anything else.') On the other, the irregularity of her birth, which might have offended provincial bourgeois mores, could be easily overlooked in the light of the introduction having been carried out by someone with the social credentials of Valentine Delessert.

In the two months preceding the marriage, Turgenev travelled continuously backwards and forwards between Baden and Paris. His first impression of his prospective son-in-law was favourable. 'I like him very much,' he wrote to Pauline. 'He's a pleasant-looking young man, with a pale face and a frank, honest expression. He reminds me of the Queen of England's late consort, Prince Albert. He has good bourgeois (in the best sense of the word) manners; he's no chatterbox, but what he has to say is worth listening to. He might seem at first a bit of a cold fish, but I think that can be put down to shyness. At any rate, and most importantly, Paulinette seems enormously taken by him; this afternoon, when he came over to meet me, she received him with a smile I had never seen on her face before… Tomorrow we are going to meet his parents, and business discussions will commence. I hope Monsieur and Madame will prove as amenable as their son gives every indication of being…'

It was a fond hope. 'With due respect to Valentine Delessert,' went the next letter, 'they don't seem quite as indifferent about money as she had been led to believe.' He soon found himself embroiled in meetings involving hair-splitting negotiations and long haggling sessions, for which no man was less suited. On learning that Gaston's father had been a notary, he proceeded to hire one of his own to represent him. But he was unable to admit to anyone in Paris, least of all to Paulinette, that the money he had, with uncharacteristic prudence, put aside for her eventual dowry had already been spent: beginning, after the dismissal of Mr P., to share his daughter's conviction that she would never get married, he had used it to purchase seven acres of the most valuable land in Baden-Baden, make advance payments to builders and architects and order the five hundred trees and shrubs he intended to plant in his garden. He had already written several times to his uncle telling him to raise money by selling some properties, but the old man made no secret of resenting his nephew's extravagance when it threatened to limit his own, and so far he had received next to nothing. There were also formidable difficulties in obtaining all the documents necessary for the marriage in France. A civil ceremony was to be followed by a religious one, and Paulinette, despite her previous enthusiasm for the Orthodox Church, was converting to Catholicism. Anguished letters sped between Baden and St Petersburg, begging Botkin and Annenkov to help him: Botkin was even asked to do without his valet, whom he had inherited from Turgenev, for a week so that the man could be despatched to Moscow to procure Paulinette's baptismal certificate, without which the marriage could not take place.

Buoyed up by his relief that Paulinette now seemed directed towards a happy, settled life, he accepted all these inconveniences with stoic patience. Only one twinge of doubt came to disturb his sense of equanimity, and that was implanted by, of all people, Mrs Innis. During his last stay at Baden before going to Paris for the wedding, he unburdened himself to Pauline.

"I found myself alone with her one afternoon. I think Paulinette was with her future in-laws. She asked me if I would like to join her for a cup of tea, and I gladly accepted; it gave me the chance, which I had been looking for, to sound her out in as delicate a manner as possible."

"Sound her out about what?"

"Well, it had been niggling around in the back of my mind that she had never expressed to me any enthusiasm about Paulinette's engagement. Even by English standards of reticence, that struck me as a little odd. My chance came when, after a few platitudes, she remarked on how pleased I must be to see Paulinette finally about to be married. I said, yes of course, I was, but was it just an impression of mine or was she herself not overly delighted? She immediately denied it, but far too vigorously, and now I wasn't going to let her off the hook.

"'Now come, Mrs Innis,' I said. 'You can be absolutely honest with me... indeed it is only what I have come to expect from you. And I promise you, I will not breathe a word of whatever you say to Paulinette. But is there something about Monsieur Gaston you do not like?'

"Again strong protestations, but not quite as forceful as before. So I insisted, this time, a little wickedly, putting her honour in question. 'You must forgive me, Mrs Innis, but I have to admit I do not quite believe you. I think – out of the best of motives, of course, your sense of loyalty and your affection for Paulinette – you are hiding something from me. May I ask you just once more if this is not the case?'

"The poor thing was in agony. She who is normally so composed, became all flustered; to give you an idea how confused she was, in order to give herself time to frame an answer, she poured herself another cup of tea without asking me if I wanted one. Then, after clearing her throat several times, she finally came out with it: 'Well, it's nothing I can really put my finger on, Mr Turgenev, but... I don't know... from time to time I detect something in Mr Bruère that... how can I put it?... well, that I don't quite trust. There! I've said it, and I probably shouldn't have. I'm sure it's all just a lot of silly nonsense... but you asked me and I've told you... and now, please, I beg you, you must forget I've even so much as mentioned it.'

"I tried to draw her out on what it might have been that had given her that impression, but she absolutely would not say another word. Instead, with effusive apologies for her unforgivably bad manners, she poured me another cup of tea and changed the subject with so deliberate a wrench that I had no choice but to not pester her any further."

Pauline smiled. "It's probably of very little significance," she said. "She looks on Paulinette almost as a daughter and surely hoped that she would marry an Englishman. Or else – and who could blame her? – there's a little bit of jealousy. She will surely miss Paulinette a lot – and also, if we are to be completely honest – a very good job, as well."

"Perhaps," Turgenev mused. "But for all her rigid ways, she's remarkably clear-sighted. And she's seen much more of him than I have."

"I trust your judgement above that of Mrs Innis," Pauline said consolingly. "So put it out of your mind."

And as he always obeyed her every wish, that is just what he did.

All the necessary documents were eventually assembled, and on 25 February, 1865, at the church of Notre Dame de Grâce de Passy, Pelageya Turgeneva became Pauline Bruère. Turgenev reported to his Russian friends that Paulinette had looked 'radiantly happy' during the service, and that he thoroughly approved of his daughter's choice. He would later admit when they visited him in Baden that he and his son-in-law had absolutely nothing in common... 'any more, for that matter,' he added to his more intimate ones, 'than I have with Paulinette.' The only potential cause for worry was Gaston's mother, a formidable product of the French provinces who, despite her over-energetic attempts to ingratiate herself with the famous foreign author, produced the opposite effect: underneath her forced pleasantries, he detected a deep disappointment that Paulinette's dowry was not larger. A Russian nobleman and a successful novelist, he read in her eyes, should surely have been able to come up with something more substantial.

Turgenev left Paris for Baden the evening of the wedding day. He had been expected to attend the reception to be held two days later at Rougemont, but 'deeply regretted' that 'an unpostponable appointment connected with the building of my house' made it essential that he return. There were, of course, other motives… chiefly a longing to return to Baden and relate everything to Pauline, who took a genuine interest in her adopted daughter's choice, and profound boredom with the Bruère family and their circle. Soon after his return, he received a note of thanks from Paulinette for the wedding, to which he replied:

'… I am glad to hear that you are settling down in your new nest. I have no doubt you will soon find it the most charming place on earth – especially when it will contain what are usually to be found in nests.

I can only repeat once more how happy I am with the choice you have made. Your good Gaston inspires me with great confidence and I feel the warmest affection towards him; tell him I embrace him as a son – and that he must always and on every occasion count on me as on a father.

I am glad to hear you enjoyed the festivities at Rougemont and regret I had to miss them. I hope you made yourself agreeable to all your new acquaintances by addressing a few gracious words to each of them (not forgetting your mother-in-law!); it is so easy to do and the rewards always outweigh the little effort involved.

I appreciate your having taken the trouble to write a few lines to Madame Viardot. It is perhaps a pity that you referred to that painful scene at Baden, since it was entirely of your making. But… that is ancient history now. Madame Viardot has told me that she hopes that one day you will realize how gratuitously cruel you were to her, but that she is delighted at the prospect of your future happiness and sends you every best wish for the future.

With all the other things on your mind, don't forget to write to Mrs Innis; I left the poor lady in tears, which women of her nationality rarely allow themselves to shed in public. She loves you like a daughter.

I hope you enjoy making Rougemont your own. Don't forget my room!

With warmest embraces to you both, (and remember to drop a line, if you haven't already, to Mme Delessert)

Your loving father,

I. Turgenev

508

Up until this moment in his life, Turgenev – in this, if in little else, a typical representative of the Russian landowning class – had never concerned himself overmuch with money matters. Nice scruples which can agitate more conventional consciences the world over were simply unknown to him. When young, he had stayed as a guest at Courtavenel for years on end without it crossing his mind that anyone might think of him as a sponger (although others had, especially Louise, who, in the memoirs she wrote long after his death, spitefully claimed that he had lived at her father's expense for over thirty years). In the reverse situation, it would never have occurred to him to have thought of long-staying guests at Spasskoye in the same light. It was quite usual for great Russian houses to harbour impecunious relatives for the rest of their lives. After his mother's death, he had become a rich man. But he had never given his finances much of a thought beyond his immediate needs; carelessly generous and a high spender on his own account, he detested arguing with his uncle, and when in need fell back on the time-honoured practice of his peers: if he required minor amounts he would sell timber; for major sums he disposed of small properties. In the six years following the Emancipation Act, he had sold 60,000 roubles' worth of land.

Now, with the need to find the money for his daughter's dowry and the expenditure on his new house, to which he was already committed, he was forced to examine his financial position and was dismayed by what he found. In a discussion with his brother Nikolai earlier in the year, he had discovered that whereas he, owning some 15,000 acres of land, received a maximum of 5,500 roubles a year in income, his brother, from roughly the same amount of property, drew over four times as much. This decided him: he would have to confront his uncle.

Two outside interventions helped to reinforce this determination. One was a rare letter from Porfiry, telling him the situation at Spasskoye was deteriorating day by day: not only was the old man depriving the peasants of as much of their rightful due as he could, but he was too lazy or indifferent even to claim from the government the substantial sums to which the estate was entitled in compensation for the loss of serfs. The other occurred during a tête-à-tête with Louis Viardot; the two men had returned from a day's hunting and were sitting in Viardot's study, smoking and engaged in desultory chatter. After a while, the older man brought up the subject of Turgenev's struggles over the marriage settlement and, more particularly, with apologies if he seemed to be prying, the matter of Paulinette's dowry. Turgenev, who, during his long absences from Paris, had left all financial arrangements regarding his daughter to his hard-headed friend and advisor, was only too happy to share his concern. He told him that the eventual agreement hammered out with the Bruère family had amounted to 150,000 francs: 100,000 down and the remainder to be paid in instalments over the next few years. When Viardot gave a low whistle at the size of the amount, Turgenev hastened to assure him that he had already spoken to a moneylender, who was prepared to advance at least half of it. "At what rate?" Viardot asked. Turgenev had sheepishly to admit that he had had no choice but to accept 10 per cent. "It will just be until my uncle has time to raise the money and send it to me," he added lamely. "Then I will pay it off."

Viardot sat up sharply and knocked the ashes out of his pipe. "This is nonsense," he snapped. "I was suspecting something of the sort and have already discussed the matter with Pauline. We have agreed that we would be happy to lend you whatever you need at any terms that seem right to you. After all, your building a house next to ours is as great a pleasure for us as it is for you."

Before Turgenev could stammer out his grateful thanks, Viardot raised a finger. "I would impose one condition, however. For your sake. Allow me to take advantage of our old friendship by reading you a little lecture. You have to deal with your uncle, and you can't do it from here. The man's making a complete fool of you. Write to him by all means, to alert him that you mean business. But then you must find the time to go to Spasskoye, have it out with him, and if he doesn't agree to cooperate, tell him he's dismissed and find someone efficient and trustworthy to replace him."

Turgenev had no choice but to comply. He dragged himself reluctantly away from Baden three times over the next four years. The first visit to Spasskoye, in the summer of 1865, seemed deceptively promising. His uncle even went so far as to admit he had been a little lax, and undertook to take steps to put things to rights. Eagerly seizing on this as an excuse, Turgenev had little difficulty in convincing himself that he would only get in the way if he became too heavily involved in day-to-day transactions; after all Nikolai lived there and must have a clearer idea than he as to what needed to be done. So he contented himself with arranging for the sale of some of his smaller properties and paying calls on his neighbours. Once again, the experience of seeing his country at close quarters filled him with gloom. He wrote almost daily to Pauline, lamenting at the end of every letter how he missed the gracious life of Baden-Baden. He knew it was absurd to compare the provincial backwater of his birth with the cultured, cosmopolitan principality where he had chosen to reside. But he looked in vain for any signs that emancipation had materially bettered the lives of the peasants…

...What profound misery everywhere! I can't step out of my door without being assailed by beggars. One wonders where they come from, the lame, the blind, the mutilated, all these decrepit wretches rendered desperate by hunger. "Save us, dear barin,*" they all cry. "Save us from starvation!" In the end it was myself I had to save by fleeing, otherwise they'd have got from me everything I own. Two priests came to visit me and complained that the peasants were far less religious than before emancipation; now they spend their days in taverns instead of bringing what money they have to the church. And who can blame them?!...*

One day, an unannounced visitor accosted him outside the house and greeted him shyly; it took him a second or two to recognize her. Feoktista! Could this ageing woman with a shapeless figure, clutching a tattered shawl over her peasant tunic, be the black-haired beauty who had shared his bed and his life for over two years? At first she was almost speechless with embarrassment, but gradually recovered her poise when Turgenev brought her inside, sat her down and asked her about herself. On being brought tea and a plate of the curd pies she had always loved, her awkwardness finally melted and she confessed she had nerved herself to come and see her old lover and benefactor on behalf of her son, who was now ten. At the time of his birth many had taken Turgenev to be the father, but she had been honest enough to deny this, without seeming very sure who actually was. Turgenev had helped her with money and arranged for her to marry a clerk in the Ministry of the Marine in St Petersburg. The baby had been left at an orphanage near Spasskoye, and then been cared for by a woman in a neighbouring village; but she had fallen ill and word had it that the boy had been taken to Moscow. Feoktista was on her way there to try and find him but, on hearing that the *barin* was back in Spasskoye, hadn't been able to resist the chance, as she said with a flash of her old spirit, to 'get a look at you.' Turgenev gave her some more money and the names of friends in Moscow who might be able to help her in her search. He also promised, if she found the boy, to pay his way through a school where he could learn a trade. When she left she had become more like her former self, and kissed him emotionally on both cheeks. After seeing her out, Turgenev went up to his room and, for no good reason that he could think of, flung himself on the bed and sobbed like a child. He was never to hear from or of Feoktista again.

The next year he didn't set foot in Russia. In fact, he hardly left Baden-Baden. Despite his repeated declarations to his friends that he would never again attempt a major work, he wrote, slowly and with great difficulty, the novel that had been in his mind for some time, and which he hoped would disperse the fog of incomprehension that had swirled around *Fathers and Children*. Meanwhile, his financial difficulties only increased. He had hoped that after his confrontation with his uncle, money to pay for the construction of his house would begin to arrive regularly. Once again he was to be disappointed. All that arrived regularly was a series of sarcastic letters from old Nikolai who, though physically going to seed, had lost none of his shrewdness; taking a high moral line that may have had some justification coming from Countess Lambert, but none from the self-serving old rascal, he assumed an inappropriate avuncular tone and reproached his nephew with abandoning his native country, making several unsubtle insinuations about his having had his head turned by an unscrupulous woman.

This drove the last remnants of Turgenev's childhood affection for his uncle out of his head. He wrote to Annenkov, asking him to find a suitable replacement and announcing that he would be coming to St Petersburg in February with the finally finished manuscript of his novel, *Smoke*. While he was in the capital, he would like to read it to a select group before going to Moscow to submit it to Katkov for publication. On arrival, he was greeted by Annenkov with the news that the man he had chosen, a certain Kiszinsky, had duly arrived at Spasskoye and been totally ignored by his uncle, who had refused to hand over the keys or have any dealings with him whatsoever. Two days later, a letter arrived…

… your gratuitously cruel behaviour towards an old man who has never had anything but your best interests at heart threatens to bring to an end an existence which perhaps has gone on too long. I have devoted the best part of my life, first under your sainted mother and then on behalf of you, to keeping up, under all the strains imposed by the wrong-headed, ill-conceived legislation regarding the serfs, which you, from the comfortable vantage-point of Paris or Germany high-mindedly supported (as long as you didn't have to suffer the consequences), a house and an estate which, over the course of so many years, have come to be home to me and mine. And how am I thanked? By your arbitrarily sending down from St Petersburg one of your 'nihilists', who presents himself here and insolently informs me that it is time to pack my bags, as from now on he will be in charge. What are you trying to do? This is the behaviour of an ASSASSIN! I demand that you come immediately to Spasskoye – never mind your literary gatherings and princely receptions. I want to hear my own nephew tell me to my face that he is turning out of the house my brother bought the man who has devoted his life to maintaining it. I repeat, I DEMAND this, otherwise I will take steps to give you financial worries that will make your present sufferings seem like hiccups…

Turgenev forced himself to make a reasonably placatory response. He urged his uncle to collaborate with Kiszinsky and assured him that he would make the journey to Spasskoye as soon as he had completed the business that had brought him to St Petersburg. He couldn't, however, resist pointing out that it was during his 'literary gatherings' that he would be arranging for the publication of his latest novel and a short story which would, he hoped, bring in a small amount of income to help compensate for all the revenues he was not receiving from Spasskoye.

The reading of *Smoke* took place over two seven-hour evenings at the end of February at Botkin's apartment, in the presence of a reduced form of the usual 'jury': Nekrasov and Panaev were naturally not present, and a couple of years earlier Druzhinin had finally succumbed to his tuberculosis.

The overall impression was favourable, but many expressed doubts as to how the novel would appeal to Katkov, who was once again to publish it in the *Russian Herald*. Turgenev proceeded on down to Moscow, where he gave another well-received reading of selected extracts, attended by the editor in person. He included one of the chapters mocking the absurdities of the self-styled progressives and avoided any of the satirical passages regarding the aristocrats and generals. Katkov was unstinting in his praise, announcing to everyone present how proud he was to have the honour of publishing such a masterpiece. Turgenev left the manuscript with him and now had to face the prospect of making the dreaded journey to Spasskoye. But he still managed to find an excuse to postpone it. The weather was exceptionally cold, even for the Russian winter, and his health suffered accordingly. He came down with a heavy cold, which he diagnosed as influenza, and took to his bed for several days. There, he received his new estate manager, who made an excellent impression on him... '*An energetic forty-year-old*', was how he described him to Pauline, '*who looks you straight in the eye. It will be a great blessing to have expert, independent advice. But I must go myself to Spasskoye and put an end to this impossible period of transition which can only be harmful to everyone concerned. I shall leave as soon as my health allows. But you cannot imagine the cold: -22° at eight in the morning, rising to -17° at midday! The very idea of setting out on a journey in weather like this would bring on an involuntary shiver in any creature other than a polar bear. But go I must...*'

He did finally set off from Moscow, but after a day's journey reached a small village from which he wrote another letter: '*I have made up my mind. I shall not be going to Spasskoye. I have been suffering from bronchitis, my foot gives me great pain, and it would be madness to undertake a journey like this in this cold, especially as I would have to make the last part in a sleigh, as the roads are virtually impassable at this time of the year. If I waited another fifteen days, perhaps the thaw would have begun, but I don't want to stay in Russia that long. And anyway I have received a couple of letters from my uncle which indicate that he is beginning to behave in a more reasonable manner. I think he has resigned himself to the unpalatable fact that the time has come for him to hand over the reins. My new bailiff also tells me there are signs that this is the case. Unfortunately it seems that the chaos is indescribable. For at least two years I shall have to keep on tweaking the Muse's ear – fortunately it looks as though literature is still 'in the giving vein'. I comfort myself with the reflection that my presence at Spasskoye would not have been of much use, except to placate my uncle, who wants very much to see me. I would happily grant him this satisfaction, but I fear it is impossible. I write him long letters every day... that will have to satisfy him for the time being...*'

It didn't satisfy him at all. In Moscow, Turgenev and Kiszinsky had worked out a settlement that they thought would satisfy the old man: he would receive a lump sum of 3000 roubles, an annual pension of 800 a year and the gift of one of the smaller estates with an estimated worth of some 20,000 roubles. The answer to this generous offer was not long in coming. Ten years earlier Turgenev had given Nikolai two promissory notes worth 10,500 roubles, with the agreement that they were to be presented only in the event of his death. It was a thoughtful gesture, intended to ensure that his uncle and family would not find themselves in financial straits if he were to predecease him. But with his usual airy disregard for the formalities normally involved in such transactions, he had put nothing in writing. Soon after his return to Baden, he discovered that, not only had Nikolai presented the bills for payment, together with a request for the accrued compound interest, but had also demanded a further 6,200 roubles, claiming this as the amount of his children's capital which he had been forced to spend on the upkeep of the estate. All in all, he declared he would settle for nothing less than a total of 28,000 roubles, and reinforced his claim with attempts to distrain on everything Turgenev owned, including the soon-to-be-completed house in Baden.

Turgenev was in despair: how was he going to pay back his loan from the Viardots when he hadn't even finished paying for his new house? Certainly not from the meagre advances from Katkov for *Smoke*. And soon there were requests from his daughter and son-in-law: Gaston had bought out the owner of the glass factory and needed money to make it a more profitable concern. The newlyweds were hoping they would soon be able to touch the balance of the dowry. Turgenev wrote to Paulinette explaining his difficulties, but was embarrassed by the fact, as obvious to everyone else as it was to himself, that the house in Baden-Baden was an extravagance he was ill able to afford. Once again Louis Viardot came to his aid, not without chiding him gently for not having gone to see his uncle in person. "You use your health too often to avoid unpleasant duties," he observed. "I hope for your sake that Nature doesn't 'cry Wolf!' on you one of these days!" The rescue operation he suggested this time was that Turgenev should sell him the unfinished house for a considerable sum – even if at an overall loss of 60,000 francs – and eventually occupy it as his tenant. Turgenev accepted the offer gratefully, keeping his disappointment tactfully to himself: when, in April, 1868, he eventually moved in, he observed ruefully to Annenkov: 'I suppose I can say I have my nest at last. Although, as it has turned out, it is not *quite* mine. Ah well, perhaps that was never meant to be!'

It was at about the same time that a settlement was finally reached with his uncle, the old man grumpily accepting a reduction in his outrageous demands from 28,000 to 20,000 roubles. By the time it was all over, Turgenev had almost ceased to care. 'I suppose you could say that I have won the battle,' he wrote to Annenkov. 'But I have come out of it with all my bones broken. The only advantage I might be able to draw from the whole disagreeable experience is that I have seen into the soul of a Russian Tartuffe. Perhaps I may be able to make something of this in a future work. Would it not be ironic if that were to be the book that would earn me enough to resolve all my financial problems?'…

He knew by now that *Smoke* was not going to do that. It earned him instead a notoriety that exceeded even that generated by *Fathers and Children*. The main subject of the book, a triangular love story set in Baden-Baden, had been in his mind for several years, but he was unwilling to let it stand on its own. The reception of his previous novel still rankled: despite his constant reiteration, through the mouths of his male characters, of the necessity of resignation in the face of a hostile world, he was unable to follow their precept; the incomprehension and scorn with which his diagnosis of the ills of Russia and the remedies he prescribed had been received, especially by the young, continued to exasperate him. He had therefore decided to intersperse the story of Litvinov, Irina and Tatyana with satirical scenes lambasting the two extremes of Russian political life, and to introduce a character, Potugin, who would play a minor role in the story, but often act as a mouthpiece for his author's views. In order that the two strands should blend as seamlessly as possible, he worked out a detailed synopsis of the novel before beginning to write it. The completion of this coincided with a visit from Botkin to the Schillerstrasse, and he welcomed the chance to submit his ideas to a critic who never let friendship interfere with rigorous honesty.

Botkin's first observation was to question the working title, which at that point was not *Smoke*, but *Two Lives*. He said it was not clear whose lives it referred to. "Perhaps it should be *Two Ways of Life*", Turgenev explained. "I mean the simple, valid life of the provincial gentry, as represented by Litvinov, Tatyana and her aunt, Kapitolina Markovna, and the glittering but hollow aristocratic society which Irina Ratmirova despises, but cannot bring herself to abandon."

"I see. But in that case you might as well call it *Two Novels*… or rather *One Novel and One Political Tract*. And the second sounds as if it's going to make the tempest caused by *Fathers and Children* seem like a spring shower."

"So you agree with Herzen. You think I shouldn't write about politics."

"I didn't say that. But your love, or should I call it love/hate, story seems so engrossing that I wonder if your readers will want to be diverted from it by what sounds to me like a continuation of your quarrel with Herzen in literary form."

"I suppose in a sense it is. I can't publish in *Kolokol*, and we have agreed not to continue our correspondence. But how can a Russian writer today produce a work which does not in some way reflect his country's troubles? I hear Belinsky every time I pick up my pen."

"You have done so before. *First Love*?"

"That was a short tale. And so long ago…"

"Five years!"

"It could be fifty. Emancipation was still to come. Hope was in our hearts. There were some people in Russia, especially young people, who actually listened to me."

"But your life is here now. You are practically an exile. Does that all still matter to you so much?"

"More than ever… and largely for those very reasons. I have to prove people like Countess Lambert wrong. I have to demonstrate that one can still engage with one's country without actually living there."

Botkin tapped the pages of the synopsis. "You'll certainly engage with this. You'll antagonize everybody."

"Everybody?! I'm attacking the reactionary right and the preposterous left. Is there no one left in between?"

"One sometimes wonders. But yes, I suppose there are. Unlike the others, we don't hear very much from them."

"And they are the ones I want to address. Potugin will speak to them. Of course everyone will say – Herzen first of all – that Potugin is me. But it's not as simple as that. Perhaps he is what I would like to be: Hamlet denouncing the rotten state and Don Quixote single-mindedly declaring what should be done to put it right."

"There will be those who say you can't put it right, or even help to put it right, from Baden-Baden."

"There will be those, certainly. I hope there will be others who recognize the value of a certain distance for seeing things in perspective. As I also hope, despite the experience of *Fathers and Children*, that people will read my book as a novel and not, as you say, a political tract."

Botkin shook his head and sighed. "I was going to try to persuade you to leave out the politics and make the story a *conte* like *First Love;* but you're obviously not going to, so let's talk about the love story. I presume your protagonists are modelled on real people?"

Turgenev laughed. "Of course! You know I have no talent for invention. I've been toying with the idea for some time now. Tatyana is a depiction to the life – or as close as I can get, anyway – of my cousin Olga, who, you may remember, I nearly married. Kapitolina Markovna, is my homage to Olga's aunt, Nadezhda Eropkina, whom everybody called Tante Nadya: her devotion to Tatyana, her complete lack of prejudices, her genuine democratic convictions, her sense of honour and morality are simply a setting-down of the qualities of that wonderful woman. It is from them and people like them that salvation for Russia must come… if it is to come at all."

"And the bewitching Irina? Do I detect in her a touch of Madame Pauline?"

Turgenev shot up in his chair and gazed at Botkin in incredulous astonishment. "Pauline?! But whatever can have made you think that? I cannot see any shadow of resemblance between them… except perhaps that everyone who crosses her path is entranced by her. But no, Irina is a manipulator: she tortures herself and others… But there's a lot of work to be done on her. You can't judge a complex character like that from a synopsis."

Botkin raised his hands in the air. "I'm sorry. I had no intention of offending either her or you. So, despite your disclaimer, is she your invention?"

Turgenev sat back and scratched the side of his nose. "Not exactly. I'm treading slightly dangerous ground here. Her circumstances reflect those of Princess Aleksandra Dolgorukaya. You remember her?"

"The Czarina's lady-in-waiting who became the Czar's mistress. Yes, of course I do. She was thirty years younger than him. And very beautiful. Everyone called her *La Grande Mademoiselle*".

"They still do. She comes frequently to Baden-Baden and is immediately surrounded by a throng of admirers – myself among them. And that in spite of the quite radical ideas she at least purports to hold. A former mistress of an absolute sovereign who likes to air republican ideals!"

"No doubt she thinks it gives her a certain cachet. I forget what happened to her after Alexander tired of her."

"There are those who say he never did… that it was she who broke away from him out of loyalty to the Czarina, leaving him distraught. At any rate, he soon recovered and transferred his affections to Ekaterina Dolgorukaya, a distant cousin, who, as we know, still enjoys them. And *La Grande Mademoiselle* very hastily married General Albedinsky, a hitherto obscure officer, who was immediately promoted to the highest positions… but always in the provinces. And there are my Ratmirovs. I hope they won't get me into trouble."

"This book promises trouble from beginning to end," Botkin said, with a grim smile. "And it's certainly not going to patch up your quarrel with Herzen. Your hypocritical windbag of a leftist… what's his name? Gubarev… is very reminiscent of Ogarev. But never mind. Go on and write it. It may turn out to be your masterpiece. Just don't expect to be loved for it."

Turgenev worked harder on *Smoke* than he had on any other of his novels. Except for a week's visit to his daughter and son-in-law at Rougemont, he never left Baden throughout 1866, and spent most of his days wrestling with his intractable subject. He allowed himself few distractions, apart from shooting with Louis and attending musical evenings at the villa Montebello. But in April, the Czar narrowly escaped death at the hands of Karakozov, a former student of Kazan University and member of a revolutionary group called the 'Organization'; a bystander, a simple peasant named Komissarov, managed to jerk the assassin's arm at the crucial moment and deflect his aim. A thanksgiving service was held in Baden, attended by the whole Russian colony, and Turgenev wrote to Annenkov describing it and asking him to send him Komissarov's photograph: 'For once there was no disagreement,' he wrote. 'All feelings melted into one transcendent emotion of gratitude and relief. One cannot but tremble at the thought of what would have happened to Russia if this ignoble crime had succeeded.' For a while he found it impossible to return to his novel and kept his hand in by starting a short tale, *The Story of Lieutenant Ergunov*, with no political implications, and sketching out a couple of operetta librettos in French for Pauline to set to music.

When he finally forced himself to return to *Smoke*, he complained it was like walking through a ploughed field after a heavy rainstorm. The assassination attempt was immediately followed by repression: Golovnin was replaced as Minister for Education by the arch-reactionary Count Dmitri Tolstoy, who wasted no time in reversing all his predecessor's liberal reforms; and *Sovremennik*, despite humiliating efforts by Nekrasov to ingratiate himself with the new ministers, was finally and definitively suppressed. In this climate, it was essential not to strike a wrong note, and Turgenev found himself deleting and revising passage after passage. In spite of this, he managed to complete the novel by January, and the readings, both private and public, that he gave in St Petersburg and Moscow encouraged him to think that it might be well received. He took Botkin's advice and changed the title from *Two Lives* to *Smoke*, after the significant passage near the end of the book where the despairing Litvinov looks out of the carriage window of the train which is taking him home and sees the smoke from the engine funnel first on one side, then on the other, depending on the direction in which the train is travelling... '*Smoke! Smoke!*' *he repeated to himself. And suddenly everything seemed to him nothing but smoke: his life, life in Russia, all that is human and especially all that is Russian. All is just smoke and vapour, he thought; everything seems perpetually to change, one image replaces another, phenomenon succeeds phenomenon, but in reality it all remains the same. Everything rushes ahead, thinking to go God knows where, and fades away leaving no trace, having achieved nothing. The wind changes, everything shifts to the opposite side, and immediately the same feverish, sterile game starts up again. He remembered all that he had witnessed over the last years, all the seemingly momentous events... and his own efforts, feelings, attempts, dreams... Smoke! Nothing but Smoke!...*

Back in Baden, he soon heard from Katkov who, after reading the whole book, predictably lost all his early enthusiasm. The editor of the *Russian Herald* had by now entirely divested himself of the last remaining fragments of his early liberal ideas and had made his paper the mouthpiece of the most reactionary elements of Russian society. He had been outraged by the book's depiction of the aristocracy and especially by Potugin's anti-Slavophil polemics. His letter came as no surprise to Turgenev, although even he had hardly expected such virulence. He read the main points out to Pauline, with whom he had discussed the novel practically page by page...

'... you have chosen to portray the representatives of all that is noblest in Russian society as despicable individuals whose arrogance is only matched by their imbecility. Furthermore, in the character of Irina, you have made such a clear

518

reference to a certain living person that the scandal caused could well lead to the suppression of my paper. I must therefore ask you to take the following steps, without which I will be unable to publish your novel:

1) show the generals in a more favourable light, allowing them some of the qualities of honour and sense of service which so distinguish their real-life counterparts.

2) either cut altogether the character of Irina or…

3) present her as in every way the worthy wife of her distinguished husband, with no immoral insinuation that she at any time betrays him with Litvinov.

4) In any event, abolish the passage in chapter 19 where you refer to her past… what you correctly call 'the terrifying story'.

I look forward to hearing, by return, your attitude to these requests, which I hope will be cooperative. I would like to be able to publish the first section of your novel in the April issue. But not as it is…'

Pauline looked at him anxiously. "What are you going to do? There'll be no book left if you do what he says. Cut Irina! She's the driving force of the novel… not to mention the most fully-rounded female character you've ever created."

Turgenev remained remarkably serene. "Of course he knows I'm not going to cut Irina. I'll just have to tone down certain passages and take out the 'terrifying story'. I knew I was playing with fire there. I'm more worried about his other complaint. He wants all the upper classes to be made perfect members of society. You notice that he doesn't say a word about Gubarev and his followers. There's the division in Russia today for you. You can be as dismissive as you like about your opponents, but your side must only be represented as spotless archangels. And where does that leave art? You'll see: the left won't make any objections to my portrayal of the generals, but they'll be up in arms over the way I depict the radicals."

Pauline was less philosophical. "But it's outrageous that he should impose changes. They can only weaken your book. And how dare he make such demands of his country's leading novelist?!"

Turgenev smiled. "That is my strength and his weakness. Perhaps he needs me more than I need him. If he becomes too intransigent, I shall find someone else to publish my book. This will be the last work I give to Katkov anyhow. But he can't find another writer who, detested though he now is by everybody, will still sell more copies of his journal than any other contributor."

"So what are you going to do? Give in to him? It's humiliating, Ivan."

"Oh, I'm not so easily humiliated. It will be give-and-take up to the date of publication. I'll concede a little here, he'll demand a bit more there. But in the end, he'll publish it. And all the changes I have had to agree to will be revoked when the novel comes out in book form. So don't worry, my dear. My precious artistic integrity, for what it's worth, will not be too badly bruised."

But the struggle was to be harder than he thought. Katkov, basking in the atmosphere of reaction which now enveloped St Petersburg and to which he had done so much to contribute, proved a tougher opponent than Turgenev had anticipated, and finally showed himself to be a dishonest one as well. When the first part of *Smoke* came out in the April edition of the *Moscow Herald*, Turgenev was dismayed to see that certain changes which he had explicitly refused to consider had nevertheless been incorporated. But his irritation was soon put into perspective by the storm caused by the book, which exceeded even Botkin's prescient forecast. As he himself had predicted, the nobility seethed with anger at the portrayal of their kith and kin in Baden-Baden and called him a traitor to his class and his country. Invitations from his compatriots to shoot in the Black Forest were no longer forthcoming. The Grand-Duchess Maria Nikolayevna, the Czar's sister, conversing with Mérimée in Paris, had been horrified by the 'immorality' of Litvinov and Irina's relationship and, to her listener's intense amusement, had called their creator 'a man execrable to women'. ('I did my best to defend you', Mérimée wrote from Cannes, 'but there are none as deaf as those who do not want to hear. But don't be downhearted: if the success of a book is to be gauged by its author being the *only* topic of conversation, your *Smoke* is assured of immortality. Cannes is full of your noble compatriots: a Princess Kochubey, a Princess Labanov… They tell me you are a most immoral man and you write novels in which none of the proprieties are respected; that you personally have behaved with *La Grande Mademoiselle,* Princess Aleksandra Dolgorukaya, exactly as Litvinov behaved with Irina Ratmirova. But in spite of it all, you are a most charming man!…')

The left was no less antagonistic. They denounced his portrayal of the spiteful, chattering pseudo-revolutionaries gathered around Gubarev as a feeble attempt by a landowner – whose liberalism, unconvincing from the start, had withered away with age – to belittle all who fought selflessly for a root-and-branch change in the governance of their oppressed country. Even Pisarev, who had been one of the few to speak up for *Fathers and Children*, suspected that Turgenev had only included the half-baked progressives for fear that his satire of the generals would make him seem a radical himself; and he complained that the spineless Litvinov was no substitute for the heroic Bazarov. But the figure that caused the greatest outrage was the outspoken Potugin; not only those with even mild Slavophil leanings, but the great mass of patriotic Russians were appalled by the denunciations of their country put into his mouth by the expatriate author. And yet there was nothing so new about these. Thirty years ago Peter Chaadaev, in his first 'Philosophical Letter', had called

Russia a *'cultural void', 'an orphan cut off from the human family'. 'To look at us,'* he had written, *'one would say that the general law of humanity has been revoked for our country. Alone in the world, we have given nothing to the world, we have learned nothing from the world; we have not added one idea to the mass of human ideas; we have in no way contributed to the progress of the human mind, and all that has come to us from that progress we have disfigured.'* Admittedly, in 1836 Czar Nicholas had ordered that the author of these words should be declared insane, put under house arrest and visited weekly by doctors. Neither the fictional Potugin nor his creator were in danger of such a fate, but Turgenev was soon to receive a visit that was to have lasting repercussions both on himself and on his visitor…

All small towns lend themselves to gossip, and Baden-Baden, with its cosmopolitan population and constant comings and goings of German princelings, Russian aristocrats, Italian adventurers, French demi-mondaines and English milords, all drawn by the mesmerizing lure of the spinning wheel, was no exception. A few chance words with a stranger over a morning coffee at the Café Weber would become, by evening, a subject for discussion and comment at the Konversazionhaus. So it was inevitable that a brief exchange between Dostoevsky and Goncharov, who was also trying his luck in Baden, should immediately reach Turgenev's ears. Dostoevsky was making a return visit to the spa with his newly-married second wife, Anna Snitkina, who had been his stenographer for *The Gambler* and *Crime and Punishment*. Although this last novel had finally brought him in some money, he was still plagued by debts and hoping to pay them off through success at the casino. Anna, who was only twenty, was at first too much in awe of her husband to dare to try and stop him.

Goncharov had made a point of telling him that he had been seen by Turgenev at the roulette tables. The author of *Oblomov* was no great friend of Turgenev's; he had even made a public accusation that *On The Eve* had been a plagiarized version of an idea of his he had discussed with its author; but he was well enough aware of Dostoevsky's pathological sensitivity to think it worth pointing out that Turgenev had not approached him because he knew how superstitious gamblers were about being disturbed while playing. When Dostoevsky mentioned this to his wife, she suggested he pay a call on Turgenev: otherwise he would think that he was avoiding him on account of the fifty thaler debt which had never been repaid. This forced Dostoevsky to admit that he had been losing heavily and that if he honoured the debt they wouldn't be able to pay their landlady. The practical Anna told him that in that case he should go to see his creditor anyhow and assure him that it was just a question of days. That way, at least a modicum of honour would be saved. A reluctant Dostoevsky accordingly wrote a note to the Schillerstrasse and received a reply asking him to pay a call a day or two later at… was it 11 o'clock as Turgenev later asserted, or 1 o'clock as Dostoevsky always claimed? Whichever it was, when Dostoevsky arrived he found Turgenev sitting down to a lunch being served to him by his butler. Immediately ill-at-ease, he muttered that he would come back another time, but Turgenev rose from his chair, wiped his lips with an immaculate white napkin and advanced on his guest with outstretched arms, offering his cheek to be kissed. Dostoevsky, although detesting this western European habit, had no choice but to oblige, but already felt defensive.

"I am so sorry I have nothing to offer you, Fyodor Mikhailovich. *Why does he always affect that high-pitched drawl when he's talking to me?* I was not expecting you... at this hour. But never mind, I hope you will take a glass of wine with me. Sit down, my dear friend, and don't be offended if I finish this delicious cutlet. Now tell me, to what do I owe the pleasure of this visit?... but before you tell me, allow me to congratulate you on your success with your new book. I deeply regret I have not found the time to read it yet... (this was not true: *Crime and Punishment* had been published in *The Russian Herald* the previous year and Turgenev had written to a friend: 'the first part struck me as quite well done, but when he starts to lapse into mysticism, it's like a prolonged colic during a cholera epidemic. God preserve us!')... but I will make reparations as speedily as possible."

"I shall greatly value your opinion, Ivan Sergeyevich." *I don't believe for a moment he hasn't read it. It's published in the same journal that serialized* Smoke. *He's just jealous that my book was so well received and his was not.* "I, on the other hand, have read your last book."

"And disliked it as much as everyone else, I imagine."

"I cannot rate it amongst your best. To be sincere, I found the passages denigrating our homeland out of place, almost scandalous."

"I see. And what was it, particularly, that offended you?"

"For a start, almost everything that came out of the mouth of Potugin, who was surely speaking for you..."

"Why do you assume that?"

"Oh come, Ivan Sergeyevich, everyone sees you in Potugin. What does he say when he's asked if he loves his country? 'I love it and I hate it.' That is the impression you have given to hundreds of your fellow-countrymen."

"And if I remember rightly, he is taken to task for that remark by Litvinov."

"Yes, because of its banality. No one would dream of calling your work banal."

"Instead they call it offensive, is that correct?"

"For those of us who love our country, with all its faults, many of Potugin's ideas are offensive, yes. For example, when he says that if Russia were to disappear from the face of the earth, the rest of the world would hardly notice the difference, for we have invented nothing... that the disappearance of the Sandwich Islands would make a greater stir..."

Turgenev looked pensive. He had finished his lunch and now offered a cigar to Dostoevsky, who refused, but took out one of his own cigarettes. As Turgenev lit both, he murmured: "How sad that there is no room in our literature for the expression of every point of view! Twenty years ago we were censored by the government; now we are censored by true believers who only want to hear the proclamation of their own ideologies. What a single-vision nation we have become! The English club in Moscow is apparently about to expel me for traducing the class into which I was born; the Slavophils, with whom you appear to have many sympathies, call me a traitor for suggesting that Russia has much to learn from European civilization; and the young progressives denounce me as an old dotard who has outlived his usefulness."

"Can they all be wrong, Ivan Sergeyevich? And only you right?"

A slight flush rose to Turgenev's cheeks and he answered sharply: "You have misunderstood my position. Perhaps deliberately. It is they who are so certain they are right. I am certain of nothing... or only of one thing, at any rate. And that is the beneficent effect on mankind of civilization. There, yes, Potugin speaks for me. I shall continue to brandish my banner with the one word, 'Civilization', written on it, and they can hurl mud at it from every side, if they choose."

"I admire your self-assurance. It is a quality that all we writers need in abundance. But I believe we must also guard against overconfidence. When, as you say, *everyone* is against you, perhaps the time has come to..."

"I have said no such thing. I am not as alone as that. My book has met with approval from many quarters – discerning quarters, if I may be so immodest. Do you know who spoke most warmly in favour of it? Aleksander Nikitenko. And why? Because there is a man who was born a serf and raised himself to become an important government functionary. He has seen Russian life from many different viewpoints. Perhaps there is a lesson to be learnt there. A lesson, if you will excuse the impertinence, that perhaps you could benefit from too."

"At least I see Russian life from the point of view of someone who lives there."

Turgenev stood up and moved over to the window. He gazed out over the garden, forcing himself to resist the provocation. Almost as though speaking to himself, he murmured: "The Salaev brothers are about to publish a five-volume edition of my collected works. I shall be reflecting on these and other subjects in a long preface, under the title of 'Literary Souvenirs', which I am now preparing. It will probably be the last thing I shall write. I shall take the opportunity to venture to offer a little advice to young writers."

"And what form will that take?"

"Above all to follow Byron's injunction: deny nothing, but doubt everything... even the values that were hammered into you during your childhood. And as a corollary to that, to beware of myopic patriotism, which paradoxically can be the worst service you can do your country." He turned round to face his guest. "No doubt this will spoil a few of your Slavophil friends' dinners."

Dostoevsky drained his glass and laid it carefully down on the table. "Before you write it," he said slowly, "I would suggest you have a telescope sent from Paris. I am told they make the best ones there."

"A telescope? What in the world for?"

"So that you can train it on Russia and see what is actually going on there."

This time there was no hiding his irritation. Turgenev turned round and moved towards the door. "I don't think that will be necessary. But let me not detain you any longer, Fyodor Mikhailovich. I must be boring you with my ruminations. You will have many things to do during your short stay here."

"I am sorry. I seem to have offended you. But I have never known you so touchy. Could it be because you are exasperated by the not very favourable reception of *Smoke*? If so, you really mustn't let yourself become downhearted by that. I make a point of paying no attention at all to what reviewers say of my work."

"I assure you that the attacks against my novel are completely indifferent to me. Otherwise I should not have gone on writing." He held the door open. "It has been a great pleasure seeing you again. And I believe you have just remarried. Please give my best regards to…"

"Anna Grigorevna."

"To Anna Grigorevna. Perhaps I shall have the honour of making her acquaintance before you leave Baden."

"If you would care to call on us, we should be delighted to receive you. But not before midday; we are late risers. And make it soon: we shall not be staying here any longer than necessary. I can't wait for the day when I shall put this godforsaken country and its people behind me. I have been cheated and robbed by these German scoundrels from the moment Anna and I set foot here. I cannot stand their appearance, their language or their manners."

Turgenev held the door open. "There again I am in entire disagreement with you. Theirs is a civilization – the civilization of Goethe and Schiller – that we barbarians can only admire and strive to imitate. For myself, I have no hesitation in saying I feel more German than Russian."

"Even after reading *Smoke*, I hardly expected to hear that. But again I seem to have offended you. I can only assure you that was not my attention." An ironic bow. *"Auf Wiedersehen*, Ivan Sergeyevich."

According to Dostoevsky, a day or two later his landlady woke him at ten o'clock to say that there was a gentleman downstairs to see him. Dostoevsky, who had been at the casino until three, told her to ask the man to leave his card, turned round and went back to sleep. Later that morning he discovered that it was Turgenev who

524

had called. "Typical!" he observed to Anna. "I told him not to come to see us before twelve, but this is his way of doing what seems to him the 'gentlemanly' thing. He has no wish to see me again, but now feels he cannot be accused of not having made the effort. What a detestable hypocrite. I am through with him for ever. I'll pay off his damn debt as soon as I have the money, but I never want to see him again."

The debt was not paid off for another eight years and even then only through an intermediary; happening to meet Annenkov on a train, Dostoevsky handed the money over, mumbling an unconvincing apology. And the two men were not to converse again until they were both invited to speak at the unveiling of the Pushkin Memorial in Moscow, one year before Dostoevsky's death and three before Turgenev's. On the odd occasion when their paths crossed over the next few days in Baden-Baden, they carefully avoided catching each other's eye. But Dostoevsky was never one to allow a grudge to go forgotten, and four years later, readers of *The Devils* had little difficulty in identifying the original of the 'famous writer', Karmazinov, who appears here and there in the book. We first see an almost straight transposition of the Baden visit, with a 'vain, pampered gentleman' offering his cheek to be kissed, complaining to his anarchist visitor that, despite his declared sympathy with all the aims of the revolutionary left, he has always been sneered at by the young radicals, and announcing that, since Russia has no future, he has become a German 'and proud of it'. Towards the end of the book, Karmazinov has been invited to read his latest work, *Merci*, at a grand reception given by the provincial governor. Having rehearsed his puns and jokes the previous day in front of a mirror, he starts to read, in a 'feminine voice with an affected lisp', a merciless parody of *Phantoms*, the story Dostoevsky had been so pleased to publish in the first instalment of *Epokha*. After delivering thirty pages of 'pretentious, useless chatter', he is interrupted by unflattering comments from the audience; whereupon he skips to the end, which nods maliciously towards the final pages of *Enough*: a short discourse on the futility of everything, ending with three repeated words: *merci, merci, merci*.

Turgenev was in St Petersburg when he read *The Devils*. He had moved from a hotel to stay with the Annenkovs, feeling more protected there from an outbreak of the dreaded cholera. He impatiently dismissed the main theme of the book, which, as he remarked to his host, illustrated so many of the reasons why he was happy no longer to live in his homeland. "This insistence on sin and possible redemption, on the uniqueness of all things Russian, on the moral squalor of radicals and revolutionaries... for me they represent the excremental discharges of a sick man. It's tragic. His first book was remarkable. But those four years in Siberia and his epileptic fits have undermined his faculties. Of course his talent occasionally shines through the gloom: he can create memorable characters – if you can bear to remember them! – and from time to time there are flashes of Aristophanic humour. But to what miserable use he puts them!"

When Annenkov asked him if he intended to take any steps to reply to the vicious caricature, he shook his head and smiled: "No, no, that would be to do him too great a favour. He'd know that he'd drawn blood. He's waited all his life to write something like this. He hated me from the first... with no great reason, I have to say. Oh yes, Belinsky and I used to tease him now and then, but we helped him too. You remember, we had his early work published in *Sovremennik*. But perhaps that's why. Passions with no existential justification are often the strongest and longest-lasting. But what disturbs me most is his personalized Christianity. It makes me almost grateful for my inability to believe. This conviction of Holy Russia's mission to save the world! I would be more inclined to think the world needs saving from the likes of Fyodor Mikhailovich, who, as his vindictive parody of me bears out, is the most spiteful Christian I have ever met."

If *Smoke* was responsible for bringing out into the open Turgenev and Dostoevsky's long-standing mutual antipathy, ironically enough it played a part in repairing the friendship between the author and Herzen. Although the most controversial passages of the novel, and especially Potugin's jeremiads, were written in direct repudiation of the measures Herzen advocated for Russia, Turgenev sent him a pre-publication copy. Resigned as he was to the loss of many of his old friendships due to political differences, he was reluctant to believe that some common ground could not still be found with the editor of *Kolokol*. The last years had been marked for Herzen by political disappointment and personal tragedy. The circulation of his journal had dropped from some three thousand in its heyday to less than five hundred. The new reactionary right in Russia no longer found it diverting to read, and the increasingly revolutionary left rejected it as out-of-date and irrelevant. Bakunin had left London, spent three years in Italy, and was now enjoying the tolerant political atmosphere of Switzerland. Ogarev suffered from epilepsy, was a virtual alcoholic and emotionally entirely dependent on his Mary. Herzen's relations with Natalie were now subject to constant strain and the twins had died of diphtheria in Paris. Hoping that a change could only improve his fortunes, he had decided to leave London after twelve years and settle in Geneva. A large colony of Russian radicals, in flight from the new oppressive climate at home, now lived in the lakeside city; he thought that by publishing *Kolokol* in French he might revive its fortunes. But it was not to be. After the attempt on the life of the Czar, he wrote an uncompromisingly denunciatory article, dismissively referring to the assassin as 'some fanatic'. To the Geneva radicals, Karakozov was their hero; one of their number wrote a furious reply, calling *Kolokol* 'a hackneyed sheet, tedious and repulsive' and branding its editor as one who, 'failing to perceive that you have been left behind, flap your enfeebled wings with all your might... Call yourself a poet, an artist, anything you please, but *not* a political leader and still less a political thinker...' In less than a year, *Kolokol*'s ten-year existence was to come to an end.

Along with a copy of his book, Turgenev enclosed a conciliatory letter, reverting to the tone of friendly badinage in which they had always communicated before their quarrel: '... So here's my new novel. As far as I can tell, it has earned me in Russia the detestation of religious believers, courtiers, Slavophils and patriots. You are not a believer or a courtier, but you are a Slavophil and a patriot, so no doubt the book will enrage you too. What's more, my uncomplimentary words about the expatriate 'progressives' will not be to your liking. However, the thing is done, and there is one crumb of comfort for me: many of the young radicals have honoured you too with the sobriquets of anachronism and reactionary. The distance between us has lessened!'

Herzen acknowledged receipt of *Smoke*, but wrote a scathing review of it in *Kolokol*, adopting a rather condescending, 'advice to an old friend' attitude. 'After his last novel,' it ran, 'the fathers have become grandfathers. And grandfathers drivel on, incoherently and endlessly. Poor Ivan Sergeyevich really didn't need to blow these smoke rings! Nature has endowed him with a wide array of talents: he knows how to write about hunting, he knows how to depict with his pen all sorts of woodcock and partridges ensconced in 'nests of gentry'. But no, he says, I want to be caustic, mordant, malicious... when he's the kindest of men without an ounce of malice in him.' Then, perhaps feeling that he had been a little too cruel to this kindest of men, he wrote to Turgenev: 'I know I have stung you a bit over *Smoke*, even though you were good enough to send me a copy. Perhaps it is time we drew up a balance-sheet of credits and debits between us, and, if you agree, settle our account. If you don't want to, so be it. Believe me, my sardonic little review was inspired by no hostile feelings; I can never be angry for more than a week at a time, and I give you my word that my irritation with you disappeared a long time ago. If you do not feel too bitter towards me – even better, if my review made you smile a little – write and tell me so. But I have to confess that I had more than enough of your Potugin. Couldn't you have cut at least half of his verbiage?'

To which Turgenev replied: 'Bitter? Towards you?! If that were so, would I have sent you my novel?... Of course you don't approve of Potugin. But far from cutting half of him, for me he doesn't speak half enough; and the general fury the character has aroused against me only confirms me in this opinion.'

And so the correspondence started up again, but without the acrimony that had entered in after the 'Affair of the 32'. And in January, 1870, they met again for the first time in eight years. Herzen had by now been diagnosed with diabetes and was in Paris with Natalie and Liza, trying to make provisions for his widely-dispersed family and consulting what passed for expert medical opinion. A tired, sick man, he had just returned from Florence, where his twenty-five-year-old daughter Tata had had a nervous breakdown after a rejected Italian suitor had threatened to blow his brains out. He had of course done nothing of the sort, but had relieved his loss of face with his cronies by spreading fabricated rumours around the town about her immoral behaviour. Tata was reported to have had visions of men waiting in dark rooms to murder her, and Herzen, remembering her mother's irrational behaviour, was terrified that his beloved daughter was lapsing into insanity.

Although Tata soon recovered, the experience had taken its toll on Herzen's already precarious health; but it was with genuine delight that he threw out his arms to welcome his friend. Turgenev was in a far from buoyant mood himself. Botkin had died in October, after a long illness that had ravaged his body but not destroyed his spirit. And only two days ago he had emerged from a deeply upsetting experience. Among his fellow-guests at a dinner party had been Maxime du Camp, Flaubert's friend, who was now publishing articles on various aspects of Parisian life in the *Revue des Deux Mondes*; an ardent opponent of capital punishment, he invited Turgenev to attend the preparations for and actual execution of Jean-Baptiste Troppmann, a twenty-year-old mechanic who, in a crime that had been the talk of Paris for months, had murdered, seemingly without motive, a family of eight: father, pregnant mother and six children. Turgenev was soon to write an appalled description of the gruesome procedure; attending a 'rehearsal' at three in the morning when the executioner tested the guillotine for the benefit of onlookers, he remarked that, 'The horses, harnessed to their carts, calmly munching hay from their nosebags in front of the prison gates, seemed to me the only innocent creatures amongst us.' Miserable with guilt at having agreed to be there at all, he ended by stating that he would forgive himself his misplaced curiosity only if his piece supplied some arguments for the defenders of the abolition of the death penalty, or at least of public executions.

With his nerve-ends thus already exposed and raw, it was no wonder that his eyes were moist as he withdrew from the long embrace with which he had been greeted. Herzen was suffering from a cold and Natalie reminded Turgenev of his diabetic condition and begged him not to keep his friend up late. He suggested that he should just stay a few minutes and come back another day, but Herzen would hear none of it. They dined *en famille* and then the two men retired to a small room to resume the conversation they had broken off eight years ago. Their attitudes had undergone slight modifications (Herzen's more than Turgenev's), but there was little change in their core beliefs; only a new readiness to be tolerant about their differences and a recognition of what they had in common... especially the realization that they belonged to a generation which, if it had not said all that it had to say, at least was not going to be listened to as once it had been.

Turgenev began by asking after Bakunin. Herzen had seen him from time to time in Geneva, but had cut all connections with him after he had fallen under the spell of the murderous revolutionary Sergey Nechaev (the model for Dostoevsky's Peter Verkovhensky in *The Devils*), whom Herzen disliked and mistrusted. The two men could only look back on their former friend with a mixture of bemused affection and resigned detachment.

"Did you hear," Herzen asked, "what he said in Berne at the Congress of Peace and Freedom? His latest enemy is Karl Marx and the International. He refused to call himself a communist because communism, he says, swallows up the forces of society for the benefit of the State. It is, therefore, the negation of liberty."

"So what does he call himself?"

"A collectivist. But, of course, his explanation of what he means by this is so obscure that it binds him to nothing."

"Between communism and collectivism," Turgenev observed, "there may be a great difference for him, but very little for me. Both hack away at the liberty of the individual. And if there is one cause that I will champion as long as I live, it is the cause of individualism." He gave his friend a quizzical glance. "And so, though you may not be so prepared to admit it, will you."

"I'm afraid you're right," Herzen admitted with a chuckle. But it's not your individualism that I question. It's your pessimism. You've swallowed too many draughts of that neo-Buddhist, that scribbling cadaver, Schopenhauer. He's eroded your belief in the ability of action to achieve anything."

"Not quite. If I may dare to bring up *Smoke* again, my hero learns from his mistakes and finds satisfaction in applying the lessons he has learnt in the West to improving his estate and the lives of those who live on it."

Herzen let out a whoop of triumph. "Condemned out of your own mouth! You give your book a happy ending – not a very convincing one, I have to say, bearing in mind all that has gone before – but a sort of happy ending, anyway. And then you proceed to nullify it."

"How?"

"By calling the novel *Smoke*. What's the use of Litvinov being reunited with his Tatyana and leading this admirable life on his estate when he himself has said, ten pages earlier, that all human endeavour has no more lasting significance than smoke billowing out of the funnel of a railway engine? No wonder our young radicals have no time for you; they're convinced they are going to change the world with their bare hands!"

"They'll find out too," Turgenev murmured gloomily.

"They surely will. But you and I mustn't let all the blows we have received consign ourselves to the enemy camp. We must believe that human development – above all the struggle for freedom – will continue, even if we disagree with the methods used."

"I'm more of the opinion of Goethe: *Der Mensch ist nicht geboren frei zu sein –* man is not born to be free. It's physiological. Throughout nature we find class-ridden slave societies. Look at bees! And of all European peoples, the Russian feels the least need for freedom. Emancipation gave it to them, in theory at least, and they're anything but grateful. Many think they were better off before, and in a way they were."

"Emancipation was only one rung of the ladder. The struggle will continue. And it's up to us to guide the direction that struggle will take... otherwise there will inevitably, sooner or later, be the terrible bloodshed we both fear."

"And you still see the peasant commune as the germ from which some kind of democratic state will spring?"

"I think there is a kernel of inherent wisdom there, yes... something from which the provincial assemblies could learn."

Turgenev shook his head. "I'm afraid the long years you've spent in the western Europe you affect to despise have erased the memory of how things actually are in Russia. You would only have to attend one meeting of the *mir* to be disabused. No one listens to anyone else's point of view. In fact no one takes the slightest notice of anything beyond his own exclusive interests."

"So what's your recipe? Although I suppose I don't really need to ask. That chatterbox Potugin of yours has told me at wearisome length. The enlightened landowners and professional men must use their knowledge of western civilization to educate the ignorant masses. Is that correct?"

"Absolutely. Because, unlike Dostoevsky, I don't believe Holy Mother Russia has some special, unique message for the world. And I don't see her as an unappreciated Venus of Milo who will dazzle all onlookers as soon as she's freed from the clutches of her wicked European stepmother. For me she's an ordinary enough wench, very similar to her elder sisters, in fact: a bit broader in the beam, a bit more of a slut, perhaps... but given time she'll make her way in the world like the others. As long as..." and he rapped his fingers on the table for emphasis, "she is allowed to take lessons from those others and learn from their mistakes."

"And suppose instead she..." Herzen had leant forward equally eagerly to underline his objection, but he was suddenly doubled up by a fit of coughing, which brought tears to his eyes and left him breathless. Turgenev sprang to his feet and took his leave, apologizing for keeping him up so late. "It's no matter," Herzen gasped. "I just need a good night's sleep. Come back tomorrow, and we'll go at it again. We're like a couple of knights at a medieval tournament, forever jousting. There's only one thing neither of us can understand, and that is why the other doesn't see what's so obvious to him."

Turgenev promised he'd come as long as Herzen was well enough. But when he arrived at the house, a distraught Natalie told him that he had come down with pneumonia and the doctors feared for his life. The bulletin was no better on the following two days. On the third, Turgenev was expected back in Baden and he took the train on which he had arranged to travel. The following day, Herzen died. He was fifty-eight. As with Belinsky, Turgenev was spared – or spared himself – the sight of the dead body of someone he had loved. It was small consolation that their last meeting had dissolved the bitterness that had eroded their friendship after the 'Affair of the 32'. 'Whatever divergences of opinion there may have been between us,' he wrote to Annenkov, 'however acrimonious our disputes, it is an old comrade and an old friend who has gone. Our ranks are thinning out. No doubt everyone in Russia will say he should have died earlier, that he survived the best of himself. But what do such words mean, what does our work mean when confronted with the silent gulf which swallows us all up? Remember what poor Botkin said the night before he died? "Even in the state I'm in, all I want is to live…"'

Although Pauline never regretted her decision to abandon the stages of the major European theatres she had dominated for 25 years, her lifelong dedication to music couldn't find full satisfaction in teaching and giving the occasional opera or concert performance in German cities. Encouraged by Clara Schumann, who had lived in Baden-Baden since 1863, she determined to develop her talents as a composer. In this she knew she could count on unfailing support and practical help from Turgenev. There were the albums of songs to lyrics by Russian poets, chosen and sometimes written by him, which he assiduously pressed on publishers in Russia and Germany. He even went so far as to suggest to Annenkov that he insert an anonymous review in a paper, praising the songs in a language that would have done honour to Schubert. There were few things his most faithful friend would not do for him, but he did balk at this, fearing, rightly, that everyone would know who had written the article and it would bring down yet another storm of abusive criticism on his head.

But Pauline Viardot's life had been devoted to the opera house, and it was there she secretly hoped one day to triumph. Here again the proximity of a world-famous writer happy to lay aside all his cares and put his time and talent at her disposal was an invaluable asset. During the difficult year of 1867, the year of the battles with his uncle and the tumultuous aftermath of *Smoke*, he found an agreeable diversion in collaborating with her on three operettas, for which he wrote the words and she the music. They were performed at first in the reception rooms of the Villa Montebello and later, when it was ready, in the little theatre in his garden, which Turgenev had had built for just that purpose. The audience, socially and artistically, was as distinguished as any to be found in the opera houses of the European capitals. The cast was, for the most part, made up of Pauline's pupils and her children, with herself, when she wasn't directing from the piano, taking small parts, to the wonder and joy of the most discriminating of her listeners. In two of the works, the major comic role was taken by Turgenev himself, who was thus able to indulge his lifelong love of dressing up and playacting.

Someone who was present at one of these performances left an account of the production. Back in 1852, when Pauline had needed to rest after a strenuous season in London and political harassment in Paris, the Viardots had spent some weeks in Duns Castle, near Berwick in Scotland; and it was during that time that Claudie had been conceived. The wealthy owners of the castle, William and Judith Hay, had become friendly with the glamorous couple from Paris, and since then had always taken a keen interest in Didie. They themselves had an only daughter,

Georgina, who had been 10 years old at the time; now aged 26, she was staying as a guest at the Villa Montebello. Desirous of escaping from the monotonous life of the Lowlands, and unenthusiastic about the suitors who were eager to capture her well-endowed hand, she nursed ambitions to become a journalist. Pauline had introduced her to her friend, Henry Chorley, and advised her to send him samples of her work for possible publication in the *Athenaeum*. With this in mind, she wrote to her parents…

Villa Montebello,
Baden-Baden.
23 May, 1868.

Dear Mother and Father,

The opening night of The Ogre *is due to take place on the 24th, and for days now nobody at the Villa Montebello has had another thought in their heads beyond tomorrow's performance. All the women in the household, from old Mlle Berthe, Monsieur Viardot's sister, who must be at least 70, to young housemaids of 16 or less, have been slaving away – cutting, stitching, patching, mending – to get the costumes ready on time. The rehearsals, which are usually held in Mister Turgenev's drawing-room, have quite lost their early carefree nature and have become deadly serious. There have been frequent clashes between Madame Viardot, who is directing, and a certain Herr Tillich, a choreographer she brought in from Karlsruhe. He is obviously not used to working with amateurs and never stops screaming at the girls, who are mostly Madame Viardot's pupils and all come from wealthy families. He complained the other day that the Swiss girls are fat, the Germans slow, the Swedes clumsy and the French never stop chattering. He's much nicer to the boys. Yesterday Madame Viardot took him to task because he was giving everyone such complicated movements that they had no breath left for singing. 'Well, madame,' he said, 'if you want them all to stand stock still for an hour, you have no need of me,' turned on his heel and stalked out of the room. But she knew he'd soon come back: the honour of appearing on the same playbill as Pauline Viardot means a great deal more to him than a fluffed glissade.*

The still centre of this whirlpool is Mister Turgenev himself. It is amazing to see this great writer throwing himself with such enthusiasm into amateur theatricals. He seems to be having the time of his life, and is always there to put in a soothing word when someone's feathers get too ruffled. I think every girl in the cast is a little in love with him… and not only in the cast!! He is playing Mikokolembo, the title role of the Ogre, and loves putting on his black costume and wearing his red beard and wig. He doesn't really have a great deal to do, which is just as well because he's not a very good actor and can't sing a note. So he mimes the part onstage while an actor sings in the wings. He keeps telling Madame Viardot he's hopeless and they must find someone to replace him; but they all know he's really enjoying himself enormously, and anyhow his presence in the cast is one of the main attractions.

As you know, he wrote the libretto and Madame Pauline set it to music. There's a complicated plot but very simple lines. An example:

Faut-il qu'à mes yeux je crois?
Oui, c'est vous, mon seul trésor,
Et mon coeur frémit de joie
Je puis être heureux encore.

Even my school French can cope with that! To give you a quick précis of the story: Princess Aleli, (that's Didie, she's very good) is in love with Prince Saphir, who has a young page called Estambardos, played by little Paul, who is only 11. Mikokolembo wants Aleli for himself... and I must say Turgenev is very convincing in this, because he obviously adores Didie. So he sends his men to capture Estambardos, and holds him for ransom: he will only give him up if Aleli promises to be his. After a whole lot of improbable comings and goings involving a kind witch (Mme Pauline, who has written a beautiful aria for herself), a band of good goblins, another of malevolent elves and all different sorts of animals, the greedy Mikolembo is lured to a clearing in a forest where especially delicious berries grow. The goblins fall on him, throw him to the ground and tickle and pinch him till he's forced to release Estambardos and renounce all claims to Aleli. As it's an operetta, it has to have a happy ending so, in a final chorus, the Ogre is forgiven for all his sins and allowed to have access to the delicious berries for ever.

I'll have to stop now, because they've just asked me if I'll help to sew some squirrels' tails on. I'm afraid when they see my prowess with needle and thread, they'll think I've been very badly brought up! I'll give you an account of the first night as soon as I have time...

For the moment, much love,

Georgina

25 May

... Well, what an evening! The charming little theatre which occupies part of a lawn at the back of Mister Turgenev's house, sloping down to a small lake, was filled to overflowing: you'd never believe all the crowned heads and famous musicians who were there. Just to list the ones I remember there was: the King and Queen of Prussia, with their Minister-President, Prince von Bismarck and Chief of the General Staff, Count von Moltke, the English Crown Princess Victoria, the Grand Duke and Duchess of Baden-Baden, the Grand Duke of Weimar, the Countess of Brandenburg as well as Franz Liszt, Johannes Brahms, Clara Schumann, Anton Rubinstein and dozens of other musical luminaries that I had never heard of. The audience was wildly enthusiastic and the applause at the end went on for at least ten minutes. The King of Prussia kissed Pauline Viardot's hand over and over again and apparently the Grand Duke of Weimar has asked her to write a three-act opera for a professional production at his theatre next season. Everyone seems to think this heralds the beginning of a new career for her as a composer.

I wish you could have been there. Apart from the music, which as you know, I'm no great expert on (it sounded very pretty, but how great it was I've no idea), it was such a splendid occasion. After it was all over, we walked in a torchlight procession – the cast still wearing their costumes – from Mister Turgenev's house to the Villa Montebello, where there was supper in the garden with cold roast beef and potato salad and gallons of chilled hock. Everyone was in the gayest of spirits... with a few exceptions. I went into the house for purposes of my own and passed a room where a small group of Russians had congregated. I hadn't been introduced to them (I'd presumed they were friends of Mister Turgenev), but they were obviously very upper crust. Everyone here is. Anyway, I couldn't help overhearing their conversation. (Well, actually I hid behind the door and strained my ears to be sure I did!) Fortunately they were speaking in French; I couldn't make it all out but the gist was that they were horrified that their compatriot had, in their opinion, made such a fool of himself. They thought it terrible that a great Russian writer should squander his talent writing tinkling verses for children and that a nobleman should make such an exhibition of himself just to please his foreign mistress. They seemed to look on it as a slight on their country. I think they exaggerated terribly. I mean, why shouldn't a writer find his relaxation in any way that's congenial to him? Although I do have to say, there was a moment when he was lying on the floor in the last scene being tickled and pinched by the goblins in a posture which I suppose really was rather undignified. I happened to look across at our Princess Victoria at that moment, and you should have seen the contemptuous smile on her lips. I'm sure what was going through her mind was something like, 'You'd never see Thackeray comporting himself in that ridiculous fashion!' But all the way through she was by far the most stuffy of the royalty present. I think her mother, our good Queen V., would have been much more jolly.

That's enough for now. I'll fill you in on all the other details when I get home. Please don't lose these letters. I want to work them up a little and send the essence to Mr Chorley.

Your ever-loving,

Georgina.

But the dark shadow of reality was soon to obliterate the never-never world of operetta. Turgenev had hoped that his Baden house, planned with such loving care for every detail, would be his nest for the rest of his life; he was to live in it for less than three years. He had been keeping a wary eye for some time on the war of nerves between France's decadent Second Empire and the rapidly accelerating military might of Prussia. When, several years earlier, his French architect had announced yet another delay in the completion of his house, he had only half-jokingly remarked that the first tenant would be a French general in the army of occupation. The eventual 'casus belli' was one of the most ridiculous in the long, ridiculous history of warfare. Prussia was plotting to put a Hohenzollern prince on the Spanish throne, vacant after a revolution, thus arousing atavistic French fears of encirclement. The inflexible elements in both countries, headed by the Empress Eugénie's clique in Paris and Bismarck and Moltke in Berlin, were clamouring for war, but it looked as if wiser heads – Thiers in France and King William I in Prussia – would prevail. But then Bismarck famously altered the tone of the 'Ems telegram': a dispassionate statement became a provocative challenge, and all possibility of turning back was lost.

Everyone in Baden seemed convinced that the Imperial armies would soon be occupying their little town, less than an hour's march from the French frontier. Only the resonant mystique of the Emperor's name could account for this. Viardot and Turgenev, who kept a closer eye on international affairs than most of the predominantly pleasure-seeking denizens of the spa, were inclined to believe the opposite. They compared Napoleon's meandering Italian campaign of 1859, ending in the Pyrrhic victory of Solferino, with Moltke's seven-week methodical destruction of the Austrian army culminating in its crushing defeat at Sadowa, and wondered what future awaited them in the German province. The Viardots were in a quandary. Louis, for all his hatred of Napoleon III, was a Frenchman through and through; Pauline had been born, educated and married in Paris and, though she had had to struggle to succeed there, at this time of crisis she felt an instinctive loyalty to her adopted country. And it was not long before there was a noticeable change in the friendly welcome which the good 'Badenburgers', as Turgenev liked to call them, had previously extended to the foreign residents who brought so much lustre, not to mention lucre, to their town. One night the household was kept awake by a group of young people playing gaudy *Schrammelmusik* on a fiddle, accordion and barrel-organ for hours on end in the street outside their house: a not very subtle indication that from now on local music was going to have the upper hand over all the imported stuff that had been swirling out of the windows of the Villa Montebello. A more pressing concern involved their finances: the days of concerts and singing lessons were over; and none of the income they had been used to receiving from properties and other assets in France would any longer be crossing the border. For the first time in their lives, the Viardots were short of money.

Turgenev himself would not have been troubled, whatever turn the war took. Russia, although favouring France as the more despotic regime – and also further away – kept itself carefully out of the hostilities. But the moment the Viardots decided they would have to move, there was no question of his remaining. He tried to persuade them to spend some months at Spasskoye before coming to any final decision. It was a dream he had cherished for many years: a natural desire to return the hospitality he had enjoyed for so long, allied to a yearning to introduce his *de facto* family to the land where he had been formed and share with them his memories. In 1868 he had alerted Kiszinsky to provisions that might have to be made for the arrival of a whole family: this will be monsieur's room, this madame's, this for two young ladies; this must be repainted, this redecorated. He had cherished the thought of Didie walking along one of the garden paths, waving to him to join her. But Pauline's practical sense dispersed all such romantic dreams. They must go somewhere where she would be able to earn money, and that could only mean England. She was in some ways better known there than in France, having a faithful audience not only in the capital but also in provincial cities like Liverpool and

Manchester. The English had a great admiration, not always reciprocated, for her. She would certainly not lack for pupils; and on the strength of her reputation and influential acquaintances, if no longer of her voice alone, she would surely be asked to give the occasional recital and concert.

For three months after the war broke out, the Viardots managed to stay on in a Baden very different from the carefree pleasure-ground they had known. The hospitals filled up with wounded French soldiers; the tuneful melodies of the Konversazionhaus orchestra were replaced with the dull boom of the artillery shelling Strasbourg. They had hoped that the Rhinelanders, with all their ties to France and suspicions of the designs of Prussia, might at least remain neutral. But the uninterrupted series of Prussian victories fostered a nascent pan-Germanic pride; and an accumulating series of small acts of spite convinced the family that their presence was no longer welcome.

In October, Turgenev accompanied Pauline, Didie and Marianne to Ostend, where he put them on the boat for Dover. He then returned by train to Baden to rejoin Louis, who had stayed behind with Paul to try and take whatever measures he could to safeguard his property from the ravages of war. The return journey involved frequent delays; to while away a forced overnight stay in Cologne, Turgenev wrote to Pauline: 'In my compartment was a lady with an outsize wig, the biggest nose I have ever seen and a forest of red hairs on the end of her chin; her husband continually referred to her as "my beautiful angel". I am not inventing!... I have naturally thought of nothing but you; this separation' (they had taken leave of each other the previous day) 'is very painful – I am going to move heaven and earth to persuade Viardot to leave Baden at the earliest opportunity...' And in this he was successful. By the middle of November, they were all once again reunited in London, the Viardots finding lodgings in Devonshire Place and Turgenev eventually settling in nearby Beaumont Street.

Turgenev's fluctuating views during the course of the Franco-Prussian war confirmed all the prejudices of his many critics in Russia, from both left and right, who could never forgive him for not taking a consistent stand, preferably in accordance with their beliefs. The shift in his opinions was reflected in a series of letters he published in the *St Petersburg Chronicle*. He chose this mouthpiece in preference to the *Moscow Herald*, in which Katkov, with the tacit approval of the government, railed against Prussia's arbitrary use of force and called on all Europe to intervene on behalf of France; this blatant call for support of an authoritarian regime conveniently forgot that its ruler was the nephew of the man who had brought more misery on Russia than any other foreigner throughout its history.

At first, as Moltke's highly trained army swept all before it, Turgenev was outspokenly pro-Prussian. 'The existence of the Napoleonic regime', he wrote, 'is incompatible with the development of freedom. This is a war of civilization against barbarism. For all the affection I hold for the French people, Bonapartism must receive its just punishment'. After only six weeks fighting, Napoleon III, surrounded at Sedan, surrendered with his army of 85,000 men. The Second Empire was over. Turgenev had no pity for the fallen sovereign: 'This miserable wretch has finally fallen into the cesspit with his entire clique. What a joy to have lived to see the day! But why is this individual treated with such respect? Let him be devoured by lice in Cayenne, that is all he deserves.'

But as the war progressed, it became harder to see in Bismarck the descendant of his beloved Goethe. For him, Germany represented the land he had known in his youth; a land of philosophers and poets, in love with dreamy idealizations and Utopian dreams. What he was discovering now was a country dominated by ruthless, brutal militarism. He was deeply distressed by the burning of the great library at Strasbourg, and opposed to the annexation of Alsace and Lorraine. 'I begin to no longer understand and, I'm afraid, soon no longer to recognize the German people. I cannot pretend that the greed for conquest that has seized the whole of Germany offers an edifying spectacle.' And in September, with the proclamation in France of the Third Republic, his allegiance definitively changed. 'It is now not Germany, but France that is fighting for freedom.' At this point, the *St Petersburg Chronicle* suspended publication of his letters.

He himself was now in the Russian capital, drawn reluctantly away from London by a renewed need for money. The success of the Prussian armies, who were now besieging Paris, had had a disastrous effect on his son-in-law's business, and every week brought a more desperate letter from Paulinette begging for help. His new manager, Kiszinsky, was not turning out as well as he had hoped, and he was receiving very little more income than he had in Uncle Nikolai's day. While in St Petersburg, he arranged through a friend for the sale of one of his properties, and wrote to Paulinette enclosing 5000 francs in advance of a larger sum which she would receive on completion of the sale; what she did not know was that he also bought 17,500 francs of railway stock, which he made over to Didie, thereby substantially increasing the dowry he had already established for her. He also arranged for the publication of another volume of Pauline's songs, despite the initial reluctance of the publisher, Johansen, who had lost money on the previous ones; it was agreed that Turgenev would finance the publication out of his own pocket on the understanding that Pauline would never know about it.

It was while he was in St Petersburg that Paris was plunged into the two-month convulsion of the Commune. Thiers, who had become chief of the executive in order to make the least humiliating possible peace terms with Bismarck, established his government in Versailles and determined to crush the heirs of the Jacobins who had taken control of Paris and shown remarkable heroism in resisting the privations and near-starvation of the long Prussian siege. But the terms he was forced to accept at the Treaty of Frankfurt only increased the Parisians' fury: apart from the indemnity of five thousand million francs, which promised to ruin an already impoverished country, Alsace and Lorraine were handed over to Germany and the victorious army was granted the right to stage a triumphal march down the Champs-Elysées. This humiliation kindled the long-suppressed patriotic pride of the Parisians. The spark that set off the conflagration was Thiers's order that the four hundred cannon stationed at the top of Montmartre, and paid for by the subscription of the inhabitants, should be removed from the hands of the National Guard. There was fierce resistance and two generals, Clément-Thomas, who had previously commanded the Guard, and Lecomte, who was in charge of the detachment sent to remove the guns, were captured by the Parisians, taken to a nearby garden and summarily shot. Paris elected its Commune and civil war broke out between the Central Committee and the predominantly royalist government stationed at Versailles. The carnage was horrendous: the communards, though less bloodthirsty than their opponents, executed a number of hostages, among them the gentle Monseigneur Darboy, Archbishop of Paris; when the Versailles army finally entered Paris in May, after a week of street fighting, 147 communards were shot against a wall at the cemetery of Père Lachaise and at least 20,000 others lost their lives.

Turgenev was appalled by the news. Never before had he been so 'Parisian' as during those two months. He wrote to Flaubert: 'Have you worked… or have you just dragged yourself from one empty, heavy day to another? I am not French, but that is just about all I have been able to do. Ah, we have some ugly moments to endure, we 'born spectators'…'

Flaubert's answer came a month later, after the uprising had been crushed. '… I spent all last week in Paris. Even more lamentable than the ruins is the *mental* state of its inhabitants. You navigate between cretinism and enraged folly… Never have spiritual interests counted for less. Never has hatred of all grandeur, contempt for the beautiful, execration of literature been so manifest… I have always tried to live in an ivory tower. But a tidal wave of shit is battering against the walls and may well bring it down…'

Hearing in St Petersburg of each day's latest catastrophe through the official French dispatches, Turgenev wrote almost daily to Pauline, sympathizing particularly with what that staunch old republican, Louis, must be feeling about the state of his country. At first, as the news issued exclusively from the government at Versailles, he, like the rest of the world, was convinced that all the barbarity was committed by the communards; later, with his habitual fair-mindedness, he was able to apportion the blame more equally. 'These fearful reports coming from Paris,' he wrote, 'absorb me completely and fill me with despair. The most recent news – the barbarous execution of the two generals – is especially deplorable as, by the use of force, it destroys all the sympathy in which France was held by the rest of Europe and plays straight into the hands of the enemies of freedom. "You see!" people here are saying, "You see where those glorious principles of 1789 lead!" What will happen to France? Could it be that the nation which we love so much, to which we owe so much, is destined to become another Poland or Mexico?' Political preoccupations then gave way to personal anxieties. 'What will become of your assets: the house in rue de Douai, the farm at Courtavenel, your shares? Here, everyone connected with financial affairs is shrugging their shoulders. "France?" a banker said to me yesterday. "A sinking ship."'

None of these worries prevented him from being absorbed back into the familiar social and artistic world of St Petersburg which, despite his frequent protestations to London of missing Devonshire Place, he found far from disagreeable. He had two sittings with Nikolai Gay, a well-known painter who had done a portrait of Belinsky, taken from a death mask and old lithographs, and one of Herzen. He was granted a long audience with Grand Duchess Elena Pavlovna, who admitted sadly that she had lost much of her influence with Alexander since the attempted assassination and the removal of her protégés from all positions of influence. He was able to do the suddenly impecunious Viardots a good turn by selling her a Rembrandt from Louis's collection. He attended a number of operas and concerts but pointedly neglected to hear Adelina Patti, who, he was horrified to report, was receiving 40,000 roubles for her appearance.

He even found, to his agreeable surprise, that the resentment aroused by *Smoke* was beginning to abate. He was invited to take part in an evening entertainment inspired by Garibaldi's intervention in the Franco-Prussian war on the side of the French. The popular Italian hero's volunteer force had even managed to win a minor victory over the all-conquering Germans near Dijon. Proceeds were to go to the wounded French. The proposed programme consisted of a heterogeneous series of 'turns', Turgenev being asked to read a passage from one of his works. When he discovered that the other contributions would have been more at home in the raucous atmosphere of a music hall than the hushed silence of the readings he was accustomed to give, he regretted having accepted and was relieved when, the authorities fearing a pro-revolutionary demonstration, the evening was called off. But the organizers managed to effect a compromise: it was agreed that if no mention were made either of Garibaldi or the wounded soldiers, the performance could proceed. Turgenev consoled himself with the thought that he would be addressing the young audience he so much wished to reach through his books. He decided to read the story *Bailiff*, the most outright of all the *Sportsman's Sketches* in deploring the arrogance of the landowners and the grovelling, sycophantic brutality of their hirelings in their treatment of the serfs.

When the evening came, he found himself in even stranger company than he had expected…

St Petersburg,
10 March, 1871.

… So after all, dear and good Madame Viardot, my reading took place, but under rather different circumstances to those I am familiar with. My name was at the head of the playbill, boldly displayed alongside 'FRESH OYSTERS'. The musical contributions were execrable – how thankful I was that you were not there! – but there was a huge enthusiastic audience made up almost entirely of young people. My intervention was preceded by a Mademoiselle Lovato, who 'performed' – I use the word advisedly – a song with the oft-repeated refrain: 'It's not in my nose that I feel that itch'. I was followed by a buxom lady with a cracked voice who gave us Schumann's lied to Heine's The Two Grenadiers, *which, as you will remember, ends with the piano evoking the Marseillaise; explosions of frenetic 'bravos', cries of* Vive la France! *lasting ten minutes.*

As for me, I have to admit that never in my life have I been the object of such – excuse the word – ovations. I only tell you this because I know it will give you pleasure. I thought of you all the time that I was standing there, embarrassed, red in the face, with what I hope passed for an impassive smile on my face, in front of that yelling crowd… The inferences of my tale were clearly to their taste, and I really believe that I read it quite well, feeling strangely calm amongst the general brouhaha, probably because of the evident sympathy of all those young people. How fickle a mistress is public taste! It seems that I have become very popular in St Petersburg…

But do not think for a minute that all this has caused me to forget where I belong. On the contrary, to the deep and unchangeable feeling I have for you has been added the impossibility of being without you: your absence causes me physical anxiety; it's as if I were lacking air, it's a hidden, muffled pain which I cannot get rid of and nothing can distract me from. When you are there, my joy is calm, I am in my element, at home, and I wish for nothing else…

It was now that the cholera epidemic struck and he took refuge, first with Annenkov and then in Moscow. His panic-stricken letter to Pauline…

'…I fear it like the Green Devil; I've spent a ghastly three nights, anguish, spasms, cold sweat, insomnia, etc.. I'm ashamed to be such a coward, but there must be some physiological cause which is stronger than I am, since no other disease inspires this terror in me…'

prompted an unusually heartfelt reply…

'Oh, my dear friend, hurry up and come back. Don't stay an hour longer than is absolutely necessary. I beg you, if you have the least affection for us, do not return via St Petersburg, or at least don't stay there.

Promise me under no circumstances to let yourself be detained in that fatal city. Please!…

 Are you going to Spasskoye? I hope not. Have your <u>young</u> portrait sent to us. And yes, write every day and come back, dear friend, come back to people who do not know how to be happy without you…'

As always, he did as he was told and was back in England at the beginning of April. He worked on a story he had had in mind for some time about the destructive power of sexual passion, featuring a woman who would make *Smoke*'s Irina seem like a Poor Clare. He spent as much time as he could at Devonshire Place, watching with concern and pride as Pauline took pupils for a quarter of what she had received in Baden-Baden and performed in concerts for a fraction of her normal fee. None of the trio was enamoured of life in London, nor of most of its citizens. 'You have to put up with them,' Turgenev remarked, 'as you do with the weather.' They admired but did not love. It was no secret between them that they were only there because that was where Pauline could still command reasonable fees. He mixed again with literary figures – Tennyson, Swinburne, George Eliot – and struck up a friendly relationship with Lord Houghton. This curious figure endeared himself immediately to the exiles for having travelled widely in France, Germany and Italy, thereby distinguishing himself from his insular compatriots. Born Richard Monckton-Milnes, poet, critic and liberal politician, who rejoiced in his sobriquet of 'bird of paradox', he had been one of the first admirers of Keats, whose work he later edited; and he still helped younger poets, especially Swinburne. Houghton was widely noted for his breakfasts – to which the only requirement for an invitation was to be famous – and in more restricted circles for his extensive collection of erotica, including all the principal works of de Sade. It was at his instigation that Turgenev travelled to Edinburgh to make a modest contribution to the festivities celebrating the centenary of the birth of Walter Scott. Excerpts from his speech were thus reported in the *Edinburgh Evening Courier*…

> Mr Torquenoff, replying in the name of Russia, said – I will not dwell upon the feelings of personal gratification to which your kind reception has given rise… hasten to say what pleasure I experience at representing on so memorable an occasion… in a city so illustrious… Russia and its literature. My country is so little known in Western Europe that it may be that I shall astonish you when I say how great has been the influence of English literature there… never greater than it is now. (Applause) Of this great influence of England… this classic land of wise liberty and free thought, (Applause) the chief founders were Byron and Scott. (Applause) All our best writers have been sincere admirers… of your great Master of Romance. Our poet, Tourhaine, above all, paid a true cultus to Walter Scott… Of all that sacred legion of great men who, though foreign to its soil, have taken part in the

intellectual development of Russia, no one perhaps has earned more
gratitude, has gained more affection, than Walter Scott, and proud and happy
am I to be this day the interpreter to Scott's compatriots of that affection and
that gratitude. (Loud cheers)

Turgenev enclosed a clipping of this piece with a letter he wrote to Pauline from
Scotland. The Viardots had gone back to the continent, first to Paris and then to
Baden-Baden, to ascertain what effect the war had had on their properties.

Caledonian Hotel,
Edinburgh,
10 August, 1871.
Midday.

*Ouf! dear Madame Viardot, how hot it is… and even worse yesterday at the 'Commemoration'. I
made my little speech in a weak squeaky voice, I floundered a couple of times, there was applause and
cheers, but let it be said between us that Mr Torquenoff was acutely aware that he was totally unknown
to everyone (in good company, at any rate, as Pushkin was transcribed as Tourhaine!) and speaking of
something to which they were quite indifferent. If I were asked to do it all over again, I should refuse, as
it is useless, if not ridiculous.*

*I am supposed to leave tomorrow for Pitlochry, where Mr Bensen has invited me to shoot grouse.
But he neglected to tell me how I was to get from the station to his house. Scottish hospitality… do you
only exist in the novels of Walter Scott?*

*I will write to you again this evening, perhaps from Mr Bensen's house, perhaps from the Pitlochry
station hotel.*

*Oh, why did I ever come to this **** Scotland?*

Allean House,
Pitlochry.
Saturday, 13 August, 1871.

Dear and good Madame Viardot,

*You have always taken such a keen interest in my 'missions of slaughter', as you call them, that I am sure
you will derive some pleasure from a short account of my pursuit of the famous Scottish grouse. Two features
are uppermost in my mind:*
1) It is abominably exhausting, a pastime for a young man, and I have not been that for a long time.
*2) You have to walk with another 'gun', as they call hunters here, and mine was young, enthusiastic and
devilishly agile. I did not take to this Siamese twin aspect, especially as he dispatched his birds with the
ruthless efficiency of a peregrine falcon, whereas I shot horribly badly: I missed my first 9 birds and only*

brought down 22 from at least 50 shots. His 'bag' – you see, I am picking up the jargon! – was 76.

The weather was superb and they served us a good lunch on the moors... but this is not a sport for me. I have never in all my hunting experience been so tired (the mountains here are very high), and I even managed to twist my ankle. No, no, long live quiet days in the Black Forest, where one is not coupled with a madman with legs like a deer's who, every time one pauses to catch one's breath, shouts: 'Come on! Come on!'...

Monday, 15 August.

I was interrupted by an announcement that dinner was nearly ready (at half past six!) and although I was dying to go to bed, had to spend a long evening – after an excellent meal, I must say – listening to Mrs Bensen murdering Schubert and Schumann (a crime that I might perhaps except from my general condemnation of capital punishment), and 'mixing' with the local gentry who included Robert Browning, whom I found exceptionally vain and not at all amusing, and his son, a nice enough young man with a huge red wart on the end of his nose.

Despite my protestations, I was out on the moors again today. It was so taken for granted that I would be present, that the honour of Russia was practically at stake. Even my poor ankle couldn't serve as an excuse. Mr Bensen kindly provided me with a pony to help cover the endless distances. Fortunately, I was not allotted my Saturday companion (the man with the seven league boots); instead I was with Mr Bensen, who is no more a hunter than he is a marmot, and Browning's son, who thinks he is (a hunter, not a marmot), but is just a simple young man with a famous, and very boring, father. There was less game, but I performed a bit better (18 birds from about 40 shots). I will not go down in Pitlochry as a 'capital shot', but at least I avoided humiliation.

I am leaving tomorrow, but fortunately received your welcome letter this morning. So... you were 'charmed' by Paris. After all the poor city has been through, that is good news indeed. I think your decision to return to rue de Douai is a good one. The evil consequences of war survive long after hostilities have ceased, and neither of you, especially Louis, would ever be able to live again in Baden the way we did for those happy six years. And while I'm on that subject, what would you both think of the idea – since you mention renting some rooms – of my becoming your tenant? It would cost me less than a hotel; and at least you would be sure that the rent would always be paid! This is an idea that has just this minute come to me. Think about it and let me know your opinion. It could be a good solution for all of us.

My friendly greetings to everyone in Baden, starting with Viardot.

I tenderly kiss your hands.

Your,
I.T.

Louis and Pauline found it an excellent solution. After years of 'keeping up pretences' in Baden and London, they finally felt they could afford to ignore the malicious whispers of a few *salons*. Louis was 71, Turgenev 53 and Pauline 50. From now on they presented the front of a common family unit. When they went out to social events or artistic manifestations, Paris soon grew used to seeing the five of them arrive together… or increasingly often, the four of them, as Louis became more and more reclusive and Turgenev adored chaperoning his three 'ladies'. If he suffered occasional pangs of regret at the loss of his own 'nest', which he had taken such pains to build, he esconced himself comfortably again on the edge of someone else's and consoled himself with the thought that only death could now separate him from the object of his lifelong veneration… and from her daughter, who was rapidly taking up almost as much room in his heart. Didie was now an attractive young woman of twenty who showed a distinctive talent as a painter and adored her 'godfather', her beloved Tourgel, whose letters left no doubt of the strength of his affection. When he was away from Paris in the following years, he wrote more often to her than to her mother. And there was the same intimate, humorous, flirtatious tone that marked his correspondence with Pauline in the fifties… in notable contrast to the dutiful, but formal letters he wrote to Paulinette, even when, after three miscarriages, she finally gave birth to a daughter, Jeanne, named after her grandfather…

Dear Paulinette,

It gave me the greatest pleasure to receive Gaston's letter with the welcome news, and to little Jeanne I return with interest the kiss that was sent to me in her name. I am very happy to hear that all went well; continue to be prudent and wise, and you'll see that you will lack nothing for your complete happiness.

I'm afraid my old enemy, gout, has attacked me again, and I am writing this from my bed. This means that unfortunately I cannot announce with precision when you can expect me at Rougemont; but as soon as I begin to convalesce, I shall not fail to let you know. One thing I would ask of you: try not to choose a date for the baptism between the 1st and 16th of September; this is the only period when I might be able to go hunting, and I would be reluctant to renounce all possibility of doing so. But in this case too, I'm afraid, Man proposes and Gout disposes!

In any case, I hope to see you soon, and in the meantime embrace all three of you very tenderly…'

I. Turgenev.

Three months after Didie's marriage to Georges Chamerot, of whom, fortunately, Turgenev wholeheartedly approved, he wrote from Spasskoye:

Dear Didie-of-my-heart,

I have just received your charming letter, and you see that if I didn't write before, at least I reply immediately after. You do not need to ask me not to forget you: you know very well that from the moment

I first saw you (you were five, weren't you?), I have been your property and you my proprietor. I will take advantage of this declaration to give you the biggest smack of a kiss imaginable, and then I will proceed.

How happy you make me when you say in your letter that you enjoy my work. I've always searched after truth in what I do, since if one can't award oneself any other merit, at least there is that. But it's not always so easy to render the truth; it must be like you with a portrait. There are certain figures I have never dared attempt, for fear of getting them wrong. There was, for example, an enchanting young girl of my acquaintance (I say 'there was' because she became a woman just three months ago) whom I would have loved to insert into one of my tales, but I lacked the artistic courage. I wonder if by any chance you know this young girl?…

You say on the first page of your letter, how good it is to be alive. Let me tell you, it is good not only for you but for all those who have the good fortune to know you and are happy just to see you live. As for your old friend, you know that you are the sunshine of his days and that without you the sky is a leaden grey. When I see you in the morning, your eyes leave me with a ray which lasts throughout the day. I cannot wait for that ray to shine on me again.

And now, Madame, as I must get used to calling you, imagine that you are sitting on the edge of the billiard table and I am standing in front of you. You are swinging your adorable little feet, as you often do; I catch them, I kiss them, one after the other – then your hands, then your face; and you let me, because you know there is no one in the world I adore more than you.

Your old godfather,

I.T.

Before taking up what was to become his permanent residence in rue de Douai, Turgenev returned in August to Baden-Baden to negotiate the sale of the Viardots' property, including his own house, which now belonged to Louis. He had hoped to stay there only for a few weeks, as everywhere he went he was haunted by memories of past, irretrievable happiness. But the business transactions, which in any case he was ill-equipped to conduct, dragged out much longer than he had thought and he was soon crippled by an especially painful attack of gout in the knee. Unable to move from his bed for three weeks, he took the opportunity to finish *The Torrents of Spring*, another story in which he examined the two aspects of love that had obsessed him all his life: the simple, spontaneous love of the enchanting young Gemma, who, though Italian, could well claim a place in his gallery of pure Russian heroines; and the sensually rapacious Maria Nikolayevna Polozova, who seduces his protagonist, Sanin, simply for the pleasure of conquest and the triumph of wresting him from his attachment to Gemma. Another Turgenev unheroic hero laments his lost love and his inability to resist the designs of a strong, unscrupulous woman.

He finally succeeded in selling the Baden properties to a wealthy Moscow banker, returned to Paris in November and moved into rue de Douai. His four rooms – living-room, study, library and bedroom – were on the third floor, reached by a carved wooden staircase. The walls were lined with green silk, the inevitable enormous sofa was covered with green velvet and even the panels of the doors were painted green. Taking advantage of Viardot's expert knowledge and fastidious taste, he began to buy some paintings, and was particularly attached to a Théodore Rousseau landscape; elsewhere a Corot vied with a marble bas-relief of Pauline in profile and a plaster-cast of her right hand. Soon after moving in he installed a speaking-tube that linked his study with Pauline's music room directly below it, so that whenever she sang he would not miss a note. Thirty years after they met, she was now the constant presence in his life that he had always wished her to be.

Over the coming years there came to visit him in these few small rooms what the Viardots must have thought of as half the Russian population of Paris. And not only his aristocratic friends, who would occasionally attend Pauline's Thursday musical *soirées*; much more often his visitors were students, exiles, unpublished writers, the often desperate, always impoverished young, seeking out their famous elderly liberal compatriot to glean from him a word of advice or a few francs with which to placate importunate landlords.

Dismayed by the shaggy, uncouth, sometimes unwashed appearance of some of these visitors, and genuinely anxious to protect her friend from the consequences of his own good nature, Pauline would remonstrate with him.

"The word will soon reach every penniless Russian student in Paris that there's a spring in rue de Douai that never dries up. Besides, by the looks of some of them, we'll have the police keeping an eye on the house soon. No one knows better than you how easily the report of an innocent meeting in Paris can become an act of treasonous rebellion by the time it reaches St Petersburg. And you still have enemies there. You must be more careful about who you agree to see, Ivan."

"I'll try. But there's something you don't realize. If you think they are using me, I am using them too... without their knowing it."

"What in heaven's name do they have to offer you?"

"Themselves. I've been thinking for some time now about a novel which would deal with the idealistic young in Russia today. A sort of sequel to *Fathers and Children*."

"You said after the way everyone lambasted you for *Smoke*, you would leave politics out of your work from now on. You kept to that in *Torrents of Spring* and look how well it was received."

"Yes, I know, that was the way I felt then. But the position is different now. It seems there is something of a sea change in the attitudes and outlook of the young.

I even sensed it in the way I was treated on my last visit. I believe now – at last – I can reach them, and I can't give up without one more effort."

"How does this 'sea change' manifest itself?"

"Annenkov spoke of it in his last letter. "Your nihilists are turning into populists," he said. "I don't think Bazarov would recognize them.""

"Populists?"

"Yes. The best of them are turning away from violent solutions and trying directly to help the peasants better themselves rather than inciting them to embark on a revolution which could only end in appalling bloodshed. With most of the blood spilt being theirs. Their new hero is Lavrov and his *Historical Letters* their new bible. Now do you see why I need to talk to these young people here? It's not enough for me to hear about them from Annenkov. I must know them at first hand, otherwise Dostoevsky will take it into his head to send me a telescope. And you know better than anyone that I cannot start an important work with just an 'idea'; I need to be struck by an image, and in developing that image some ideas may creep in behind its back. These young people who come to see me are worth more to me than any amount of letters telling me what their contemporaries are up to in Moscow and St Petersburg. But now that I have stored their faces and stories in my mind, it will be useful to talk to Lavrov, who is expected here in Paris very soon."

"Who is this Lavrov?" Pauline asked. "Will I be allowed to meet him, or will you try to smuggle him in some time when I'm out, as I gather you have done with some of the others?"

Turgenev gave her a reassuring smile. "On the contrary, I think he would be an ornament at one of your dinner parties. He's no starving, embittered student. He's only four or five years younger than me. He was an artillery colonel who taught mathematics in the St Petersburg military academy. Word got out that he was a sympathizer with the 'Land and Liberty' movement and after Karakosov's assassination attempt he was banished to the Vologda region. There, by one of those mysteries that are inexplicable to anyone outside Russia, he succeeded in publishing in a small journal, under a pseudonym, a series of what he called 'Historical Letters'. It seems hardly an exaggeration to say that these are changing the political face of Russia."

"What did they say to do that?"

"The burning conviction behind them is that every educated man and woman in Russia would enjoy none of the comforts and advantages they so effortlessly take for granted were it not for the toil of the illiterate masses. They therefore owe those masses a debt which it is now time to repay."

"How?"

"By making any sacrifice necessary to improve their lot. Giving up their comfortable lives and going to live with the peasants, teaching them to read and write, ensuring they have decent medical care, informing them of their rights and gradually preparing them for revolution."

"Ah! So revolution is still essential?"

"Apparently he believes so. I, as you know, do not. That is something I look forward to discussing with him. But he emphasizes that the task of the educated for the moment is to enlighten the people, not enflame them. In this he differs from our friend Bakunin who is still exhorting every man, woman and child to take up arms tomorrow. If the young people who come to see me are anything to judge by, Lavrov is having the sort of impact on them that Belinsky had on my generation. And in that too he differs from Bakunin. Michel is always preaching, laying down the law, telling people what they should do; Lavrov is more Socratic: he wants to draw out of people what is already there inside them. You should have seen the look of veneration in the eyes of one of my visitors. 'For us,' he told me, 'the *Historical Letters* were like the gospels, they stimulated us both ideologically and emotionally. The style was so abstract that each of us could take whatever we wanted and make it our own. They solved,' these were his actual words, 'they solved the problems of life for us.'"

"Blessed be the man who can do that! Yes, I think I should like to meet him. But you say he was exiled."

"He escaped from Vologda after four years and made his way to Zürich. But he is expected here very shortly, and has already written to me to say he hopes he can meet me."

Lavrov made a favourable impression on Turgenev from the moment he met him at the end of 1872. A short, stout man of fifty, his only distinguishing physical characteristic was a luxuriant and perpetually unkempt black beard. A pair of watery pale blue eyes seemed to peer vaguely out into the world as if bemused by its incomprehensibility. The potential awkwardness of a first meeting between the theoretical revolutionary and the urbane man of letters was soon dissipated when Lavrov recounted his brief flirtation with Bakunin in Zürich. The inveterate firebrand was trying to recover some of the authority he had forfeited by having become, and so clearly been seen to become, the dupe of Sergey Nechaev. This terrifying young man, who proclaimed that the true revolutionary should have no personal interests or sentimental attachments of any kind, neither of friendship nor love, that might distract him from his single aim of pitiless destruction, had easily convinced Bakunin that he was the head of a vast revolutionary organization in Russia; and that he had been arrested, tortured and incarcerated in the Peter and Paul fortress, from which he had made a miraculous escape. None of this was true. What was true was that he had planned and executed the murder of one of his followers, who was becoming suspicious of him and whom he falsely accused of preparing to betray his comrades. Bakunin readily accepted his story that this was vicious propaganda put out by his enemies and enthusiastically took the promising disciple under his wing. It was not long before the ruthless young fanatic was leading the ageing anarchist by the nose. It took a year before some of the truth began to sink into Bakunin's reluctant consciousness and another three months before evidence of Nechaev's treachery and financial chicanery led to the final breach. In the meantime, most of the rest of the Russian exiles, who had seen through Nechaev's machinations long before, began to keep Bakunin at a distance; Marx used the episode a couple of years later to engineer his expulsion from the First International.

Lavrov had not been in the Swiss town for more than a few days before he received a visit. Dazzled at first by the man's legendary reputation, boundless enthusiasm and enormous charm, he made the fatal initial mistake of mentioning that he had it in mind to start a journal: it was to be called *Forward!*, and would aim to fulfil more or less the same function as Herzen's *Kolokol* in its days of glory. Turgenev was unable to hide a smile when told that Bakunin had immediately welcomed the idea and suggested that he become a collaborator. Lavrov, who was completely without funds, needed above all some form of financing, and with that in mind initially welcomed the idea. They agreed to think it over, Bakunin said he would draft a proposal, and they would meet again in a couple of days.

"May I hazard a guess at what took place at that meeting?" Turgenev asked. "He arrived at least an hour late, seized your hands in an iron grip and proclaimed how proud and excited he was at the idea of the two of you being joint-editors of 'our paper'."

"How could you possibly know?" Lavrov asked, dumbfounded. "I know that news travels quickly in this claustrophobic world of ours, but it happened so recently. Who told you?"

"No one told me. I have known Michel all my life and I truly believe he can no longer surprise me. I take it that I was not far from the truth."

"The only detail that escaped you was that, before I could say a word, taking our co-editorship for granted, he insisted on having the right of approval on all articles. Including my own! And on seeing my stupefaction (I was unable at first even to stammer out a definitive 'no'), he added: 'Otherwise *Forward!* will inevitably become a wishy-washy version of *Kolokol.*'"

Turgenev smiled. "How did it end up? Did you just agree to go your separate ways?"

Lavrov shook his head reflectively. "Oh no. When I gave a blank refusal to his terms, he stalked out in a rage, vowing that I would regret my decision. And in a pamphlet that came out a few days later, he denounced me by name as doctrinaire, patronizing and ineffectual. It had a rather unfortunate effect. As there are quite a lot of young people in Zürich who share my views, they took strong exception to this article and came to blows with several of Bakunin's disciples in cafés all over the town. The police had to intervene and it didn't do my position in Zürich any good. That's one of the reasons I've come to Paris."

"Apart from trumpeting his opposition to you, did he put forward any beliefs of his own?"

"Oh yes. He clearly hasn't learnt much from the Nechaev episode. He declared that young Russians must go to the people with one aim and one aim only: to incite them to partake in immediate revolution. What I had had to say in my *Historical Letters* were recommendations that could only be explained by a craven fear of the results of such action. Spreading literacy was a waste of time under an autocracy, since all the masses required was their instinctive drive towards violent insurrection. And those of us who thought otherwise were tainted by a bourgeois arrogance that took it for granted that our values were superior to those of the people."

"He has learnt nothing," Turgenev mused. "Unlike Herzen who, for all the differences between us, was beginning at the end of his life to come round to what I had been trying to convince him of for twenty years. That your average muzhik is every bit as conservative as his former masters. His whole dream is to become as much as possible like them."

"That is true of some of them no doubt. But by no means all. And it is to the others that the privileged and the educated must go to enlighten them, to prepare them for the coming of socialism, whether it arrives by means of revolution or not."

"And you think there is fertile ground for the seed to fall on? I would like to think you are right, but it requires an optimism of which I fear I am no longer capable. But you must tell me about these young people with their sense of mission. I have the highest admiration for their dedication, even though I can't help feeling they are doomed to failure. It was even in the back of my mind to write a book about them…"

Turgenev was to see Lavrov frequently over the next years. Expecting a firebrand, he had found a deeply reflective man whose views coincided closely enough with his own to make the occasional differences matters for amicable discussion, rather than impatient breakdown. 'He is a pigeon' he confided to Annenkov, 'who would like to pass for a sparrow-hawk.' When a small London press agreed to publish *Forward!*, he guaranteed him a subvention of 500 francs a year on condition that it remained a secret between the two of them. As Pauline told him with a mixture of affection and exasperation, the fact was that at this time he was leading a double life. If the cream of Parisian society, entranced by his charm, fame and polyglot culture, competing for his attention at one of Princess Rakhmanova's soirées or hanging on his lips at the embassy dinners presided over by his friend, Prince Nikolai Orlov, had known of the unkempt, bedraggled figures who climbed the wooden staircase of rue de Douai, they would have bewailed the end of the world as they knew it.

lowly – more slowly than any of his other works – the novel that was to become *Virgin Soil* began to take shape. By the middle of 1874 he had decided on the main strands of the plot and made a list of the characters, with little biographies attached to them. He was determined to avoid the tendency to caricature, which had earned him so many brickbats over *Smoke*. This time the men and women who fleshed out his story, however extreme their politics, were to be real and recognizable. With no doubt in his mind that this would be the last important work he would write, he took endless care over details. 'I don't want to disappear from the surface of the earth,' he confided to Flaubert, whom he was visiting at Croisset, 'before finishing this new long novel of mine. I think it may dispel many past misunderstandings and place me where I think I belong. I hope it will be an answer to those of my fellow-countrymen who proclaimed after *Smoke* that I was alienated from Russia and had nothing more to say.'

Flaubert, the only French writer for whom he had unqualified respect, had become an invaluable confidant. The relationship between the two men, born out of mutual professional admiration, had developed into a close friendship. They wrote regularly and saw each other whenever Turgenev could find the time to visit him in his Normandy home, or Flaubert was ensconced in his Paris apartment in the rue Murillo. At the dinners with their friends they would talk in general of literary matters; but when alone they would often read extracts from their most recent work and occasionally offer advice, which was invariably well taken if not always followed.

On this occasion he was visiting Flaubert prior to embarking on a three-month journey to Russia. The two men had revealed to each other the main lines of the books on which they were about to start, in each case the most ambitious of their entire *oeuvre*. The French author, contemplating the mammoth research that would be necessary for *Bouvard et Pécuchet*, was always a little jealous of his friend's absences. But when he teasingly suggested that Turgenev's journey was an excuse to avoid the daily grind of writing (from which he himself hardly ever deviated), he was met with an answer of unexpected seriousness: "No, it is absolutely necessary for me. I must make the places and people in this novel as immediately recognizable as you made Yonville-l'Abbaye and its inhabitants in *Madame Bovary*. But you were talking about something with which you and your readers had been familiar all your lives; Yonville, you once told me, was almost a replica of a town half an hour's drive from where you were born."

"And your book is set in St Petersburg and the Russian countryside. What could be more familiar to you?"

"It's not the setting I'm worried about. It's the characters. I know more or less what they are going to do, but I don't really know yet who they are. The young, that is. The older people I am familiar enough with. The government servant with an assured future, Sipyagin, and his wife, for instance: seemingly broad-minded, pretending to understand and even share some of the anger of the young, liberal in conversation – even flirtatious on her part – but the moment talk gives way to action, reactionary and ruthless. Oh, I can do them all right. And some of the young too, I think. Those I see in Paris have been a great help to me, but most of them are exiles. They are not living at first hand the turmoil of thwarted hopes that is Russia today."

"Your protagonist, if I understand him right, is a not unfamiliar figure in your work. Could I call him the 'superfluous man' thirty years on – sickened by what he sees around him, brimming over with idealism but unable to decide where or how to focus it?"

"Yes, and my ideas are fairly clear about him. Nejdanov is what I call one of the 'romantics of realism'. They aspire towards the real as the Romantics did towards the ideal. But they have no time for poetry (Nejdanov even writes some, but is ashamed of it). They are looking for something splendid and meaningful. But they are constantly brought face to face with the fact that real life is not splendid and meaningful, it's prosaic and uninspiring. That's the way it is and always will be. Hence their miserable dissatisfaction with themselves… and their absurdity."

"In your terms, Hamlets who want to be Don Quixotes."

"Exactly."

"So who do you expect to have trouble with? Who do you want to track down in Russia?"

"The ones who do know where they are going. The ones with no doubts. The ones who frighten me."

"Be careful, my friend. They may not be very anxious to be seen with you. And the authorities may be even less anxious for you to be seen with them!"…

One of the aspects of populism that Turgenev was most interested in investigating was why so many young girls had joined the movement… and what sort of girls they were. His visitors in rue de Douai had all been male. He considered passing through Zürich on his way to Russia; of the large group of exiled students there, the majority were women, as one of the new laws promulgated by Count Dmitri Tolstoy, who had succeeded the liberal Golovnin as Minister of Education, was to forbid girls to enter Russian universities. But he was dissuaded by Lavrov, who had heard that his former secretary had been beaten up by the extremists and feared that neither age nor reputation might protect Turgenev from some sort of verbal, if not physical, attack.

He found what he was looking for in a place were he little expected it: Spasskoye. Porfiry had in his care a young woman from a family of rich Moscow merchants who had fled her background and was now acting as his assistant. "You wouldn't believe it," he told his half-brother. "There is nothing she is not prepared to do. Gently wash the filthiest of bodies, clean and dress suppurating, gangrenous wounds, spoon soup into mouths exhaling the foulest breath, wash a lifetime's growth of coarse matted hair free of lice... I have never known a nurse with half her dedication. The people round here are convinced she is a saint. How long she will survive is another matter. She insists on dressing in rags, even in the coldest months of winter and eating only enough to barely keep her alive. And with all this, she will not hear of a compliment. When I try to praise her for her self-abnegation, she puts a finger to my lips and gives me a mysterious smile. I have just had to compel her, almost physically, to take to her bed for a few days. She says there is nothing wrong with her, and medically I cannot argue with her. It's just that her body cannot begin to compete with her spirit."

When Turgenev asked if he could talk to her as soon as her condition permitted, Porfiry said he very much doubted if she would allow it: being in the presence of someone so famous would surely make her embarrassed and self-conscious. So the two of them hatched a plot whereby Turgenev would seemingly casually come round to Porfiry's *isba* when she was convalescing and stay for a few minutes. Warned that if he started asking probing questions she would fall mute and probably leave the room, he carefully confined himself to chatting with Porfiry about local conditions, occasionally addressing a question to her as if for confirmation. Only as he was leaving, feeling that he had broken down some of the nervous mistrust she had displayed at first, did he feel he could ask her one question which had been preying on his mind ever since he had heard her story.

"May I ask you if there was one moment in Moscow when you decided to make this radical change in your life?"

She thought for a moment and then the nearest thing he had seen to a smile hovered around her thin lips. "It wasn't a moment, Ivan Sergeyevich," she answered. "It was a decree."

"A decree?"

"Yes a decree, issued by the Chief of Police, shortly after the assassination attempt on the Czar."

"Saying what?"

Now the smile was unmistakable. "Giving orders to all his subordinates to ensure that the girls in their districts didn't cut their hair short, but put it up into a chignon. And wore crinolines..."

On another occasion, he went out to dine with neighbours with whom he had little in common except proximity. Tiring of the local gossip which had monopolized the conversation at the dinner table, he remarked, with all sincerity, on the excellent quality of the food that had been served.

"Ah, that's our Sofya," his hostess volunteered brightly, sharing a mysterious smile of complicity with her husband. "We brought her with us from St Petersburg."

"She must have attended one of the finest cookery schools. I haven't eaten better in Paris."

"To the best of my knowledge, she's never been to any school at all."

"Then where did she learn to prepare dishes like that?"

"Presumably from her family's cook. Or possibly even in Paris."

Turgenev looked at her husband. "I think Lizaveta Yurevna is pulling my leg."

"Only very gently," his host replied. "You see, our 'cook', Sofya Timofeyevna, is the daughter of General Khodarkovsky. His wife is a friend of Lizaveta's and she asked us to do her a favour. Sofya is one those deluded young girls who has got it into her head that it's her duty to devote her life to helping the poor. There's a regular outburst – almost an epidemic – of this sort of thing going on at the moment. A very admirable desire, of course, but it's not enough for her to donate some money to some charitable organization, as our sort of people have always done. Oh no, she said she had to go to live like the poor before she could know in what way she might help them. Her mother, in despair, asked my wife if she would take her on as a cook. At least she'd be sure that she lived in a decent house and would be properly fed and clothed."

His wife took up the story. "Of course I thought she would live with us and occasionally go down to the kitchen and supervise the menus. I was only too delighted to help. After all, the Khodarkovskys are one of the best families of Moscow. One of the wealthiest too, I might add. We even thought…" her husband, seeing her look over at their son, a handsome, silent young man of about twenty, coughed and she failed to finish the sentence. "Instead, from the moment she arrived, she has insisted on living in the servants' quarters, dressing like them, and refuses to take any part in our life at all. The only time I see her is in the mornings when she comes to take the day's orders."

Turgenev toyed with the stem of his wineglass and gave his hosts a quizzical glance. "You can't help admiring somebody with such inflexible principles, can you?", he asked.

His host didn't disappoint him. "I can," he retorted. "If you ask me, it's just a form of immaturity and self-indulgence. Think what it's doing to her poor family. And I shouldn't be at all surprised if our servants didn't feel embarrassed by her presence amongst them."

His son spoke up for the first time. "With respect, father" he said, "I don't think you're right about that."

"How would you know?" his father almost snapped.

"Well, when Matvei brought me my boots after cleaning them this morning, it just came into my head to ask him, quite casually, about Sofya. You should have seen his face light up. 'Oh, we all love her, young master,' he said. 'We were quite worried at first. We thought she'd put on a whole lot of airs and all that. But she doesn't. Not at all.' Then he gave a big grin. 'And we all eat so much better now.'"

His father frowned. "It would be better, young man, if you didn't interfere in matters which don't concern you."

"Yes, of course, father. I'm sorry." And the boy looked down at his plate and didn't open his mouth for the rest of the meal.

But Turgenev couldn't let the matter drop. "Nevertheless," he said, "I would be most interested to meet this young lady."

His hostess flung up her hands. "There you are, you see. That's what we're talking about. The only time since she arrived here that she has behaved like someone of her class was this morning, when I was dictating this evening's menu. I said we must serve something especially delicious tonight because we were going to be honoured with the presence of our great writer, Ivan Turgenev. You should have seen her! She practically dropped the pad she was writing on. She blushed all over her face and murmured something about how much she loved your books. I thought I saw my chance. I told her that after she had supervised the preparation she should change into something pretty and join us for dinner. I thought that was a nice gesture on my part. But you know what? She wouldn't hear of it. Absolutely refused. And nothing I could say would make her change her mind…"

Turgenev sniffed an opportunity he was determined not to miss. A couple of days later, on the pretext of a hunting excursion, he made his way to the back of his friends' house and spoke to a servant-girl who was bringing in laundry. It was a scorchingly hot day and he proffered a limp excuse about having tripped and lost all the water from his flask. He didn't want to disturb the master and mistress, as they would feel obliged to entertain him. But could someone bring him a drink for himself and also his dog, whose tongue was conveniently hanging out. He believed there was a cook called Sofya Timofeyevna (he had carefully memorized the name), perhaps she'd be so good as to…

To his surprise and relief, it worked. Only a moment after he had sat down at a wooden table in the shade, a young girl appeared, carrying a tray with a jug of kvass and a large bowl of water. She was wearing a simple black tunic, with a muslin scarf knotted around her head; but she might have been 'dressing down' for a costume ball for all that she looked part of her surroundings. She put the tray on the table, picked up the jug and was about to pour the visitor a glass when she glanced at his face. Transfixed, the jug poised in mid-air, she gasped: "Ivan Sergeyevich! Is it you?"

Turgenev got to his feet with a reassuring smile. "Don't be nervous, Sofya Timofeyevna. I'm afraid I have unscrupulously engineered this meeting. I was hoping I might have a few words with you."

She glanced guiltily around, then, seeing there was nobody about, perched on the edge of a chair and blurted out: "I shouldn't be doing this. But it's such an honour... I mean, your books have meant so much to me..."

"It is you who honour me," he said, resuming his seat. For a silent moment they gazed at each other, he noting the short cropped hair, strong aquiline nose and large grey eyes, she returning his glance with undisguised adoration. "Was there one you liked most?"

She thought for a moment. "*On the Eve*, perhaps." *Ah yes, of course, there she is, my Elena, 12 years on.* "And I loved *Fathers and Children*, but..."

"But?"

"Oh, it's not for me to say, but I wish you'd let Bazarov live. We so need people like him..."

"If you really feel that, perhaps you can help me."

"How can somebody like me help you?"

"By telling me about yourself. You see, I am trying to write a book which follows on from *Fathers and Children*. Not about the same people, but about how the young have developed, post-Bazarov, if you like. And what you are doing by coming to work here, and above all why you are doing it, is of fundamental importance. I don't live in Russia any more, you know, so daily life here is not constantly before my eyes. And I like to catch my characters alive."

"There is nothing particularly special about me. Hundreds of people are doing the same thing, and hundreds, perhaps thousands, more will."

"I know. But I have the privilege of talking to you. Perhaps I should add that nothing you tell me will be disclosed to anyone."

A peal of laughter revealed how attractive she could be when she felt at ease. "Except to all your readers."

"Ah, but they won't know my source. I was really referring to your present employers."

"I have nothing particular against them. They are decent enough people, by their own lights. As are my parents, by theirs. It's just that I feel stifled around them."

"Stifled? Can you be more specific?"

She leant her elbows on the table and dug her knuckles into her cheeks. "I don't know if I should tell you this, Ivan Sergeyevich. But it's as if I knew you a little through your books, and therefore feel you will understand. I'm ashamed to say it, but all my adult life I have been unhappy. Not unhappy for myself... that would be the basest ingratitude. But I've often felt as if I was suffering for all the oppressed, all the wretched in Russia. No, suffering is not the right word. Angry, indignant, rebellious, that's what I've felt. I looked around me and felt only disgust for all those plump, tranquil, self-satisfied people. And for myself above all. I burned with desire to do something. I felt I'd give my life to be able to change things. Instead, I was a well-brought-up young lady, a potential bride with a considerable dowry… in other words, a parasite, doing nothing and powerless to do anything. But that's enough about me. You don't want to…"

"On the contrary, I cannot hear enough. May I ask you one more question – rather a personal one?"

"Certainly."

"Do you have faith?"

"Religious faith, you mean?"

"Yes."

"Not that God will do it all by himself. I have faith in truth, and in justice. But the day of truth and justice for all will not come just by going to church on Sunday morning." She stood up. "I must go now. They'll be wondering in the kitchen what I'm up to. It's been a great honour talking to you, Ivan Sergeyevich. I admire you so much."

"No more than I admire you… and the sacrifice you are making."

"It's no sacrifice. I am happy here for the first time in my life. I am learning something new every day. At home, every day was the same."

"At the end of the summer, will you go back to Moscow, back to your family?"

"Oh no. I shall stay here."

"But they won't need a cook here in the winter."

"I shall find something else to do. I am already taking off a few hours teaching some of the kitchen-maids' children to read. Perhaps I will go and work in the local school. It's run by the deacon, so you can imagine what he teaches. There is so much need around here for people with a little education. I won't have any difficulty in finding an occupation."

Aware that the subject of his book might reawaken the dozing watchdogs of censorship, Turgenev had decided it should not take place in the actual present but a few years earlier, in 1868. This hardly made it a historical novel, but he accepted the experienced Annenkov's observation that, given the myopic vision of most of the censors, events taking place 'in the past' were more likely to slip through the net. A further discussion with Lavrov, soon after his return to Paris, confirmed the wisdom of this decision. The fierce reactionary tide in Russia showed no signs of ebbing. The authorities saw enemies of the state everywhere, especially since they were not, with some justification, at all clear as to who these enemies were. The struggle between the populists and the revolutionaries for the allegiance of Russian youth had not ended with the break between Lavrov and Bakunin. After Nechaev had been arrested in Zürich, extradited to Russia, tried and sentenced to life imprisonment in the Peter and Paul fortress where he died, unrepentant, ten years later, his place at the extreme edge of revolution had been taken by Pyotr Tkachev. This son of minor nobility, now in his late twenties, had been inspired, like so many others, by the *Historical Letters*. Exiled to the provinces for a tenuous connection with Nechaev, he had escaped to Switzerland, where for a while he had collaborated on *Forward!*. But he soon lost patience with Lavrov's gradualism and founded his own paper in Geneva, *The Tocsin*, in which he had just written an open letter to Lavrov proclaiming the necessity for immediate revolution. He foresaw that, as improvements were introduced into agriculture and industry, a conservative landed and bourgeois class would very soon be formed. Revolution, organized by an underground intellectual élite, had to strike before then, or too many interests would be threatened and it would be doomed to failure. *'That is why we cannot wait. That is why we assert that in Russia revolution is urgently necessary, and necessary precisely now. We do not admit any postponement, any delay. Now, or not for a very long time, perhaps never. Now circumstances operate in our favour, in ten of twenty years they will be against us.'*

Turgenev asked Lavrov about Tkachev. "He shares Nechaev's singlemindedness," he was told, "but not his inhumanity. I don't believe he would ever betray his comrades as Nechaev did. I respect him, but fear that if the course he advocates is followed, the consequences will be appalling."

"In Pushkin's words: 'God spare us from ever seeing a revolution in Russia. It would be absurd and pitiless'".

"It's as true now as then. I would try and convince Tkachev that there *is* still time for a peaceful solution. We would argue all night over it, but he was immovable. He would say that it's not theory and thought that steer the course of history but passion. This provides historic leaps forward when autocratic regimes go through a period of weakness. It happened for a while after the Crimean War and emancipation. But now reaction has settled in and the muzhik is far too passive to initiate anything himself. Yes, I would tell him, but he can be nudged and helped and instructed and shaken out of his passivity by a dedicated young intelligentsia."

"You think so?" Turgenev asked. "I would like to believe you are right."

"We shall soon find out. The battle is now joined. We will see who makes the greatest appeal to the Russian young. I am cautiously optimistic. I believe the example of Nechaev has convinced many of them that savage cruelty and the suppression of all natural human feelings is not the way to create the better world they are so anxious to bring about. I am hearing that many thousands of them are preparing to leave their families and go out into the country to share the lives of the peasants."

"They have my admiration and my blessing," Turgenev said. "Which do not, alas, alter my conviction that the end result of all their efforts will be a fiasco."

For four years Turgenev juggled with ideas and themes and characters for his book. Often on the point of abandoning it, he would always resume, driven by the conviction that it was his duty to make one final effort to communicate with the great mass of his countrymen who, he was sure, identified with neither the reactionaries nor the revolutionaries. The massive amount of work involved went some way towards allaying the sense of guilt he could never quite shake off over his failure to participate in the everyday life of his country. By the beginning of 1876, he finally felt he had all the material he needed and could see how he wanted to handle it. Knowing that the only place where he could write with undisturbed concentration was Spasskoye, he arranged to spend the summer months there and completed the first draft in six weeks. The only major interruption was his decision, long in maturing, to dismiss Kiszinsky, who had followed in the grand tradition of intendants of Spasskoye by systematically stealing from him. He confided in a letter to Flaubert:

'...I have never in my life worked as I have since arriving here on my monster novel. Sleepless nights, bent over my desk. I have toyed once again with the fancy that one can say things... not that have never been said before – I have no illusions about that – but at least say them in a different way. And at the same time I have been overwhelmed with financial and administrative matters, which take more out of me than goodness knows how many pages of scribble. Amongst other ungrateful tasks, I have had to show my estate manager the door, having discovered he has stolen from me something in the nature of 130,000 francs, a not inconsiderable proportion of my entire fortune. And so the other day I had the pleasure of watching from a window as the wretched man in whom I had had such confidence piled his belongings on to carts and drove away. You will not be surprised to hear that during this process I recognized several items which in fact belonged to me. Unable to bear the thought of another confrontation, I waited until he had vanished from sight and then dashed into the road, waved my fist after him and indulged in some venerable Russian oaths. Why have I been so stupid? Laziness, I suppose, led me to place a blind trust in the fellow, even though I often had the feeling, looking into that bushy-bearded, smooth-tongued countenance, that it belonged to a scoundrel. Ah well, too bad. Let him digest my money as best he can!'

While he was always happy to converse with Flaubert over matters of style, there was no replacing Annenkov for critical appreciation of the content of his work. His hope was that, in portraying the young revolutionaries with a critical but evidently sympathetic eye, he would avoid the contemptuous abuse he had incurred for his portrayal of the inconsequential chatterboxes grouped around Gubarev in *Smoke*. On his way back to France, he handed his friend the completed manuscript of *Virgin*

Soil and waited in some trepidation for his opinion. To his relief, this was generally favourable, but as usual Annenkov had some wise suggestions to offer. "This should get you into less trouble than *Smoke*. You haven't lambasted either the right or the left with such scorn. But you've still made judgements about Russia and her lack of civilization which, true as they may be, are simply going to fit arrows into your enemies' bowstrings. I've marked the most blatant; look through it and see if you can't cut, or at least modify, some of them."

"Very well. But tell me, how will the young see themselves reflected? I have tried to neither mock them nor idealize them.

"And you've succeeded. Not, I think, that that will make you wildly popular. The theme of your book is very clear: they are setting out, even if from the best of motives, on an impossible task, which is doomed to failure."

"But is it clear where my personal sympathies lie?"

"It will be to the best of them. The others will attack you as before. But at least at the end, the man who ends up as your hero, Solomin, comes from the same stock as they do. He may be a bit wooden – he's not a type you will have had much contact with – but his strength and sober common sense should appeal to all but the most violent. Your young women, especially Marianna, will earn you lots of feminine admirers. And I like the way you keep your Nechaev figure off the page. They all talk about him but we never meet him. That's good, as well as being wise. Now all we have to worry about is getting it published. In the present climate, the censors will not love you for the way you depict the figures of authority. Unless it makes your artistic conscience bleed, make those cuts I suggest."

Turgenev returned to Paris and spent three months transcribing, correcting and editing. Having broken definitively with Katkov over *Smoke*, he had been publishing over the past eight years in the *European Herald*; this liberal journal had been founded in 1866 by Mikhail Stasyulevich and rapidly became the favoured forum for leading authorities on artistic, political and social questions. Turgenev soon enjoyed a friendly and constructive working relationship with his new editor that he had not known since the early days of Nekrasov's *Sovremennik*. Stasyulevich had announced the appearance of the first half of *Virgin Soil* in the January 1877 issue. A month before, Turgenev feared that all his efforts to write the book he hoped would represent the summation of his life's work had been in vain. On December 6th over 200 students and workers met in the Cathedral of Our Lady of Kazan, where they prayed for Chernyshevsky, whose fragile health was succumbing to the rigours of north Siberia. They then marched out and paraded down the Nevsky Prospekt, waving red banners inscribed with the outlawed words *Land and Liberty* and shouting 'Long live the People!' and 'Death to the Czars!' Although they were soon rounded up and the ringleaders imprisoned, news of this, the first mass manifestation of open defiance to the government, was the talk of St Petersburg; it was scarcely the moment to choose to submit to the censors a novel which cast so critical eye on the upholders of authority and so sympathetic a one on the revolutionary young. But fortunately for Turgenev, Stasyulevich had overridden his objections and insisted that the book was too long to be published in one issue, and would have to be divided in two. The censors had been presented with the first half, where the overall slant of the book was not yet clear, and had seen their way to passing it. When it came to considering the second part, the vote was divided evenly between for and against; the matter then passed to the Minister of Education, who had the deciding voice; it is unlikely that Count Dmitri Tolstoy pronounced that publication should proceed on account of his admiration for the novel; more probably he was acute enough to foresee that passing half a book by Russia's most famous author and rejecting the other would attract national and international ridicule.

Annenkov's notion that *Virgin Soil* would meet a more favourable critical reception than his friend's two previous novels was soon belied. The accusations from the right took familiar forms. Turgenev's care to avoid caricaturing his representatives of the upper reaches of society, as he had with the generals in *Smoke,* earned him no new friends: Sipyagin, the 'future minister', who flirted with liberal ideas as long as they were confined to the drawing-room, his beautiful wife, hiding her frigid, ambitious, vengeful nature under a veneer of flirtatious charm, even Kallomeitsev, their viciously reactionary neighbour, were all familiar, easily recognizable individuals; this only made their creator's patent dislike of them all the more reprehensible. The conspirators, different as they were from each other, were not, as they should have been, portrayed as dangerous criminals, to be exterminated like vermin. And, perhaps worst of all, that the book's heroine, Marianna, daughter of a general, should not only reject society but conspire to overturn it, was an insult to the nation's womanhood. Was nothing sacred any longer? Once again the author was branded as a traitor to his country and his class. Katkov vented his spleen at having lost his most eminent contributor by calling him 'the lackey of Europe and socialism.'

But it was the hostility from those he had hoped this time to reach that broke through his carefully constructed shield of fatalism and left him emotionally shattered as never before by the reception of a book. Journal after journal hurled invectives at him. What right had he, from his life of self-exiled ease, to ridicule young people who were prepared to sacrifice their comforts, their freedom and sometimes their lives for the great cause in which they believed? What had happened to the champion of emancipation, who now portrayed the muzhiks as nothing but gross, ignorant, drunken savages? What led him to believe that a few weeks spent every couple of years in his homeland entitled him to interpret all the complex issues raised by the 'going to the people' movement, which few if any of his countrymen yet fully understood? Would it not have been more becoming to have kept quiet? Or written a novel set in China, about which he was probably just as well informed? In *Annals of the Fatherland*, Mikhailovsky wrote: 'Turgenev found himself in the position of an artist who sets out to paint a forest but has no green on his palette. What is the result? Red birch trees and blue pines!'

Towards the end of the Baden-Baden years, Turgenev had published his *Literary Reminiscences,* which included a few pages reflecting on the reception of *Fathers and Children.* Ending with words of advice to young writers, he had recommended that they should never seek to justify themselves. 'Whatever libellous stories they may tell about you, don't try to explain a misunderstanding, don't be anxious to say "the last word". He now took his own advice. Hard as the barrage of hostile criticism hurled against *Virgin Soil* hit him, he maintained, at least in print, a stubborn silence. Only with those closest to him did he occasionally lower his guard. To Pauline, who told her friends at this time that her old admirer had become 'the saddest of men', he vowed that he would never write another word of his own; if his writing hand began to itch, he would translate his French friends into Russian and his Russian friends into French. Pauline had heard this before, but knew it was not the moment to remind him of it. With Flaubert, he was sure of a sympathetic ear. Shortly after publication in Russia, he wrote: 'My book seems to give much pleasure to my friends, and very little to the critics or the public. The papers find that I am used up and – a familiar ditty to you – belabour me with my past things (my *Sportsman's Sketches,* your *Madame Bovary*). They want us, expect us, to write the same book twenty times!'

But the fatalistic resignation he displayed to his friends was only a brave front to conceal an overwhelming sense of melancholy, the worst he had suffered since the Paris winter of 1856/7. The hostile reception of his novel was not the only cause of this. There were his ever more frequent and painful attacks of gout, which he now referred to as 'Katkovitis'; compromising his ability to accept invitations, even to Croisset or to Nohant to visit George Sand, where he was always a welcome guest, they added to his sense of being a prisoner in Paris. His journeys to Russia became less regular, but his increasing sense of alienation from his homeland transcended the physical; it was now accompanied by an erosion of the belief that had sustained him all his life: that there was, there had to be, a gradual, democratic, non-violent way for his country to move into the future. But he had always been convinced that reform must come from above; and with the dismissal or retirement of all the liberal elements around Alexander, the possibility of this had receded into the furthest reaches of improbability. He was as violently opposed as ever – and this he had make clear in his novel – to the revolutionary alternative. So had he always been wrong? Autocracy or revolution – was that the stark, inescapable choice? The failure of *Virgin Soil* brought him face to face as never before with the isolation of his position and the inescapable awareness of belonging nowhere. The Baden years had afforded him the illusion that this was not true; the five-year effort the writing of his book had required had put it out of his mind. While it lasted, the demands of creativity had rejuvenated him; but when the results proved so barren, the old sense of futility was no longer to be held at bay.

The moments of bleakest desolation he reserved for his diary... '*17 March, 1877, midnight. I am sitting again at my desk. Down below my poor friend is singing something in her completely cracked voice, and it is darker in my soul than the darkest of nights. It's as though the grave were in a hurry to swallow me up. The day, a fleeting instant, departs... empty, without purpose, without colour. And now it's time to throw myself once again on my bed. I no longer have the right to live, nor the taste for it. There's nothing more to do, nothing more to expect; nothing more even to wish for.*'

There remained the small, regular pleasures. He never missed the Thursday evenings at rue de Douai: his tall, elegant frame could be seen leaning over the piano as Pauline played, scrutinizing the score through his lorgnette, or, when Didie and Marianne joined their mother to sing, seated at the right end of the front row of chairs, legs crossed, nodding his head to the rhythm of the music. His attendance was regular too at the Sunday afternoon family gatherings, when games were played, charades enacted, little playlets performed in a small-scale imitation of the glory days of Baden. And, as in Baden, many Russian visitors to Paris, who had hoped to pass an evening with their illustrious compatriot discussing finer points of politics or literature, were chagrined to see him on hands and knees, with Didie on his back enacting Penthesilea. Henry James, on the other hand, who since 1875 had become a frequent visitor, found such scenes 'strange and rather sweet... a striking example of that spontaneity which Europeans have and we have not.'

Turgenev's fictional silence lasted longer than on any of the previous occasions he had vowed to write no more. It was to be three and a half years before he again published some tales. But underneath the seemingly total acceptance of the failure of *Virgin Soil,* his writer's pride was never totally extinguished. And in what could be seen as poetic justice, it was to be a new pattern in the endlessly shifting Russian political kaleidoscope that would bring it to the surface...

If the authorities in St Petersburg had set out to mount a defence of the writer whom they still regarded with wary suspicion, they could scarcely have been more effective. During the three years that the 'Going to the People' movement lasted, the police had arrested over 1600 young people, of whom some 250 were women. Many of them had been denounced by the very peasants they were trying to help, as had happened to one of the conspirators in *Virgin Soil*. Now, in 1877, counting perhaps on euphoric patriotic fervour aroused by the outbreak of the pan-Slav war against Turkey, it was decided to stage two massive public trials, known, from the number of the accused, as the Trial of the 50 and that of the 193. In what amounted to a masterstroke of self-damage, these were, exceptionally, declared open to the public, who, it was assumed, would thereby see with their own eyes the mortal threat to the very fabric of society posed by these young people. They were also widely reported in the press. The result was the exact opposite of what had been intended. The defence lawyers were as able and eloquent as the prosecution was inept. For the first time ordinary Russians could hear or read of the degrading conditions in which the great mass of the peasantry lived and of the selfless, if ineffective, efforts that young people from every class of society had made to better them. The women made a particularly strong impression. It was no longer so easy for respectable pillars of society to illustrate Turgenev's ignorance of the state of affairs in Russia by declaring how false the character of Marianna was because young ladies of good society 'didn't do that sort of thing'. These young ladies stood at the bar and spoke proudly of what they had done, or tried to do.

The majority of the accused were eventually acquitted, although many were later secretly rounded up again by the police and sent into exile. And Turgenev, while steadfastly refusing to commit himself to any more major work, could begin to view the hostile reception to *Virgin Soil* with greater objectivity. He arranged with the willing Annenkov for some thoughts he had put to paper to circulate among both reactionary and liberal circles in Moscow and St Petersburg. '*With the exception of a few, a very few, private opinions, I received nothing but contumely and abuse for my last novel. As I live most of the time abroad, it was widely assumed that I know nothing about life in Russia or the people who live it. I therefore had to invent everything, with the result that no aspect of the book was credible. I may perhaps be forgiven, therefore – although I am sure I will not be – for pointing out that after certain trials which have recently taken place in my homeland, my 'fabrications' have been revealed to be nothing more sinister than the simple truth. And it is now being reported to me that those who sat in judgement are not, of course, admitting that they might have been in some way mistaken, but have simply renewed their attack from a different direction. Now they claim, not that I invented a plot which was quite beyond belief, but that it was in all details so true to life that I must have been a clandestine participant in the organizations I was depicting. How else can I have been so well informed?*'

His damaged self-confidence received further balm from the favourable reception of his book in western Europe. Such was his reputation outside his own country that in less than a year after its appearance in the *European Herald* it had been translated into nine languages and won a wide readership in France, Britain and America. Flaubert was unsparing in his praises, both to his friends and to the author himself; 'I have just finished *Virgin Soil*. Now, that's a book! It banishes all other recently read work from the mind. What a painter, what a moralist you are, my very dear friend! Too bad for your compatriots if they do not find your book a marvel. That is my opinion, and I'm not the easiest person in the world to please!'

On 24 January, 1878, a year after the publication of *Virgin Soil*, and a day after the end of the Trial of the 193, a 29-year-old woman named Vera Zasulich stood in a line of petitioners waiting to be received by General Trepov, the St Petersburg Chief of Police. This notorious sadist had just had a student who had been imprisoned in the Peter and Paul fortress for taking part in the demonstration outside the Kazan Cathedral savagely flogged because he had not taken his cap off when the general passed him on a visit. When her turn came, Zasulich, who had been in Nechaev's circle, calmly drew a pistol out of her overcoat pocket, pointed it at Trepov and pulled the trigger. Her aim being weaker than her determination, she only wounded him, but made no attempt to escape, submitting to arrest without resistance. Her trial was followed with intense interest and, three months later, amidst thunderous applause from a packed courtroom, the jury, emboldened by the defence's revelation of the many inhuman acts committed by the general, chose to ignore the irrefutable evidence, and acquitted her. The authorities, fearing that something of the sort might happen, had ordered the police, in the event, to re-arrest her the minute she left the building. But such was the size of the crowd that engulfed her that friends were able to spirit her away and within a few days she had reached safety in Geneva.

Turgenev made an exception to his habitual condemnation of the resort to violence and greeted the news with open delight. He received a visit soon after from Lavrov and was surprised by the man's guarded enthusiasm. "I am, of course, very happy for the young woman," he explained. "But this is going to give Tkachev and his comrades the *cause célèbre* they've been waiting for. The Trials of the 50 and the 193 showed the populists as sympathetic but not very effective; now the most clearsighted, not to say ruthless, of our friends are going to look on the Zasulich affair as the absolute confirmation of what they have been saying all along: assassination is the only action that will bring results. And the government has already taken the first, inevitable step to combat this: all incidents of conspiracy, resistance to authority and plotting or committing acts of violence will now no longer be tried by jury but by a military tribunal. We are in for violent times, my friend."

He was not wrong. 'Land and Liberty' split into two factions: one group remained sympathetic to the Lavrovian line and still believed in working with the peasants and urban poor to prepare for constitutional reform from above if possible, or eventual insurrection from below if not; the other faction, calling itself 'People's Will', committed itself to breaking down the government's resistance by planning assassinations of its leading representatives and eventually the Czar himself. In

August, 1878, N.V. Mezentsev, the head of the Third Department and another brutish general, was killed on a crowded St Petersburg street by an ex-artillery officer, who pulled his droshky up alongside, leapt out, ran the general through with his sword, sprang back into his carriage and drove off. Like Vera Zasulich, he also managed to escape and eventually reached London.

Other generals and high functionaries were targets in the following months for assassination attempts; but in April, 1879, the stakes were raised. A thirty-year-old teacher, Aleksander Soloviev, was able to fire three shots, all of which missed, at the Czar while he was taking a recreational walk in the palace grounds; the guards who eventually overpowered him managed to wrench away a phial of poison before he could drink it, and after a summary trial he was hanged. Two months later, a mine was laid on the tracks over which the Imperial train was scheduled to pass on its way from Odessa to Moscow. The explosion duly took place, but the carriage blown up contained the royal baggage, not the royal person.

The Czar's luckiest escape took place in February of the following year. A member of 'People's Will', Ivan Khalturin, gained employment as a carpenter in the Winter Palace. Day after day he smuggled in sticks of dynamite in his toolbox and hid it under his pillow until he had amassed over fifty kilos. On a night when Alexander was giving a dinner with many members of the imperial family in honour of the Czarina's nephew, who had just been created Prince of Bulgaria, he detonated the charge in the basement under the first-floor dining-room. But the train bringing the principal guest had been delayed, and the Czar and his suite were waiting in another part of the palace. The gigantic explosion was heard all over the city and caused extensive damage: six members of the imperial guard who were waiting in the room directly above were killed outright and nearly fifty others seriously injured. No member of the imperial family or entourage received a scratch.

Turgenev, still convinced, despite Lavrov's admonitions, that lasting reform could only originate with the Czar himself, was horrified. Once again, as after the St Petersburg fires, he watched helplessly as moderate opinion veered off towards the extreme fringes: all but a handful of the men surrounding Alexander insisted on repression as the only antidote to revolutionary violence; and all but a handful of those seeking change were now convinced that any chance of the introduction of gradual liberal reforms had now evaporated. One evening, at a reception at the Russian embassy, he was taken aside by the German ambassador to France, Prince Hohenlohe. Bismarck, the master player in the great game of European diplomacy, was surreptitiously tinkering with the *Dreikaiserbund,* the alliance between Germany, Austria and Russia, favouring the former and distrusting the latter. Swirling brandy around in his glass with studied nonchalance, Hohenlohe, using *Virgin Soil* as a pretext, asked the novelist whether he thought the increase in revolutionary activity in Russia was likely to result in any marked changes in government policy.

"I would like to think so, Your Excellency," Turgenev replied. "But I have just returned from St Petersburg, and I see very little likelihood of that. I'm afraid the Czar and his closest advisors do not understand the nature of what is going on in Russia. They can't see the difference between a hundred or so conspirators, of 'nihilists', if I must use that word, and the great mass of educated people who are convinced of the necessity for liberal reforms.

"What form might those take?" the ambassador asked.

"Surely the time has come for some sort of constitution. Not necessarily as liberal as in western Europe, but allowing a degree of representation. For example, the *zemstvos*, the elected provincial assemblies, should have control over local finances and administration. It would be so easy for the Czar to win all hearts by making just a few such concessions. This is the moment. I cannot exaggerate the desire of the Russian people for this. But Alexander, who is told every day that it was concessions that led Louis XVI to the guillotine, refuses to see it. He, who started with such admirable intentions, seems to have become indifferent to the desires of so many of his people. He only listens to a small coterie, which tells him he must treat the extremists and the liberals in exactly the same way. This exasperates the moderates. And their discontent is fanned by the arbitrary measures he allows to be passed: nine hundred young people are languishing in his prisons, and God knows how many others have been exiled. And very few of these are conspirators or revolutionaries. Some are men and women who have dared to express their desire for a constitution; others have been arrested because some over-zealous police chief didn't like the way they were dressed."

"Do you foresee any possibility of a *coup d'état*?"

"Not of a successful one, no. Not at the moment. That's why it is of such paramount importance to act now, while some moderate change is still possible. If this opportunity is lost, sooner or later there will be a terrible catastrophe…"

Prince Hohenlohe wrote that night, in his diary: 'If I were the Czar of Russia, I would entrust the forming of a cabinet to this man…'

But that was not quite what Alexander had in mind. The days when the Czar had revered the author of the *Sportsman's Sketches* were long gone. Turgenev, on a visit to Croisset just before leaving again for Russia, confided to his host that he now feared another sentence of exile. "Every time I cross the frontier, I wonder whether I shall be able to leave as easily."

Flaubert was inclined to pooh-pooh the idea. "That was 25 years ago. You're an internationally famous figure… the first novelist ever to be made a Doctor of Civil Law at Oxford University. They would never dare lay a hand on you."

"I wish I were as sure as you are. You know my departure last time was rather precipitate."

"Why?"

"Well, I had been received with the greatest warmth, both in Moscow and St Petersburg, by students and young professors, who said the most flattering things about me. Far above my deserts. But after all the abuse I had suffered, I can't deny it was rather gratifying."

"How do you account for this sudden change? Two years ago, they were hurling insults at you."

"I put it down mostly to the effect of the assassination attempts. Young people are now having their noses rubbed in the consequences of following the Nechaev and Tkachev path. It is one thing to preach violence, another to see the results. Perhaps they are now wondering if the advice of a decrepit old liberal is really to be treated with such scorn. One of the students, proposing a toast, called me his generation's 'spiritual predecessor'. I tell you, I had to choke back the tears."

"And that was enough to antagonize the authorities?"

"Well, that wasn't all. The journal that publishes my work, the *European Herald*, gave a banquet for me at the Hermitage, and in a modest reply to all the compliments I had received, I made a reference – nothing specific, mind you, – to the need for a constitution, indicating it as the next great step after emancipation. Afterwards a number of people came up to me and asked me to return to Russia to head a pro-constitutional party; others suggested I founded a political review with the same end in mind. I told them, of course, that all that was quite impossible. I lived in France and was a writer, not a politician. But just a day or two later I received a visit one morning from one of the Czar's aides-de-camp."

Flaubert raised his eyebrows. "And what did he have to say?"

"He didn't waste words. He asked me, very politely, when I was planning to leave Russia."

"What did you tell him?"

"He barely waited for an answer. But I have to admit that the moment he left I started packing my bags. Not very brave, perhaps, but in the event I think I was wise. Just two days after I left, a man fired three shots at Alexander. Although I have consistently declared my horror at these atrocities and repeated that all reform must be initiated by the Czar, they would be quite capable of linking me to it in some way."

Flaubert fingered his moustache thoughtfully. "It sounds as though I was a bit hasty in suggesting you had nothing to fear. The more I hear about this journey of yours, the less I like it. Don't go. Stay with your friends. We need you. Especially me. In a week or two I'll have finished the religion chapter of my book, and I'll want your opinion… and criticism. You know there's no one in the world I listen to as I do to you. Put off this journey, for a while at least."

"In many ways I wish I could. For the first time I shall be going without a definite date for my return. But I must go... for reasons which I cannot explain to you because I cannot entirely explain them to myself. All I can tell you is that it has not been an easy decision, and I shall leave with a heavy heart..."

The previous spring, collecting some letters from the *poste restante* after a week spent with his daughter and her family in Rougemont, Turgenev had gazed in puzzlement at the writing on one of the envelopes. It looked familiar, but at first he couldn't place it. Then he remembered, and opened it with eager fingers. By the time he had read the letter through, he had to blink away tears from his eyes...

Yasnaya Polyana
6, April 1878.

Ivan Sergeyevich,

Thinking back in recent days on our former friendship, I discovered, to my surprise and joy, that I no longer felt any animosity towards you. God grant that you may feel the same! In all truth, remembering how good you are, I am sure that your hostility vanished long before mine. If this is so, shall we shake hands and will you consent to forgive me for all the wrong I have done you? For me it is natural to remember only your qualities, for you have been very good to me. It is to you, I well remember, that I owe such literary reputation as I have and I have not forgotten that you liked my writings and even my unworthy self. In all frankness, if you can forgive me, I offer you all the friendship of which I am capable. At our age, only one thing is of value: affectionate friendships between men. I would be very happy if such a friendship could be re-established between us.

Lev Nikolayevich Tolstoy

Turgenev was overjoyed. He had often thought of the 'Troglodyte' and read all his works with a mixture of admiration and exasperation. The early chapters of *War and Peace* had disappointed him: he wrote to Annenkov that the pinpoint details of St Petersburg social life seemed a waste of the great talent he had always discerned... 'paltry and trivial... extracting psychological platitudes from his characters' armpits... and those young ladies, self-conscious Cinderellas'. But he was soon caught up in the sweep of the giant novel and pressed it on all his friends: 'Astonishing passages... the nocturnal troika race, the wolf-hunt made me shiver with excitement... in confrontation with his fellow-writers he is an elephant in a menagerie'. His only serious reserve concerned the passages of philosophizing, especially the forty pages of the second epilogue, which he found extraneous and facile: 'He leaps on to some hobby-horse of a universal system, some all-embracing truth, in this case historical determinism, and rides it until, hey presto! , every problem in the world is solved'.

Anna Karenina came in for some pungent criticism too: 'Despite truly magnificent set-pieces like the horse race and the hay-making, there is much that is sour: this is the fault of Moscow and his isolation, Slavophil nonsense and Orthodox old maids… and so we have gossip, the Arbat, Katkov, bad manners, conceit, the officer caste, cabbage soup and an absence of soap. In a word, the most gifted writer in Europe stuck in the native swamp of barbarism.'

But no such thoughts affected the welcome prospect of seeing his cantankerous friend again. He wrote by return…

50, rue de Douai,
Paris.
8 May, 1878.

Dear Lev Nikolayevich,

I received your letter today and read it with great emotion and joy. It is my liveliest wish to renew our former friendship and I eagerly grasp the hand you offer me. You are absolutely right in thinking I have no hostile feelings towards you. If they ever existed, they disappeared long ago; what remains is the memory of a man to whom I was sincerely attached, and a writer whom I was fortunate enough to be the first to hail and whose every new work awakens in me the keenest interest. I rejoice with all my soul at the end of the misunderstanding which came between us. This summer I hope to go to Orel province, in which case we shall no doubt see each other. While awaiting that happy event, I send you all best wishes and once again clasp your hand in friendship.

Your devoted,

Ivan Turgenev

Four months later, he stepped down from the train at Tula station to find Tolstoy waiting for him on the platform, having made the journey from Yasnaya Polyana to greet his guest personally. After a long embrace, they drew back and sized up in an instant the changes that seventeen years had wrought. Turgenev found Tolstoy little changed: the voluminous beard was streaked with grey and the hairline had receded, but there was little fat on the bulky figure and the eyes still flashed with the same impetuous fire. He was introduced to his companion, Tolstoy's brother-in-law, Stepan Behrs, and the three men climbed into the carriage which was to take them to Yasnaya.

When they arrived, Tolstoy's wife, Sonya, surrounded by her six children, was waiting in the garden to greet the guest about whom she had heard so much. She was in a fever of curiosity. Who was this man on whom her husband would at times lavish extravagant praise, at others cover with ignominious abuse? They had never met before, but Turgenev knew who she was: the daughter of André Behrs, who had been his mother's doctor and briefly lover, and was the father of his half-sister, Varya. She was immediately won over by the elegant appearance and charming manners of the new arrival, which offered a stark contrast to the simple country clothes and brusque behaviour of the husband whom she nevertheless still adored. Turgenev was soon surrounded by a chattering group of children, who ranged from the 15-year-old Sergey to the infant Andrey. They all felt instantly at ease with this exotic stranger. After he had distributed some chocolates he had brought from Moscow, they asked him if he would join them in the game of croquet they had been playing before his arrival. Waving aside Sonya's remonstrations that he must be tired after his journey, he immediately accepted and was soon hunched over the ball, frowning in concentration. In between shots, he waddled from hoop to hoop like a giant penguin, mallet slung over his shoulder, reducing the children to ecstasies of laughter. In fifteen minutes he had established himself as a favourite uncle.

As they were about to sit down to lunch, Turgenev looked around and remarked that there were thirteen of them. "Anyone who's afraid of death, lift your hand," he said, raising his own. Knowing that the master of the house's unorthodox brand of Christianity deplored superstition, no one dared move. "It looks as if I'm the only one," Turgenev observed sheepishly. Tolstoy, mindful of his duties as a host, reluctantly raised his and muttered: "Well, if it comes to that, I don't want to die."

Towards the end of the meal, the second eldest son, Ilya, pointed to the two gold watches that Turgenev carried in the pockets of his velvet waistcoat and asked him why he needed both. "So that I can compare them and be sure I always know the right time," was the reply.

"In the old days you wouldn't have cared about that," Tolstoy grunted with a chuckle. "You were always late for everything."

"I still am," Turgenev admitted, with his most disarming smile.

He then reached into another pocket and brought out a finely engraved silver snuffbox. After offering it to everyone, including the children, he took a pinch. Tolstoy asked him: "Don't you smoke any more?"

He shook his head. "I'm not allowed to."

"Doctor's orders?"

"No. There are two charming young ladies in Paris who have told me that if they detect the scent of tobacco on me, they will not allow me to kiss them."

The older children's sniggers were soon suppressed when they caught their father's eye. Tolstoy stood up abruptly and suggested the two of them retire to his study.

Alone for the first time, both found themselves unexpectedly tongue-tied. After

Turgenev had complimented Tolstoy on his charming wife and attractive children and Tolstoy had asked after the Viardots and his Russian acquaintances in Paris, there were moments of uneasy silence. In the old days they would have eagerly discussed each others' books, but both were wary of entering this potential minefield. Turgenev was able to praise the aspect of his colleague's works that he genuinely admired, while withholding for the while his strictures; Tolstoy had detested *Smoke* and written off *Virgin Soil* before he had even read it. The fundamental attitudes of the two great Russian writers could scarcely have been more divergent: on one side the European sophisticate, content to present the world as he saw it and leave any conclusions to his readers; on the other, the man who believed that writing a book that did not have a didactic purpose was an exercise in futility. Aside from their own works, it was hard for them to find any common ground on literature in general. Having suffered and survived many self-lacerating attempts to find a faith that could answer his needs, Tolstoy was now on the verge of a fully-fledged spiritual crisis: the search for the good, the right life, which was to remain with him for the rest of his days, required first of all the attainment of humility; the letter to Turgenev had been a step in this direction. He had come to the conclusion that the true aim of all people of good will should be to establish the kingdom of God on earth. He had broken resoundingly with the Orthodox Church, claiming it distorted the message of Christ; all that insistence on suffering in this life being rewarded by bliss in the next was an immoral stratagem to justify the injustices of the existing social order. In his search for humility, he had tried to submerge his justified pride in his great novels by belittling the importance of all literature. When Turgenev asked him what writers he now admired in Russia, he was met with a dismissive, "I don't bother with most of them. I have little time for such things."

"What occupies you then? Local issues? Your school?"

An impatient grunt. "That was one of those youthful impulses one soon grows out of."

"Do you still arbitrate between the peasants and the landowners?"

"Not for fifteen years. All either party was interested in was making the most for himself by cheating the other."

"How do you pass the time, then... when you're not writing?"

Tolstoy took his time before answering, his eyes scrutinizing his companion's face, trying to ascertain what lay behind the question.

"I search for the reason why we are on this earth. At our age, is there anything else worth bothering about? Do you not give it any thought?"

Turgenev tried to make light of it. "Oh, I used to, but I gave it up a long time ago."

"Why?"

"Because I came to the conclusion that as there is nothing we can know, acting as though there were can only lead to madness."

"I can partly agree with you there. I sometimes think I am going mad."

"Then allow me the impertinence of suggesting you spend less time tormenting yourself with abstract thought and more sitting at your desk and writing. Your work is so splendidly sane." Seeing Tolstoy's brow furrow, he immediately added: "But I had better not pursue that line too far or we will end up quarrelling again."

Tolstoy allowed himself a smile and thumped his palms down on the arms of his chair. "That's more than possible. Let us go for a walk. Our friendship always thrived in the open air!"

As soon as they stepped into the garden, they found the whole family waiting for them. Pressed by the children to join them for another game of croquet, Turgenev would willingly have accepted, but Tolstoy told them his guest had not come all the way to Yasnaya to play with them and that they were going for a walk in the woods. On their way, they came across a plank that had been laid across a chopping block to form a seesaw. They both climbed on and swung themselves up and down, accompanied by clapping and cheering from the children. At one point, as Turgenev was up, he looked down at the countess and said: "This is where I was when I first met your husband…" And as he sank to the ground, he added: "And this is where I am now."

As they entered the woods, Tolstoy, more perhaps from a sense of obligation than genuine interest, asked his companion about his work. Turgenev told him that he had written his last novel. "To keep my hand in, I scribble down from time to time some very short pieces – observations, really – which I call *Senilia* and other people have called *Poems in Prose*. Stasyulevich wants to publish some of them, but I don't think they're worth it. We'll see." His attention was caught by a choral burst of birdsong, and he began to identify them. "You hear that? That trill interrupted by a long wheeze? That's a greenfinch. And that flutey, twittering one up there… a linnet." Tolstoy was not to be outdone. After a while they came to a clearing where a bony old nag was grazing as the peasant who owned him dozed on the ground with his back against a tree. Tolstoy went up to it, put his arm round its neck, rubbed its nose and began to talk into a scrawny ear. Then he put his own ear to the horse's mouth and listened with seemingly intense concentration. "What is he telling you?" Turgenev asked. "He's saying that being old isn't so bad, as long as you have enough to eat and you don't think about dying." Turgenev smiled and remarked: "I believe, in a previous existence, Lev Nikolayevich, you were a horse yourself."

At dinner there were guests: Prince Urosov, the Vice-Governor of the Tula province, whom Turgenev had known in his youth, together with his wife. After the meal, Tolstoy asked Turgenev if he would read them one of the *Poems in Prose* he had told him about. Turgenev said he would be glad to, but the only one he had on him was one he had written just a few days ago and was rather sad. Perhaps it would upset the children. Tolstoy shrugged this off, observing that children should not always be protected from the darker side of life. And so Turgenev pulled on his spectacles, the children sat on the carpet around his feet, and the adults settled back in their chairs as he began to read *THE DOG*.

There are two of us in the room: my dog and I. Outside a furious storm is raging.

The dog is sitting in front of me, looking straight into my eyes.

I also look into his eyes.

It's as if he wants to tell me something. He can't make himself understood, he is dumb, he doesn't understand himself. I understand him.

I understand that at this moment one and the same feeling exists in him and in me and nothing separates us. We are identical; in each of us there is the same flickering little spark which burns and glows.

Death will come and will sweep us away with his cold wings, with his wide cold wings...

And that will be the end!...

And who, after us, will decipher this enigma? What was the difference between those sparks that burned in each of us?

No! it is not an animal and a man who are looking at each other.

It is two pairs of eyes, the same eyes, fixed on each other. And in each – in the animal as in the man – there is one and the same life, fearfully seeking a refuge in the proximity of the other.

A long silence followed the end of the story, no one quite knowing what to say. As Tolstoy stared straight ahead of him, his expression indecipherable, Sonya felt it was up to her as hostess to risk an opinion. She gave Turgenev a warm smile and clapped appreciatively, a gesture which was only taken up by the children, who joined in enthusiastically. "Thank you, thank you, Ivan Sergeyevich," she said. "That was really beautiful..." turning to Princess Urosov. "Didn't you think so, Natalya?"

The Princess's pursed lips signalled her disapproval. With a little grunt and a nod, she turned to her husband. "What did you think, dear?"

Urosov straightened up in his chair. "I have to disagree with what I take to be the moral of the story." He appealed to Turgenev. "Am I to understand that you see no difference between a human being and an animal? And that you do not believe in the existence of an afterlife?"

"As to your first question, there are, of course, differences. But if humans have an immortal soul, I see no reason why animals shouldn't. And for your second, I neither believe nor disbelieve. I simply don't know."

The pious prince shook his head. "I had hoped that age would have brought you wisdom, Ivan Sergeyevich. But I see now that you will die as you have lived: the most likeable of pagans."

Sonya now felt she had to elicit some sort of an opinion from her husband.

"Lyovochka, what have you to say?"

Turgenev intervened. "He doesn't have to say anything. It's a negligible trifle, which I have no intention of publishing and will probably throw into the wastepaper basket tomorrow. It's not worth even the consideration of Russia's greatest writer."

Tolstoy managed a grateful half-smile and rose to his feet to indicate that, as far as he was concerned, the evening was over. He walked over to Turgenev and put his hand on his shoulder. "I have only one thing to say. Whatever one may think of the content of your work, when it comes to style, you are the master of us all."

The following day, Tolstoy had organized a shoot. Sonya, ever more appreciative of her guest's flattering attentions to her, elected to accompany him rather than her husband. Their prey was woodcock and Tolstoy had placed him in what he assured him was usually the best possible position. But in the event, hardly a bird came within his range. While they were waiting, staring into an empty sky, Sonya asked him why he had almost given up writing. He gave her a sad smile and confessed, in a low voice: "This must remain between you and me. Please don't tell Lyovochka. But in the past, when the desire to write a book came upon me, I was seized with a kind of fever. Like when you're in love. But now I am old, and I can neither write nor love." At that moment, Tolstoy, who was behind some bushes about fifty yards away, fired twice and brought down two birds. "There you are, you see. He's the lucky one. Fortune has smiled on him all his life… not least in providing him with such a charming wife." When it was time to go back to the house, Tolstoy had eleven woodcock in his bag and Turgenev had managed to kill only one… which his dog had been unable to retrieve as it had fallen into the branches of a tree.

In the evening, the elder children had invited some of their friends to meet the guest who, by now, had completely won their hearts. Turgenev, as always in his element in the company of the young, had everybody, with the noticeable exception of the head of the family, hanging on his lips with tales of life in the French capital.

He imitated and made fun of the Parisian women, comparing what he saw as their shallow, insincere attempts to please with the dignified simplicity of their Russian counterparts. He spoke of his friends among his fellow-writers and described how the 'realism' of Flaubert, the Goncourts and 'perhaps, humbly, myself', was being developed by younger writers into what was being called 'naturalism'. When Sergey Tolstoy asked him what that meant, he answered that the naturalists felt they could write about subjects that had hitherto been considered unacceptable. "Like what?" the fifteen-year-old asked. Seeing Tolstoy's eyes flash in warning, he extricated himself by citing as an example a story called *Le Maison Tellier*, which the young Guy de Maupassant had dedicated to him: "But it may never see the light of print, because it takes place in an establishment which I shall not describe here."

Resisting a chorus of "Yes, yes, go on, please!" he deftly moved on to the subject of the music-halls and the dances that were popular there. "Have you heard of the cancan?"

"No, what is that?" He looked around and pulled the eldest daughter, Tanya, to her feet. Linking one arm in hers and sticking the other hand through the armhole of his waistcoat, he started to sing and perform the relatively sedate version of the famous dance before, ten years later, the Moulin Rouge immortalized the high kicks and splits. All the company, with the obvious exception, clapped in rhythm and sang along until the exhausted, red-faced 60-year-old collapsed in a chair, breathless but relishing the laughter and applause with which his performance was ecstatically greeted.

He left the next day for Spasskoye and wrote to Tolstoy: '… I can only repeat once again what I told you before leaving: what a good and pleasant impression my visit to Yasnaya Polyana has left with me and how happy I am to see that the misunderstandings which had come between us have disappeared without leaving a trace, as though they had never existed. I feel very strongly that the life that has aged us has not slipped by in vain, and that you and I have become better people than we were seventeen years ago.' Tolstoy, perhaps more realistically, wrote to his disciple, Strakhov: 'Turgenev has been staying with us, as kind and brilliant as ever. But, between you and me, he is a bit like a fountain into which water has to be pumped; one is always afraid that it will run dry and there will be nothing left.' And his diary for the last day of the visit ended: 'Turgenev – cancan. Sad.'

t was as well that he knew nothing of a friendship that was soon to develop between the fountain and a new source of sparkling water. In the last weeks of 1878, a letter had arrived in Paris for Turgenev from a Russian actress in St Petersburg, whose name was unfamiliar to him. After a long preamble introducing herself as a member of the Alexandrinsky Theatre Company and apologizing that someone so insignificant should importune such a revered international figure, she came to the point...

'*1879 is my benefit year, which means I can choose, within reason, any part in any play that I would like to perform. I have long been in an agony of indecision about this, but all was resolved a week ago when I read your* A Month in the Country. *I feel the part of Vera might have been written for me, and it would be the greatest honour in the world if you would allow me to interpret this beautiful role.*

There is only one problem, and that is that the directors of the theatre, who agree enthusiastically with my choice, would like to make a few cuts here and there (mostly for censorship reasons) and shorten a few of the speeches. I hardly dare to ask this of you, but my desire to play the part is so great that I have summoned up the courage to do so. Of course, if you agree, we would send you all the suggested alterations for your final approval...

I cannot describe the breathless anxiety with which I await the courtesy of your reply. If your answer is yes, it will mark the most glorious moment of my career (I am 25, but I have been on the boards since I was six); if no, I will manage somehow to swallow my disappointment and hope only that one day when you are in St Petersburg, I may have the great honour of making your acquaintance.

Your devoted admirer, whose heart will remain firmly lodged in her mouth until she hears from you,

Marya Gavrilovna Savina

Turgenev replied by return...

50, rue de Douai,
Paris.
17 December, 1878.

Dear Marya Gavrilovna,

I cannot say whether I was more charmed to receive your letter or amazed to hear that someone was

579

interested in reviving my old play. You are so young that I think perhaps I ought to warn you that I wrote it, if my memory serves me, in 1850 and it was not performed until 22 years later, when it opened in Moscow to hostile reviews and ran for 5 nights. Do you really want to climb into this creaky old vehicle (older than you are, in fact) for so important an undertaking as your benefit performance. There are surely innumerable plays more worthy of your talents (I haven't had the pleasure of seeing you on stage, but if they are giving you a benefit at only 25, you must be remarkably gifted). And then you tell me that you want to play Vera. Are you sure you don't mean Natalya Petrovna, who is the protagonista assoluta *of the play. You would surely be wasted in such a small part as Verochka.*

However, if you really intend to proceed in this quixotic enterprise, please be assured that you have my full permission to make any changes, without any further consultation, that you or the directors require. I can only imagine that they will improve this long-forgotten effusion of my theatre-loving youth.

I shall be visiting Russia some time during the year, though I am not sure yet of the exact dates. If you would not find it tedious to share for a few moments an old man's company, I should be entirely delighted to make your acquaintance,

Wishing you the greatest success in your venture,

I remain,

Your devoted,

Iv. Turgenev

Turgenev finally left for Russia at the beginning of February, 1879. After a busy two weeks in Moscow, where he was feted by his fellow-writers, university professors and a host of student admirers, and gave a number of speeches, several of which were later published in various journals, he left for St Petersburg. The afternoon of his arrival at the Hotel de l'Europe, a pageboy came to his room to inform him that there was a visitor waiting below who was very anxious to see him. When asked who it was, the boy announced in a reverential whisper that it was 'la Savina', the famous actress of the Alexandrinsky Theatre. Curiosity instantly overcoming fatigue, Turgenev asked for her to be shown up.

From the moment she walked – or rather, made her entrance – into the room, he was struck by the force of her personality. By no means conventionally beautiful, he could well imagine that theatre audiences would be unable to take their eyes off her. She was of under average height, with a slim, wiry body, short black hair parted down the middle, restless, penetrating dark grey eyes in a sharp pointed face and an energy which coursed through every word she spoke and every gesture she made. The only aspect that at first made an unfavourable impression on him was a harsh, unmelodious voice; it immediately flashed across his mind that this must be a severe handicap in her profession; he was later to find out that it brought instead a reality to her performances that took them off the stage and into the audiences' experience.

For the first few minutes, lacking her habitual confidence in the presence of the famous figure, she talked without drawing breath, excusing herself for disturbing him so soon after his journey, expatiating on how words failed her (they didn't) to express what it meant to her to be talking to a man whom she had admired all her life... Turgenev didn't interrupt, but let her carry on until she suddenly clasped her hand to her mouth and groaned that here she was in the same room as Ivan Sergeyevich Turgenev and all she could do was babble on like a fishwife behind a stall. He ushered her into a chair and gently began to put her at her ease. "It's a privilege for me too to meet such a famous actress."

She laughed this away. "What a comparison! I'm talking to a man whose name is a household word throughout Russia."

"I'm afraid in a lot of households it's a name to sling mud at. But tell me, how is my poor old play being received?"

She settled back in her chair and, finding herself on familiar ground, immediately regained her poise. "It's an extraordinary success. There are queues outside the theatre every night and people are offering fortunes for tickets. And this is the real reason for my coming to bother you." She leaned towards him, her eyes beacons of supplication. "Do I dare to ask you if you would attend a performance?"

He pretended to a reluctance he didn't really feel. "Oh dear! I think I would be embarrassed by it. I wrote it so many years ago. Can it have anything to say to people today?"

"There's a very easy way for you to find out." She laid a hand lightly on his knee. "Please, Ivan Sergeyevich! Nothing in my career would mean as much to me as your presence in the audience."

"Then I will certainly come."

She clasped her hands in front of her mouth, and rose from her chair. "Thank you, thank you, thank you. And now I won't keep you a moment longer. Just leave me a message at the theatre which evening would be suitable, and I'll arrange for a box to be reserved for you." A hurried, timid kiss on the cheek and she was gone.

Hotel de l'Europe,
St Petersburg,
10 March, 1879.

Dear and good Madame Viardot,

How long would we have to live before we could understand the behaviour of our fellows – at least in my country? The only possible answer is: forever. Two years ago I was a reviled, despised, almost hated man. Today, apparently, I am something of a hero.

In Moscow I was received in the enormous Assembly Rooms of the University with acclamation from over a thousand students. Everyone on their feet, endless hurrahs, hats flying in the air. Then a young student delegate made an enflamed speech which continually bordered on the impermissible (authority to hold the meeting had only come through the previous day), and the poor rector, sitting in the front row, was white in the face and trembling with apprehension. In my reply, I did my best not to set a match to all this tinder, while still trying to avoid banalities. Afterwards they all followed me into the adjacent rooms, the girls seizing my hands and kissing them. Pandemonium! If a colonel of gendarmes hadn't come and gently but firmly seized me and deposited me in my carriage, I think I should still be there.

I understand the cause of all this, which has little or nothing to do with my merits; on the eve of reforms, always promised and always postponed, on the eve of the birth of a meaningful political life, all these young people are charged with electricity and I am a potential detonator. It is my liberal opinions which are behind all this at least as much as my writings. If these poor young people don't give vent to their feelings they will explode! This doesn't prevent me from being extremely touched – and totally worn out – by what is happening to me so unexpectedly.

I arrived in St Petersburg three days ago and have been allowed no respite. On the contrary! The day after I arrived there was a dinner at the Borel restaurant with 80 guests and almost as many speeches! Yesterday I was asked to address an Institute for Young Ladies, which was holding a literary soirée. Tomorrow I have been invited by Marya Savina (you remember the young actress who wrote to me in Paris?) to attend a performance of A Month in the Country, *with a reception afterwards. She came to my hotel to see me the other day and I found her most charming. Who knows how good an actress she will turn out to be.*

But oh, what an exhausting life! Decidedly not what our English friends would call 'my cup of tea'.

I enclose a photograph which was taken of me the other day and Annenkov considers a very good likeness. I think I just look old and tired, but I leave it up to you to judge.

And with that I embrace you all and remain, as ever,

Your devoted,

I.T

On March 15 he crept surreptitiously into the empty Director's box at the Alexandrinsky and skulked in a dark corner at the back until the play began, hoping that no one would be aware of his presence. But as soon as the house lights went up after the last act, it became clear that Savina had made sure that everyone knew he was there. The entire, wildly applauding audience, at an almost imperceptible signal from the actress, turned to face the box and started to shout in unison: "Author! Author! Author!" As Turgenev stood up in acknowledgement, Savina beckoned to him to join the cast on stage. But after a brief wave and grateful bow, he hurried backstage before anybody could accost him.

There he found the atmosphere he had found so congenial when he used to go round to take his place on the third paw of the white bear in Pauline's dressing-room: actors, stage hands, dressers, wardrobe mistresses, scurrying about, smiling, laughing, grumbling, joking – all part of the intangible euphoria that permeates a successful theatrical production. He greeted some of the actors, complimenting them on their performance, and gradually made his way to Savina's dressing-room. He found her alone, sitting in front of her mirror, just beginning to remove her make-up; she turned to face him in silence, all eloquence contained in her half-opened mouth and the anxious interrogation of her eyes. He moved towards her, bent down to kiss her cheeks and looked at her, shaking his head. "Verochka! Is it possible that all those years ago I wrote this Verochka? I don't remember paying much attention to her; my thoughts were all concentrated on Natalya Petrovna. But now you've revealed her to me. It's all due to you, not me. You are the real Verochka, you have brought her to life. What a great talent you have, what a rare, extraordinary talent!"

Tears filled her eyes and she clasped his hands. "You have given me the courage to ask you a great favour. I didn't think I'd dare, but after what you've just said…"

"What is it? If there is anything I can do…"

"Tomorrow I have been asked to take part in a gala performance in aid of the Literary Fund, which helps artists and writers who are in need…" She paused and looked up at him, dabbing a little more greasepaint off her cheeks.

Turgenev thought he understood. "And you'd like me to be there. But of course. Not as a favour to you but as a pleasure for me."

"Well that's not all. You see I…" She hid her face in her hands to hide her non-existent blushes. "I took the liberty… oh, will you ever forgive me?… of saying that you would read a scene with me from your *Provincial Lady*, which I am thinking of reviving next year."

Turgenev was taken aback. "You want me to read alongside you? But I'm no actor. Oh, I've taken part in a few plays as an amateur, but I'm really no good at all. I would just ruin your performance."

She brought his hands up to her lips and kissed them. "On the contrary, I know you will inspire me to give of my very best…"

Turgenev had almost forgotten *The Provincial Lady,* a Mussetesque comedy he had written before *A Month in the Country.* In the scene Savina had chosen, the heroine, Darya Ivanovna, ward of an old countess who has married her off to a worthy but dull civil servant, is trying to persuade the countess's son to find a job for her husband in St Petersburg, thus enabling her to exchange a dreary provincial existence for the glittering life of the capital. The middle-aged Count flirted with her when she was a young girl, and she now returns the compliment with interest; so successfully, in fact, that he falls in love with her.

Savina read the part with all the fire and charm for which she was famous, but she didn't receive much help from her partner. Appearing for the first time before an audience with a consummate professional, Turgenev suffered a stage fright beyond anything he had ever imagined. Annenkov, who attended, told him afterwards that he looked like a shambling bear let out of the zoo with its keeper, mumbling into his beard and casting embarrassed sideways glances at his partner, who would reply with an encouraging flash of her eyes. But it made no difference. Savina had arranged for their scene to be the last event of the evening, and when they finished the whole house rose to their feet and shouted in unison: 'TUR-GE-NEV! TUR-GE-NEV!' He managed to mutter a few words of thanks before Savina, noticing the tears coming into his eyes, led him off the stage.

Later they dined together, and she told him that Dostoevsky, who earlier had read a passage from *The Brothers Karamazov*, had come to see her in her dressing-room. "I'm afraid he was a little jealous of your success."

"That was silly of him. It wasn't my success, it was yours."

"It was your name they were shouting."

"Yes, that would be enough to upset him. But what did he say? Did he congratulate you?"

"Oh yes, very flatteringly." With affected coyness, she lowered her glance. "But I don't think I had better tell you the rest."

He made no attempt to hide his curiosity. "You can't leave me in suspense like this. Don't worry, by now I am quite immune to Fyodor Mikhailovich's barbs. Tell me what he said. Please!"

She looked across at him under her lashes, her eyes brimming over with mischievous glee. "Well, his exact words were: 'Every word of yours, Marya Gavrilovna, is like finely-carved ivory. But as for the old man – he lisps.'"

A few days later she received a gold bracelet, in which he had had their two names inscribed on the inside, and a photograph of himself with the inscription: 'In memory of our joint reading, and with my thincere devotion, I. Turgenev.

50, rue de Douai,
Paris
18 March, 1879

My dear good Tourgline,

Thank you for your letter and photograph. I reply with the certainty that this will find you happily ensconced in St Petersburg, where these new triumphs of yours are going to make you put down roots. All very well, as long as it doesn't make you homesick when you're back in Paris. You're not going to abandon us, are you? I'm afraid you'll get bored here, no longer surrounded by a fever of admiration – only by the same old faces (each day a little older, or anyway a little less young), who will be happy to see you, but tranquilly so… a few eccentric friends, a few good new acquaintances, a lot of tedious ones, and always the same routine at the same hours, everything as it always has been…

But it will make us so happy to welcome you back… if you ever have the strength to tear yourself away from all those young creatures yelping and bounding around you, not to mention the attentions of beautiful and adoring young actresses! Not a word, I notice, about the probable date of your return – if I know you, there will be a second letter, then a third and then… an attack of gout! May heaven grant that my presentiments are unfounded. I shall not have total ease of mind until I see you walk through the door.

Your expression in the photo is relaxed and happy. One sees in fact that you are happy. It's good to think that 'the man already dead', the 'tattered old heap of rags', as you were referring to yourself last winter, has become young and frisky again. If you dare ever again to talk about yourself in those terms, I shall sit you down, force you to read your own letters and put the photograph in front of your face.

Ah, how many interesting things you will have to tell us! I want to hear everything, remember, everything.

As the Schubert song says: 'If only I were a little bird…'

100,000 tendernesses,

Pauline

Soon after their return to Paris, the Viardots had started looking around for a country replacement for Courtavenel. In 1875 they settled on a property at Bougival, situated on a wooded hill overlooking the Seine, only 45 minutes west of Paris. The house, called *Les Frênes* after the surrounding ash-trees, was set in a large garden replete with moss-covered fountains and statues. Turgenev immediately set about building, less than fifty yards away, a small residence for himself, half Swiss chalet and half dacha, which was completed the following year. But he kept a large study on the second floor of the main house, where the Viardot family would often congregate on summer afternoons, Pauline embroidering or studying a score, Didie at her easel in the large bow-window and Marianne reading aloud from some French or English novel.

It was here that Turgenev spent the summer of 1879, working on another edition of his complete works, to be published by the Salaev brothers in ten volumes, and revising and adding to his *Reminiscences of Belinsky*. He also made strenuous efforts to popularize Tolstoy's work in western Europe, approving of the English translation of *The Cossacks*, deploring the French version, which he and Pauline retouched themselves. He sent copies of *War and Peace* to all the leading critics and literary figures of France, including Taine and Renan, as well as Daudet and Zola. Later he wrote to Tolstoy enclosing selective quotations from Flaubert, who had just finished the novel. <u>Included</u>: '*It is of the first order! What a painter and what a psychologist! The first two volumes are* sublime... *I even found things that reminded me of Shakespeare. I uttered cries of admiration while I was reading.* Omitted: '*The third volume falls off terribly. He repeats himself. And philosophizes. Finally one sees the man, the author and Russia, whereas up to then one had only seen Nature and Humanity.*' But Turgenev's efforts coincided with a period when Tolstoy was once again belittling his literary achievement, claiming that it even embarrassed him to reread what he had written, let alone have others discuss it. He wrote Turgenev an indignant letter accusing him, even if from the best of motives, of making fun of him and asking him not to mention his work ever again. 'You know very well that everyone has his own way of blowing his nose, and let me assure you, I will blow mine exactly the way I want to.' Turgenev wrote a dignified letter back – 'I thought that you had long since got rid of this kind of egocentric feeling'- and continued to promote his work.

Turgenev had admitted to Flaubert his ambiguous feelings about the journey he was to make to Russia at the beginning of 1880 and he was to write in the same vein to Annenkov: 'I haven't the least idea how long I shall be staying, but only hope the decision will remain in my hands and not be appropriated by the authorities. The reasons which drive me to go are diverse and personal. I cannot say the choice I have made has been an easy one; in many ways it has been very painful, and has left me with an inexplicable feeling of melancholy...' Amongst the personal reasons, and certainly not of the melancholic variety, was his eagerness to see Savina again. They had written to each other regularly over the preceding months, he often failing to maintain a suitably grandfatherly tone, she unfolding the vertiginous details of her romantic life and even occasionally soliciting his advice. He invited her to dinner the day after arriving in St Petersburg and they made plans to see each other at least once a week until he moved down to Spasskoye in the spring. But he soon began to suffer recurring and violent attacks of gout – probably, as Pauline mercilessly reminded him, owing to overindulgence at the numerous dinners to which he was invited – and he refused to allow her to come and see him when he was incapacitated. To her offers of playing nurse from time to time, he proffered an unambiguous refusal. He loved to be cosseted by his Parisian 'ladies' when he was suffering, but this was different.

On his way to Spasskoye in May, he stayed a few days in Moscow to confer about the celebrations surrounding the unveiling of a monument in honour of Pushkin. This was to take place on June 6, the day of the poet's birth. The whole of the Russian literary world was involved: Dostoevsky, Ostrovsky, Goncharov, the Aksakovs, Annenkov, Katkov, Pisemsky and Fet, among many others, would all be present. Tolstoy had of course been invited, but no reply had been received. It was already being predicted that the event would provide the background for an epic struggle between Westerners and Slavophils, who would each interpret Pushkin to suit their own purposes: for the former, he was the writer who had represented the continuation on Russian soil of the great European tradition dating back to Shakespeare, Cervantes and Rabelais; to the latter, his inspiration had been purely and exclusively Russian. Turgenev was asked to make one of the two main speeches of the evening; the other would be delivered by Dostoevsky. Battle was joined!

Before reaching Spasskoye, Turgenev stopped off at Yasnaya Polyana to sound Tolstoy out about his intentions. It was no great surprise to find out that his intention was not to attend. Proclaiming that he had a horror of all official functions, he was deaf to Turgenev's plea that the absence at the ceremony of one of the great 'trinity' of Russian novelists would gravely diminish the importance of the occasion. "Nothing would induce me to travel to Moscow for such a farce," was his succinct comment. "Pushkin himself would be horrified. It will simply be an occasion for lots of second-rate *littérateurs* to babble endlessly on… chiefly about themselves. All my absence will mean is that there will be one babbler the less."

Working fitfully on his speech at Spasskoye, Turgenev found inspiration sadly lacking. He had lost the habit of writing regularly and his thoughts kept straying back to St Petersburg and Savina; he had written to her suggesting she visit him, but had received no reply. And then, on May 8, he opened a newspaper and was shattered to read that Flaubert had been struck down by a cerebral haemorrhage and died within a few hours. He wrote to Marianne, who sent him some obituary clippings from the French papers: 'After your family and Annenkov, he was, I believe, the man I loved most in the world. And now he has gone to that country from which no traveller returns. The last time I saw him, at Croisset, he was nearing the end of his novel and thinking of future works… he sometimes used to say he thought 'Bouvard' would kill him. Perhaps it did. If only he had been able to finish it!…'

And to Flaubert's niece, Caroline Commanville: 'The death of your uncle has been one of the greatest blows I have ever suffered in my life. I cannot reconcile myself to the thought that I shall not see him again… It is one of those sorrows for which one doesn't *want* to console oneself…'

He tried to return to his Pushkin speech, but with even less enthusiasm than before. One morning, after gazing glumly at his notes, he glanced through the morning's post and recognized a familiar handwriting. Tearing the envelope open, he read that Savina was about to travel to Odessa to take part in a theatrical season there. Seizing a piece of notepaper, he wrote: '… on your way, why do you not stop off at Orel and spend a few days with me at Spasskoye. It would give me more pleasure than I can express to show you my birthplace; for all the headaches it has caused me, it is as much a part of me as an arm or a leg, and to share it with you would be an enchantment. You have been much in my mind these past weeks; of all the memories of Petersburg, the dearest and best are of you. You see, I don't find it easy to forget you – but then I don't really want to. I feel I can say without fear of misunderstanding that I have truly come to love you; you stand for something in my life with which I could never wish to part...'

She declined, ostensibly for reasons of time, but suggested he join her train at Mtsensk and travel with her until they reached Orel. Enthralled by the prospect of this romantic adventure, he readily agreed; so the night of 16 May, 1880, saw a sixty-two-year-old elderly gentleman, a little stiff from gout, waiting with an absurdly beating heart on the platform of Mtsensk station for the Moscow/Odessa train to arrive. And sure enough, when it drew up, the smiling face of the young actress was framed in a compartment window, with an outstretched finger beckoning him to board.

When trying to remember over the following days exactly what had passed between them during the mere half-hour it took to reach Orel, Turgenev could summon up only a jumble of uncoordinated memories. At first a few conventional questions from him about the plays she was to perform in Odessa were followed by equally banal ones from her asking how he had found Spasskoye after a long absence. When, while answering her, he had repeated his desire that she should come one day to see for herself, he had seized her hands, covered them with kisses and gazed into her eyes with a fierce longing he made no attempt to hide. Far from showing any signs of embarrassment, she kept her hands in his and looked back at him, lips slightly parted, with an expression in which teasing flirtation and genuine emotion were perhaps inextricably entwined.

They had been sitting opposite each other, but now Turgenev moved over next to her, putting an arm round her shoulders. At first she looked straight ahead of her, seeming to be only half listening to the rather incoherent words tumbling out of his mouth; but when he murmured into her ear, "Marya Gavrilovna, you have become something in my life from which I never want to be separated," she turned towards him, gave a slight shake of her head, whispered, "Perhaps it's my sin, but neither do I," and touched his lips with hers. He instinctively put his hand behind her head to prevent her drawing away and slid the other down the front of her jacket until he felt the swelling of her breast. An involuntary tightening of her hand on his arm signalled that this did not displease her. But at that moment a sharp whistle and sudden application of brakes indicated the train was pulling into Orel station. He got to his feet and they looked at each other in silence, the rise and fall of their chests betraying their agitation, until the train came to a stop. He climbed out of the carriage and she followed him down on to the platform. He was about to envelop her in an overpowering embrace when he saw they were being watched by the stationmaster, whom he had known since he was a junior ticket-clerk. He hurriedly kissed her hand and helped her back into her carriage. As the train drew slowly away, she remained leaning out of the window and waving a handkerchief until the station and the solitary figure on the platform receded from sight.

Spasskoye,
17 May,
12 noon.

Dear Marya Gavrilovna,

I have been back in my house only an hour and a half and already I am writing to you. After leaving you, I spent the night at a hotel in Orel – a good night because I never stopped thinking about you, a bad night because I never closed my eyes… Today is the day I hoped you would be spending with me at Spasskoye. If you had been here, at this moment we would be sitting on the terrace admiring the landscape, I would be talking to you about this and that and, in my thoughts, in an overflowing outburst of gratitude, I would be kissing your little feet over and over again. That is what I had dreamed of. Of course, one ought to chase such dreams away, but it is not easy…

When, last night, you had climbed back into your carriage and were leaning out of the open window, I stood there in front of you, unable to think of a thing to say. Then I suddenly blurted out the word 'desperate'. You seemed to think it applied to you, but what I had in mind was something quite different: the truly 'desperate' temptation to snatch you off the train, take you into the station, and then…

Alas, prudence had the upper hand. The station bell rang, and ciao! as the Italians say. But just think of what the papers would have made of it! I can see the article, with the headline: SCANDAL AT OREL STATION. 'An extraordinary event took place yesterday: the writer T…, an elderly man, abducted the famous actress S…, who was on her way to Odessa for the start of a dazzling theatrical tour; as the train was about to pull out, as if possessed by the devil in person, he dragged her through the window of her compartment, and despite the desperate resistance of the artist…, etc., etc.. What a bombshell, what a rumpus this would have caused throughout the whole of Russia! And yet, as so often in life, it could easily have happened…

Just now, from an ingrained sense of duty, before picking up my pen I glanced at the draft of the speech I have to make for the inauguration of the Pushkin memorial. But as I was reading it – with little satisfaction – I sensed that deep down in my soul only one note, always the same, was resonating. I noticed that my lips were murmuring: 'If you had been here, what a night we would have spent! And what would have happened afterwards? God only knows!…' I remember you said something about my being your 'sin'. Alas, you have no need to reproach yourself with that. And if we let another two or three years go by, I will be a really old man. As for you, you will have definitively embarked on the strada maestra *of your life, and nothing of our past will remain. Your whole life is ahead of you; mine is behind me, and that half-hour spent in the railway carriage, when I felt almost like a young man of twenty, was the last flicker of the lamp. I find it hard to explain to myself the feeling you have aroused in me. I don't know if I am in love with you. In the past, it was different. That indefinable need for fusion, for possession, for the*

589

gift of oneself, when sensitivity itself disappears in a sort of delicate flame… I am no doubt talking idiotic nonsense, but I would have been unspeakably happy if, if…

Knowing now that it will not be, I am not exactly unhappy, I don't even feel especially melancholy, but I deeply regret that that wonderful night is gone for ever without having brushed me with its wing. I regret it for myself and – I dare say it – for you as well, for I am convinced that you would not have forgotten the happiness you would have given me.

I wouldn't write all this to you if I didn't feel that this was a letter of farewell. Our correspondence will certainly not stop here. Oh no! I hope that we will frequently exchange news of ourselves; but the half-open door, that door behind which something mysterious and marvellous appeared, is closed for ever. The bolt is drawn. Whatever happens, I will never be the same again, and nor will you.

Nevertheless, consider me

Forever yours,

Ivan Turgenev.

P.S. Please do not be alarmed about the future: you will never receive a letter like this again.

Three weeks later, Turgenev returned to Moscow for the Pushkin memorial celebrations; these lasted three days and centred round the unveiling of the statue on Strastnaya Square. As he placed a laurel wreath at the foot of the monument, there was a spontaneous outburst of cheers and applause from the vast crowd filling the square. The next day he gave his speech to the Society of Lovers of Russian Literature. To the end he had remained vaguely dissatisfied with it, sending the last draft to both Stasyulevich and Annenkov and accepting without a murmur all the alterations and cuts they recommended. He had never felt comfortable speaking in public and was afraid of appearing pedantic or portentous. And then again, perhaps his thoughts had been more on Savina than on Pushkin. The speech was greeted with its due share of applause (even Katkov raised his glass in a gesture of reconciliation, which Turgenev ignored), but without the enthusiastic warmth of the previous day. He had never seen life or literature in terms of superlatives, and that was what his audience wanted to hear. He praised Pushkin for the power and simplicity of his language, for his versatility in the many forms in which he expressed himself, and for his introduction of the European model into Russian literature. But he specifically stated that, even if only because of his early death, it would be an exaggeration to give him the same prominence as a 'national' poet which the British gave to Shakespeare and the Germans to Goethe. His closing words appealed more to the head than the heart: 'It is said that everyone, on becoming literate, starts to read Shakespeare. Let us hope we shall be able to say the same with Pushkin: that our descendants, standing before the statue we unveiled yesterday, will by that very act become more Russian, more educated, more free!'

It was with philosophic detachment rather than any rancid sense of envy that he listened to the tumultuous ovation awarded to Dostoevsky's speech the following evening. The content was not surprising, but the delivery – broken voice, hypnotically staring eyes, grandiloquent gestures – was electrifying. Knowing that his fellow-Slavophils outnumbered their adversaries, the speaker allowed no misgivings as to plausibility (some might say truth) to temper his passionate advocacy. He even made a gesture of generosity to his old enemy, mentioning Liza in *A Nest of Gentry* in the same breath as *Evgeni Onegin*'s Tatyana as models of the purity and modesty of Russian women; Turgenev blew his rival an appreciative kiss. But as the speech wore on and the orator felt his audience identifying with and glorying in the rhetoric, the tone grew more apocalyptic: Pushkin became little more than a pretext for his messianic fervour.

It was, as Turgenev wrote to Stasyulevich, a 'clever, brilliant and cunningly skilful speech. But shot through with falsehood. Like a good politician, he gave the public what it wanted to hear. Even the reference to Tatyana could hardly bear examination: is it only Russian wives who remain faithful to their elderly husbands? The inescapable leitmotif was the superiority of everything and everyone Russian. Pushkin's genius symbolized the Russian soul destined to fulfil the ultimate aim of creating 'universal man'. (Whoever he is. Wouldn't you rather be just a Russian?) Without Pushkin, we were asked, how would we ever have gained our belief in the independent destiny of Russia in the family of European nations? For it is we Russians, we were told, who will bring about the final reconciliation of Europeans' contradictions, and their sickness of heart will be cured by contemplation of the Russian soul, universal and all-uniting… And so it went on, with everyone standing and cheering and stamping and clapping and weeping, and all I could think was, 'If only Belinsky were here to hear this. What an article would have appeared in the next *Sovremennik*!' I am tempted to write one myself, but will resist. It would only be taken as a spiteful revenge for my caricature in *The Devils*.'

But the next thing Turgenev was asked to write about Dostoevsky was his obituary. On 28 January, 1881, just two months after finishing *The Brothers Karamazov,* the novelist succumbed to a series of haemorrhages. Stasyulevich wrote to Paris asking for a piece for the *European Herald,* which Turgenev at first agreed to do. But after a few days he thought better of it. It was for him an impossible task, requiring a degree of hypocrisy of which he was incapable. He wrote to Stasyulevich: 'What is expected of me is not literary memories of my relationship with the dead writer, but an appreciation of his work. Now first of all, it is very difficult for me to do that; and secondly, I'm afraid the public in its present mood, especially so soon after the Pushkin celebrations, would inevitably claim that I had again seized an opportunity to talk about myself…'

A month later, another death in his homeland came as a far greater blow. In line with the spasmodic changes of direction which had characterized his reign, the Czar had recently favoured the rise of Mikhail Loris-Melikov; this remarkable Armenian, who had been one of the most successful generals in the Turkish war, was now appointed head of the Supreme Executive Committee, a new body entrusted with two specific functions: first to capture and put on trial all who preached or practised violent revolution; second – and this was a totally new conception – to examine the grievances from which the violence sprang. Within a few weeks of his appointment he had submitted to Alexander a proposed series of reforms which would surreptitiously have opened the way towards something resembling constitutional government. This had the effect of galvanizing the hard core of 'People's Will', now led by the lucid, single-minded Sophia Perovskaya, daughter of a former Governor-General of St Petersburg and a celebrated society beauty. Moderate reform was the last thing the radicals wanted: it would decimate their support amongst people who hitherto had seen no solution but terrorism.

And so, on 1 March, as the Czar Liberator, having handed Loris-Melikov the document outlining the reforms with his signature attached to it, was driving back from his usual Sunday morning visit to the riding-school at the Mikhailovsky Palace to admire the horsemanship of his guards, Perovskaya's cell moved into action. A first bomb was thrown which only damaged the Czar's carriage, killing one of the crowd and wounding several others. Alexander, although urged by the colonel commanding the escort to immediately climb into another carriage and drive on, insisted on getting out and walking over to inquire after the casualties. This provided the opportunity for a second conspirator to hurl his bomb at close range. The Czar's mangled body was taken back to the Winter Palace where he died two hours later.

This was the event that Turgenev had dreaded above all others. His letters reveal the extent of his anguish and fear for the future. 'What will happen,' he wrote to Annenkov, 'if attempts are organized on the life of the new Czar? In that case we can only blindfold ourselves and run to the furthest edge of the world, there to wait for the muzhik's slipknot to tighten round every civilized neck.' His sympathy with Vera Zasulich did not extend to the Czar's assassins, whom he described as 'monsters of imbecility and irresponsibility, whose action no sensible mind can possibly approve. By murdering the most generous sovereign who has ever ruled over Russia, they have only done harm to the revolutionary cause and invited the authorities to stamp down ever more brutally on those who were working for moderate change.' Drawing on a brief meeting he had had with the then Czarevich, now Alexander III, when invited by Nikolai Orlov to a reception in his honour at the Paris embassy, he wrote an anonymous article in French for the *Revue Politique et Littéraire*, in which 'wishful' tended to predominate over 'empirical' thinking. 'If the nihilists imagine that the new emperor can be induced by fear to grant concessions and even provide a constitution, they are making a big mistake, in complete ignorance of his character. Any attempt at intimidation will only stop him on the liberal path where his nature would lead him; if he does take some steps, it will not be because, but in spite, of the fact that they have threatened him.'

But the steps that were taken led in a very different direction. Loris-Melikov was immediately singled out as the prime cause of the tragedy. The minute he heard of the assassination attempt, he had hurried to the Winter Palace in the hope of seeing the wounded Czar. On his way in, he was greeted by a nobleman who pointed to the blood on the floor that had dripped from Alexander's body and said to him: "There's your constitution!" As the result of a campaign of denigration whipped up by Katkov, he was forced within two weeks to offer his resignation, which was immediately accepted. The man the new Czar now turned to was his former tutor, the arch-reactionary Procurator of the Holy Synod, Konstantin Pobedonostsev, who was to exercise his gloomy influence well into the reign of Nicholas II. To bury the illusions of all, who, like Turgenev, hoped that some of the proposed reforms might still be implemented, the new Czar set his name at the end of April to a manifesto in which he declared to his loyal subjects: 'The voice of God orders us to place ourselves with assurance at the head of absolute power. Confident in the supreme wisdom of Divine Providence, full of faith in the justice and the strength of the autocracy which we have been called upon to affirm, we shall preside serenely over the destinies of our Empire which from now on will only be discussed between God and ourselves.' The Russian age of reform was over before it had begun.

The news of Alexander's assassination reached Turgenev as he was writing a letter to Savina, once again inviting her to spend a summer week at Spasskoye. After breaking off, he returned to it two days later and even used the 'terrible news' as an added incitement... *As all theatres will probably be closed for about three months, my invitation to you seems very opportune. How beautifully we should pass the time! Do not wait for my arrival in Petersburg to let me have your decision. In any case, it is scarcely a month before I shall see you. You say at the end of your letter, 'I kiss you warmly'. What does it mean? As it was then, on that June night, in the train? Should I live for a hundred years, I will not forget that kiss. I dare to believe that this was in your mind.*

Dear Marya Gavrilovna, I love you very much – much more than I ought to, but that is not my fault.

I return your kisses with all the warmth of which an old heart is capable,
Do not forget your
Ivan Turgenev.'

In her reply, she made a promise that this year she would accept his invitation; he wrote back expressing guarded delight but wondering how she would keep that promise. Once again, the first weeks after his arrival in St Petersburg proved difficult: the inevitable gout attacks reoccurred, she was often away performing in Moscow and only paid flying visits to the capital, with many people to see besides her elderly admirer. She repeated her desire to come to Spasskoye, but was never able to fix a date. Nevertheless, he was determined that everything should be ready for her arrival if she eventually decided to come. He had finally found a competent and honest estate manager in the person of Nikolai Shtchepkin, grandson of the great actor Mikhail Shtchepkin who had performed in many of his early plays. He now wrote to him, telling him to hang new curtains in the main guest bedroom, install a new bath, buy fine wine and make any other arrangement necessary to ensure the comfort of such an important guest. He had also invited his friends the Polonskys to stay for the summer. Yakov Petrovich Polonsky was a poet and painter who had been one of the early contributors to *Sovremennik*. Their friendship had deepened over the years, especially since Polonsky's marriage to Zhosefina Antonovna, a talented amateur sculptress; they had two small children, of whom Turgenev became very fond. In his last years, the Polonskys were closer to him than anyone in Russia, apart from Annenkov. Although announcing to these people that Savina would be arriving later in the summer, he told each of them privately that he was sure that in the end she would never come. He expressed himself in even stronger terms to Didie, who, before he left France, had appointed herself his 'duenna' and insisted that he communicate to her full details of everything that took place between her beloved Tourgel and the young Russian actress.

> *Nevski, 11,*
> *St Petersburg,*
> *22 May, 1881.*

… you can imagine with what pleasure I received your letter yesterday. It is good and kind and tender like yourself. Except, of course, for your inquiries about Mlle Savina! But here I can reassure you. She reappeared for a moment but is about to leave again. I am almost certain she will not come to Spasskoye; and even if she does, it will not be hard to keep the promise I made you: that little flame was extinguished some time ago. The histrionic element became too blatant; she lives only in the theatre, on the theatre and for the theatre. Once in a while the actress disappears and then, hey presto!, reappears a second later as… an actress. My thermometer as regards her has fallen below 'tepid'. Her fish-like mouth, vulgar nose and raucous voice make me forget her eyes, which are beautiful and lively, but not kind. 'Sie ist vergessen und bald verschollen', which means, in case your German has grown rusty, 'She is forgotten and soon will have vanished for ever.' I can almost hear you saying: 'There's men for you!'…

Fish-like mouth, vulgar nose and all, he met her in Moscow on his way to Spasskoye and happily heard her swear with her hand on her heart that she would join him there in the middle of July. And this time she was true to her word. If it were not quite what he had so often dreamed of – entertaining the whole Viardot family – her visit brought him five days of rare happiness, the melancholy falling away from him like a heavy cloak that slips off the shoulders. The time passed in a succession of events, grave and gay, that afterwards, when he had time for reflection, made him think that that was how his life could have been if he had not gone to the opera on a certain evening in the autumn of 1843. In the mornings they would walk in the garden and he would point out to his guests the places that had been of particular significance to his childhood, like the tree-stump from which he had watched in horror the long duel to the death between an adder and a toad. Or he would drive them around the countryside in his droshky looking, as Savina remembered, 'amazingly handsome in a big straw hat, a Parisian brown knitted jacket with silk sleeves and a loosely-tied kerchief instead of a tie. He drove the horse with great pleasure, like a child, and the smile never left his face. In the woods he gathered flowers more eagerly than the rest of us and chatted away incessantly.' Lunch was served on the terrace, with Savina entertaining the table with a succession of tales of backstage life. Turgenev would then retire to his study, where he was putting the final touches to his story *The Song of Triumphant Love*. One afternoon Savina went swimming in the lake, and Polonsky, who had passed that way 'by chance', as he assured his sceptical host, teased an envious Turgenev by recounting how desirable she had looked in her bathing suit.

That evening, when the others had gone to bed, Turgenev took Savina out on to a balcony to savour the scent of jasmine and lime and listen to what he called 'the voices of the night'. They talked until the sky began to lighten in the east, Savina relishing the chance to discuss her turbulent emotional life with her attentive admirer. Her divorce with her hated first husband, a second-rate actor and skirt-chasing drunk, being just about to come through, she was in a fever of indecision about whether she should yield to her current lover's ardent appeals for her to marry him at the earliest opportunity. She was unsparing in her description of his attractions: Nikita Nikitich Vsevolozhsky was the nephew of the Director of the Imperial Theatres, but had broken away from his background and become an officer in the hussars. Young, rich, handsome, seemingly assured of a brilliant future, it was he who had been waiting for her in Odessa the year before. The most assiduous of lovers, whenever he was in St Petersburg he came to the theatre every night, or, if he was on duty, sent baskets overflowing with flowers.

After this description, Turgenev could only wonder why she hesitated.

She hung her head, as though pondering her reply, although she must, he thought, have gone over the reasons a thousand times to herself. "It may be too soon," she finally said. "I've just got used to my independence and I'm afraid of giving it away too quickly. And then, you know, I've played many different parts in my career, but…" she giggled, "an army wife!? And I sense he would be jealous of my work. When he was younger, his uncle hoped he would succeed him, and his experiences then made him very cynical about life in the theatre. He says he wouldn't interfere with my career, but once we were married I wonder how long that would last. And you know, Ivan Sergeyevich, I'm a theatre animal first and foremost, and a woman second. You can understand that, can't you? It doesn't sound so terrible to you as it might to others."

Turgenev smiled. "Far from terrible, it sounds all too familiar. I can't disillusion you about that. The life of the theatre makes demands that very few are able to understand, and even fewer to accept. But perhaps I should add one thing. This will be a problem whoever you marry… unless he's an actor, and that creates difficulties of another kind: rivalry, jealousy… Do you think any of your admirers would be any different? I assume," he added, with a gentle smile, "that your Nikita is not the only one!"

He saw in the flickering candlelight on the balcony that she had lowered her head and was biting her lip. "I'm sorry," he put in quickly, "I do not want to seem to be prying into your affairs, which are of course no concern of mine. It was just that…"

She reached over and squeezed his arm. "No, no… it's so good of you. And it means so much to me. There's no one else I can talk to as I can to you." She stopped for a moment and looked away. Then, without turning back towards him, she continued: "There is someone else, but perhaps I shouldn't mention him…"

Turgenev maintained what he hoped was an encouraging silence… and he didn't have to wait long.

"He's a much older man…"

"How much older?"

"He's over forty!"

"That old! Is he in a wheelchair?"

Again she leant over and laid her hands on his knees. "Oh, I'm sorry, forgive me. It's just that I never think of you as old. For me you could be my age… except that I could never talk to someone in his twenties as I can to you."

"Well then, tell me about him."

"He's a railway baron. Impossibly rich."

"Does he know about Vsevolozhsky?"

"Yes. They even met once in my dressing-room."

"Doesn't he mind?

"No. He even said that if I married him I could keep Nikita as a lover. But of course I would never do a thing like that."

"What is his attraction, then? Apart from his wealth."

She shook her head and gave a mirthless laugh. "Apart from his wealth, nothing. Unless you call his obsession with me an attraction. But, you know, my dream has always been to have my own company. And he's more or less told me that he would finance that. Can you imagine? I could put on any play I wanted. Play any part I wanted. Direct, if I wanted…" Her voice trailed away and she was silent for a moment. Then she turned to Turgenev. "Now I have shocked you, haven't I?"

He leaned back in his chair and clasped his hands behind his head. "One of the few advantages of old age is it becomes increasingly difficult to be shocked. Surprised? Occasionally still, yes. But shocked? Very rarely. And certainly not by you. I only want what will be best for you. You have a classic choice – it is the subject of countless plays, isn't it? – between the head and the heart. For my part, I would counsel you to follow the heart… but you must not take too much notice of an incurable old romantic like me. Especially one who wonders after a long life whether he has ever understood anything about love."

"But love stories are intrinsic to everything you've written. Beautiful love stories."

"And all, to a greater or lesser extent, unhappy ones. I have never seemed able to capture the other sort. Perhaps because I have no personal experience of them. Look at Rakitin in *A Month in the Country*: he is me. I have always portrayed myself as the unsuccessful lover in my works."

Her smile was teasing, but hugely affectionate. "Nevertheless, Rakitin was full of good advice to others. And I would enormously welcome yours."

"Well, I'm afraid the best I can do is suggest that you wait before making a decision. Time is sometimes a wise counsellor. But there again, I might be accused of partiality…"

"Why?"

"Because if you are not married to either of them, I can perhaps hope to go on seeing you from time to time and sharing moments like these, which blow a breath of life on the dying embers of an old man's heart."

He held out his hands, drew her to her feet and kissed her hands ardently. "And now we must go to our beds, otherwise we shall cause a scandal in Spasskoye. It would not be the first, but the others were so long ago. And tomorrow we have a busy day."

She threw her arms round his neck, planted a lingering kiss on his lips and hurried back into the house. He went slowly up to his bedroom, but it was a long time before he fell asleep.

The occasion that would cause the 'busy day' was the wedding anniversary of the Polonskys, which Turgenev had planned to celebrate in lavish style. An exquisite dinner for his closest friends and neighbours served with champagne in the garden at the back of the house was followed by a surprise which he had succeeded in keeping from everyone. After a brief speech, in which he extolled the couple's talents as artists but singled out their gift for friendship, he called on everyone to drink their health. The toasts finished, he clapped his hands and fifty peasants in traditional costume burst out from behind the bushes. The men, carrying fiddles, balalaikas, accordions and drums, formed a half-circle around the young girls, who grouped themselves into an expectant tableau. A moment of stillness and silence. Then an introductory couple of fierce spread chords, and the singing and dancing began. Gone within seconds was the soporific torpor of the hot summer night; in its place, the plangent harmonies of the music, the stamping of feet, tossing of heads and twirling of arms. Savina was entranced. Before long she was clicking her fingers and nodding her head to the rhythms, revealing, as Turgenev whispered to Zhosefina Polonsky, 'the gypsy blood stirring in her veins.' Finally she could sit still no longer; a quick interrogatory glance at her host, who nodded with immediate understanding, and she leapt from her chair to join the dancers, who immediately gave her pride of place. After she had lead them to a triumphant conclusion, they all swarmed around her in complete ignorance of the fame of the *barin*'s friend; laughter and kisses and mutual compliments were exchanged before Savina, her cheeks flushed from exertion and pleasure, could tear herself away and rejoin the enthusiastically applauding guests. Sitting back down next to Turgenev, she whispered in his ear: "That was worth an ovation at the Alexandrinsky."

When the other guests had departed, Turgenev was reluctant to let the evening end. He invited Savina and the Polonskys into his study and read them the story he had just finished, *The Song of Triumphant Love*, which he had dedicated to the memory of Flaubert. His listeners were taken aback by the contrast between his habitual realism and the grotesquerie of this new tale, which told of the love of two men for a girl in 16th century Verona and contained elements of oriental magic, hypnosis and somnambular eroticism. Written at a time when his thoughts were constantly reverting to Savina, it appeared to move her deeply. At the end, when the girl feels the first stirrings of a new life within her and Turgenev read the ambiguous last words, *What did it mean? Could it be...'*, she sat in silence for a few seconds, then stole over to his chair, sat astride his knees and planted a lingering kiss on his forehead. To cover his confusion, Turgenev fell back on his customary self-deprecation. Patting Savina's hand, he turned to the Polonskys and asked them if they thought such a bizarre tale was worth publishing. Savina didn't give them time to answer. "Oh, but I believed every word of it," she said. "And I think it could make a wonderful play." She seized his hands and gazed entreatingly into his eyes. "Would you adapt it for me, Ivan Sergeyevich?"

Turgenev shook his head. "Who would ever believe such a fantastic concoction? They would laugh me – and I'm afraid even you – out of the theatre."

"You're wrong, you're wrong!" She jumped to her feet and appealed to the Polonskys. "Isn't he wrong? The events may be fantastic, but the three people are so *real*..." especially, she might have been thinking, the unsuccessful suitor, so besotted with the beautiful Valeria who has married his best friend, that he resorts to magic in order to possess her. And as Savina sat the next day in the train taking her back to Moscow and Vsevolozhsky, might her thoughts not have lingered on the significance of the epigraph from Schiller, with which the author had prefaced his story? *Wage Du zu irren und zu träumen! (Dare to err and to dream!)*

For the month after her departure, not only Turgenev but the whole Spasskoye household suffered from the absence of the dynamic young woman who had infused such life into the placid country routine. He wrote to her frequently, constantly reviving memories of those magical five days ('Since you left, our life here has grown very dull. The room where you stayed is and will remain for ever "the Savina room".'), wondering if and when they would next meet ('And by then, will you be Madame Vsevolozhskaya?'), and repeating his avowals of devotion ('Do you remember that radiant, burning kiss which suffused my whole being on the balcony? I cannot forget it; the thought of it sends my head spinning even at a distance of 3000 versts.') But mentally he was already drifting towards his other life, his 'real life'. 'Although materially I am still here, my thoughts are already there. I feel my French skin pushing up under my Russian skin, which is ready to be discarded.'

At the end of August, he took his leave of the familiar sights of his birthplace, unable to avoid wondering whether he was looking on them for the last time. In St Petersburg, where he stayed for a few days on his way home, he thought it as well to prepare his 'ladies' for his return...

Grand Hotel d'Europe,
St Petersburg,
27 August, 1881.

My beloved Didie,

Yes, you may give me as many slaps as you wish for not having immediately replied to your sweet letter from the seaside. For me it will be no punishment. As you know, I do not have a great admiration for Victor Hugo, but he knew what he was talking about when he said, more or less: 'Better to receive slaps from that hand than caresses from any other.'
This letter will probably arrive in Bougival only the day before I do, but I know you and your mama are devoured by curiosity (mixed with a discreet measure of malice) about my friendship with Madame

Savina, so I will keep you up to date until my return (by which time everything may well have changed again, so tempestuous is the said young lady's emotional life at this period). You will remember that I described to you the conversation we had when she was my guest at Spasskoye in July. Her choice was then between two pretendants, personifying, as I believe I put it, the claims of the head and the heart. I saw her again the other evening, and she couldn't wait to confide in me. She has suddenly, for the first time in her life – or so she says – fallen obsessively in love. (Not with me, I need hardly add.) But it is to me she pours it all out, in a very lively, graphic fashion. You will think I might have been expecting something else, but not at all – and I found it most diverting. Just imagine that, despite this new passion, she feels obliged by some kind of point of honour and other psychological and social reasons to go to Perm, on the Siberian border, to join lover number one, Mr N.V., who is still begging her to marry him, in order, she says, to compel her to give up the theatre. But if the new Romeo (who happens to be a married man with three children) had kept an appointment he had made with her in Moscow and pressed his suit, she would – she swears – have renounced everything there and then – career, Mr N.V., everything – and left with him for the end of the world. But he didn't appear and she claims to be relieved. Her conscience is at peace, but she is overwhelmed with sadness and everything seems stale and meaningless.

At a bit of loss as to what to say, I tell her rather piously that a good action, even if involuntary, needs no other reward and that a duty accomplished is invariably followed by a feeling of melancholy. After which, to lighten the atmosphere, I take advantage of her sense of humour and tease her a little. She responds well to this; it lets the sceptical side of her nature get the better of the romantic, and she is able to laugh at herself – which doesn't stop the tears coursing down her cheeks the next minute. Well, enough of the little Savina. As you can see, I didn't have to bother with the promise I made you. And anyway, I am, as always,

Your ever-faithful old,

I.T.

Back in France, Turgenev couldn't dismiss 'the little Savina' from his mind, although he was less inclined to discuss her with his 'ladies' in person than he had been by correspondence. She wrote to him frequently, having now cast him as her 'confessor' and revealing every new twist of her amorous entanglements. Vsevolozhsky seemed to be cooling off, not, she assured her sceptical friend, because he suspected any of her other liaisons, but only because of his jealousy of her life in the theatre. He had suggested they postpone the marriage date until she had made up her mind. Turgenev pretended to be indignant: '*This is impossible behaviour,*' he wrote. '*It sounds to me like an excuse. And after all the allowances you have made for him! I fear you are risking uniting your destiny with that of a man with whom you have very little in common. This would make sense if there were any strong passion, but it seems there is none. In any case, you must stand up for your freedom as an artist. I do not know whether not to do so would be worse for you yourself or for the vast legion of your enthusiastic admirers, of whom, as you know, you can count me as one of the foremost…*'

In her next letter, only a week later, she announced that, exhausted by the relentless grind of theatrical life combined with her emotional insecurity, she feared for her health and was considering abandoning the stage for some months and going to Tuscany for a rest. His genuine concern was seasoned with the wild, impractical idea of joining her there…

…now you are dreaming of quietly slipping off abroad. For my part, I am dreaming how good it would be to travel around – just the two of us – for at least a month in such a way that no one would know who or where we were. My dream, at least, will surely remain just that. But my imagination cannot help painting pleasant pictures. For instance, you mention that you might be going to Florence. Many, many years ago, I spent ten unforgettable days in Florence. The city left the most poetic impression on me, even though I was there alone. What would it have been like if I had had a travelling-companion who was agreeable, sweet-natured and beautiful. (Oh yes, that's essential!) I was not yet forty – a respectable age – but I still felt very young. Certainly not the ruin that I am today.

But the past cannot be restored. Surrounded by the wonders of Florence, my heart was in love… but it was a love without an object. No, that's not true: I was in love with Florence. Oh, those beauties in stone!

You are a beauty, and not a beauty of stone. But you cannot warm to my rays. You need a hero; and above all, one who is young. What's to be done?'

What was not to be done was to harbour so much as a passing thought of making a journey to Italy. In the late winter months of 1882, the tranquil life of Paris and Bougival suffered three unwelcome shocks. Marianne, after breaking off a brief engagement to Gabriel Fauré, had married the pianist and composer, Alphonse Duvernoy; her subsequent pregnancy proved very difficult, and the doctors couldn't hide their fears for the lives of both mother and child. Louis suffered a stroke, which left him a permanent invalid. And a few days later a miserable, frightened Paulinette arrived in Paris with her two children. She had written a desperate letter to her father telling him that Gaston had become dangerously violent and she feared for her life. Although suspecting that she was exaggerating, he had told her to leave Rougemont unobserved and come to him in Paris. She arrived the next day and he put the three of them up in a hotel in nearby Place Clichy. Having arranged for Fräulein Arnholt, who had been Didie's and Marianne's governess in Baden, to look after the children, he settled Paulinette down in his study and asked to hear the whole story. He had known for some time – and been constantly reminded by his daughter's letters – of the dire financial situation of the Bruères. Gaston had proved a disastrously incompetent manager of the glass factory and was now bankrupt, having spent all his wife's dowry, along with the considerable payments his father-in-law sent regularly. What he had not known was that the marriage itself was in a state of crisis beyond repair. Seven years ago Paulinette had given birth to the long-awaited son, Georges-Albert, but this had not had the desired effect. Gaston had taken to drink and, as she now informed her alarmed father, had threatened her on more than one occasion with a pistol.

He settled into the corner of his sofa and looked across at her sitting upright in her chair, hands folded primly in her lap. Twenty years slipped away as though they had never been, and he had to make a quick mental calculation to arrive at the astonishing fact that she was now 40. Perhaps reading his mind, she looked at him with a sad smile and said: "I'm sorry Papa, I'd hoped that the days of these sort of conversations between us had gone for ever."

Returning her smile, he murmured, almost to himself: "Nothing goes for ever... except life. But that's neither here nor there. We've faced some difficult situations before. Let's see what we can do about this one. For a start, I assume there is no possibility of your going back to Rougemont and trying to patch things up."

"I wouldn't dare be seen there again. When he gets drunk enough, he's quite capable of killing me. And his parents would always support him. They hate me... almost as much as I hate them. They want to take my children away from me."

"Have you given them any reason? Have you had anything to do with any other men?"

After a slight hesitation, "No."

"You don't sound too sure. You must tell me everything. If we have to consult lawyers, I need to know the exact situation."

"There is a man who has been paying some attention to me. But I have given him no encouragement."

"Do you like him?"

A blush. "Well, yes, I do rather. But I promise you, there has been absolutely nothing between us."

"Could Gaston suspect there had been?"

"No, otherwise he would have said something when he was drunkenly waving that pistol about."

"Very well. So we have nothing to fear from that direction. And any rate, I would imagine that at your age you are no longer much troubled by feelings of that sort. Well, there is no alternative: we must start proceedings for a legal separation. And in the meantime, we shall have to look for a safe hiding-place for you and the children. If Gaston finds you, he will have full legal right, under French law, to take them away from you."

"Couldn't we stay in Bougival for a while?"

Turgenev thought for a moment and then shook his head. "No, it would be the first place he would look. We will have to find somewhere he will never suspect."

"But just for a few days, until we do."

"It's not possible. My chalet is too small and I couldn't ask Madame Viardot to let you stay at the big house. She has too many things on her mind. Monsieur Viardot is bedridden after a stroke. And Marianne is having a very difficult pregnancy."

She gripped the arms of her chair, bit her lip and her eyes began to fill with tears. Remembering how easily she had relapsed into a sulky mood, he tried to make light of it. "But don't worry. I'll find somewhere safe for you to go."

"It's not that. It's… it's…" *words couldn't find their way past the constriction in her throat…*

"Well, what is it?"

… and when they did, they came out louder than she probably intended. "All you can think of is Marianne's pregnancy. Is that so important at a moment like this?"

"She's in danger of her life."

"SO AM I!" It was the first time in her life that she had shouted at him, and it left him speechless. She turned away and stared down at the floor. "But I don't suppose that matters much to you…"

"Paulinette!"

Months, years of solitary suffering swept away all the inhibitions of childhood. "It never has, has it? It's always been Didie and Marianne, Didie and Marianne… when it wasn't Madame Viardot herself. I always came last. Even your grandchildren come second to Didie's little Marcelle. It's always been the same.

Always. Everyone loved you, but they had lots of other people to love them. I only had you. And you had so little time for me…" She covered her face with her hands and gave way to violent, uncontrollable sobs that racked her whole body.

"Paulinette, that's not true!"

Only huge, gasping sniffs could now halt the flow of words that had echoed around her mind so many hundred times. "There was no room for me at Baden-Baden, was there? Even when you had your own house. At my wedding you had to leave the same night to get back to Madame Viardot. I suppose she couldn't have done without you for another twenty-four hours! So at the reception afterwards, when everyone was wanting to meet my famous father, I had to find excuses for your absence. I bet you were there all night for Didie's wedding party… charming everyone, no doubt…"

"Now listen…"

"No, Papa, just for once, you listen to me. I'll never dare talk to you like this again. Oh I know you did what you thought was best for me. You were so pleased when I finally got married. 'There', I'm sure you said to yourself, 'I've finally got her off my hands'…"

"That is monstrously unfair. You gave me every indication that you were very much in love with Gaston."

"Yes, I suppose that's true. But it was still very convenient for you too, wasn't it?" She blew her nose long and hard and her tone became more pensive. "And as for love, there is only one person in the world that I have ever really loved… apart from you."

"And who was that?"

"Porfiry."

"Porfiry!? Don't be so silly! You were just a little girl… nine years old."

"I know I was. But I discovered very early what love really meant. And I've never found it since. And never will. He was everything to me. Nothing mattered except what he said to me and what I could do for him. And what did you do? You took me away from him and sent me to live in Paris as Madame Viardot's unwanted extra daughter."

"You know very well why I did it. So that you would be brought up with everything that is best in the European tradition, instead of living as little better than a peasant in a backward part of Russia."

"I'm sure you did, Papa. But you made it impossible for me ever to really love again."

"That's absurd, my child. You had a crush on an older man who was fond of you and enjoyed playing with you. It happens to many little girls of your age. It has nothing to do with mature love. And you should see Porfiry now. He has a stomach the size of the Pantheon dome and is more or less drunk from morning to night. He would have made a fine husband for you!"

604

"I'll bet he wouldn't try to kill me. And I'd bet too that he'd be a kind, loving father to my children."

"Well that's as may be. But this is no time for fanciful hypotheses. We have some real decisions to make. And I have had an idea. I think it would be best – and don't tell me it's because I want to get rid of you – if you and Jeanne and Charles-Albert left the country for a while. Wherever you went in France, it wouldn't be too difficult for Gaston to find you. And before we can obtain a legal separation, he would automatically be granted custody. You can imagine the influence your mother-in-law would exert."

Paulinette's mouth crinkled up in a moue of distaste. "But where could we go? And how would I pay for my keep? I have no money at all."

"If you agree, I'm going to talk to Fräulein Arnholt. When she's not in Paris, she lives in Switzerland, and I am sure she could recommend a decent and not too expensive *pension*. Once there, you'd be beyond the reach of French law. As for money, I will of course provide you with whatever is necessary."

"Oh Papa, this is going to cost you a lot – what with lawyers and everything…"

"I'm afraid it is. But don't you worry about that. I'll find something to sell… that can always be managed. The important thing is for you and the children to be safe and sound."

She got up and flung her arms around his neck. "Oh, thank you, Papa. I'm sorry I said all those terrible things. I know I exaggerated, but I've just been so miserable lately, and I never have anyone to talk to. You've always been so good to me, and I love you so much. You do believe that, don't you?"

He put his arms around her shoulders and drew her tightly to him. "Yes, my dear daughter, I do. But the important thing is that you believe that I love you too."

In reply she could only nod her head vigorously, blinking through her tears, and cover his cheek and neck with kisses.

Turgenev spoke the next day to Fräulein Arnholt, who suggested a possible solution. A friend of hers owned the Kronen-Hotel in Solothurn, a Roman town at the foot of the Jura. An exchange of letters revealed that Frau Hubermuller had a set of rooms which she could offer at a moderate price; a week later Paulinette and her two children were established there. Turgenev sold his Théodore Rousseau landscape and his horse and carriage, and was able to send a regular sum of 400 francs a month to his exiled daughter over and above her board and lodging. In the meantime, he started talking to lawyers about how to to obtain a judicial separation which would prevent Gaston from laying hold of either her children or her money.

At the beginning of March, Marianne finally gave birth to a healthy baby girl, who was called Suzanne. With two of the crises resolved – even Viardot's condition was grave but stable – Turgenev's thoughts began again to turn to Russia… and to

Savina, the two images being by now inseparable. He wrote to her at Merano, in the south Tyrol, where she had gone for her health, announcing that he was planning to leave at the end of April and stay until October. He also reminded her of her promise to revisit Spasskoye. But she surprised him by announcing her own arrival in Paris; the pure Alpine air had not had the desired effect and she wanted to consult some doctors in the French capital... and also, perhaps, confide to her friend yet another complication in her turbulent love life; although still engaged to Vsevolozhsky, she had conceived a passion, fully reciprocated it seemed, for the dashing general Mikhail Skobelev, who had won a heroic reputation in the Turkish War. Always dressed in a dazzling white uniform and riding a white horse, he was known to his adoring troops as 'The White General'.

On the evening she arrived in Paris, Turgenev presented himself at her hotel with a pot of superb azaleas in each hand, the attached note saying: 'Bloom as these bloom!' They had only time for a brief conversation, but he was secretly disappointed to learn that, little as the trip to Merano had done for her health, it had had a tonic effect on her fiancé: Vsevolozhsky had suffered unbearable pangs of deprivation and jealousy while she had been away, and immediately on her return they had fixed the wedding date for July.

"And your immortal warrior, as I seem to remember your calling him?"

She gave him a luminous glance in which amusement and nostalgia seemed equally mixed. "He turned out to be mortal. He has become converted to Panslavism, and is preaching the inevitability of an all-out war between Slavs and Germans." A little giggle. "I thought I should lose you forever if I were seriously involved with a man like that. And, wedding or not, I still intend to come to Spasskoye, you know."

He expressed the hope that he would be able to make the journey, and admitted that he had been suffering from severe pains in the chest. "But, you'll see, the spring will drive them away. And we must be together once more at Spasskoye. After that, I shall have to call you Madame Vsevolozhskaya. Things will never be the same again."

She patted his hand. "They will always be the same. Between us, Ivan Sergeyevich, nothing will ever change."

But there was one change that crept up on them by stealth. Eager exchanges of views on theatre, music and literature began, with dismal regularity, to be supplanted by the more prosaic but pressing topic of the state of each other's health. At first Turgenev minimized his own sufferings, which were becoming increasingly severe, and busied himself in finding a doctor who could diagnose Savina's ailments – real or imagined, he could never quite decide. A certain Doctor Hirtz was tried, but could find nothing much wrong with her and was summarily dismissed. After

606

consulting his acquaintances among the medical profession – which by now included most of the doctors in Paris – Turgenev was given the name of Jean-Martin Charcot, who for some years had been carrying out his experiments in the therapeutic use of hypnosis. Having made an appointment, Turgenev accompanied her to the Salpêtrière Hospital and waited while the great doctor examined her. Afterwards, while she was dressing, the two men spoke and Turgenev was relieved to hear, rather as he had expected, that there was little wrong with her. Charcot suspected that the recurrent sense of languor of which she complained was in all probability the result of her unaccustomed professional inactivity: nothing, in short, that a resounding success in the theatre or the unravelling of her amatory entanglements wouldn't cure. He confided in Turgenev, for whom he professed a sincere admiration, that he would prescribe a treatment for her that was entirely anodyne and would merely serve to make her think she was not wasting her money. When Turgenev told him that he would be paying his fee, Charcot gave him a keen glance and asked him about his own health. Turgenev told him that he had been suffering for some time now from recurrent pains in the shoulder and chest, together with breathing difficulties. He was immediately given an appointment for the next day. After a lengthy examination, Charcot diagnosed *angina pectoris* and told him he must remain lying down in his room for at least ten days, while taking certain medicaments and having red-hot needles inserted into his shoulders.

He was thus compelled, rather reluctantly, to invite Savina to come and visit him at rue de Douai. Pauline and Didie, devoured by curiosity which they kept well hidden under conventional good manners, received her downstairs and exchanged a few minutes of polite conversation about the theatre in Russia, and had she been to see any plays in Paris, and what part was she going to tackle next, and how they wished they could attend one of her performances, they had heard so much... Then, leaving Viardot, who had remained motionless and virtually speechless, stretched out on a divan, they led her upstairs to the patient's bedroom and, after exclaiming to him how charming and delightful they found her, left them alone. Neither was comfortable. The easy spontaneity which had characterized their relationship from the very first meeting was quite absent. She found the small, overheated room oppressive and couldn't fail to notice his frequent spasms of pain whenever he attempted the slightest change of position. He tried to strike the flirtatious, bantering tone that usually came so naturally to him, but found it hard to find the pitch. Their intimacy, he mused, belonged to Russia, and was not easily to be transplanted. He asked her if, now that her marriage to Vsevolozhsky was definitely to take place, she had been able to banish all her doubts; she assured him with a bright smile – behind which he saw the actress more than the woman – that she was very happy and convinced that she was doing the right thing. As he started to revert to the old question as to whether her husband would allow her to continue in the theatre, they were interrupted by Marianne who, unable to bear missing her chance of taking a glance at Tourgel's friend, came in with tea and cakes. She apologized for not having been there to greet Savina, but explained that most of her time was now taken up by the six-week-old Suzanne. There followed fifteen minutes of obligatory baby-talk between the two women before Marianne excused herself and left them alone again. As Savina was explaining how she had made the continuation of her career a condition of marrying her Nikita, she was again interrupted, this time by what she described to the Polonskys after her return as something between the cawing of a crow and the braying of a donkey. It was Pauline, in the music room downstairs, attempting a group of Schumann lieder. Turgenev proudly showed her the outlet of the speaking tube he had had installed. After allowing just enough time to avoid giving offence, Savina, with the excuse of not wishing to tire him, took her leave, promising to return soon.

She never did, and it was to be the last time they were to see each other. He pretended, on receiving a letter from Polonsky immediately after her return to St Petersburg, to be furious with her.

Moved by pity, and surely a touch of jealousy, she had drawn, Polonsky wrote, a most dismal account of the great Russian author's Parisian existence: '... Surrounded by old people and confined to one rather shabby little low-ceilinged room... never a minute's privacy without one of the Viardot women interfering in one way or another... completely under the influence of Madame Pauline, subjected to a kind of sentimental slavery, she thinks you are losing all your identity, all your will...'

'Savina is an idiot,' came the immediate reply. 'She only saw one of the four rooms I have at my disposal, and that was my bedroom, which is no smaller or with any lower a ceiling than the usual Parisian bedroom. Not only does the music coming from below not irritate me, I spent two hundred francs on installing the tube which would enable me to hear it. Certainly Viardot is very old, but I am no rumbustious puppy myself, and I only see him for five minutes a day. As for Madame Viardot and her wonderful daughters, yes, they attend to my slightest need and I count myself blessed by their constant presence. One can pity me for my illness, which is, I believe, incurable. From every other point of view, I am the most fortunate of men.'

But it only needed a letter from Savina to dissipate his irritation and bring all the old feelings flooding back. 'Next month,' she wrote, 'I shall be married, but you must promise me that that will not change anything between the two of us. You cannot know how difficult it was for me to say goodbye to you in Paris, nor everything that I was feeling at the time. Since you came into my life just three years ago – is that really all it is? – I am quite literally a changed woman. And it is not conceit when I say that I know it is a change for the better...'

'Your letter,' he wrote back, 'fell into my grey existence like a rose petal on to the surface of a muddy river. As for our effect on each other, you have given me far more than I have been able to give you. I know for certain that if our two lives had converged earlier... But what good is that? I am like my poor old German composer Lemm, in *Nest of Gentry*: I am looking into a dark grave, not a rosy future...'

A month later, on the occasion of her marriage to Vsevolozhsky, he wrote her a letter that did not brim over with enthusiasm. 'I congratulate you, not only on the marriage itself, but because you have had the courage finally to extricate yourself from the false situation in which you found yourself and which caused you so much torment. That was what I had in mind when I said I trusted in your wisdom. I sincerely wish (and have hope that my wish will be fulfilled) that you will never regret your decision...

'I read that your 'immortal warrior' is no more. What an untimely end! How cruelly Fate mocks our great Russians. To have this hero die in a hotel which is little better than a brothel!

'But enough of these sad topics. I beg you to remember your promise to send me a plaster cast of one of your hands. While waiting for it, I kiss your living hands and then all the rest of you. "'All?" you will ask. "In my new situation?" "Yes, all," I reply. "Or as much of you as you will yield to my lips..."'

It was the end of May when Turgenev wrote to Polonsky that he believed his illness to be incurable. He gained this impression from Charcot, who told him that medical science was virtually impotent in the face of this disease. "If that is the case," Turgenev had gone on to ask him, "how long can I expect – or hope – to live with it?" The doctor – whether from humanity or ignorance (his diagnosis turned out after all to be incorrect) – had fallen back on the safe medical formula: "If there are no further complications, there's no reason why you shouldn't live for a good number of years." For the next twelve months Turgenev's mood, principally conditioned by how much pain he was in, veered between cautious optimism and gloomy resignation. His letters, especially to Savina and the Polonskys, and entries in his diary, which he now began to keep regularly, record these frequent oscillations.

At the beginning of June, he was 'packed into his carriage like a trunk', as he put it, to make the journey to Bougival. The doctors thought the move out of his cramped quarters in rue de Douai might improve both his health and his spirits. But the beauty of the late spring countryside and the fresh country air failed to produce the desired effect. 'I still cannot stand or walk,' he wrote to Savina, 'without causing almost unbearable pains in the left side of my chest. I am beginning to believe that it is impossible for me to get completely well. This illness is one of those from which many artists, writers and other hypersensitive people tend to suffer after the age of sixty. It sticks to them, like a faithful wife, until the end of their days. One must reconcile oneself, though it is not easy to do so…' As the likelihood that he would ever see his birthplace again receded, so did his longing for it grow. 'If only this illness had waited for another brief year, I should have managed to go to Spasskoye… I have made so many plans – literary and business ones, and… plans of all sorts! Now all this has melted away and I feel totally extinguished…'

Word of his condition soon reached Yasnaya Polyana and the resulting letter displayed all Tolstoy's warm-hearted compassion and congenital lack of tact: 'The news of your illness has caused me terrible grief, especially when I was assured that your condition is serious. I understood then how much I loved you. I felt that, if you were to die before me, I should suffer the most acute distress… But perhaps it's all doctors' lies and we shall see each other again soon at Yasnaya or Spasskoye. Please write or have someone write to me with full details about the state of your health. I embrace you, my dear and cherished old friend…'

Turgenev managed a positive reply: 'As far as I am concerned, I think I shall go on living for some time yet, although I have already sung my little song. But it is you who must live for a long time, not only because life is, after all, not such a bad thing, but to complete the work you have been called upon to achieve, and for which we have no other master but you.' Tolstoy availed himself of this opportunity to send his friend a copy of his *Confessions*, which was not the sort of work Turgenev had in mind at all. Written at the height of one of its author's most self-flagellatory periods, he seemed almost to revel in stripping himself bare and accusing himself of every crime known to man – drunkenness, fornication, gambling, even killing. Turgenev confided to a friend: "I am at a loss as to how to respond to Lev Nikolayevich. The manifest sincerity of the work is astonishing, but it is all built upon a false premise and leads to a total negation of almost every facet of human life. It has a nihilism all of its own. It makes me very sorry for him. He is without doubt the most remarkable man in Russia today, so we must continue to put up with his idiosyncrasies; and after all, as the French proverb has it, everyone has his own way of killing his fleas.'

Turgenev was persuaded to consult another famous French luminary, Doctor Jaccoud, but his report to Pauline after his visit was scathing: "After he had examined me most perfunctorily, his only recommendation was that I should eat virtually nothing except an occasional spoonful of broth, while drinking as much milk as I could manage to consume. And for that expert advice, he charged me 400 francs!"

"At that price, you had better do what he says."

"I'll be damned if I will. It can only make me feel weaker than I do already – if that were possible."

A few weeks later a physician he had often consulted in St Petersburg was in Paris on a visit and came to see him. "I don't know why you bother him," Pauline had remarked tartly. "What's the point of seeing another doctor if you're not going to do as they tell you?" "Because I have great faith in Bertenson," Turgenev had replied. "Whatever he suggests, I shall follow to the letter. I promise you."

Feeling more at home with a fellow-countryman, and knowing how doctors love to hear critical assessments of their colleagues, he related the milk story to Bertenson. To his astonishment, the doctor, instead of expressing his incredulity and shaking his head over the state of French medicine, nodded in agreement and announced that was exactly what he would have prescribed. At this point his patient had no choice but to comply; and for the next three months Turgenev existed on 12 glasses of milk a day and a cup of broth in the evening.

Whether because or in spite of this ascetic diet, a gradual improvement did take place. One of his most frequent correspondents now was Zhosefina Polonskaya; convinced, like nearly all his Russian friends, that he must be detached from Pauline Viardot's clutches, she offered to come to France to look after him. In August he wrote to her assuring her that, were he the sole heir to an imperial throne, he could not be more cosseted, and that his 'ladies' would deeply resent any interference from outside. But, 'I have not lost hope of getting to Spasskoye, if not in the autumn, then in the winter,' he wrote. 'I see no reason why I should not live another twenty years. The point is, is it worth it? At the moment, my state of mind is very peaceful. I have accepted the thought that my condition will not make any significant improvement, but find that it is not too bad to be an oyster. After all, I could have gone blind. Now I can even contemplate working again.

'I have in mind a tale based on the story you told me last summer, do you remember? About Yevlagiya Kadmina, the actress, who committed suicide by poisoning herself on stage. Someone you knew – a professor of zoology, wasn't it? – who had never met her, became infatuated with her after her death... to such an extent that he was committed for a while to a mental hospital. I would like to take this as a basis for a semi-fantastical story à la manière de Edgar Allan Poe. I already have several ideas for it and the thought of returning to work helps to lift my spirits. Who knows? It might even have what Charcot would call a therapeutic effect on my poor suffering body.'

In effect, he worked with unremitting concentration on the story, which he at first called 'After Death', though Stasyulevich later changed the title to *Klara Milich*, after the eponymous heroine. In less than two months he had completed the 60-page tale; unlike most of the rest of his work, it was written while he was constantly in Pauline's company, and he would often discuss some detail or other with her.

One morning she opens *Le Temps* and gives an exclamation of astonishment. "Your story is becoming more topical than you would have wished," she says, handing him the paper. On the front page, underneath a large photograph of a beautiful woman, he reads:

RUSSIAN ACTRESS COMMITS SUICIDE

The famous actress from St Petersburg, J.N.Feigina, currently appearing at the Comédie Française, *was found dead in her apartment in the rue Montagne Ste Geneviève yesterday morning. The police have ruled out any suspicion of foul play. It is assumed that the unfortunate woman took her own life after indiscretions about her relationship with a nephew of the former Emperor were exposed in a widely-read Paris newspaper.*

He shakes his head in disbelief. "Poor woman! I knew her slightly and have seen her perform several times. What a sad end!"

"There seems to be an epidemic among your country's actresses! I hope your little friend Savina doesn't catch the disease." Turgenev gives her a reproachful look. "I'm sorry, I shouldn't have said that. But why do you think she did it? Is what they say in the paper true?"

"Oh yes, it's been common gossip for some time now. The *Figaro* ran a series of articles that left it in no doubt that she had become the mistress of the Duc de Morny. She was a beautiful woman, and proud too. The thought of having sold herself to such a stupid, vile creature, of reducing herself to the level of the most vulgar courtesan, must have been too much for her. Add to that the ease with which Russians convince themselves to commit suicide…"

"But the man in your story who falls in love with Klara after her death – is he going to commit suicide too?"

"No, Aratov will die of grief, havng discovered love when it was too late."

"Like Evgeni Onegin!"

"Ah, you mustn't put me in that company. And I haven't quite finished the story yet. But I'll cheat and tell you that Aratov's dying words to his distraught old aunt are: "Don't you know that love is stronger than death?""

He reaches out to her and takes her hand. She squeezes it, then gets up hurriedly and moves over to the window so that he shall not see her tears.

Klara Milich was finished at the end of September and was published in the January edition of the *European Herald*. Turgenev noted in his diary: 'My story appeared in St Petersburg and Moscow at the same time and, it seems, found favour in both cities. Even Katkov's journal managed to praise it. Incredible!' But the next day, after a sleepless night of constant pain, he added: 'Perhaps I wrote *Klara Milich* just a matter of days before dying myself. Not a cheerful thought! Nothingness terrifies me. And, what's more, I want to live. But... come what will!'

In November, it was time to return to Paris. His condition was unchanged. 'I should be fine,' he wrote to Savina, 'except for the fact that I still cannot stand or walk without causing almost unbearable pains in the left side of my chest. But in four days I shall be 64, so I have no right to be demanding. In fact, I have become very humble, dear Marya Gavrilovna. So much so that when I recollect last year's antics at Spasskoye, I ask myself – was it really *me*, that grey-haired but still young man, who could be set on fire by one kiss from delightful lips? All this has been deposited in the archives of memory – where, by the way, this particular memory has first place and is kept on the very best shelf.'

Henry James had come down to Bougival to pay him a visit, and Turgenev suggested he accompany him back to the capital. The Viardot family were all taking the train, but he felt he'd be less jolted around in a carriage. James was delighted to accept the opportunity of having Turgenev's company all to himself for two precious hours. Then 39 and still little known in France, although he had already published *Portrait of a Lady*, he had taken pains to cultivate the friendship that dated back to a first visit in 1875, to the 'green room' of rue de Douai. The two writers, separated by twenty-five years, were drawn together by similarities in their approach to literature and, on a more personal level, by the fact that they were both almost professional *étrangers*: the American domiciled in London, the Russian in Paris. Both wrote about their countrymen with a perception enhanced by distance. James made a point of announcing his presence whenever he was in Paris, and Turgenev was happy to introduce him into his circle. Thus James had climbed up on Sunday afternoons to Flaubert's fifth-floor apartment on the rue du Faubourg St Honoré, had once or twice attended Pauline's Thursdays, which he described as 'rigidly musical and to me, therefore, rigidly boresome,' and had partaken of lunches in the company of Russian visitors and the young French writers, whose naturalism he viewed with wary suspicion. Turgenev liked James well enough and could not fail to be flattered by the younger writer's admiration; but he was not greatly struck by his books. James, on the other hand, would have been hard put to it to say which he esteemed more: the work or the man.

He always remembered the one-and-a-half-hour journey from Bougival to Paris, charmed as ever by his companion's spontaneous flow of conversation in idiosyncratic but fluent English, broken only by spasms of pain at any violent jolt of the carriage. When they reached the exterior boulevard they parted company, as each was heading in a different direction. The American remembered that as he stood in the chill November air taking his leave at the carriage window, he became aware that a small fair was taking place under the bare trees of the boulevard; and that what was to be his final farewell to a man he loved and respected above most others was punctuated by the nasal voices of a Punch and Judy show.

James would write a long obituary article for the *Atlantic Monthly*, opening with the words spoken by Ernest Renan on the platform of the Gare du Nord before the train carrying Turgenev's coffin started on its long journey to St Petersburg. '*His conscience was not that of an individual to whom nature had been more or less generous; it was in some sort the conscience of a people… No man has been as much as he the incarnation of a whole race: generations of ancestors, lost in the sleep of centuries, speechless, came through him to life and utterance.*' And the article ended: '*He was the most generous, the most tender, the most delightful of men; his large nature overflowed with the love of justice; but he was also of the stuff of which glories are made.*'

For a few weeks, Turgenev was able to resume a subdued version of his regular Parisian life. He received visits from Russian friends, among them Herzen's daughter, Tata, with whom he had remained on friendly terms after her father's death. She was trying, indefatigably if not very successfully, to continue Herzen's crusade against absolutism and he was able to help her by introducing her to many of the exiled Russian revolutionaries. He had also taken a liking to her constant companion, Prince Aleksander Meshchersky, a geographer by trade and passionate musician and pianist by inclination. He invited them regularly to the Viardot 'Thursdays' and hoped – as it turned out, in vain – that they would marry. Although he rarely left the house, he managed to drag himself to one of the Lamoureux concerts to hear the first performance of Marianne's husband's opera *Sardanapale*; delighted that it was well received, he nevertheless confided to his diary that the music was 'mediocre'.

Maupassant came to see him and read him his first full-length novel, *Une Vie*, which he found 'remarkable'. Desirous as ever to forward the career of anyone in whom he detected talent, he sent a copy off to Stasyulevich, recommending that he should publish it in the *European Herald*: 'I cannot exaggerate my enthusiasm for this book. Nothing like it has seen the light of day since *Madame Bovary*.' He even considered translating it himself, which would have made publication in Russia certain; but what time he had was already fully taken up in preparation of another edition of his collected works, this time for a new publisher, Glazunov of St Petersburg. He therefore entrusted the task to one of his penniless exile friends, who proved totally incompetent; the job was then passed on to Adelaida Lukanina, another protégée of his, but this time a skilled professional writer. Admitting his mistake, Turgenev paid for both translations out of his own pocket.

But even this limited activity took place against a background of constant pain. The doctor he was seeing most of now was a brilliant young man of thirty-two called Paul Segond, who was also a friend of Claudie and Georges Chamerot. Segond had been keeping his eye for some time on a large abdominal neuroma, and in January, 1883, informed Turgenev that it should be removed. This would normally not have been a particularly serious operation, but all the doctors agreed that, given the patient's age and his already precarious condition, it would be too dangerous to use chloroform. Turgenev therefore agreed to submit to the operation with no anaesthetic except a little ether. When the time came, he neither moved nor cried out. How he was able to do this was recounted to Edmond de Goncourt by Alphonse Daudet, who visited Turgenev in rue de Douai a few days after he had returned from the hospital.

"There was a happy atmosphere in the house – flowers everywhere, sounds of young voices down below and our friend up there stretched out on his divan. But what a difference! How weakened and changed he was! Hardly recognizable. He had been totally conscious throughout the twelve minutes the operation had taken and told me about it with all his usual lucidity. 'To keep my mind off the pain,' he said, 'I thought of our dinners. If, God willing, there are to be others, I felt it would be of interest to you all to know the precise nature of the experience. So I concentrated on searching for the exact words to describe it. As the steel cut through my skin, it reminded me of the circular motion of peeling a piece of fruit; then, as it dug into my body, I thought of a knife slicing a banana.'"

Goncourt winced. "My God, metaphors, at a time like that!"

Daudet nodded. "Remarkable, no? Even under such pain, he was taking care to describe the event with the same devotion to detail he would have lavished on a scene in one of his novels."

"How is he now? Is he making a good recovery?"

"It seems so. Apparently the operation was a complete success. He's already able to walk a little. In fact, he accompanied me downstairs and showed me some of the paintings in the hall. Most of them were of Russia: a halted troop of Cossacks, a waving field of corn, stifling summer days on the steppes – they might almost have been illustrations to his books. Old Viardot was down there, silent and suffering. His wife's voice could be heard singing from a nearby room. And there was our Muscovite, surrounded by the arts he loves, smiling at me as he said goodbye."

The 'Muscovite' might have been living in Paris, but his thoughts constantly reverted to his native country. He still wrote frequently to Savina and Zhosefina Polonskaya, playing down his ill-health to the one and describing it in minutest detail to the other. To the Polonskys, who were to spend the summer again at Spasskoye, he wrote: 'When you arrive, give my greetings to my house, the garden, my young oak – and to my country, which I shall probably never see again.'

With Savina, he was a little more sanguine. 'I am fit as a fiddle but condemned to immobility, for I can neither stand nor walk. The prospect of our meeting in St Petersburg is more and more veiled in mist. I do not know what will happen to me or when I shall see you. That is why it is not very pleasant for me to think about this enigmatic future. And yet, the devil can play all kinds of tricks – or so I should say if I could believe that even the devil intervenes in human affairs. But he imitates his master and leaves these things to run as they will…'

Daudet had been right: the operation was a success. But the constant, excruciating pains in his shoulder and chest which, belying Charcot's diagnosis, turned out to be due to cancer of the spinal cord, became unbearable. In order to snatch a few hours of sleep he ignored the doctors' recommendation and had recourse to ever stronger doses of morphine, often administered by Pauline; these began to bring on wild hallucinatory fits which made his worried entourage begin to wonder whether he was going insane.

MONTAGE OF BRIEF SCENES

INT. RUE DU DOUAI, TURGENEV'S STUDY – DAY

Turgenev sits at his desk, leafing through a book. His lips move as he reads.
A KNOCK ON THE DOOR.

TURGENEV

Come in.

Pauline shows in the Russian ambassador.

PAULINE

The ambassador has come to see you, Tourgel.

TURGENEV
(with a gracious gesture)
Won't you please sit down.

Pauline moves towards the door.

PAULINE

I'll leave you two alone.

The ambassador is clearly nervous at the idea of remaining alone with Turgenev.

AMBASSADOR

Ah no, madame. Please stay.

Pauline looks at both men and then takes a seat on a chair near the door.

PAULINE

Very well. But you must pretend that I'm not here. Then you will
feel free to speak…
(a ravishing smile)
… your barbarous language.

Throughout the ensuing dialogue, which takes place in Russian, Turgenev keeps very still to avoid causing himself pain. He remains perfectly courteous and never raises his voice above a low monotone.

TURGENEV

How kind of you to come and see me, ambassador.

AMBASSADOR

My pleasure, Ivan Sergeyevich. I am glad to find you looking so well.

Turgenev gives him a long look.

TURGENEV

I am well enough. But, you know, I cannot move very far. May I ask
why you find it necessary to keep me in chains.

AMBASSADOR

I beg your pardon?

Turgenev holds out his clenched fists and pretends to find it impossible to separate them.

TURGENEV

I have no intention of trying to escape. I await His Majesty's pleasure.

The Ambassador looks hopelessly at Pauline, who gives him a sweet smile and shakes her head to indicate that she hasn't understood a word.

Ivan Sergeyevich, I…

TURGENEV

But if there is to be too long to wait, may I ask you a favour?

AMBASSADOR

(humouring him)

Of course. Anything I can do…

TURGENEV

(with a gentle smile)

How kind you are. Well then, next time you come, would you be good enough to bring me a phial of poison?

The Ambassador gazes at him, speechless.

TURGENEV

What was it that Emma Bovary used? Arsenic, wasn't it?

CUT TO:

INT. RUE DE DOUAI, TURGENEV'S BEDROOM – NIGHT

Turgenev is lying on the top of his bed, screaming and writhing in agony.
He seizes the bell-pull and tugs at it over and over again.
LOUD RINGING OF BELL

One by one, three or four servants in nightdress come into the room and stand by the door, gazing at the frightening spectacle. None of them dares approach the bed.

TURGENEV

(in between screams)

Keep away from me! I know who you are. You're all conspiring to kill me.

Pauline, wearing a long black nightgown, appears in the doorway and starts to move towards the bed.

Ha! There is Lady Macbeth!

With surprising strength, he wrenches the heavy metal ball off the bell-pull and hurls it in her direction. Fortunately it goes nowhere near her. Undaunted, she walks on towards him, holding out her hands in a supplicating gesture.

PAULINE

Tourgel...

TURGENEV

No! Keep away! You don't deceive me. You look like the innocent flower, but I know... you're the serpent under it.

She has now reached the bed. Her tenderness and concern penetrate even his delirium. He grows calmer. She takes his hand and strokes it.

PAULINE

Tourgel... my poor Tourgel...

CLOSE-UP *of his ravaged face staring up at her with uncomprehending eyes...*
BLACK-OUT

Fragments of these delirious moments would sometimes remain lodged in his mind. But he could never be sure if they were lurid images from nightmares or had actually taken place. Anxious to know the truth, he would question Pauline about them; but to spare him embarrassment, she would fall back on evasive replies. One morning when she came to visit him in his bedroom, she found him very weak and still in pain, but philosophically calm. He asked her point-blank if he had ever threatened to kill her.

"It's of no importance," she answered with a smile. "What you say at those moments has nothing to do with you. They're too much morphine speaking, not my Tourgel."

"Which is your way of saying that I did. My God, with all you do for me! It's better that I get out of everyone's way. I am nothing but a burden to all of you. It's time to end it. Help me over to the window, and I'll throw myself out."

"I will do nothing of the sort. You're far too heavy. Besides, you'd hurt yourself."

A momentary look of puzzlement. Then he started to shake with laughter he could not control, even though it made him grimace with pain. He seized her hand and lavished kiss after kiss on it.

But laughter was a rare commodity in rue du Douai that spring. Pauline herself was nearly worn out from the strain of looking after her helpless husband and her suffering friend. At the beginning of April, the doctors told her that Louis would almost certainly not survive longer than a month. She didn't convey this to Turgenev, but to spare him the pain of witnessing the death of his old friend, suggested that he move back to Bougival, where they would join him as soon as Louis was well enough. Always preferring the country to Paris, he accepted willingly, especially when Pauline told him that Didie and her family would be often at *Les Frênes*.

On the day of his departure, Turgenev was laid on a stretcher and carried down the stairs. As they reached the first-floor landing, a hoarse voice called out from one of the bedrooms: "Wait, wait!". The door opened and Louis came out in a wheelchair pushed by a servant. With an imperious gesture, he indicated that he wanted to be placed alongside Turgenev's stretcher.

For a long moment the two men, aged 83 and 65, looked at each other in silence, unable to find the right words, or indeed any words. Finally, each extended a withered arm and grasped the other's hand.

Turgenev was the first to speak. "*Au revoir, mon vieux.*"

Viardot slowly shook his head. "*Adieu, mon ami.*"

He sat stiffly upright in his chair, watching through tear- dimmed eyes as the stretcher bearing his old friend, and the rival for his wife's love, continued on down the stairs and out into the street.

Ten days later, he was dead.

The fact that Turgenev was expecting the news didn't lessen his grief. But there was a part of him that envied the old man. 'How I would like to rejoin my friend,' he wrote in his diary. A week after Louis's death, Pauline, having arranged for her unrepentantly atheist husband to be buried after a civil ceremony in Montmartre cemetery, came to Bougival to look after her other patient. Didie and Marianne were there most of the time too. In the few moments when he was free from pain, Turgenev relished participating in the happy family life surrounding him. He continued to work on his new collected edition, and received visits from both Annenkov and Stasyulevich, two of the very few of his countrymen who saw and appreciated the dedication with which Pauline looked after their ailing friend.

Annenkov had been summoned by Turgenev, who wanted to appoint him his literary executor. He had been on holiday in Baden-Baden, but came post-haste to Bougival as soon as he heard that his friend was asking for him. On being shown into Turgenev's study, he found him stretched out on another enormous divan; but there, all resemblance to times past ended. Could this shrunken, emaciated figure be the same man who, only eight months ago, had recounted every detail of Savina's visit to Spasskoye with such boyish enthusiasm. Despite his best efforts to summon up a warm smile of greeting, his anguish clearly communicated itself to Turgenev. The sick man's eyes filled with tears; and when his lifelong friend bent down to embrace him, he gave way to a fit of uncontrollable sobbing.

After he had recovered, he motioned Annenkov to a chair and told him why he had asked for him. He described his delirious fits and the dreadful visions that haunted him. "I am afraid of going insane," he explained. "That is why, when I give you my instructions, you must write down every word. The next day I may something completely different. If this pain will give me a moment's respite, I want to record some of these visions I have. Last night, for instance, I was at the bottom of the sea, and I saw monsters and foul creatures tangled together, which nobody has yet described because nobody has survived the spectacle."

He raised himself to a sitting position and shook his head apologetically. "But enough of all that. This is no way to greet an old friend after a long journey. We'll get down to business tomorrow." He rang a little handbell. "My good Antoine will help me down into the garden." Throwing off the quilt that covered the lower half of his body, he swung his legs gingerly to the floor and looked down at them. "You see why I can't move very far by myself. How can one live with legs like a grasshopper's?" The male nurse came in and helped him to his feet. As they moved to the door, he flashed a mischievous smile at Annenkov. "I want to hear all about Baden. You must tell me everything: the music, the gossip, the scandal…"

When they talked the next morning, Annenkov was surprised at how much thought his impractical friend had given to what would happen to his modest fortune after his death. Turgenev was worried by the contradictions between the laws and customs of France and Russia, and foresaw the confusion and endless litigation that could – and eventually did – ensue. He had already made a will, leaving his entire property – including the Bougival chalet – to Pauline, together with the income from his literary production. He had also, some years ago, made over to the Viardots securities to the sum of 100,000 francs, the interest on which was to be used for Paulinette's maintenance payments, with power to Pauline to make larger distributions at her discretion.

That left Spasskoye; and here he was tormented by the fear that he had left matters too late. He couldn't bequeath the estate to Pauline because under Russian law inherited patrimonial property had to pass to members of the family. So he instructed Annenkov, as soon as he returned to Russia, to arrange for the sale of the property. The proceeds could then be transferred to France, and would pass to Pauline and her daughters. Together they drew up a document authorizing Annenkov to oversee the sale. But it didn't occur to the two intellectuals to have the document witnessed by a notary, so it was to prove legally invalid. Spasskoye passed to two obscure relatives of Turgenev's whom he barely knew. Both Paulinette and her husband tried separately to contest the will in the French courts, but neither met with any success.

Stasyulevich made the journey from St Petersburg in August, and was surprised to find so sharp a mind in so ravaged a body. One afternoon he and Turgenev sat in a shady corner of the garden of *Les Frênes*, the only background to their quiet conversation the click of mallet on ball, interspersed with occasional hoots of laughter from the young members of the Viardot family playing croquet on the lawn. As they sipped tea and nibbled the cakes that Pauline had brought out to them, Stasyulevich thought of the fury directed at their hostess by many of Turgenev's fiercely proprietorial friends at home: how they accused her of monopolizing their great writer, how much happier, they claimed, the dying man would be if he were at his home in Spasskoye. 'Who there,' he asked himself, 'would surround him with the love and attention he receives at all times here?'

They talked of the new Glazunov edition and Turgenev told him exactly what he wanted included and what omitted. He also went through the minor changes he had made here and there, and they discussed a few further corrections which he had in mind. Stasyulevich asked permission to publish some of the *Poems in Prose* in his journal, and Turgenev gave his reluctant consent. "But only the ones I authorize," he insisted. "Some of them are too personal for publication." The editor then went on to test the waters as to the possibility of future work. He had published, to general approval, a couple of tales Turgenev had written before *Klara Milich*; set in the Russian provinces in pre-emancipation days, they had been grouped under the general heading: 'Extracts from Memories – My Own and Other People's'. Stasyulevich tried gently to encourage him to write some more. "Perhaps you would repeat your early success with the *Sportsman's Sketches*," he suggested. Turgenev gave him a wry smile. "You mean end my career as it began? A charming idea, Mikhail Matveyevich. But it comes too late. I have sung my little song. Perhaps there is still time to change a note or two here and there; but anything new is out of the question. In my condition one should meditate on the past, satisfy the demands – such as they are – of the present and never think of the future… with one little exception, which I now want to bring up with you. It's about where I am to be buried."

"Oh, come now, there's plenty of time to think of that."

"Perhaps. And, more likely, perhaps not. In all events, I wish you to know my feelings. I want my bones to rest in my native country. I would really prefer to be buried in Spasskoye, but I suppose, with the little reputation I have, some will want it to be in St Petersburg. I used to think that I would like to lie at the feet of my master, Pushkin. But I do not deserve that honour. So will you, together with Annenkov, please use all your influence to see that I am buried in the Volkov cemetery near my friend Belinsky. We were parted too soon in life; let us remain close to each other in death."

Stasyulevich tried to make light of the matter. "I will do what I can, Ivan Sergeyevich. But you probably don't know that the Volkov is in very poor condition. There is talk that sooner rather than later it may be condemned; then all the coffins there will have to be moved somewhere else."

"Never mind that. I have led a peripatetic life. If I have to resume my travels after my death, it's all the same with me."

As even the act of writing could send stabs of pain shooting through his chest, he now nearly always dictated his letters, either to Pauline or to one of the two nurses – one male, one female – whom she had hired to ensure that he would never be left alone. But one night, unable to sleep, he seized a pencil and a notebook which were always on his bedside table and wrote, by candlelight, in a barely legible hand:

Dear and good Lev Nikolayevich,

I have not written to you for some time because I was, and, to speak frankly, am on my deathbed. I cannot get better, it's useless even to think of it. I write to you now above all to tell you how happy I am to have been your contemporary and to put to you my last, sincere request. My friend, return to literature. That gift comes to you from the same source as all the rest. Ah, how happy I would be if I thought this letter could have some influence on you. I am a finished man, the doctors don't even know what name to give to my sickness. Gouty stomach neuralgia! I can neither walk, nor eat, nor sleep. It even bores me to have to repeat all this. My friend, great writer of the Russian land, hear my prayer. Let me know if you have received this scrap of paper and allow me to embrace you once more, you, your wife and all your family. I cannot go on, I am tired…

References to his conviction that he was a dying man appeared regularly now in his letters and his diary. When he heard of Wagner's death in February, 1883, he noted: 'That Wagner should make his escape upon the first attack of an incurable illness is another sign of his unfailing luck.' To the Polonskys, he wrote: 'My longing for death keeps growing.' And yet, despite his disclaimer to Stasyulevich, there were moments when he still felt he might have work to do. One afternoon in August he called Pauline to his bedside and asked her, in a trembling voice, if she would help him. Thinking he was referring to some physical requirement, she sat on the side of the bed, took his hand and answered: "Of course. What can I do?"

"You're going to think this very odd," he began, blinking away the tears that flooded into his eyes. "But I have an idea for a story, only I don't feel strong enough to write it."

"You'd like to dictate it to me, is that it?"

"Yes."

"Well, you know my Russian is very limited… mostly to the lyrics of operas and songs. But I'll do my best."

"No, no," he said, shaking his head. "If I try and write it in Russian, it will tire me out too much. I will always be searching for the right word, the exact phrase, and not be able to find them. What I thought was… I'll just recount the story in my own words in one or other of the languages we both speak – whichever comes into my mind first… we'll start in French, a little German here, a bit of English there…"

"But nobody will publish it like that!"

"Ah, but when it's finished, I'll ask you to write it all out in French. It won't be very long… no more than twenty pages. Then I'll have someone – Grigorovich, perhaps – translate it into Russian."

"All right, let's try it. When do you want to start?"

"Now. I have the beginning all clear in my head."

"It's amazing," Pauline confided to Didie that evening when they were alone. "He dictates it to me fluently, hardly stopping to change a word. And it seems to act like an analgesic; while his mind is on his story, either he doesn't feel the pain or he's able to forget about it."

"We must try to keep him writing, then. After all, that is what has always defined him as a man. Every other day he says he no longer has any reason to live. Work could provide him with one. What do you think of this story? Will it be worthy of him?"

"Well, I certainly can't judge its style… with this mumble-jumble of languages, there *is* no style. But the idea is promising. It's based on a real incident, apparently. The main character is a noble who's fallen on hard times after emancipation and scratches a living by trading in horses, most of which he steals. He seems to be an arrogant, very unpleasant character, but as usual Ivan lends him a certain fascination. I believe he's going to come to a bad end. But I'm not allowed to know how."

"Does it have a name?"

Pauline wrinkled her nose. "He wants to call it *Une Fin*."

Didie shook her head decisively. "I don't like that. We'll have to persuade him to change it…"

The next morning, when Pauline went into Turgenev's room to start the morning's work, she found him propped up in bed, his arms lying limp and helpless by his side, one hand clutching a crumpled sheet of notepaper. As he turned his head slowly towards her, she noticed that the expression in his eyes, which usually lit up with pleasure when he saw her for the first time in the day, was weary and dispirited.

Dispensing with her usual bright greeting, she asked him: "What's the matter? Bad news?"

For answer he handed her the sheet of paper.

She took it and read: '*Dearest Father, forgive me for bothering you once again. I know you are not well, but I am desperate and only have you to turn to. It's been more than a year now that I have been rotting away here in Solothurn. I feel I must get away and go somewhere where I can find a job and earn my living. But to do that I need a little money, and what you kindly send me is only just enough for the three of us to get by on. In fact, I have already incurred a few debts... not very big ones, but I don't see how I will ever be able to pay them off. Please my dear, kind father, you who have done so much for me, don't let me down now. Give me the means to get out of this dreadful place in a decent, upright manner. After that you can leave me to my miserable fate.*

I am writing also to Madame Viardot to tell her of my intentions and ask her pardon for my ungrateful behaviour in the past.

Dearest Papa, please try to understand. I am so unhappy, so bitter, and my life at the moment so horrible that I don't know where to turn, except to you.

I hope you are feeling better and beg you to reply as soon as you can,
P.B.

Turgenev raised his head an inch or two from the pillow. "What am I to do?" he asked in a hoarse whisper.

Pauline crumpled the sheet of paper into a ball and threw it down on the bed. "Nothing," she said flatly. "You have done everything you could for that young woman. Now it's time she did something for herself. Why doesn't she find a job where she is?"

"What could she do in a place like that?"

"What could she do anywhere? Teach languages. That's all she's equipped for. Let her find someone to take care of the children for a few hours a day and go out and give lessons."

Turgenev nodded helplessly, but she could see that he was not entirely convinced. She pressed home her attack.

"You know what she's angling for, don't you?" He shook his head. "She's hoping that you'll write to her, telling her to come back to Paris and you – or I – will use our acquaintances to find her some work. For what other reason would she write to me after all these years? She has a nerve, I'll give her that. But I'm not going to allow it. She has always dragged you down, and she'd do so again, even if she didn't mean to. All of us here are trying to help you get well. The last thing we need is for Paulinette to come bothering you with all her troubles... most of which she has brought on herself."

"So what I should say to her?"

"Nothing… for the moment. When you're feeling better, we'll think up something. Then you can write back to her. And now, let's go on with your story. I can't wait to know what happens. Let's see…" she consulted the previous day's pages, "we finished with our hero's neighbour coming to tell him he's sure Platon Sergeyevich has kidnapped his beloved 15-year-old blonde daughter. They're both on their way to Platon's house to look for her…"

Turgenev nodded and tried to pick up the story. But for the first time since they had begun, he stumbled, tried to correct himself, and lost the thread. Finally he patted her hand and asked if she would mind if they continued tomorrow.

"Of course not," she said. "But only if you'll promise me not to torture yourself over Paulinette."

He smiled weakly and said he'd try. In fact, he never answered his daughter's appeal. The last letter he wrote to her was a scrawled note accompanying the regular monthly payment:

Dear Paulinette,
Here enclosed is the 400 francs. My health is not improving and I spend my days in bed.
I embrace you and your children,

I. Turgenev.

Une Fin lived up to its title. It was Turgenev's last work. As soon as it was finished, Didie read it in its multi-lingual form. She sang its praises, which meant more to its author than any critical acclaim, and duly tried to persuade him to give it another name. But for once he didn't give way to her, explaining that 'An End' had no personal reference. "At least, my dearest Didie, that was not my intention. If Fate proves otherwise, so be it. The 'end' I refer to is that of an entire way of life, the way of life in which I was brought up. The aristocracy led charmed lives for hundreds of years, but their time is running out. Of course, there are good landowners who care about the peasants and do their best to improve their conditions; I hope with all my heart that no harm will come to them. But the others – like my Platon Sergeyevich – have never accepted emancipation. They feel cheated out of what they consider a natural right. And I fear that, sooner or later, many of them will meet a fate worse than perhaps they deserve; once the underprivileged become aware of the power of numbers, who knows when the bloodshed will stop? And so my narrator looks at Platon's mutilated body lying in the snow, his head split open by an axe, and thinks to himself: 'That's how they end!'

Only a few days after finishing the story, the slight recovery that its writing seemed to have brought about evaporated. He had enjoyed the experience of dictating *Une*

Fin to Pauline, and even suggested they start on a novel using the same method. He managed to dictate a list of the principal characters, with short biographical comments on each. Then the pain returned with redoubled fury and the moments of incoherence became more and more frequent. Dr Magnin, the local Bougival doctor, told the Viardots that it was unlikely he could survive more than a week or two. The family took turns to sit with him, day and night. There were occasional moments when he would address them with some wild, rambling remark. Louise, who had never been close to him, happened to be staying; when she entered his room, he recognized her immediately and said: "Look, Louise, look over in that corner. Do you see it?"

"See what?" she asked.

"Why, my leg, of course. Don't you see it hanging there? And all these coffins in the room. What do you make of those? They're too soon, you know. They've given me three more days to live."

But most of the words that now issued from his lips were in Russian, which made it hard for the Viardot family to know what was passing through his mind…

WHAT SHALL I BE THINKING?

What shall I be thinking when the time comes for me to die? – if I am capable of thinking!

Will I be thinking that I have not taken the best advantage of life, that I have neglected or overlooked the possibilities it offered me, not known how to enjoy its gifts?

'What, Death already? So soon? Impossible! But I haven't had time to achieve anything… I've only been serving my apprenticeship!'

Will I remember my past? Will I let my thoughts dwell on the rare luminous moments that I have lived, on images and faces dear to me?

Will my bad actions rear up in my memory? Will the burning anguish of late repentance invade my soul?

Shall I be thinking of what awaits me beyond the grave? For that matter, will anything at all await me?

None of all that. I think I will make an effort not to think at all, force myself to concentrate on some trifle, with the sole aim of distracting my attention from the threatening dark gradually spreading out in front of me.

A dying man once, in my presence, never stopped complaining that he was being prevented from cracking hazel

nuts. Only, in the depths of his dimming eyes, one could see
something struggling and trembling, like the broken wing of a
bird wounded to death.

He still received the occasional visitor. On 29 August, Maupassant came to see the writer he revered and the man he loved. He had intended to talk about his long story, *Yvette*, which Turgenev had promised to have published in Russian translation; Maupassant had already been paid in advance, not, as he thought, by Stasyulevich, but by Turgenev himself. But he soon realized that the constant pain made concentration impossible for the sick man; after only a word or two, his mind began to wander.

But an instant of lucidity seemed to return as the visitor began to take his leave. He stretched out an arm to detain him and fixed him with a feverish intensity which Maupassant had never seen in his face before.

"My dear Guy," – the voice was low but steady. "The next time you come to see me – if there is a next time – I have a great favour to ask of you."

"Anything… anything at all."

"I want you to bring me something. But first you must make me a promise. You must not breathe a word to anyone – especially the ladies here – about what I am going to ask you."

"It will be a secret between us. You have my word. Now tell me, what would you like me to bring you?."

The pleading in the eyes was more eloquent than any words.

"A revolver."…

Four days later, Prince Meshchersky arrived unexpectedly at *Les Frênes*. Not knowing of the precipitous decline in Turgenev's health, he was keeping an appointment that had been made some weeks earlier. No one in the Viardot household had thought to put him off. He was to describe the events of the next forty-eight hours in a long letter he wrote over a week later to Tata Herzen…

'In his last hours, Ivan Sergeyevich spoke mostly Russian, so I was the only person who was able – sometimes – to understand him. The whole Viardot family was in the room most of the time: Madame Pauline, of course, her son, Paul, her two daughters, Claudie and Marianne, and their husbands, Chamerot and Duvernoy. I tried to translate to them what he was saying, but it was not easy, as much of it was incoherent. He seemed to be returning to childhood, and often spoke as though he were talking to a peasant or his babushka. He even quoted lines of poetry that he must have learnt as a small boy. Towards the end he became aware of who the people were in the room, but still addressed them usually in Russian. He was clearly trying to take his leave of them all. At one point he said to Chamerot: "Yes, you have a Russian face, so embrace me in the Russian way and believe in me. You must all believe in me, because my love

has always been sincere and I have tried to live honestly. The time has come to say goodbye, like the Russian Czars of ancient times…Czar Alexis… Czar Alexis the Second…" he insisted on this, which was odd, because there has been only one Czar Alexis. Then he saw Madame Pauline coming close to him, her cheeks streaked with tears, and he said, very clearly but still in Russian: "Ah, here is the Queen of Queens. How much good she has done!" She whispered to him: "Tourgel, do you see us?" He stretched out his arms as though he wanted to take all their hands and answered, this time in French: "Yes, but you are not all here yet, come closer, so that I can see you all… warm me with your bodies…" At this point Claudie broke down and flung herself across his chest. He smiled and stroked her head, but his mind wandered again; he seemed to assume the identity of a Russian peasant taking leave of members of his family. He made a particular point of giving advice to a young woman, presumably the peasant's daughter, and her illegitimate son: "Yes, he is your sin, but that's of no matter… just see that he becomes a good man and an honest one. Bring him up in such a manner that he too knows how to love…" After that, he relapsed into silence, except for the occasional incoherent mumbling, and he died the next day at two in the afternoon.'

On 7 September, a memorial service was held in the Orthodox church of Alexandre Nevsky in the rue Daru. Edmond de Goncourt, who was present, noted in his diary: *'The religious ceremony around Turgenev's coffin brought out of the houses of Paris a world of giant-sized figures with flattened features and Eternal-Father beards: a whole little Russia that one had no idea lived in the capital. There were also many Russian women, German women, English women, pious and faithful readers coming to pay homage to the great and sensitive novelist.'* It was assumed that the coffin would then be immediately transported to St Petersburg; but that was to reckon without the heavy mist of suspicion which again hung over the Russian capital: the struggle between Turgenev and his homeland had not terminated with his death. No arrangements could be made until authorization for the transport of the coffin had been received from the Ministry of the Interior. In the meantime Lavrov was grasping at every opportunity to embarrass the Russian government. A declared atheist, he had gone to the service at the Alexandre Nevsky, bringing with him a number of fellow nihilist exiles; they set down a wreath with a card saying *'From the Russian refugees'*, and then waited outside to applaud the coffin as it was carried out of the church. On the same day, no longer bound by his promise, he wrote a letter to the French left-wing journal, *La Justice*, revealing that Turgenev had helped finance his review, *Forward!*. Katkov, seeing a chance to pursue his enemy even after his death, published this, without comment, in the *Moscow Herald*. Stasyulevich, in all good faith, denounced Lavrov's letter as calumnious, but the revelation was enough to have Alexander III's ministers wondering what effect the funeral of so dangerous a revolutionary would have in the already inflammable atmosphere of St Petersburg. It was to be three weeks before the authorization was to arrive.

The day of departure was finally fixed for 1 October, and the coffin was taken to the Gare du Nord, where Pauline had arranged for a temporary mourning chapel to be installed in one of the station warehouses. The gloomy atmosphere of the building was dispelled by the gentle light emanating from twelve large crystal chandeliers, each holding sixteen candles. The walls of the chapel were covered with black velvet. On the coffin itself was a large green wreath with the inscription '*From the Viardot family*'; also the scarlet gown and black mortarboard Turgenev had received for his Oxford doctorate, describing them to Annenkov as 'somewhat inappropriate for a Russian face.' Pauline had issued the invitations: most of the leading figures of the musical and literary Parisian world were present, including Zola, Daudet and Goncourt, the survivors of the *dîners des cinq*. But among the over four hundred people who came to pay their respects were refugees and exiles who had received no invitation but had heard about the ceremony by word of mouth. A Russian journalist working in Paris noted that, while the official mourning was led by Prince Orlov, the Russian ambassador and representative of the Czar, a line of dishevelled figures filed past the coffin who, in their own country, would have been arrested on sight. 'Glory to all those,' the article ended, 'around whose tomb this fusion *in extremis* of vain political passions can be obtained!'

Four men had been invited by Pauline to deliver prepared speeches: two Frenchmen and two Russians, representing the poles between which the dead writer's life had veered. As well as Ernest Renan, quoted by Henry James in his obituary, there was Edmond About, writer and journalist, president of the Literary Society of Paris, Grigori Vyriubov, a positivist philosopher and Herzen's literary executor, and the painter Alexis Bogoliubov, president of the society, founded by Turgenev, for the support of indigent Russian artists in Paris. The speeches were long and all, while extolling the stature of the writer, dwelt principally on the qualities of the man. The ceremony, which had started at three o'clock, ended shortly before five, only because it was at that hour that the train was due to leave.

Despite many attempts to dissuade her, Claudie had announced that nothing would stop her accompanying her Tourgline to his last resting-place. Her husband accordingly agreed to go too, as did Duvernoy, representing Marianne, who was still too taken up with her baby daughter. Fortunately for the three of them, who had never been to Russia and didn't speak a word of the language, they would have Stasyulevich, who was again in Paris, as chaperone. Pauline announced that the two deaths, coming one so soon after the other, had left her without the strength to undertake such an exhausting journey. There may have been other reasons: she was well aware of the hostility many Russians felt towards her, the 'tyrannical foreign mistress' who had deprived Russia of one of its living glories; she had no desire to return to the scene of some of her greatest triumphs only to be snubbed by the very people by whom she had once been so rapturously acclaimed. She may also have remembered a *Poem in Prose*, which Turgenev had written five years earlier…

WHEN I AM NO MORE…

> *When I am no more, when everything that was me is dispersed in dust, o you, my unique friend, loved with so deep and tender a love, you who will surely survive me, do not come to my grave… there is nothing for you to do there.*
>
> *Do not forget me, but equally do not try to remember me during your daily tasks, pleasures and cares… I do not want to trouble your life, disturb its even flow. But, in the lonely hours, when that sadness familiar to tender hearts comes unexpectedly upon you, take one of our favourite books, and find in it the pages, the lines, the words which – you remember? – made sweet silent tears rise at the same instant to our eyes.*
>
> *Read them, close your eyes and give me your hand… hold out your hand to your absent friend.*
>
> *I will not be able to press it in mine; my limp hand will be under the earth. But, today, it makes me happy to think that then, perhaps, you will feel your hand brushed by a gentle caress.*
>
> *And you will see me, and tears will flow from your closed eyelids like those that once, moved by Beauty, we shed together, o you, my unique friend, you whom I loved with so deep and tender a love.*

Pauline did not have to wait long before receiving from Claudie a vivid account of Turgenev's final return to his homeland…

St Petersburg,
Thursday, 11 October, 1883,

Dearest Mama,

I know you will be waiting anxiously for news of our sad journey, so I'll try and put some of it down on paper while it's still fresh in my memory. Forgive me if I am not always very coherent, but the last – what is it? – ten days (it seems like ten weeks) have left me more tired than I ever suspected it was possible to be.

It took us an entire week to reach St Petersburg. We made normal progress until we crossed the

Russian frontier, but after that we slowed to a crawl, stopping, it seemed to me, at the station of every town, if not village, in north-west Russia. The government was evidently terrified at the thought of the trouble the return to his country of one of Russia's greatest sons might arouse. Much of what I am now about to say comes from Stasyulevich, who has been endlessly kind in keeping us informed about what was happening. Apparently they were convinced there would be anti-governmental demonstrations every time the train stopped. Certainly we saw from our carriage that, amongst the hordes of people packed on the platforms, there were almost as many policemen as civilians. As it was, no unpleasant incidents occurred. Often, small religious services were held on the platforms themselves. But the amount of paperwork was not to be believed: dozens of documents had to be drawn up and read and signed and stamped every time before permission was granted for the train to move on. Sometimes we were held up for seven or eight hours. Stasyulevich said we might have been transporting one of Russia's legendary brigands, rather than the remains of a great writer.

When we finally got here, permission to hold the funeral didn't arrive for three days. But the day before yesterday it finally took place. There was a memorial service in the Cathedral of Our Lady of Kazan, at which not one representative of the government was present. After that, we started on the long funeral procession to the Volkov cemetery. The weather was perfect: cold, but with a bright sun and brilliant blue sky. This wonderful city, which of course you once knew so well, looked unbelievably beautiful. Georges, Alphonse and I walked directly behind the carriage bearing the coffin, with Stasyulevich, Annenkov and other friends of Tourgel's I didn't know just behind us. Mama, you simply wouldn't believe the size of the crowd. Every pavement was crammed to overflowing with people, some clapping, some cheering, some weeping. Every window along the route – and I mean every window – had three or four heads sticking out of it. The procession itself stretched for miles. There were apparently 176 deputations from every kind of artistic, literary and civil institution. Each one brought its own wreath. There was one from the Society for the Prevention of Cruelty to Animals with a card which read: 'To the Author of 'MUMU''. Annenkov told me that political prisoners from all over Russia had clubbed together to raise a subscription for a wreath with the inscription: 'From the dead, for him who is Immortal.' I heard this morning that it is estimated that 400,000 people turned out. You remember how often we heard Tourgel lamenting that he was not appreciated in his native country?!

Once again, there were policemen everywhere, and at the graveyard there was a detachment of 500 Cossacks. But at no moment during the entire proceedings was there any hint of trouble. Which means, I suppose, that everybody had come to pay their last respects to the writer they loved, not to make political gestures. Just before the internment, there were speeches around the grave, and then the coffin was lowered. I stepped forward and looked down at it for a moment, and thought of you and said a little prayer. And then they started shovelling in the sand and it was all over.

Yesterday evening, there was a gathering organized by the Literary Fund, at which many of his friends and fellow-artists paid some kind of tribute. It was all in Russian, of course, so I didn't understand very much. But I have to say that one contribution stood out: that of Marya Savina. She was pointed out to me at the funeral, and I was told she would play Verochka that evening in a memorial performance of A Month in the Country. I must say, last night she looked quite destroyed by exhaustion and grief. But as far as I could tell, she read the last lines of Tourgel's Faust superbly. I suppose she chose that because

632

of the famous passage about constant renunciation and fulfilment of duty being the two patterns of behaviour that should determine our lives; she probably thought of it as T.'s moral bequest to posterity. Perhaps it was, but it makes him sound so terribly serious. It's a little difficult to reconcile with the Tourgel we knew and loved. At any rate, I remembered from the French translation you gave me not long ago that the last word of the story was 'Adieu!' And as she pronounced it, the tears cascaded down her cheeks and she sank into a chair, made a gesture to silence the applause and remained there with her head in her hands, her shoulders heaving, for minutes on end. In all fairness, I have to say that I do not think there was any acting in this. She seemed utterly desolate.

I must stop now and fall into bed. We leave early tomorrow morning. Assuming that we proceed a little faster than we did on the outward journey, we should be back in Paris by the beginning of next week. Goodnight, dearest Mama. I cannot tell you how glad I am I insisted on coming, painful as so much of it was. It's been an experience I will remember for the rest of my life. I only have one wish – alas, an impossible one: that Tourgel had been there and then been able to recount it all to us in his inimitable way. As it is, when I am home, I will fill you in on some of the details there have not been time for in this letter.

Your ever-loving,
Didie

There was one detail that Didie didn't report because she was unaware of it: on the day of the funeral, 'The People's Will' clandestinely circulated a leaflet in honour of the dead man… 'A gentleman by birth, an aristocrat by upbringing and character, a gradualist by conviction, who feared and distrusted revolution. Nevertheless, he was sympathetic to several of our aims and ideals, helped many of us individually, and thereby, perhaps without knowing it himself, sympathized with, and even served, the Russian revolution.'

Katkov, whose *Russian Herald* had ignored the funeral, printed this pamphlet on the front page. All right-thinking members of Russian society were thus able to heave a sigh of relief and tell themselves – and each other – that they had been right all along about Ivan Sergeyevich…

THE THRESHOLD

I see a huge, imposing building. In the front wall, a narrow door, ajar; from behind it, wisps of gloomy smoke. A young girl stands at the threshold… a young Russian girl.

From the interior depths of the building, carried on a draught of icy air, comes a slow, hollow voice.

"You who aspire to cross this threshold, do you know what awaits you?"

"I do," replies the young girl.

"Cold, hunger, hatred, mockery, scorn, injustice, prison, sickness, even death?"

"I know."

"Are you prepared to be rejected by everybody? Are you prepared for total solitude?"

"I am. I expect it. I shall bear all suffering, all blows."

"Even if they come, not from enemies, but from family, friends?"

"Yes, even then."

"Very well. Are you prepared for sacrifice?"

"Yes."

"Anonymous sacrifice? You will die and no one... no one will even know whose memory to honour."

"I am not concerned with gratitude or pity. I am not concerned with fame."

"Are you ready to commit a crime?"

The young girl bows her head.

"Even that."

The interrogating voice pauses for a while. Then:

"Do you know that you may one day no longer believe in what you believe now; you may come to think that you have been duped, that you will have thrown away your young life for nothing?"

"I know that too. And knowing it, I still wish to enter."
"Enter!"

The young girl crosses the threshold. A heavy curtain falls over the door.

From somewhere behind her, a grating voice proclaims:
"Fool!"

To which another voice, coming from who knows where, replies:

"Saint!"

SELECTED BIBLIOGRAPHY

Biographies

Frederick Brown. *Flaubert: A Life* (London, 2006)

E.H.Carr. *Michael Bakunin* (New York, 1937)

Gustave Dulong. *Pauline Viardot: Tragédienne Lyrique* (Paris, 1987)

April Fitzlyon. *The Price of Genius: A life of Pauline Viardot* (London, 1964)

Joseph Frank. *Dostoevsky: A Writer in his Time* (Princeton University Press, 2010)

Remo Giazotto. *Maria Malibran* (Turin, 1986)

Aileen Kelly. *Mikhail Bakunin: A Study in the Psychology and Politics of Utopianism* (O.U.P., 1982)

P. Larionoff – F. Pestellini. *Maria Malibran e i Suoi Tempi* (Firenze 1935)

David Magarshack. *Dostoevsky* (London 1962)

André Maurois. *Tourguéniev* (Paris, 1931}

V.S.Pritchett. *The Gentle Barbarian* (New York, 1977)

Leonard Schapiro. *Turgenev: His Life and Times* (New York, 1978)

E.K.Séménoff. *La Vie douleureuse d'Ivan Tourguenieff* (Paris, 1933)

Henri Troyat. *Tourgueniev* (Paris, 1985)
   Tolstoy (Paris, 1965)

Avrahm Yarmolinsky. *Turgenev: the Man, his Art and his Age* (New York, 1959)

Other sources

Isaiah Berlin. *Russian Thinkers* (London, 1978)
   The Sense of Reality (London, 1996)

E.H.Carr. *The Romantic Exiles* (London, 1933)

Alfred Cobban. *A History of Modern France. Vol.2: 1799-1945* (London, 1961)

Edward Crankshaw. *The Shadow of the Winter Palace: The Drift to Revolution, 1825-1917* (London, 1976)

Alphonse Daudet. *Trente Ans de Paris* (Paris, 1888)

Richard Freeborn. *Furious Vissarion: Belinski's Struggle for Literature, Love and Ideas* (School of Slavonic and East European Studies, 2003)

Edmond et Jules de Goncourt. *Journal: Mémoires de la Vie Littéraire Vols 5 et 6 1872-84* (Paris, 1935)

Nora Gottlieb and Raymond Chapman (ed. and tr.) *Letters to an Actress: The Story of Turgenev and Savina* (London, 1973)

Henri Granjard. *Ivan Tourguénev et les courants politiques et sociaux de son temps (Paris, 1954)*

Henri Granjard et Alexandre Zviguilsky (ed.) *Lettres inédites de Tourguénev à Pauline Viardot et à sa famille* (Paris, 1972)

Constantin de Grunwald. *Le Tsar Alexandre II et Son Temps* (Paris, 1963)

Alexander Herzen (tr. Constance Garnett) *My Past and Thoughts* (London, 1974)

Alphonse Jacobs (ed) *Gustave Flaubert-George Sand: Correspondance* (Paris, 1981)

Aileen Kelly. *Toward Another Shore: Russian Thinkers between Necessity and Chance (*Yale University Press, 1998)

Arthur P. Mendel (ed.) and Irwin R. Titunik (tr.). *P.V.Annenkov: The Extraordinary Decade. Literary Memoirs* (University of Michigan Press, 1968)

Frank Friedeberg Seeley. *Turgenev: A Reading of his Fiction* (Cambridge University Press, 1991)

Hugh Seton-Watson. *The Russian Empire, 1801-1917 (O.U.P 1967)*

George Steiner. *Tolstoy or Dostoevsky – An Essay in Contrast* (London, 1960)

Alexandre Zvilguilsky (ed.) *Ivan Tourguénev: nouvelle correspondance inédite. Tomes 1 et 2* (Paris, 1971/2)

Alexandre Zvilguilsky (ed.) *Gustave Flaubert-Ivan Tourguénev: Correspondance* (Paris, 1989)

Turgenev's works

I have read all the novels and tales, but not the early poetry nor all but a couple of the plays. Not speaking Russian, my sources have been twofold:

In English I have read the works published by Penguin Classics, translated by Richard Freeborn, Isaiah Berlin and Gilbert Gardiner. I crave their understanding – or that of their estate - if a quoted phrase or two here and there uses their exact words.

The rest I have read in French from the three-volume *Pléiade* complete edition, the bulk of the superb translations having been done by Édith Scherrer and Françoise Flamant. All translations from the French are mine.

Finally I must acknowledge my huge debt to the annual *'Cahiers'* put out by the *Association Des Amis D'Ivan Tourguéniev, Pauline Viardot Et Maria Malibran*. Article after article, written by experts in their various fields of many nationalities, have been of invaluable help to me. My particular thanks to M. Alexandre Zviguilsky, President of the Association, who was kind enough to grant me, many years ago, two or three hours of his valuable time; and to Mme Tamara Zviguilsky for her painstaking research into the life and character of Varvara Petrovna, Turgenev's mother.

ACKNOWLEDGEMENTS

My warmest thanks to Wendy Dallas who, with her long experience in publishing, was able to help me with a multitude of little details. She gave unstintedly of her time and expertise, and I couldn't be more grateful.

Also to my old friend Rhoda Billingsley, my unofficial editor, who read the first draft through in record time and made many suggestions for cuts, most of which I accepted.

I am also enormously grateful to Gillie Elliott for all the research she did into the – to me – mysterious world of self-publishing and the consequent precious advice she was able to give me.

Amongst other friends who have read parts of the book and made helpful suggestions and/or encouraging comments are: my wife Giulia Patriarca, Jane Kramer, Bill Pepper, Carlos and Lin Widmann and Gerald Peacocke. My grateful thanks to them all.